Recollections

Sidney Gabrel

Recollections

Matador
9 De Montfort Mews
Leicester LE1 7FW, UK
Tel: 0116 255 9312
Email: matador@troubador.co.uk
Web: www.troubador.co.uk/matador

ISBN 1 904744 16 8

Cover design: Troubador Publishing

This is a work of fiction. All characters, locations and events are imaginary,
and any resemblance to actual persons, locations and events in purely coincidental.

Typeset in 10pt Plantin Light by Troubador Publishing Ltd, Leicester, UK

Matador is an imprint of Troubador Publishing

Contents

Contents

Contents

Contents

Contents

Introduction

Great credit must be accorded to my niece, Katie, for inspiring and encouraging me to write these short stories.

When I used to recount episodes in my life, she urged me to write them down for posterity. Even though we are only one generation apart, the backgrounds to some of the stories were as of different world to her and very much alien to her children. After she had read the first few, she expressed extreme delight, not only in their contents but also in the manner and style in which I had recorded them.

She confessed that some made her laugh outright, whilst others caused her to weep in sympathy at the pathos. She further encouraged me by volunteering to type my hand written manuscripts on a word processor which she had recently acquired.

At first, only a few stories were involved, but with encouragement and inspiration, I wrote more at about the same rate as she typed them. Whenever she handed me a batch of typed stories, I handed her a further batch of hand written manuscripts to type. The more I wrote, the greater were her expressions of appreciation which installed in me the first aspiration of having the stories published. Credit must also be given to my dear wife, Dora, who often reminded me of incidents that made the theme for further stories.

When I had recorded a total of 155 short stories, I then commenced the arduous task of finding a publisher. I had been pre-warned that this would be difficult, if not impossible, as publishers at large do not welcome short stories and especially those written by first time, unknown authors.

Some of my recollections go back to my very early childhood, some 75 years ago, and some reflect experiences as a youth including those during World War 2 and some quite recent.

Further encouraged by the very enthusiastic reception by readers of the published book, including among them, doctors, solicitor, builder, car mechanic, taxi driver, teacher, postman and others in all walks of life, I wrote a further 45 short stories, making a total of 200 and drew an illustration for each and every one.

When the first edition print ran out, I decided to publish this enlarged, fully illustrated edition.

I hope and trust that you will find all these concerted efforts worthwhile and enjoyable.

Megillah Purim

The weather here in west Essex has just simply been awful. For the last 140 days and nights or so, it has precipitated continuously in one form or another. Rain, gales, sleet, blizzards, hail, snow, drizzle, showers, storms, rain and yet more rain. However, as if by some miracle, the precipitation eased somewhat on the eve of the festival of Purim. What we had instead, was a saturating and penetrating misty drizzle. The temperature was just at or a little below freezing. The very air itself was frozen. Icy dampness clung to every surface, roads, pavements, walls, street signs. Lamp posts had a mournful halo around their lights. Trees, shrubs, hedges and even the solitary intrepid soul venturing out on some urgent mission soon had their clothes saturated and their spectacle lenses misted over. It was an evening when even my dear beloved wife, Dora, would not be so heartless to send me out. When the time came to light the festival candles and to close the curtains, I glanced out of our front bay window to observe the dismal scene outside, I noticed a furtive movement in our immediate neighbour's front garden which was heavily overgrown with large assorted shrubs.

I called Dora over and together we kept watch on the suspicious character. He was wearing a dark duffle coat with its hood concealing his face. What sort of person would venture out on such a horrid evening and loiter about in someone else's garden?

Several times he approached the neighbour's front door and peered through the letter box. He also attempted to look through chinks in the curtains. He had a bulky case with him which could be containing house breaking implements or even a weapon.

We tried phoning our neighbour to warn him about the potential dan-

1

ger but there was no reply.

Dora decided that we must take immediate action. She decided to 'phone the police but just at that moment the person may have become aware of our observation and started to walk swiftly away.

In such moments of crisis, Dora is very decisive and instructed me to follow the suspect at a discreet distance and to point him out to the police when they arrive.

Who said that she would not send me out in such horrid weather? She told me to hurry and to be careful. I quickly donned a heavy dark overcoat and pulled a thick black woolly hat down on my head. As a precaution I took with me a heavy walking stick for self defence should it become necessary.

Meanwhile, Dora had given a detailed description of the suspect and the direction he had walked off in.

In the short while I had donned my hat and coat and grabbed the walking stick the suspect had disappeared into the mist. I began to peer into nearby front gardens in case he was hiding among overgrown shrubs.

The police arrived in a few minutes and asked why I was peering and searching in the front gardens. I told them that I was looking for a suspicious character. They told me that in fact they believed that I was the suspect and that I fitted the description just given to them by a concerned resident. They asked me for identity but I had none on me.

They also asked what sort of pleasure I derived from peering through letter boxes and through chinks in other peoples curtains and frightening the lives out of lonely old women. I assured them that I was not such a pervert. They then asked why I was carrying a heavy stick when obviously I was not disabled. Did I intend to carry out a violent robbery on some defenceless person?

I tried to explain the true situation and told then that the person who phoned them was actually my own dear wife and it was she who had sent me out so attired and armed.

They said that no decent loving wife would send her husband out in such terrible weather and then phone the police about a fictitious character in the neighbourhood. I told them why Dora had sent me out just when she was about to light the Purim candles. They scoffed and said that they had heard of Christmas candles but never of Purim candles. The situation got more tangled when I tried to explain why Dora was going to light Purim candles and what Purim was all about.

I told them about Queen Esther and the King of Persia which is now called Iran. They asked me what had happened to the Ayatollah. I also told them about the wicked Haman and why even today, we Jews dress up in fancy costume.

2

They said that they had heard some good excuses in their days as police, but this excuse for going armed and acting in a suspicious manner was the best they had ever heard.

Eventually with Dora's help, I got the matter sorted out. The next day, we went to warn our neighbour about the suspicious character that had been seen in his front garden. He said it must have been his insurance agent who had an appointment with him at that time but due to the bad weather our neighbour's train had been delayed and he had arrived home too late to meet the insurance agent.

Car Accident

We are now the proud possessors of a brand new coloured TV set. It has a large screen, sharp brilliant colours, crystal clear 3D sound, full remote control and also incorporates what is known as Teletext. At the touch of a button, all sorts of information is available, latest news, weather, sport, finance, politics etc., but most important of all, subtitles to all programmes. Because of my impaired hearing, this is most useful.

You may very well be asking yourself, how is it that a couple of old age *schnorrers* like us, who have never bought a brand new item for the house before suddenly become the owners of such a fully paid up brand new luxury item.

It's true, ever since we were married, many years ago, we only bought second hand furniture, cookers, radios, heaters, refrigerators etc.. When we were married, we were very poor (sob, sob); our wedding reception was a modest, self catering affair in Dora's parents' house. Our honeymoon was spent in a run-down farm deep in the country. We did not buy new clothes for the wedding, we wore our normal everyday clothes. All our wedding presents were measly useless items. One was a second hand electric clock which promptly caught fire as soon as we plugged it in. Other presents, were bric-a-brac which the presenters' grandparents had discarded as being 'old fashioned' dust collectors.

In those days it was impossible to rent accommodation, so with the very little cash we had, we put a deposit on a small house in a decrepit London suburb and furnished it with second hand furniture. That was 45 years ago. The furniture etc. that we bought for virtually nothing and some that was scornfully given to us at the time, was 55 years old or more. Those items today, are over 100 years old and much sought after costly antiques

4

(which now cost us a fortune to insure) and which are the envy of those who scorned us at the time for being *schnorrers* for buying old things and for taking in what others were discarding.

Never before, did we own a new TV set. We always bought 'reconditioned' sets. Now we own a brand new fully paid for set which is the envy of those who considered us *schnorrers*.

We will let you know how this came about. Dora is a very clever shopper, always with an eagle eye for a bargain. A couple of weeks ago, she saw an advert in a local free-give-away newspaper that a super cut price store had opened about 45 minutes drive away. The prices of the goods on offer were very cheap compared with those in the local shops but the offer only applied to items bought in large quantities.

When we arrived in our 15 year old second hand car, the super cut price store's car park was virtually empty. As I dislike shopping in any kind of store, I let Dora go in to find the bargains on her own whilst I found a quiet, remote part of the nearly empty car park in which to wait for her. I thought that I would take the opportunity to have a nice relaxing snooze in the warm, bright, sunshine. I had hardly drifted into a relaxed happy dream when I was rudely awakened by a violent shudder. Virtually, out of the blue, a big 1930's style American car had reversed into the back of my car. My first reaction was anger but then I thought, maybe this is some form of robbery. My apprehension was not lessened when the driver got out of his car. He looked a shabby form of Al Capone. Instead of the language I expected to hear, the man was genuinely apologetic. He straight away confessed that the accident was entirely his fault and that he would pay fully for the damage to my car. He said that because he had not been feeling well, he had not been concentrating. When he reversed, he had assumed that that remote part of the car park was empty and he did not notice my car. He said that he would prefer that I did not put my claim through my insurance company and that instead he would settle up immediately I let him know how much it would cost to repair the damage. This proposition suited me, as due to my age and the age of the car I might find it difficult to re-insure if I made a claim and also, I would lose my no claims bonus when and if my policy was renewed. He said that as he was out and about a lot I could best contact him through an answer phone agency. He gave me their telephone number and told me to leave a message for Alec. For the moment I thought he was going to say Al Capone.

Within a couple of days I obtained a repair estimate and duly left a message for Alec on his answer phone agency number. Dora was sure that I would not hear from him. She said it was obvious that he was a smart Alec and had made a real fool of me. She quite rightly pointed out that I had not obtained his name and address, noted his car licence number, taken details of the damage to both cars, made a plan of the accident location, etc. What bargains had Dora bought? A hundred weight (112lbs) of porridge in a sack; 12x5 litres of bleach and 1 gross (144) rolls of assorted coloured toilet paper!

Quite to our mutual surprise, 'Alec' did respond to the message we left on his answer phone service. We told him how much it would cost to repair our car. He promised to deliver the money the following day and asked us if it would be acceptable to pay in cash.

Right on the dot, 'Alec' called and paid the full amount in brand new bank notes. We gave him a receipt for the money and he left hastily saying that he was not feeling well. I immediately phoned the car repairers and made arrangements to have the necessary work done.

About 2 hours later, two police detectives called and asked us if we knew a man of Alec's description who drove an American style car. You can imagine the thoughts that ran through our heads. Was this a set-up? Was Alec a drug dealer or a gun runner and would we be accused of aiding and abetting?? We decided that honesty would be the best policy. After all we had done nothing wrong and we did not know anything about Alec or his business. We asked the detectives why they were making these enquiries. They explained, that a man with Alec's description had suffered a severe heart attack in his car about a mile from our house and that he had died before he had been got to hospital. There was no identifying evidence on the body or in the car except the receipt which we had given him for the cash. They had hoped that we would be able to help identify the dead person.

As soon as they left, Dora said we should get rid of the money as soon as possible as the banknotes may be forgeries. She said that with the money we should by a lovely TV set she had seen in the super save cut price store. She said that with the money she had saved on her shopping and with the money we would save on the TV set, we would be able to pay for the car repair. I pointed out that the store would have one of those machines that detect forged bank notes and we would be in big trouble. Dora, for ever resourceful said, we will pay for the set cash-on-delivery, the van driver would not have such a machine with him. When the set was delivered, the van driver said that before he could accept the cash he would have to check that they were not forgeries with a little machine he kept in his drivers cab. With our hearts beating madly, he said that the notes were fine. He said that he hoped we were not offended but he had to check because so many people had tried to pass forged money to him. So now you know, how it is, that we, notorious shnorrers own such a lovely fully paid for TV set with Teletext.

6

Blackie's Burial

When our beloved and affectionate 17 year old cat, 'Blackie' died on 17th January 1992 after a short illness, we buried her in our back garden. Several of our neighbours attended the burial as they all knew 'Blackie' and were very fond of her. Her name was particularly appropriate as her coat was jet black without even a single white hair. It is very unusual for black cats not to have even a single white hair. Even the pads of her paws and the roof of her mouth were black.

The miserable cold drizzly weather did not deter the mourners from attending the burial and to pay their last respects to a much beloved cat. No doubt, despite the fact that the burial was non-denominational (being an animal, Blackie had no religion) several silent prayers were said on her behalf. Among the mourners, was a good friend and neighbour, Mrs Irma McLaren. Actually, it was her son who dug the grave, because, due to an attack of Lumbago, I was not able to do so myself. Irma knew 'Blackie' from the day she was born among a litter of five assorted coloured siblings. 'Blackie' was the smallest of the litter, she was so small, that she was nicknamed 'Tuppence'. Irma, lived next door to the house in which Blackie' was born and watched her grow up from day to day. 'Blackie' was very friendly with Irma and visited her often by entering her house almost at will through her back door. When 'Blackie' grew up, she ventured into other neighbours' houses through their back gardens.

Eventually, she plucked up courage and made herself acquainted with us using the back gardens as a means of access. Although, 'Blackie' became acquainted with most of the immediate neighbours she never lost contact with Irma. In the course of time, her owners decided to move and as they realised that 'Blackie' would be unhappy to leave her surroundings they asked us if we would 'adopt' her. 'Blackie' readily accorded to this idea and made herself at home but did not forget her old friend, Irma, who she continued to visit regularly.

In recent years, Irma developed Arthritis in her joints, especially in her knees and ankles which made it very difficult to walk even within her own home. She knew I had a similar condition and asked me how it was that I seemed to have recovered; once you have developed arthritis, you have it for the rest of your life. I explained that at first, I took powerful pain-killer tablets but I stopped taking them as I realised that in the course of time, I would have to take progressively stronger drugs to suppress the pain.

I decided to apply ice packs to my swollen, painful joints. In just a few days, the swellings subsided and the pain greatly diminished. Irma, said that she would try the same.

About two weeks later, she excitedly phoned me and said the treatment was very effective.She had tried it on her knees and the pain had virtually gone. She said that she would now try it on her ankles and as soon as she could walk again, would come round to thank me personally. She was extremely excited at the prospect.

Two weeks ago, her son, the one who dug the grave for little 'Blackie' came round to tell us that Irma had been admitted to hospital and had died the previous evening. She died of a previously undetected and therefore untreated cancer of the liver. We have just returned from Irma's funeral at which were several of the same neighbours who attended 'Blackie's' burial.

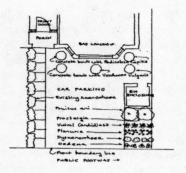

Town Planners

In the past, each borough council in the United Kingdom issued their own building regulations. This caused problems for architects who were asked to prepare building plans and specifications in various different boroughs.

In order to overcome this problem, the government introduced national building regulations that would be applicable anywhere in the United Kingdom.

The technical-legal lawyers who compiled these regulations did so in very legal jargon which was incomprehensible to most people including those most concerned with their application and implementation.

The legislators appreciated this problem and when the new regulations were published they were all accompanied by explanatory notes and illustrations that made their interpretation quite clear.

The regulations covered all aspects of building in a comprehensive and logical manner. They were so comprehensive that they had to be published in six hefty A4 sized volumes. Never-the-less, despite this mass of legislation, it was fairly easy to ascertain what the building regulations required and to comply with them.

But town planning laws are quite a different proposition. They are far more condensed but far more vague and very controversial. Vague requirements like "New erections or extensions to existing erections shall not adversely affect neighbouring properties" or, "New erections shall be sympathetic aesthetically with neighbouring structures and the neighbourhood generally" are open to wide variations. How should a new house be designed if the neighbouring houses are slum dwellings? The problem is exacerbated as most town planning officials whose duties are to advise their elected committees whether or not to approve an application are not

9

trained building designers and many town planning committees do not include a single architect among their members.

Most town planning committees rely heavily on the recommendation of their officials as whether or not to approve a design.

A basic problem for applicants and their architects is the undue power that officials wield. If an official says to an applicant, "We suggest that you do so and so", it is virtually a command because failure to comply with his 'suggestion' means he will recommend that the application is rejected. The rejection can be discussed with the official and/or his superior and a compromise arrived at. But this will mean at least one month delay, more probably, two or three months as committees meet only once a month and in the summer, take a holiday. If a compromise cannot be arrived at, it is possible to appeal to the appropriate Minister of State who will appoint an inspector to look into the dispute and advise the Minister accordingly. This will take at least six months. As time is money, it is far more prudent to comply with the town planning official's 'suggestion' however galling it may be.

A lot of bad design that is blamed on architects is actually the result of town planner's 'suggestions!

Many of the town planners are not only not trained in building design but many are not even qualified as town planners.

So now, you may appreciate my anger and frustration when I applied upon behalf of a client for a house he owned locally to be converted into four self contained flats. Basically, the council could not refuse as for many years, at least twenty, the house had been multi-occupied by tenants who shared a bathroom and WC. There was no proper privacy, no fire spread prevention, no car parking and no bin enclosure.

The council could not object to the basic proposal as the premises had under the law, 'Existing usage rights.'

The young official whose duty it was to examine the proposal had a fetish about the front garden design. I had shown a four bin enclosure tucked neatly out of sight but he insisted that it be located alongside and facing the front access path. When I pointed out to him that this would be unsightly and unhygienic he said that a suitable creeper could be planted that would conceal the enclosure. I asked him, how will the tenants be able to get access to their bins if a creeper was concealing the stores. He said simple, the creeper can be held aside whilst access was made to the bins.

Next, he asked for a row of fir trees to be planted along the front of the building, he said to give privacy to the ground floor tenants. He insisted until I pointed out that the council would be legally liable for building subsidence because fir trees would grow in a few years to be forty feet high, about twice the height of the house and would certainly undermine the

10

foundations and destroy the drains. The only privacy the ground floor tenants would get would be the width of the tree trunks.

He went on and on with all sorts of stupid and impractical 'suggestions'. He eventually said that it was no good me just showing areas of the front garden designated for flower beds, flowering shrubs and trees. I was to mark on each plant and describe them by their Latin designations. I resignedly complied with his 'suggestions' about the planting in order to get the application approved as soon as possible.

I carefully drew each and every proposed plant and alongside annotated a description in Latin-

PITYRIASIS CAPITIS	*DYSMENORRHOEA*
PROPHYLAXIS VULVAL	*CANDIDIASIS*
ERYTHEMA MULTIFORM	*PRUITUS ANI*
PROCTITIS	*AMENORRHOEA*
OEDEMA	*PEDICULOSIS CAPITIS*
VERDUCAE VULGARIS	*PROCTALGIA PLANNURIA*

Approval was speedily granted, the plan was duly sealed with the Council's official seal and signed by the town planning committee chairman and the Mayor.

The plan contained a condition, that if any of the above should perish within 5 years they are to be replenished.

I can now admit that I awaited this approval with great apprehension and anxiety in case any of the officials or committee members would recognise the above as being medical terms for-

Dandruff	Painful periods
Preventative Vaginal Thrush	Rash
Anal irritation	Anal Itch
Absence of periods	Water retention
Head lice	Warts
Pain in the Anus	

11

Menieres Disease Syndrome

Some while ago, a builder called to see me about a site he was tendering for and as I had previously been involved on the same project he needed some background knowledge of previous events.

He was a hale and hearty man, about 40 years old and in apparent robust health. I willingly imparted the information he required but refused his invitation to visit the site with him. I explained that for the time being, I was not travelling anywhere. I was not even strolling round the corner to pick up an evening newspaper as I used to in case I suffered an attack of Menieres. He was surprised, he said that I looked quite healthy and asked what were the signs and symptoms of the condition. The only thing he had noticed about my health was that I was obviously hard of hearing. This is a polite form of informing someone that they are deaf. I told him that he was fortunate in as much as I could comprehend what he was saying.

I was in partial remission of the condition but was deaf to certain frequencies. He had a loud voice which included frequencies I could hear.

Some people, I could not hear at all or they sounded as thought they were speaking incomprehensible Swedish. All music sounded to me like Chinese military marches on an off radio station.

He asked if the condition was due to old age. This was an oblique way of reminding me that I had passed the use by date. I told him that it affected people of all ages but the only other known case to me was a man of about his own age who until his first attack had been a fitness fanatic and played tennis every day.

This aroused his curiosity still further and pressed me for more details. I told him that it all started a few months earlier when we had visitors. I suddenly felt the hubbub of conversation unbearable and discreetly retired to rest for a while on my bed. Shortly afterwards, I felt that the room was spinning round at a fantastically fast speed. First of all, I thought that if I lay still the spinning would stop but it simply went on and on with the feeling that the slightest movement of my head would make it worse.

The spinning continued relentlessly and then I had the uncontrollable urge to vomit. I felt that I was vomiting my very guts out.

Eventually I attracted the attention of my wife who came in to see what the matter was. She said she would try to assist me to get to the bathroom as I had the urge to vomit more, but due to the spinning sensation I could not move. One of our visitors was a trained nurse. When she saw what was happening she gallantly rose to the occasion and promptly left.

Dora, then frantically 'phoned our doctor and described the condition. The doctor said that as it was a Sunday afternoon and as he did not have nor could he obtain the appropriate pills there was no point in him calling. He assured Dora that the attack would pass over and that I should come and see him at the surgery the following morning.

The attack did pass over and I was left with profound deafness, to such a degree that I could not even hear myself speaking. However, the deafness did not preclude me hearing terrific noises in my head. There were loud whirring and buzzing noises accompanied by ghoulish shrieking sounds and banging as though I had an iron bucket over my head upon which some sadistic torturer was smiting with a hammer. In addition, I had the sensation that my brain had swollen and was painfully pressing against the inside of my skull. My ear drums became very painful and very sensitive to sounds, even the gentle sound of a cup being placed on a saucer was torture to my inflamed ear drums.

It was very irritable when people tried to speak to me and I was, on a few occasions, unreasonably rude to well meaning friends who only tried to have polite conversation with me.

What concerned me most, was that in subsequent attacks, the spinning effect hit me so suddenly that I fell uncontrollably to the ground. It was for fear of such attacks that at the time, I felt unwise to move out of the relative safety of my home.

I noticed that the builder's ruddy face had gone white and that he had beads of perspiration on his forehead. He asked to be excused as he urgently had to contact his doctor and convey these symptoms to him.

I assured him that even though the medical profession did not know why this condition affects people, they know how it effects them and it is certainly not an infectious disease. He said he appreciated that it was not infectious but the problem was he is a confirmed hypochondriac and he wanted to forewarn his doctor as he was certain to suffer all the symptoms within the next couple of days. He said it would have been better if 1 had not described the condition to him.

13

The Bespoke Overcoat

During one of our visits to Barney's widow, she asked if we could sell his overcoat, all she expected to get for it was ten pounds. This may sound a lot for a second hand coat but it was actually a bargain in a way. There was however one snag. Barney had not been taller than 4'7" (1400 mm) and had been very tubby and squat. Despite not wishing to speak disparagingly of the dead, he was not quite your average size figure.

Barney and his wife had lived all their married life in a slum dwelling in 'Brady Street Buildings' in the heart of the Jewish part of the east end of London off the Whitechapel Road.

He left school at the age of 14 and was apprenticed to a Saville Row tailor whose clients included gentry, aristocrats and notabilities. He remained with the same firm all his working life. Like many tailors, he was never exceptionally or even well dressed himself.

However, when he retired at the age of 65, he decided to make himself an overcoat which was to be at least as good, if not better, than any he had ever made for any of his firm's clients. He used the heaviest Melton cloth he could buy, the very best silk linings, the strongest cottons and he patiently hand stitched every seam. When he had finished it, it was a work of art. Unfortunately, he never lived to wear it, he died of a massive heart attack soon after.

It was this coat, which his employers would have charged at least £300 for to one of their clients, we were piteously being asked to sell for a measly £10. The linings alone would have cost much more to buy, However, we could not refuse to do this favour for his widow. We thought that somewhere, there must be someone of the same unfortunate stature who would be willing to pay a measly £10 for such a wonderful coat.

14

On our journey home with the coat, Dora had one of her many inspirations. "It could fit Mrs Shaul's husband, Thomas!". Thomas had also retired recently, having worked as a ledger clerk in the same Clerkenwell transport company since he left school at the age of 14.

On his mantelpiece was an oak cased Westminster chiming clock suitably inscribed by his former employers commemorating the great historic event in his life.

We first showed the coat to Mrs Shaul who was very keen and was even willing to pay for it herself out of the money she earned doing housework for some of the neighbours.

As soon as she went home, she told Thomas to come over to us to try on the coat. The Shauls only lived a short distance away. Thomas came over after first polishing his shoes and changing his tie. All his movements and speech were slow and deliberate, not that he spoke much. When replying to questions he responded after much deliberation in monosyllabic words. He even had the ability to make the affirmative 'yes' appear to be a speech. When he walked, he did so at a funeral pace with his arms hanging limply at his sides. He tried the coat on in front of a full length mirror, which in his case, was 1 1/2 times full length (may I be forgiven for speaking disparagingly of those who are now dead but were not dead at the relevant time).

The coat fitted perfectly, it was as if it had been made specifically for him. Even Thomas appeared to agree. We told him not to take the coat off but to wear it returning home so that Mrs Shaul could see what a wonderful fit it was. We said that Mrs Shaul could pay us whenever it was convenient.

We ushered Thomas towards the front door and as he raised his arm to operate the front door latch which was just above his eye level, the sleeve naturally rolled back slightly revealing about 1 inch (25mm) of his shirt sleeve. Without much ado, he wheeled round and took the coat off saying in his inimical manner, that the sleeves were too short.

15

The Chamber Pot

It is ironical that the only souvenir we have of Thomas Smith is an old chamber pot that we now use as a plant holder. We have no photographs of him, just the rose decorated chamber pot. He owned the house next door to us which he let off as furnished flats.

We first became acquainted when we chatted over the garden fence. The conversations usually were about gardening and plants about which Thomas knew quite a lot as he used to a commercial horticulturist in his younger days. It was one of his several unsuccessful enterprises. All his life, he tried hard to make big money but did not succeed. The most successful of his enterprises was the purchase and renting of sub-standard rent controlled dwellings, which, because of their low or even negative returns could be bought cheaply. The house next door was one of such dwellings.

We chatted when he came each Monday to collect the rents. These chats developed into friendship and in due course we learnt a little of his interesting history.

He was born circa 1890 in rural Essex. His father was the local policeman but as Thomas was one of many children he felt neglected by his parents. Because of his father's low pay and many children he experienced great poverty as a child.

Even as a child he strove to make money. One of his jobs was to drive the local doctor's pony and trap when he was visiting patients. Unfortunately the doctor appeared to be absent minded and often forgot to pay Thomas his 6d wages (2½p) for his days labour.

As soon as he could, at the tender age of sixteen, he escaped from his impoverished surroundings by enrolling into the army cadet corps which opened up a whole new world to him. After two years in the cadet corps he enrolled as a private in the regular army in a cavalry regiment. He served during the 1914–18 war but fortunately he did not have to endure the trench warfare because he had become the personal chauffeur to a general.

One of the first things he did when he was demobbed after the war was to invest his demob gratuity in buying for a total of £150 three dilapidated cottages in a terrace in a street not far from the centre of the market town of Romford in Essex. The cottages had no front gardens. The front door opened straight off the pavement into the living room which in turn opened onto a rear kitchen extension. A rickety, steep staircase led up to two tiny bedrooms.

The cottages were sans all facilities, no electricity, no hot water, no bathroom but it did have an outside water closet at the rear. Other features were-rising damp, sliding sash windows which permitted a plentiful supply of fresh country air even when they were closed.

Thomas had speculated that with the return of millions of young men from the war there would be an enormous demand for houses and rents would shoot sky high. He therefore did not mind that at the time of purchase, the rents, exclusive of rates, were only five shillings a week (25p). What he did not foresee was that the rents in 1918 were to be frozen at that level by the government and then only increased by small amounts spread over several years as and from 1970.

As the years progressed, Thomas's hope of making a profit on the houses rested increasingly on the tenants leaving and then selling with vacant possession and no rent control. Unfortunately, the tenants had no desire to leave despite the lack of facilities. It-would have been impossible to rent a dog's kennel let alone a house for a few shillings a week. His next hope rested on the ageing tenants dying but the Spartan conditions seemed to prolong their lives.

One tenant lived to over 100 years, another to over 80 whilst the third who did die left the tenancy to her unmarried daughter who had lived with her. This was in accordance with the law. The daughter's name was Gertrude. We never got to know what her surname was.

Over the years, a strange peculiar relationship developed between Gertrude and Thomas. We doubt it had a sexual basis. In respect for the dead, we wont comment about what Thomas once confided to us, but it would only be honest to admit, that Gertrude presented a forbidding, gaunt appearance. She was a most devout Catholic, dressed entirely in black even though she was not a widow. As far as we knew she had never married. Conversation with her was very difficult.

One day, Thomas 'phoned to tell us that Gertrude had died from a heart attack in her sleep. He had a shock when he called on her to collect the rent and found her dead. How or why he had entered the house he did not explain.

17

A few weeks later he 'phoned again and asked if we would accompany him to Gertrude's house to clear her belongings out. After discovering her body, he was reluctant to go into the house on his own. He said that Gertrude had left a will in which she bequeathed all her wealth and possessions to her church. The solicitors had told him that the church representatives had taken all that they wanted and that Thomas could have the remainder in lieu of the accrued out-standing rent that was owing to him.

Thomas said that he was extremely angry that Gertrude had not honoured an agreement that they had made, that each would leave all their wealth to the other in the event of death.

We advised Thomas to revise his will as having Gertrude as his sole beneficiary may cause complications when probate was made. He said that it would not be necessary as he had never intended leaving her anything at all in his will.

It was hardly worthwhile clearing out the few pitiful items that the church had not taken. There were about ten long black dresses, five black hats with big brims, black shoes, well washed underwear, bedding, some well used pots and pans but all the ornaments crockery and cutlery were gone. Thomas put the items in a couple of black bin liners and was about to leave when he spotted the chamber pot under the bed. He said, "Sid, you collect old things, you can have the pot for a fiver'. The price was OK as the pot was obviously old but I was reluctant to handle it as it apparently been in good use because of the only WC being outside the house. However, in the circumstances, I stooped to retrieve it from under the iron bedstead with its sagging springs but as I lifted it a piece of linoleum, approximately 300×300mm was dislodged. We could then see that a similar size section of the floor board underneath could also be lifted. Thomas asked me to remove the floor board to see what was underneath. When we did so, we could see a tin box about 200×200×150mm high in the space between two timber floor joists. I handed the box to Thomas who excitedly opened it and we could then see a thick wad of the old fashioned white five pound notes, which are now worth at least twenty pounds each to collectors and dozens of gold sovereigns. Thomas quickly closed the tin and said, with a very mournful face and tears welling up in his eyes, "Please leave me alone so that I may, in solitude, reflect upon a good friend I have so tragically lost after many years of acquaintance. I will be in touch with you in the future and don't forget that you owe me five pounds for that lovely chamber pot".

In the subsequent meetings neither of us mentioned the tin box even when I paid Thomas the five pounds for the only souvenir we have of him.

The Fence

I am writing this episode despite a splitting headache. The cause of the headache started a short while ago when my dear wife says "Why are you stuck indoors on such a lovely day, why not repair the broken garden fence at the bottom of the garden?" I reminded her that it had been blown down during the big gale during the winter and that I was waiting for our neighbour to do something about it because, according to the deeds of the property, it was his responsibility to keep that particular fence in a good state of repair. Dora said that is very well but the fact remains that the wreckage of the fence is lying in our garden and that it is not only unsightly but there is also a loss of privacy and security. In turn, I reminded Dora that the remains of the fence happens to be lying in our garden because our good neighbour had transferred it there from his own garden one dark night when we were not at home.

Originally it had blown into his garden. Dora does not believe in strife between neighbours and decided to use her skills in diplomacy and her charms on our Asian neighbour to persuade him to honour his legal obligations to reinstate the fence. She said he appears to be a simple man and no doubt does not understand such matters.

After a lengthy but friendly conversation with our neighbour, Dora returned triumphantly and said that he was most considerate and appreciative of her explanation and was most willing to co-operate and to fulfil his neighbourly obligations. He said that as his brand new Mercedes was not appropriate for carting the old fence away he would be pleased if I were to kindly oblige by removing it especially so, having in mind that it was actually lying in my garden. Dora had gladly agreed on my behalf to such a reasonable request.

19

In the event, it cost me quite a bit to get a removal contractor to cart it away and to dump it. Dora had also agreed on my behalf that I would pay for the new fence posts and panels. She said that the neighbour had no idea at all what to buy or even where to buy it.

In return, the neighbour had generously agreed to pay a full half of the labour cost in erecting the fence.

I told Dora that her agreement did not sound very clever to me. She said "I knew you would not appreciate the clever part, the labour would cost us nothing if you were to do all the work yourself'.

Whilst I was struggling with the posts and the panels in a rather stiff breeze, our considerate neighbour sent one of his young sons out to help me. I said it would be very helpful if he would hit it with the hammer when I gave a signal by nodding my head. His father was most apologetic and said his son did not understand English very well. He said he would gladly have given me a bandage to bind my head wound if he had one in the house.

Christmas Day, 1968

My mind goes back to Christmas morning 1968. During the night there had been an exceptionally heavy snowfall. It lay deep and undisturbed, when at about 6am. there was frantic knocking on our front door. I realised at once that it could not be Father Christmas with a belated gift for us.

I hurriedly put on my pyjamas and dressing gown and went to open the door. It was a neighbour from across the road. She said that she thought that her husband was dead and as she did not have a telephone, would we please 'phone his doctor. His doctor said that as the snow was at least one metre deep and as the council had not yet made any effort to clear the roads, he would find it almost impossible to reach his patient without the assistance of the emergency services. He said he would make all efforts to arrive if the patient was still alive but it would be pointless, if, as suspected, he was already dead. Even Dora could not fault such logic and she volunteered that as I had been a first aider during the war, I would go and confirm if Ernie was dead or not. I had never before in my whole life been assigned such an honour and great responsibility.

I struggled through the deep snow and entered our neighbour's house. Ernie looked dead to me but that was not surprising as he looked dead even when he was alive. His eyes were open and he had his usual expressionless look on his face. He did not respond when I shouted his name and asked if he was alright. I touched his face which was cold but by then, so was mine. I could not hear any breathing. I tried to take his pulse but found access to his wrist difficult because he appeared to be wearing three pair of pyjama jackets each with longer sleeves than the other. I decided that he was probably dead and that it was not worthwhile calling on the emergency services on such a freezing cold Christmas morning.

21

My observations were relayed back to the doctor who promised to come round as soon as the roads were passable and to confirm my decision by issuing a death certificate so as to permit funeral arrangements to be made.

Because I had demonstrated such efficiency in declaring the death of my neighbour, the doctor asked me to lay out the body. I mentioned that this was something I had not done before but would be willing to try if he would kindly instruct me. He said I should close his (the dead person's) eyes and straighten his limbs. Fortunately, Ernie lay in bed stiff as to attention with his arms straight. I never did recover the two coins I used to keep his eyes closed.

A few days later, Ernie was cremated. His widow said that at a funeral of a friend, he had made an off-the-cuff remark that the cremation service was short and sincere.

I decided not to make any similar remarks at any future funerals I may attend.

Subsequently, when I recounted my experience to friends, I enquired what else I could have done to ensure that Ernie was actually dead and not just in a deep coma. One said I should have taken a dog into the room. If it howled, it would be a sign that the person was dead. He was not sure if such a service was available on the NHS (National Health Service).

Nicknames

When I was young, that is in the 1920's, my family lived in the east London borough of Stepney in a wedge of slum streets bounded by Whitechapel Road, Commercial Road and Jubilee Street. It was inhabited 99% by Jewish immigrants, mainly from eastern Europe. They were largely self sufficient with virtually no contact with the indigenous surrounding population.

They had their own shops, own doctors, own hospital, own cemeteries, own factories, own shoe repairers etc. They only spoke Yiddish and read their own Yiddish newspapers and books and it was not until I commenced infant school that I heard English being spoken.

The schools were run by the local authority as education was compulsory for all children and the state provided teachers were English speaking non Jewish un-married women, mainly spinsters, because married women in those days were not allowed to teach.

These strange looking women with their incomprehensible language and strict discipline were very formidable creatures in the eyes of the Jewish infants who were dragged by their mothers screaming (the children) to school.

In the evenings and on Sunday mornings, the children were sent to the homes of the learned religious men who would teach them the elements of the Hebrew language and to recite prayers in Hebrew by rote without understanding.

This dual culture and education confused me and for quite a while I spoke an incomprehensible mixture of Yiddish/English and Hebrew. Neither my parents nor my teachers could understand me.

When I was about five years old and still talking 'in tongues', my mother consulted a local rabbi fearing that she had given birth to an imbecile. He

23

assured her that there was nothing to worry about and that I may turn out to be normal eventually. I feel she was never sure, even when I was grown up.

It was quite common in this self enclosed Jewish community to identify others by *nicknames*, in Yiddish.

At birth, all Jews are given religious Hebrew names. Surnames were not used except for secular purposes. Sons were named after the name of a deceased close relative (never after any living relative), for example, Yakov ben Yitzhak (Jacob the son of Issac). This may eventually have been anglicised to Jack Jackson. Daughters were similarly named after deceased female relatives.

Despite this, the quaint use of Yiddish nicknames prevailed, many being uncomplimentary. One small sized woman was known as der fiertel tuches (the quarter arse), a man with the Hebrew name of Shmuel (Samuel) was called Shmiel (fool).

Women were often known by their husbands nick name, the name of Shmuel's wife would be Mrs Shmuel.

One notorious character was known as der Shicker (the drunkard) and another, very uncomplimentarily, as der Hauker (the hunchback). A simple minded person was nick-named, Kapusta (cabbage). Other names are not mentionable in polite society.

My father's nick-name was 'the Dardenelle'. He obtained this because of his war service in World War 1. He was born in a small river side village in Bielorussia, now known as Belorus and emigrated as a young unmarried man to Palestine which was then under Turkish rule.

When World War 1 commenced, he went to Egypt which was under British rule and volunteered for the British army in order to help drive the Turks out of the Holy Land. The British did not know what to do with the horde of foreign speaking Jews who were volunteering for the British army so they formed special corps commanded by British officers. My father was *enrolled* into one such corps known as the Zionist Mule Corps. The British generals found this corps useful in supplying the front line troops in the Dardanelles who were trying to relieve the German pressure on the demoralised Russian army in the South of Russia.

The campaign failed after sustaining heavy casualties and the troops withdrawn.

In the confusion of the withdrawal, my father found himself on a British warship bound for this country where he was eventually demobilised.

He was also Known as Henoch the Bukker (baker) but as I have always had impaired hearing, even as a child, I once told my teacher what I thought to be my father's name. The teacher, Miss Pearce, a righteous middle-aged spinster, severely punished me for pronouncing such irreverence.

I shan't say what my Yiddish nick-name was.

Junk

We bought our Victorian house where we now live 40 years ago.

The name of the vendor was Richard Dadd, he had lived in the house for many years and had inherited it from his father who bought it when it was built in 1904. He was married with a sweet young daughter but he was very neurotic.

For some reason or another, he seemed very eager to get away from the property. Along with the house, he sold us some old furniture and carpets which today could be considered as antiques. He said that the items were too large for his new modern house.

Some while after, when I went into the loft to lay thermal insulation, I found a lot of junk, including a dismantled piano, a circular table with a single but massive pedestal leg, a child's Victorian pram with one wheel missing, a Victorian curtain rail complete with wooden rings, some musty books, an old leather covered album with family photos and a peculiar oil painting depicting fairies in a garden, everything was painted in great detail. All the items were thickly covered in dust.

I 'phoned Mr Dadd and asked if he wanted any of the items; I had in mind particularly the photos which I presumed were of his family and may have been of sentimental value to him. He said he was not at all interested in the items, he had deliberately left them behind. He added, the painting had been done, so he had been told, by his grandfather's father who had suffered a mental breakdown and had painted it as therapy whilst in a mental institution. He would rather that his wife and daughter were not to know about it. In any case, he did not like the painting and would not hang it up even if he had room for it. He said I could keep all the junk including the family photos and the painting.

25

Dora took a dislike to the painting and insisted that I should get rid of it as the frame had wood worm holes. I took all the junk into the garden and burnt it.

Forty years later, I recalled the incident whilst watching a TV programme called 'The Antiques Roadshow' in which members of the public are invited to bring their antiques for experts to evaluate. These experts became very excited when a man brought in an oil painting which he says he found in his garden shed. It was entitled 'Halt in the Desert'. It depicted people around a desert camp fire, some were in European clothes whilst others were dressed as Arabs. The experts immediately identified the painting as being by a Richard Dadd and was painted by him during his middle east tour. They said he subsequent became violently insane and murdered his father.

He was incarcerated in a hospital for the criminally insane for the rest of his life. Whilst in the asylum he continued to paint and gave his paintings to any of his relatives who bothered to visit him. During this period of his life, his paintings were peculiarly detailed.

A short while after the programme, the painting was sold at auction for £1,350,000!

Maybe, on a bright moonlit night, I will steal quietly into our garden and see fairies dancing over our poor little cat's grave where I scattered the fire ashes.

Tina

When I married Dora, she brought with her as part of her dowry a small, obnoxious, smelly Yorkshire terrier whose name was Tina. She looked like a dirty dark grey floor mop sans handle with glimpses of black beady eyes. At first it was difficult to tell which part of the mop was the front end until she started to yap which she did very frequently. The other end frequently emitted most obnoxious silent smells.

Anything was a good enough excuse to start her yapping and once she started nothing could stop her.

One of her objectionable habits was to roll herself in anything smelly and then to yap in sheer delight. Cow dung, horse manure, other dogs messes were all a heavenly joy for her to roll in.

One day having taken her on a visit to Hyde Park, we returned in the evening on the number 25 bus. The journey from Hyde Park to Beacontree Heath where we then lived is a long and tedious one but we used it as it was convenient, involving no changes and was the cheapest form of transport.

The route is uninteresting and the tedium is increased by the fact that even though it was a Saturday evening and there was virtually no traffic the bus followed the week day rush hour schedule which allowed for traffic jams and a crawling pace.

London Transport Board regulations required passengers who wished to smoke and/or those with dogs to use the upper deck of two storey buses. Thus, even though both Dora and I are non-smokers, we had to take Tina with us to the upper deck and endure other peoples tobacco fumes. It was a warm and humid evening and despite several of the windows being open we found the atmosphere most irritating.

27

Tina

At Stratford Broadway, east London the usual crowd of losers from the Clapton dog track meeting clambered onto the bus. One of them, a large muscular unshaven man sat down on the vacant adjacent seat and immediately lit up a foul smelling pipe. This was a good enough signal to Tina to start yapping furiously. The man continued to puff out smoke and Tina continued to yap. After about ten minutes the man quietly asked, "Can't you stop that bloody thing from yapping?" I told him that we could not stop her yapping as she was not used to seeing people smoking and that, in her way, she was trying to tell you that you were on fire. He smiled sardonically and replied, "Well if you can't stop her yapping I certainly can". With that he grabbed little Tina and in a flash threw her out of the moving bus window.

I was absolutely astounded and he sat there with a self satisfied look on his face. Other passengers who had seen what had happened rang the emergency bell and the bus stopped. I was aware of the raised hubbub in the bus and slowly I also became aware of Dora shaking my shoulder and saying "Wake up, we're at the terminus and if we don't get off soon the bus will take us to the depot".

I awoke and found most of the passengers had already left the bus but the pipe smoker was fondly stroking Tina's head and she obviously loved the attention she was receiving.

An Early Morning Encounter

Very early each morning, providing it is not raining, I take a 30 minute stroll around the local streets which are very quiet, most people are still asleep and there is very little traffic, if any, around. While I perform this constitutional, my wife is preparing breakfast.

My route usually takes me past the wrought iron gate to a local park. We have several excellent parks in the borough but this particular one is the smallest of them all but it leads directly onto and into the fringe of Epping Forest.

Apart from a wide variety of mature trees, this part of the forest contains three large lakes, several glades, grazing cattle, much wildlife and a fast flowing river. Dogs just simply love being taken for walks there.

As the gates are opened at 6am several local people take their dogs for a run in the park before going to work.

As I was passing the park gate one dark and very misty morning I was not unduly surprised to see an elderly lady emerging from the park but I was most surprised to see that instead of having her dog on a lead she was carrying it. It was a large dog and must have been very heavy especially for such a small elderly, frail lady. My first gallant instinctive reaction was to offer to help her as I assumed the dog may have been injured and could not walk. The swirling mist made it difficult to see clearly and I was still some distance away. As I got nearer I started having second thoughts. If the dog is injured and in a distressed state it may bite a stranger who suddenly appears out of the mist and starts holding him. I also started to remember my lumbago and arthritic knees, would I be able to carry such a large and heavy dog even if it permitted me to?

Before I could get within talking distance, I noticed that the woman had put her burden down and it stood absolutely still without moving a muscle. It did not even glance up at its owner nor at me as by this time I was quite close. Just as I was going to ask the woman if 1 could be of any help, I could see that the dog was actually standing on a wooden trolley with small pram wheels. I did not have the opportunity to say anything because the lady started to walk away from me pulling the trolley but not till after she spoke to the dog "There dear, did you enjoy your walk today?" She and the dog disappeared like ghosts into the swirling mist. The dog was still standing stock still.

A House In Islington

The client was quite excited when he 'phoned. After much searching he had found the house of his dreams. It was a three storey Georgian house in a street in Islington that was beginning to be gentrified. It was going at a reasonable price freehold. He said that he had set his heart on it and would buy it what may. It overlooked a lovely square and had a sunny aspect. I said that it seems a bit pointless for me to do a structural survey if he was going to buy it in any case. He replied that even though the price was reasonable he thought he could get a good discount if a survey pointed out defects.

After surveying the property but before writing the report I 'phoned the client to inform him that I found very little wrong with the property. I agreed that it would make a very pleasant residence and wished that I could buy a similar property for myself. However he insisted that I write the report but to make it appear as bad as possible. I told him that as a professional surveyor I could not write any report that contained false information. Eventually my written report was sent to the client and I enclosed my account.

A couple of days later, a very irate client 'phoned to ask why I had written such a rotten report about the property he so desired to buy. I reminded him about his instructions. He said true, but he did not expect such a bad sounding report. His wife had read it and was disgusted that he should even think that she would live in such a horrible hovel. Finally he added, "Don't expect me to pay for such a useless misleading report!"

The Lawyer

I don't like going to parties for several reasons. I don't like dressing up and wearing a tie. Being a non smoker I find the tobacco fumes encountered at most parties very, irritating.

Because of a hearing defect I cannot comprehend what people are saying if there is a hubbub in the room. I also have a low resistance to the effects of alcohol and after just one or two drinks, all I want is to go to sleep. In addition, parties go on till much later than my usual bedtime and I am not used to eating late meals.

In summation, parties are a torture to me and make me most miserable. I avoid going to them as much as I can but there are a few that I cannot avoid.

One of my valued clients insisted on me attending a party he was giving. He was, and still is, a very rich and influential person. He was inviting other rich and influential people as well as the professionals he associated with in his business. He told me that it would be a good opportunity for me to get to know potential clients and to discuss problems with other professionals such as bank managers, financial investment advisers, insurance brokers, lawyers, solicitors, debt collectors, structural engineers, quantity surveyors, project managers, computer experts, town planners, town clerks, antique experts etc. He wanted me to be there as his architect. I could not refuse.

At the well organised party in the client's town centre pent house flat, each guest was given a badge bearing his name and indicating their profession. The host encouraged everyone to circulate and converse. It was certainly an animated party. People were circulating, people were conversing, people were exchanging business cards. I never got round to speaking to any of the property tycoons and they in turn, unfortunately never got round to speaking to me. I had a few enquiries about how to combat rising damp, ineffective WC cistern, blocked drain, condensation, peeling paintwork, neighbours intrusive extension, weeds in the pathways, double glazing etc. but no new commissions. All I really yearned for was some fresh air and peace and quiet.

Amidst all the hubbub I noticed a man quietly resting in a comfortable armchair and no one was approaching him. Being intrigued, I introduced myself and noticed that his badge described him as a lawyer, I told him just how wearisome I found the party to be and asked why it was that no one appeared to be interested enough to ask him legal questions. He said, "Do you really want to know the reason?" I replied affirmatively. He said "It's quite simple. All the people here know that if they ask me questions that I will charge for the advice I give".

Within a week I received a fee account from him for advice given at a party on a certain date at a certain address.

A Day At The Races

What a day? A day I will never forget and Dora will make sure that I don't.

Several years ago, Dora received an invitation from her friend Hilda to visit her in the small village of Isleham in Cambridgeshire.

Hilda had been evacuated there as a child on the outbreak of the war in 1939 and had made friends with several of the village girls with whom she had continued to keep in contact. When her husband died, she decided to retire to the peace and quiet of Isleham. The village had one church and three chapels but twice as many pubs. These 'pubs' were actually peoples own front rooms licensed to sell alcoholic beverages. There was no cinema or other place of public entertainment. Hilda wanted Dora to visit her in order to keep up-to-date with events and gossip.

Whilst I was needed to drive Dora there, I was not actually welcome to sit in on the gossip. The two women therefore decided that I should visit the nearby Newmarket races. A local bus gathered people from the local villages and took them to the races and then home again. I protested in vain even when I claimed not to have any money to bet on the horses and that in any case I knew nothing about horse racing or betting. Dora said that she knew I did have money on me but I said I was keeping that in reserve in case I needed to buy petrol on the return journey. She said, "Lend me ten pounds and I will give it to you for you to spend on the races". She then added, "You've got nothing to lose because it is now my money you will be gambling with. If you win, we will go fifty-fifty on the profits".

My next problem was, which horse to bet on? I had no idea of form. I examined the bookies boards and noticed that one horse was called Flatcap. It so happened that I had donned a tweed flat cap for my visit to the country. It was an outsider at 20–1 but I put the whole of the ten pounds on it to win. To my absolute delight and to everybody else's surprise it came in first. I now had £200 and should have quit there and then but the gambler's bug had got me. I could not resist betting in the next race on a horse called Trilby. I usually wore a dark coloured trilby when attending weddings and funerals. At 5–1, I won the incredible sum of £1000. £500 for me and £500 for Dora! I could just visualise the delight on her face. I searched the names of the next race for any horse with a name associated with head gear but to no avail. I was then inspired when I spotted the name of a horse with the name of Overcoat. I said to myself hats and coats go together. This was surely a sign that it was the horse I should bet on.

I realise now what a fool I was to place the whole of my £1000 on the horse but at 5–1, it was a cert to win. I got nothing.

When I told Dora, she was furious. She would not listen to reason when I reminded her that all I had really lost was the initial ten pounds which she reminded me that I still owed her.

She asked what horse had actually won the race. I told her that it was a hopeless outsider at 15–1 by the name of Yarmulka. Dora nearly exploded. She screamed, "You idiot, don't you know that Yarmulka is the Yiddish word for skull cap?"

The Sabbath Day

My father was an observant Jew but not extremely so. Never in his life did he profane the Sabbath day except on one occasion. This was in September 1940 when the Germans were intensively bombing London particularly the east end where we lived.

Due to an emergency caused by bomb damage at the Jewish bakery where he worked, he was obliged to work over Friday night into Saturday morning, the Sabbath day.

I was 16 years old at the time and working for John Lewis Partnership in Oxford Street. It was quite normal in those days to work a six day week and it was considered very liberal of John Lewis to allow its employees to work only up to 1.00pm on Saturdays.

On the relevant Saturday morning I went to work as usual. On my return journey home, I bought the mid-day edition of the Evening Standard. The front page news was of a day-light bombing raid by a single German bomber which dropped its load of five bombs on east London homes near a disused fire station. I became very apprehensive as our home was near a disused fire station. The journey home seemed to last forever. As soon as I turned the corner into Jewel Street I could see the devastation. Our house, number 13 was completely demolished and the two adjoining houses in the street were badly damaged. As I approached, I could see rescue workers frantically digging into the rubble. Neighbours had told them that my father who worked night shifts and never worked on a Saturday must be buried somewhere in the rubble.

I rushed round to the bakery where my father worked and was relieved to confirm that he was still alive. By comparison, the loss of our humble home was secondary. The rest of our family had previously been evacuat-

36

ed to the country. Our next immediate concern was for our pets. Our wire-haired terrier dog was unharmed, no doubt, due to previous experience, he went into the Anderson air raid shelter at the bottom of the garden as soon as he heard the air-raid warning siren. He was most intelligent. Possibly the cat had followed him there as she was also unharmed.

We tied a luggage label onto the dog's collar, addressed to our family in Isleham in Cambridgeshire where they had been evacuated. We then took him to Liverpool Street station where the guard on the next train kindly agreed to see that he got off at the correct station. We 'phoned the sole policeman in Isleham who informed our family who were not on the 'phone about the bombing and the pending arrival of the dog.

We realised that virtually nothing could be salvaged from the pile of rubble that had been our home. Even had we salvaged anything, we had nowhere to keep it. All we owned were the working clothes that we stood up in.

We obtained shelter for the next two weeks in a local school whose pupils had been evacuated. We slept on the floor of the assembly hail which was crowded with other homeless people. There was no privacy at all. Breakfast of hot porridge and a mug of strong sweet tea was provided by the Women's' Voluntary Service.

Whilst we searched for alternative housing, I returned each evening after work to feed our cat who had taken up residence in the air-raid shelter. Soon her feeding time was shared by several other ravenously hungry bombed out homeless cats.

One evening, when I turned up with scraps of food, there were no cats.

Three Bibles

In the 1960's, despite 30 years of religious suppression, derision and persecution in the Soviet Union, a resurgence in Jewish religion and interest arose. This led to an expression of a desire to emigrate to Israel. Such emigration was actually in accordance with Soviet law and was in compliance with United Nations declarations relating to family re-union to which the Soviet Union had ascribed its name.

Never-the-less, such applications for citizens to emigrate from the 'Soviet Paradise' alarmed the authorities who had always denied that any of their 'contented' citizens would ever wish to leave.

The authorities decided to discourage such 'aberrations' by accusing the applicants of having committed serious crimes and inflicting severe punishments.

In June 1970, the authorities accused twelve such applicants of plotting to seize a twelve seater civilian aeroplane in Leningrad and to flee in it to Sweden.

In a trial held in secret they were found guilty, as all accused in the Soviet Union were in those days, and sentenced to long terms in 'strict regime' labour camps but two were sentenced to death.

These deterrent sentences were broadcast on Christmas Day 1970. The Soviet authorities, no doubt, had calculated that the western world would be engrossed in celebrations and would not notice, whilst 'the message' would be received by Soviet citizens who don't celebrate Christmas on 25th of December.

Unfortunately for the Soviet authorities, their plan back-fired on them. Even though newspapers had not been published on Christmas Day, the TV news was very active. Because there was little else to report, they gave repeated prominence to the impromptu protests that took place in the swirling snow outside the Soviet embassy in London.

Thus began an ever increasing protest and action movement, worldwide in which my wife and myself participated. Each individual and each group carried out their protests in the way they felt most appropriate. Some concentrated on writing individual letters to officials and politicians; to those who became known as prisoners of conscience and also to those who had applied for emigration but whose applications had been refused and were known as Refuseniks. There were also mass meetings held in large city centres. The situation became well known and still persists even though it has eased somewhat with the abolition of the Soviet regime.

All the accused in what became known as the 'First Leningrad trial' served their lull term of about eleven years in most dreadful prison camp conditions.

Under the Soviet regime there were no remissions for good behaviour, only extensions for bad or uncooperative' behaviour.

As the result of the protests in the 'West', the death sentences were commuted to long prison terms. Among those sentenced were two non Jews, Yury Federov and Aleksi Murzhenko who were close and true friends of their co-condemned and also a Jew, Yosif Mendelvich. They were finally released in 1981.

When their incarceration began, my wife and I decided that it may give them moral encouragement if they were made aware that many people in the West knew of their situation and were trying to help.

In those days, censorship in the Soviet Union was very strict. A few innocuous personal letters might be allowed through but it was impossible to send any printed matter however harmless. As the three prisoners were religious, we decide to send each one a copy of the bible containing both the Old and the New Testaments printed in Russian. We knew that in the ordinary course of events, such bibles did not stand a snowball's chance in hell of reaching Soviet citizens let alone prisoners in a strict regime labour camp. We thought that if the bibles were signed by important people and sent through official channels they may get through.

We were fortunate in obtaining three suitable bibles and then we commenced obtaining appropriate signatures.

Among those signing were the then Chief Rabbi of Great Britain and the Commonwealth; the Archbishop of Canterbury, Cardinal Hume; the President of the British Methodist Church; the two local MP's; the Local European Parliament Member; various local councillors including the leader of the Council; the Chairman of the Council of Christians and Jews; local church dignitaries and others. However, there was yet another church dignitary whose signature we wanted and that was the President of the

Baptist Union. Unfortunately for us he operated from Bristol. He said that he would be glad to sign and suggested that we meet him when he will attend an ecumenical evening service in the Westminster Cathedral in a few weeks time. He said that anybody who was anybody in the church would be there and we would be able to get several signatures in one go.

The appointed day was freezing cold and the pavements and roads were covered in slippery slushy ice. Before starting out on our journey across London by public transport, we both dressed up warmly in woollies and then donned khaki coloured voluminous quilted coats. Dora wore well worn fur lined suede boots and I put on a recently purchased pair of brown Dr Martin boots with thick soles so as not to slip on the ice.

We arrived before the agreed time and expected to be introduced to Dr West, the President of the Baptist Union.

To our dismay we found that this was not possible for quite a while because the ecumenical service in which he was participating had already commenced.

A sidesman, dressed in a medieval pages costume advised us to wait until the service was over and to follow the participating clergy into the vestry where they will change out of their vestments.

We patiently and respectfully waited in a pew at the rear of the vast cathedral. Even though several hundred people were in the congregation, the cathedral was only partially filled. Possibly, the horrible weather had kept many more away,

In nearby pews, there were about 20 Wino's and like us muffled up against the cold. Occasionally, one or another would delve into a plastic shopping bag and take a deep swig from an unlabelled bottle. They were obviously enjoying their spiritual intake. Instead of Amens an occasional snore or quiet belch could be heard from among their ranks. From our attire, they seemed to have accepted us as fellow beings.

As soon as we perceived that the service had ended, we rushed down the aisle towards the front of the cathedral where the participating clergy had formed themselves into a procession. At the head was the Cardinal, then the Archbishops, then the heads of denominations followed by minor clergy interposed by a full choir and men swinging censers all dressed in full ceremonial robes and insignias.

Whilst they were solemnly walking in grand procession a mighty organ played a triumphant tune and all the congregation were smiling and shaking hands with one another as tokens of fellowship and friendship.

We duly complied with the sideman's suggestion and followed immediately behind the procession.

No doubt, we must have looked out of place dressed as we were. I forgot that I was still wearing a woollen bobble hat in West Ham colours. In one hand I was carrying a Tesco plastic-shopping bag bulging with the three large bibles.

As I had never worn Dr Martin boots before, I was unaccustomed to their springiness. This together with their newness and my arthritic knees caused me to stagger from side-to-side however much I tried not to.

Having followed the clergy into their changing rooms, we were made most welcome and duly obtained Dr West's signature and those of several others.

Strangely, none objected to Dora being present whilst they were changing clothes!

Despite our efforts, we could not find a means of surely getting the bibles to the prisoners. We had to wait till they were released and emigrated before we were able to let them have the bibles.

Charity

Our street which is in a suburb to the east of London is very interesting because it contains such a mixture of races and religions. There are Muslims, Hindus, Sikhs, Parsees, Buddhists, Uhais, Christians and Jews. They are of various income groups, professionals, shop keepers, unemployed, unskilled, inventors, retired and entrepreneurs of varying success. There are others which I have not listed.

It was therefore not surprising when recently two elderly Asian lathes, dressed in beautiful Saris, each with a large pimple on the centre of their foreheads which I understand indicates they are of a 'high caste', rang our doorbell.

Because my deaf aid was not working properly, I could not understand what they were saying. As we get on well with all our neighbours whatever religion, race or income group I asked Dora to help. She ascertained that the local Hindu people wanted to build a Temple in which to worship and they were asking for donations towards the building fund. Dora said it was a most worthwhile cause and in the spirit of inter-racial harmony she would be pleased to make a generous donation. The women beamed on hearing such a declaration. Dora explained that as Jews, we in turn would welcome donations from other religions for the urgently needed repairs to the local synagogue. She asked the ladies to set such an example which she would gladly match to their fund. Thereupon, one of them handed Dora a five pound note. Dora turned to me and asked if I had ten pounds on me. I handed her the requisite note and upon seeing this the ladies faces lit up. Dora benignly placed the five pound note into the collection box proffered by the women.

Needless to say I never got my ten pounds back.

The Samovar

I used to correspond with someone who lived in Kiev in the Ukraine which until recently formed part of the Soviet Union. I used to write in English and my pen pal got someone he knew to translate into Russian.

The Russian language was widely used in the Ukraine. For my convenience, my correspondent got his acquaintance to write to me in English.

One day, there was a ring on my front door and when I opened it there was a black man smiling at me. He said, "You do not know me but I am the person who translates your letters to so and so in Kiev". He went on to explain, that by nationality he was Nigerian but for many years he lived in Poplar in east London. He spoke perfect English with a slight cockney accent. For some reason or another, the Nigerian government decided that he should study engineering in the Kiev University. They paid his educational fees and gave him a generous grant.

He said that my pen pal would like to send me a gift but had no idea what I would like. I told him that the only thing I would like from Kiev would be a genuine antique Samovar, but I would certainly not want my correspondent to pay for it. My visitor said that he was friendly with an old woman who lived in a remote village and that she had a very old family heirloom. As she had no one to pass it onto he felt sure that she would be glad to sell it. He said that she would be over the moon if she was given fifty pounds sterling. That would be an undreamed of fortune for her. He said that if she agreed, which he was sure she would, he would bring it with him when he next came to visit his family who still live in east London.

A couple of months later, he came again, without any prior warning as on his first visit, but this time he brought his Ukrainian born wife with him.

43

She was as fair as he was black but she spoke no English.

He had brought a fair sized cardboard box with him with Russian wording on it and after we had tea and exchanged pleasantries he extracted a lovely brass Russian style Samovar which he held up for me and my wife to admire.

Soon alter, he got up and said that he had to dash to keep an appointment. I handed him fifty pounds in cash for which he profusely thanked me on behalf of the old village woman.

I was very pleased with the purchase. I would have expected to pay at least £100 in a London antique shop for such a fine Samovar.

After our guests left, I took the Samovar out of its box and was amazed to see a two pin electric plug at its base and inside an electric coil similar to that in electric kettles. Also on the metal base were Russian wording which translated read 'Made in the USSR'. The USSR did not come into existence till 1920. When the Russian wording on the box was translated, it just simply read, 'Electric Samovar'.

Nips

I don't know how our family's wire haired terrier got his peculiar name but I do know that we acquired him from a young man who had received his army call-up papers and had no one else to care for his pet. Maybe it was Nips previous owner who named him so.

Nips was most intelligent and affectionate. He amused the family and visitors by mimicking words but unlike some birds who mimic words, he associated the sounds with actions. He knew that if he said 'hallo', he would be rewarded with a pat and praise. If he said, 'I want one', he would be rewarded with a biscuit. Eventually, he had quite a vocabulary and associated them all with the expected reaction. With a bit of prompting, he would even sing 'God save the King'.

During the German blitz on London, he quickly associated the sound of the air raid warning with a hasty exodus of the family into the Anderson air raid shelter situated at the bottom of the garden. With his keen hearing, he was able to hear the warning in an adjacent district several minutes before we could hear the local siren. This was eventually to save his life, but that it another story. As soon as we saw Nips rushing to the air raid shelter we followed him.

The air raid shelter was a very crude affair. It consisted of curved galvanised iron sheets covering a dug-out about 750 mm deep below ground level. The excavated soil was piled on top as extra 'protection'. It was damp and in the winter, it was cold and there was only room for a maximum of six adults sitting hunched up under the curved corrugated sheets. However, it gave shelter from shards of flying glass and falling plaster if we had remained in the house during air raids. Nips must have felt a sense of assurance being with the family during the air raids with all the noise of bursting bombs and anti-aircraft guns and also the acrid smell of burning buildings. No doubt, he was just as apprehensive and tensed up as we were. We would sit up in the shelter until we heard the all-clear siren. There was no room to lie down and only fitful sleep was possible. When the bombs fell very close my father would utter a quiet prayer in Hebrew, usually, the Shemab, which sounds like 'Shemah Yisroel, Adenoi Elohanu, Adenoi Echad'. Translated, means, 'Hear oh Israel, the Lord our God, the Lord is One'.

During 'bombers' weather' the raids would continue all night up to day-break, every night for weeks on end. In some raids, the Germans used up to 1000 bombers at a time. It was a period when the ordinary citizens of London earned the praise of people all over the world for their stoic heroism.

One night, there was a particularly heavy air raid concentrating on the London docks which were about two miles from our house. It was amazing how inaccurate their bombing was because relatively few of the bombs actually fell in the dock area. Most of the bombs fell in the surrounding residential areas, including ours.

The Germans did however succeed, possibly just to set fire to a large timber yard about a quarter of a mile from our house. Once the German bombers saw this enormous blaze they concentrated their bombs at and around the fire in order to create a fire storm. Many of their bombs fell close to our house and each time one did, our dug-out shelter trembled. After a while, my father gave up saying his prayers because the more he said them, the closer the bombs appeared to fall. We just crouched there waiting for daybreak and the end of the raid.

After an intense of bombing and anti-aircraft fire I heard an intense 'Shemah' being said with such pathos that it penetrated the snooze I had fallen into. As if by response, the bombing stopped and soon after the all-clear siren sounded.

Nips was the first out of the shelter. When we emerged, we noticed that all our windows had been blown out, most of the roofing slates had been blown off but the house was still standing. Debris was everywhere and because it was fairly dark it appeared that the whole of London was ablaze around us.

We then noticed, just a few yards away from our air raid shelter the fin of an unexploded bomb protruding from the ground.

My father said to me, no doubt your 'Shemah' saved our lives. I replied, "It was not me, I thought it was you".

Sde-Boker

In the summer of 1970, my wife and I were on holiday, staying in a friends flat in Tel-Aviv. One day she said to us, tomorrow is BenGurion's birthday but for security reasons they are not publicising the fact that a big birthday party is being held for him in the Kibbutz at Sde-Boker which he helped to establish and to which he retired. His wife, Paula is buried there. She suggested that we should go and told us which bus to catch to get there direct.

So bright and early, very early, we caught the bus and alighted at the Kibbutz Sde-Boker (Sde-Boker is Hebrew for morning field).

At the Kibbutz we were informed that we should have stayed on the bus as the birthday celebrations were actually being held at a desert site about two miles away. We were also informed that there would not be another bus going that way for another three hours. We were advised to "make a tramp" which is the Israeli wording for 'get a lift'.

As we waited at the side of the road a couple of army vehicles passed but did not stop, presumably they are forbidden to give lifts to civilians although it is not forbidden for military personnel to accept lifts in civilian vehicles.

Eventually, a small dusty car pulled up and asked where we wanted to go. We explained our dilemma. The driver told us that we were lucky that it was he who stopped to give us a lift because security at the celebration site would be very tight and without a special pass we would not be admitted. However, he explained that he was a life long friend of David Ben-Gurion and that his wife had been friends with Paula Ben-Gurion since school days. They knew all the influential people who would be there and would try to get us admitted. After travelling a short while through the

47

desert the driver stopped the car so that we could admire a particular geographical feature. Being a keen amateur photographer, I got out of the car to photograph the feature. When I returned, the driver questioned me about my hobby and I showed him the various photographic apparatus I carried in my very large ex army shoulder bag. I showed him two spare cameras, interchangeable lenses, light meter, collapsible tripod, packs of various films and the bottle of water I carried in case of emergency.

As soon as the couple saw the contents of my bag there was a sudden change in their attitude. They became much more relaxed and talkative. Whereas previously they only spoke in Hebrew between themselves they now spoke only English.

They explained that when they first picked us up they had suspicions that we may be terrorists or saboteurs and that the heavy bag I was carrying may have contained arms or explosives. They had determined to hand us over to the first military or police unit they came across and that originally they had no real intention in getting us into the celebrations. We further allayed their apprehension by showing them the contents of Dora's shoulder bag which consisted of warm woollies against the cold desert night temperature.

When we arrived at the celebration site the elderly couple did indeed seem to know everybody. After they conversed with a group of armed men at the entrance and glances in our direction, we were welcomed to enter and to enjoy ourselves.

There were performances of biblical songs and dances by the Kibbutz children. Quartet concert by Kibbutz members and other entertainment including recital of poems in praise of David Ben-Gurion and his late wife Paula. There was also a spectacular fly past by the Israeli Air Force. After a while, we realised that we appeared to be the only nonIsraelis present

My camera soon became very busy as we recognised famous Israeli personalities present. The whole of the Israeli cabinet and members of the Knesset (Parliament) were there as well as top Generals. We recognised their faces from photos in the newspapers and on TV.

As I seemed to be the only photographer present, they all willingly posed to be photographed.

Suddenly, out of the blue, an army helicopter appeared and landed a short distance away. Out of it stepped General Moishe Dayan, the hero of the six day war, smiling broadly and walking directly towards me. He obviously did not want to miss a photo opportunity. My camera was clicking away madly and I became concerned that I may run, out of film. Fortunately, I did not.

Food and non-alcoholic drink was abundant, served by pretty Kibbutznik girls.

There was a wonderful festive atmosphere. Actually, it was festival time, apart from it being Ben-Gurion's birthday, it was also the festival of Chanucha (tabernacles). Jews all over the world erect temporary structures and partake of meals therein to commemorate the 40 years during which the Hebrews wandered in the Sinai desert before being allowed by God to enter the Holy Land after being led out of bondage in Egypt by Moses (Moishe in Hebrew).

The Kibbutzim (Kibbutz members) erected an enormous Sukkah (tabernacle) on the celebration site wonderfully and colourfully decorated with fruit and other produce of the Kibbutz.

As evening fell, we made enquiry as to our return to Tel-Aviv. We were told that the last bus would be leaving in a few minutes but if we wished, we were welcome to stay as the celebrations would go on all night and that we could catch the first bus in the morning. We preferred to depart immediately and boarded the bus.

In Israel, it is normal to pay the fare to the driver on entering the bus. We asked what the fare was but the driver gave some incomprehensible reply in Hebrew and pointed to the last two remaining vacant seats. We gratefully settled down in self satisfaction but absolutely fatigued. We looked out of the window and there, not far away, was the man in a pink sports shirt and a gun in his holster who had never been far away from us during the whole day We tried to chat to him a few times but even though he was polite he made out that he only knew a little English.

Just as the bus was about to draw away, an elderly couple boarded the bus and after a brief conversation with the bus driver who pointed to where we were sitting they explained to us that all the seats were reserved for VIP's and that the seats we occupied were reserved for them. They told us that they understood the situation but we were welcome to stay on the bus. We completed the tedious sleepy journey sitting on the bus floor whilst the bus resounded with the contented snores of the VIP's including those of the couple whose seats we had temporarily occupied.

Mr And Mrs Katz

Although I only heard them addressed as or referred to as Mr and/or Mrs Katz they did have forenames. I can't say Christian names because they were both Jewish. His name was Louis, an Anglicised form of Liebel which is Yiddish for a 'small lion' although, but unlikely, it could also mean 'waist' or 'jacket'. Her forename was Sarah or Sara, which is Hebrew for 'princess'.

He was a tailor by trade, tall, handsome and very friendly, always well dressed. She was exceedingly short, tubby and I never saw her when she was not wearing a full wrap round floral decorated overall with the string bands done up in a bow in front of her round stomach.

They had one child only, a daughter, Celia (Latin for 'Heavenly). They absolutely doted on her.

Most tragically they were all to meet untimely deaths. They lived in a tiny terraced house behind the Royal London Hospital which is situated in Whitechapel Road, Stepney, east London. Until about 1935, the street in which their house was situated was named Oxford Street and from time-to-time, they received mail that was intended for an internationally famous shop in London's famous shopping street also called Oxford Street. In order to avoid such confusion, the street in which the Katz's lived was re-named Stepney Way.

Their house was exceedingly small. The street door opened direct off the pavement into a narrow passageway that led to the rear room which was used as a kitchen/dining/living room. In the corner was a vintage gas cooker. In front of the window was a small pine table. There was a built-in cupboard in the fireplace alcove. The fireplace itself was not used because the incidental heat from the gas cooker was sufficient to keep the tiny room

50

exceedingly warm. The seating provision consisted of 4 rickety dining chairs.

The concrete floor had a decided slope down to the rear wall which apart from a vertical sliding sash window, contained a door which in turn, led onto a concreted small yard. In one corner of the yard was an old chipped and cracked ochre coloured ceramic kitchen sink with a single cold water tap. There was no room for the sink in the kitchen itself. In the further corner was the premises sole water closet. To reach the closet one had to walk through a flock of chickens and if the WC door had not been properly shut, one had to shush the chickens out of the closet itself before it could be used for normal function. The chickens were kept to supplement the meagre war time rations.

Apart from the aforementioned, the ground storey contained one other room. This was the front room, or as most popularly called, 'the parlour'. This room was not used but kept as a memorial to their dead daughter. It was the room in which Celia had entertained her friends including her boy friend to whom she was eventually to become engaged.

A narrow, steep, rickety staircase led up to the first floor storey which consisted only of two tiny bedrooms. One was that used by Celia but kept intact also as a memorial and the other was the Katz's matrimonial bedroom which was so small that is could only contain a double bed, a dining chair and a wardrobe with a mirror on its door. There was no bathroom or internal WC.

During the German blitz in 1940 on the East End of London, the Katz's along with Celia and her fiancee sought shelter each night in London's deepest tube station known as the 'Bank because it was situated close to the Bank of England's city offices. It was considered to be the safest air raid shelter in London and hundreds of families flocked there each night.

One evening, whilst Mr and Mrs Katz prepared the blankets on the concrete railway platform for the night's sleep. Celia and her fiancee wandered off to the ticket concourse where the youngsters met. Unfortunately, by a million to one chance, one of the German bombs fell down a ventilation shaft and exploded in the ticket concourse causing many casualties, mainly youngsters. It took Mr and Mrs Katz a few moments to reach the concourse but Celia was already dead. For some peculiar reason, her fiancee who was very close to her in the crowded concourse was virtually unharmed although very dazed and shocked. In the short while it took for Celia's parents to reach her, someone had removed her wrist watch and much treasured engagement ring. The Katz were devastated but this did not stop them from having their constant rows which arose out of the most trivial matters. Mr Katz was a bit of a hypochondriac but did not always like or agree with what was prescribed for his complaints. Once we visited him when he was an in-patient at one hospital but unknown to the medical staff there, he was taking the medicine prescribed for a different condition at another hospital. His wife smuggled the wanted medication in and secretly took away the unwanted.

The cupboard in his kitchen /dining room was crammed tight from floor to ceiling with medications prescribed by various doctors and hospitals but not consumed.

One day when his wife went to collect his prescription from the local pharmacist, she was knocked down by a reversing truck whose driver said he did not see her because she was so small.

Despite their lives of constant quarrelling and bickering, Mr Katz was heartbroken at her death and died soon after.

As far as I know, there were no other relatives in this country but I heard them speak of distant relatives living in Paris.

Mr Katz and my father were born in the same village in Belorus by the name of Wielien on the river Notec 16 3 1'–53 about 50 miles north of Poznan. They grew up together and when they were about 18 years old, they both emigrated to avoid the pogroms and to seek new lives. Mr Katz came direct to London and settled in the tiny house in 'Oxford Street' whilst my father went as a pioneer to Palestine. During the first world war he left Palestine and *enrolled* in the British Army and took part in the Dardanelles campaign and was brought to this country where he was subsequently demobbed.

It was by sheer chance, after many years, that he met up again with Mr Katz in Stepney, east London.

The Vase

It all happened like a dream. I was browsing round a local bric-a-brac shop when I spotted a ceramic vase that looked interesting. It was about 250mm high and about 120mm diameter. It was ochre coloured with Chinese looking figures on it. It also had Chinese looking writing on the base. To me it was nice but not extraordinary. I assumed it was Chinese but it may even have been Japanese or Korean, I would not know the difference. For its size, it was fairly heavy but not unduly so. Upon asking the price, I was told sixty pounds and as though mesmerised I agreed to buy it even without haggling. On refection, I realised that when I was asked £60. they expected to receive £50.

I told the shopkeeper that I did not have the money with me but I would return in a short while and pay in full. He said, "No bother, guvnor, I consider it as sold and I will put it aside till you return."

Almost immediately I had second thoughts. What have I committed myself to? Why was he so keen to make the deal? Was I being over-charged? What would Dora say?

As I was staring at my impulsive purchase in walked two Chinese gentlemen dressed in European clothes. It was not long before they spotted the vase I was holding and began a very excited conversation between themselves. In a form of desperation and as a gesture of politeness I handed the vase to them and asked if they could read the Chinese wording on the base. They read out the wording but I was no wiser. They must have thought I was the shopkeeper and asked me how much the vase was. As a spontaneous joke I said "Only £260. after another animated conversation between themselves in Chinese they responded by offering £160. First of all I thought that they too were joking and then from their inscrutable faces

I realised that they were serious. I accepted their offer with alacrity. They appeared to be very pleased with their purchase, one of them pulled a fat wad of ten pound notes from his pocket and paid me in full. They hurriedly left the shop and I never saw or heard from them again.

Whilst all this was going on, even though it might not have taken more than five minutes the shopkeeper stood with his mouth open in astonishment. I then said, I can settle up with you now and handed him sixty pounds out of the £160 I had just received. I then offered him a further £10 for use of his premises in order to conduct a private deal. He refused the extra ten pounds and said, "I should be paying you for having witnessed such a brilliant transaction". He said that none of his mates in the pub will believe him when he tells the story.

When I returned home triumphantly and told Dora what had happened she said that I was a fool and if she had been with me she certainly would not have allowed me to sell the vase to the Chinese gentlemen. I thought to myself, as I dare not say it aloud, if she had been with me she would not have allowed me to buy the vase in the first instance.

X-Ray

Alter enduring a painful knee for several months I eventually went to see my doctor. He gave it some painful prods and twists and told me I would have to have it x-rayed and wrote a certificate for me to present to the hospital when I went for the x-ray.

Before leaving for the appointment, Dora insisted on me changing my underwear, "Just in ease" she said. This alarmed me but she assured me that it was just in case they admitted me as an in-patient or if I needed an urgent operation. She gave me a strong cup of tea so as to fortify me for the ordeal, packed a cheese sandwich in case I should feel hungry and ensured that I wore my rain coat because isolated thunder showers had been forecast.

When I had 'phoned the hospital for the appointment they told me to report to the chest clinic at the rear of the hospital. The only car park for visitors and patients was near the front of the hospital so I had a long walk to the rear of the extensive hospital grounds. My knee was most painful and my discomfort was increased by the raincoat as it was a most hot and humid day.

There were signs, directions, instruction and warnings everywhere but no indication of where the chest clinic was. There was a forest of signs of No Entry' – 'Entry Forbidden' – 'Staff Only' – No Entrance' 'Exit Only' – No Parking' – 'Staff Parking Only' – 'Wheel Clamping in Operation' – 'No Loitering' – 'No Litter' – 'No Noise', etc. But no direction to the Chest Clinic.

Every other department seems to have been sign posted. I continued to hobble painfully towards the rear of the hospital ground and the signs simply multiplied 'To Main Stores' – 'To-Laundry' – 'Gardeners Stores' – 'To

Incinerator' and so on. The further I progressed, the more ramshackle the buildings became. The scattered buildings were inter connected by rusting, ramshackle corrugated iron covered walkways. The doors to the ramshackle building had signs, No Entry' or 'Exit Only'. I wandered, how does anyone gain entry to any of these buildings. Maybe they are unoccupied because nobody has ever found a door with a notice 'Entry'.

I also started to wonder, did I hear the appointments girl correctly, is there a chest clinic here after all in this ramshackle hospital, if so, why is it so isolated from the main building, was somebody playing a wicked joke on me?. I decided that having come so far I would persevere, the hospital grounds must surely come to an end sooner or later.

The disintegrated asphalt road (there was no footpath) was edged with 'Slow' signs, '5mph mm', Dead slow' and then signs saying 'Ambulances Only', 'Hearses Only' and then another ramshackle structure with a notice over the door saying 'Mortuary' but the door itself bore two signs, No Entry' and Exit Only.

Each hospital sign was a different size, fixed at different heights, of different alphabets and different colours. At last, when I had almost given up and the pain in my knee had become unbearable I spotted a sign on a ramshackle building reading 'Chest Clinic'. After a moment of elation I wondered if it was a mirage induced by the humid heat and overpowering pain in my knee.

The building was set back from the road beyond on an enormous green edged with signs 'Keep off the grass'.

Eventually, by a long tortuous and circuitous route I reached the building without setting foot on the grass. Just as I was about to enter I suffered a minor pang of panic. What was I doing entering a Chest Clinic when all I needed was to have my knee x-rayed?

Was I at the wrong hospital? My chest was OK or had the doctor noticed something so serious that he was afraid to tell me the truth and kidded me that it was my knee? Was Dora in on the secret when she made me change my underwear? Was she also afraid to tell me the dreaded secret? What was the real reason behind the cheese sandwich, was it actually a barium sandwich disguised as cheese?

With all these thoughts crowding in on me, I entered the Chest Clinic.

The staff were very pleasant and polite and sympathetic. I was attended to immediately. I wondered, did they treat everyone with a painful knee in such a prompt and considerate manner?

It was suggested in the most politest manner that it would be helpful if I were to take my raincoat off before entering the x-ray room. I was surprised that they had not asked me if I had eaten my 'cheese' sandwich yet. The radiographer was a nice young man who spoke with a slight lisp and a nasal accent and had a gold ear-ring in his left ear. He could see that I was very tensed up and perspiring profusely. He told me to relax, not to worry, the process would be absolutely painless and would be over in a very short while but I was not to move whilst it was in progress.

He then said that I should take my trousers off. I panicked, why does he want me to take my trousers off if this is a chest clinic? He then asked me to lie on the couch. However, I thought that I may as well get it over and done with and find out what the truth is. He then asked me to turn over, face down.

At this point, I frantically asked if it would be possible for a female radiographer to do the necessary. He said certainly, if it will help calm my nerves.

It only took a few seconds. As soon as it was over, I raced back to my car and quickly started the engine. It was only then that I had realised that I had reached the car in record time despite my swollen knee. How I did it, I don't know even now. I also became aware that I was still perspiring profusely, the car was oven hot as I had parked it in the sun with the windows closed and I was wearing my heavy raincoat.

It was with some trepidation that I unbuttoned my coat and with great relief noted that in my panic, I had not forgotten to put my trousers on before leaving the clinic.

On leaving the car park, I read a sign that I had not noticed before, 'Beware, thieves operate in this car park'.

I thought they must be short of medical staff and operating theatres. Thank goodness, I had only come for an x-ray!

A week later, I went to see my doctor. The results of the x-ray had been sent direct to him. He told me that they showed a slight amount of arthritic wear but at this stage did not warrant an operation.

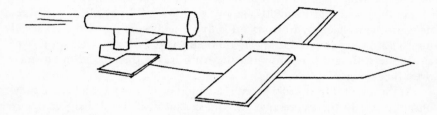

Doodlebugs

During the latter part of World War Two the devilish Germans developed and began to use the V1 terror flying bomb. They were also fast developing the V2 weapon which was a rocket borne high explosive bomb that could reach all parts of London when fired from the German occupied continent. Neither of these weapons could be aimed accurately but the Germans were satisfied as long as they reached any part of London. Their intention was simply to terrorise the inhabitants of London. They also relied on the fact that neither were considered interceptible nor destructible. This was true of the V2 rocket bomb but the Royal Air Force did devise means of intercepting or prematurely destroying some of the V1 flying bombs. These consisted of a 500lb high explosive bomb onto which they fixed short stub wings and a ram jet engine. There was no crew and no guidance system. The Germans just pointed the bombs towards London and put in just enough fuel to reach the sprawling metropolis. When the fuel ran out, the bomb stopped flying and dropped down. The bomb could fly faster than most fighter planes available at the time and radar was still in its infancy. Even though the RAF and its anti-aircraft guns prematurely exploded some of the missiles, most got through to their target.

Unlike manned planes, they could fly in any weather, day or night.

The first that people in London knew of the approach of one of these missiles was when they could hear the distinctive throb of its ram jet engine. The terrifying moment came when the engine sound stopped. If it was close, the explosion would be close. It was quite common for people, even if they were not religious to pray for the sound to continue. If it did, and you heard the resultant explosion, you knew that your prayer had been answered, if you were unfortunate in hearing the engine stop and not heard the explosion then someone else's prayer had been answered. Not everybody can be obliged.

Once the approach of a flying bomb was heard, there were only a few seconds in which to take shelter. Some people sought shelter under a sturdy table, some under a desk or work bench, some under the stairs but my family's shelter was a dug-out covered with corrugated iron sheets at the bottom of the garden.

One night, I was aroused from a deep slumber by the sound of an approaching flying bomb. When I looked out of the window I could see one approaching, its fiery trail very distinctive in the dark. I could also see the fiery trail of incendiary bullets being fired at it from machine guns deployed in the local park. Why they wanted to shoot it down once it had reached London, I don't know, it was bound to come down in any case!

I shouted a warning to the rest of the family and made a dash for the shelter. Halfway there, I was fast over taken by my mother who was severely crippled with arthritic knees and normally could only walk very slowly and painfully. When we got to the shelter, we found our faithful guard dog already there. Because of his acute hearing, he had heard the bomb approaching long before we did and without bothering to warn us first had made his way to the shelter.

Never-the-less, he was please to see us and to have our comforting company in that cold dark shelter.

That raid was soon over. It was a lone bomb which we heard explode in the distance. The mournful all-clear siren sounded without first giving a warning of the approaching bomb.

About 2500 V1 bombs and 1590 V2 rocket bombs fell on London sometimes at the rate of 500 a week.

Hamstring Injury

I did not obtain my hamstring tendon injury through participating in some energetic sport. It occurred when I was gently doing some gardening. Actually, I was tidying the flower bed under which we had recently buried our beloved cat, Blackie. I was preparing the bed for spring planting. I had already forked it over and was smoothing the surface with a rake when my left leg slipped on the slight slope at the edge of the bed. It was only a slight slip but it resulted in a searing pain up the back of my calf. As a consequence, I keeled over and went sprawling over the newly prepared flower bed just over the spot where Blackie was buried.

The agony was awful, I cried out in pain and beat the ground with my fists. Dora came out when she heard me shouting and said she did not realise just how much Blackie meant to me.

The next day I hobbled painfully to see my doctor. My leg had swelled up till the skin was stretched and shiny until it looked like a pink balloon. I was scared that it may burst and the accumulated fluid would flood out of my trouser leg. I could just visualise a child saying in a loud and penetrating voice, "Look Mummy, that man is peeing on the pavement."

Due to the swelling and tenderness I could not wear normal trousers and had to wear shorts. As it was raining when I went to the doctor I wore a raincoat. The receptionist gave me a hard stare and said "What is your problem?".

The doctor prescribed water tablets to reduce the swelling. No sooner had I taken the first one that Dora made a dash to the loo.

Blackie

It all began about 20 years ago when a pathetic looking skinny young cat began haunting our rear garden. At first, we only got brief glimpses as it fled whenever we appeared at the rear door but slowly it became more emboldened and watched us from a safe distance. It became progressively bolder and eventually permitted us to stroke her. She obviously enjoyed this attention and rolled over in sheer delight purring very loudly. Although, at first, we did not feed her in case the food would entice her to leave her own home. She cried so pitiably and loudly that we felt sorry for her and started to think that perhaps she is a stray. We started giving her leftovers from our own three moggies who were most fussy and wasteful. She gulped this food down and loudly cried for more. She ate enormous portions, almost as much as our three grown cats ate altogether. This feeding became a regular habit. The amount of food she gulped down at each meal was enormous. Although we fed her, we did not allow her into the house.

One day, whilst gardening, I put my heavy duty gardening gloves on the ground whilst I went to fetch something from the shed. To my astonishment, I saw Blackie, for that was the nick-name we had accorded her disappearing through the adjoining gardens carrying one of the heavy gloves in her mouth. I noted the direction she went in and made enquiries at neighbours. We soon ascertained who her owners were.

They were very embarrassed and apologetic. They said that 'Tuppence', their name for 'Blackie' was an inveterate kleptomaniac and ever since she was a tiny kitten had been bringing various items home. Usually, they had no idea from where she had taken them. We took the opportunity to raise the rather delicate question about Blackie's apparent hunger. They were a nice, pleasant, middle-aged couple and genuinely appeared to be astonished when we described the enormous amount of food that she ravenously consumed. They assured us, that 'Blackie' ate at least as much at home, they seemed to be so sincere, that we were inclined to believe them although their facts seemed to be incredible.

A few months later, the couple contacted us and told us that they had sold their house and would be moving shortly. They said that they appreciated that 'Blackie' had some sort of affinity with us and would not be happy to move away. They asked if we would 'adopt' her. We gladly agreed.

Almost immediately 'Blackie' appeared at our back door and nonchalantly strolled into the house and without even looking round went straight up to my favourite armchair and ensconced herself thereupon as though it had been her own personal chair for years. Her manner made it quite clear that she would stand for no nonsense from the three long residence cats, they would have to accept her or lump it. They accepted.

Before long, an irate neighbour rang our doorbell and said that our cat had picked up from her lawn an item of intimate underwear and had carried it back in our direction. To our embarrassment, there it lay near our rear door. Whilst we handed it back with due apologies, she tactfully approached the subject of our not feeding the cat adequately.

Although Blackie was a lovely and loving cat she was murderous as far as birds were concerned. She caught and killed birds of all sizes, from small sparrows to largish Jays. One day, a neighbour told us how he had seen her catch two birds at the same time. She had pounced on them and had one pinned to the ground under each of her two front legs. They were still both alive and if she had released one in order to deal with the other she would have lost it. The neighbour said that he managed to rescue both the birds who flew away.

She would catch as many as one a day and bring their corpses home and lay them as a gift for us in appreciation for having adopted her. She rarely ate the birds. She did not hunt them because she was hungry but just for sport. When she did eat any, she ate the whole body including the head and feathers but always left the claws.

One morning I went into the garden and even though it was quite warm, the whole lawn appeared to be covered in a light sprinkling of snow. On closer inspection, it was not snow but white down which had come from two white doves whose corpses lay nearby.

We knew which neighbour kept white doves and we certainly did not wish to cross her path because we feared that if we did, she may do harm to Blackie. I therefore carefully collected each tiny item of down and buried the corpses deep down.

One day, when I was about to bury the corpse of a Blackbird that

Blackie had deposited on the lawn I noticed that it had a small metal ring on one of its legs. I removed the ring on which were the words "Inform British Museum London SW7-XE03661" I did so and in return got a computer printout of the museums record which stated that the bird was a +1 year old female Blackbird, ringed on 20 Feb '79 in Wanstead (which is not far away) that it was found on 19 July '83 at our address, duration 1610 days and that it "had been taken by a cat".

We were only aware of Blackie ever catching a mouse on one occasion. She had brought it home from some neighbouring garden and it was already dead. After playing with the corpse for some while she ate it but it must have died from poisoning because soon after Blackie became seriously ill and nearly died.

Income Tax

I feel that I am on the verge of a nervous breakdown. I've gone off my food, normally I have a good appetite. I don't sleep well, normally I sleep like a log. I can't concentrate and am very irritable. In my own modest estimation, I am normally a placid, pleasant and efficient person. You may very well wonder what caused such a change. The simple but absurd reason is the local Inspector of Taxes. Yes, I can expect many to say, we all have our problems with our Inspector of Taxes but my problem is that I do not have any problem. I have not had a single squeak from any office dealing with income tax, no tax demands, no forms, no requests for information; nothing. I have written several times asking for a tax return form, but no response. I have asked them if there is any tax due or overdue, still no response. What are they up to? What fiendish scheme are they hatching in their multi-storey modern office block.

Several times I have slowly passed by their local headquarters and confirmed that they have not moved away from the address I send my correspondence to.

For about 30 years I practised as a one man self employed architect. At first, my tax assessment was reasonable but with successive years my assessment increased logarithmatically until I was obliged to engage an accountant to explain that in no circumstances should I be obliged to pay more than my total income. The more I paid, the more they demanded. Amid the welter of correspondence I discovered that just by chance, I was being subjected to what they described as a 'random in depth investigation'. I was assured it was nothing personal, it could by chance have happened to anyone.

The questions were sent one by one to my accountant who sent them

64

onto me. I replied to my accountant who in turn replied to the local Inspector of Taxes who was in charge of this random investigation in depth. As soon as I answered one question, another would be submitted. All this time my accountant's fee was piling up. He was earning more out of me than I was earning. They asked 'how much a week do I spend on meat' 'how much on vegetables' 'what membership fees do I pay to any club or religious organisation' 'what is the value of presents I give when I attend a wedding etc.?' When I protested at this line of questioning they assured me it was nothing personal.

This investigation eventually merged with a blatant wrongful assessment of the tax due on a private property disposal by my wife. My accountant pointed out that under the law the profit should be charged at 25% but the tax inspector was charging something like 68%.

My accountant concluded that the tax inspector was after promotion and was going to make this point of contention a legal test case. He reckoned that with the unlimited resources of the Inland Revenue, he would easily be able to crush any feeble resistance I may put up. My accountant recommended that I employ a solicitor who specialised in income tax. He in turn recommended that I engaged a barrister who is a specialist in this section of the law. Eventually, the matter came before a Tax Commissioners Tribunal with tax experts, solicitors and barristers employed by both parties. By now, I had become a 'party' to this contest. I won the case resoundingly but it greatly impoverished me. I had planned wreaking vengeance on the inspector concerned but the conniving so and so eluded my anger by conveniently dying suddenly of a heart attack.

As my life has always been a struggle especially with officialdom of one kind or another, my mental and physical constitution became conditioned to dealing with problems, not only my own but those of my clients. Thus, when the Inland revenue changed their tactics and failed to arouse my adrenalin by sending me any correspondence what-soever despite my frantic appeals, my constitution re-acted accordingly.

I don't know how long I will be able to stand this strain.

Parachute Mines

When my family was bombed out in the east end of London, we were allocated a small flat in Holborn which was nearer the centre of London. Up till then, the more central parts of London had been comparatively free of bombing, but soon after our move, the Germans switched from their terror bombing of the east end of London to fire raids on central London. Vast areas of the City of London were razed to the ground in horrific fire storms. Holborn, being on the verge of the City received many of the bombs which may have been intended for the more central areas. The German tactics were first to drop clusters of magnesium incendiary bombs and then to aim high explosive bombs so as to deter fire fighters putting the blazes out.

The incendiary bombs themselves contained a small explosive device which detonated when the bomb had nearly burnt itself out. This also was intended to deter fire fighters approaching too close.

Most of the fire fighters were just ordinary citizens of both sexes and of all ages and were known as 'fire watchers'. The only implements they had available were sandbags and stirrup pumps which directed a feeble jet of water. Its water supply was from a two gallon iron bucket which had to be replenished from the nearest domestic supply. If the fire watchers could not control an outbreak, they asked an air-raid warden to summon a proper appliance with a trained crew. This may consist of a powerful pump manned by a crew of the regular fire brigade or an appliance known as a Green Goddess, named after its colour, manned by hastily trained volunteers. They obtained their water supplies either from the mains or from giant water tanks formed out of the basements of bombed out buildings.

One evening, when the air raid warning had sounded, a small group of volunteers gathered in the recessed porch of our small block of flats and waited to deal with any fire bombs that may fall in the vicinity. We did not have to wait long before a cluster of fire bombs hit the flank wall of our block of flats and bounced off to fall onto the pavement where they burst into flames but did not ignite anything. We smothered them with sandbags and waited for them to burn themselves out harmlessly.

Whilst waiting, we returned to the covered porch because razor sharp jagged pieces of shrapnel from anti-aircraft shells were falling all around us. Suddenly someone cried out, "There's a parachutist coming down" and pointed to a dark object slowly descending from the smoke filled sky. There were fires burning all around us and the nearby City of London appeared to be burning.

The parachute drifted to roof level of a nearby building and as a group of us rushed towards it with the intention of helping the parachutist if he happened to be one of ours or to detain him if he was an enemy airman. One second, all we could see was a parachute but the next second we could see that the object descending upon as was not human but a large black cylinder. The cry went up "Parachute mine" and as one, we turned and fled. These parachute mines were intended to explode at ground level, they contained 1500lbs of high explosive, and they wrought absolute devastation especially so, on residential property. I don't know about the others, I ran and ran until I had no breath in my body and collapsed to the ground where I waited for the explosion.

I had previously seen the effect that these fiendish bombs had wrought. Before being made homeless by a 'normal' high explosive bomb, I served although just 16 years old as a volunteer in a light rescue/first aid unit in Stepney in the east end of London. During one bright moon lit night we were sent to aid an incident just outside our area. When we arrived in our tiny canvas covered pick-up truck the scene was most eerie. At least two whole blocks of two storey houses had been flattened to the ground as though a giant bulldozer had run over it. Not a single wall had been left standing. Here and there were small groups of rescuers digging with their bare hands in the tangled rubble of bricks and timber. Seeing our vehicle arrive, one such group asked if we were first alders and if so, could we convey a seriously wounded woman to hospital urgently. We picked our way cautiously over the rubble towards the group taking a stretcher with us. Apart from the bright moonlight the area was lit by the flickering yellow flames of ignited fractured gas pipes. The flames leaped up to six-seven feet. Even though these gas pipes were aflame, there were no fires, just dozens of flickering flames. We had hand torches but they were useless because by some ridiculous regulation they had to be masked allowing only a tiny beam of light to come out.

We placed the woman on to the stretcher. Under the conditions, it was useless to try to give the woman any first aid. She was thickly covered in mortar dust and her face was covered in chicken feathers, no doubt from a pillow and was stuck with congealed blood. There were four of us to carry the stretcher. As we lifted her up she asked "Are my children OK?" What could we say? Not far away were two small bodies wrapped in grey blankets. The men who had rescued her indicated with a shake of their heads that the children were dead.

As we carefully carried the woman across the rubble the sky was further illuminated by searchlights seeking the bombers who had returned. Anti-aircraft guns were firing from a nearby park and the shrapnel from their bursting shells was raining down all around us. we could hear the drone of a bomber approaching and then the terrifying whine of a falling bomb. One of the stretcher bearers lost his footing on the rubble and stumbled. This sudden loss of balance caused the rest of us to stumble and fall onto the rubble. Goodness only knows what further injuries this caused the patient.

When we got back to the first aid station after unloading the woman at a nearby hospital the man in charge asked what I had done to my leg. I looked down and my left leg was dripping with blood. I had apparently injured it when I stumbled in the rubble. He instructed the truck driver to take me to the, local hospital. As the truck turned a nearby corner, the front fell into a recently formed bomb crater. I clambered out and walked to the hospital where the wound was washed and dressed. Before being bandaged, the nurse applied a yellow powder, she said it was something very new and very effective. It was an early use of anti-biotic, Penicillin.

I therefore, had good reason to fear the parachute bomb we saw descending from the sky. Most fortuitously, the parachute had become entangled on a lamp post with the bomb's detonator just inches from the ground. It was soon made harmless by an army bomb disposal team and life in the street returned to 'normal'.

The Eye Test

Subsequent to my attack of Meniere's disease syndrome I was left completely deaf for a while.. The only sounds I could hear were the pounding and shrieking noises inside my head. After a few weeks a little hearing returned to my left ear. I had to rely on Dora for hearing purposes like a blind person relies on a guide dog. When someone 'phoned. Dora would speak on my behalf. When someone asked me questions she would reply. If 1 belched, she would say, "Excuse me".

One day Dora decided I needed an eye test and as I could not do so myself, she arranged an appointment. Naturally, she accompanied me to the optician. We had known him for many years, ever since he emigrated here from the Soviet Union. He never lost his thick Russian accent.

When Dora explained why she was accompanying me, he burst out in laughter. Somehow or other, he found deaf people to be very funny. Dora was shocked. I did not know why he had suddenly burst into laughter. Dora asked what's so funny about a deaf person wanting an eye test? She pointed out, that it would not be funny if a blind person required a hearing test. He became serious and led me to a chair and put one of those complicated spectacle frames on me. After selecting a couple of lenses from a case containing dozens of different lenses he asked me to read a test sheet with random letters of various sizes. Dora put her spectacles on and commenced reading the sheet. The optician said that he wanted me to read the sheet, not her. Dora pointed out that because I was deaf she had to reply on my behalf.

What happened next was very embarrassing for Dora. The optician tried again. He shouted direct into my ear, "Can you read the sheet?"

I replied, "No thanks, I went just before I came out".

Dora blushed but the optician burst out laughing again.

Wind

Apart from meteorological winds there is another type of wind that has a great influence on weather, climate and ecology and health. This type of wind is never mentioned in polite circles, if one is to believe it, it does not even exist in certain social strata. In other, less sophisticated circles it is called by a name which rhymes with tart and cockney's blandly call it a raspberry. The unmentionable word is actually a proper Anglo-Saxon word, derived from the German, 'farzen'. Even the Greeks had a word for it, 'perdein'. There is no reason why I or any other decent, law abiding citizen should not pronounce or write it, because it is not a swear word or blasphemous. It can be found in any proper English dictionary with a description like:-'A discharge of wind from the Anus'. There is no reason to believe that even though the word may never pass the lips of those in high society that they have not actually made such a discharge from time-to-time and no doubt enjoyed doing so. There is nothing to be ashamed of, it is a result of the natural process of the digestion of food. Air contained in food and drink is expelled during the digestive process either through the mouth when it is called a 'belch or by the aforementioned discharge. Sometimes the latter is augmented by gases produced by the complicated digestive process and has its own particular odour. This discharge of gases apply to both sexes and all ages and all races and religious affiliations. It also applies to all animals, those who keep pet dogs will be particularly aware of this fact. It applies not only to pets but also to all domestic and wild animals. As the worlds human population increases at an ever increasing pace so does that of the domestic animals that are nurtured to meet the nutritional needs of the humans. In some countries, the animals outnumber the humans.

70

Wind

Scientists have measured (I don't know how, perhaps they were attached to gas meters) that a cow emits 150 litres of wind each day, that is 1050 litres a week or 54,600 litres a year. It would be interesting to learn how many litres of milk she yields as a percentage of gas. If you take a meadow containing, say, 100 cows, the gas being emitted would be enough to turn a windmill to produce sufficient electricity for a small town. Instead it is all allowed to go to waste but even worse, it adversely effects the protective Ozone layer which surrounds this earth's fragile balanced ecology.

Scientists have predicted that before long this will result in the earth's climate warming up and causing the ice at the North and South poles to melt. When this happens, the melted ice water will flood the dry areas and the evolutionary process will have to be reversed. How many times in the billions of years of the existence of this planet has this progress and regression occurred?

One has to remember, that it is not only humans and domestic animals that this concerns but all animals and possibly also birds, fish and insects. Plants certainly both absorb and emit gases.

This is a serious and vital problem and we owe it to future generations to come up with a solution soon and so we can all start, at least, by pronouncing the word that fears to hear its name.

Passing of wind can be of great personal benefit. Despite the odium concerning this activity it does no doubt give great pleasure and relief to the participant and thus relieves mental and physical tensions. It would be even more beneficial and enjoyable if people could remove from their minds the associated idea that it is somewhat sinful and /or unhealthy. Passing of wind is nowhere condemned in the holy scriptures and no authority has ever claimed that it is unhealthy. If anything, it is unhealthy to suppress such a natural function.

Many people suffer with obesity which in turn causes or complicates diseases. Very few people who are overweight are content with the condition and would gladly lose weight but find that diets don't help or are only effective temporarily. Passing of wind could help such people on a permanent and easy basis. They only need to eat 'sensibly' but also to increase considerably their consumption of items that produce wind, such as butter beans. When wind is expelled from the body, it takes with it a considerable amount of heat. On being expelled, the wind is about 100°F (37°C). The heat was derived within the digestion system which breaks down the body fat and converts it into energy and heat. The more wind that is expelled, the more fat has been consumed and converted into heat.

Butter beans are notorious for creating wind and therefore the more butter beans that are consumed the more wind will be created and the more body fat consumed to heat it.

Wind

People have been brain-washed to consider the wind's odour to be obnoxious. In order to overcome this psychological barrier a group of scientists and agronomists have been secretly working on developing a butter bean that will result in giving off sweet smelling odours.

Another benefit of blowing wind is that its odour discourages bed ticks which in turn induces asthma. In recent years there has been an enormous increase in the cases of asthma among all age groups. The cause of asthma has been attributed to air pollution from vehicle exhausts but recent research has proved this not to be the case. Scientists should now compare the incidence of asthma with the consumption of butter beans in various regions of the country and in different countries.

The perceptive author, Emile Zola wrote extensively and frankly about wind in his novel *Earth*. One incident in the book describes how a corpse laid to rest emitted wind and scared the life out of the mourners present. In another, he described a village competition in which the participants have to blow out the most number of candles but not by using their mouth.

In India there is a religious sect that considers that the life spirit in contained in their wind and consequently believe that the more wind they retain within their body, the longer they will live.

A recent census indicates that the community is exploding.

A Ghost

I don't believe in fairies, I did not even when I was a young child. I also don't believe in witchcraft, demons, ghosts, spirits, the supernatural, fortune telling, UFO's, astrology, corn circles, etc.

I had none of these influences in mind when I set out one warm sunny morning to carry out a structural survey of an empty house in Manor Park, east London for a prospective buyer. I first checked that I had the address, had the key, had the route, had the necessary instruments and tools, torch, notebook etc. and that I had left a note as to where I was going and who to contact, should I not return about the time anticipated. The latter being important in case of an accident in an empty property. Once, I had, due to a defective lock become locked into an isolated industrial building on a day when the temperature was below zero. I panicked because I had forgotten to leave a note of the address or who to contact. By a lucky stroke (I don't believe in luck either)! managed to attract the attention of the police who released me with the aid of powerful bolt cutters.

When I started the survey, I commenced in a methodical manner beginning with the exterior. Orientation, access, storeys, adjacent properties, fences, gardens, outbuildings, slopes, ground levels in relation to damp proof course, drains, chimneys, roofs, gutters, walls, windows, doors, trees, bushes etc. So you can see I had plenty to occupy my mind and senses before I entered the house.

I proceeded with the survey of the interior with the same methodical manner. The loft, ceilings, walls, doors, windows, floors, chimney breasts and fireplaces, decorations, stairs, sanitary fittings, light points, socket outlets, plumbing, ironmongery, heating and hot water etc., etc. I left the cellar till last. As I went down the steep cellar steps I noted that they were rickety and should be replaced. I carefully inspected the exposed ground floor joists for signs of woodworm, I noted the incoming gas, water and electricity mains and was about to note the meters when I suddenly felt a clammy cold envelope me, holding me in a frozen embrace. I then clearly heard a horrid groaning and whimpering. This seemed to go on for ages, I could not move or speak, my vocal cords seemed to be paralysed. The sensation left as suddenly as it started. I left the cellar in a panic, snatching my case of instruments and tools and left the house as quickly as I could.

I felt shaken and sat down on the front garden wall to recover in the warm sunshine before attempting to drive home. As I sat there, a postman went by and asked if! was feeling ill. I said I was alright but was just feeling faint after surveying the house. I could not tell him what had actually happened, I would sound such a fool. He said, "Have you also heard Mrs Jones's ghost?" He went on to explain that a previous occupier had fallen down the cellar steps and broken a leg and an arm. She was unable to attract attention and died in pain after a few days.

I duly wrote my report but could not in all honestly include anything I firmly did not believe in.

Plus-Fours

I was 16 years old when my family's house in Stepney, east London, was completely destroyed by a German bomb. It was on a fine Saturday morning in September 1940 whilst I was at work. Everything was gone and all 1 possessed in the world were the clothes I stood up in.

I found temporary shelter in a local school where I was allocated a space on the assembly hall floor on which to sleep among about 100 other bombed out people. There was no privacy and I slept in the same clothes I wore during the day. I washed and shaved wherever I could. Baths could only be taken at the municipal communal baths but this was fraught with danger as there were constant air raids and as soon as the air raid warning siren sounded the bath attendant would throw the door open and bellow "All out".

One advantage of staying at this temporary shelter was that a hot breakfast was provided. It consisted of a large enamel mug of hot, strong, sweet tea which was very invigorating after a rough night on the hard wood parquet floor (no mattress) and a large bowl of thick hot porridge. You were welcome to second helpings.

The shelter was organised by the air raid wardens and the breakfast by the Women's Volunteer Service.

Such was the spirit of the population, that despite all this hardship, I went to work as though everything was normal. Getting to work from east London to west London was far from normal or easy. After a nights bombing, the roads were covered in rubble and broken glass, firemen's hoses would be strewn across streets where many buildings were still blazing. Some roads were closed due to unexploded bombs suspected of having delayed action fuses. Buses were frequently diverted and long stretches of the journey sometimes had to be traversed by foot.

At the time, I was employed as an office boy in the in-house architects department of a large, well known, departmental store in Oxford Street. The office was situated in a lovely house at the rear of the main store overlooking Cavendish Square.

A few weeks after I was bombed out, the departmental store itself sustained severe damage when it caught fire during an air raid.

The water damaged goods salvaged from the fire gutted buildings were brought in and place on display in the upper rooms of the house in which I worked. Some of the goods were not badly damaged, in most cases, the wrappings had got slightly wet.

It became known that the staff would be given priority in purchasing these goods before they went on sale to the public. They were to be sold very cheap, as the firm was receiving generous compensation from the government. Moreover, they were to be sold without clothing coupons having to be surrendered. Clothes were very severely rationed at that time.

The staff were served in order of seniority. I don't know about the chairman but first came the directors who carried away enormous quantities, then likewise, the managers, then the supervisors, then the seniors and then nothing, everything worth buying was sold. Even though I was desperate for a change of underwear let alone other items of clothing I was not given the opportunity to buy anything, not even a single handkerchief. Such was the pecking order of the day and in the spirit of the day, I accepted it as normal. After all I was only the office boy, the lowest of the low.

One day I heard that a voluntary organisation had collected clothes and was handing them out from the People's Palace theatre in Mile End Road to those, who like myself; had been bombed out. The People's Palace was actually a municipally owned concert hall situated not far from our bombed out house. Miraculously, it was not destroyed by all the surrounding bombing.

I did not have any clothing coupons because my ration book was buried under the rubble of what had been our house. Even if I did have any coupons, I would not have had any spare money to buy clothes because my salary as an office boy was only fifteen shillings a week (75p) and out of that, I had to buy my lunches and pay my fares to work. Fortunately, food in the soup kitchens called civic restaurants in those days was very cheap, stodgy and filling.

When I called at the Peoples Palace, a young curate was in attendance. I told him that the only clothes I possessed were those I was wearing and he agreed with me that they were beginning to give off a strong unpleasant odour. He asked the caretaker to switch on the lights so that he could select some items for me. The caretaker gave me a sour look and refused to do so. He said it was not his job to switch on the lights. He said he would get into trouble because of the blackout regulations. The curate failed to point out that it was broad daylight. However, he went into the hall and by the light that filtered through the open door gathered up some items and gave them to me.

I decided to wear my newly acquired clothes for work the next day. As soon as I entered the office, the manager wearing a smart outfit he had bought in the fire salvage sale called me aside and told me that I was not suitably attired for work in such a prestigious establishment. I wondered what was wrong. The clothes had obviously come from a well-to-do family and fitted fairly well. The Sherlock Holmes deer stalker hat was very comfortable, the heavy Harris tweed jacket with leather patches on the elbows was only slightly too large but I will admit that the two inch (50mm) gap between the tops of my socks and the bottom of the plus-four legs were unusual.

Now for the younger generation in particular I must explain that before the 1939–45 world war 2 it was almost de-rigour for golfing gentlemen to wear plus-four trousers on course. These trousers made from tweeds with a bold brightly coloured plait were cut in a baggy fashion and did up just under the knee with a clothe strap and metal buckle. The name plus-four derives from the fact that the tailor allowed an extra four inches (100mm) of material at the bottom of each leg so as to form the distinctive bulge just above the knees.

For grammatical reasons the plural of plus fours is knickerbockers. It would therefore display a persons ignorance if they were to say that someone was wearing knickerbockers as it would imply they were wearing more than one pair of trousers.

The office manager was a kind hearted God fearing man and as amends pointed out that the firm made special provision for staff to buy a suit made-to-measure in their tailoring department complete with button up waist coat and a spare pair of trousers in their standard dark grey hop sack material and it would only cost me three pounds. He knew full well that three pounds was four weeks of my gross salary.

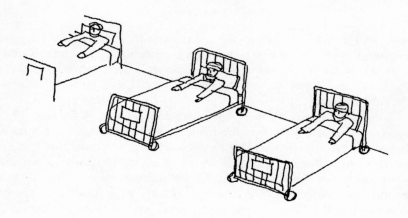

Mastoiditis

Mastoiditis is the inflammation of the mastoid bone which is situated immediately behind the ear lobe. With the advent of antibiotics, operations to remove this condition are far more rare than they used to be. If not treated effectively and timely, the infection, caused by bacteria can enter the blood and/or brain with disastrous results . In pre Penicillin days an infection often led to impaired hearing or complete deafness. It used to be a very serious condition and the chances of survival quite small.

By the age of seven, I had had five mastoid operations as they were then called. I don't know at which age I had the first but I must have been very young. I recall that I was taken by the nurses into an adjoining ward where a conjuror was entertaining the children. I must have been very young as I was placed in a cot. I did not see much of the show as I soon fell asleep. I was too ill to stay awake.

I remember very little of the five times and five operations I had for mastoiditis but I do recall a few incidents. About 1930, I was in a hospital, I don't know which one and my bed was adjacent to a large open fireplace with a blazing coal fire which was used to heat quite a large ward. I was told that I must go to sleep otherwise Father Christmas would not be able to come down the chimney and leave a gift for me. Normally sleep was no problem for me, the condition seemed to induce almost continuous sleep.

However, later that evening I awoke and was amazed to see Father Christmas entering the ward but not by the chimney but through the door and he had his arm around one of the nurses. At the time, I thought the nurse may have been his mother. I pretended to sleep and I received my present.

Another incident I remember was being in an all children's ward.

Mastoiditis

Possibly, it was in the Throat, Nose and Ear Hospital in Grays Inn Road, London. Discipline was very strict. Plain, painted walls, green up to dado height, deep cream above, highly polished floor, no pictures, no toys, no books. Not a single wrinkle in the bed covers, no talking, no playing, no comics, no visitors. There were heavy, adult size earphones dangling over the head of the bed but I could not listen in because of the thick bandages wrapped round my head. When I first gained consciousness after my operation I saw a pair of nurses wheeling a trolley from bed-to-bed and re-dressing the children's operations. As they did so, each child yelled in pain so when the trolley reached my bed, I pretended still to be asleep. The ruse worked, the trolley moved on to the next bed whose occupant wailed aloud. On the third day, the trolley passed me by again but no sooner had they finished treating the adjoining patient that they turned sharply around and caught me watching.

Re-dressing the wound involved removing the thick layers of bandages, then the lint which was impregnated with pus and then removing a long gauge bandage which had previously been packed inside the wound cavity to soak up the pus. The wound was very tender and painful as there were no effective pain killers in those days except morphine. The wound cavity was then re-packed with a bandage soaked in an antiseptic solution and thick crepe bandages wrapped around the head and secured with a safety pin. It was a very unpleasant procedure both for the child and nurses. The pus stank to high heaven.

I was in that ward for five weeks. After a while I was able to sit up and see the other children but was not allowed to talk to any.

Every day, at least one of the recent entrant was prepared for the mastoid operation. A nurse would crop the hair on one side of the child's head, the side that was to be operated on and then shave it down to the scalp using an open cut throat razor. This was rarely done without a few nicks in the process. Next, the whole of the shaven area was mopped with a strong solution of iodine. The pain was excruciating. Strangely enough, I don't remember this being done to me although it must have been as it was standard procedure. I do however remember lying fully conscious on the operating table prior to the operation. I was taken into the theatre about 30 minutes before the operation. I saw the operation theatre sister preparing the instruments. She took them out of a stainless steel container in which there was boiling water and laid them on a white ceramic tray along-side my head. Every so often she would smile encouragingly to me but said nothing. She did however speak to an assistant nurse telling her that I only stood a 50-50 chance of surviving. Fortunately, I did not really appreciate the significance of her remark. However, she was right. Very few of the children taken out of the ward for the operation returned to their bed.

Mastoiditis

After a while, several men in white aprons entered the theatre. Whilst two held my arms and legs down another placed a pad of cotton wool over my nose and mouth and started to drip chloroform from the bottle thereon. Someone else taunted me and told me to shout. I soon saw psychedelic patterns swimming in front of my eyes and my tormentors voice receding into the distance. As soon as I stopped protesting and struggling they knew I was anaesthetised.

I endured five weeks in that strict regime ward and then for several months after attended out-patients to have the cavity wound inspected and re-dressed.

The Raid

In the 1930's, the streets in Stepney in the east end of London were always lively. Hordes of children would be playing various games in a multitude of groups. Football played with a ball composed of rags tied up with string, the teams varying in size and members frequently interchanging sides. The goals were indicated by piles of clothing laid in the road. There was no referee and score was kept but there was a lot of shrieking. Cricket was played with a home made bat cut out of a plank of wood. The wicket would be chalked on a brick wall and the ball would be nothing harder than a tennis ball in case it hit a window. Each player was an umpire and the game ended when the owner of the ball felt slighted and would go home taking the one and only ball with him. There were also hop-scotch games marked out in chalk on the York stone pavement slabs. This was mainly played by girls as were the skipping exhibitions. Boys would also play games flipping cigarette picture cards. These could be picked up free from the many cards thrown away by adult smokers who despite the abject poverty could afford to smoke quite heavily. These cards are now valuable collectors items. There were also leap frog games and piggy in the middle games all accompanied by shrieks of the participants. There were many other games such as ring-a-ring-roses but once a year, during the Jewish Passover festival there were games involving trying to throw hazelnuts through holes cut in the lids of matzo boxes. Matzos being the unleavened bread eaten during the seven days of the festival in lieu of ordinary bread. Every so often a couple of boys would have a fight, watched and urged by their friends. The fight would stop when one started a nose bleed.

Toys were almost totally absent, cycles were an unknown luxury but occasionally a home made soap box on pram wheels would be pushed around by envious friends. All activities were accompanied by appropriate shouting. Periodically, some of the games would be temporarily disturbed by street traders pushing their wares on flat topped two wheel barrows hired for a shilling a day (20 shillings to the pound). Their shouts proclaiming their wares were added to those of the children. On offer were fruit, vegetables, slices of large red melons, fish. In addition there was the milk man with his large galvanised iron urns from which he ladled warm fresh milk into the buyers own jugs. Occasionally, the 'Stop me and buy one' ice cream man with his peaked cap would traverse the streets with his pedal driven insulated cart. One favourite trader was the toffee vendor, Jubilee Max, who sold a variety of home made toffees. Out of goodness of heart, he would from time-to time give a 'taster' to one of the pathetic hopeful band of children who would trail round the streets with him.

Street musicians would wander through the streets hoping to be rewarded here and there with a penny or two. Cripples claiming to be war veterans displaying terrible deformities or amputations would beg for charity. During the day, the streets were a lively mass of noisy humanity.

Policemen were very rarely seen, at least in the streets populated by Jewish immigrants from eastern Europe. Despite the poverty, crime was virtually unknown. Motor vehicles very rarely traversed the streets, the vehicles normally seen were horse drawn coal carts. The dung dropped by these horses was quickly gathered from the granite set paved roads for use in window boxes.

Two sectors of Stepney were inhabited almost exclusively by Yiddish speaking refugees from eastern Europe and their English born offspring. The larger and more densely populated sector was north of Whitechapel Road bounded on the west side by Middlesex Street, more commonly known as 'The Lane' in which a famous street market was held each Sunday morning. The north and east was bounded by the Great Eastern Railway line which ran into Liverpool Street Station.

The smaller of the two sectors was contained within a triangle formed by Whitechapel Road, Commercial Road East and Jubilee Street.

The Jewish community was virtually self sufficient and had very little contact with the surrounding non Jewish areas. The language barrier was a powerful dividing force.

It was on an ordinary day after school when the Jewish children were at play in the street that the raid took place. The raiders consisted of some 30 children on roller skates from an adjacent non-Jewish district. They were armed with sticks and raced in a tight phalanx through some of the Jewish streets. The raiders were accompanied by a pack of excited dogs who had picked up a kitten and were tearing it apart as they ran along. The raid was over in a few minutes. Apart from the kitten, there were no serious injuries.

The Raid

People were just shocked at the sudden, unexpected but well organised raid.

As evening drew on the noise subdued somewhat. The cobbled roads and York stone paved footways imbued a quieter, more romantic atmosphere. Having fed their families, mothers brought chairs out and sat in groups outside their front doors which opened straight off the public pavements. What they gossiped about, goodness only knows but whilst they did so, they were able to keep an eye on their children who were not yet tired enough to go to sleep in their bug ridden, over crowded insanitary homes. The later and more tired they were, the more chance they had of getting of to sleep.

Meanwhile, the men folk would gather in groups in somebody's dwelling to discuss their prime problem, employment, or rather the lack of it. They would also discuss politics and most likely end up playing cards or dominoes. The air would become thick with cigarette smoke. No one ever smoked a pipe.

In the street, a lamp lighter would trudge from lamp post to lamp post turning the gas jet into a comfortable yellow glow which was so weak that it only illuminated a circle of about two meters diameter around the base of the lamp.

Our Poltergeist

Soon after we moved into our house in Kensington Gardens, Ilford, Essex, Dora got chatting in the street to an elderly neighbour. She was very interesting and had a vast knowledge of the borough and some of its more notorious residents. She told Dora about a serviceman, who during the war murdered several prostitutes in the most brutal manner. She spoke about the 'brides in the bath' murderer as though she was on first name terms with him. She even told Dora in which shop he had bought a tin bath in which to drown one of his brides and then had the effrontery to return the bath for a refund as being unsuitable.

She said that she had been a friend of Edith Thompson and frequently travelled up with her to the City where she worked as a book keeper for a wholesale milliner. She was amazed when Dora asked who was Edith Thompson. She said, you ought to know, she and her husband Percy used to live in the very house that you have just bought. Her husband was a shipping clerk in the City but she didn't travel up to work with him because she wanted to travel separately in order to read those trashy, cheap romantic novels. She was always reading them. She was very snooty but he was nice and friendly but too trusting. He never suspected that his wife was having an affair with the much younger merchant seaman, Frederick Bywaters who came to visit them whenever he returned to England. Possibly Percy got to know him through his work in a shipping office. She then told Dora, that young Frederick who had an intense passion on Edith, knifed Percy to death on the corner of Kensington Gardens and Belgrave Road when the couple were returning late one evening from a visit to the Criterion Theatre in the west end of London.

Apparently, Edith used to write love letters to Frederick whilst he was away at sea. In some of the letters she said that she wished she could be free of her husband so as to be able to live with Frederick as husband and wife.

Because of the contents of her letters to Frederick which the police discovered, she was jointly charged with him in the murder of Percy on 3" October 1922.

Frederick confessed to the murder but Edith's counsel pleaded that her letters were just romantic day dreams, fantasies; she did not love Frederick and did not wish to have Percy murdered.

Nevertheless, both she and Frederick were found guilty of murder and sentenced to death. All appeals failed to reprieve and she was carried semi-conscious to the scaffold.

She told Dora that Edith's restless soul still haunts the house which we had recently moved into.

When Dora told me this I said that it did not worry me because I don't believe in ghosts, fairies or Father Christmas.

In the ensuing weeks, Dora was convinced that Edith's tormented spirit haunted the house. She said at times she felt the room enveloped in a cold clammy atmosphere and that ornaments had been thrown over. I told her that I would insulate the loft and draught proof the windows and that in any case I did not like the ornaments that the kitten had playfully knocked over during the night. I eventually convinced Dora that there were no poltergeists in the house when I showed her a local history book that I borrowed from the library that clearly gave the Thompson's house as being number 41 Kensington Gardens which is further down the road and across the street. However, our house did actually have an interesting historical connection but that is another story.

The Gambler

When a distant relative, Morris, had a heart attack, his doctor advised him to refrain from any stressful activity and to lose some weight. He did not have to worry about stress at work because he hardly did work. Not that he had any private income but he subsisted on unemployment pay and a little that his wife earned at part time jobs.

He did however, indulge in a very stressful activity. He was an inveterate and compulsive gambler specialising in horse racing. His knowledge of this subject was encyclopaedic and he had instant recall of any detail. In fact, this was the only subject he could speak about apart from his 'illnesses' that prevented him from working. Unfortunately, his impressive knowledge of horse-racing did not prevent him losing most of his meagre income when it came to placing bets. Despite his bragging of the few occasions he did win, family and friends regarded him as a joke and cited him as a warning to the younger generation. He was pathetic. Not long after his heart attack, he told me that in accordance with his doctors advice, he was no longer gambling with his own money but in order not to waste his vast knowledge of horse racing he was setting up as an agent betting with clients money and only taking a small percentage of their winnings as a fee. He quite frankly admitted that as a gambler in the past he had been a dismal failure despite his vast knowledge but he had devised a foolproof system. First, he was not gambling with his own money and therefore could not afford to be reckless because, if he did not have a good record and reputation he would not have any clients. He said that he had now gone into partnership with a young man who was a computer wizard. He reckoned, that combining his vast knowledge with the icy cold logic of a computer they could virtually eliminate most risks and beat the bookies at their own game.

He said that he and his partner had tried the system many times and the results were staggering. On paper, they would have won a fortune if they had actually put some money in but as the idea was not to involve their own money they were just practice 'dry runs'.

He did not convince me even though his logic was sound but I could not refuse when he asked me to be their first client. He said that he did not require a big stake and if I won, he would not ask for any further stakes but re-invest the money I had already won but never more than 50% so that there would always be a jackpot available. I silently said farewell to the ten pounds I handed him.

Subsequently, about once a week, he would 'phone me to report excellent results and the amount available in the jackpot which I could withdraw at any time I wished. The news of his new venture and his new found success quickly spread among his relatives and friends and his former detractors plied him with money. The few who asked to be paid their jackpot or part thereof were promptly paid.

Soon friends and friends of relatives clamoured to join the bonanza. His esteem among relatives rose sharply and he became much respected. His period of glory did not last long. Before he died, he left a note in which he confessed that there was no new system, no partner, no computer but he had enjoyed spending all the money that his former detractors had willingly poured into his lap through their greed.

The Hearing Therapist

No sooner had the Hearing Therapist carried out the first adjustments and inserted the expensive hearing aid into Harold's ear his whole world had changed. He delighted in hearing sounds that he had not heard for many years and was overwhelmed at understanding what was being said to him. He no longer had doubts about the wisdom of having spent so much money on such a tiny, inconspicuous object. Now he knew that he would not be cut off from other people by that wall of muffled incomprehensible speech. No longer would people have to shout at him as though he was an idiot.

He could not refrain from expressing his delight to the Therapist and his assistant/receptionist. He invited the therapist to a pub lunch and drink to celebrate. The Therapist readily agreed but only on condition that he paid. He asked Harold to call him by his name which was Frank. He said that he was pleased to pay for the lunch for more than one reason. First, he admitted to having made a 'small profit' on the sale of the hearing aid, secondly, he was glad that Harold was pleased because satisfied customers, or rather 'clients' were a good source for introducing further 'clients' and also, he very much wanted to tell him something that was on his mind and wished to disclose before it was too late, as both of them were getting on in years.

He asked Harold if he recognised him, Harold said that his face was somewhat familiar but could not place him. Frank said, "You would no doubt instantly recognise my feet. I attended your chiropodist clinic for years until you retired, not that I really needed treatment but because I just wanted to see you from time-to-time". Then Harold was amazed to hear him say, "You obviously don't realise it but I was, or rather still am your wife's husband". Harold said, "I don't believe in ghosts, my wife's first husband had been dead for about 50 years". He then joked, "Maybe there's something wrong with this hearing aid you sold me; the first time in years I can both hear and understand what people are saying but I can't believe I'm hearing right".

Frank assured him that there was nothing wrong with the hearing aid and that he was hearing the truth. He said that Frank was not my name until I 'died' some 50 years ago, I used to be called Malcolm and I used to be a bank clerk. Harold was astounded, as far as he was aware, only he and his wife Milly knew this fact, how could this stranger have known Malcolm's details. After he gave a few more facts that only Malcolm would have known, Harold became convinced that there was something in Frank's claim.

Frank asked if Milly was still alive and when told, yes, said, "I don't suppose she has changed her character". After glancing at his watch he said, "I can't stay much longer, I've another appointment soon." He then hurriedly went on to explain. "Before I met Milly, I was the only child in a well-to-do, respectable family. I had been to university and graduated with an economics degree and was set on a career in banking like my father. Milly enticed me into marriage and quite falsely told me that she was pregnant. I did not know at the time, but she was an assistant in a millinery shop but she put on airs and graces and fooled me in believing that she came from a wealthy background. My parents were furious when I told them that I was going to marry Milly because I loved her and that she was bearing their grandchild. Even though I was blinded by love they were not. They could see right through her, that she was a fortune hunter and they suspected that she may not even be pregnant. Milly refused to be examined by a gynaecologist appointed by my parents. Despite all this, I went ahead and married her in a registry office. On my salary at the bank, I was able to buy a nice house in a respectable neighbourhood on an endowment mortgage, that is, if I were to die, the outstanding mortgage would be paid by the insurance company. In fact, he said, it is the very same house that you are now living in. In addition, at Milly's insistence, I took out a life insurance policy for £5000 which was a fortune in those days.

After a short while, Milly did become pregnant and bore a son whom we named Samuel". He said, that even though he was officially dead he had closely followed Samuel's career as an operatic singer.

"I had a reasonable salary at the bank but Milly was a wastrel and a slut. Because of her vicious tongue, all communication.between myself and my family were terminated, they did not want to have anything to do with the woman I had married. She used to row with them like a fish wife and even accused them of stealing things from her, even things she never owned.

They never had the opportunity of seeing Samuel their one and only grandchild.

The atmosphere between Milly and myself got steadily worse. She rudely insulted all my friends who consequently lost contact with me. She nearly lost me my job by 'phoning my boss and rowing with him. Eventually, we were rowing virtually non-stop. I hated the very thought of returning home after work.

Soon after Samuel was born, I decided to take Milly and Samuel on a holiday to a remote island off Greece which had been recommended to me by a colleague at work. He was told about it by someone who used to go there regularly every year. He agreed to come with us. It was indeed an idyllic place for a holiday. Although it was rather select it was inexpensive. Milly lost no time in rowing with the hotel owner and with the staff She loved bullying and bossing people about and being snobbish to the other guests. To me, it was most embarrassing and I was glad to escape into the sea and to swim among the rocks."

Harold heard all this in amazement, this was certainly his Milly and she had not mellowed one iota in all the years. Frank continued. "One day whilst swimming among the rocks I came across the body of my office colleague. Apparently, he had slipped on the rocks and had fallen unconscious with his face in the water and had drowned. His face was badly gashed and one arm appeared broken. Despite his facial injury, I recognised his distinctive bathing costume. I was about to drag him to the shore when I remember reading about a similar incident in a novel. I quickly changed costumes with him in the shelter of the rocks and placed my signet ring on his finger. I waded back to shore, picked up my colleagues clothes, dried myself and returned to his room.

Soon after 'my' body was found and Milly began to blame each and everyone for the accident. Milly identified the body as being 'me'. Whether she realised the truth, I do not know but she had a strong financial incentive to identify the badly bruised body as being mine. 'I' was duly buried on that idyllic island but no gravestone was ever erected. I, as Frank returned to his bed-sitter and suffered a 'nervous breakdown' caused by Malcolm's untimely death. I changed my profession and eventually became a Hearing Therapist".

Having got all this off his chest, he glanced at his watch once again and said, "I must hurry, or I'll miss my next potential client". Laughingly he said, "I always like to be dead on time".

When Harold returned to have his hearing aid adjusted a couple of weeks later, the receptionist told him that Frank had passed away, he had suffered a massive heart attack.

Roscoff

I don't know what Roscoff in Brittany, France, is like now that it is a main port for giant cross channel car ferries. When I was last there about 40 years ago, it was a quaint fishing village. Very few English tourists visited the village. Any that did go to Brittany tended to visit more fashionable adjacent resorts. The main roads and railway bypassed the village. We first became interested in Roscoff when I was studying French and wanted a place where I would be compelled to speak and listen in French with native residents. This is difficult in say, Paris or Nice because, if you tried to converse in French you would more likely than not find that the person you spoke to is a foreigner themselves.

In order to practise my self taught French I used to converse with the colourful onion vendors who used to call at virtually every house in this country. They wore the distinctive Breton beret and a striped Tee shirt. Their vehicles were old bicycles heavily laden with purple tinted onions and sometimes also garlic. Two such vendors used to call on us regularly over many years. We bought fairly large quantities as we ourselves enjoyed their produce but we also bought on behalf of friends and relatives. Our custom, was therefore quite welcome especially so as we were also quite hospitable to them. Whichever one was the first to call on us in the season, would assure us that the other was not coming that year and would explain why in French which was interlaced with the local patois language which they knew I would not understand. They were both colourful characters, one was called Henri and the other Francois.

Through them we learned that the onions and garlic they sold were actually grown by themselves locally around their own village of Roscoff and when ripe, they would be shipped in bulk to Plymouth where they

91

would arrange to cart their own required quantity to the locality where they operated in Great Britain. Each had their own area but sometimes such areas overlapped as in our case.

The onion growers come vendors in those days were known here as Onion Johnnies. They would come over along with their families on the onion boats and set up in a lock-up garage, disused shop or even as locally, in the loft of a public-house. Whilst the men went out selling their wares, the rest of the family would stay behind stringing up the onions and garlic for the next day.

The selling season usually started about June and ended in time for the families to return home in time for Christmas, whilst here the children attended local schools.

One day, I told Henri that I wanted to spend a holiday in France but I wanted to go somewhere English tourists do not frequent so that I would be able to practise my French. He told me, that his own village of Roscoff has only two English visitors each year, a doctor and his wife from Cardiff. Subsequently we discovered that what he told us was correct but he failed to tell us that virtually everybody in the village spoke English. They had all, at one time or another spent a six month period in Great Britain in connection with the sale of onions and also their children, had spent 6 months a year in an English school. What we eventually found to our amusement was that each spoke English with the local dialect of the area in which they sold onions.

The journey to Roscoff was rather painful and impressive.

We changed trains in Paris but only 1st class carriages from there to Roscoff had upholstered seats. We sat all night on wood slatted seats which left deep impressions on us.

Roscoff was indeed a very picturesque fishing village and our room in the Hotel Du Centre overlooked the harbour. In the mornings we could see fishermen bringing fish direct from their boat into the hotel for the same day's meal. In addition, the village had its own lobster farm.

The only other residents in the hotel were French people from Paris who delighted in spending the annual vacance in Roscoff especially in the Hotel Du Centre because they considered the village as being unspoilt by tourism and the food in the hotel as being par excellence. As far as that was concerned, we struck lucky as it was also fortunate that the visitors from Paris could not speak English.

The area around the village was split up into small plots on which the onion Johnnies grew their wares. The plots were served by narrow dirt tracks only accessible by horses pulling small carts. We were able to amble along these lanes all day without the nuisance and annoyance of motorised vehicles.

The sandy soil on these plots was very poor but the farmers laid a thick bedding of sea weed which they gathered onto their horse drawn carts from the abundance swept up daily onto the fine white sand of the adjacent beaches. It is this sea weed which gives their onions and garlic the lovely purple tinge.

The sea water was quite warm because the gulf stream impinges on that part of the Brittany coast.

Henri asked us to visit his cottage so that he could return the hospitality he received when he visited us. He lived in a centuries old stone cottage which seemed not to have been changed from the day it was built. Sans water, sans electricity, sans gas, sans everything except an abundance of mellowed charm. The large, low ceilinged living room which was entered direct off the country lane contained a double brass bed. Even though it was June, a log fire burnt in the large open stone fireplace. Henri served us with large mugs of the delicious strong coffee that only the French seem to be able to make.

We spent a long evening with them and it was about midnight when we got back to the hotel which was in darkness and locked up for the night. We, naturally apologised to the manageress for disturbing her sleep and explained why we were so late. We don't know why but she pointedly asked, "Did Henri serve you brandy?'

The next morning whilst we partook of continental breakfast on the hotel terrace overlooking the harbour, the manageress asked Dora if she was not feeling well. Dora said that she had spent a restless night because she could hear an elephant constantly turning over on the roof. - The manageress, like everyone else in the village understood English quite well but as she thought Dora was using a colloquialism asked me to confirm in French. The manageress and the Parisians sitting at adjacent tables all looked up in surprise at the steeply sloping hotel roof. I was most embarrassed but Dora was quite adamant, she was sure that she heard an elephant continually turning over on the roof all night.

One afternoon there was a lot of excitement in the harbour. A small fishing boat had been brought in managed by a boy of about 15 years of age. His middle-aged father, the only other occupant on the boat had had a heart attack and died at sea.

Roscoff had a lobster farm and most of its produce was sent direct to Paris packed in ice but some of it came straight to the kitchen of the Hotel du Centre. It was not unusual to have a whole giant lobster served as an hors-d'oeuvre at the evening meal. On the first occasion we were at a loss as to how to tackle such a formidable prehistoric looking creature. Dora who was sitting opposite me said that she would watch what the French couple sitting behind me did and she would copy them and then I was to

93

copy her. On another evening we were served with cockles in their shells. All the French people had come prepared with pins which they had inserted into their lapels. The waitress was puzzled why we were not also so equipped.

Our wine consumption at meal times soon became a matter of great amusement to our fellow diners. Whereas they appeared to consume a whole bottle of wine at each meal, our bottle was sufficient to last a few days between us. At the first meal, we asked the waitress for water. Because I had such a terrible accent, she thought that she had misheard me and called the manageress who spoke excellent English over. At first, the manageress also thought that she had misheard me and then incredulously and in a lowered tone explained that nobody drank water with their meal but if we insisted, she would get us a bottle of mineral water.

Because Dora and I both had rapacious appetites and being naturally fast eaters we got through our meals very quickly. We finished eating whilst the other diners were still tackling the second course. When we got up to leave, several of them could not believe that we had completed our meal and signified that there were four courses.

At the table adjourning ours was a family from Paris. An elderly lady, her daughter and her husband. We got quite friendly with them even though they could not speak a word of English. One evening, the old lady was gabbling away in French to Dora who does not know the language but claims she can understand what is being said by the tone of voice and facial expressions. Dora responded by smiling broadly and saying "Very good, very good". I had to intercede and tell Dora that the old lady was describing the horrible way her sister had recently died of cancer.

We were amused when at meal times, the old lady would take out her full set of false teeth and place them on the table and replace them on completion of the meal.

One day, Henri invited us to visit the local clinic where he worked from time-to-time but first made us promise not to tell any of the patients what he did for a living in England.

He met us at the door of the formidable looking premises which abutted onto the sea shore. He was wearing a long white medical style overall and stethoscope. The patients assumed that he was a medical orderly of some sort.

The clinic specialised in treating patients with various rheumatic complaints and who came from all parts of France. The treatment consisted mainly in spraying the patient with warm sea water mixed with mud from the adjacent sea shore. The water was naturally warm because the gulf stream impinged on that part of the coast.

Vera

Vera was in her early sixties but she looked about ten years younger. Her hair had not turned grey, at least not to be noticed. She had a slim shapely figure and was always neatly and sensibly dressed. What was most noticeable was her abundant energy, cheerfulness and zealous effort to help fellow beings, especially old age pensioners. She would do shopping for them, care for their front gardens, trim their hedges, get their prescriptions, take their pets to the Vets, take their dogs for walks and many other odd jobs that could be of help. She did not expect any financial reward for these services and would not have accepted even if she had been offered. She chatted to all the neighbours but did not gossip. All the neighbours admired her.

Those who spoke to her noticed that in recent times she had become progressively hard of hearing. When anyone suggested however gently that she should entertain the idea of an hearing aid, she laughed the matter off and assured everyone that there was nothing wrong with her hearing.

However, her husband noticed that she increasingly suffered with bad headaches. Being a retired optician he naturally suggested that she should have an eye test. Vera scoffed at the idea that there may be something wrong with her eyes. She said that she could see perfectly both at long and short distance.

Eventually, as her headaches became more and more frequent and more intense, Vera went to see her doctor, one of her very rare visits. He referred her to a local hospital who carried out a brain scan. A week later, Vera went again to the doctor to find out the result of the scan. As she had inwardly feared, he told her that the scan had revealed a brain tumour. The tumour was quite advanced and was inoperable. The doctor said that although the tumour was inoperable and terminal the painful headaches could be repressed and until the end came she could lead a normal life.

He offered suitable counselling but Vera was the type of person who could take such news in her stride. She thanked her doctor for being so frank but refused the counselling. She then determined to do the things that she had always promised herself. With her husband's willing agreement, she bought each of her children and 'grandchildren expensive presents. She gave them each a lump sum, equivalent to what she would have left them in her will. This did not deprive her husband in any way as he already owned their house outright and had a very generous pension.

She next went with her husband on a never to be forgotten holiday to the Holy Land, something that they had both wished to do for many years.

They perused the catalogues and bought all the things that they should have before.

Then Vera indulged in what she had always wanted to do, ever since she was a schoolgirl. She ate what she fancied in any quantity she felt like. For all her adult years, Vera had eaten very frugally in order to retain her shapely, slim figure and now she did not need to be concerned. She wound down on her charitable works.

Despite all, Vera remained cheerful but slowly and surely what she had always avoided all her life came about, she started to put on weight quite noticeably. All her body increased in size but not in height. Vera had to discard her nice clothes and buy those advertised as being for the fuller figure. Eventually, her weight increased from about 9 stone (57kg) to about 15 stone (95 kg).

She became so heavy that her knees and hips quickly developed arthritis and she could not walk about, not even in the house. Despite all this, she still remained cheerful and kept on eating. The more she ate, the more she wanted.

Finally, her internal organs began to dysfunction as a result of the overweight, abuse and strong drugs and she passed peacefully away.

Several weeks after the funeral, Vera's husband opened a letter addressed to her from the hospital. In carefully worded officialese they regretted that the results of Vera's scan had been confused with that of another patient with a similar name. Vera's scan had proved negative and they suggested that she should consult an optician as her eyesight may very well be the actual cause of the pains in her head. They apologised for any inconvenience caused.

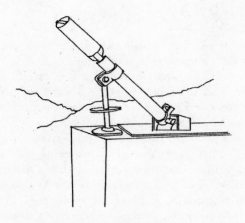

Safad (Zefat)

When we first visited Israel, we made the journey by boat because Dora had a fear of flying which she has since overcome. We travelled by train to Marseilles and there boarded the newly commissioned single class Israeli Moledet' (Homeland) liner. Apart from Dora's fear of flying, it was the cheapest means of getting there.

The boat sailed the following morning and at breakfast we learnt that several hundred Jewish refugees had embarked secretly during the night and were concealed in a lower deck until we were well clear of territorial waters. The refugees were from Algeria. A steward had told us that the majority of the refugees were children because Algerian Jews tended to have large families, ten children to a couple being quite common place. Many of the older men were blind.

We immediately remembered that in our cases were many gifts to be distributed to orphanages in Israel. Among these gifts was a box of blow-up balloons that made a whistling sound when the air was released. We asked a steward to distribute these gifts to the pitiful, impoverished children below. It was not long before the ship resounded with hundreds of these balloons sounding off. The din went on and on and several fellow passengers ominously said that they would like to get their hands on the idiots who gave the balloons to the children.

Some bright spark in the newly formed Israeli Zim shipping line had carefully scheduled the boat to arrive in Haifa on Saturday morning when the port was closed for the Jewish Sabbath Although we could see the Israeli coast quite clearly the boat had to sail back and forth for a whole day so that we could disembark the following morning.

In order to extend our holiday with the finances available, we had pre-arranged to stay privately with a lady in a room in her flat on Mount Carmel which towers above the port of Haifa.

As soon as we had deposited our luggage in our room we set out on our first objective. We had solemnly promised Dora's elderly father that we would visit the graves of his grandfather and other relatives who were buried in the cemetery of Safad. In bygone generations, it was the fashion for religious elderly Jews to leave eastern Europe to die and be buried in the Holy Land. The belief was that those nearest to the Temple Mount in Jerusalem would be the first to be resurrected when the Messiah came. Even though Safad was some distance from the Temple Mount in Jerusalem, it was an important place for pious Jews to live and die in because it contained the grave of the much revered, saintlike, 18th century Cabalist Rabbi Yitzhak Luria known as the Lion of Safad. It also contained the ancient synagogue of Arieh Hakadosch (the holy lion).

We caught an inter-city Egged bus to Safad which is about 35 miles to north-east of Haifa, 4 miles from Lake Tiberias (Yam Kinneret), four and a half miles from the Lebanese border and four miles to the Jordanian border. It was an extremely hot day. We found out later that a Khamsin desert wind was blowing. Every time the bus door opened, in came a blast of hot air similar to that experienced when an oven door is opened. Very few people were about. The next day our hostess told us that about the worst place to go when a Khamsin wind is blowing, is Safad. She said that everyone who can, takes it easy when a Khamsin is blowing.

Safad is a very picturesque town built on a 4000ft hill. It is very popular with artists. Because of its dominating position, it was a prime objective for the invading Syrian army in 1948 when the State of Israel was proclaimed. The Syrian army was well equipped and highly trained and they considered that they would have no problem in capturing Safad which they knew was defended only by a handful of poorly armed volunteers with little or no military experience.

The Israeli in charge of the defence of Safad was also too aware of the odds against them and in desperation devised a ruse to overcome them. The most powerful weapon the defenders had was a home made mortar. He fired this with a loud as possible explosion and then with a handful of other defenders holding white flags descended into the enemy camp. He told the Syrians that there was no point in defending the town because a secret atomic weapon they were harbouring had accidentally exploded and the whole town and surrounding areas were now highly radio active. Anyone staying in the vicinity was doomed.

As soon as the Syrians troops heard this, they dropped their weapons and fled with their officers leading the way. By the time that they realised that they had been fooled, regrouped and returned, the defenders had been reinforced and were now well armed with the weapons abandoned by the Syrian troops. The Syrians did not capture Safat. On a ridge of the hill overlooking the plain below is the mortar weapon used to set up as a memorial and is called the 'Davidka' (little David).

Touring Salad involves walking up and down steeply sloping roads and to do so in a Khamsin is very exhausting indeed. Because sensible people were taking a siesta whilst the Chamsin was blowing it appeared at times, that we were the only ones in town.

Having done a bit of sight-seeing, we set out to find the cemetery in which Dora's antecedents were buried. We had been advised to make enquires at the ancient Arieh Hakadosch Synagogue. The official there was very co-operative, he looked up some ancient documents and located the graves for us. As we could not read Hebrew, he asked his young son to go with us, the cemetery was situated at the foot of the hill and was reached by a steeply sloping rough path. The young boy led the way and was nimble footed like a mountain goat We were not so agile and being worn out by the preceding unaccustomed clambering on the steep roads of the town, gave up half way down. Perhaps, without the Chamsin, we might have managed it. We decided that we would try again another time, but 30 years later, we have not yet done so.

The climb down to the cemetery was not the only problem we encountered. We stopped several people to ask them the way to the ancient synagogue but none spoke English. Finally, one young man understood our request but reacted angrily. "Why do you want to visit an old synagogue, why visit a synagogue at all? Have you nothing better to do?" He said that if we had nothing better to do, we should visit and admire the lovely new synagogue which in any case was much nearer. Whilst we were trying to explain the reason for our request a small group gathered and apparently a lively discussion ensued between them as to whether we should visit the old or the new synagogue or any synagogue at all. We slipped away and found our own way there.

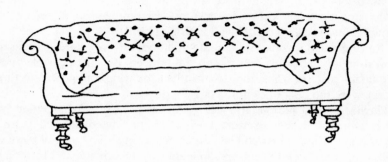

The Chesterfield

Before we went on honeymoon, my wife and I bought a small three bedroom end of terrace house in Beacontree Heath, east London and agreed with the vendors that they would vacate the premises before our return. They complied with this agreement but when we went to take possession we found that they had left behind several items of tatty furniture. When we contacted them we reminded them that the contract was for the house to handed over with vacant possession. They said that meant with no living being and did not include furniture. They also said that as far as they were concerned the items were ours and we could do what we liked with them. We were dismayed at their belligerent attitude, prior to the sale they were so pleasant and friendly.

We burnt most of the unwanted items but as we were short of money we retained some pro-tem till such time that we would be able to replace them.

Among the items we retained was a rather incongruous couch and

two matching armchairs. These were exceptionally tatty as the vendor's two Labrador dogs had used them as beds. The upholstery was filthy and the seats sagging. They looked less unappetising after we cleaned the upholstery and temporarily covered them with table cloths given to us as wedding presents.

We then encountered another shock, the vendors had not left the premises void of living beings, we discovered that the house was infested with bed bugs (cimex lectularins). The local council fumigated the house and eliminated the infestation at first attempt.

After living five happy years in the house, we decided to move home but did not wish to take the furniture that we had 'inherited' from the previous owner with us. We therefore took all the items into the garden and burnt them, that is all except for the large couch which was too heavy for us to move on our own.

Fortunately, this problem was overcome when a snooty, close relative kindly offered to take the couch off us completely free of charge. We were glad to see the back of it.

A few weeks later, the relative gleefully 'phoned to tell us that when they stripped the covering off the couch to re-upholster it, they consulted an antiques expert who confirmed their anticipation that it was indeed an original Chesterfield made couch. He said it was an exceptional example of one of his early couches, made about 1880 and the frame was 'signed' with his name as an indication of authenticity. He told them that it was unusual for a Chesterfield of that age to be completely free of any wood-worm attack. It still had its original horse hair stuffing, its original hand made springs and original castor wheels. He reckoned that even in its stripped down condition a dealer would gladly give at least five hundred pounds for it (that was in 1954).

My relative decided that they would have it reupholstered by an expert recommended by their friend as its value would be increased tremendously and that they will keep it as its value would be enhanced by each passing year

I ruefully looked at the modern couch that we had bought in its stead. It had already started to sag, its upholstery looked drab and its latex foam filling was powdering and seeping -through the covering.

Dora consoled me, she said that we had pulled a fast one on our snooty relative when we burnt the two matching armchairs!

Tell Tales

During my long career as an architect I undertook from time-to-time structural surveys on premises on behalf of would be purchasers.

Professionally, this is a dangerous practise as in a short time one has to discover and report on defects that the purchaser would be able to notice at leisure possibly with the assistance of family members and friends. The odds are very much against the surveyor who may eventually face charges of negligence or incompetence. Even if innocent, such charge can prove to be expensive both in money terms and time involved. In fact, I ceased doing surveys when advised to do so by a friendly solicitor who worked for a firm who specialised in defending surveyors being sued. Her wise words were, "Get out while you're winning".

However, I must express my appreciation to those vendors who inadvertently rendered valuable assistance in noting defects in their property. One obvious example is when the vendor is very insistent that I do not carry out the survey at certain times. The way I overcame my suspicion was to call at the premises during such a period to inform the vendor that I was just passing by and wanted to confirm the agreed appointed time. Such visits are useful to determine if there is neighbour problems or problems in the neighbourhood. Sometimes I would call on a neighbour with the excuse that I had mistaken the number of the house and explain why I was calling on the house being sold. Neighbours at times can be very helpful especially so, if they are not on good terms with the vendors.

Vendors who place anti down draught devices on chimney stacks point out that they are experiencing problems. Odd walls that have been rendered indicate rain penetration. New air bricks indicate dry rot in floors. Lopped trees indicate possible problems with blocked drains or foundation settlement.

If the house is vacant, see if any of the letters on the door mat are from firms specialising in treating rising damp, dry rot or woodworm.

A smell of fungicide or insecticide gives grounds for suspicion. Freshly plastered walls up to one metre above floor level is a dead give away of rising damp. Freshly papered walls in a house that has been decoratively neglected gives cause for a rational explanation. New floor boards or new skirting warrant explanation. Carpets that are closely tacked down along certain edges indicate possible problem.

One tactic to be used against the vendor, is suddenly, in the midst of general conversation to ask if his woodworm, dry rot, rising damp certificate is readily available. Such a question confuses an inexperienced vendor.

When surveying one must also be aware of tricks. In one house, there was a generous provision of 13 amp socket outlets in each room but upon investigation I found they were not wired up. In another house one wall was adorned with a giant Union Jack. Pulling it aside revealed a large damp patch. My suspicion was aroused in a house which had a musty smell which indicated woodworm. I suspected the attack was in the corner of a room in which an old lady sat knitting. The corner was dark and when I asked if she would mind if I had a quick look at the floor boards under her chair she appeared not to hear despite the fact she was wearing a hearing aid. I knew that a call of nature would soon induce her to leave the room. I made out that I was finished and went into the next room. No sooner had I done so I heard her leave and as soon as I heard the bathroom bolt operated I returned and confirmed my suspicion of wood worm. It was so bad, it was a wonder that the legs of the old lady's chair had not gone through the floor.

One vendor claimed that he had lost the key to a locked bedroom and another had packed a bedroom with so much furniture and lumber that I could get no further than the doorway. In both cases, a note of suspicion was included in my reports.

In one instance, I was called upon by a vendor to enable him to fool a surveyor. His house had been subject to severe settlement cracks. He had had his foundations underpinned and cracked bricks replaced. However much he tried, his bricklayer could not disguise the new bricks and the new pointing. They stood out like jagged streaks of forked lightening. The bricklayer had tried all the tricks of the trade but the new bricks and the pointing stood out. I advised the opposite, I told the bricklayer to wire brush the existing bricks and pointing to remove surface dirt and weathering. The result was that all the bricks and mortar, both old and new looked the same. Apparently, this ruse was successful. I hope the surveyor concerned will never discover my part in the deception.

Street names can also be helpful. It pays to make enquiries at the local council offices if any of the local street names suggest that trees may have been removed or pits filled in. Such names are Forest Road, Chestnut Avenue, Willow Tree Walk, Pitfield Street or Lakeside View.

Houses built on such sites may be prone to foundation subsidence or ground heave.

Bedroom Furniture

Soon after we moved into our four bedroom, Victorian, terraced house, Dora decided that we should furnish the spare bedroom in case we received overseas visitors. She over-ruled me when I pointed out that if we did not make provision, we would not feel obliged to put up such visitors.

We brought very little bedroom furniture from our previous house because Dora had decided when we moved in there, to have as much furniture and cupboards built-in' as we could. Our Victorian house had no such luxuries. We replied to an advert in our local newsagents window. It offered a large wardrobe and dressing table for £75.00. The advertiser turned out to be a student in a nearby bed-sitter. He explained that it was not actually himself who was selling the items, but his mother who lived in a village in Essex. We asked that if that was so, why did she not advertise locally. He said that his mother had a certain social status to uphold locally and did not wish it to be known that she was selling off some of her furniture. He explained that his mother was actually a titled lady. We 'phoned Lady 'X' and made an appointment to view the furniture.

Although the appointment was for 3pm, Lady 'X' did not turn up till 3.30pm. She was rather inebriated or more truly, 'drunk as a lord'. She lived in a large Georgian house which was very dilapidated both outside and in. She must have been very eager to get rid of the items as she had them standing in the hall ready to be taken away. Both the wardrobe and dressing table were in sound condition but were crudely painted apple green colour. The brush marks were all too obvious and there were streaks of paint running down the speckled mirrors.

We paid a local builder £15.00 to transport the furniture for us in his van. The items served us well as they were both most commodious but when a snooty relative offered to buy them from us for £100 Dora was very tempted and said make it £90 and its a deal. Dora always loved haggling, she was good at it.

When we visited the relative a few weeks later she showed us what she had done to the items. She and her clever teacher husband had stripped the paint and revealed the beautiful satin wood underneath. They had also had the mirrors re-silvered. The transformation was wonderful, even Dora agreed but said that the painted finish would have been easier to keep clean.

Six months or so later, our snooty relatives called round and showed us a Sotheby's catalogue in which was a coloured 'photo of the two items. They were described as being designed by Owen Jones in 1873 for Eynsham Hall, Oxfordshire and were in immaculate original condition. Dora did not seem to have noticed the suggested auction price but said, she's not all that clever, after all, we made a profit when we sold the items to her.

Luke

We got to know Luke as being the local odd job man. He did not mind doing any odd job however small or unpleasant but he hated gardening. His own garden testified to his dislike. However, he would not mind cutting down trees or digging compost pits or emptying compost pits.

He willingly undertook to do any job including window cleaning, painting, repairing paths, washing cars, etc. but his problem was actually to carry out the work. He suffered with an extreme form of lethargy which involved long periods of deep slumber.

Even when awake, he looked sleepy, his eyes were puffed and half closed, he spoke slowly and hesitantly as though just awaken from a dream into the world of reality. His skin had the appearance of ingrained dirt, his clothes were shabby as though he habitually slept in them, which he most likely did. We never knew him to wear a tie even when he attended his father's funeral to which he arrived when the service was nearly over. We first knew him when he was about 30 years old and by then he was married with five children, 4 girls and one boy, all bright and cheerful and healthy.

Luke subsisted basically on unemployment pay supplemented by the various additional benefits that the state allocated to men who were not employed and had a wife and five children dependant on them. In addition, he augmented his income with that which he earned by doing odd jobs.

Possibly, he did the odd jobs in order to get out of his own house which quite frankly could do with a large number of odd jobs, such as cleaning, painting, tidying, repairing and decorating. We noted with amusement that his wife employed another odd job man to clean their windows.

We once asked him how it was that he was eligible to draw unemployment pay for such a long period of time when there were many vacancies locally for people with his qualifications. He told us that it was not his fault really that he was unemployed. He did try to get a job but firms would not employ him even though they were desperate for labour. He said they seemed to object to his extremely shabby appearance and his apparent lack of sleep. Despite this, he did occasionally get a regular, 'permanent' job but they did not last long. One such job was for a long distance lorry driver. He turned up late on his first day but before starting out on his long journey he took his loaded lorry home to show his wife what a lovely vehicle and costly load he was responsible for. His wife gave him a hefty but belated breakfast to speed him on his way. Luke decided that a short rest before his task would not come amiss. The outcome was that three days later the police awoke him and told him that his employers were rather concerned as they had received no news about their expensive lorry and its load for three days. They feared that perhaps there had been an unreported hijack

On another occasion he got a job cleaning the bedding department of a large well know departmental store in Oxford Street, London.

Luke greatly admired the department's showpiece of a four poster bed with satin silk sheets and pillows which was prominently on display in a window fronting the prestigious Oxford Street. As Luke's cleaning duties took place during the night when the store was closed, he was tempted to fulfil a long held desire to sleep on such a bed. He just meant to lie down for a few minutes to savour its delights. He took his motor cycle boots off and placed them beside the bed, he then placed his leather jacket and motor cycle helmet on a nearby chair and closed his eyes in ecstasy.

The departmental manager who had employed him had great difficulty waking him up the following morning whilst a huge amused crowd gaped through the shop window. Many thought it was a publicity stunt. Once, when we visited Luke to arrange for an odd job to be done he invited us to take a seat. Just as I was about to sit down on an arm chair, he said, "Just a moment, I think the baby may be under these clothes". Indeed it was. I was very careful in selecting another chair as they were all draped in clothes. Nothing appeared to have been put away in cupboards or wardrobes. As we looked around the room we could see that it contained expensive looking furniture. Luke explained that he had bought it on hire purchase from a well known departmental store. We asked how it was that in his impecunious situation he was given such credit facilities. Apparently, someone who he met regularly at the local Social Security office gave him a glowing testimony and an iron tight guarantee on headed paper that he had purloined from a titled gentleman's house.

The departmental store had tried to re-possess the items but gave up after three court attempts when Luke failed to appear. The court was reluctant to issue an arrest warrant as they did not wish to deprive five young children of their dutiful lather.

One of the odd jobs we asked Luke to do was to clear a blocked drain. After poking about and rodding and plunging, he said that he would have to dig a hole to expose a section of the underground drain. He explained that this would not have been necessary had the house had a manhole. He said that once he had exposed the drain, he would carefully chisel a hole in the top in order to gain access to the blockage.

As soon as he had cut this hole, the blocked sewage that had then built up in the vertical stack pipe spurted out covering Luke with it's smelly contents. We gave him an ample supply of paper kitchen towels and a bucket of warm water to cleanse himself.

He then said that having cleared the blockage, but before reinstating the drain, he would have a break for lunch. Thereupon, he took a packet of sandwiches from his tool bag and commenced to eat. Dora timidly asked if he would like a cup a tea.

Luke loved to mess about with old clapped out cars which he tried to rehabilitate and also with old noisy motor bikes. There were at any one time about five motor bikes in various stages of dismemberment in his front garden. Out of the five he sometimes got one to function. His pride and joy were his knee length motor bike boots, leather jacket and helmet. One day, when he was deeply depressed about his lethargy and inadequacy, he decided to commit suicide. He felt that he had failed as a father to provide for the forthcoming Christmas and New Year. He donned his leather jacket, motor bike boots and treasured helmet and went deep into the local Epping Forest and sat down with his back against a tree in the position near the lake where he had spent so many contented hours in trying to catch fish. He had written a farewell letter to his wife and children and carefully placed it in his leather jacket pocket in which he had also previously placed the pills he was going to take. He considered that this was the most reasonable, honourable thing to do. All his worries vanished, he seemed strangely relaxed and could almost imagine heavenly music and angelic choral song. He closed his eyes and waited to be welcomed into the next world which he was sure would be Heaven. In the morning he was rudely awaken by a Policeman asking if he was ill. He told the Policeman that he never felt better when he was alive. The Policeman looked at him curiously and asked if he should not be taking pills for his condition. Luke replied that he had not taken all the pills required before passing over.

He then glanced down, and on the ground near him was the unopened packet of pills he had brought with him. Meanwhile at home his wife was frantically searching high and low for her birth control pills.

Luke

One day, whilst I was out, Luke called to tell Dora that subsequent to his failed attempt to commit suicide, the local housing authority had decided to re-house him and his family. He asked if he could leave his newly acquired Rolls Royce in our front forecourt until he got settled into his new house and insured the vehicle. Dora readily acquiesced thinking of what an impression such a prestigious vehicle would have on neighbours and visitors. Six months later, we are still waiting for Luke to remove the clapped out Rolls Royce hearse.

The Inventor

Our local council in conjunction with a charity housing association had provided flats at the bottom end of our street for political refugees from eastern Europe.

My first encounter with one of them was when a smartly dressed well coiffured, white haired gentleman presented himself without a prior appointment at my front door. He bowed deeply, smiled and uttered what I presumed to be his name. He said, 'Please" and walked straight in before receiving a reply. Without being requested he ensconced himself in my favourite armchair and said, "Thank you".

In very poor, highly accented English, he confirmed that I was who he assumed I was. He then kindly proceeded to explain the purpose of his visit but before doing so, he lit a cigarette in a long cigarette holder and said, rather than asked, "Do you mind?"

He said he was from Poland and that he was an inventor and had many inventions to his credit. He had heard that I was an architect and that he would welcome my endorsement of an interlocking building block that he had invented and in return he would be willing to accept my investment of £5000 for a partnership in the venture. He ignored my declaration that I was no longer an architect, that I had retired a few years previously, that even if I had still been a registered architect I would not be permitted by my institute in endorsing building products or having financial interest in such and he also ignored my declaration that I did not have £5000 to invest. He carried on as though I had not spoken and produced papers from his smart briefcase. He shuffled them about and from time-to-time thrust one or another to me to emphasise a certain point he was making in his very broken English.

111

From the glimpses I had of these papers I gathered that he had submitted an application for a provisional patent and that the patent office, whilst registering his application was saying that they needed more information before proceeding and that the information submitted should be in more comprehensible English.

When I mentioned this to the inventor, he said that they were all idiots, with the emphasis on the 'ots'. He said that the patents office employed a lot of foreigners who could not speak proper English and all they really wanted was to get hold of the details of his inventions. He said that he would not supply same until he had secured sufficient financial backing to proceed with a full application. That, he explained, was the main purpose of his visit.

I tried to explain that it was very unlikely that anyone would invest in his invention unless he first obtained a full patent.

In confidence, he told me that the main constituent of his building block was sawdust but he had not yet decided on the bonding agent. He said that the beauty of the block lay in the type of sawdust to be used, which he refused to reveal and the fact that they could be cut using ordinary carpenter's tools.

I told him that architects would not be able to specify his block or the Council's building inspectors accept them, unless he obtained a certificate from the British Standards Institute. In order to obtain this, he would have to furnish the results of tests carried out by independent testing stations approved by the BSI. Such tests would include water absorption tests, durability tests under differing weather conditions and temperatures, comprehensive and tensile strengths, fire resistance tests, thermal insulation tests etc.. He just dismissed these as unimportant details which could be dealt with in due course.

He then said that he understood that I would want to confirm my investment with my wife but meanwhile, would I be kind enough to get someone to type out his own specification details because his handwriting was not too good and whilst doing so, correct any small grammatical errors and spelling mistakes which he might have inadvertently made. His specification was difficult to read and was incomprehensible.

We gathered that he stayed at home working on his inventions whilst his wife slogged away in a factory as the breadwinner. She was convinced that he was a genius and that one day, he would capitalise on his inventions and they would be multi-millionaires. If only he could get the required financial backing. He also told us about some of his other inventions for which he could not find any financial backers. One was for a giant parachute to be fixed on top of passenger planes that could be opened and lower the plane gently to the ground should the engines fail. He said the principle could also be applied to war planes. Re had been in touch with NASA in the United States as he reckoned that such a parachute could also be used in the event of a space rocket failing. NASA kindly replied that they can't consider the proposal until such time that he obtains international patents on his idea.

His idea of ejection seats for cars had been rejected by all the major car manufacturers on the grounds that it would be safer for people to remain in their cars in the event of an accident rather than ejecting about in roadways where there may be fast moving vehicles. He could not understand why the car manufacturers would not accept his idea of burglar proof locks. They reckoned that they were so efficient that the car owners would not be able to get in either, nor would any occupants be able to get out easily because the locks were designed to be operated from the outside only.

The inventor was particularly proud of his anti-mugging device. This consisted of a revolver strapped under the clothes onto the chest. In the event of being mugged, the victim has only to pull a cord concealed in his or her pocket to fire the gun. I asked hint what would happen if the mugger attacked from the rear, he said quite simple, have another gun strapped to the back.

His latest and finest invention was a device to couple lengths of pipes together in lieu of welding. This was particularly applicable to gas and oil pipe lines. He approached the Russian Embassy in London and they said that as he would not divulge details to them, he should see their experts in Moscow and describe his invention to them. They were particularly interested as at that time they had signed a contract to supply vast quantities of gas from their Siberian oil fields to Western Germany. The contract was vital to their economy.

Dora loaned him the few hundred pounds he needed for his Moscow visit. He assured her that he would pay her back several times over from his first royalties. She is still waiting.

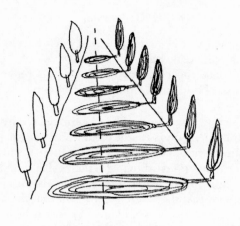

The Lodger

We first got to know Brian through a mutual acquaintance who told us that
he was very unhappy in his present lodgings and would very much like to
move in with nice friendly people like ourselves.

Before we accepted the suggestion, we met Brian several times and satisfied ourselves that he would be compatible. As far as we could ascertain
he had lost his wife in tragic circumstances and could not bring himself
round to re-marry. We had suitable accommodation in the house which in
prior times had been occupied as two self contained flats. Brian agreed,
that in exchange for the accommodation, light, heat and full board, he
would furnish light duties such as window cleaning, gardening, car washing, decoration, feeding the cats when we were out and chauffeuring etc.
The agreement worked out mutually well for all of us. He stayed with us
for many years but we never got to know much about his past except for
the vague mention of being a widower and having served in the Royal
Navy during the war. We never even got to know his age or his birthday.
He never received post. He went and came as he pleased but we had no
idea where he went. As we only paid him spending money, we provided all
his basic needs including clothes, we assumed that he had some private
income or pension.

He was completely honest and trustworthy and dependable. One day,
Dora arranged that we and her brother and his family would spend a day
visiting Cambridge. As Dora's brother had four young children, there were
too many passengers for one car so it was agreed that Dora's brother
would take all the adults in his car and that Brian would drive the four children in my brand new Rover. I had no qualms about this, as Brian was a
very careful and capable driver and he loved driving my luxurious saloon

with auto gear box and power steering. He had no car of his own.

The outing was very successful and we returned late afternoon along the Al road with the setting sun flitting between the trees growing at regular intervals alongside the road giving an hypnotic and stroboscopic effect.

Brian arrived home first and opened the front door with his own key but no sooner had he stepped onto the front door mat that he fell face down. At first, we thought that he may have tripped over but then we noticed he was unconscious but before we could phone for an ambulance he recovered. Despite his refusal to receive any medical attention, we summoned the emergency doctor service. Alter examining him, the doctor said he could find nothing wrong and that he should consult his own doctor as soon as possible as he may have suffered a Petit Mal which we later discovered meant a minor epileptic fit.

If he was subject to such fits, he should not be driving and this fit may have been induced by the stroboscopic rays of sunshine on the return journey. The fit could easily have happened earlier whilst he was driving. Needless to say, we never permitted him to drive our car again.

Our Namesake

When we moved into our house at No. 48, we were not aware that a person with an identical first name and surname lived at no 8 in the same street. He and his wife were long time resident when we moved in.

I had my bank accounts transferred to a local branch. The first we knew of our namesake was when I received a statement of account from my bank. The balance was far more satisfactory than I anticipated because we had a lot of expenditure in moving home. However, I was perturbed to note that the bank was making regular direct debit payments to several organisations unknown to us. With the knowledge that I was comfortably in credit, I 'phoned the manager to complain about the mistakes including the fact that they had addressed my statement of account to no 8 instead of no 48.

He was most apologetic and assured me that it would not happen again.

A few days later, an elderly gentleman called at our house and handed me a buff envelope and said "I think that this was meant for you but it was delivered to my house at No. 8 by mistake". It was in fact my own statement of account but the balance, although still in credit, was so, only marginally. The neighbour apologised for opening the letter and explained that as it bore his name on the envelope he opened it quite innocently. He had not noticed that it was addressed to no 48. He only found out about his namesake when he phoned the manager of his bank to complain about the wrong balance and wrong payments. He also found out that we both share the same bank branch.

Until he died a couple of years later, the local regular postman had a fixation and delivered all the post addressed to our namesake to our house

116

but fortunately not visa-versa.

Because our neighbour was ex-directory, we received many 'phone calls intended for him. He was very active in the local community and had many acquaintances. Sometimes Dora had a long friendly conversation on the 'phone with a caller before realising that the call was not intended for her.

However, the confusion did not cease immediately on the demise of our namesake.

Because he was so well known locally, we received a lot of 'phone calls and letters of consolation when his death became known. Some of the callers had quite a shock when I answered the 'phone. One woman timidly asked where I was and I told her, "In the lounge".

On the day of the funeral, the street was choked with mourners' cars, none of which left room for the hearse to park outside no 8. Because of the congestion, it had to park temporarily outside our house.

Just at that time, one of our friends passed by and was severely shocked when she saw the hearse parked outside our house.

A few days later, she received another shock when she met Dora by chance in the street. Dora was going to a protest meeting which had been organised by a woman's group she belonged to whose members wore black when attending such protests.

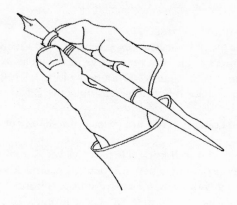

Divine Inspiration

I am not at all religious but am very interested in all religions. Even though by birth I am Jewish, the majority of my acquaintances are not Jewish. Several of my closest friends consider themselves good practising Christians and are regular churchgoers. A few are either Christian clergy or full time missionaries. Surprisingly, none of them overtly try to convert me or my wife but we have no doubt that they would dearly love to do so. We very much appreciate their restraint and their sincerity.

One non-Jewish acquaintances who was a work colleague, who like me was not religious, did from time-to-time accompany his wife to church just to please her. He would rather have stayed at home and done some gardening, etc.

One Monday morning he came into the office looking very peculiar and not well. He assured us that he was not ill but suddenly slumped over his desk and sobbed bitterly. Slowly and hesitantly he told us that when accompanying his wife to church the previous day he suddenly felt the presence of Jesus. He could not describe it but he was sure that

Jesus himself embraced him and he felt a changed person, he felt that he must now follow Jesus and do his bidding. He said that he was crying because he knew so little about Jesus and about Christianity and he did not know what to do or say. It took quite a while for his colleagues to realise he was sincere and to stop teasing him. He was very emotionally upset and very confused. He was in contrast to some other 'Christians' who told us that either Jesus or God spoke to them and told them what to do, but we noticed that in each case, Jesus or God told them to do what they wanted to do in any case.

The restraint on the part of our Christian friends to openly try to convert us directly did not stop them from passing our names and addresses to Christian missionaries who would place us on their regular mailing lists or to send missionaries to chat to us.

Apart from being intrigued by religions I was also interested in studying foreign languages including French, German, Russian, modern Hebrew and Yiddish.

Anyone who has studied a foreign language will appreciate that, in order to build up a vocabulary it is useful to commence reading books in that language as soon as the basics have been absorbed. They will also appreciate that this process is very slow and frustrating when most words have to be painfully looked up a bilingual dictionary.

I decided to combine my interests in religion and languages by exploiting the fact that I could first read a verse of the bible in English and then read the same verse in a bible of the language of my choice. It was not difficult to get copies of the bible in the desired language. I had only to mention my interest and one was promptly produced as if by a miracle.

Even though my prime interest was in learning foreign languages I could not help taking note of what I was reading especially so, as I was reading each verse several times over. When something struck me as particularly interesting I jotted it down on a scrap of paper. Eventually, I had dozens of such scraps and stuck related ones onto sheets of paper. When I mentioned some of my findings to friends, they showed great interest and suggested that I should write a book on the subject.

I thought to myself, no harm in recording what I and my friends had found to be interesting, so I began writing. As I was working professionally during the day, I wrote most of the book in the evenings. My writing table is in front of a window facing west and one evening, as I wrote, the setting sun glistened on the gold nib of my fountain pen. I suddenly felt that I was completely enveloped by some mysterious force which compelled me to continue to write. Not a sound was to be heard except a steady quiet buzz in my head, the birds fell silent and there was a pure clean sensation in mind and body. All I was aware of, was the gold nib of my pen gliding swiftly over sheet after sheet of writing paper. The nib appeared to be an instrument of pure gold fire and the words came effortlessly.

Suddenly, I seemed to come back to earthly life and I felt that some force had divinely inspired me to record my religious message to the world.

I did not mention my out-of-world experience to Dora but waited patiently for her to type the chapters that I had written. I wondered, was it just pure chance that I had married a champion typist?

After a while, Dora entered the room brandishing the sheaf of papers which I had handed her and I waited with baited breath for her comments. She asked, "Have you gone nuts? What a load of twaddle and your spelling mistakes are more atrocious than ever, what came over you?"

The spelling mistakes alone convinced me that I had not been under any form of divine inspiration.

The Austin 7

In February 1951, Dora decided that we should acquire a motor car. We advised a local second hand car dealer of our requirement and stipulated that it should not cost more than forty five pounds. This may not sound very much for a car but in those days, it was more than a months salary for me. Within a few days the dealer phoned to say that just by chance that very day, he had bought in a lovely car, in beautiful condition, a good runner and it was a mere forty five pounds. He advised an early inspection as such cars were in great demand.

New cars were virtually unobtainable. Civilian car production had ceased at the beginning of the war in 1939 and only recommenced at the end of the war in 1946 and even then, the few produced were sold as exports. One had to have very strong connections in high places to have the privilege of buying a brand new car even if one had the money. Most of the second hand cars available were those that had been laid up for the duration of the war as petrol was not available for civilian use.

We hastened along to the car dealers plot and as we approached we saw a little car with a tattered canvas hood wedged between giant army surplus lorries. At first we laughed at the notion of being seen driving around in such an ancient looking car, after all, we had a position to uphold in our street in Beacontree Heath, east London. We were one of the few who owned, albeit on mortgage, our own house and I was the only person in the street who worked in an office and wore a tie to work

The car had certain unique features, it had a crash gear box, that is, the gears were not synchronised, this meant that when changing gears the speed of the car and the revs of the engine had to be judged just right by the driver or the gears ended up in a mangled up condition. On the steer-

121

ing wheel was a lever marked ignition advance and retard but it did not seem to make any difference to performance when I advanced or retarded it.

The choke was a simple device and consisted of a piece of string attached to a hinged flap on top of the carburettor. When the string was pulled, it opened the flap and increased the air inflow. The petrol tank was situated immediately above the engine, no petrol pump was required as the fuel dripped directly into the carburettor. The petrol gauge was a wooden stick with inches marked on it. The car did have a speedometer but this indicated whatever speed it fancied and was situated for some unknown reason out of the drivers sight on the passengers side of the car. The brakes were operated by cables which tensioned against the chassis, but as the chassis was so flimsy all the cables did was to flex the metal work with very little effect on the brakes.

I first became aware of the braking deficiency when driving along the local shopping parade at about 15 miles per hour. A child darted out from the crowded pavement and when I applied the brakes there was very little reaction. In those days, my reactions were much quicker than they are now, I turned the steering wheel violently and did a sharp 'U' turn and stopped on the other side of the road. The child was unhurt but nearby women onlookers were screaming hysterically. Out of the crowd, a huge burly man whom I presumed was the child's father came hurtling towards me and before I could say or do anything he grasped my hand and said " Thanks, you deserve a medal for your brilliant driving and your bravery of driving against the flow of traffic in order to save my little boy's life". There was also a round of applause from the onlookers. Dora was very proud of me.

The brakes of the car were so arranged that the foot pedal only activated the brakes on the front two wheels and the hand brake the two rear wheels. In an emergency both the foot and hand brakes had to be activated simultaneously. The wheels had wire spokes and very little tread on the tyres. The car even had a feature that modem cars lack, even the most expensive ones, that is a top hinged outward opening windscreen. This was very useful in very misty or foggy weather, especially when the fog was polluted with smoke from chimney stacks was really thick and dirty. The car had two outside mirrors fixed onto the front mudguards. Moreover, the car had charm and character and age, it was a 1929 model. Even in 1951, it was considered vintage.

However it lacked certain fixtures which today are taken for granted. The twin doors did not have locks, just latches but even these were superfluous because it was quite easy to step over the closed doors. Locks were not needed as car thefts were virtually unknown in those days.

It had no heater or demister and no windscreen wipers. A neighbour who was a lorry driver kindly obtained a wiper from the firm where he worked and fitted it on for me. It was a powerful wiper and with each sweep of its blade the car rocked from side to side.

It had no ignition key. To start the engine a switch on the dashboard was activated and then the engine turned by a brass handle permanently fixed at the front of the car. The engine usually needed several turns and when it started it would whirl the handle round swiftly and with the power of the engine. If the starter's hand was not withdrawn quickly enough it could easily be smashed by the handle.

All signals had to be given by an arm stuck out of the side of the car. There were no electric or mechanical signals. In cold weather, drivers gave vigorous signals if only to keep warm and in the hot weather would stick their arms out to cool down.

The retractable canvas hood had a tiny aperture at the rear to serve as a rear window but as this was so small and obscure it was useless. When we first bought the car, the hood had a single slope from windscreen up to the rear of the car and then the hood dropped vertically in a most incongruous shape. Another neighbour kindly reshaped the hood for us with new canvas but forgot to form an aperture in the rear. As we had the car during the spring and simmer months only, this did not matter much as we usually drove with the hood down.

A colleague at work who was a car enthusiast warned me that the king pin in the front steering gear was missing and that any moment I could lose complete control of the car. One day I said to Dora, I would like to see the maximum speed that the car can do so we went for a drive along the Eastern Avenue arterial road. I asked Dora to keep an eye on the speedometer as it was out of sight from the drivers seat. On a clear straight stretch of the road I put my foot down hard on the accelerator and twiddled the ignition advance and retard lever. Dora started calling out the speeds which varied with alarming alacrity, some of the speeds were excellent but I had difficulty in hearing Dora's voice because of the wind, we had the hood down in order to reduce wind resistance.

Just as we reached maximum speed a sporty cyclist with shorts and bent down handle bars glided past with a cheerful "Good day".

Sometimes our dignity and social status in the street would be dented somewhat when we were towed home. Once it was by one of those enormous vehicles which takes crates of empty milk bottles back to the bottling plants and once by a motor cycle.

For some reason or another, the car seemed to attract attention. If we drove past a bus queue, conversation would stop and heads swivel in disbelief

Once a policeman on traffic point duty signalled me to pull over and after staring at the car said "Its OK sir, I just wanted to make sure it was not an hallucination". On another occasion when driving across Hackney Downs in east London to visit Dora's parents in Stoke Newington, some local children started to chase us and throw stones. We avoided pulling up alongside double decker buses as we soon learnt from hard experience that people on the upper deck were bound to throw rubbish down on us. Finally, after some hair raising experiences due to the dismal brakes we decided to dispose of the vehicle. We offered the car back to the dealer who originally sold it to us but he sadly shook his head and said that he would try to sell it on a commission basis if we were to leave it with him. He advised us not to stick out for the price we had paid because with the approaching winter it would be impossible to sell the car at all.

Within a week, on a very rainy day, he turned up and said that he had sold the car and paid the money due to us. Because of the heavy rain he was soaking wet, he must have walked to us and as we had not asked him to sit down he leaned against a newly papered wall. When he had gone, there on the wall paper, was his outline complete with his large brimmed hat. He said he had sold the car to a district nurse from Devon who asked for an assurance that the car could do that journey. He told her, "Only if you put some petrol in the tank".

Our Dragon

When we moved into our house about 40 years ago there was already an established straggly privet hedge some 40' (1200mm) high and 20'0" long along the front garden boundary with the neighbouring house.

With each succeeding trim, it became progressively bumpier, I tried to keep it straight but failed miserably. I then had an inspiration. Why not exaggerate the bumps and form the hedge into the shape of a monster. Eventually the shape of a dragon emerged with an upstanding stubby tail, ridges along its back and a big round friendly smiling face with large ears.

I found this a lot easier to keep in shape than a straight hedge where even the slightest irregularity showed up.

One day, this unusual and unique hedge came to the notice of the local press who published its photo on the front page. As a result, a lot of people from neighbouring streets came to view the monster. Sometimes coaches with elderly people or children would specially come down the street to see our dragon. Coaches carrying what appeared to be foreign tourists also stopped to take photos. It wasn't long before a Japanese photographer asked permission to photograph the hedge. He had seen a photo of it in a London newspaper and wanted to send photos to various overseas publications. He promised to let us have copies of any published but we never received any although we heard that the photos were published in several countries. So our 'dragon' achieved international fame!

Whilst I was trimming the hedge one day, a woman stopped to chat. She told me that whenever she felt depressed, she deliberately came to see the dragon because his friendly smile always cheered her up. She even confessed to speaking to him at limes.

We often see passing couples nudge each other and point out the dragon and openly laugh. He certainly has a therapeutic effect on people. Visitors both to our house and to adjoining houses who cannot remember house numbers use the dragon as a landmark. One day, we heard a crash in the street and when we looked out of the window we saw that two cars had had a head-on collision. Apparently, the attention of one driver was distracted by the image of a dragon.

A neighbour's funeral cortege passed down our road recently. The cortege consisted of the hearse and ten fully laden limousines. In accordance with custom it proceeded at a slow walking pace preceded by the chief undertaker dressed in tailed morning suit and top hat with long black crepe ribbon. Each step he took was recorded by a sharp tap the road with his silver knobbed walking stick. Looking out of our window we could see that as each limousine passed our front garden the passengers saw the smiling dragon, their gloom ridden faces suddenly changed to smiles and laughter. No doubt our deceased neighbour would have appreciated that if he could have seen it.

The Dog

A couple of years before our friend Ernie died at the grand old age of 81 years, he asked us to act jointly with his solicitor as executors of his will. He told us that for several years past, he had been simplifying his estate so as to make its disposal easy for probate. He had no outstanding debts or mortgages.

When he died, his solicitor confirmed that we indeed were joint executors with himself and that in recognition of our friendship, Ernie had left us the generous sum of £50.00 each in his will.

The solicitor also confirmed that the bulk of the estate was in the form of cash deposited with a building society and apart from a few small bequests he had left the remainder of his wealth to a society for the blind. All in all, Ernie had died a fairly rich man and had surprised everyone concerned including all his relatives both close and far to whom he left nothing

Apart from the cash, he had left two properties. One was his own house in a very desirable district and the other was a derelict shop with an occupied flat over. The solicitor said that he would have no difficulty in disposing of the house and contents but there was a complication concerning the shop and flat over. It was situated in a slum district on the south side of the river Thames and was occupied by a controlled tenant, that is a tenant who paid a derisory rent controlled by rigorous and penalising regulations administered by a local authority with a genetic hatred of anyone who was not a controlled tenant, especially landlords.

At the behest of the tenants, the local authority had served several notices on Ernie requiring him to carry out repairs and maintenance the costs of which far exceeded the rent due.

Much of the repairs required were in respect of damage caused by the tenant's family. The shop was not in use as the windows were boarded up as a consequence of repeated vandalism and no shop keeper wanted to trade there because of the local reputation of mugging, looting and robbery. The tenant's sons were unofficially using the shop premises as a motor bike repair shop.

Ernie could not find any insurance company willing to cover the premises and also could not find any buyer even though he had offered the property at a give-a-way price. The tenant was also months in arrears in rent. The solicitor advised us that as joint executors of Ernie's will, it was our duty to inspect the property, interview the tenant and submit a written report for consideration by the joint executors. He told us that if we failed to fulfil our duties as executors it would be a serious misdemeanour subject to severe penalties.

Dora decided that I would honour our obligations and sent me on my way with a caution, "Be careful". I had prepared myself with a clipboard, pad, pencil and a road map with my route clearly marked in red. It was a fine sunny Sunday afternoon.

The river Thames is a great divide in London. Even though I had crossed the English Channel several times, this was the first time I had motored across one of the Thames bridges. For the first five minutes, all went to plan, then I started to hit diversions and one way routes until I had completely lost my orientation. The road signs were useless, they all pointed to districts I never knew existed. However, eventually, I found the property but by now I was feeling frustrated and exhausted.

I was greeted at the door by a man with a collarless shirt open at the neck, a waistcoat but no jacket, loose fitting trousers that appeared to have been slept in for many months. He looked at me and asked if I was from the 'social'. When I replied "no" he asked if 1 was a sanitary inspector. I told him that Ernie had died and that I was one of a trio of executors and that I had come to make a report with a view of disposing of the property. He said what a shame, he and Ernie had always got on well, knew him for years, " He was a real gent, it's a shame he's gone but we all have to go at some time or another".

Apparently, he had misunderstood what I had told him and asked me if I was the new landlord. I tried to explain the situation again but with doubtful result. Our conversation was made rather difficult due to the loud revving of a motor bike engine and the even louder thumping of music from the shop.

I asked if it would be okay for me to have a quick look round the premises so as to report back to the other executors. He replied, " Okay by me son (he kept addressing me as son, even though I was at least as old as he was and even though he had at least a weeks growth of a stubbly beard) but I must warn you, my dog don't like strangers, he was trained as a guard dog and is very fierce".

His dog was a massive shaggy Alsatian type of dog with a heavy leather collar with spiked studs. He did not display any aggressive attitude to me, in fact he kept sniffing at my trousers from all directions and wagging it's tail. I realised the dog must have got the smell of our cat who often sits on my lap. I knew that dogs wagged their tails when they were pleased so I patted him on the head and called him "Good boy".

Thereupon I entered the premises, the dog following close by and continuing to smell all parts of my trousers in an embarrassing manner but still wagging his tail. I nervously kept repeating "Good boy".

The premises were in deplorable, dilapidated condition and very dirty, neglected and smelly. There were several grown up children in punk clothing and haircuts. I thought, I would not like to meet them on a dark night or come to think of it, even on a bright day. They just lounged about glaring at me suspiciously.

I quickly made notes on my. pad, thanked the tenant for his cooperation and thankfully went to make my exit not forgetting to reaffirm "Good boy" to the dog who was still sniffing my trousers and wagging it's tail.

It was just as I was passing out of the street door that the attack came. Without any warning what-so-ever, the dog pounced, bowled me over and tore away at my legs ripping my trousers to pieces. Fortunately the wounds were not serious. The tenant said. "Sorry, son. I did warn yah".

The Field Sergeant

I had heard of the army rank of Field Marshal but was amazed when Ernie told us that during the 1914-18 war- he had been promoted to the rank of Field Sergeant, He said that it was an almost unknown rank but was one which was awarded on the field of baffle for exceptional and exemplary conduct in the face of the enemy. It was a way a General could express his admiration immediately for behaviour he considered went beyond the normal expectancy of duty. Once awarded it could never be withdrawn except by Court Martial.

Ernie then proceeded to describe how he had earned this exceptional honour which was so rare as to be virtually unknown.

He told us that before the war broke out, he had been a regular soldier in a cavalry regiment. When war was declared, the British army was rapidly expanded and there was an increasing demand for drivers and chauffeurs, In its unfathomable wisdom, the army decided that in light of Ernie's experience with horses, he would make an excellent chauffeur for a General. He was given a crash (no pun intended) course in driving and a brand new staff car and was allocated to a particular General who happened to have known Ernie in the cavalry,

One day when the battle front was rather fluid and undefined, the General instructed Ernie to drive him to a particular army headquarters in Belgium. Ernie had been there a couple of times before but suddenly the route he had taken did not seem to be as familiar as it should have been. He drove on hoping to see a familiar landmark or someone to ask but there were no familiar landmarks and there was a strange absence of human beings, neither soldiers nor civilians.

He knew he was very close to the HQ and turning a sharp bend in the

130

narrow country road, saw with great relief the gates to a large country house with sentries on duty. He called out cheerfully to the General, "we're here sir." The General replied, "Thank goodness, I thought you had lost the way".

As they got nearer to the gates, Ernie perceived that the sentries wore German uniforms. He had to make an instant decision. He could turn the car round but as the road was so narrow and the car large and cumbersome, it would take a while, in which case, the Germans would become suspicious and capture them. Equally, if he put the car in reverse, the Germans could fire and kill them. He decided to bluff them. He shouted to the General to turn his peaked cap back to front because German caps had no peaks. Ernie did likewise. He then drove steadily up to the gates. The sentries saluted smartly thinking that a German officer was approaching, The road in front of the gateway was much wider than elsewhere. Ernie very slowly and deliberately turned the car round and very slowly and deliberately drove the car away. The Germans were puzzled and could not work out why the car was driving away. When they did realise what was happening the car was round the bend and speeding away. When they had put a few miles between them and the camp, the General ordered Ernie to stop and said. "I Should have you court marshalled for endangering my life and liberty, but as it is my- birthday, I promote you to Field Sergeant."

Ernie said that one day, he will show us his army discharge papers in which his promotion is recorded. Although we believe him, he never did show us the papers.

Whilst he was on the subject of his war experience he pointed to a large scar on his left cheek and asked if we knew how he came about it. He said that at some time during the war he had found himself in Cairo and one day, when he was walking through the streets he was surrounded by Arab children and Arab men pestering him for money. There must have been at least twenty of them each with outstretched hands and shouting.

He should have known better, but just having had a good lunch and a nice cold beer he felt in a good mood. He put his hand in his pocket and pulled out the five coins therein and handed them out to the nearest boys.

The pestering continued but even more persistent and louder. He turned his pocket linings out to show that he had no more money on him but to no avail. He eventually lost his good humour and when one evil looking Arab man thrust his hand. right close to his face, Ernie swiftly swept it aside. The man's hand stank. In a flash, the man produced a knife and lunged it into Ernie's face and neck, just missing his jugular artery.

He also recalled the period he spent as a boy cadet attached to a regular cavalry regiment before the 1914-18 war. He was born and bred in a small village in rural Essex. His prospects were that like those of all the local children, he would leave school at the age of 13 years, semi-illiterate and doomed to be a casual farm labourer. Life in the village had been so for generations but Ernie was determined to escape this pre-destined fate. By sheer determination he managed to get accepted as a boy cadet in the cavalry regiment which was stationed in a nearby town. He was a strapping lad and most enthusiastic to learn. At the passing out ceremony which was held in a church and attended by top army brass and important local dignitaries, each cadet was required to kneel at the alter individually and to repeat an oath of loyalty.

When it was Ernie's turn, he forgot that he was wearing full ceremonial uniform and when he knelt down, his rather large bottom came down heavily onto one of his spurs. His involuntary oath was not that which the padre required or approved.

The Tinker

Every evening, sharp at 8pm Ernie would open the first of at least two large bottles of strong cider and declare it was "Opening time". At the same time, he would scatter a handful of chocolate drops around the room to keep his dog busy searching for them.

After a glass or two, he would ask, "Have I ever told you about so and so?" On this occasion, it was, "Have I told you about the tinker?" and knowing that he had not, immediately proceeded to tell us.

Once he started telling one of his tales, he did not like to be interrupted as it broke his train of thought. Although we would have liked to have clarified some details of this interesting episode we contained our curiosity.

Ernie said that after the war (he did not say which war, he had served in the 1914–18 war) he had undertaken the management of a pub that primarily served the bargees and others working on the adjacent canal. He did not clarify in which district the pub was situated in nor which canal. Trade was rather good, not only in beer and tobacco but also other items which could not be sold openly over the counter.

Very often, a bargee would come in and offer some item or another which they claimed 'had fallen off the side of the barge'.

One evening, a tinker stopped off for a drink at the pub. He was already well intoxicated. Everybody knew him well, he was quite notorious, traded his wares along the tow paths shouting obscenities and blasphemies at all and sundry.

His goods were strapped onto the back of his horse which had an old battered flying pan tied to its tail. He asked Ernie if he would like to buy a couple of sacks of sugar. Ernie could only guess as to how he had come by such a commodity, it certainly could not have been by legal means. In those days, sugar was strictly rationed and anyone caught dealing with black market goods were bound to receive a very severe punishment quite often, imprisonment.

One problem was that the tinker was asking a very high price but Ernie found that the more the tinker drank the lower the price of the sugar became. Finally, when the tinker was virtually out of his mind they agreed a price which Ernie found agreeable. He paid the tinker who went staggering out of the pub.

A few hours later whilst Ernie was still working out his likely profit on the deal and having stowed the contraband safely away in the back room, two policemen arrived. They asked Ernie if the tinker had called at the pub that evening. Ernie quickly denied that he had. The police explained that they had just fished the tinker and his horse out of the canal and they knew that somewhere along the tow path he had disposed of two sacks of black market sugar.

Ernie expressed his regret at the tinkers fate but dared not ask if the tinker had drowned. He assured the police that he had not seen the tinker and was certainly not foolish enough to have bought any black market sugar off him. He told the police, "I've nothing to hide, you don't need to get a search warrant, you can right - now search these premises from top to bottom". The police said that they believed him and left without searching the premises. No sooner had they left, that Ernie sold the sugar to the next bargee passing by. It was with a light heart that he admitted the police who returned a short while after with a search warrant.

Hearing Aids

All sorts of euphemisms are used for difficulty in hearing. Hard of hearing; impaired hearing; defective hearing; loss of hearing; distorted hearing and hearing impediment. Very rarely is the word deaf used although in very severe cases, presumably because the person concerned would not hear in a any case, the term, profoundly deaf is used.

As I grow older, I find that an increasing number of my age group have hearing problems in varying degrees.

Sometimes deafness comes on suddenly and because of the trauma, the condition is acknowledged. In the cases where deafness is progressive, there is a reluctance to accept the fact that hearing is not as good as it should be. Such was the case of Cedric. At first, one would only have to repeat something occasionally but eventually almost everything that was said to him had to be repeated in ever increasing loudness. On other occasions, even after repeating something it was obvious that he had not heard because he would, out of politeness, just smile and nod his head affirmatively or give an irrelevant reply.

When we first suggested that he should see an ear specialist, he replied that there was nothing wrong with his hearing. He said that when people spoke clearly like they do on radio and TV he has no problem in hearing them. We tried to tell him, so did his neighbours, because he turns the sound volume up high.

It was most embarrassing to hold conversation with him in public places because everyone around, except him could hear what we were saying.

Very often, he would not hear us when we rang his door bell and to overcome this, we would 'phone through first to tell him we were coming

135

but the problem arose quite often when he could not hear the telephone ringing even though the 'phone was in the same room.

When we took him anywhere in my car, he would remark, "Lovely quiet engine".

Eventually, he came round to accepting the fact that his hearing was not as good as it used to be but he still would not consult an ear specialist or consider wearing a hearing aid.

One day when my wife was trying to make herself audible to him in a restaurant, an old man from a nearby table cane over and said to him, "You should get yourself one of these" pointing to a protrusion in one of his ears. He continued, "I used to be deaf like you but since I've had this, my whole life has changed but it cost me £700 and its worth every penny".

This seemed to have impressed itself on Cedric who consulted a private hearing therapist. A couple of weeks later Cedric turned up with a flesh coloured protrusion in his left ear. He said that it looked similar to the one worn by the old gentleman in the restaurant but this one was much superior and cost £1150.

At last we thought, we can now converse in a normal manner but Cedric still could not hear us. He told us that the hearing therapist had explained that it would take a while for him to get used to it and if, up to 30 days after purchase, he was not satisfied, he could have all his money refunded. Meanwhile, at the therapist's suggestion, he paid a £50 premium to insure the aid against loss or damage and bought some spare batteries at 50p each. The batteries only lasted for 10 hours use. He also sold him some other gadgets totalling some £200. He had a special telephone installed with a sound control but discovered it only turned the loudness of conversation down but not up.

Just before the 30 day guarantee period expired, Cedric went back to the hearing therapist and said that he could hear less when wearing the hearing aid than without. He said the only difference was that when he ate anything, it sounded like thunder in his mouth and that periodically, the hearing aid emitted a piercing shrill whistle in his ear that made him feel dizzy.

The therapist was most understanding and said, certainly, he could have all his money back on the hearing aid but would he not first like to try out an improved model that has only just come onto the market. It fits right inside the ear and cannot be seen at all and is so technically advanced that it adjusts itself automatically to the person's individual requirements. He could have it on a 30 day approval period but it would cost just a little bit more, about £2000.

After a short while Cedric told us that the new aid was no better that the first one and that he was going to return it and get his money back He said he felt that he was being conned and would insist on the immediate return of his money.

When we saw him about two weeks later, his hearing was still bad, we asked if he had experienced any problems in getting his money returned. He said, "Not exactly, I accepted his suggestion that I should try two of the latest models, one in each ear". He replied "Yes" when we asked if it would be £2000 each.

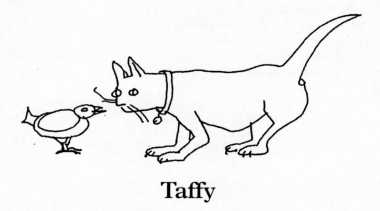

Taffy

A young Welsh couple lived next door for a few years. They were both school teachers in a local school but they decided to return home to their native Cardiff. They consulted a vet about taking their two grown kittens on such a long journey. He prescribed a sedative. It worked wonderfully well on Hezikiel the pretty tabby but it had a most unexpected effect on the black, gawky moggy, Arbuthnot.

Why they named him so, goodness only knows. Hezikiel went into a deep peaceful sleep but Arbuthnot reacted most peculiarly. He went into what looked like a fit. His eyes rolled, he staggered around blindly and struck out at anyone who came within reach.

The couple were most alarmed and realised that they could not transport him in that condition. They asked us if we would care for him until he recovered and until they could return to collect him. Twenty years later, we still await.

Arbuthnot recovered from his condition the next day but we were left with the problem of his peculiar name. We consulted an encyclopaedia and discovered that there had been a John Arbuthnot, 1667-1735, a Scottish physician to Queen Anne and the creator of the national character of John Bull. We could not see any relevance. In any case, we could not very well poke our head out of the window and call "Arbuthnot, Arbuthnot, your dinner's ready", at least not in this district. We decided to re-name him Taffy for obvious reasons, the most important of which was that we already had a cat called Toffy.

Taffy was a loner. He went for long walks through the rear gardens and soon had a routine of calls on neighbours who he got to know would give him tasty morsels of food. One neighbour told us that he insisted on Loch

Fynne kippers cooked in butter whilst another neighbour told us he would not touch cream unless he personally saw her opening a fresh tub. Despite all this pampering he remained lean, angular and gawky.

Although he caught mice, he did not interest himself in birds. It was therefore with great surprise, that one day I spotted him walking through a neighbour's garden with a bright coloured bird in his mouth. I don't know how I did it, but in a flash I had leaped over the dividing garden fence which was some 4'0" (1200mm) high and grabbed hold of Taffy. He was so surprised by my sudden appearance that he dropped the bird who remained petrified on the ground. Even though I have a phobia about handling birds, I picked up the poor creature and wondered what I could do with it.

With four cats in the house, it would not be practical to keep it. I remembered that a neighbour a few doors away had a similar budgie so I took it along and asked if they would mind looking after the bird until I could make enquiries to ascertain who had lost it. Actually, the neighbour was a retired vet and after examining the bird declared it was not injured in any way what-so-ever. Possibly, because it was Taflys first bird, he did not know how to kill or maim it.

The neighbour said that it would make a nice companion to his own budgie and went to put it in his own bird's cage. When he entered the room, he saw Taffy excitedly inspecting the empty cage.

The Hermit

Neighbours caught glimpses of him very early at daybreak when he would quietly and assiduously plant shrubs in his front garden. Each shrub would be neatly labelled and watered in. A few days later, he would dig them out again and re-plant them in a different order. Without any apparent reason, he would at a later date remove them and plant completely different shrubs and always at daybreak. He did not tend his rear garden at all, it had long become an impenetrable jungle of brambles and bindweed. This early morning activity was about all they ever saw of him for over 40 years.

On some mornings, he would operate the water company's stopcock which was situated in the pavement in front of his house. The mains water supply to his four bedroom terraced house had long been cut off. His electricity and gas supplies had also been disconnected many years ago. How he managed to live in such deprived conditions is unimaginable.

He had inherited the house from his parents and had lived on his own ever since his spinster sister died some 25 years ago. Well actually, he did not live entirely on his own because he shared the house with at least 100 pigeons. These entered and left the house at will through two sliding sash windows which were permanently open because the sash cords had long ago rotted away. The pigeons also entered and left the loft space through holes in the slated roof. No maintenance had been carried out to the property for about 50 years.

Nobody had seen him bring shopping home nor had he ever put refuse out to be collected.

The front door had been boarded up where a glass panel had been broken by vandals.

On the rare occasion that neighbours had seen him out, he ignored any

attempt at conversation and would not respond to even the slightest cour-
tesies. He had a thick mop of straight grey hair and his deep set dark beady
eyes were always focussed far away.

The postman was never seen delivering mail. Neighbours complained
to the local council about the smell that emanated from the premises and
the nuisance caused by the pigeons but they seemed to be helpless in the
face of the hermits intransigence. He would not respond to notices nor
open the door to callers.

One day, Dora was amazed to see a clean, tidy but very elderly lady
emerging from the house. Unlike the hermit, the lady was most keen to join
in conversation. She said that she was a close relative and had just delivered some cooked food to the hermit who was bed bound because he had
injured a hip whilst carrying a heavy wardrobe down the stairs. She said
that he had refused to have a doctor or any other medical attention. He had
never in his life consulted a doctor or attended any hospital or clinic. She
said he was a most obstinate and obdurate person.

A couple of weeks later there was some excitement down the road.
Somebody or another had alerted the police who broke in and found the
hermit dead in bed. He had died of a heart attack in his sleep.

The house still stands dark and neglected with the garden overgrown
but now the open windows have been closed and the holes in the roof
repaired and the 100 pigeons or so disconsolately perched on the roof
ridge, on the chimney stacks and on the window ledges.

The Smuggler

One of the many enterprises undertaken by Ernie in the inter-war years was that of market gardening including cut flowers and plants for sale to the general public.

Just outside his property was a plot of land which did not seem to belong to anyone in particular. In order to present a pleasant entrance to his small holding. Ernie planted daffodil bulbs on the plot.

Early each spring there was always a lovely show of joyous golden daffodils. Being of an enterprising nature, Ernie popped up a notice '1/- (one shilling = 5p) a bunch.'

One day, a smart looking couple in a posh car pulled up and asked Ernie how many blooms in a bunch. He replied, "Its up to you, for that money you pick your own". They paid him a shilling and started to pick the flowers. A short while after, Ernie returned and was astonished to see that the couple's car was full of daffodils. In exasperation he sarcastically asked, "Would it help if I loaned you a pair of shears?' to which they replied affirmatively. The man said, "Don't be upset, I can do you a big favour". Ernie replied, "What, come back with a lorry?" The visitor then pointed out to Ernie in case he had not noticed that he spoke with a slight accent. Ernie had noticed but in his ignorance took it to be a posh London accent. The posh gentleman went on to explain he was actually a Dutchman but he lived in England a lot of the time because his wife was English. Ernie's eyes lit up in recognition, "Oh, are you from Holland?" as though that was the reason for the man's greedy behaviour.

The Dutchman went on to explain that in Holland he was in a similar sort of business, raising tulips for cut blooms and selling tulip bulbs. From the car he produced a catalogue of wonderful tulips, prize winning blooms.

Ernie gasped, he had never seen such wonderful blooms before and he gasped once again when he saw what was being charged for the bulbs.

The Dutchman told Ernie not to take any notice of the prices in the catalogue, he said that he could supply them at a fraction of the price. He explained, that for prestige purposes he had to price them high to impress would be purchasers at flower shows where he often won prestigious prizes. In a lowered voice and with a conspiratorial glance over his shoulder, he said that income tax was very high in Holland and import duty in England forced the prices up.

He then quoted such a low price to Ernie that Ernie gasped again. The price was subject to a minimum quantity and that cash was to be paid on delivery.

The Dutchman told Ernie that he was to turn up at a certain fixed time in the dark at a certain spot on the nearby shore of the Thames Estuary. Ernie was to carry the sacks of bulbs away in his own lorry. Because of the tides and the danger of being discovered it was agreed that the transfer of bulbs from the Dutchman's boat on to Ernie's lorry was to be done swiftly, silently and without lights. Both Ernie and the Dutchman turned up bang on time, the Dutchman in his posh car and Ernie in his lorry. Soon after the Dutchman flashed his pocket torch into the darkness of the misty estuary, a rowing boat appeared, unloaded several sacks and then returned for reloading from his supply ship which was some distance away enshrouded in the mist and darkness.

After several such journeys Ernie checked that the correct number of sacks had been unloaded and paid the agreed sum in cash to the Dutchman. After quickly checking that the money was correct, the Dutchman swiftly departed in his posh car.

Ernie asked the boatman to help him load the lorry. No sooner had they finished and before the Dutch boatman could return to his ship, several bright torches switched on and a voice called out, "Don't move, we are His Majesty's Customs Officers."

The boatman who could not speak English nor able to give an address was kept in jail overnight whilst Ernie was bailed to appear in court the next day.

Ernie decided to make a good impression on the magistrate. He carefully groomed himself and put on his best suit which he normally wore for weddings and funerals. He also hastily arranged to be represented by a solicitor.

When Ernie's solicitor had completed his eloquent representation the magistrate curtly said, "Poppycock, I don't believe a single word except the defendant's own confession that he had intended to avoid paying import duty on the goods." He ordered the bulbs to be confiscated and destroyed also that Ernie should pay the customs duty on the import and imposed a hefty fine.

He said that if it had not been for Ernie's exemplary war service he would have imposed a long prison sentence. He added, looking straight at Ernie, "The way you dress you are obviously a spiv living on your wits and avoiding honest work. It is deplorable that you exploited this poor, hard-working Dutchman here who I find completely innocent and feel nothing but pity for him in his desperate, destitute state and his inability to comprehend the dangers you, through your insatiable greed had led him to."

At the Seaside

Our friend George had been made redundant from the Civil Service at the early age of 50. He had been employed as a supervisor for building works in or around Royal Palaces. It had been a very interesting and easy job. Finding himself unemployed at the age of 50 worried him because he had been in the Civil Service all his working life, albeit as a 'temporary' civil servant and thought that he would not be able to compete at his age in the wicked commercial world. He did, however, mysteriously mention that the redundancy was largely based on medical grounds which he never defined. However, his worries did bring on a heart condition. His doctor said that it would be alright for him to work but it must not be of a stressful nature.

After a while, he did find suitable employment that was easy and did not involve undue stress. His new employers were aware of his condition and went out of their way to ensure that he suffered as little aggravation as possible. When his doctor assured him that it would be O.K to drive his car provided he relaxed and drove carefully he suggested that Dora and I together with him and his wife go, in his car and spend an easy relaxing day at Southend-on-Sea-

We jumped at the suggestion. We often went there and enjoyed a fish and chip lunch at a sea front open air cafe in adjacent Westcliffe. Dora even offered that I pay all the expenses involved. George and his wife, Mary, occupied the two front seats whilst we sat in the back. As we drove along Mary frequently punctuated the conversation with single words that were out of context. It was some while before we realised why she said, Red; Amber; Green; as we approached traffic lights. George was apparently completely colour blind! He had never mentioned this as though it was some deadly sin to be ashamed of.

145

Having cleared the local roads and got onto the arterial road to Southend, we joined a steady stream of traffic heading in the same direction, taking advantage of the wonderful weather.

George proclaimed that he was going to take it nice and easy and will not join in the general speed of the traffic. He said that he will drive slow enough to comply with his doctors instruction and to enjoy the scenery. He slowed down to about 25 miles per hour, humming to himself and every so often interjecting "Just look at those idiots racing to an accident" or, "These youngsters have no manners or courtesy", when frustrated drivers passed him hooting and making rude hand signals to him.

After a while a police car signalled to him to pull over. George asked, "Any problem officer?" The reply was, "Yes, you are ". George was asked why he was crawling along and causing frustration to drivers behind him who were caught in a mile long tail back. George explained that he was not in any particular hurry and wanted to enjoy a relaxing day at the seaside. The police officer warned him that if he did not drive with consideration to other road users, he would be enjoying a relaxed day in a nearby police cell.

George continued his journey at a reasonable speed muttering, "No wonder there's so many people with heart conditions when they can't relax, we are forced to drive like maniacs". When we arrived at Southend, George approached the sea front via some confusing back streets. We were most surprised to find plenty of parking space on the sea front itself considering that it was such a lovely day and so many people were driving in. George said that even though they drove expensive cars people were too mean to put money into the parking meters. He fed his parking meter with enough money to last the whole day and said, "Now we can relax and have a nice day".

After a most enjoyable fish and chip lunch followed by ice cream in one of those sea front cafes which advertised that they served 'children's portions', we ambled along the mile long Southend pier, but because of George's heart condition, we took the pier train when returning. George said, "I should not have had the fish and chips and ice cream, its just about the worst thing I could eat for my condition."

After about 3pm, we ambled back to the car so as to make a relaxed journey home before the homebound traffic started. George's car was the only one in the entire road and a tow-away vehicle was about to hitch it up. George asked the nearby policeman what was wrong and pointed out that the time on the meter had not yet expired. The police officer told him that all parking meters along the sea front had been suspended for the remainder of the day since 2pm. There were notices all around the town. The town's annual carnival was about to take place and he told George that if

146

he did not make a fuss he would be allowed to drive his car away provided he did so immediately.

George was quite upset but said he would not allow such stupid officialdom to spoil his day. He would return home by country lanes and thus avoid the noisy speedy traffic on the arterial road. He said we could pass through some lovely ancient villages on the way. All went well until some yobs overtook George, flashing their headlights and hooting wildly and making rude gestures and calling out obscenities in connection to Georges apparent age and slow driving. This incensed

George who told Mary to take the offenders registration number. He said that he doubted that the offender's car was even taxed and insured and possible might even be stolen. Mary said that she can't note the registration number as they were too far ahead and the road was winding. George said that he would soon see to that and put his foot down on the accelerator. The car leaped forward but when the yobs could see that George was pursing them, they too accelerated. Soon both cars were speeding at dangerously fast break neck speed through the narrow country lanes. We pleaded with George to slow down but the devil seemed to have got into him. We feared that either we would be involved in some horrible accident or that George would have a heart attack or possibly both.

However, fate intervened in a most bizarre manner. There was a terrible grinding noise and to our astonishment we saw the front part of the car containing George and his wife parting from the rear part in which we were seated. The two parts quickly came to a standstill and fortunately no one was hurt although all of us were shocked.

Subsequently we learnt that George had bought the car from a local dealer who had acquired it from a person who specialised in repairing cars that had previously been in serious road accidents. He would weld the front undamaged half of one such car onto the undamaged half of an identical car whose front half had been damaged. George was fined for driving a vehicle that was unfit for use on the public highway and driving it in a dangerous manner. His driving licence was suspended for a year and he was ordered to take another driving test and have a health test at the end of that period. So ended a lovely relaxing day at the seaside.

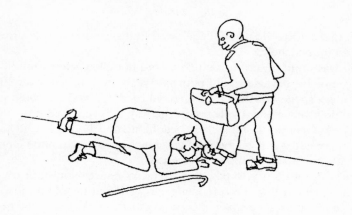

Mugged

Until he retired several years ago, Manny worked as a London double decker bus driver. He found life as a pensioner rather boring and started to join various organisations to pass the time away. The rheumatoid arthritis which he had suffered with for many years suddenly became much worse and he was only able to walk with the aid of a walking stick.

One of the organisations he joined was a local Jewish old peoples club. At first, he found this rather boring as most of the members were women in wheel chairs or hobbling about on Zimmer frames. Most of their conversations were about their wonderful daughters or their brilliant grandsons. However, he discovered that on a Friday afternoon, a few of the male members gathered informally to discuss religious topics. Although Manny was not religious he was keen to learn more about his own religion and he loved to listen to debates. For example he was intrigued to learn that in the original Hebrew version of the bible a true translation would read: "In the beginning, God created the sky and the earth". Because of the Christian belief in reward and punishment, the word, 'sky' was translated as 'heaven' as a counterpoint to hell. In the Old Testament, hell is not mentioned at all.

He had heard of Isiaih's exhortation to 'beat your swords into ploughshares' but was amazed when someone pointed out that another prophet, Joel (3-10), had equally exhorted "Beat your ploughshares into swords". He wondered why he had never heard Joel quoted by religious preachers. All his working life he had been an ardent trade unionist and supported the five day working week but he considered that trade unionism and religion were incompatible because the ten commandments said "Six days thou shall labour".

It was also pointed out that a glaring misinterpretation was the "Red

Sea" in Exodus. There is no doubt it should have read the "Reed Sea". In the original Hebrew the words are quite different.

There were no orthodox Jews among the group which was split approximately 50–50 among believers and sceptics. It was run very informally, people voicing their opinions on any aspect appertaining to religion and not always to Jewish religion. Occasionally, a more learned person would attend to give a lecture.

As was to be expected, reference, quite often was made to the bible. Manny began to consult his own copy of the bible which had been given to him when he was bar-mitzvah at the age of 13 years and which had remained un-opened ever since.

On his way to the bible club one Friday afternoon, Manny put his bible in a brief case because it was raining and en-route called in to the local sub-Post Office to buy some postage stamps. There were some youths loitering about outside and he did not notice that one of them, a black boy, was following him when he left the Post Office. Just as he was walking slowly and painfully through an underpass to reach the club, the youth violently pushed him over and snatched the briefcase. Instead of running off with his spoil, he started to kick Manny's head many times as hard as he could. He only ran off with the briefcase when he was aware that someone was approaching, it was another black youth who followed the mugger to his home and alerted the police.

Manny was taken to the hospital but was dead on arrival. The youth was found guilty and sentenced only to five years on the ground of diminished responsibility. He is now free having served 3 years.

He showed no signs of remorse at his trial and possibly has resumed his diminished responsible muggings.

The Bookie's Runner

By the time I had got to know him, Peter had become a self made successful manufacturer employing many people. He was a highly respected member of the local community and had a happy family. Few knew of the desperate poverty he had been born into and in which he grew up.

He was born in Bethnal Green in the east end of London in a notorious violent street where the police dare not venture alone.

He never knew what his father's trade was, that is if he ever had one, he was never employed, unless being a bookies runner was considered employment.

Off-course betting was strictly illegal but very prolific in the slum streets of east London. Each bookie had his own recognised patch and his own heavies to safeguard it.

The bookies usually transacted their business in alleys with look-outs to warn them of any approach by the police. Being an illegal business, it thrived on trust and honesty of the participants and woe behold anyone who broke the unwritten code.

Apart from the street betting, there was a parallel trade in betting on the shop floor in factories, warehouses etc. For this, the bookies employed trusted 'runners' who entered work places and took bets on behalf of the bookies and in the event, would deliver any winnings. If any of these runners defaulted they had retribution waiting from both the bookies and the punters.

Peter did not know how or why his father had so defaulted but he knew that one day the bookie called to 'see' his father. The conversation was quiet but never-the-less very menacing.

The bookie complained that it had been a very bad week for him. An unusually large number of punters had hit lucky and two of his runners had gone off with some of the punters winnings, one of them being Peter's dad. The bookie said that he immensely disliked people who ran off with his punters' money but being kind hearted and as a gesture of friendship, he was going to make a proposal which he felt that Peter's father would be stupid to refuse.

He suggested that he would forget Peter's dad's misdemeanour if he were to visit the other defaulting runner and break of one of his arms. He assured Peter's dad, that he was under no obligation to accept, but if he did not, he would ask the other runner to do it to him.

Peter's dad willingly accepted, such were the times and traditions of the day in Bethnal Green. The bookie reminded Peter's dad that he had a good honest reputation to live up to in the neighbourhood and would not want anybody else to be likewise tempted.

He told Peter's dad who the other runner was and where he lived. After fortifying himself with a couple a of good pints at the local pub, Peter's dad set off to redeem his obligation. He knocked loudly on the designated door and was astounded when a giant of a man agreed that he was Mr So-and-So. Peter's dad had not reckoned on such adverse odds but realising what any default in his contract with the bookie entailed piled ferociously into this opponent. He was not sure if he actually broke his opponents arm but in the ferocity of his desperation he inflicted grievous bodily harm. In turn, he too, was badly injured.

When he reported back, the bookie was astounded to see the extent of his injuries. Upon further enquiries, he ascertained that Peter's father had attacked one of the defaulting runner's sons who was a professional wrestler. The bookie told him not to be such a schmuck in the future.

The Writing Bureau

Auntie Sadie had a very hard life. Her late husband was an invalid for as long back as I can remember and was not able to work. For the last couple of years of his life she nursed him night and day.

We were therefore glad for her when she met and married a widower, Solly Sussman. They set up home in his flat. Although he appeared to be devoted to Sadie, I took an instinctive dislike to him. I can't explain why this was so, but perhaps it was his envious nature. He disliked anybody who was younger than himself or in better health He lived in a rented flat and expressed his dislike of anybody who owned their own home even if it was heavily mortgaged. He disliked anyone who had, or who he suspected had a larger income than his. In fact he disliked virtually everyone he came into contact with and that included me. Therefore, the feeling was mutual.

Because of Aunt Sadie, who adored him, I suppressed my feeling and forced myself to be exceptionally polite to him.

Upon our first visit to the newly married couple, I expressed my genuine admiration of a small walnut, bow fronted ladies' writing bureau. Solly said that it was unique because he made it himself as part of his completion of his apprenticeship as a master cabinet maker. He boasted that they don't make items like that these days because they do not have such highly skilled persons such as himself. For a change he was not envious but derogatory. Sadie was full of admiration. It was therefore with great surprise when, during our next visit he called me aside and told me that he would like to take Auntie Sadie on a nice overseas holiday but he did not have the money. He then said that in order to do so he would be willing to sell his writing bureau for a mere £650, a fraction of what it is worth. He asked if I knew anyone who might be interested. I told him that I would not mind buying it for myself. He was very pleased at this because he knew that I would treasure it and keep it as an heirloom in the family. I had no idea what such a unique item was worth but I reckoned that such a hand-made item today would cost much more than £650 to make even if the skilled craftsman could be found.

Shortly after, when I was showing the bureau off to a friend she said, "What a coincidence, we bought an identical bureau recently'. I assured her that it could not be identical, perhaps similar, but not identical. She was adamant and told us where she had bought it. Out of curiosity, I went along to the furniture department of the local departmental store and lo and behold, there on prominent display was an identical bureau priced at £350.

I asked the departmental manager if it was reproduction or a genuine antique. He said it was a very good reproduction made by a factory in De Beauvoir Square, Hackney, east London who specialised in repro' furniture. If we were interested for the same price we could have it finished in Cherry wood, Yew, Mahogany, light Oak, dark Oak, satin wood, Walnut or Rose wood.

He said that despite the price they were selling fast and in fact not long ago they had sold one in Walnut to an elderly gentleman who was a skilled cabinet maker who confirmed that they were well made and good value for money and had the previous day come back for another one.

The Frying Pan

We were most surprised when Joyce rang our door bell and asked if she could stay the night. She was the sole child of our friends who lived only a short walking distance away. They were a very happy and close family and lived in a nice three bedroom house.

She had brought a night bag with her and was obviously very upset. We first of all assumed that it was a family tiff and that after a cup of tea and a chat, she would return home.

We told her that we would first have to 'phone her parents and tell them where she was. She said that her lather was not at home and her mother was in hospital. We asked when she expected either of them to return. Her answer was that her father was most likely visiting her mother who would most likely be an in-patient for some while. She told us that her mother had serious head injuries and was being kept under close observation for possible brain damage.

She started sobbing and it was difficult to obtain further information but through persistence we ascertained that when Joyce returned from work a couple of days previously her meal was not quite ready. In her anger she had hit her mother with a heavy frying pan and knocked her unconscious. Her mother was detained in hospital and the following morning, full of remorse and regret Joyce went to visit her but instead of consolation and apology attacked her again.

Her father ordered her to leave home immediately and never to return and that is why she was asking for our hospitality.

We explained why it would not be convenient for her to stay with us and we arranged for her to stay at a nearby guest house, bed and breakfast. Then rather fool-heartedly we offered that she could come to us for an

154

evening meal when she returned from work each day. We paid in advance on her behalf for a weeks stay at the guest house as she said she had very little money.

She went to see the Social Security and told them that her father had forced her to leave home but she did not earn enough to stay at a guest house and also to continue with her dancing lessons. She had aspirations to become a ballet dancer although it was obvious she did not have the appropriate physique.

The Social Security said that they were not empowered to assist her financially because she was in full time employment but if she was fired by her employer and became unemployed, they would be able to help. They would be able to pay for her training for a professional career as a dancer and also pay her rent for a furnished flat. They emphasised that they would not be able to help if she left her employment voluntarily.

At first, her employer refused to fire her, she was a - good hairdresser and popular with the clients but he did so when Joyce threatened to deliberately upset some of the clients.

In subsequent conversation with her father, we ascertained that she suffered with a recently acknowledged medical condition known as PMT (pre-menstrual tension) which can turn normally placid females into violent attackers. We had wondered why such a pretty, pleasant girl never attracted a steady boyfriend.

One day Joyce called to thank us for our help. Her Mother had just phoned to say she can now return home. Her Father is in hospital with severe head injuries and is likely to be there for a very long time.

Henry

We heard Henry or Enoch as he preferred to call himself before we saw him. We heard joyful singing coming from the roof next door and when we went to see what was up, we saw Henry light footedly in white plimsolls flitting about the roof re-fixing loose and dislodged tiles.

We asked our neighbour who was training to be a priest in the Elam Church if it would be in order if we asked his roof repairer to refix some loose tiles on our roof He told us that Henry was a long standing member of the church he attends and would do a conscientious job without overcharging.

Upon his recommendation we engaged Henry and when he had finished the work we invited him to have a cup of tea with us. We were curious to find out why he appeared to be so happy. Perhaps he had won the football pools or had hit it lucky with some floozy. He said he was happy because he had joy in his heart and was not afraid of falling of a roof because he trusted the Lord to protect him. He added, that even if he did fall off a roof one day, he would still be happy because it will be what the Lord wanted. He told us that our young neighbour had been largely instrumental in rescuing him from a life of sin and debauchery and depression and led him to the light of his life.

He suggested that we too should accept the lord into our lives but we politely declined saying that we were at this present moment in time quite content to have had the loose tiles fixed.

Just before he left he said, "I was speaking to a very good friend of yours yesterday ". We could not think who it could have been. We have very few friends and none that we could think of who 'would claim to be a very good friend. When we enquired, he said, "He is also a good friend of mine

Abraham. I speak to him every day and I also speak to our other mutual friends, Isaac, Jacob, Moses and King David ". We asked him to give them our regards next time he speaks with them. We paid and he left, but through our neighbour kept in touch with Henry from time to time especially so, when our roof needed attention.

We felt flattered to have a roof repairer who had such influential friends in very high places.

We learnt that Henry was a very popular and successful Sunday school teacher. The children loved his cheerful method of teaching. He also spent many weekends preaching in the open air to day trippers near Southend-on-Sea pier. On the return journey from one such expedition, his home made soap box was lifted off the roof of his van and smashed into the windscreen of a following car. He assured the driver that it must have been the Lord himself who saved him from more serious damage or injury.

After the Lord took Henry's wife to his bosom, he decided to go and live with his son who had settled in Australia and who was active in the Elam Church there. When he attended his first Sunday service in his son's church, he thought that the guest preacher was somewhat familiar. When he asked the preacher if they had ever met before, he said "yes, we certainly did. It was I who nearly arrested you for trying to smuggle bibles into East Germany. I was the KGB officer who warned you to turn round and take the bibles with you. Fortunately, you did, but I did confiscate one bible for my own curiosity and through reading it I accepted the Lord and now here I am."

Mrs Barnet

As Mrs Barnet was an elderly and long standing friend of my parents, my wife and I we visited her soon after she came out of hospital after a serious operation. We did not know what the operation was for, but as the condition was not specifically mentioned we presumed it was for cancer. She lived in a granny apartment which was part of her elder son's house.

She was wizened, small but sprightly despite her age and illness. Her husband had died many years ago and single handedly without any state help had brought up her two sons. The elder had become a fairly successful business man and the younger obtained a doctorate in philosophy and a permanent post as lecturer at Cambridge University. Mrs Barnet could never understand why her son, who was called a doctor would never prescribe a medicine for her.

When we arrived, she already had a visitor, an elderly neighbour. They were exchanging stories and descriptions of their illnesses, each trying to outdo the other in horrible details and self pity. Alter a short while listening to their exchanges, we began to feel quite queasy.

In an effort to change the conversation, Dora suggested that I tell them a joke we had recently heard about a childless couple. The elderly pair were very eager to hear the joke, possibly because it gave them the opportunity to withdraw from the contest of telling the most lurid descriptions of their medical conditions. The atmosphere immediately became most convivial and even before I started telling the story they began laughing. I had my doubts that they would appreciate the subtlety of the humour.

I began, "There was a couple who could not produce a child," this opening seemed to amuse them very much and they roared with laughter. I continued, However much they tried they remained childless". The laughter increased and I sensed that they thought that was the joke. When their laughter subdued a bit, I persevered and explained that they were already middle aged and the woman was near the end of her child bearing period. More laughter and by now, the hysteria had caught hold of my wife, Dora who also burst into uncontrollable laughter. I went on amidst the laughter to tell them that a wise and friendly doctor said it may help the wife to become pregnant if they took in a young lodger. By now all three women had tears pouring down their cheeks and gasping for air and clutching their stomachs because of the pain produced through such hysterical laughter in which I had now joined. I could hardly get round to the punch line when I saw that Mrs Barnet had stopped laughing and her face had gone deathly white. We then all stopped laughing and called her son in. He immediately phoned for an ambulance and she was whisked off to the hospital from which she had recently been discharged. They found some internal stitches had become undone and that she had severe internal haemorrhage.

She recovered but never got round to hearing the end of my story.

Secrets

The initial stages of many building projects are often shrouded in great secrecy involving subterfuge and conspiracy. This applies to proposals both small and large. It is understandable that freeholders do not wish to alarm leaseholders or tenants especially so, when a tenancy or lease is due to expire shortly. Prospective purchasers of sites or properties would not wish to let vendors know of contemplated enhancement etc. etc.. So it was no surprise when a developer for whom I had already carried out several projects, commissioned me to act as architect in a feasibility study of a town centre site on condition of observing the utmost secrecy. The site was in Ilkley, a lovely little town on the Yorkshire moors, about 16 miles from Leeds.

The client wished to avoid any information or rumours getting about as it could increase the asking price of the site and/or alert protest groups. If protests were made, it would most likely lead to a public town planning enquiry with its consequent costs and delays. A public enquiry would also inform every other potential developer of the inherent possibilities of the site. I understood that my client was the sole potential purchaser and the site was considerably under-valued. My responsibility for absolute secrecy and discretion was made quite clear to me. Actually, I never met the client even though I had acted as his architect several times. I received his commissions through a quantity surveyor who acted as his project manager.

In order to prepare a feasibility report on the site, it was agreed that the project manager and myself visit Ilkley as tourists and gather the necessary information surreptitiously.

The client informed us that getting town planning approval should not be difficult provided the project was kept secret because he had already discussed it with the leader of the local council who is very keen on the proposed development and in due course will assist the town planning application through quickly, provided that any publicity does not lead to protests and a public enquiry.

The councillor had arranged for us to discuss the project with the council's Chief Town Planner who also acted as Chief Architect and Chief Borough Engineer. It was agreed that the meeting was to be held in great secrecy and confidence. Such a discussion was necessary to ascertain the Council's requirements regarding car-parking, road access, plot radio and exterior materials etc. etc., without which, it would not be possible to prepare a reasonable viability report.

We caught the first flight from Heathrow airport to Leeds, each taking a small night case in which we concealed our measuring rods, note books, etc.

Emerging from Leeds airport we took the first taxi in the rank and asked to be taken to Ilkley, where the project manager had pre-booked us into a two star hotel in order to avoid anyone suspecting that we were on business with expenses paid.

After a short while, the driver asked "It is the Grey Stones Hotel that you will be wanting?' Although surprised, we wondered whether he had just made a lucky guess or did the hotel have a reputation for putting up two middle-aged men travelling on their own. After we confirmed that that was the hotel we required he asked, "Would it be about the cinema site you come about?" We proclaimed ignorance of any such site and said that we had just come as holiday makers. We were now really worried, what did the driver know? Was he an agent provocateur sent by the client to test our reliability? We said that we had heard such a lot about Ilkley moor and about Ilkley itself that we just simply had to come and see for ourselves. The driver was cynical, he was obviously Jewish and in turn so were we. He said, "What would two healthy young prosperous London Jewish boys be doing in Ilkley out of season carrying only a small night case each if they were not interested in the development of the cinema as a supermarket?" We maintained our pretence. Seeing, that he was not going to get any more information from us he desisted in further questions. Possibly at that stage, he may have known more about the project than we did. He then gave us renderings of Chasanic (synagogue) music in a fine tenor voice, presumably to convince us of his Jewishness. We booked into the hotel and immediately left to keep our secret appointment with the Chief Town Planner. We dare not ask the hotel enquiry the way to the Town Hall but when we reached the town centre we asked an elderly gentleman sitting on a park bench where the Town Hall was. His reply was to the effect that as we Londoners knew everything he was not going to tell us. We were thankful that he had not asked us if it was about the proposed supermarket. We presumed that he just guessed that we were from London. Actually, as we soon discovered, the Town Hall was right opposite where we were standing.

We told the young girl at the enquiry desk that we had an appointment with the Chief Town Planner. We had half expected her to ask if it was about the cinema site but she did not. She very courteously escorted us to the Chief Town Planners office and introduced us as the people from London about the supermarket site.

At that stage we felt like asking if there was anybody at all, in Yorkshire who did not know about us and about the site.

We had a very useful and informative discussion with the Chief Town Planning Officer who was obviously well briefed by his staff and by the leader of the council. We received more information than we had ever hoped for. Never-the-less, we still had to see the site for ourselves. We declined the Chief Town Planners offer to get one of his assistants to escort us. We remembered the warning from our client, that the cinema staff must not get the slightest inkling of what was afoot. It only needed just one vital member of the minimum staff employed to get wind of the proposed development and leave, for the cinema to have to close and then the reason would immediately be known all over town.

To check dimensions of the site, we walked steadily around the site, heads down, counting the pavement slabs. We knew that each slab was a standard 2-0' (600mm) wide. We took note of ground slopes by counting the number of brick courses involved and knowing that each course is 3" (75mm). We took note of heights of adjacent buildings and their fenestration.

Next, we had to see the inside of the cinema to get an idea of the construction for demolition estimate. To do so, we nonchalantly bought tickets and entered. Nobody asked us any questions except do we want cigarettes, chocolate or ice-cream?

As we came out, a woman in usherette uniform said that she would be glad when they demolished the cinema and she would not have to see the same poxy films over and over again.

Next morning back to London to prepare our viability report. The scheme went ahead without any undue problems.

The Winner

Acquaintances will no doubt be surprised that somewhere or another I have a certificate to the effect that I came first in an inter Inner London Metropolitan Councils swimming event. They will have good reason for their surprise because I am not and never have been an athletic type. Physically, I was not natures choice to be an athlete. As a child, due to a series of illnesses and operations I was a skinny, weak runt with little stamina. As a teenager, through assiduous concentration on a diet I became exceedingly overweight, or to put it slightly mildly, I was fat. My reflexes were exceedingly slow and also, I was a physical coward. For my height, I was on the average, on the short side, besides, unlike most of my contemporaries, I took no interest in sports. Football heroes meant nothing to me.

However, in order not to waste my physical attributes I took up swimming. I found that once the art of relaxing was acquired swimming required little effort and my surplus fat helped to keep me afloat and to combat the cold water. I enjoyed lying on my back and skilfully flipping my feet in the water. I also was rather good at plunging into the swimming pool from the edge and then gliding from the impulse through the water with my arms outstretched in front of me for a considerable distance. Most of the distance was covered under water and this naturally involved holding my breath for a long time.

Although not of Olympic standard my talent was duly noted by the swimming coach/chief finance clerk of our London Borough at which I was at that time employed. He implored me to participate in a forthcoming swimming gala representing our Borough Council. I duly discovered that he was only able to enrol two other participants but they were good, very good. One was a free style champion of some sort and the other was

163

an excellent acrobatic diver who practised intensely all the year round so as to show off at the swimming pool during his two weeks at Butlin's holiday camp.

Although he was about twice my age, about 50, Peter was athletic and lithe, a veritable bronzed Adonis.

Just after Christmas and not long before the swimming event, Peter went for his daily training session at the local swimming baths. As usual, he asked for a ticket to the second class pool, there were two pools. He was issued with a ticket and a towel. He entered the second class pool and handed the ticket to the attendant/life guard who handed him the tagged key to a clothes locker. Peter swiftly changed into his well used swimming trunks and carefully placed his clothes, wallet and spectacles in the locker and tucked the key into the small pocket in his trunks. He stood for a while at the edge of the pool which was supervised by the attendant/lifeguard deciding whether to start off with a spectacular double somersault or to swim a couple of lengths first just to warm up. Fortunately he chose the latter and plunged in from the edge of the pool. To his horror and shock he discovered too late that instead of 4'-0" (1200mm) water depth there was only 2'-3" (700mm).

The pool had been emptied over the Christmas holiday and was in the process of being refilled. He was badly bruised and was unfit to participate in the swimming event. The other entrant had caught 'flu and also could not participate. That left me as the sole representative of my Council and I was determined to do my best. As I was the only participant in the plunging contest I was awarded first prize which is my valued certificate of excellence.

You Know

One afternoon Malcolm a young voluntary church social worker unexpectedly called on us. He was accompanied by another young man. He asked if we would mind if they could come in for a short while for a friendly chat and if possible, a cup of tea.

We knew that Malcolm quite often took people seeking help to his own home in connection with his voluntary counselling social work. For some unexplained reason he said that it was not convenient at the time to take Richard to his home. We guessed that Richard had a problem but from his cheerful demeanour we had no clue.

The conversation over tea and Dora's home baked sponge cake was light hearted and cheerful. After a while, Malcolm told us that something terrible had happened to Richard that very same morning. Thinking that this was a prelude to another joke, I jested, "He didn't marry Dora, did he?" Malcolm persisted and told us that Richard's young son of five years had been run over and killed earlier in the day by a lorry. We then realised that he was serious and felt awful. Malcolm explained that he did not wish to inform us sooner because he had hoped that by a general cheerful conversation, Richard's thoughts on the terrible event might be distracted for a while.

We commiserated with Richard and apologised for our frivolity but he said that there is no need to commiserate, we should in fact, congratulate him "Because you know Jesus has taken him unto his bosom, you know". He had a habit of saying "You know" both at the beginning and end of every sentence and sometimes also in mid sentence. We don't suppose that he was even aware of the habit. We told him that we were glad that he found such comfort in his faith and we nearly added, "At this joyous occasion" but refrained just in time as he may have thought we were mocking him. He described how he witnessed the accident and just as the giant vehicle ran over the child's body he saw a look of heavenly delight on the child's face. He was sure that "Jesus was embracing him, you know, just as the lorry was crushing the life out of his body, you know". Its not often that Dora is lost for words and all she could reply, was "Yes, we know".

Richard told us what a lovely and loving child he was and said, "You know, he had a hole in his head, you know". We replied that we did not know. He told us that when his son was about 3 years old he had a tumour on his brain and the surgeon removed about a 2 inch (50mm) diameter part of the skull to remove the tumour. He said, "You know the operation was a complete success, you know, but he was left with a 2 inch hole in his head, you know". He continued, "You know, the doctors fitted a silver plate over the hole, you know, and from time to time, removed the plate, you know, to have a look inside, you know".

What can one say on such occasions? His seriousness intermingled with "You know" was indeed a strange mixture and regretfully, we just about refrained from bursting out laughing.

He told us, that at school "You know, the other boys would tease him, you know, and would ask, you know, to look inside his head, you know. This used to make the boy very unhappy". With a big smile on his face, he said, "You know, our Lord Jesus Christ must have realised just how unhappy he was, you know, and called him you know, I am, you know, the happiest man on earth, you know".

The Solicitor

Bernard and I went to the same east London secondary school. In fact, we were in the same class. Whereas he excelled himself in English and History, I concentrated on carpentry and technical drawing etc.

In August 1939, our education was suddenly interrupted when our school was evacuated to a small village in Cambridgeshire. There was an attempt to keep the evacuated school functioning but in the circumstance this was difficult. After a few months, upon reaching the then school leaving age of 15 years, we both returned to London to commence earning a living as was expected of us.

It was about ten years later that we met again by chance. We were sitting opposite each other on a London underground train. Recognition was mutually instantaneous. His face had not changed except that he wore a moustache and he appeared a lot taller than when I last saw him. He had lost his east London accent and was smartly dressed. He was wearing a bowler hat and was carrying a leather brief case and rolled umbrella.

By contrast, I still spoke with a pronounced east London accent and my appearance was far from sartorial and I was carrying some shopping in a plastic carrier bag.

He told me that when he left school, he got a job as an office boy in a solicitors office and through evening classes he qualified as a solicitor and recently had commenced his own practice but pro-tem he was working at home.

I told him that likewise, I had entered an architect's office and had qualified after studying in evening classes and that I too had my office at home.

He promised that he would recommend me when any of his clients needed the services of an architect. I likewise promised to refer people to him if they should be requiring the services of a solicitor.

It transpired that we lived fairly close together although he got off the train the station after mine.

We kept in touch, as apart from appearances and speech, we had a lot in common.

One day, I wanted to consult him rather urgently about a legal matter and he arranged that he we meet at his younger brother's house where he was helping to arrange a birthday party for his brother's young son.

When I and my wife arrived, the party had already commenced and was very lively and noisy.

Bernard's wife suggested he should get a chair for Dora from an adjoining room. As he was carrying the chair, his younger brother stopped him and said "Ill carry that, its a heavy chair". Bernard told him that he was quite capable of carrying the chair but his brother insisted on doing so telling Bernard that the strain was no good for his heart. Even at school, Bernard had had a weak heart for which he was excused sports etc.

Bernard insisted that he did not need help, but his brother snatched the dining chair from his grasp. There had always been some animosity between the brothers which in later years was accentuated when Bernard became a professional man but not rich, whilst his younger brother had married a rich man's daughter and became a rich business man but jealous of his brother's social status. The tug-a-war between the two continued with ever increasing temper until Bernard collapsed with a heart attack from which he never fully recovered. He died a comparatively young man. Dora did not get her chair and I never got any clients recommended by Bernard even though I had sent several to him.

The Site

Martin Baxter was a very successful wholesaler of children's clothes. His warehouse was a continuous hive of activity, all directed and controlled from his chaotic office situated right at the centre. His need to expand his premises was most pressing, but it was to be carried out without any interruption to his present business. Apart from a rear extension in a congested area he also wanted his large damp derelict basement made useable. The toilet facilities were to be increased and improved. Obtaining Town Planning approval was tricky and complying with the Building Regulations and Fire Brigade requirements were also very complicated. In addition party wall agreements had to be arrived at with owners of adjoining properties. Preparing the building contract documents and choosing a suitable contractor to carry out the works had to be done with careful consideration. Close co-operation and co-ordination with the builder and the wholesaler's staff had to be organised with the greatest of diplomatic skill. Just doing the plans was possibly the easiest part of my duties as the architect. It was therefore, no great wonder that Martin, (as he preferred to be called) expressed his sincere appreciation when all went, as the saying goes, 'according to plan'.

His day to day business was not interrupted and due to the extensions, actually increased.

As architects are not allowed to advertise, it is quite essential to have such satisfied clients in order to receive recommendations. Because Martin's customers were all business men, I did, through that project receive several further commissions.

Not long alter completion of the works, Martin consulted me once again but before revealing what he had to say made me solemnly agree to keep the information he was about to impart an absolute secret and I was not to mention it to anyone not even to members of his own family.

He then told me that through contacts, he was being given the first option on buying a 5 acre site suitable for housing development. It was part of an estate of a recently deceased titled person and had to be sold quickly to pay towards death duties.

This was in the late 1970's during a building boom and developers were desperately outbidding each other in order to get hold of any site suitable for development. Martin said that his contact had told him that it was essential to sign a contract as soon as possible in order to avoid the site going to someone else.

He asked me how many houses could be built on a 5 acre site. I politely replied "As long as a piece of string." I explained that the answer lay almost entirely with the local council who, under the town planning law would have already designated the use of the site and its development density. I also told him that other factors would have to be considered before I could give him a sensible and reliable answer. Such factors would include the shape of the site, road access, site slopes, sewer provision, protected trees, size of houses, etc.. I told him that only the local council could give me the answers to these questions. He said that he could not risk approaching the council as the availability of the site may then become known to local developers and they would gazump the price.

I said, that if he told me the council involved, I could make discreet inquiries and pretend that my interests were actually in a nearby site. He thought that was a brilliant idea and he then revealed that the site was on the perimeter of a small village near Selby in North Yorkshire. He showed me photos of the site that his contact had loaned him. It certainly appeared to be in a pretty area.

He was even more pleased that by coincidence, I knew someone who worked for the Selby Council in their Building Surveyor's department. We had worked together in a London Council's office and I'm sure he would respect the required confidentiality.

When I phoned my acquaintance his immediate response was "Surely not another enquiry about the so and so site adjacent to the so and so village, we've had at least a dozen from would be developers from down South. We tell them that in all fairness, the local developers have refused to buy the site because it is over a disused coal mining area which is subject to severe and unpredictable ground settlements."

I passed this information on to Martin who felt sick with disappointment and with the knowledge that his 'reliable' contacts had tried to deceive him.

I explained that under these circumstances any houses built on the site would have to have special foundations and the drains would have to be suspended from beams. The extra building costs would be enormous. Because of this, building societies may be very well reluctant to grant mortgages, insurance companies would impose harsh conditions and it may prove most difficult to sell the houses. In other words, I warned him that if he went ahead, he most likely would badly burn his fingers. He thanked me for my advice like a mourner thanks a counsellor.

I too should have received consolation as through my conscientiousness I had talked myself out of a very nice commission.

A few days later, Martin phoned me up quite triumphantly. He told me that he had so connived it, that someone who had gazumped him on a previous project, was confidentially informed that he, Martin, was about to buy the site. The man had with amazing alacrity signed a contract to purchase the land, Martin was as pleased as though he had himself won a fortune on the pools. He said "One bad deed deserves another." However, it was not long before I had another call from Martin and I immediately knew something was wrong when he commenced "Mr Baxter here."

He was boiling with anger. He had just heard from his 'reliable' contacts that hardly had the ink dried on the purchase contract that the site had been resold to some other developer at an enormous profit. He concluded "Thank you very much for your invaluable advice, I'll know where to go next time an opportunity from my 'reliable' friends arises."

I was very sorry that our, up till then, most amicable relationship should end in such acrimony due entirely to good intentions.

My first meeting with Martin was in rather unusual circumstances. When I first met him, he was stark naked with half a banana in his hand. His first words to me were, "Would you like a banana?" Perhaps, a little elucidation will help to dispel any hastily arrived at conclusions.

I was introduced to Martin by Thomas who had employed me as his architect several times. When Martin said that he needed the services of an architect, Thomas was only too glad to recommend me. Thomas told me that the most convenient time to meet Martin and discuss the proposed project would be on a Friday afternoon, when a group of them gathered in the public Russian Vapour Bath in Bethnal Green. The group had been meeting thus, for many years and had formed an unofficial friendship club. Of course, all were male and several, like Martin and Thomas were business men, others were street traders and taxi drivers. One of them was a fruiterer who always brought along bunches of bananas and handed them out to 'club' members.

To enter the vapour baths, I too, had to strip naked but modestly, I used a towel to conceal the parts that normally are not seen by my clients.

Maybe, if we had not been introduced in such an informal manner, we may not have parted in such a regrettable manner.

Cockey

It has been said that whatever or whoever a chick sees when first emerging from its shell is taken as being its mother. It must therefore be assumed that the first thing young Cockey the cockerel saw when he emerged from his shell was not a hen but young Jimmy.

Young Jimmy and his family used to live just a few doors away from us when I was first married. My wife and I, and no doubt all the neighbours were amused when we saw young Jimmy being taken to school and Cockey following him like a young puppy. The family tried to dissuade Cockey following them but to little avail. He always found means to do so. The teacher eventually resigned herself to seeing Cockey perched on a desk near young Jimmy who spent more time surreptitiously feeding Cockey than attending to the lessons. After the initial distraction caused by Cockey's presence in the class, the children soon accepted it as normal and ignored his clucking and occasional strangled attempts at crowing.

The teacher could not evict Cockey as he was difficult to catch and even if she could get hold of him she could not just simply put him out of the window because she could be accused of being cruel. In any case, if she did put him out of the window, he would only cause a distraction to the whole class or he would just simply fly in again through another window.

Cockey was therefore just accepted as a member of the class even though he was never entered into the register. After school, it was also amusing to watch Cockey participating in street games with the children. He was quite good at the running games but became very vicious when a football was used. He did not mind small tennis balls but he would viciously attack any child kicking a football. Presumably, he might have instinctively taken the football as being a hen. He had never seen a hen in his life,

172

but to him a football might have been a hen without legs. His instinct was to protect the ball against the children who kicked it. He could, with his sharp spurs and beak inflict painful injuries on any foolhardy child who he saw kicking a football.

As he had never seen another chicken, he assumed that he was just another child in young Jimmy's household and the family accepted and treated him as such. He ate with them, but never partook of fowl, slept with them, watched TV with them and helped in the garden by pecking at everything he possibly could.

Jimmy's father, the head of the family worked for the local council and earned a reasonable and regular wage. He was a nice chap but had one peculiarity as possibly we all do. He was very mean when he had to spend money on food. He scrimped and scraped although Cockey never went hungry. The neighbours were always willing to give him tasty morsels. Jimmy's father was very thin through lack of nourishment and so was his wife but the children were well fed because they received school dinners and milk. His wife told us that she actually looked forward to going into hospital for under-nourishment because, whilst there, she received good, plenty food. The only time he was lavish with food was Christmas time when he went berserk. All his married children and his grandchildren would gather together for the festival and he provided a plethora of food and drink. Expense was no object. The highlight of the feasting was a sumptuous dinner when the whole family sat round the table and ate till they felt that their stomach was bursting.

After the meal, they all settled down to relax with expensive liqueurs, brandies and cigars and cheerful.chatter.

Jimmy suddenly remembered that it was an extremely cold evening and went to let Cockey in to warm himself in front of the cheerful log fire. Despite being called several times he did not respond. Meanwhile his dad was helping to clear and wash up the dinner items and dispose of the well picked chicken bones.

Protests

In 1970, my wife and I, first became actively involved in protest demonstrations against the Soviet persecution of their Jewish citizens. It was in the dark days of KGB terror when Soviet citizens were being incarcerated in freezing Siberian gulag prison camps for very little reason and quite often for no reason what-so-ever apart from the perpetuation of a regime of terror and oppression.

For quite a while rumours were reaching the west of a campaign specifically aimed at Soviet Jews. It commenced with show trials of prominent Jews and Jewish intellectuals who inevitably pleaded guilty and were immediately executed. The campaign was conducted against Jews in every strata of life including doctors who were accused of poisoning their patients. All that was needed to send someone to their death or 20 years minimum in a labour camp was an accusation, however ludicrous by a malevolent or envious person. Spouses were blackmailed to give evidence against each other and children were encouraged and rewarded in school to report 'misdeeds' of their parents.

Whilst we were aware of these happenings, there was little we could do to aid our co-religionists let alone Soviet citizens in general.

Writing to such people would immediately put them at risk of being accused of being spies or American agents. Likewise, we could not name individuals when writing letters of protest.

The first opportunity to protest came when on Christmas Eve 1970, the Soviet news media announced that as a result of a trial that had recently taken place in Leningrad, eleven persons had duly been found guilty of an attempt to hijack a civilian plane and fly it to Sweden. The Soviet authorities were aware at that time that hijacking planes was a very sensi-

174

tive issue in the West and that little sympathy would be accorded to the person accused of hijacking. They also knew that almost everybody in the West would be pre-occupied with celebrating Christmas and that newspapers were not published on Christmas Day. Two of the accused were sentenced to death and the others to up to 15 years in 'strict regime' labour camps.

Unfortunately for the Soviet authorities they had not reckoned on the fact that TV in the West did not close down on Christmas Day and that nearly everyone was at home to watch it. As there was little other news to report, great prominence was given to the Soviet announcement and the spontaneous protest demonstration that took place outside the gates leading to the Soviet embassy in London. At that time, there were no organisations in existence to co-ordinate actions by individuals who wished to demonstrate their revulsion at Soviet oppression and cruelty. We felt that a demonstration was needed to express our feelings and we phoned friends who we knew felt the same way as we did.

They in turn contacted their friends in order to mount a protest demonstration outside the Soviet embassy. Locally, we organised several car loads of people who came along with their improvised, home made banners and congregated outside the Soviet embassy. It was a bitterly cold day with snow flurries and because local authority workers were on festive holidays the roads were not de-iced and were very slippery.

The setting and the weather gave TV news reporters a wonderful opportunity to cover the event which was repeated in each news broadcast on all channels.

The result was so embarrassing to the Soviet authorities that they were compelled by the adverse publicity to commute the two death sentences to long terms in labour camps. All the condemned served their full sentences before being released.

Once it was shown that demonstrations could produce positive results, individuals combined to form groups and the protests continued in many forms all over the country but particularly in London. It inspired similar organisations in other countries.

We participated in many further demonstrations in aid of other individuals and Soviet Jewry in general. One such event was a 7 day, 24 hours a day protest outside the Soviet embassy in London. I can't remember on whose behalf the demonstration was being held but Dora kindly had volunteered to do the Friday night shift and naturally expected me to accompany her as her minder.

Protest placards were already in place and we were furnished with a plastic bucket filled with sand and several flaming torches, sufficient to last through the hours of darkness. The shift was quite interesting. The weather was fine and all night through, people were walking up and down the street, many walking their dogs. It was amazing how many people appear to be insomniacs. Every so often, a burly man would come out of the Russian embassy to check that we were still there.

Several people stopped to enquire what the protest was about. We were surprised when a large official looking Rolls Royce stopped, it had some insignia protruding from the roof but from the angle where we were squatting we could not see what it was. The passenger got out and told us that he sympathised with our protest and asked to sign the petition that was to be presented to the Russian Ambassador. He explained that he was the equerry to a senior member of the Royal Family who also sympathised with our protest but protocol forbids him to sign such petitions. Just as daylight was beginning to break, Dora said that we could dowse the flaming torches. I pressed them one by one into the sand in the bucket but one unexpectedly ignited the plastic bucket. It flared up like an incendiary bomb and in turn ignited a couple of the placards. There was an enormous blaze and there was nothing to hand to put the fire out with. We were alarmed when suddenly a policeman appeared. We had visions of being arrested and possibly accused of attempted arson against the Russian embassy which by international law was actually Russian territory. Would we be tried by a Russian court in which we were bound to plead guilty and sentenced to 20 years in a 'strict regime' labour camp in Siberia?

Surprisingly, the policeman did not mention the blaze which had commenced to burn itself out, he asked if we had witnessed a vehicle collision which had taken place a short distance up the road. Quite truthfully, we had not.

We thankfully handed the charred remains to the next shift.

Badminton

When the Welsh couple who lived next door moved back to south Wales they promised to keep in touch with us. They also left us with one of their two grown kittens because the sedative which he had been given for the long journey had not functioned properly. They promised to arrange for his transport to Wales in the near future. They never contacted us about the cat, whose 'temporary' custody lasted some 14 years until he died of old age. We named the cat Taffy as we already had a similar black cat called Toffy. Even though they did keep in contact with us, they never mentioned Taffy or asked about his welfare. In turn, we, that is my wife Dora and myself, did not mention him in our letters as we had become fond of him and were apprehensive that they may ask for his return. After a couple of years of polite exchange of letters we were surprised to receive an invitation to visit them. They said that if we accepted, they would send us train tickets and that we could stay with them for a week. They told us that they lived in a pretty village outside of Cardiff and that the climate at that time of the year was very pleasant. They were keen to show us the dilapidated farm house they were rehabilitating and were sure, that being an architect I would be interested in seeing the project. They were carrying out most of the work themselves in their spare time which, being teachers, they had plenty. Almost as an aside, they asked me to fetch with any instruments I may need to advise them on treating the rampant dry rot, woodworm and rising damp.

We were interested but had our doubts about the weather. Our previous experience in Wales was of continuous heavy rain. As that was in north Wales, we thought we would try our luck in south Wales where we were told that the climate was quite different. When we received the train tickets we were most surprised to note that they were first class! We had never travelled first class before.

The first class train compartment only had one other passenger. We immediately noticed his very smart clothes, bowler hat and rolled umbrella and briefcase with the letters 'ER' embossed in gold.

He was very friendly and talkative and said he was glad to have companions to talk to on such a long and dreary journey to a dreary destination.

He handed us one of his embossed visiting cards. I can't remember his name but he was an important civil servant in the Department of the Environment.

In exchange I handed him one of my cards which impressed him very much. He noted my qualifications and that I was an architect in my own practise. He was very interested as he said that his work often involved new building projects and alterations to existing ones. He also said that he regretted not having become an architect himself and hoped that one day his young son may become one. He asked me how one trained and qualified as an architect, how long it took and how did architects go about getting work. I told him that architects were not permitted to advertise or tout for work but had to rely basically on their reputation and recommendations by previous satisfied clients.

Dora introduced herself as my personal and managerial assistant (how true!) and that actually we were on our way to consider whether or not to undertake a big renovation project on the personal mansion of an important client who we, for confidential reasons, could not name. She said he was a multi millionaire and that he had insisted that we travelled first class and stayed at a five star hotel, all at his expense. She said that he had used me for the design of several of his supermarkets in various parts of the country and even though I did not normally undertake such small projects, I felt that I was under an obligation to do so, especially as we were on such friendly terms. This impressed our fellow traveller who mumbled something that he may be able to use his influence to get some projects put my way.

Dora was thus encouraged in her unappointed role of PR and went on to explain that even though my practise was not large it was in great demand because clients took particular note that I personally attended to each and every detail however small. She pointed out that in most large architectural practises, unqualified and inexperienced assistants were often employed to carry out the work whilst the principals charged fees as though the work was done by fully qualified experienced architects.

I was quite embarrassed by the glowing description of my qualifications, experience, expertise and capabilities and successes. She described projects which I found difficult to identify but I could not contradict or correct her in front of this important person who might be able to get some commissions passed my way.

After a long while, the compartment door was slid open by a railway employee, who asked "Anyone for Badminton?" Dora brightly responded "how can anyone possibly play Badminton on a train?" He explained that the train only stops at Badminton station if anyone wishes to alight there. Very few people use the station when there is no event there.

I was most embarrassed but tried to pass it off as a joke.

I never received any commissions from or through our fellow traveller and the weather during our whole stay in South Wales was horrid and Taffy's name was not mentioned, not even once.

Hard Of Hearing

One of Shakespeare's characters says, "If music be the food of love, play on, give me excess of it". Indeed, if music is the food of love I've been undernourished all my life. The trouble is that to me, music is not sweet, relaxing, inspiring, exciting, emotional, sentimental or any of the other virtues ascribed to it. To me, music of any kind is an irritating noise. People who do not appreciate music are described as Philistines. I am not a Philistine, I have never been to Philistinia and have never met anyone who has. Maybe, I might have Philistinian genes in my blood because several other members of my family suffer with the same affliction, that is tone deafness that prevents us appreciating the fine points of good music.

Possibly the earliest memory is that of my mother singing a lullaby and me wishing that she would give over and let me get to sleep. I am not sure that even in my infancy I was tone deaf or that my mother was, possibly it was a combination of both. My father was definitely tone deaf and on the few occasions I did hear him sing it was like a well worn and badly cracked gramophone record.

My hearing problem was compounded when I was a young child when I underwent five mastoid operations that left me completely deaf in my right ear. I did not realise until recently when I suffered a serious attack of Menieres disease syndrome that I was tone deaf in my one and only functioning ear. This came to light when I consulted an ear specialist and had my hearing tested on an audiogram. This revealed that my hearing in the high frequency range of sounds was very impaired and explained why music that was so sweet to others was just an annoying and irritable noise to me and why, whilst being able to hear what some people were saying, I could not understand a single word. We have a neighbour who frequently drops in for a chat and I have to ask Dora what he is saying. In his case it does not matter much because, in turn, he has impaired hearing and can't understand what I am saying. We both pretend to hear each other. When listening to people, I do catch the odd words and out of them, I endeavour to compile a complete sentence. This of course, takes a few seconds. Sometimes my compilation is correct and sometimes incorrect which either produces annoyance or laughter and is the reason why some deaf people are accused of hearing only what they want to hear. I don't suppose there is a single person who would laugh at seeing a blind person stumble or fall but most people are quite ready either to laugh at a deaf person or to be outright annoyed.

I was the only pupil in school who was told by the music teacher to keep my mouth shut during singing lessons whilst, at the same time he was exhorting the other pupils to open their mouths wide.

Because my right ear does not function, the protruding flap is normal size and flat against the skull whilst my left ear flap is larger and protrudes in order to catch as much sound as possible.

Another disadvantage of being deaf in one ear is the difficulty of hearing anyone speaking to me on my right side. In order to catch their words, I have to swivel my head right round in order to have my left ear facing them. For some reason or another, some people get embarrassed when I swivel my head round to face backwards. Not being able to hear properly explains the reason why I make so many spelling mistakes. Because I not able to catch the fine differences between the sounds of certain letters of the alphabet causes words to be misspelt. It is also embarrassing not to be able to catch people's names let alone remembering them.

Sometimes, when I take my car to be tuned in my local garage, the mechanic will say, "Ah, that's the trouble, can you hear that tappet?" I dare not reply that I could hardly hear the engine, let alone a tappet.

In my case, hearing aids did not help much, that is they do not help me much but my immediate neighbour appreciates it when I use one as then, the sound volume on the TV can be turned down to normal. All that any hearing aid does is to amplify the sound, so if I use one, all it does is to amplify the distorted noises that I hear. Hearing aids do not rectify the loss of frequencies suffered. However good they are, they add their own distortion to the distorted noises heard.

It is difficult to listen to music in concert halls because I can easily hear the low frequency sounds emitting from the audience (it is amazing just how much noise a quiet, attentive audience automatically makes) but cannot hear the higher frequency sounds of some of the orchestra's instruments. After all, the audience outnumber the flutes, violins etc. many times over. Although I did try to impress girlfriends by taking them to classical concerts, I preferred listening to the rousing, thumping sound of a military band playing well known marches. Maybe, after all, I do have Philistinian blood in me!

Even after 45 years of marriage, Dora still sits on the wrong side of me in situations where it is difficult to hear, such as on crowded buses or trains or in rooms where there are a lot of people talking with a loud background noise. It is very painful to keep twisting my head right round!

The Titter

For some reason or another, Frank decided he could confide in me and obtain sound advice. I was an assistant in the local council's architects' department and he was the foreman electrician in the council's maintenance section. Occasionally, in the course of work, we met in order to discuss some technical problem. I presume that it was because of the way I helped to overcome technical problems that he developed a trust when discussing more personal matters.

Although he was respected by his more immediate colleagues because of his honesty and technical knowledge, he was to a certain degree held in ridicule for his fanatical adherence to a strict religious sect which forbade amongst other things for its members to partake of alcohol, tea, coffee, to listen to the radio or watch TV.

He was happily married with a teenaged son and daughter. He told me that he was having problems with his son who was exhibiting a peculiar interest in women's' breasts. I assured him that it was quite normal and natural for young boys to be intrigued with women's breasts. He said that his son's interests in breasts expressed itself in an embarrassing manner. He would stare fixedly at the breasts of women visitors to the house and would also do so even in church. He made it obvious when he looked down women's cleavages and recently had even tried to fondle the breasts of women in the street.

He said that his son spent hours depicting women's breasts in all shapes and sizes and had also secreted under his bed newspaper cuttings on which he had coloured in various colours the breasts on women's' photographs even those fully clothed.

I asked him if he had consulted a psychologist. He said that he had not done so as he expected that the psychologist would only attribute the condition to his strict religious background. He also feared that his son would be prescribed drugs which are forbidden by his sect and may become dependent on them eventually leading his son to become institutionalised.

I suggested that he put bromide in his son's tea in order to suppress his sexuality but Frank said that his sect forbade tea or similar drinks.

I had to confess I did not know what else to suggest and tried to console him with another instance of a boy of the same age who developed an obsession with glass bottles. His parents found it most embarrassing when he stopped for ages in front of off-licence shops and gazed lovingly at the bottles. He knew the shape, size and colour of every bottle on display. Somehow or other, he managed to bring home hundreds of bottles which his parents had to consign to the garden shed in case visitors got the wrong impression. He asked me if he grew out of the obsession but I replied that I did not know as I had lost contact with the family when they moved away. A short while after, he asked if I would mind drafting a letter of application for his son to copy for a job in the local county court. A friendly neighbour who knew of his problem had told him that the court urgently needed a replacement titter to replace the one who had recently left due to ill health. The applicant must be young and fit and must be available to take up his duties immediately. His neighbour said that physical fitness was important as it is frequently reported in the local press "A titter ran round the court". It was difficult to suppress laughter whilst I explained that his neighbour had taken advantage on his naiveté in order to play a cruel joke. However, Franks son did soon find a job with a local builder as a labourer. He was very happy in his work which included the removal of chimney breasts.

Tarzan

I don't know why or how it came to be that my parents' dog was named Tarzan but that was his name. My cousin had him originally when he was a puppy. Tarzan was always very playful and grew very fast. It was not long before he found he could easily leap over the garden gate and roam the local streets at will.

He was of mixed breed and soon demonstrated that in his genes were those of a breed used for herding cattle. He demonstrated this at a very early age by snapping at the heels of young horses being trained by the police at a nearby horse training school.

Naturally the police were not very pleased with this and made dire threats to my cousin if her dog should continue his unwelcome behaviour. My cousin realising that she could not prevent Tarzan from leaping over the garden gate and attacking the police horses, offered him to my parents who had not long before lost their own dog.

He was a good and faithful companion to my parents who being retired were at home all day, every day.

The high-light of the week was when my father took Tarzan with him shopping in the local market. However deep in sleep Tarzan was, he would leap to life whenever the words like 'walk', 'market' or 'shops' were mentioned in conversation . He would grab his lead and take it to my father.

He also liked to lie in front of the fire resting his head on a cushion thoughtfully made for him by my mother. Somehow or other, he sensed when my father went to the small shelf whereupon he kept his collection of prayer books and bibles. He knew that my father objected to having a dog in the room when he was reading from his holy books and without being told to do so, Tarzan would dutifully pick up his cushion and take it with him into an adjoining room returning only when he heard the word 'Amen' and the book being replaced on the shelf.

Both my parents were very hard of hearing and one day when I was visiting them, the front door bell rang but I noticed that neither of them, nor the dog took any notice. They had obviously not heard.

I told them that someone was at the front door and that the bell had just rung. Immediately my father sprung up and ran to the front door making barking sounds. Tarzan looked on very interested to know who was at the front door. After all, he was their watch dog.

When my father returned to the room I asked why he was making barking sounds when he went to answer the door. He said he was showing Tarzan what he should be doing but he doesn't catch on.

As a treat, from time-to-time, I took Tarzan on a long walk in Epping Forest the fringe of which was not far from where I lived. This part of the forest abutted directly onto a golf course from which it was separated by tall iron railings. Some vandals had cut an opening in the railings through which a herd of heifers which normally grazed in forest clearings had strayed. A handful of golfers were trying to herd the cattle back through the gap in the railings. As soon as Tarzan sized up the situation his herding instincts sprang up and before I could stop him, he joined in the exercise. The young heifers panicked at the combined efforts of men and dog and stampeded off the golf course back to the forest meadow. There must have been about thirty of the beasts each weighing something like a ton racing towards where I was standing. Fortunately I just managed to reach and climb the only nearby tree. When it was over, Tarzan came looking for me very pleased with himself.

Funerals

The streets in the predominantly Jewish part of the east end of London in the 1920's and 1930's were theatres that never closed and where the residents, young and old were the players. The activity ebbed and flowed depending on school hours, Sabbaths, festivals and the weather but it never stopped. The majority of the players were children who swarmed over the pavements and cobbled roads indulging in a wide variety of games any of which automatically involved shouting at full throat.

Quite frequently, a sliding sash window would be opened and a woman's voice would shout instructions to her child to run immediately to the corner shop and buy a certain item of grocery. The bulk of the shopping was purchased item by item as and when required and continued all day and well into the evening. Even when the tired shopkeeper closed the door of the shop, someone or another would suddenly discover that they had run out of something or another and knock on the shopkeepers back door. There were no supermarkets and all shopping was done at the corner shops.

In addition, there was a continuous procession of costermongers selling fruit, vegetables and fish etc. off flat topped two wheeled barrows. These were favourite with the housewives who would be enticed out of their homes by the costermongers fruity cries that could be heard above the hubbub of the shrieking children.

Depending on the weather, in the summer, ice cream vendors would trundle through the streets with their ice boxes mounted on tricycles and in the cold weather, coalmen, selling sacks of coal from carts drawn by tired old horses. Each vendor had his own distinctive cry. There were also milk men with large metal urns doling warm milk by the ladle full into jugs proffered by housewives attracted by their 'Milko' calls. The children were particularly intrigued by the horse of one milkman who continuously blew wind. Maybe, that was how the milk was kept warm. The milk was to nourish babies and children but was also the source of tuberculoses (consumption) which was very rampant in those days. The children could safely play on the manure strewn roads as there was virtually no mechanical vehicle.

Occasionally the local doctor would call in his car on a patient and immediately a crowd would gather around the patient's door. A home call by the doctor signified that the patient was dangerously ill or else the family would not have expended 2/6d (twelve and half pence) on such a luxury. Inevitably, such a visit by the doctor would shortly be followed by the patient being carted off by ambulance to hospital. The gathered crowd would long speculate on the patient's chance of survival as hospitals in those days were mainly for the desperately sick and dying. Dreaded word like, 'cancer', 'consumption', 'heart attack', 'double pneumonia' would be uttered sinisterly and the street noise would, for a while, become somewhat subdued.

Men did not actively take a major part in the street theatre, presumably, they were either working long hours in the sweat-shops or frantically seeking work in such establishments. When they did come home from work they were too tired to partake in any activity except to eat in order to replenish expended energy, to sleep in order to rejuvenate the body for another days work and also to produce more young participants for the street theatre.

The highlights of the street theatre apart from the shrieking, hair pulling fights between women were the funerals. These were of two distinctive types. Christian funerals and Jewish funerals, the two could not possible be confused.

From time-to-time a Christian cortege would pass from a neighbouring, mainly Christian district, through the adjacent predominantly Jewish streets. In such an event, all street activities would come to a standstill while the cavalcade passed by. The cortege would be preceded by a tall funeral director dressed in morning suit and top hat with a long black crepe ribbon trailing down the back. He would slowly and deliberately stride along the granite cobbled road tapping each step with his black silver topped staff.

The open flower bedecked hearse was drawn by four fine black prancing horses with tall black plumes fixed to their heads. The hearse was followed by many beautiful shining black landaus each drawn by prancing black horses with tall black plumes.

The street performers for a while stood in petrified awe at this impressive display of respect to the dead. Each and every mourner in the cortege was dressed entirely in black, even babes in arms were dressed in black. Women sobbed silently into black lace edged handkerchiefs.

As soon as the cortege had passed by I, in accordance with previous instructions from my father, dashed out with an iron pail and shovel and gathered the rich harvest deposited on the road by the lovely black horses for use in our pathetic window boxes. The manure tended to be too strong for the weak struggling nasturtiums but added piquancy to the general atmosphere inside our over-crowded slum dwelling.

The cortege proceeded to the church where a solemn lengthy boring service would be held and where the deceased as with all those who pass away are eulogised to high heaven. From thence to the cemetery. Cremations were very rare in those days. All then returned for the funeral breakfast which may have been held in the deceased front parlour, or, if that was too small, in the local pub, where the mourning could proceed with consoling beverages whilst the piano (Joanna) would jingle out tunes of enlivenment.

Such a grand send off obviously cost a lot of money and this was usually forthcoming from an insurance policy into which the deceased would have paid weekly contributions assiduously in preference to any other obligation or commitment. A good funeral was the highlight of any decent cockneys life.

By contrast, a Jewish funeral was somewhat different. In accordance with Jewish tradition and custom, a funeral is held either the same day as death or the next day.

There is therefore no opportunity for any elaborate preparation or lying-in-state or wake. Every male adult Jew was a member of his local synagogue and part of his weekly contribution to the synagogue was a sum that ensured that he, his spouse and offspring would be given a free funeral which would be arranged by the burial society. Having received a doctors death certificate the society would obtain the necessary secular burial permission, provide a plain, nailed together, sawn wooden coffin, unpolished with no handles, covered with a shabby black cloth. If the deceased were to be buried the day following death they would provide a religious Jew to keep watch over the deceased body during the night. This is reminiscent of the days not long past when newly dead people were snatched by thieves for use in medical dissection. They would also provide a hearse (a converted black painted van) and a limousine for the immediate family. All the other mourners had to find their own way to the cemetery and as none of them owned cars, it was usually by public transport or a hired London Transport bus. The grave was also provided free by the burial society and the service would be conducted by the Rabbi of the deceased's synagogue. For some reason or another the body guard, the hearse driver, the pall bearers, the grave diggers and the Rabbi all expected to be tipped by living relatives for services rendered to the dead.

The female mourners were expected to loudly wail and lament and they certainly did so to an extreme extent. If their cries did not reach heaven then nothing did. Lamentations were usually accompanied by admonishments to those they considered had failed the deceased. Blood curdling curses against those who they considered had done wrong to the deceased and also curses against many others. By-standing women who may not even have known the deceased felt obliged to join in the wailing and cursing. Black cloaked and bonneted elderly women would pass among the mourners and onlookers with small wooden boxes marked 'Charity' into which coins would be thrust as a superstitious token against any possible evil befalling them the donors.

At the cemetery, the Rabbi would make a very emotional eulogy and would continue until every woman was crying their heart out and at least one had fainted from hysteria.

For religious reasons, Jewish graves face towards Jerusalem so that on the day of resurrection the rising dead would know in which direction to travel.

By custom, no flowers or wreaths are provided or presented. The chief male mourners have an item of clothing rent as a token of their grief. Men with the name of Cohen are not allowed near the grave (except in the case of members of their own immediate family) because they are deemed to be descendants of the priestly tribe of Cohens who officiated in the temple in Jerusalem and must therefore not be defiled by the dead.

Women were not generally allowed to go near the open grave because in their hysterical state some have been known to throw themselves onto the coffin as a demonstration of their grief. This makes it difficult for the grave to be filled in.

It is the custom for the men present each to cast at least one shovel full of earth onto the coffin until the grave is filled up. On one occasion I duly did my duty, but because I was suffering with an inner ear condition which adversely effected my sense of balance, I nearly toppled into the open grave. What would people have thought if I had fallen into a grave of a woman I hardly knew?

Before leaving the cemetery, all wash hands under running water.

Back in the house of mourning, by tradition, all mirrors are covered over. The family hold a formal initial seven days of intense mourning called Shiva (Hebrew word for seven). Friends and relatives call to extend sympathy and condolences and prayers are held at least once a day.

As soon as the funeral vehicles have left the street, the theatre once again resumes its normal activity.

The Siege Of Sidney's Street

The siege of Sidney Street in Stepney, east London which took place about 76 years ago is quite well known but few know or remember about the siege of Sidney's street in nearby Ilford which took place only six years ago.

The Sidney Street siege took place when a band of armed anarchists were cornered in a first floor flat in a multi-storey block of slum apartments in a depressing street in a slum area of east London.

The anarchists were led by a wanted, Russian born, criminal, who had been nick-named 'Peter the Painter'. Winston Churchill who was then the Home Secretary, had called on a brigade of the Guards to assist the armed police who were besieging the premises in which the anarchists had taken refuge. The anarchists took advantage to escape the siege when a fire broke in the apartment.

The story of the siege received wide national and international news coverage.

The siege of Sidney's street however, was somewhat different. Sidney's street is the almost unknown middle class street of two storey terraced houses erected in 1904 and named Kensington Gardens, Ilford in the county of Essex.

On Saturday the 23rd March 1988, Sidney and his wife, Dora, were relaxing after lunch and watching a romantic film on TV. More precisely, Dora was watching whilst Sidney blissfully snoozed in his armchair.

The peaceful atmosphere was disturbed when the 'phone rang.. Sidney heard but continued to pretend to be snoozing. Dora answered. It was her niece asking if we were alright. Dora assured her that we were both in good health. She asked if we were in any danger. Dora said no more than usual. Her niece then asked what the situation was regarding the siege. Dora

191

asked, "What siege?" Her niece then said, "Don't you know there's a siege in your street?" Dora then shook me and said "There's a siege on". I replied that I was not interested and if she was, she should change to another TV channel. She then told me that the siege was actually in our street. Her niece had seen it on the TV news and had just 'phoned to tell us.

We looked out of the window and low and behold, the street was filled with police cars and vans parked at all angles and there were dozens of police, many armed crawling though front gardens and taking up sniping positions against a nearby house on the other side of the street. Apparently, what had happened, was that a disgruntled man had 'phoned a national newspaper to say that he had a gun and was holding a woman and her baby hostage. He was doing this as a protest against the local council who had obtained an eviction notice against him for persistent non payment of local council rates on his own house in nearby East Ham where his wife and child lived. The house under siege in our street was that of his 'girl-friend' and her child.

The newspaper had alerted the police who made a silent approach so as not to startle and excite 'the gunman' who appeared at the window holding a knife to his hostage's throat and warned the police to keep away. He subsequently reappeared at the window holding a gun which subsequently turned out to be an imitation one. One false or misleading move on his part could easily have led to him being shot by one of the police marksmen.

Apart from the woman and child, he was also holding a male resident as hostage. The police considered the situation as most serious and dangerous. They mustered 250 police officers, most of them armed, brought a mobile command post with very high police officers in charge and also specially trained sharpshooters.

The street was sealed off, no traffic or person allowed in or out and residents warned to keep away from their windows. One women who had just previously popped around the corner to buy a bottle of milk for her baby was allowed back but she was surrounded by a phalanx of police officers wearing body armour.

The siege commenced at 1pm and continued until 8pm. Local traffic including bus routes were diverted and this caused congestion over a wide area.

The siege came peacefully to an end when the hostages came out and said that the gunman was fast asleep. He had fallen asleep watching a film on TV.

This episode cost the local police £250 000 including the services of a helicopter and specially trained dogs. He was charged and eventually tried.

He was not jailed but placed on probation to be of good behaviour. We next saw him about 3 months later on a very hot afternoon walking down our street accompanied by his girlfriend', her baby in a pram and the resident who had all been his 'hostages'.

I called Dora to the window to have a look. I said, "Disgusting, they are all stark naked", but Dora corrected me by pointing out that they were all wearing shoes and socks, even the baby!

The Bungalow

When I set up practise as a full time self employed architect, I was glad to receive any commission what-so-ever, it did not matter how small, humble or dreary. I was therefore delighted to be asked by a local doctor to design a retirement bungalow for him.

He had thought his requirements out quite carefully and his brief was precise and clear.

The site was a plot of land immediately adjacent to his existing four storey, end of terrace Victorian house. As he was fast approaching retirement, he and his wife, found his existing house too large, cumbersome, uncomfortable and inconvenient.

His plan was to have a small, compact, modern, comfortable, easily maintained bungalow built into which he and his wife would move. He would then lease his existing house but retain the sub-basement storey for use as a surgery for his private patients. So far, so good and most promising for a brilliant, young and eager architect such as myself.

We readily agreed conditions of employment which were those as recommended by the Royal Institute of British Architects. I was to design the bungalow and to obtain the required planning and building regulation approvals. The doctors said that he would not need me to obtain tenders or to supervise the actual works as he felt quite capable of doing so himself. The builder who carried out his odd jobs had agreed to do the work at a very competitive price.

When I inspected and measured the site, I pointed out that it was too small on which to erect a detached bungalow but it was sufficient if the new dwelling was to be designated as a single storey 'granny extension' to the existing house. This would overcome several problems such as down draught for the open fire which he stipulated and certain complex town planning and building regulation requirements including separate off street car parking for which there was no room and was not required by the doctor.

I pointed out that an extension to the existing house would fall within the 'permitted development' regulation of the town planning acts whereas a detached bungalow might not receive approval on grounds that it was inconsistent with the general existing properties. He readily agreed.

I then pointed out that due to the close proximity such a development would have to the public thoroughfare it would lack privacy. To overcome this, I suggested that the windows facing onto the public thoroughfares should be as few and as small as aesthetically possible and that all the principal rooms should open onto an internal private fully paved courtyard with an ornamental fountain therein. I said that such a courtyard would ensure his privacy whilst enjoying the maximum benefit of sunshine and shielding from street noises. Again he readily agreed and asked that all the rooms have French doors opening onto the courtyard. He was very excited and was going out to the garden centres to view appropriate fountains, statuary and associated fish ponds.

He quite unashamedly expressed his gratitude and praised my brilliance and conscientiousness. I modestly concurred with his astute assessment and sentiments.

He next handed me a brochure that had been given to him by a colleague describing a heat exchange unit which was designed to reduce the temperature of a larder by extracting heat therefrom and pumping the heat to warm adjacent rooms. He was very insistent that I incorporate such a unit into the design despite the fact that I pointed out that the heat from a larder could not possibly be sufficient to heat the much greater volume of the habitable rooms. Apart from anything else, this involved planning the bungalow around the unit instead of being able to site the unit in an appropriate position adjacent to the kitchen.

When I had completed the design the doctor told me that those having a new home built should plan the furniture layout therein by sticking cut out outlines of the furniture onto the plans. He invited me to measure the furniture items he wanted incorporated in his new compact home and to make cut out outlines.

I was shocked at the amount and cumbersome sizes of the furniture he had in mind. I reminded him that his brief was for a small compact home and the agreed design could not possibly accommodate the furniture he indicated. After lengthy consultation with his wife a much reduced list was produced. After juggling about with cut out outlines of the reduced furniture I had to tell the doctor that it was still not possible to incorporate the items into the new design. His wife said that she would not move into the bungalow unless all the items she had listed could be incorporated. She said that she had a lot of visitors and that the large sized furniture were legacies from her parents and she will not part from them.

The doctor said the solution was simple; just make the rooms larger. I pointed out that the restricted size of the site made this impossible. He replied, not if the size of the internal courtyard was reduced and if the bedrooms were moved to the first floor. Again, I referred to his original brief which was for a compact single storey dwelling suitable for his retirement. A two storey dwelling would involve a staircase which is not helpful to aged people as he should very well know.

As he was adamant, I revised the design again and quickly submitted it for town planning and building regulations approvals were duly granted. Because I had on several occasions pointed out to the client certain problems regarding his instructions, my status in his estimation was somewhat reduced. His wife said, "It is a bad state of affairs when your own architect won't let you have your own furniture in a two storey bungalow of your own design".

Several weeks later a builder phoned me and asked me to alter the design. He was not the original builder the doctor employed. I asked the current builder what happened to the original one. He said that he and the doctor had dismissed him. The new builder said that what had been erected so far is very different to my approved design and the council wanted a fresh application submitted and approved or they would serve a demolition order on that already erected. He said that the doctor and his wife somehow held me responsible for the difficult situation they were now in. I told him that I could not possibly take instructions from a third party and if the doctor were to approach me direct, I would most likely refuse to act again on his behalf.

Hotel Seaview

The Hotel Seaview in Westcliffe-on-Sea no longer exists. It was demolished several years ago and replaced by a five storey block of 'desirable' flats. The hotel is gone but memories linger on. The hotel was situated on the sea front. Actually, sea front and Seaview are both misnomers because the water involved is the Thames Estuary. The water is salty and tidal and the nearest shore opposite the hotel is that on the Isle of Grain, some 4 miles away. On a clear day and with the aid of binoculars the oil refinery on the Isle of Grain can be seen. Westcliffe is contiguous with the better known and more popular Southend-on-Sea with its $1^{1/2}$ mile long pier jutting out into the estuary.

Westcliffe is considered to be the more genteel of the two resorts, especially so, as it abuts onto Leigh-on-Sea which has an even more genteel reputation.

As Westcliffe (note the 'e' suffix) is only 40 minutes drive from where we lived, my wife Dora and I decided to spend a few days relaxation there. We booked into the Hotel Seaview because the hotel terrace directly overlooked the Estuary and the sea front promenade. The promenade is usually busy with day trippers and the sheltered beaches full of families enjoying the shallow, calm water. The estuary which leads to the London docks is well used by commercial ships and also pleasure and private boats. Therefore, even though rather genteel, it is quite lively and only a short walk away from the exuberant facilities of Southend to which the more livelier day trippers are attracted.

The three storey hotel had about twenty bedrooms and was owned and rim by a husband and wife team who were both Jewish. Nominally, it was a Jewish hotel in as much as the majority of the guests were Jewish and although not strictly kosher, served Jewish style food. The atmosphere was informal, easy and friendly. The guests were gregarious and talkative and mainly elderly.

The rooms were old fashioned but comfortable. The bathrooms and WC's were not en-suite. The food was good and plentiful.

On Saturday evenings, the proprietors arranged for free in-house entertainment by local amateurs. The weekend that we were there, we were entertained by an enthusiastic young group, obviously homosexuals but very hilarious. We doubt if most of the residents were even aware of the group's sexuality.

It was not long before we got to know our fellow residents. There was the fat woman, Mrs Alexander. She was so fat that when she went to the toilet, she had to ask another female resident to accompany her so as to take her bloomers down and then to pull them up again when she had finished. The longer stay residents knew this and made themselves scarce as soon as Mrs Alexander showed signs that nature was calling. One night she fell over in the corridor on her way to the WC and because of her size she could not get up. There was no one strong enough in the hotel that night to pick her up so she laid there until the following morning when outside help was available. Mrs Barnet was the first to discover her on her way to the WC but said that because she had a weak heart she had a job to climb over Mrs Alexander so as to answer her own natural requirements.

Early one morning, Mrs Alexander ponderously got out of her chair which was the signal for all the other women to make a hasty exit. I thought she would surely not have the effrontery to ask me to take her bloomers down. I was shocked when she came direct up to where I was sitting and she asked me if would be kind enough to help her to get to another hotel as she felt that the women in this one were not friendly and that the food portions were not as large as they should be for the money being charged. Dora and I did accompany her to the hotel she wished to go to but if she had fallen over on the way there would have been little we could have done except shout for help.

Mrs Conn was a bore of the first order. She was full of self pity and never tired of talking about her favourite subject, which was herself. She too was very much over weight although not in the Mrs Alexander league. She had had a heart attack and her doctor told her that unless she changed her diet and lost a considerable amount of weight there would most likely be another attack. He had given her diet sheets to adhere to. She was very sorry for herself, she told us that on such a diet life was not worth living. She bored us with detailed lists of each meal and how unsatisfying they were. The hotel proprietors had been given copies of the diet sheet and prepared special meals accordingly for Mrs Conn. We could not help noticing that although she ate these meals she bribed the staff to serve her second and even third helpings. On several occasions we spotted her in seaside shelters heartily tucking away at slabs of chocolate and seaside rock.

Doris was about 40 years old and she told us that she was recuperating from a nervous breakdown after her fiancee had broken off their engagement. They had been engaged for about ten years.

Mrs Edwards was very thin and gaunt with a terrible nervous face twitch and stammer. She too was recovering from a nervous breakdown. In fact, both she and her husband had both had nervous breakdowns caused by the cost of their daughter's wedding. The groom's parents had made such exorbitant demands that they far exceeded what they could afford and were now facing bankruptcy.

Mr Fine was a jovial man. He seemed to be a permanent resident and was glad to find someone new each week to talk to. He had apparently made a lot of money by buying condoms wholesale from the London Rubber Company (condoms used be known as French letters but now, because of the European Union it is not considered correct to call them as such) and re-sold them at a considerable profit to people who were not in a position to buy them in a shop. He sent them to customers who had responded to his advertisements in his national press. Many of his customers were in Ireland and in remote villages and hamlets around the country. He said he was surprised at the number of requests he received from residents in retirement and nursing homes. He should not have been surprised because the proprietor's wife told us that she was annoyed with Mr Fine because she had found him one day in bed with the young chambermaid. She said she was no prude but she objected to him having sex with her staff during working hours when she was paying her wages.

Mr Grundy's mournful face belied his jovial character. He was always telling jokes. He told us that he stayed at the hotel because he enjoyed the food and the atmosphere. One day he called me aside and apologised for pointing out that I was 'Rather thin on top'.

I told him that I had consulted my doctor who assured me that there was no cure and that I would waste my money if I tried out patent restorers. Mr Grundy agreed. He said that there were many charlatans about and he himself had spent a fortune in trying to restore his lost hair. I was puzzled because, even though his hair was grey, he had a very distinguished head of hair. I asked him why he had spent a lot of money on hair restorers when he had such a good mop of hair. He laughed as he removed his wig and revealed a shining bald patch. He told me that he had several wigs all similar but the hair trimmed to varying lengths to give the impression of haircuts and growth. I agreed with him that his wig was very realistic and impressive and by far the best one I had ever seen. I told him that I had seen wigs that were so obviously false that they were laughable. He said, "There are wigs and there are wigs but it largely depends on your supplier."

He told me about someone he knew who went to West Germany to have hair implants done. It took ages, was very painful and cost the earth but all his hairs came out the first time he washed it and left him with scores of regularly spaced holes in his head. For some reason or another he could not recover his money or sue for damages.

He confidentially whispered into my ear that if I was interested he could get me a wig of similar quality to his own from his usual supplier who was a friend and it would be a fraction of the normal retail price but the transaction would have to be cash. He said that if I was not 100% satisfied, I need not buy. I could see no harm in it. When I tried the wig on, Dora thought it looked very natural and that I should go ahead and buy it. After I paid the cash I asked if he could get me another one to match but with the appearance that I had just had a haircut. He said certainly, and he would contact me as soon as his friend obtained a suitable one. I asked if it would be possible to deal direct with his friend. He said he doubted if I would wish to do so because his friend is a mortuary attendant and in any case, he would be reluctant to deal direct with the public.

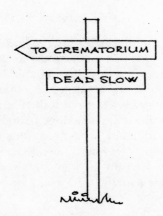

The Crematorium

It used to be quite common for promoters of civic buildings to hold architectural competitions for the design of their project. In this manner, they had the advantage of being able to choose a design from among possibly up to several hundred entrants. There was usually a cash prize for the winner and the two runners up. Generally, the winner was also given the opportunity to carry out the work at the usual fee.

This competition system afforded young and unknown architects the opportunity to crash in on a successful career.

It was with this in mind that I entered a competition to design a crematorium. I obtained the details and requirements and the rules.

As I had no knowledge of crematoria, I had not even been to a funeral in one, I commenced my research. I was surprised at the number of books on the subject of disposal of the dead in my local municipal library. They had been borrowed many times previously. I wondered what sort of people would be so interested in such a morbid subject.

Surprisingly, the library of the British Institute of British Architects was not helpful. Most of the designs of crematoria in their books were based on classical architecture and quite unsuitable for the present day.

I decided that visits to crematoria might help so one fine sunny afternoon I took my wife out to the local crematorium which is set in the midst of an enormous old cemetery with large, ornate and well tended tombstones. The atmosphere was quiet and peaceful and the crematorium was set in a beautiful well kept garden of remembrance. As we sat on a bench admiring the garden we saw a man clambering over the rock garden taking photographs. When we came near, he smiled politely and said, "Nice day." We were very annoyed at his impudence and Dora asked him if he

201

was not ashamed at desecrating such a revered and beautiful garden. He was most apologetic and explained that he was the manager of the crematorium and one of his duties was to submit at monthly periods photos of the garden of remembrance to the appropriate council committee.

He discreetly and solicitously enquired if there was anyone in particular that we were remembering. I explained the reason behind our visit. He was intrigued and suggested that he would recommend that I visit the crematorium in Southend which was newly erected and was a show-place with the latest techniques. He said the manager there was a friend of his and told me to mention his name when I asked for permission to make a visit.

As soon as he parted, Dora exclaimed, "What a kind helpful gentleman, I knew he was different as soon as J noticed his photographic interest in botany. I'm glad that I introduced ourselves."

The manager of the Southend crematorium was likewise helpful. He arranged for us to be taken on a conducted tour of his recently opened crematorium.

Our guide first showed us the modern and pleasant chapel and demonstrated how, after the service, the coffin would gently and silently glide through a hatch and then the velvet curtains would close across the hatch opening whilst solemn piped music was played.

All the activities were closely monitored and co-ordinated on closed circuit television.

We were then taken to see 'behind the scenes.' Contrary to popular belief, the corpse is not cremated as soon as it passes through the hatch. Actually the coffin is lowered on a hoist into a basement room and is stacked along a wall with all the other bodies whose funeral service was held that day. The cremations usually take place after nightfall so as not to distress mourners and nearby residents.

If the cremations are properly carried out, there is a minimum amount of smoke emitted but there is a little vapour. There was no morbid atmosphere, the place resembled a modern bakery. In fact, our guide, who operated the ovens told us he used to work in a bakery but had to give up when the flour dust affected his lungs. He explained that the ovens were worked in rotation. They were pre-heated by gas burners until the fire brick lining was white hot. The lid of the coffin was removed and the body, together with the coffin was slid into the oven. After a short while, the coffin and the body would burst into flames and be consumed very quickly. The oven would be allowed to cool down and the remains removed. The remains consisted of the coffin ashes and the fragments of calcinated bones. These were passed along a conveyor belt along which powerful magnets removed any metal objects such as the remains of the coffin screws. Next, the bone fragments were passed through a mincing machine to grind them into a powder. The bone powder together with coffin ashes were then placed in an urn, labelled and placed on a shelf to await collection or instructions to dispose of them.

Our guide was not amused when Dora spotted a small amount of ashes on one of the work benches and exclaimed, "Oh look, someone's elbow bone.

Although I put my heart and soul into the competition design I did not win, my effort did not even get a mention in the judge's opinions on the range of designs submitted. It was, as you might say "a dead loss".

Langsamer John

My wife and I, willingly agreed when her nephew suggested that we share a holiday in Switzerland with him. He spoke perfect German which would be very useful as we were to stay in a private chalet and our hosts could not speak a word of English.

The chalet was in the small village of Spiez in the German speaking Berner Oberland canton situated on the west shore of Lake Thun between Interlaken and Thun.

Dora's nephew Sidney had stayed with the family previously and heartily recommended them.

We raised no objection when he asked if he could bring a friend of his own age to make up a foursome.

It was agreed that his friend, John, buy the tickets and that we would meet at Victoria Station a half hour before departure time to catch the boat train and thence by 3rd class train through France to Switzerland.

We became alarmed when John did not turn up on time and did not appear till about one minute before the scheduled departure time. He ambled towards us at the ticket barrier as though he had all the time in the world and then started to search for our tickets in his pockets and hand luggage.

This was just the first of the many instances of his irritating, languid and indifferent manner that was to mar our otherwise most enjoyable holiday.

When we arrived in Zurich after a long and tiring journey we deposited our luggage in the station left luggage office and we strolled around the town whilst waiting for our connection to Spiez. John wandered off to find a Post Office as he had promised to 'phone his parents as soon as he had arrived. They were anxious as this was his first holiday without them and they obviously were aware of his shortcomings. When we went to retrieve our luggage,

Sidney had an altercation with the attendants who tried to overcharge by about ten times. They knew that we had just arrived and thought that we were not acquainted with the currency nor could understand the language.

Once again, John arrived at the last moment when we were to catch the local train to Spiez. He said he had been delayed because when he left the station he had found himself in a street where virtually every shop was selling watches. He bought himself a wrist-watch in the first shop he came to. It was much cheaper that in England but he found that as he walked down the street, the same watch was progressively being offered at a lower price. He had gone back to the first shop for a refund but the staff who spoke perfect English when he bought the watch suddenly could not understand what he was saying.

We hoped, that with the new watch, he would be able to keep better time but to no avail. He had bought the watch as a present for his father who had given him the money.

The chalet was very pretty and our hosts were very friendly and hospitable. Mr Hoffenburger was a small, meek man who worked on the Swiss railway of which he was rightly proud. All his conversations were about the railway system and was very useful in advising us where to go and how to get there. He said that all the trains and interlinking cross lake boats left punctually looking at John who our hosts soon nicknamed Langsamer John (pronounced Lungsummer) meaning slowcoach John.

Our hostess was a buxom hearty woman who laughed at everything we said, not that she understood a word but the sound of our language was very amusing to her. When our conversation was translated by Sidney, she laughed even louder and slapped the nearest person heartily on the back. Unfortunately for John, he was usually the nearest one to her. When he asked us not to say anything when she was standing near him she found that amusing too. She always served him his meal first because she knew he was the slowest eater and always finished last. Each time she served him with a dish she heartily slapped him on the back and wished him 'Gut appetit' which nearly caused him to choke. Our hosts had two sons, one was still at school and the elder was apprenticed to a local baker. Early one morning we met him out delivering the bread after working all night baking. He was wheeling a bicycle up a steep slope and on the bicycle was strapped two panniers loaded with bread and towed behind was a small wagon also loaded with bread. The first few days in the chalet were not very happy ones for John. Besides the back slapping he had developed a cough which he at first attributed to the timber of which the chalet was built but later realised it was due to the acrid smoke from our host's pipe tobacco. He soon became immune to this irritant.

He next suffered a bad bout of what we termed 'The Swiss roll.'

Mrs Hoffenburger often served a local dish which she called 'Rershty'. It was a pasta doused in oil and garnished with herbs. It was very tasty but, as we found to our great discomfort, very indigestible. The first night that we had the dish, I felt a discomfort in my stomach which I found was relieved if I turned over but the discomfort soon returned and subconsciously I turned again. As the discomfort returned at ever increasing frequency I suddenly found that I was turning over very fast. In the morning, we all confessed to the same symptoms but John had it much worse than us and we had to call in the local doctor. About the only thing that we found that John did fast was this Swiss roll and the associated dashes to the toilet. When our host's younger son told his teacher that his parents had English visitors and that they were either qualified professionals or training to be so, he brought home a message that the Headmaster would be honoured if we were to pay a visit to his school.

Because of the mountainous terrain and the climate, schools in Switzerland have long winter holidays but make up for this by very long hours in the summer months.

When we entered the school, we were treated like royalty. As we entered each class, the children would spring to attention and lustily sing a song of welcome, (so we assumed) and the teacher demonstrated a lesson. In every class we visited, the teacher would yell to the children in German, "Reply in high German." This is because the Swiss speak their own corrupted form of German known as Swiss Deutsch. Subsequently, when we walked through the village, children would point us out to their parents as the distinguished visitors to their school.

John rather disillusioned them one day, when as a result of the Rershty, he violently vomited in the high street.

Switzerland consists of 22 cantons, that is political districts about half of them being predominantly of the Catholic religion and the other half non-Catholic Christian denominations.

When we asked our host one day the best way to get to a certain beauty spot he became very vague and obstructive. He mentioned all sorts of difficulties and problems and suggested that we visit another beauty spot which he considered to be much better. Eventually, we discovered the reason for his reluctance to assist us was that the place we wished to visit was in a Catholic canton and he was very much an anti Catholic. On the first Sunday morning we stayed with them, our hostess asked if we were going to church. We said that we were not churchgoers. She said that she understood as many young people these days did not attend church regularly. She asked if we were Presbyterians and when we replied no, she went through a long list of other denominations to which we answered no to each. She then looked hard at us and asked if we were Catholics. We assured her that we were not. She then implored us to tell her what we were. We told her that we were Jews. At that she burst out laughing hysterically and thumping John on his back. With tears of laughter running down her cheeks and gasping for air she called out for her husband to hear. When she told him that we claimed to be Jews he also laughed hysterically and said, that if we had been, he would have slung us out of his house even in the middle of the night. In between thumps on his back John said, "Is this true or am I having a Rershy nightmare?"

Our hosts sent us on our way saying its the best joke they ever heard and could not believe that we kept such a straight face whilst telling it.

This experience, however, did not stop us eating in Methodist run restaurants run for abstainers which served nice meals at reasonable prices.

At one restaurant, the waitress who recognised us immediately as English tourists excitedly asked us repeatedly if we wanted 'Pommes frites' with every dish we ordered. The portions were enormous and as we were about to leave the waitress asked "Plus de ponimes frites?' For a change, John reacted quickly and thinking that she was asking if we were satisfied, he replied, "Yes please." When the four large portions of chips were served we told John that he could eat them all himself whilst we went for a stroll. It took him about an hour to get through them.

One day our host told us about a crystal clear lake on top of a mountain but warned us about swimming in it as the water was very deep and very cold. When we got there, John decided that in spite of the warning he would take a dip. He went in and shouted that it was not exceptionally cold but as a precaution he would soon come out. As the only other swimmer there, I was glad as I did not feel heroic enough to risk swimming in a freezing cold lake.

John's shout attracted the attention of a herd of pigs in a nearby field. They were, apparently, a local attraction and when called by tourists would come to collect tit bits of food.

They apparently could swim, and evidently enjoyed doing so. They dashed into the lake and surrounded John, grunting for their expected rewards. John found it difficult to leave the lake and I had visions of trying to save him whilst hemmed in by a herd of greedy swine.

In Matthew 8-30 it describes how a herd of 2000 swine dashed into the lake of Galilee and drowned. This seems strange when apparently swine can actually swim and enjoy doing so. We found Swiss shop keepers very annoying. If you stopped even momentarily near their shop, they would dart out and pester you to buy. If you did buy something they would pester you to buy more. Just before we left, I went into a clock shop and chose a cuckoo clock to give as a present. The assistant demonstrated it and took it behind the counter to wrap it up. When I got home, to my disgust she had wrapped up a rusty broken clock and not the one I had paid for.

Yankel the Yank

In June 1967 the Israeli armed forces captured the Sinai Peninsula in a brilliant six day campaign. My wife and I were fortunate to be among the first civilians to be permitted to enter the Peninsula after its capture.

We had virtually no idea what-so-ever what to expect. The tour had been hastily organised by the Egged bus and tour company in Israel.

We left Tel Aviv about 5 a.m. in a convoy of four coaches, each with it's own driver, guide and mechanic. Although there were no medical staff there were several doctors among the passengers who consisted of a mixture of Israelis, Americans and a sprinkling of English, French and Swedes. Our guide spoke English.

Our first stop was in Beer Sheva for an early breakfast. Whilst we were queuing at the self service counter we could hear the excited chatter of a group of Americans just behind us. They were talking about their home town, Castro Valley. Dora turned round and asked them if they knew her cousins Harold and Phyllis Tannin who lived in their town. They said they certainly did, they were close friends and neighbours and they would have been on tour with them but had to drop out at the last moment. Dora said that she and the cousins corresponded regularly but had never met.

The convoy continued in a south west direction through the Negev Desert and entered the vast and remote Sinai desert through which Moses led the Israelites from bondage in Egypt to the promised land.

The route the convoy took had no proper roads and proceeded along the dried out beds of river wadis. The 'road' was indicated by white painted boulders spaced about five meters apart along the sides of the 'road.' It was dangerous to stray off the indicated route as there were many live and

208

unmarked land mines about, evidence of which was shown by the bleached skeletons of camels that had not heeded the warnings.

It was soon after we entered the Sinai desert that we became aware of the person we nick-named Yankel the Yank. By the way of interest, the word 'Yank' is a contraction of 'Yankee' which was the name attributed by the French to early English and European settlers in America. Later it was applied to all inhabitants of the USA. Yankel is my own diminutive form of Yank.

Yankel asked the guide to switch on the air conditioning to alleviate the desert heat. Although the desert day temperature was very high we did not feel uncomfortable because of the dryness of the air. Yankel pointed out that in the States where he came from, all coaches operated the air conditioning even when the temperatures were nowhere nearly so high as here. Yankel persisted in his demands even though the guide tried to explain that under the circumstances it was better not to operate the air conditioning. Yankel continued by reminding the guide that the brochure advertising the tour said that all the coaches were air conditioned and as a citizen of the United States he insisted on his contractual rights. The guide relented and switched the air conditioning on. Within a few minutes we were all covered in a film of fine yellow dust which had been picked up from the river bed through the air conditioning intake which was situated under the coach. After that episode we settled down to admire the majestic and enchanting scenery. On each side of the wadis arose steep granite mountains, each of a different hue; red, blue, purple, lavender and pink. The beauty was continuous and hypnotic. Occasionally, we would pass a lone Arab rider on a camel.

We realised why we had a mechanic on each coach. In the event of a breakdown there was nobody to help. There were no garages, no filling stations, no service areas, no refreshments, no water, nothing but rocks and sand. The coaches carried its own stock of food and water but in the event of a breakdown they would have to rely on the Israeli air force spotting them and directing relief.

We continued south westward through the Mitla Pass and saw evidence of the tremendous battle that took place there. For mile after mile the sides of the wadi were littered by unending relics of armed vehicles and transports and were littered with unexploded ammunition. If there was an Armageddon, it had taken place here.

We passed through the battle zone and reached the northern part of the Gulf of Suez. Here we joined a proper road and continued southward along the coast road.

On the other side of the Gulf we could clearly see, even without the aid of binoculars the Egyptian oil fields.

Even though both Egypt and Israel were still at war with each other, there was an undeclared truce in this area for mutual benefit.

I always thought that a mirage was something in the mind especially of those who may have been desperate for water but we did see at least one mirage. It could not be the figment of my imagination as everybody else on the coach saw it too and none of us was desperate for a drink. Right there in the middle of the desert was a beautiful lake of crystal clear shimmering water. The guide assured us that there was no lake there and that it was indeed a mirage.

We continued along the coastal road and stopped for the night at the oil camp at Abu Rudeis oil-field on the shore of the Gulf of Suez. The accommodation was that as provided for the oil workers and was rather primitive. To avoid embarrassment, men slept in bunks or on the floor in one hut and the women in another. Before I went to sleep I left the hut to do something I had long wished to do. I wanted to see the desert sky at night. To see nature's splendour that was not possible in the light polluted sky in and around London. I wanted to see the firmament from horizon to horizon but it was not meant to be as the security lights around the camp perimeter blotted out the sky.

During the middle of the night I was awoken by a commotion. There was screaming, sirens sounding, lights on everywhere and armed soldiers dashing about. There was an alarm and everybody thought the worst. When things calmed down, it appeared that Yankel the Yank had suffered an attack of cramp in one of his legs to which he was very prone. He had woken up and had cried out instinctively for his wife. Someone thought he was being attacked, switched on the lights and called for help. The soldiers guarding the camp had assumed that it was an enemy attack and searched for the attackers.

The sanitary provisions were very crude and the ablutions consisted of a trough of water and the showers were completely in the open with 12 shower heads controlled remotely. After the women had had their shower it was the men's turn. We formed an orderly queue and the first twelve stood under the showers. As soon as they had soaped themselves down the water stopped flowing. Yankel the Yank stormed off to get the flow re-started, which it soon did. We completed our shower but by the time Yankel returned the flow had stopped again.

After a hearty breakfast, we continued westward along a wadi to the St Catherine's Monastery which is situated in a valley at the foot of the reputed Mount Sinai. There is no firm evidence that this was the actual mountain described in the Old Testament on which Moses received the ten commandments.

We stayed the night in the Monastery which was not prepared to receive so many visitors at once. The accommodation was most crude; soiled and lumpy mattresses and old iron bedsteads, just one WC which was continuously becoming blocked up and one cold water tap in the open courtyard for ablutions.

About 3am we started our climb up Mount Sinai. Before we started, the guide implored Yankel the Yank not to join the climb. He explained that it was very hazardous and not at all suitable for anyone over the age of sixty. Yankel insisted on going, saying that he was as fit as anyone half his age.

As there was no moon and as most of us had not been pre-warned to take with a torch, we stumbled up the hundreds of crude and large granite steps formed for the pilgrims by a monk appropriately named Moses.

We reached the peak of the mountain just as the sun was rising over the adjoining mountain peaks. One of the guides donned a prayer shawl and led the morning prayers.

We did not stay long as it was essential that we completed the descent before the heat of the day.

At a short distance down Yankel had another of his cramp attacks and could not walk any further. The guides had to carry him down and this delayed the return to the Monastery and the commencement of the next leg of our journey which was to take place along a river Wadi. Due to the delay, part of the journey was after nightfall which, combined with the lack of moonshine, made the journey most dangerous. If one of the coaches had strayed off the marked route it could easily break an axle and get stuck in the sand or overturn.

When we finally reached the coastal road that ran along the Gulf of Eilat everyone heaved a sigh of relief The guide gave up a prayer of thankfulness and Yankel vowed to give a donation to his synagogue when he got home to the States. So that no one should not be aware of his vow, he made it over the amplified address system in the coach.

We proceeded along the coastal road that ran along the Gulf of Eilat and the Straits of Tiran till we got to Sharm el-Sheikh. It was actually when the Egyptians installed their heavy artillery at the Straits of Tiran and threatened to sink any boat going to the Israeli port of Eilat that the six day war commenced. A blockade is akin to a declaration of war. The use of the port of Eilat was essential to the existence of the State of Israel. We flew back from Sharm el-Sheikh to Tel-Aviv on the Arkia internal airways.

Due to the many hours sitting on the coach over bumpy roads, climbing a granite mountain in plimsolls, sleeping on hard floors or lumpy mattresses I developed a bad attack of Lumbago.

So a good and memorable time was had by one and all with no small thanks to our United States citizen, Yankel the Yank.

ENQUIRIES

Chutzpah

Not many people know that the plural of the word 'Chutzpah' is
'Chutzpot' but then I don't suppose on the other hand that many people
know the meaning of the word 'Chutzpah' even though in recent years
they may have heard it being used. It is a Hebrew word, that like many foreign words became incorporated into the English language. It is difficult to
define, so I will try to explain by instances personally experienced during
a visit to Israel, the home of the word. One Saturday, my wife and I spent
the Sabbath day on the beach of Kiryat Yam which is near Haifa. The
beach is served by an infrequent bus service which is not scheduled. It
seems to run whenever a driver feels like doing so, or when he fancies a dip
in the lovely warm Mediterranean himself. As there may be a long wait, we
went to make enquiries at the bus route terminus where there was a timber kiosk with the word 'Enquiries' written in several languages.

Inside was an elderly Jewish man with a long beard and a black hat
intensely reading a book. It took a little while to politely attract his attention. He looked up at us rather annoyed and we asked him when the next
bus was due to leave for Haifa.

He looked at us blankly and replied in Yiddish, "Ich Veis?" which literally translated means "I know?"

It is a trait among Jews to avoid direct replies to questions by responding with a question which can be illustrated by the following story:-

A judge in a Tel Aviv court put the question to the accused: "You are
accused of stealing a chicken, do you plead guilty or not guilty?"

The accused: "Why should I want to steal a chicken?"

The Judge: "Mr Levy, please stop responding to questions in this court
by asking another."

212

The accused: "Who me?'

Israelis are curious, uninhibited and sometimes even rude. If they are curious they will not refrain from asking a direct question which in this country would be considered rude. At first, we were very annoyed at such questions but we soon found out that a truthful reply was not really expected. A very large proportion of Israelis can speak English, a relic I suppose of the English mandate period. If they meet an English person they jump at the opportunity to practice their English with a native born speaker. Often, this was to our advantage, as not knowing any Hebrew, we found many people who went out of their way to answer our questions. Very often, our questions were duly answered by other questions, such as "Do you know Mr So and So who lives in England?' Another frequent question was, "So what do you do for a living?" Closely followed by "And how much do you earn?" Other questions "Do you own your own house and how many rooms does it have?' "What sort of car do you have?"

Complete strangers that you meet in the street would ask such direct questions and not consider it rude.

In response to an enquiry about a bus route a stranger asked us the usual line of questions and then added "How many children do you have?" We should have known better but we replied "None." He said "What a shame, don't catch the bus you asked for and come with me because I know a good doctor who specialises in such problems."

It would appear that all doctors in Israel specialise in something or another. One day, when we were in Tel-Aviv, our young niece who was at the time about 13 years old was violently sick in the street. She had eaten exactly the same food as ourselves so we were rather concerned and were about to ask someone where we could find a doctor when right nearby we spotted a doctor's nameplate written in English, 'Dr So and So, specialist in children's ailments."

Israel is a photographer's paradise. Sunshine virtually all year round, all day long. Varied scenery. Historical buildings. Religious sites and sights. Mixed races. Modern structures. Colours galore.

The problem is not to find something or somebody photogenic but to exclude shots so as not to run out of films.

People are not reluctant to be photographed. and sometimes are too eager. Scenery has to be photographed quickly before the inevitable group of children start posing and blocking the view. Spying the camera, adults would invariably start smiling and children would pester you to take their photo'.

In Beersheva I wanted to photograph a Bedouin but he deliberately kept turning his head away and indicating that he did not want to be pho-tographed. Dora said, "It must be something to do with his religion, some religions regard photos as being akin to their immortal souls." A nearby Israeli suggested that I should pay the Arab. So with trepidation I offered him a shekel which in those days was worth about 2/6d or 12½ pence in today's currency. This was quickly accepted and he happily posed exposing a set of really rotten teeth. I must have paid him much more than he expected because he insisted I also photographed his son, who likewise exposed a set of rotten teeth and his camel who had a fine set of teeth.

Strolling through the streets of Jerusalem on a Saturday morning we came across a young boy leading a fully grown sheep on a lead. It was obviously his pet. With the historical background of Jerusalem behind him it made a wonderful picture. He did not mind being photographed at all. He asked if he may have a copy. This was unusual, as most Israelis don't ask for copies even though they gladly pose. I gladly agreed and asked him to write his name and address in my note book. He refused, saying that it was the Holy Sabbath day and it was forbidden to write things down but told me to do so instead.

There is a district in Jerusalem, Mea Shearim (100 gates) in which extremely religious Jews live. The atmosphere is fantastic and it is like leaping back at least a century in time. All modernity are espoused by the inhabitants who wear old fashioned clothes. Even in the middle east heat the men have their heads covered and the women, even young girls wear skirts down to their ankles and long sleeves. It could easily be a setting for the Fiddler on the Roof musical.

We asked an elderly Jew the way to a certain ancient synagogue. He deigned not to reply but said in Yiddish, "Gay freg der goy dort." (Go and ask that non Jew there) pointing to another man on the other side of the street. We could hardly believe our eyes. He had pointed to another religious Jew in the traditional Hasidic outfit of long black beard, side burns, black hat, long black coat with the titses (religious fringes) hanging from under his vest. His object of derision was presumably of a slightly different and in his estimation inferior denomination. I photographed both. As there was so much to photograph, I always had my camera and flash gun at the ready. In a Tel-Aviv street one evening I spotted an elderly Jewish man in the traditional Hasidic clothes sitting on a low stool under a street lamp intensely studying what I assumed to be a religious book. It was a delightful picture of piety. I set my camera and began to focus when Dora said, "He is a religious man and may well object to being photographed". Regretfully I relented and started to put my camera away when the man looked at me, he had, obviously, been aware of my intention to take his photo' and said "Noo?" You can't look this word up in any dictionary but it obviously meant, "Well get on with it". The shot made a wonderful picture!

In Tel-Aviv we were invited to attend two weddings. The invitations did not come from either of the parents but from a mutual acquaintance who assured us that as long as we took our camera with it would be OK. We took the chance, the worst that could happen would be that we would be slung out for being chutzpardick.

The first wedding was very colourful. It involved bride and groom of families who emigrated from Morocco. They are known as Sephardi (Spanish or Portuguese descent) Jews with their own customs and traditions. Whilst the official photographer was sweating away taking the requisite photos', I was circulating and taking what I considered to be interesting and picturesque shots. After a while the official photographer approached me and started to shout in Hebrew. Our acquaintance explained that the photographer objected to me taking photos and taking away his livelihood. I tried to explain that the photos were entirely for my own personal use and would not be sold or given to anyone else. He reluctantly accepted this.

The next wedding was between Ashkenazi Jews (of European origin) and was more like the Jewish weddings I was accustomed to in England but the girls seemed to be more exotic and more beautiful. In order to avoid another possible scene with the official photographer, told him that I was not in any way in professional competition with him. He looked scornfully on me and said "If I could not compete with an amateur like you I would give up photography."

When we stayed in Tel-Aviv we rented a room, bed and breakfast privately. In the opinion of our landlady, we did not do justice to the enormous traditional Israeli breakfast and she tried to make amends by packing sandwiches for our lunch. Out of politeness, we accepted the sandwiches although we really did not want them. We decided to give them to the beggar who regularly sat on the corner of the nearby street market. We normally gave him some small change but on that morning we decided to give him the sandwiches instead. He accepted the two packages rather doubtfully and asked, "Are they kosher?"

So in summation, 'Chutzpah' may be interpreted loosely as 'cheek' 'arrogance' 'insolence' or 'taking liberties'.

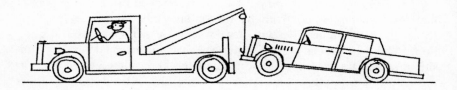

Car Accidents

I am a very careful driver and this is reflected in the fact that in 50 years of motoring I have only been involved in five accidents and in none of them was any person or animal injured or killed. In fact, one of the accidents I was not even in the car at the time.

Several years ago, a heavily pregnant visitor to our home suddenly decided that she would have to enter the maternity hospital rather urgently. The hospital was in another part of London and in the control of a different health authority. They said that they could not fetch her from a district outside their control. Our own local health authority said that they could not in the circumstances despatch her in an ambulance to a hospital outside its control. The problem was decisively resolved when my dear wife Dora volunteered that I should take the woman in my car.

About halfway to the hospital I was stopped at red traffic lights but could not proceed because the starter motor had apparently jammed and stopped the engine. The lights changed to green and the motorists behind became very agitated and annoyed. Fortunately, help came from a kindly policeman who helped me push the car round the corner. This was accomplished with great difficulty because the power assisted steering did not function when it received no power from the engine. By now it had started to rain quite heavily but by another stroke of fortune I found myself near to a public telephone box. I phoned for a taxi and despatched my passenger who I hardly knew on her way before my number of passengers doubled in number.

I next phoned my motoring organisation and asked for breakdown assistance. They said that none of their own vehicles were available but they would get one of their local approved garages to tow me in and get me mobile again. It was not long before a pick up truck arrived, not a low loader but the type with an over hanging crane. The driver was in a bad mood and very gruff. Apparently he was not at all pleased to be sent out on a job in such a downpour. I told him that the car was fitted with an automatic gear box and the makers had advised in their handbook that the car should not be towed more than a short distance. He snarled that he knew what he was doing and hitched the car up so that it was towed on the two rear wheels. He then thrust a form at me covered with small print on both sides and asked me to sign. He said it was my authority for him to tow my car away and without which he could not proceed. As his garage was approved by my nationally well known and long established motoring organisation and under the difficult circumstances I found myself in, I signed it and made my way home.

A few days later, late in the afternoon, I received a call from the garage, informing me that my car would be ready for collection any time after 6pm.

I went along, it was already dark and the garage was closed but my car was standing in the forecourt with the ignition key in the lock. To my horror, I noticed that the front of the car was badly damaged. Luckily, I had a witness with me.

I got an estimate from a local firm who reckoned it would cost £400 to remedy the damage.

When I contacted my motoring organisation they said that they could not compensate me because I had signed a document absolving the garage from any responsibility whilst the car was being towed. They would not listen to any reason. However, they quickly changed their mind when I threatened to report them to the relevant advertising control authorities on the grounds that an intensive advertising campaign that the motoring organisation were running emphasised that in the event of a breakdown their service was free. I told them that as I now had to pay £400 because of their service I don't consider it to be free.

Their solicitor phoned me up to assure me that I would be paid the £400 in full and that the problem was due to a misunderstanding.

Needless to say, I am now registered with another motoring organisation. I never found out what eventually happened to the pregnant woman but it was not only her who nearly had a baby on that rainy day.

As the accident was not my fault, I did not lose my no claims bonus but I did lose it on only one occasion even though the accident was not my fault. I was negotiating the busy Gants Hill, Ilford, roundabout when a black car to the left of me suddenly accelerated and turned sharp right in front of me. It was so sudden that I could not avoid hitting him. The driver was a black man and he started to shout that it was my fault. He reached inside his car and brought out a writing pad and pen and told me to make a full written confession and a promise not only to pay for the damage to his car but also to compensate him for all consequential losses arising out of the accident.

I obviously refused and we began to exchange details. He gave me his name and address in Handsworth near Birmingham. I then noticed what appeared to be snowflakes all around his car. Although it was quite a dark night the roundabout was fairly well lit up and I was able to see that the 'snowflakes' were actually flakes of white plaster painted black on one side. I then looked carefully at his car and could see the rust holes that the plaster had filled up but had fallen out on the impact.

I lost my no-claim bonus, not because the accident was attributed to me but because the driver had given me a false name and address, his car was stolen and was not taxed or insured.

I did not lose my no-claims bonus on the three remaining accidents but being self-employed, I lost the value of the time involved in making insurance claims and arranging for the damage to be repaired.

Early one morning I cleared the mist that had gathered on the outside of all the car windows and set off on my journey. I had not gone far when I halted at a junction with a major road and was waiting for a break in the traffic when another car bumped heavily into my rear. The windows of the other car were heavily misted up and the driver was a woman. She immediately accused me of rolling back into her car. I pointed out that there was no backwards slope to the road and even if there had been one, I could not have rolled back because my car had an automatic gear box.

An elderly lady sitting in the rear passenger seat of the offender's car then interceded and said she had seen it all. She would be a witness that the accident had not been her daughter's fault at all. I was too gentlemanly to point out that her eyesight could not be too good because she was wearing and peering through thick beer bottle bottom type spectacle lenses.

The other two accidents were similar to the first I described in as much as that the vehicles travelling on my left hand side suddenly accelerated and turn sharp right in front of me. In one case it was a small car and we were both travelling fairly fast, the small car which I hit sideways on went rolling over and nearly ended up in front of fast traffic going in the opposite direction. The sole occupant stepped out of his badly damaged car completely unhurt although slightly shocked. He accepted full responsibility for his stupid mistake which was witnessed by a motor cyclist travelling just behind me.

The other accident was when a lorry turned sharp right in front of me without giving any previous signal. The driver said he had turned his indicator on well before making his turn. I pointed out to him and he agreed that his indicator, although working was only winking at about five second intervals. He said that he had actually complained to his manager before setting out on his journey that his indicators were not functioning properly. The accident was witnessed by two builders repairing a front garden wall nearby that had been damaged by a previous accident.

Five accidents in fifty years is not bad, that is an average of one accident every ten years and most of my motoring is in heavily congested city centre areas.

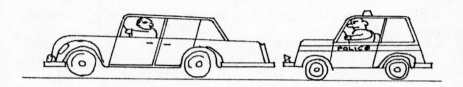

Dangerous Driving

I ant by nature law abiding. I have never committed a legal offence not even by incurring a parking ticket. I am also a very careful driver. I have also always purchased safe cars and carefully kept them in safe driving condition. I am courteous and considerate to other drivers on the road. It was therefore with some surprise that I was asked to stop by a police officer.

It was not long after taking delivery of a new powerful Rover 3500. I considered the powerful 3.5 litre engine as a safety asset in as much as when fast acceleration is required, for instance when overtaking, it can be accomplished, safely and swiftly. I did not want the power for speed for its own sake. The car also had very efficient brakes. In short, a safe car in good condition and a safe driver who made a point of never drinking any alcohol before getting into the car.

The incident took place in good weather on a fairly clear local arterial road.

I became aware in my rear mirror of a small white coloured car travelling very close behind me with it's bonnet just a few feet from the boot of my car. It was potentially dangerous because if I had to brake suddenly he would most likely crash into the rear of my car.

If I accelerated, so did he, if I slowed down, he did similarly, I signalled to him to overtake and though there was plenty of room to do so he kept following me with no safe braking distance between us.

When we were stopped at red traffic lights, I decided to shake him off by using the power of my 3.5 engine to accelerate away from him as soon as the lights changed to green.

I accelerated from nil to 70 miles per hour which was within the legal speed limit in a spectacular fashion leaving him far behind. I then slowed down to a more comfortable speed and to my dismay I saw him again in my rear mirror driving very close behind me.

I knew that there were some drivers who prided themselves that their cars could keep up with much more powerful models on the road. In the past, I dealt with such drivers by giving them the satisfaction of overtaking me. They were happy and I would be pleased to have got rid of potentially dangerous drivers. However, this driver showed no inclination to overtake me. His obvious desire apparently, was to drive close behind me which I understand is called 'tailgating.' I next decided to get rid of him by pulling in and stopping in the next lay-by but kept in mind that if he were to show any criminal intent, I would keep my windows closed and doors locked and would use my superior speed to tear away from him.

When I pulled into the lay-by, so did he and it was only then that I noticed that he was a policeman in uniform and that the car was a police panda car which is not normally used for traffic control. He did not even have a blue flashing light nor did he sound his two tone siren.

He indicated that I should wind my window down and asked me to switch the engine off. He asked me for my driving licence which I fortunately did have with me. He asked if I was the owner of the car and the index number. He also asked if I had been drinking and smelt my breath.

I enquired if there was a problem. He said that he had noticed that I had been driving erratically. Sometimes slowing down and sometimes accelerating and then I shot off at an alarming rate at the traffic lights.

I told him that the erratic speeds were due to the fact that I saw someone in my rear mirror driving dangerously close behind me and that I had sped away from the traffic lights so as to get away from him.

I pointed out that at no time had I exceeded the speed limit on that stretch of road, that I had not broken any law and that I had not driven dangerously.

He said that as he did not have a companion in the car to verify his accusations he would be taking no further action.

On reflection, I suppose that I should have taken his number and the index number of his car and reported him to the police for dangerous driving. Still, it is always easy to be clever after the event. That was the one and only time I have ever been stopped by the police when driving a car. Not a bad record in nearly fifty years of driving.

The Civil Servant

I readily agreed when my good friend, John, asked if I would mind if his daughter put my name forward as a character referee on her application form for a job in the Civil Service as a short-hand typist.

John himself had been a Civil Servant for many years until he had been prematurely pensioned off on health grounds. I was somewhat flattered by his request having regard to the fact that he had many important and influential acquaintances whom he could have asked. I knew the family well. They were honest, sincere and hard working and I had no doubt that his daughter would be a suitable applicant-

I had, in the past, been asked by many people if my name may be put forward as a character referee. In most cases, I heard no more. In a few cases, usually where a commercial employment agency was involved, all I had to do was tick off the appropriate answers on a pro-forma and return it in a pre-addressed and stamped envelope.

Only in a very few cases was I actually required to submit a written testimonial.

After about three months, I was phoned by a lady who said that a Mr. So and So, OBE, of the Ministry of Defence would like to interview me about John's daughter's application. I was not keen to spend half a day travelling up to Whitehall or where-ever else the MOD's offices were just to answer some Civil Servant's stupid questions. I started to explain that as I had strained a ligament in my leg, I could not travel and would a written testimonial do instead. The lady said that that would not be necessary as Mr. So and So, OBE, would prefer to interview me in my own home. This suited me fine and I made an appointment.

Mr. So and So, OBE, arrived bang on time. I glanced out of the window whilst Dora was letting him in to see what sort of car he had arrived in but there was no car in front of the house. He said that he had come by train and had walked from the local station.

It was hard not to laugh as he looked just like the stereotyped bumptious Civil Servant that appears in farces and comedy shows. Black bowler hat, neatly trimmed moustache, black jacket, striped trousers, black shoes and socks and a small pink carnation in his button hole. He was carrying a black leather briefcase with gold embossed letters thereon. He spoke in a clipped precise manner and with an accent I could not place.

He said he was Mr. So and So of the MOD and that he was there to interview me with regard to John's daughter's application for a job in the department that was involved with the development of the Blue Streak rocket project. This puzzled us as we had read in the papers that the government had decided quite some while previously to abandon the project.

He then asked me to identify myself and to prove who I actually was by production of a passport etc. He then asked me to identify Dora and if I wished her to be present during the interview. There was no apology or reason given for this approach and I became annoyed at his attitude. I told him that in light of the security of the circumstances would he, in turn, provide evidence of his identity. To my fiendish delight, he searched his pockets and brief case and could not produce a single suitable document.

I suggested I could phone his office and verify who he was but he said his secretary who could normally do so was on leave that day and no-one else would be prepared to respond to questions on the phone.

I was now, not only a bit triumphant over this pompous ridiculous looking character but also a little suspicious. If the project was so secretive so as to warrant a Civil Servant to make a house visit and interview could this person be an agent working for the Russian secret service trying to find out character defects so as to use them as possible blackmail in order to obtain secrets?

I was also suspicious that the whole affair might be an elaborate practical joke and I was being set up for a big laugh.

The way Mr. So and So was dressed and acted reinforced my twin suspicions. I carefully eyed his brief case to try to ascertain if it contained a concealed tape recorder and/or camera.

Although Dora later claimed that she too was suspicious she chatted away merrily and I was afraid that she may say something that could be mis-construed. I continued with the interview because I did not want to prejudice John's daughter's chance of getting the job.

I tried to answer his questions politely but with the minimum of information.

Many of his questions were more concerning myself personally and/or

223

any possible romantic attachment to John's daughter. It was difficult to restrain my annoyance at his line of questioning but I realised that it was possibly necessary. He even asked questions about my personal finances and my relationship with Dora.

I was glad when the interview finished. As we lived some distance from the local station I offered to give him a lift which he declined to accept but not before ascertaining that the car was fully paid for.

Strangely, I noticed that he did not walk in the direction of the station.

I knew someone who had dealings with the Special Branch of Scotland Yard and from him I obtained the name and phone number of a Detective Sergeant who I phoned. I told him about this suspicious character and he promised to investigate and phone me back. I never heard from him.

When I next met John, I told him about this strange experience. He was puzzled as his daughter had been given the job almost as soon as she applied several months previously, neither of the two other referees she had given were approached.

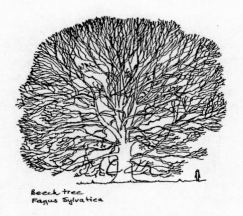

Beech tree
Fagus Sylvatica

A Day's Outing

The word 'outing' these days appears to have assumed a completely different connotation to that when I was a child. In those days, it meant an excursion away from home, usually to the countryside or seaside.

One day, the head teacher of the primary school I attended announced that there would be an outing on a certain Sunday. Children would be conveyed by coach and given a bag containing fresh fruit but they would have to bring their own packed lunch and also pay the nominal sum of sixpence ($2^{1/2}$ pence in today's currency).

The nominal payment was in order to meet certain legal insurance requirements even though the bulk of the cost was being met by a charitable fund that wished to see the poor slum dwelling children in the east end of London to get away from the grimy, disease ridden, polluted streets of their environment even if it be for only one day and to let them breath some fresh air.

I asked my mother if I could go but she said it would be a waste of sixpence as I could go and play in the local park for nothing. She said that if I went the other children would want to go and if they were not to be included they would be upset.

I was bitterly upset but my class was very excited and were discussing what they would do and what games they would play. I joined in the discussions even though I knew I would not be with them. I did not want them to feel sorry for me.

On the morning following the outing, the teacher dropped a bombshell. She asked the class to write an essay (it was called a 'composition' in those days) on the outing the previous day.

I was in a dilemma. I could not just write that I did not go on the outing. I did not wish to bring attention to the fact that I was the only child in the class whose parent did not allow him to go. I decided instead to use my imagination.

·I got high marks for my effort and the teacher called me to the front of the class and asked me to read out aloud what I had written. I took this to be most complimentary.

As I was reading my composition, the class began to snigger. The more I read, the more they laughed. The teacher smirked. I did not know whether or not to be pleased. I could not understand the cause of the laughter and was afraid to ask. All this came back to me recently when I was returning in a chauffeur driven limousine from the funeral of a very close friend. The car was gliding along a road through Epping Forest. All the trees were a glorious red autumn colour. I spotted a road sign pointing down a narrow country lane to 'Burnham Beeches' a local forest picnic and beauty spot.

Then I remembered quite clearly as though I had only written it yesterday my composition headed 'My outing to Burnem Beaches' in which I described my exciting day at the seaside, swimming and building sand castles.

The Wrist-Watch

During the last war, new wrist-watches were almost impossible to buy. Virtually all the watches made in the U.K and those imported were consigned for use by the armed services. However, soon after the war ended, the War Office sold a mass of surplus equipment through the commercial market.

I was therefore, glad to be able to buy a new, fairly good quality, wrist-watch even though it was encased in an inelegant stainless steel case with a large three pointed arrow and stock number impressed into the back plate. Subsequently, it gave me many years of reliable service and I still use it today nearly fifty years after! Like all watches in regular use, it eventually required cleaning.

At that time I was working in the City of London and in the window of a well known jeweller I noticed an impressive looking piece of apparatus with a notice nearby claiming that all watch repairs and cleaning on the premises were timed electronically.

Although their charge for cleaning the watch was almost double that elsewhere and they took about twice as long to do it, I reckoned that it would be worthwhile.

I duly left my watch with one of the assistants who was very smartly dressed in black jacket and grey striped trousers and who called me 'Sir' although I was nowhere nearly as smartly dressed as he was. It should have been me calling him 'Sir.' Still, that is the way of the world. It made me feel important.

When the time came to collect the cleaned and electronically timed watch I was most politely informed by the very smartly dressed assistant that there had been an unforeseen difficulty and that I should call again in about two weeks time. When I did, it was the same performance.

On the third occasion the suave gentleman kindly informed me that there would be yet another delay. At this, I lost my respect for him and my temper. In a raised voice so that all the other customers could hear I accused them of having lost or purloined my watch and that if they did not return it when I next called in a weeks time I would stand outside their shop with a placard warning other customers of their shoddy behaviour and that I would collect the names of any other disgruntled customers for a joint legal action. This threat seemed to have done the trick. Within a few days I received a most apologetic phone call from the shop's manager informing me that the watch was cleaned and ready for collection.

At last, I was able to use my reliable watch once again. It kept excellent time and it was many years before it required cleaning again. It never did require repairing.

A very embarrassed assistant explained that all the repairs and cleaning of watches taken into the shop were actually done by an old but very skilled watch-maker in the nearby Whitechapel district. He had given them excellent service for many years but quite unexpectedly had suffered a severe heart attack. My watch, with several others was in his back street workshop at the time and it was some while before they could retrieve it.

I asked about the electronic timing. He was rather vague and pointed out that they still had the apparatus in the window.

The Convalescent Home

Now that I'm in the autumn of my life and fast approaching it's winter season, I have difficulty in not increasing my already surplus weight. This contrasts strangely with my childhood when I was so emaciated that I had to be sent away for a whole year to recuperate in a convalescent home.

My emaciation was not caused by lack of nourishment. Even though I had been brought up in grinding poverty and deprivation there was always an abundance of food because provisions were so very cheap to buy and were plentiful. Evidence of this could be seen in my siblings and friends.

My emaciation was caused by a combination of conditions. Up till the age of seven years, I had undergone five major operations the chance of survival of any one was very small. But I survived. Recuperation from these operations was hindered by my childhood environment. My parents were illiterate immigrants in the notorious slums of Stepney in east London. Our home was a two bedroom 'apartment' with a living/kitchen/dining room and a WC two floors up shared with two other large families. There was no bathroom nor hot water and no garden. Playspace was either the dung strewn cobbled road or the reeking rear concreted yard onto which opened two WC's for the tailoring sweat shops that abutted thereon. The yard was also used to house five stinking, overflowing dustbins around which there was always a host of buzzing blue bottle flies The yard was also the toilet for any of the unfortunate miserable cats in the apartments.

Our home was inhabited by nine persons, my parents, my mother's parents and five children. Being the eldest son, I was given the privilege of sleeping at the foot of my grandparents double bed. If they had a restless night for whatever reason, so did I.

The Convalescent Home

Apart from the nine human inhabitants we had a host of bed bugs which emerged after dark to feed on and torture the humans and to ensure that they enjoyed a restless night. It was not just our home that was infected with bed bugs. I don't suppose that there was a single home in the east end of London that did not have its ample share of these foul smelling blood sucking insects. There was no way of getting rid of them or avoiding their nasty, itchy, swelling bites. Nothing could stop the bugs reaching their human targets. Bed legs were rested in tin cans filled with paraffin to stop them climbing up from the floor. Bed springs and frames were also daubed daily with paraffin. With fiendish cleverness, the bugs would crawl upside down along the ceiling and then drop down onto their sleeping victims.

These days in east London, we do get some days or nights when there is a mist which sometimes are mistakenly called, even by weather experts, fogs. In the 1930's, London fogs were real pea-soupers, smoke particles suspended in the misty air to such an extent that at times it was impossible to even see your own hand held six inches in front of your face. These smoke particles would lodge in peoples lungs causing terrible bronchial problems. In those days, you did not have to be a tobacco smoker to be liable to get lung cancer.

My school's doctor strongly recommended that I be sent to a convalescent home. Out of the hundreds of deprived and poverty stricken children attending my local primary school, I was selected as the most urgent needing recuperation. As my parents were practising Jews, they would not consider me going to a convalescent homer unless it was a Jewish one. My mother took me along to the offices of the Jewish Board of Guardians which were situated in Middlesex Street, east London. The street is more popularly known for its Sunday morning street market, as 'The Lane.'

The Board's own doctor examined me once again and agreed that I was an urgent case for a convalescent home in Broadstairs which is a seaside resort on the east coast of Kent, situated between the more popularly known resorts of Margate and Ramsgate. I can't remember how I arrived there or who I travelled with, but suddenly, I found myself among about a hundred other children of about the same age and among strange adults in strange surroundings.

This was not too great a shock for me as during my short life up till then, I had spent a great proportion of my existence in various strange hospitals. I was not really homesick as many of the other children were, as I found my own home and family a bit strange. I was not close to my siblings and parents. I was naturally stoic even at that tender age. At least, in the convalescent home, I could understand and be understood in English, whereas at home, my Yiddish speaking parents and siblings could not

230

understand my English which I had acquired in my long sojourns in hospitals. My siblings mocked and derided me as a foreign speaking intruder who from time-to-time came to stay with them.

Because the children in the home were mainly long stay residents it was run on the lines of an orphanage. Food was adequate but not tasty and second helpings were rarely afforded. The regime was strict. The staff displayed no affection to the children. The matron who was in charge of the home was a tyrant, smacking children on the face for the slightest offence. She was old, small and offensive.

Occasionally, we were given treats. Once a local farmer donated his bruised, surplus apples which the sister threw onto the playing field and for which we had to scramble and compete to pick up.

The home kept its own chickens. If any of the hens strayed and laid an egg where it should not have, the child finding the egg would be rewarded by having it hard boiled for breakfast the next day. I don't know who had the other eggs the chickens produced. One day, I discovered in a cupboard under the stairs, a galvanised iron dust bin in which eggs were being pickled. I took one out and claimed that I had found it under a bush. The next day I was served with a hard boiled egg but when I opened it, I found it was bad inside.

Sometimes, we were taken for a walk along the seafront or to play on the sandy beach. If on the way we passed a nun (there was a nearby convent) we were told by the older children to keep our mouths shut or the nun would count our teeth. I wonder what the nuns thought when they passed a file of Jewish children with their mouths tightly clenched shut.

There were also regular nit inspections when a visiting nurse would pass an iron comb dipped in disinfectant through our tangled hair to see if any of us had any nits or lice.

Strangely enough, even though we were all there on poor health grounds we were not given any medical inspections. It was also strange, that even though all the children were there for long periods, no attempt at all was made to educate us, not even reading to us from story books. Of course there was no TV in those days and we had no access to radio. When we left the home, we were all that much retarded educationally compared with our contemporaries.

We were not allowed to have our own spending money but we were permitted to visit the tuck shop once a week and to spend a limited amount out of the spending money provided by our parents but held in trust on our behalf by the Sister in charge.

On several occasions when I went to the tuck shop I was told that my spending money had run out and therefore I could not buy any sweets.

Parental visits were only permitted once a month but for some reason

231

or another, my mother came only once to see me in the 12 months I was resident there. When I saw her, I knew who she was and I think she recognised me, but because of the language barrier we could not communicate. It was a true case of 'my mother does not understand me' syndrome. Even when her English improved, I don't think she ever understood me. One day, it was noticed that I had a high fever and was covered in red spots. I had caught scarlet fever and was immediately whisked away to an isolation hospital. I still don't understand, how it was, that out of more than a hundred children, I was the only one to catch the disease.

The regime in the children's ward of the isolation hospital was even more severe than in the home and many were to times when I wished to return to the home. After about two weeks, I recovered from the fever and was discharged but not back to the home but into the charge of a local woman who was to care for me. Here, it was heavenly. The woman displayed affection and she had a dog with which I could play. But this heaven was not for eternity. I was returned home to my hostile siblings, to the ever present bed bugs and to my bewildered parents who could not believe that this weird, foreign speaking creature was their own son. In time, they slowly came to accept the possibility and perhaps wondered if I had along the way become a changeling. I must confess, that often, I did.

Auntie Leah

As a child, I was somewhat deprived in as much as that I only had one aunt, that is Auntie Leah, my mother's elder sister. There had been another sister but she died before I was born, her name was Rachael. She was survived by a very young son, Victor, who was duly brought up by Aunt Leah who had no children of her own. So, I not only had one aunt, I also only had one cousin. Although I never heard it spoken of, I believe Aunt Rachael died of cancer which at the time was an unspeakable word.

Victor's father also died when he was very young whilst he was on army service during the first world war. I have a photo' of him in uniform, he was a tall, fine looking man.

My father had no relatives in this country. Those that he did have were all murdered by the Nazis in their home country, Belarus. Not a single one of them survived, not even a child.

Auntie Leah was married to Burman. That was his surname and everybody including Leah called him Burman even to his face but sometimes, he was called 'Leah's fancy man.' In a way, he was good looking and dressed very smartly. He even owned his own morning suit which he needed for his work as a waiter.

He did not wear it often as he rarely worked because of his flat feet. He could not stand for long or walk very much because of his flat feet and therefore could not work often, if ever, as a waiter.

My parents said he was a loafer and was living of the income Auntie Leah earned in her shop. She had a shop which principally sold 'fancy goods' or in reality, goods that most people did not fancy, or did not have the means to purchase such as ornamental novelties. Her shop was not exactly an emporium but was the tiny front room of her tiny house in

Redmans Road in Stepney Green, in the east end of London. Actually, the district was known as Stepney Green and just round the corner where she lived was a public park known as Stepney Green.

I used to like visiting her as sometimes she gave me a tin whistle that had gone a bit rusty in her show window and could not be sold or some other unsaleable item out of her stock. After all, it was not the value of the item but the thought that counted. Moreover, I liked going there because cousin Victor owned a cat's whiskers wireless set with an enormous horn. I was intrigued by the noises that seemed to come out of it as if by magic.

Auntie Leah had a badly ulcerated varicose vein leg which she would treat with exhausted tea leaves. It never cured her condition but at that time, there was no cure for it.

She had emigrated to this country from Poland as a very young child but never learned to read English. She took advantage of my visits to ask me to read out aloud to her any correspondence she had received. I learned later, that she did the same with my siblings so as to cross check that we had read it correctly.

She died sometime during the war. I do not know when or cause of death. Her death may have been caused by her ulcerated varicose veins. We were not informed because Burman did not inform us. He was annoyed with us. When we were bombed out of our house, I cycled past his flat to let him know that we were unharmed and where he could contact us. As he was not at home, I left a note. Apparently, he took objection to being notified in such a manner. He thought that we should have informed him of our change of address in a formal manner through the post. He never spoke to us again. So my one and only uncle became incommunicable! And my one and only aunt was dead.

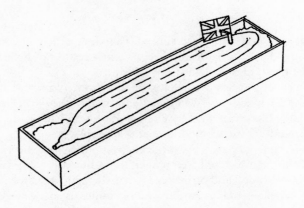

The Cucumber

The house directly across the road from us which had previously been occupied by an elderly lady and her equally elderly lodger had been converted by its new owner into two comfortable, self contained flats. The conversion was tastefully done and well equipped.

They were immediately sold on a 99 year lease. The ground floor flat was brought by George, a 30 year old bachelor and the first floor flat by Elizabeth, also about 30 years old, a recent divorcee who worked for a firm of accountants. They were both very well paid, especially George who had some particular expertise that was in high demand in the print trade and worked night shifts.

It was not long before we got to know them both quite well when they enthusiastically joined the local ward of our own political party.

They proudly showed us their flats. Elizabeth confided that she had a new boyfriend and hoped to marry him soon and set up home in her flat.

George told us, that even though he loved his doting parents, he was an only child, found he had to get away from them as they stifled any attempts of his own of a love life. They still saw each other regularly.

George became very popular in the local party political ward and was soon appointed social secretary, an office which he carried out most successfully and energetically. Although he had not had any previous gardening knowledge, he transformed his garden into a picture. He spent a lot of money on its landscaping and on buying plants and tools etc.

We were surprised, when after only a few months, he started to redecorate his flat and we were shocked to see the transformation. The developer had chosen bright and cheerful decoration but George had replaced it with most morbid colours. He had the ceilings painted black and the walls

235

re-papered with deep, purple coloured wallpaper. All the exposed paint-work he painted a dark battleship grey. We just could not believe it but he took it as being an enormous improvement.

He was an enthusiastic collector of old 8mm films and had a large library of them which he sat watching by himself in the dark. He also accumulated a large library of videos. Whereas Elizabeth had a constant stream of visitors, nobody ever seemed to visit George.

After a couple of years we noticed a sudden and sharp decline in George's health. He suffered frequent colds and flu, his rotund boyish face became pallid and dull and he lacked his usual vitality. He took a lot of time off from work, neglected his garden and his duties as social secretary in the local party.

We were sorry when he told us that he had been diagnosed as having a certain form of Leukaemia and had to have regular chemo-therapy treatment.

It was about this time that both his parents died within a short space of time apart.

I can't remember the sequence of events but it was also about this time that Elizabeth started to receive 'heavy breathing' phone calls that soon became sexually insulting and physically threatening. The caller seemed to have a good knowledge of her movements.

She also started to receive filthy and threatening letters through the post which became progressively worse. She finally decided to refer the matter to the police when she received a long package in the post. It contained a long green cucumber with a union jack stuck into the end of it. One day, when I returned from a business visit, Dora told me that the police had called and questioned her about my activities. They asked if I was secretive and locked myself away for long periods. They also asked to look at my stationary stock especially my index cards. They explained that some of the filthy messages had been written on such cards but they did not match those that I used.

They told Dora that Elizabeth had suspected that I was responsible for the filthy phone calls and dirty letters. She based this on the fact that as I was self employed, I was at home most days and could easily observe her movements and those of her visitors. She had apparently overlooked the fact that because George was on night shifts, he was at home most days.

When she finally accepted the fact that it was not me responsible, she showed us one of the least embarrassing of the letters she had received. It was certainly not my handwriting and compared with a note we had received some while before, it matched George's completely. George died of Leukaemia, a short while after and the offending phone calls and letters ceased.

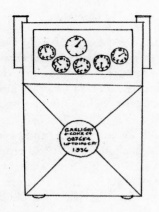

The Gas Meter

As an architect, I had dealings from time-to-time with the local gas board. Sometimes it was to discuss the installation of new service pipes, that is mains entering a site, sometimes about gas piping within a building and sometimes about the provision of appliances.

The local gas board is housed in a huge modern office block.

Usually my dealings commenced with a letter to them outlining the subject matter. Very often this produced no response except possibly a formal acknowledgement of receipt. When I encounter such a situation with any organisation, I pursue the matter by telephoning. On one project where a response was urgent. I duly 'phoned the local gas board and was asked by the operator for my full name, telephone number and address followed by a request for a description of my enquiry. This was annoying as it was time consuming and she obviously could not understand what I was talking about. Eventually she put me through to someone who asked exactly the same questions. He said that I had been put through to the wrong extension and put me back to the switchboard. It was not the same operator but once again she asked me the same questions before putting me through to another office. The person there also asked me the same questions. When I told him that I had already given the required information three times, he said, "I can't help you unless you tell it to me." When I had given the same information for the fourth time, he said that I had been put through to the right office but the official who dealt with that particular matter was on leave and would I 'phone back on Monday . I ascertained the name of the official I was to contact and his 'phone extension number.

On the Monday, I 'phoned the gas board and I asked for the extension number and the person I wished to speak to. The operator asked for my name which I gave her and then she started to ask the other questions. I told her that my 'phone number, address and the details of my enquiry were private and would she please put me through to the extension number I asked for. She said she could not do so unless I first provided her with the requested information. I told her to stop being officious and to put me through to the required extension. She said that as I refused to give her the information she required she could not connect me and promptly cut me off.

I immediately 'phoned back and asked to be put through to the telephone supervisor. I was asked for my name, 'phone number, address and the nature of my enquiry. I told her that I wanted to make a complaint about one of the operators. She said that if I could not give her the details requested she could not connect me and promptly cut me off. By now I was most annoyed. As an architect, I deal with many different organisations but have never experienced such obstructive behaviour. I decided to call personally at the gas boards offices and to demand to see the manager in charge of the telephone operators.

As soon as I entered the imposing office block a uniformed cominissionaire directed me to an enquiry desk where I was asked to complete a questionnaire which included, my name, 'phone number, address and the reason for my enquiry. When I had done so, the desk clerk asked who I wished to see and what time was my appointment. When I told him that I did not have an appointment, he said I would have to make one by 'phone or post and return. He then gave me a card. I asked what it was for. He said it was an exit card and without it I would not be allowed out of the building.

When I went out I made my way to the giant car park only to find the gate locked. I found the car park attendant's office and asked for the gate to be unlocked as I wished to leave. The uniformed official told me that he was only a relief attendant and that I would have to wait until the official car park attendant returned from lunch because he had the key with him.

By eating humble pie, I eventually got in touch with the official I wished to negotiate with.

A short while after, I received a notice from the gas board informing me that in accordance with an act of Parliament they are obliged to replace any domestic gas meter that was more than a certain number of years old and that the meter serving my home comes within that category. An appointment was made for a certain day but they could not give me a time. The day came and went but the gas board did not come. A few days later, a card was put through my letter box informing me that they would be coming to change the meter the following day.

This time, they did come and put a new meter in and left the old one in the porch. They told me it was not their job to take the meter away but someone would come the following morning to collect it.

I asked about a meter reading before it was taken away. They said it was not their job to read meters but it would be read as soon as it was taken back to the depot and that I would be charged accordingly.

As I am a cautious person by nature and by now not being too friendly disposed towards the gas board, I took my own meter reading just in case something went wrong. I also took note of the meter number.

In due course, I received the quarterly bill and when I checked it, the reading for the old meter was very much higher than it should have been.

I adjusted the account according to my reading and enclosed a cheque for the reduced amount. I next received an account for the extra claimed by the gas board and a warning that it should be paid within seven days.

I wrote them a letter telling them that their reading was wrong and that no sum was due to them. They then told me that when the meter was returned it was read by a very experience meter reader and his reading was verified as correct by his supervisor. In the circumstances they cannot except my reading as correct. I got several written warnings about the disputed amount and also some unpleasant 'phone calls. Eventually I got notice that if the outstanding sum was not paid forthwith, they would cut off my gas supply and they would only reconnect if and when I paid the outstanding account plus the costs of both disconnecting and reconnecting the supply.

I decide to take the bull by the horns as they say and I wrote on my professional headed paper direct to the gas board's chairman at head office in London and marked it private and for his personal attention. In my letter I described the sequence of events, commencing with my problem in trying to 'phone the local offices of the gas board and told him that if he doubted my experience he should personally 'phone and ask for the official I had tried to contact. I also assured him that my meter reading was correct and that I could indisputably prove it. I also offered to donate £1000 to a charity of his choice if I did not do so.

Apparently, he must have checked out the problem of the 'phone operators and also, he must have been impressed by my confidence regarding the meter reading because within a couple of days I was swamped with 'phone calls and personal visits from all sorts of managerial officials from the local gas board headquarters. They told me that the Chairman had sent a note to them marked 'Report back to me personally.'

One of the local managers implored me to accept the fact that their meter reading was correct and to settle the account or they would most reluctantly have to cut off my gas supply.

He said that their meter reading had been checked and re-checked and found to be correct. I asked him where the meter had been read and he said in the depot where all returned meters were kept. I suggested that they may have read the wrong meter. He said that it would be virtually impossible because of their strict registration and meticulous records combined with specialised expertise.

I warned him that if they cut of my gas supply I would sue them for damages and compensation.

He asked why I was so confident. I told him because when they had not collected the old meter within seven days, I put it in my cellar for safety and there it still is complete with its embossed registration number and correct reading. He asked if he could take the meter back with him for checking. I told him only after I had received an unambiguous apology from the Chairman himself. This was forthcoming in next to no time.

Balls

I dislike shopping very much, whether I go on my own or accompany my wife, Dora. On the other hand, Dora loves shopping, and whenever I can, I get her to buy the odds and ends that I require. Of course, certain items I do buy myself, like cars, TVs and video recorders and expensive cameras, but if I can, I leave things like clothes etc. for Dora to buy for me. However, I do accompany Dora when she intends to buy heavy and/or bulky items, but even then, I patiently wait outside the shop until she has completed the purchases. On one such shopping expeditiuon I waited outside the local supermarket until she emerged. I relieved her of a good part of her burden, and we commenced crossing the busy main road to a side street where I had parked our car.

Fortunately, there is a pedestrian crossing just outside the store but as the road is very wide at that point, the crossing is in two parts with a island refuge in the centre of the road. The refuge also contains a tall lamp post from which are suspended large orange globes to indicat that it is part of a pedestrian crossing.

We had safely negotiated the first part of the crossing and reached the refuge but before the queue of cars that had stopped to let us cross could re-start, a motorist came along on the off side of the cars and drove at full speed onto the island refuge which was only protected by a flimsy illuminated bollard.

The bollard was crushed aside and the car hit the lamp post at full speed. No attempt had been made to slow down or to brake.

By a miracle, neither of us was hurt but we were shocked and annoyed, especially so, as we were bombarded by a shower of large orange balls which were bouncing all around us. We stood petrified and weighed down by large shopping bags filled with porridge, bottles of oil, bottles of bleach,

241

bags of flour and toilet rolls.

Just by chance a very high ranking police officer was passing by and seeing that there had been an accident stopped to take details during which he asked Dora if I was her husband. She said, "yes, but only through marriage."

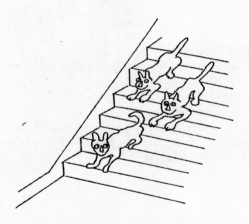

Cat Burglar

We were pleasantly surprised when one day two complimentary tickets to the Ideal Home exhibition in Wembley were slipped through our front door letter box. There were no indications who they were from and we assumed they were part of a promotion scheme. Anyhow, we weren't going to look a gift horse in the mouth as the saying goes.

We went to the exhibition straight from work and as we were recently married and set up home, we saw a lot that interested us. We were surprised to see a near neighbour also at the exhibition.

By the time we returned home it was quite late and were shocked to find the front door open. The rear door was also open. We had been burgled. The intruders had entered by forcing a window at the rear.

We were next alarmed by a loud thudding noise from the bedrooms on the first floor. I grabbed a poker and started to make my way upstairs when I was nearly bowled over by our cat, Minnie rushing down the stairs hotly pursued by about seven eager tom cats. It's amazing just how much noise a pride of cats can make when they are intent on the reproductive process.

Minnie had not been spayed as we obtained her as an adult cat from a baker who was about to dispose of her because of her propensity to reproduce the species rather than to catch the mice and rats that infested his baker shop. It did not take the police long to arrive as they were already in the street summoned by other neighbours who had also been burgled the same evening.

They told us that at least eight other adjacent houses had been burgled. They comforted us by telling us that as well as having cash and jewellery stolen all the other houses had been wantonly vandalised. They told us that we were lucky as we had not only not had anything stolen by also our house had not been vandalised.

We assumed that when the intruders entered our house and left the doors open as a quick means of escape in case of need, Minnie and her entourage had entered and the noise they made caused the burglars to panic and flee.

The police told us that all the householders who had been robbed had received complimentary tickets to the Ideal Home exhibition. The tickets themselves had previously been stolen.

Nice

Many years ago, Dora and I shared a very enjoyable holiday with our friends Don and John in Nice in the south of France. It was not that we were rich, but the pound sterling in those days went a lot further than it does nowadays. In order to economise, we travelled third class all the way. We went by steam train to Dover and then across the channel in a small, crowded ferry with no facilities that tossed and pitched so badly that virtually every passenger was violently seasick. It was in the days before the modern giant car ferries and Hovercraft. The only facility provided was a rail to lean over in order to vomit direct into the sea. The ferry was so crowded that often the vomit was blown back onto other passengers.

The journey across France, Calais - Marseilles - Nice was in a crowded carriage with wood slatted seats designed to torture passengers and to make them thankful for the journey's end. It was a pleasure at times to get up and offer your seat to an unfortunate passenger who did not have a reserved seat on the long journey.

As the train progressed south, it became noticeably warmer but it was not much use to open the carriage windows as this allowed the dirty smoke from the steam engine to blow into the carriage and add a sooty film to perspiring faces.

These conditions were part of the norm and part of the holiday adventure.

We had, on recommendation, pre-booked into a minus five star hotel which was not far from the plus five star Negresco hotel where the rich and famous stayed. So on our return, we could truthfully boast that we stayed quite close to the Negresco.

The small hotel was owned and managed by a friendly Frenchman who could speak fairly good English. His staff all appeared to be members of his family. Even though we arrived very late in the evening, he gladly cooked and served us with an excellent meal at a very reasonable price.

As we turned in for the night, he strangely said "Goodbye." We took it that he meant, "Goodnight", but in the morning we realised that it was "Goodbye" because he had sold the hotel and the new management and staff took over in the morning. It was obvious that they did not have the slightest idea of how to manage and run a hotel. They were very willing to learn and asked us what to do. At times, it was quite hilarious, especially so, as they knew no English at all and we relied on John's scant knowledge of French.

One day, whilst wandering through the back streets of Nice we came across a small clothing shop with the proprietor's name 'Pizan' on the fascia board. This intrigued us as it was Dora's maiden surname. We went in and spoke to the proprietor using John as our translator. The proprietor was intrigued as the name, Pizan, was very rare. He invited all four of us to come to his flat at 8.pm on the coming Friday evening to discuss the matter in detail and to exchange family details.

John insisted that even though no mention had been made of a meal, it was customary in France, especially on a Friday at 8.pm to give their guests a sumptuous meal. He said it would be inconsiderate of us to eat before going there and not doing full justice to French hospitality and cuisine.

So with rather empty stomachs and great expectations we presented ourselves promptly at 8.pm on Friday evening. It appeared that we were too punctual and the maid who admitted us, asked us to wait a short while in the ante chamber: There was a hive of activity, the maid kept dashing backward and forward carrying trays of food and crockery. Wonderful smells assailed our sensitive nostrils. At last, our host welcomed us into his reception room and introduced us to his peroxide haired wife and pretty little daughter.

It soon became clear from the discreet burps and suppressed belches that they had just finished a heavy meal. We were invited to partake aperitifs.

It was not long before the rumbling of our empty stomachs joined the cacophony of sound emanating from their stomachs. Having exchanged family details, it did not appear that they were related to Dora despite the unusual surname.

John who had a rapacious appetite started to agitate about returning to our hotel on the excuse that we were all very tired. Our host would not agree and kept giving us small, sweet liqueurs which on an empty stomachs soon went to our heads.

When we finally managed to get away about 11. pm our host and his family insisted on escorting us back to our hotel, no doubt, more to walk their meal down than to ensure our safety.

Our hotel was in darkness, the manager, no doubt, was already in bed, so there was no hope of getting a meal there. We waited a short while and sneaked out in search of a late night restaurant which we soon found.

As it was a very warm evening, we seated ourselves around one of the tables on the pavement outside a restaurant which was still very lively.

We agreed that due to the late hour, it would be best if we had a light meal which Don insisted on ordering. He said that during the war he had served in many foreign countries and could make himself understood in sign language. The non-English speaking waiter could not make out what Don was trying to convey and with a despairing shrug of his shoulders and an upward glance for help to the dark sky he went inside the restaurant. I jokingly said that he will most likely end up serving us a chinaman. To my utter surprise the waiter returned with the manager who was a chinaman. We had noticed, the restaurant was an Indo-Chinese one. Fortunately he understood a little English and we got the sort of meal that we wanted. In a quiet undertone, the manager warned us not to get involved with a soldier sitting at a nearby table. He told us that he was in the Foreign Legion and had drunk too much and was likely to be violent. We gladly accepted his advice. The next day, whilst taking a coffee in a pavement cafe, an Arab peddler approached us and offered to sell a rug. Don said, "Leave this to me, I know how to deal with such Arabs, after all, I served in Egypt and Iraq during the war." He asked the Arab how much he wanted for the rug and offered him about 25% of the asking price. Neither of them understood what the other was saying but wrote the figures down on a piece of paper. After a long while the Arab said, "OK." agreeing to a figure of about 30% of the asking price. Don then indicated that he was not really interested in buying the rug and said "Imshee", which in Arabic means bugger off or words to the effect. In a flash, the Arab whipped out a vicious looking knife and held its point to Don's neck. Don quickly got the message and paid up. He was also charged custom duty on it on his return to England.

The person who recommended us to our hotel also recommended us to a small restaurant. It was approached through an uninviting courtyard and consequently was only frequented by locals. The food was excellent and very reasonable. As it appeared that we were the only tourists to visit the restaurant, we attracted attention. Whatever we ordered to eat or drink was commented on openly by the other diners. When we placed vegetables on the same plate as the main item it created great mirth. It was as though we had poured hot custard onto our meat. They laughed when we shared a single carafe of local wine between us and were very amused at John's primitive French.

The owner not only cooked the food but also served it. Whenever he dived back into his kitchen we cold hear him conducting a lively conversation in French. From the tone, it seemed as though one moment he was scolding, the next praising and a times even affectionate but we could not hear any response. Eventually, we realised why, he was speaking to his sole companion, an Alsatian (German Shepherd) dog.

When we were relaxing one day at an open air cafe, we noticed that the second cup of coffee we ordered was considerably more costly than the first. We brought this to the notice of the waiter who explained that the second cup was ordered when the orchestra inside the cafe which could be heard outside was playing. For that service, there was a surcharge.

The next day, being that much wiser, we delayed ordering our second cup until the orchestra took a short break. The bill was still higher and when we queried it the waiter explained that because we had delayed ordering, the clock had passed 3.pm and after that time, there is a surcharge.

John and I were nearly lost at sea. We were both good swimmers and because the sea was so calm and warm we ventured out much further than the other bathers. We kept looking back using the tower of the Negresco hotel as our landmark. When we next looked back we could not see the Negresco at all. All around us was only sea and sky. Using our instinct and by luck we soon again saw land but no Negresco. We found ourselves about a mile along the coast.

Dora and I were amused when we noticed a widely advertised brand of soft drink by the name of 'Schitt'. We amused ourselves by ordering "Two Schitts please." The waiters used to puzzle why we giggled when we did so. Luckily we were always served with the soft drink. I resolved to photograph one of the adverts to bring back as a souvenir. The adverts were on the front of most buses. In those days I used a complicated camera that was difficult to set and focus so having got everything ready I asked Dora to let me know when the next bus carrying the advert was approaching. She duly called out "A Schitt is now approaching." She was reproached by a passing very smartly dressed Englishman who said "There is no need to be so vulgar."

John was a customs officer and as such had a special passport that enabled him to clear customs controls without any hassle. When we were packing for our return journey he warned me that despite our friendship he would not help me if I got into trouble at customs. I told him that I would not dream of smuggling anything home and if he wished, he could inspect my luggage. After we had passed comfortably through English customs, I asked him to let me have the expensive camera I had bought in France and had accidentally left in one of his cases.

Lesbos

Lesbians derive their description from the reputed behaviour of women in ancient times on the Greek island of Lesbos. When we moved into our present terraced house, the two adjacent properties were owned by a pleasant, jovial builder who had converted them into four apartments each, which he let off furnished. The conversions were not thorough as the four flats had to share 2 bathrooms and two WC's between them. Instead of producing friction, this arrangement actually caused a feeling of friendship and neighbourliness between the tenants. This was enhanced by the fact that none of them considered their sojourn as a long stay or permanent. The rents were cheap which assisted them to save for a deposit to buy a house or flat. Many were young couples, recently married and/or recently moved into the district. Apart from sharing the sanitary facilities they also shared the gardens. It was when I was in my own garden that I was able to chat with them and to get acquainted. Quite often, they would ask to borrow gardening implements and I would give them surplus seedlings etc., as well as free advice.

As neighbours, we got on exceedingly well and amicably. When the landlord died, his widow took over the management of the properties and carried on in the same manner. However, in the course of time, we noticed a steady change in the type of residents. Instead of young married couples, the flats were being occupied by a couple of girls until virtually all the flats except one, were occupied by women.

The woman who cleaned and tidied the common parts, such as the hall and stairs on behalf of the landlady once remarked that Terence being the only male amidst all the young females was a lucky chap. We expressed our doubt saying that we suspected that the girls were most likely Lesbians and that he would be more likely to be frustrated than lucky. She said she doubted if they were Lesbians as they all spoke good English without a trace of foreign accent. She also asked, if they were actually Lesbians, what was going on in their own country that caused them to flee here.

We believe that she had great doubts about our explanation. She had never heard anything like it before but she said that she would take care next time she went in there.

When we spoke to the landlady, she told us that at first she had not suspected anything. She had let one of the flats to a delightful, pleasant, couple of girls who had come down from Manchester to work in London. They were excellent tenants and when they recommended a couple of their work mates for the next flat that became vacant, she was glad to accept especially so, as she did not have to pay an agent's fee. As further flats became vacant, she accepted more of their workmates or friends. They were all excellent tenants, quiet, clean and prompt with their rents. It was only after her cleaning woman told her what we had said that she realised what had happened.

The first couple had got a job as chauffeuses with a ministry in Whitehall and they had recommended their friends who also worked there. Later they confided in us, that the manageress in charge of the ministry's car pool was a lesbian and she only engaged lesbians as drivers. There were very few male chauffeurs employed in her department.

Some of the girls were exceedingly pretty and beautifully dressed. Some were not so young and not so pretty. One was actually very ugly and squat and very strong. It was nothing for her to come home from work with 1 cwt (approx. 50kg) sack of coal slung over her shoulder. On another occasion, we saw her lift without any difficulty a tiled fireplace surround which two of the landlady's workmen had difficulty in moving. She had a very pretty blonde friend, who we knew as Jeanette, until she told us that actually it was John who liked to dress up as a girl. One couple, a little older than the others, were a local school's head mistress and her deputy. Another resident we were surprised to see one day driving a bus locally. They were all very industrious.

We got to know them and to like them quite well as we had the previous tenants.

One day, there was a commotion. One of the young girls rang my bell and asked me to help. One of the girl's jilted lover had come round to settle matters with her ex lover's current mate. She had been refused entrance and had climbed up an adjacent drainpipe and entered the premises through a first floor window.

The girls in the house were scared because the intruder was armed with a large knife which she had threatened to use on the current partner. When

I entered the house through the front door. I heard a terrible row in progress. About six of the girls were screaming abuse and using such foul language that I had never heard men use. The amazing thing was that as soon as they saw that a male had entered the house, they became coy and quiet. The intruder apologised for the bad language and meekly left through the front door replacing the knife in a leather sheath.

One day, the girl who occupied the flat adjacent to our lounge said that she was going to give a birthday party the coming weekend and as it would inevitably become a bit noisy she would like us to come to the party and join in the fun. She assured us that she was also inviting Terence so that we should not feel isolated among the other party goers who she said that we might find to be a bit peculiar. We told her that we were quite broad-minded and as a matter of fact we let on that we were quite aware that they would be Lesbians. When she realised that we knew that she and the others were Lesbians she blushed deeply as she had assumed that we were ignorant of the fact.

The party was an eye opener. The girls came in pairs. One of the pair was very pretty wearing a beautiful party frock whilst her partner was smartly dressed in an expensive lounge suit complete with black bow tie and looking most handsome. The party soon got under way. The drinks flowed freely and the music was loud. It was not long before the participants began to lose their inhibitions and hands were wondering in most unusual places but not, may I assure you, in my case, or Dora's or Terence's. After a while, Dora and I had had enough and decided to discreetly return home but Terence whose face was aglow with excitement implored us to stay. We told him that we were not used to such noise or the thick tobacco smoke but there was no reason why he should not stay on, which he did.

Terence was easily old enough to be any of the girl's father or even grandfather. He was a bachelor and despite his age in excellent physical condition. He went in for hill and mountain climbing and for relaxation went in for Scotch dancing. One day, he asked me to measure him up for a kilt to be used in connection with his hobby. He had found a firm in Scotland that made genuine kilts, all you need do to have one made to measure was to send them the money through the post together with waist, hips and length measurement. Even though Terence was exceedingly fit he had a paunch. His waist was much larger than his hips. The kilt maker assumed that he got the measurements reversed and made the kilt the other way round. There was one other problem about measuring him for the kilt. He had been advised that the length should be measured from the waist down to two finger widths below the knees. The problem was that he had no defined waist and particularly no knees. His legs went straight

Lesbos

down without any knobs for his knees.

When he finally got the kilt corrected he went to a Scotch dance. The kilt was a bit on the short side and he wore a mackintosh(rain coat).

There was a bit of a dispute with the bus driver who at first accused him of being indecently dressed.

One day, I heard Terence calling me to the rear garden. When I went out he was leaning over the garden fence. He said, "Thank goodness, you're in. there's a woman inside me who wants to come out". I told him to stop shouting because all the neighbours would hear. I told him that I can't help him and unkindly suggested that he should have an abortion. I was beginning to become a little confused myself.

On one occasion, the landlady had let a two bedroom ground floor flat to four young ladies. It later transpired that they were all married but had conspired to leave their husbands simultaneously. Subsequently, there was a sequence of cars parked outside the house with what we assumed were private detectives taking notes of coming and goings. If they took notes of Terence's activities, they were wasting their time and their client's money.

Eventually, the landlady sold the premises to a developer who made a proper conversion of each house into four self contained luxury flats and sold them to ordinary people like ourselves.

The Nag

Ernie thanked us profusely for coming to see him on such a miserable, cold, drizzling November evening. He seemed to enjoy our company and the opportunity to tell us of his experiences in life. Precisely at 8pm as he does every evening he 'opened the bar'. There were always a variety of drinks but for himself, Ernie always drank two large bottles of strong cider. Dora had her usual whisky and I, because I was driving, an orangeade.

After his first glass, Ernie said, "This weather reminds me of the day I acquired a horse". He then asked if he had told us about the horse but without waiting for a reply he proceeded to do so.

He said that it was on such a miserable November evening that he discovered a scraggy, sore covered horse tethered outside the canal side pub that he was managing in the depression years. The horse was obviously sick and was coughing badly. Ernie knew that it did not belong to any of his regular customers and he ascertained that neither did it belong to any of the casuals drinking at the time. At least, they all denied that it belonged to them.

Ernie felt sorry for it and offered it some odds and ends to eat but it refused, it even refused to accept some cubes of sugar.

He was at a loss to know what to do even though he had served in a cavalry regiment during the war and was well acquainted with horses, that is with healthy horses and their constant attention of the regiment's veterinary officer.

In the morning, it was still there, still coughing and still refusing to accept food. No one had claimed it during the night. It had obviously been abandoned to die. The police were not interested, they had no facilities for sick and abandoned horses and they certainly did not want the sick horse to come anywhere near their own healthy horses. They told Ernie to call in a vet and if the horse was not claimed within seven days, legally, it was his property.

Although Ernie liked horses, he certainly was not keen to spend his scarce, hard earned money consulting a vet about some other person's sick and dying horse.

However, one of his regulars came to his rescue. He told Ernie that he had recently inherited a nearby field and whilst his family was deciding what to do with the field, Ernie could keep the horse there. He said that the previous owner had kept a horse there, the field had a shelter and a running brook. The arrangement was, that when the horse died, Ernie would be responsible to dispose of the corpse.

For the first couple of weeks, Ernie would visit the field to see if the horse was still alive. He was amazed to see that it was and that it had stopped coughing and that it accepted the titbits he brought along.

From time-to-time, the owner of the field told Ernie that the horse was doing well and enjoying itself and that, meanwhile, it was OK leave it there.

This was a relief for Ernie who had been worried about the cost of disposing of the horse that was now legally his when it died.

About eight months later, Ernie was surprised when a gypsy horse dealer asked him if he was interested in selling the horse and was even more surprised at the generous amount offered. Ernie was suspicious but could not refuse the temptation. Cash was paid on the spot and the transaction confirmed by the traditional clasp of hands. The gypsy had a few pints before setting off to take his purchase away. He told Ernie that it had been a pleasure to do business with such a gentleman and to keep him in mind if he ever came across such a fine horse again in the future.

A couple of days later, the Gypsy returned to the pub and ordered a pint of beer and told Ernie to have one himself. Ernie enquired as to what he owed such a pleasure. The gypsy said that he wanted to congratulate Ernie. He went on to explain that he had been a horse dealer all his life and before that, his father had been. The family had been horse dealers going back for generations but this was the first known time that any of them had bought a dud. He told Ernie that he and his sons have been trying to catch the horse and put a halter on him for a couple of days without success. He had never seen such a wild and wily horse and doubted that if he ever did catch it that he would be able to tame it. He ominously said that he may even haveto leave the horse in the field until it died.

The Village Doctor

Ernie often told us about the hard life endured by the poor people in his home village in rural Essex at about the beginning of the century.

He told us of the deaths of babies through pneumonia which was known at the time as the poor man's friend. Life was harsh, children were wanted, not only for natural love but also for labour and as a safeguard in old age. In those days, there was no welfare state and no birth control aids. Beyond a certain number, depending on the child's sex, children were an unbearable and un-needed burden. It was quite well known, but not openly spoken about, that unwanted babies would be given a hot bath by their mother and then left naked by an open window during the night. Pneumonia was the inevitable result about which the doctor could do nothing but eventually issue a death certificate stating 'natural causes'. There were no antibiotic drugs and no intensive care wards in the hospitals.

The local doctor used to employ Ernie as the driver of his pony and trap when doing his rounds for which he was paid 6 pence (2 1/2p) for the day but the doctor often forgot to pay him. Ernie did not mind too much, as the job gave him prestige among his 12 year old peers. Many of the doctor's calls were in connection with such cases of infantile pneumonia.

One day, Ernie was surprised when he drove the doctor on an emergency call to his own home. It transpired that Ernie's eldest brother who was a braggart had been passing by the Smithy's shop where he saw six local men struggling to place an anvil onto a cart. His brother sneered at the locals saying that he on his own could get the anvil onto the cart. He explained that he would be able to do so, not only because he was strong and healthy but because he would use his brain. He told them to stand aside and watch what a combination of skill and cleverness could achieve.

To the utter astonishment of the locals, after flexing his muscles, he smoothly lifted the anvil and gently placed it on the cart. The locals gave him an involuntary applause but soon after had to carry him home because he had ruptured himself. It took Ernie's brother at least a year after the operation to recover from that episode.

Normally, Ernie did not work for the doctor on Sundays except in the case of emergencies but one Sunday, the doctor asked him to be available as he was expecting guests to arrive from London and he wanted Ernie to collect them from and to return them to the local railway station. He told Ernie that as that alone would not warrant a day's pay of sixpence, he would require him to work between times in his vegetable garden. Because it was Sunday and as the doctor was a religious man he promised Ernie that the cook would provide him with lunch.

Ernie was curious and asked the cook what was for lunch. She described a sumptuous meal that really made Ernie's young mouth water. He thought he would make the most of such an opportunity by really working hard and raising an appetite that would do full justice to his expectations.

At the exact time that the cook had indicated, he called at the rear kitchen door and told the maid that he was ready for his meal. She told him to wait at the door whilst she went to see the cook. The wonderful smells of food wafting out through the door nearly caused Ernie to faint from excitement. The maid returned and handed Ernie a brown paper bag in which were cheese sandwiches and warned him not to make a mess whilst eating them in the garden.

From time-to-time, Ernie also helped the doctor's gardener in the heated green house in which he saw exotic plants growing but also fruitful grapevines. Grapes in the village were an unknown luxury and Ernie was determined to taste some. He could not do so whilst the watchful gardener was about so he sneaked back after dark. He picked up an empty seedling box and filled it with bunches of ripe grapes. As he was making his way out, the gardener unexpectedly returned. Ernie had to get by him in order to reach the door. As the gardener got near where Ernie was crouching under a bench, he rose suddenly and quickly pressed the tray of ripe grapes into the gardener's face. In the confusion, Ernie escaped sans grapes.

The gardener told Ernie that he knew who the culprit was and would get his revenge at the first opportunity.

Jerusalem

When Ernie heard that we were going on a visit to Israel he implored us to take him with. At first, we had our doubts, because, although he was fairly active, he was 84 years old and on our previous visits to Israel we had been very active. We thought he would be a hindrance to our plans. He guessed what was in our minds and promised that he would not impede any of our activities. He had seen the coloured slides of our previous visits and was intent on seeing Jerusalem before he died. He said that if we did not take him with, he would go on his own and we would miss the benefit of his company.

Despite his age, Ernie was a good companion and always had an entertaining tale to tell. He also assured us that he would pay his full one third share of any expenditure. This, he adhered to, to a certain extent although he often conveniently forgot to pay even after we reminded him of the day's expenditure. He had asked us to pay as and when the need arose and that at the end of the day he would settle up with us. It amused us to note, that whereas we drank low cost soft drinks, he would drink large glasses of brandy. It was amazing just how much strong alcohol he could consume without it apparently affecting him especially so when we were bearing the bulk of the cost.

The day before we started our visit, he came over to settle accounts. We had booked and paid for his air fares and medical insurance etc. Even though he was 84 years old, he still drove his own car. After he had settled up he suggested that we should drink to the success of our venture. Knowing that he was driving, I suggested a low alcohol beer but he said that it would not be proper to launch such a tour on low alcohol beer and future success would be assured if we toasted the occasion with a little brandy.

I got the brandy bottle out and three small glasses. Ernie said that brandy should always be drunk out of a large glass so as to be able to savour the aroma. He picked up a tumbler and said that that would do. Just as I was going to pour some brandy into his tumbler, he took the bottle from me and said, 'Let me pour, as I am driving, you may tempt me by giving me too much". he then proceeded to fill the tumbler to the top. I naturally assumed he was joking but in almost one gulp drank he the lot. He did not seem to be effected by it and declared that he always drove better after a drink. I was alarmed and offered either to drive him home or to call a cab. He refused both offers and refused to let me hold his car keys. Short of alerting the police, there was nothing I could do.

When we met the next day to commence our journey, he said to us, "You know there's no fool like an old fool, after I had that drink at your house yesterday, I did not remember a thing, I could not even remember my drive home, I did not remember arriving home and do not remember anything about the rest of the day !"

When we saw the long queue at the airport awaiting security and boarding, Ernie said, "Leave this to me". He beckoned over a uniformed member of the air line staff and told her that he was an invalid. She immediately produced a wheelchair and took Ernie straight onto the plane and as we were with him, so did we.

We were amazed at Ernie's energy. Even though we were about 30 years younger than him, he had no difficulty in keeping up with our activities. He had a wonderful time, he even went into the sea for the first time for about 30 years. He saw sights that he had only previously dreamt of seeing.

It was also particularly enjoyable, because it was the first holiday for many years that he had not spent on his own. For some unknown reason, his wife refused to go on holiday with him.

After a few days, he even discarded his walking stick which previously he had heavily relied upon. Unfortunately, he had to resort to it soon after his return to England.

One day, when I said that I wanted to photograph a particular recent archaeological excavation, Ernie said that he would prefer not to come with me. Dora decided, that she too, would prefer to relax and they both spent the day on the Tel-Aviv beach.

Upon my return, we all went out for a meal and whilst we were chatting Ernie said "I am rather confused, when we go into a Church, I have to take my hat off, when we go into a Synagogue I have to put my hat on, what do I have to do when I go into a Mosque?". Without much thought I said, "You take your trousers down". This was followed by an embarrassed silence by both Dora and Ernie and I wondered if I had been too crude. Later, when we were on our own, Dora said that she was not going to tell me till we got home, but whilst she was on her own with Ernie he had confessed to being an active homosexual even at his age now. At first I thought she was having me on. There was nothing about Ernie that would suggest he was a homosexual, after all, we had known him for 20 years. He was married and had two grown up children and was very masculine in appearance and actions. Dora said that she had promised Ernie that she would not tell me till we returned to England but my statement about Ernie having to take his trousers off caused her to break her vow in order to avoid any further embarrassment whilst we were on holiday. He had told Dora that he had acquired the deviation whilst he was a full time army cadet and that it was further developed in the many years he had served as a regular soldier.

Marriage had not altered his pre-disposition and he had never revealed it to his wife although he suspected that somehow or other she knew.

He told Dora that he had carried on his homosexual activities under the guise of employing young men in his various business enterprises. When one of them was hospitalised, he visited him and told the nurse that he was the boy's godfather. He asked the nurse if she could draw the curtain around the bed so that the other patients would not be able to observe how emotionally upset he was. As soon as the curtains were drawn, Ernie undressed and got into bed with the young man.

He said that he generally made contact with suitable young men in public toilets and asked Dora to discreetly enquire where he may seek such contact in Israel.

He told Dora that the previous year when he was on holiday in Malta, he found himself alone with a young Maltese man in a lift. Ernie made certain suggestions and the young man in return flashed a knife in Ernie's face and threatened to cut his throat before they reached the first floor.

Apart from this proclivity, he told us many amusing stories which we regret not having taped because it was not only the contents of the stories but the way he recounted them that made them so amusing.

He told us how in the 1920's he took his wife on a luxury cruise. All the other passengers appeared to be well-to-do and the majority of them were elderly ladies. One group were chatting one day and asked Ernie what he did for a living. He replied rather evasively that he was in the conveyancing business. They exclaimed, how nice, a solicitor, very interesting. He did not demur. The next day, the same group was showing each other their passports and the interesting visa stamps therein. When Ernie's wife showed her joint passport, they noticed that Ernie was described as a ·bus driver. Realising that his pretence had been exposed, every time Ernie passed this group he said "Honk, honk".

Even in the worse days of the 1920–1930's depression, Ernie would never despair and would try his hand at anything to make some money.

Once he tried his luck as a salesman of unbreakable glass tumblers. The firm that produced them gave him an impressive demonstration and then sold him a gross (144). At the first public house that he tried, the landlord dropped one of them and it just shattered into smithereens. He had very little luck elsewhere.

When he tried being a builder, he found it difficult to obtain work. He would walk down a street until he found a roof in a bad state of repair. He would point out to the occupier the obvious defects and agree a certain amount for each slate he replaced. Very often the defect was not a broken slate but one which had slipped down. Ernie or one of the young men working for him would refit the existing slate but turn it over so that the shiny underside was uppermost. He would do the same to a few other slates whilst he was on the roof and charge the occupiers for supplying new slates. He had such an honest and earnest face that no one doubted he was telling the truth.

When he had the opportunity, he would surreptitiously form small holes in the woodwork with a sharp bradawl and inform the occupier of the premises that there was an infestation of woodworm and if he did not have it treated at once, it would spread throughout the property.

He tried his hand as a nursery man raising seedlings for sale in local shops. One day, he found that the local Woolworth's had brought their supply from a rival. Ernie sprayed the rivals displayed seedlings with a weed killer and returned a few days later to re-stock the shop which was a good outlet for him.

However, he was most successful when he tried buying up large dilapidated houses and letting them off as sub-standard furnished flats. By this means, he managed to acquire a few properties and a steady income.

A few weeks after our return from Israel, Ernie 'phoned us and said he would like to see us as he has decided to die. When we arrived to see what his curious call was all about, we found that he had moved his bed down to his lounge. He was sitting up in bed looking quite fit and cheerful. He told us that he felt that he had lived long enough and had decided to die before he became crippled and mentally enfeebled and would be treated with the indignity accorded to such persons. He said that he would stay in his bed until he died with his full faculties intact.

A week later, he asked us once again to visit him as he felt he was beginning to die and would not last much later. He was still lucid and we told him that if he would get out of bed and see a doctor, he could still have many more years to live. He said he would not see a doctor as they had no time for elderly people and would only prescribe something to finish him off. Although we tried, we could not see any logic in his conviction about doctors.

He told us that he was beginning to have hallucinations and could clearly see projected onto the wall opposite, images of Jerusalem and thought that he would not last more than a week. He told us, that a goody-goody religious neighbour had come to visit him a couple of days before to see how he was getting on and to pray for him. Ernie said, "You know what I did, I sold her my old clapped out car for twice as much as I would have got from anyone else, not bad for a dying man, eh?"

A few days later, his wife 'phoned and said that Ernie had passed away.

On the reading of his will, Ernie had, after making provision for his wife in trust during her remaining lifetime, left all his estate to an Exserviceman's organisation. His wife said that she could not understand it as he had had no connection with it.

The Demon Drink

Several houses down our street were split up into four flats but the flats were not sell contained. They shared certain amenities such as bathrooms, WC's entrance hall, staircase and garden. In order to circumvent the then current tenant protective laws, the flats were let furnished. Generally, this suited the tenants who could get accommodation without waiting a long time and the rents generally, were reasonable.

Hilda was one such tenant of the terraced house just a few doors to our own. Whereas most of the other tenants in such accommodation were mainly young, recently married couples, she was on her own except for her dachshund dog. She was about 50 years old.

She wore expensive, 'sensible' clothes and had a dignified appearance. We often wondered why a woman of her age should be in such a type of accommodation.

We got on speaking terms when a small package intended for her was wrongly delivered to our house. She had an important job in the civil service and took her dog with her to work. We noticed how fond she was of the dog as she bent down to pat him every few yards or so on her way to the local railway station when going to work. It was not long before we realised that whilst she was patting the dog she was simultaneously depositing empty bottles against fences and under hedges. All the bottles were from various forms of alcoholic beverages, some were small Vodka bottles, some Whisky and some cheap wine bottles.

She was disposing of the empty bottles in this manner so as not to draw attention to her alcohol consumption by placing the bottles in the communal bin where she lived.

Our suspicion that she was an alcoholic was soon confirmed when her elderly parents enquired at our house if their daughter, Hilda, who had recently left home was settling in OK in her new accommodation. During conversation, it appeared that they were not so much concerned about their daughter's welfare than to besmirch her. The mother seemed to take a particular delight in this exercise. As we became more acquainted with Hilda we became more acquainted with the degradation and misery caused by alcoholism. It is a far cry from the jollity of inebriation as heaven is from hell. Alcoholism is a hell into which some people are cast not by their own fault, but through inherent genes passed on through the female side of the family but skipping alternative generations whilst other alcoholics are self induced.

Hilda blamed her addiction on an unhappy marriage but possibly her fate had already been pre-destined or maybe, the unhappy marriage was caused by her pre-destination. Her colleagues at the ministry were very sympathetic and supportive. They covered up her absences and failings. Quite often they would 'phone us and ask us to see if she was OK as she had not been into work for a couple of days and had not 'phoned in.

The man in charge of her department had arranged for her to go on a rehabilitation course but to no avail, the alcohol had already, irreversibly, damaged her kidneys, liver and brain. On one occasion when one of her colleagues asked us to see if she was OK we found her lying semi conscious on the landing near the bathroom door. Her little dog was lying across her body, silently and mournfully protecting and comforting her.

Once, she asked us if we knew who a large pair of muddy men's boots which she had found near her bed belonged to, or if anyone had been making enquiries about them.

Apparently, she often got so intoxicated in a pub she frequented, that she had to be brought home by fellow imbibers. The good Samaritans also frequently stayed the night with her. One such night visitor, during the small hours felt the irresistible urge to visit the shared bathroom but forgot which door opened onto Hilda's bed-sitting room. By mistake, he entered the bedroom of a young couple and when the young woman awoke and saw a naked man trying to get into bed with her she started to scream hysterically. This aroused the neighbourhood and the police were called. Because of the commotion the landlord got to know of the affair and gave Hilda notice to quit on the grounds that she kept a dog on the premises in contravention of the tenancy agreement.

Her fellow tenants had up till then, also been sympathetic and had not complained about her misbehaviour which at times caused a great nuisance.

It was fortunate, that at that time one of her drinking partners, possibly the naked man or the one who forgot his boots asked her to many him and to live in his house. We imagined that her mother would not have been too pleased if and when she learnt that the man was a council dustman or an environmental cleansing operative as they are now known. When she was leaving, she asked us to accept a gift in appreciation for our help. She gave us a Victorian, oak banjo style aneroid barometer that had been given to her father by his tailors, Harry Hall, in appreciation of his valued custom. The barometer was in good condition except that the thermometer was broken. She had snapped the glass and consumed the methylated spirit therein because, unlike the methylated spirit obtained commercially it had not been adulterated with an emetic.

For a while, we were puzzled about the many large tins of brown shoe polish we noticed in her bed-sitter, but one day, someone explained that alcoholics resorted to shoe polish sandwiches in order to get satisfaction from the unadulterated methylated spirit therein.

After she left, we lost touch and do not know her fate or that of her faithful dachshund. We only hope that they lived happy ever after but we doubt it.

The Wedding

There were no wedding bells to mark the happy occasion because the ceremony took place in a registry office. The office was situated in what had previously been a fine country mansion set in well maintained grounds. There had been certain complications attached to the marriage. Both bride and groom, now in their thirties, had been married previously.

The groom was Jewish, that is, that his mother was Jewish and that his mother's mother had been Jewish, so by Jewish tradition, he was Jewish even though his father was not and that he had never observed the Jewish religion. He was British by nationality because he had been born in London although both his parents were Russian. He was born in London because at the time both his parents were working as translators in the Russian Trade Mission in Highgate, North London. To have been allowed to live and work overseas, both his parents must have proved to the KGB that they were ardent and reliable communists and to be trusted and not to abscond. When the groom was still a baby, the parents returned to the Soviet Union taking the child with them. He was raised and educated in the Soviet Union. When he was about thirty he used the technicality of his birth in London to obtain a British passport and come to live in England bringing with him his Russian born non-Jewish wife and her two children by a previous marriage. She and her children were observant members of the Russian Orthodox church.

The couple were separated not long after settling down in England and eventually divorced. The marriage had not been a happy one especially so, alter he brought his invalid mother and her aged mother to live with them. His father did not come as he had divorced his wile when she became an invalid through Parkinson's disease and had in his dotage married a very

265

much younger woman. Being an ardent communist and a confirmed atheist he preferred to remain in Moscow with his young wife and her two children through a previous marriage. He had declined on the grounds of health to attend the wedding.

The groom's mother did not attend the wedding because she had become hospitalised and her mother did not attend on the grounds that she was dead and buried in a Jewish cemetery.

After the divorce, the groom met and fell in love with the Polish born bride when he visited Poland where he had gone to meet his father clandestinely because in those days, the KGB would not permit the groom to re-enter the Soviet Union.

I hope that so far, the reader finds the facts simple and clear. He obtained permission for his loved one to come to England to be married here. As she was a Catholic and had previously been married she could not obtain permission to be married again in a Catholic church. She came to England leaving behind, pro-tem, her two children from her previous marriage.

Although the groom could not speak Polish and although the bride could not speak either Russian or English, they somehow or other managed to communicate quite well. Love finds a way.

The bride's previous and divorced husband had been living in England for quite a while before the wedding and had obtained British citizenship. He had kept in touch with his divorced wife because of their common interest in their two children whom he continued to help maintain. There had apparently been no acrimony in their divorce and he continued to be very fond of his previous wife and their children.

Because of the good relationship he had been invited to the wedding.

When the congregation, or audience, or assembly or whatever is the correct collective noun for the people attending a wedding in a registry office is termed were seated, the Registrar entered the room accompanied by her male clerk. With a very pleasant smile she commenced the proceedings with a short introductory explanation.

As the law requires that those taking a marriage vow must understand what they are undertaking, an elderly uncle of the bride who spoke both Polish and English sat at the Registrar's table to act as translator on behalf of the bride. The bridegroom did not need a translator as he himself was an English/Russian/English translator by profession.

As the Registrar read out the vows in English which were to be repeated by the bride she looked at the uncle who was acting as the translator and nodded her head as a signal for him to translate into Polish for the benefit of the bride but the translator just sat there in silence with a broad benign smile on his face. She repeated her signal a couple more times without any appropriate reaction.

The bride's previous husband went up to the translator and asked why he was not translating the vows. Apparently, the batteries in the translator's hearing aid had run down suddenly and he could not hear a thing. As there was no-one better qualified to take over as translator, the brides previous husband acted as the translator although his comprehension of English was not very good but his Polish was excellent. The Registrar also had difficulty in pronouncing the bride's Polish name and her clerk who was not acquainted with the east European custom of writing the surname first, followed by the patronym and given name, had entered her name the wrong way round on the certificate.

As soon as the ceremony was completed, those present formed a ring around the newly married couple and sung a cheerful and rousing song in Polish.

The ceremony was followed by a very pleasant reception and meal in a local Chinese restaurant at which many toasts were drunk in vodka.

Several years later, the bride's own children came to live with them, and the family live very nicely and amicably together. The brides ex-husband still regularly visits them and is concerned about his own children's education and welfare.

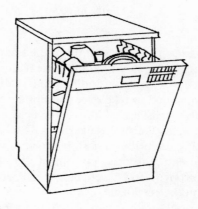

The Dishwasher

Dora has a very efficient dish washer but it is not one that you can buy but one that clears the dining table, clears the scraps off the plates, thoroughly washes all the crockery and utensils, dries and finally stacks and stores everything in its proper place. No doubt, you have guessed, the dish washer is none other than me, myself. It's not that I have always been a dish washer but have carried out the task for the last five years.

It started on a bleak winter's afternoon when snow had fallen the previous day and through semi-thaw and re-freezing the snow had turned into ice which turned roads and footpaths into extreme danger zones.

Whilst the main roads had been gritted, the side streets remained as treacherous traps for the foolhardy and unwary. Dora had received a telephone call informing her that someone she knew who lived about half mile away had some jumble for a charity sale Dora was helping to organise. Dora volunteered to pick it up immediately and to take it to the hall where the jumble sale was to be held.

Despite my warning about the treacherous conditions on the roads and pavements, Dora persisted in going. She said she would be OK, she would dress up warm with her padded duffle coat over several woollen cardigans, wear a padded ski style cap with an anti-glare peak, put on her fur lined boots and as a precaution against slipping on the ice, she wrapped her boots in old towels tied on with string. She said that her mother had taught her that when she was a child.

She went out looking like an over grown, misshapen, Donald Duck but her improved footwear worked wonderfully. Whilst others slid and slipped, she glided past confidently and swiftly. People looked at her in amazement. She soon reached the house where she was to collect the jumble and as she strode up the front path, she tripped over a small step that had been concealed by driven snow. As she fell she instinctively stretched out her right hand to prevent her face hitting the frozen path but in doing so she fractured a small bone in her wrist. This is quite a common type of fracture and is known as a Collis fracture. Her doctor sent her to the casualty department of the local hospital who put her wrist in plaster and her arm in a sling. As she could no longer do the washing up, the task naturally fell to me even though her wrist mended quite soon, I am, five years later, still the dish washer.

Goodness only knows, what I might have been today if her injury had been more serious.

Ginger

One bitterly cold winters evening, we came across a small crowd of people watching a couple of youths rescuing a small ginger kitten from a chimney. A woman told us that it had been up there for three bitterly cold nights. She had 'phoned the local RSPCA (Royal Society for Prevention of Cruelty to Animals) but they refused to do anything, saying that eventually, it will find its own way down. She did not know who the kitten belonged to, neither did anyone else in the crowd but an elderly lady said that she would care for it whilst the owner was being found.

This was not the first time we had heard of the callousness of the RSPCA. A few months before, we had reported to them a squirrel trapped up a telephone post when it had apparently been chased by a couple of cats who were persistently waiting at the foot of the pole for the squirrel to descend. The RSPCA said that as squirrels were considered wild animals, there was nothing they could do to help. However, British Telecom came to the rescue and brought the animal down and conveyed it to the local park, from where, it no doubt came.

A friend, who lives quite close by, told us of her experience with the RSPCA. She noticed that her immediate neighbours loading their car with lots of luggage, obviously intended as a long holiday. A couple of days later, she heard their cat mewing from inside the neighbours house, she looked through the letter box and saw their ginger cat in a very distressed state. Our friend fed the cat through the letter box each day, but what she could not do, was give it something to drink. She realised that without liquid the cat would die so she contacted the RSPCA of which she was a member. The inspector came after a couple of days and was in a furious temper but clothed in a very smart uniform.

He also peered through the letter box and confirmed that the cat was indeed in distress, but, instead of the expected reaction he told our friend to mind her own business, he said that the cat belonged to the neighbours and they could do what they liked with it.

One day, we noticed a ginger cat sheltering under a hedge in our front garden and as it appeared to be hungry, we gave it some scraps left by our own cats which it ravenously consumed. We placed an advert in local newsagent's windows that we had found a ginger cat but no-one responded.

When our local, regular, chatty postman saw us one day feeding the cat, he said he knew who it belonged to, he said he was very fond of cats and knew many on his round. He gave us the address but said it was no good going there as the cat's owners had moved away and had not left a forwarding address. We knew that the address he had given us was the same as the family who had left the ginger cat locked into the house when they went on holiday.

We decided that we would not 'adopt' the cat who, had apparently been abandoned by its owners. We already had three strays who we 'adopted'. They were all black and would not likely take to a cat of a strange colour. A young couple who lived in a bed-sitter flat next door to us readily agreed to adopt the stray, but after just a few weeks they informed us that their marriage had broken up and that they were separating and that neither of them could take Ginger with them. We quickly overcame this small problem when the young bachelor who took over their flat agreed to take Ginger over also. But as fate had it, he too had to relinquish the adoption after a short while because, on the death of his father, he had to return to Ireland to take care of his family's small farm. He said that a domesticated cat like Ginger, would not be able to survive the aggression of the hardy farm cats who would not take kindly to a softie English cat.

This time, we could not find anyone to adopt Ginger, so he became the sixth member of our family.

Although he was subject to a little bullying from our three black cats, particularly, the small she cat, he was begrudgingly accepted by them.

One of our young nieces was very fond of him. When she came to stay with us, she dressed as a nurse and bandaged Ginger up as though he had been in an accident and wheeled him around in a child's toy pram. He loved this attention and meekly allowed her to bestow all manner of indignities on him. Because he was younger, he outlived two of the three black cats but eventually, he himself became terminally ill. One day, the vet said he would die very shortly and as he was not in pain he suggested we let him die naturally rather than have him put to sleep. The vet said that he would die in a few hours.

Ginger lay down on a comfortable bed we made for him in his favourite corner and curled up. We supposed that natural instincts let him know that he did not have long to live. We left him in the corner when we went to bed expecting him to die sometime during the night.

However, about 5 am. we were awoken by his loud cries outside our bedroom door. Ginger had decided that as a condemned person, he was entitled at least, to a last good meal and drink.

He died peacefully in his sleep a few days later.

My War Service

The second world war had been in progress for three years and five months when on my 18th birthday I received my national call-up papers. Up till then, the war had not gone well at all for the Allies. In fact, it had gone very badly. The War Cabinet's hopes lay largely in my recruitment.

Initially, I was to undergo a medical examination which was expected to be just a formality to certify that I was actually still alive. The demand for fresh recruits for the armed forces was so great that even men with flat feet were being compulsorily recruited. I did not anticipate any problem with my medical. Many of my friends had already been called to the colours and I considered myself to be at least as fit as any of them including Mark who had been accepted for flying crew in the Royal Air Force, which demanded the highest standard of all. The medical examination was carried out on a conveyor belt system. Around the perimeter of the hall was a line of trestle tables behind each of which sat an army Officer or Sergeant. At the first table, proof of identity was taken. This was not difficult as each person in those days had been issued with a national identity card. The medical examination was progressive as one went from table to table. Height and weight was noted. Eyes examined (blindness was no excuse for not being called up). Chests examined. Another part of the anatomy was held whilst you were required to cough. Feet examined and somewhere along the line, ears were peered into with the aid of a conical shaped torch.

When the Officer peered into my right ear, he became quite perturbed. In an accusative tone he informed me that the whole of the inner ear was missing. I told him that I had had five mastoid operations on that ear when I was a child but I could hear quite well in my other ear.

He asked me if I wanted to go into the armed services. I told him that

I did not mind but if I had a choice, I would like to go into the Royal Engineers where I already had two friends. He appeared to be at a loss as what to enter on my medical report card. He scribbled something down and directed me to another table on the other side of the hail. The Officer there asked me if I had ever been treated for mental disorders of any kind. I assured him that I had not. He then told me to place my hand over my hearing ear and asked me if I could hear him speak. I told him that I could. He also peered into my right ear and again asked if I had ever been examined by a psychologist.

Included in the series of tests was the one where you sit with your legs crossed and a doctor taps each leg in turn with a rubber headed hammer just below the knee cap. In my case, there was no jerk as was expected. The officer who conducted this particular examination kept repeating it without my legs jerking until black and blue bruises started to appear. He also asked me if I had ever been treated for any nervous or mental complaints.

After completing the round of the tables I was directed to one near the exit door, which was actually the same one through which I had entered. Here, I was handed a green card which certified me alive but grade IV, the very lowest grade before the death certificate!

None of the armed services would accept anyone on that grade. I was informed that I would be of most use to His Majesty's Armed Forces by not serving.

I next applied to the Ministry of Labour and National Service to be given work of National importance to the war effort. As at the time I was working in a drawing office as an architectural assistant, they directed me to work for the D.C.R.E, "B" NW. London (District Command Royal Engineers "B" North West London). This suited me as it was the sort of job I had hoped for had I been taken into the army. I was to work in a drawing office alongside conscripted and volunteer servicemen and servicewomen preparing building plans etc., for the needs of the Royal Engineers.

It had the advantage that I would not be subject to military discipline even though army officers were in charge, I would also be able to continue living at home and to continue study at evening classes for qualification as an architect. Maybe grade IV was not all that bad and I continued to be fit and healthy and not subject to any treatment for mental disorders.

At first I was assigned to an office in Ebury House, Allington Street, London SW1 which was situated between Victoria main line railway station and Buckingham Palace but one of its more important features was that our office on the second floor directly overlooked the flat roof at the rear of the Victoria Palace Theatre where the chorus girls stripped and sunbathed in between rehearsals. During these periods, full use was made of the powerful telescopes on the theodolites that otherwise were used for surveying building sites. One drawback was that the images seen in these instruments are for some obscure reason, upside down but that did not matter as the girls left little else to the imagination. I suppose it could be considered that this was their small contribution to the war effort.

After a few months in the Victoria Office, I was transferred to the office situated in the army barracks on Bittacy Hill, Mill Hill, London NW7 which was much more inconvenient for me to travel to work each day but instead of a view over the roof of the Victoria Palace Theatre, it looked over the nearby gas works and its giant gas storage holder.

Our main task here was surveying and recording army installations that had been erected over a large area during emergencies in great haste and no records kept. We also surveyed sites and planned new army installations such as additional barracks, offices, gun sites, barrage balloon sites, ammunition stores etc. etc.

Here, theodolites were used for their proper purpose and almost unbelievably surveys were done with iron chains. These chains actually consisted of iron links about 200mm long joined together by iron rings onto which were attached bronze tags marked in 'poles', 'rods', 'links' and 'chains'.

On one survey, the chain got caught on some obstruction and in the effort to free it, one of the links broke. The Sergeant in charge of the survey party decided that in order to avoid awkward questioning he reassembled the chain without the broken link. That chain must have been used on countless subsequent surveys but we never heard of any complaints.

In order to get admission to army installations, civilians such as myself were issued with special passes which had to be regularly renewed. One day, arriving at an AA (anti aircraft) gun site which was situated in Regents Park, London, I realised that I had submitted my pass for renewal and did not yet have a new one. It would not have reflected well on me if I had to return with the survey party without completing the task we were sent to do. The Sergeant in charge said that he needed me in order to do the survey properly according to army manuals. He said, that we would survey our way in. We had done this before but just for fun. It consisted of taking measurements and notes of the road in front of the entrance gate to the site. Details would be taken of the gate itself and whilst the armed sentries watched similar measurements and details taken just inside the gate. Once inside we would continue with the real survey.

The ruse worked again and whilst we were taking measurements all around the site, we noticed an AA gun with most unusual features. I have never heard about it since and as it may still be on the secrets list, I will not describe it. We got chatting to the crew manning it who described in great detail its features and capabilities.

Suddenly, a sergeant and two gunners came running up armed with rifles and fixed bayonets which they held most threateningly to our chests. He demanded to know what we were doing there. We explained our purpose but he demanded to see our passes. The two military personnel had no trouble but I remembered that I did not have my pass and had visions of being arrested as a spy and shot at dawn. In desperation I searched my wallet and the nearest thing I could find to identify myself was a public library ticket. I flashed that at the Sergeant and said, 'Here is my pass". He apologised for the incident and explained that the gun was experimental and top secret and that they could not be too cautious who took note of it.

Only a couple of years later, after the war, I had another experience in Regents Park but one of a much more pleasant nature. I had taken Dora there when we were courting, or was it that she had taken me there? We did what most courting couples do in Royal Parks but scrupulously avoided infringing any of the park regulation as posted at the entrance gate. It was bliss, it was springtime, the air was full of blossom perfume, the birds were singing and we even heard bells ringing. When it got fairly dark and I was beginning to feel hungry we went to leave the park but found the gate locked. The bells we heard were apparently the warning that the gate was about to be locked. It was a tall and beautiful wrought iron gate. We found a more secluded part of the park railings and after helping Dora to climb over, I did so myself without injury to either of us and to our clothing.

However, back to how I helped to defeat the might of the evil German forces.

One day, we were instructed to survey a farm that had been requisitioned by the army for use for storage purposes. We found the lane that led to the farm but unlike most army sites it did not have sign boards pointing the way.

After travelling about 100 yards down the lane two armed soldiers suddenly appeared in front of us with rifles aimed at our chests whilst two others did likewise behind us. We were asked for our identity and purpose of visit. The Sergeant said he could not accept the passes we had because only a very special pass was acceptable at that site. We asked to see an officer and explained the situation to him. We had never heard of the very special pass demanded and we doubted even if the colonel in charge of our section had heard of it or else we would have had one issued. The officer 'phoned the colonel and after a lengthy conversation with him agreed to let us proceed with our survey but first he insisted on having us searched right down to our underwear and the soles of our shoes examined. The soldiers who had metal studs in their boots had to don thick rubber over shoes.

The officer said under no circumstances were we to light matches or smoke and that we were to be as quick as possible and to leave immediately.

Once we saw what was stored in the giant barns we did not have to be told to leave immediately. There were thousands of tons of high explosive ammunition piled up to the rafters.

Prior to 'D day', the invasion of the Allied forces into Nazi occupied Europe, there was a vast influx of United States service personnel most of all, if not all, spent time relaxing in London. Many over-indulged in alcohol or overstayed their permitted leave and as a result were arrested by the US military police and detained for court martial or return to their unit.

The central place for such detention was a multi storey building in South Crescent, Store Street, off Tottenham Court Road, London WC1, I believe the building is now occupied by the Building Centre.

The premises had been converted into an American style prison, the cells, each occupied by about ten prisoners were just cages built of stout iron bars facing onto a central passageway. There was no privacy at all for the prisoners.

When I called to carry out a survey for building alteration purposes, the atmosphere was not depressive, in fact quite the contrary. If a prisoner wished to go to the toilet, he had to attract the guard's attention by rattling his enamelled mug on the iron bars. The other prisoners thought it was hilarious to do the same simultaneously so that the guard would not know which prisoner actually had the urge to relieve himself. The result was that the victim would relieve himself out of one of the windows.

The building was so arranged that all the cells faced onto a central courtyard at the foot of which was stationed an armed guard. At first, I could not understand why the guard stood there under an opened umbrella on a sunny day. Apparently, the prisoners were not permitted to smoke but they could chew tobacco to relieve their craving for nicotine. This resulted in frequent jets of brown sticky saliva being expertly aimed through the open windows onto the unfortunate guard on duty at the foot of the light well. What amazed me was the sumptuous food served to the prisoners. They had at one meal alone what the British civilians had rationed to them for the whole week and they also had items that the British civilians did not see at all, such as bananas, oranges and ice-cream.

Because I was a civilian I was required to volunteer to act as a Fire Watcher, unpaid, after working hours at place of work and in addition, as a Stretcher Party First Aid volunteer in my spare time in the locality where I lived. Also, at the time that the centre of London was subject to intense fire bomb raids and we were temporarily living there, I also volunteered to serve in my spare time in the AFS. (Auxiliary Fire Service).

In the spring of 1945, the work that I was engaged in changed in nature and we began to design demobilisation centres which included medical examination halls similar to that when I received my call up papers.

Krasnaya Presnaya

1969 saw the beginning of the struggle to assist the oppressed Jewish people in the Soviet Union. Only then, were trickles of information penetrating the iron curtain, only then, were the pathetic pleas for help beginning to be heard. At first many disbelieved that the Jews in the Soviet Union were being oppressed and others were cautious about taking any action in case it aggravated the situation. In addition, there were the strong and vocal apologists who felt it was their duty to discount such reports.

The pro-Soviet propaganda was all pervasive and persuasive. It was in this atmosphere that Dora and I joined other isolated but concerned individuals in trying to help our brethren in the Soviet Union. Each evolved their own means and methods but swiftly evolved into combined actions through mutual interest.

At first, the struggle would appear to be hopeless. Just a handful of ordinary people against the might of the Soviet Union which had done so much to destroy the invincible conquering Nazi war machine and that had occupied vast areas of Europe. In addition, the Soviet Union had the dreaded KGB and it's many agents and sympathisers overseas. The Soviet Union had unlimited funds at its disposal but we only had our own meagre means.

Our battles evolved in the form of protests and demonstrations and letters to the press, informing the public of the perilous situation of the Jewish people in the Soviet Union.

The Soviet government was very sensitive to this exposure as they had never before experienced anything like it.

Protests were held outside their embassy in London and demonstrations where ever any of their representatives or delegations were visiting.

The Soviet authorities very much disliked these demonstrations as, when their representatives returned home they reported to friends and relatives what they had seen and heard. These reports trickled back to the Jews and encouraged them in insisting on their rights in accordance with the written Soviet constitution and laws and also their rights under the various international treaties of human rights signed by the Soviet government.

Thus, when we heard in October 1974 that the London Borough of Hackney Council would be receiving and hosting for a week a fraternal delegation from Krasnaya Presnaya, a suburb of Moscow with which Hackney was twinned, we decided to hold a demonstration to highlight the plight of Soviet Jewry generally but also that of a Jewish family who lived in that district. (Krasnaya in Russian means, Red, Bright, Fine, Revolutionary whilst Presnaya means Fresh).

Out of courtesy we wrote to the Mayor of Hackney informing him of our intention and to ask if he would arrange for us to hand a letter to the leader of the Russian delegation. We assured him that as with all our demonstrations, it would be silent, dignified and peaceful.

The Mayor's reaction was, that if we agreed not to hold a demonstration, he would ensure that we would meet the leader of the Russian delegation in order to hand him a letter and as he himself spoke fluent Russian, he would act as our translator. He suggested that the best time for us to do so was on the 20th November 1974 when the delegation was to be formally received by the full Council in the Town Hall followed by an informal tea during which he would introduce us.

He suggested that we meet him beforehand to discuss details and wrote giving us a date and time.

When we turned up for this preliminary meeting we found the Town Hall to be in almost total darkness but there was a doorman on duty. We told him that we had an appointment with the Mayor. He surprised us by asking us if it was to do with the Russian party. We were surprised that a doorman would be acquainted with the purpose of our meeting. When we affirmed, he said, "Upstairs, committee room 2".

As we approached the committee room, the imposing mahogany door swung open and a man lurched out, the slightly worse for drink, and asked what we wanted. We told him that we had an appointment with the Mayor. He turned round and through the open door in a booming voice called out "Arthur, two of your mates here to see you". He then lurched off in the direction of the toilets undoing his fly as he went.

In the few moments it took for the Mayor to come to the door, we could see a very lively party in progress in the committee room with an abundance of drink and food and someone trying to do a Russian Kazatzka dance. The Mayor asked what we were doing there. We reminded him that we had an appointment but he said that it was for the following evening. We showed the letter that gave the date of the meeting for that same day. He glanced behind him to make sure the door was closed and said quite unexpectedly "There are no Russians in there and there is no party". If indeed it was a normal Council Committee in progress, it was certainly a strange one. We noticed that all down the Mayor's tie were fresh drips of food on top of old stains. The Mayor was not in his ceremonial attire.

Whilst ushering us out of the Town Hall, he reminded us that there was to be no demonstrations and that we were to stay close by him during the whole of the formal Council reception and meeting to be held on 20th November 1974.

At the meeting and reception it was not a case of us staying near him as his staying near us. He neglected all his other obligations and duties to stay as close as possible to us during the whole evening.

Every so often when we saw that the leader of the Russian delegation, Mr D.G Borisov was not engaged, we asked the Mayor to introduce us but he insisted each time that it was not opportune. As the evening progressed, we had the suspicion that he had no intention of introducing us, so we made the reasonable excuse that we had to go to the toilets. At this, he nearly went into a panic and called a young man over and asked him to escort us to the toilets and to bring us straight back to him.

The young man had urgent need to occupy one of the WC cubicles and whilst he did so, Dora and I slipped back without him into the reception and went straight up to the leader of the Russian delegation. We handed him the letter we had prepared in a sealed envelope but before we could say anything he said in perfect English "Is this about the Jewish family you want me to help ?" We said "Yes" and he assured us that it would receive his personal attention. We had decided, not to press the question of Soviet Jewry in general but to bring his attention to one particular family domiciled in his district of Moscow who had been denied the constitutional right to emigrate.

After we had passed our letter to Mr Borisov we returned smartly to the Mayor and said that as it was getting late we have to leave immediately. He wished us bon voyage but did not ask if we would like to meet Mr Borisov before we left. He most courteously escorted us to the Town Hall door.

About a month later we were most surprised to receive a registered letter from Mr Borisov signed in his capacity of 'Chairman of the Executive of the Krasnaya Presnaya District of Moscow'. He assured us that he had studied our letter very carefully and had approached the relevant authority to have the Smelyansky family's application to emigrate re-examined".

We replied immediately by registered post to the address in his letter heartily thanking him for what he had done.

A short while after, our letter was returned to us by the Russian Postal Authority on the grounds that the address was not correct. We confirmed the address with Hackney Council who assured us that it was correct and it was the same one that they regularly used in correspondence with their twinned city. We returned the letter for redelivery and on 13th May 1975 received confirmation from the Russian Post Office that it had been delivered. In June 1975 we heard that Councillor Arthur Super who had previously been the Mayor of Hackney was going to visit Mr Borisov in the course of his civic duties. We handed a pretty silk ladies scarf to Councillor Super and asked him to present it to Mrs Borisov as a token or our appreciation for what her husband had done. He was not at all keen in doing so saying that he doubted if she would accept.

We wrote to Mr Borisov explaining what we were doing and received a polite acknowledgement.

On the 26th August 1975 on his return from his Moscow visit, Councillor Super wrote that Mr Borisov had indeed refused to accept the token gift and denied having met us during his visit to Hackney. He was also unhelpful concerning the Soviet Jewry problem. It was many years later that the Smelyansky family was permitted to emigrate in order to be re-united with their family in Israel.

Arthur Super retired in 1979 from the Hackney Council and worked voluntarily as treasurer for the National Council for Soviet Jewry which was the umbrella organisation for all the voluntary Soviet Jewry groups in Great Britain. He had since died.

The Reward

When the car body repairer 'phoned to let me know that my car which had recently been damaged in an accident in a deserted car park was ready for collection, Dora said that she would like to accompany me to collect it. She said that after I collected it from the repairers situated in East Ham, I could drop her off in Barking where she would like to do some shopping.

We walked down to Ilford High Road, where we could catch a bus that would take us direct to East Ham. As we approached we saw a large brown suit case tied up with rope to the bus stop.

I said to Dora, I don't like the look of that, its very suspicious, it may be a bomb, let's carry on walking to the next bus stop. Because I said it may be a bomb, Dora naturally said, "It can't be, who on earth would want to blow up a bus stop?"

Anyway, she said, "Somebody may have lost the case and there may be a reward in returning it". I politely pointed out that anyone losing suitcase would not tie it up first to a bus stop. Dora persisted, she said, "OK", and agreed that we walk onto the next bus stop, but as we would be passing the local Ilford Police Station which is just a hundred yards or so up the road, we could leave the case with them and claim any reward that may have been offered to the finder.

I have to admit, it is far easier to agree with her than to try and install sense.

We carried the case into the Police Station and told the young constable on duty at the enquiry counter that we had just found a case and would like to claim any reward for its safe return to the owner.

The constable was polite and pointed out that there were already about eight people waiting and if we took a seat, we would be seen to in due course.

282

We said that we could not wait and would therefore forego any possible reward and just leave the case to be reclaimed by its owner. The constable said that that would not be possible as it was his duty to record full particulars of finders, location of find etc. etc. so would we please take a seat and wait. We replied, that if that was the case, we would return the case to where we had found it. He said that if we did so, he would be obliged to arrest us for not properly reporting lost property, for refusing to give the particulars required by law, for returning property, knowing or suspecting that it had been lost and if we returned the case to the bus stop, for abandoning property on the public high way to the danger of the general public. He further added that if the case should contain a bomb, there could be much more serious charges involved. He assured us that it would be in our best interest to take a seat and await our turn in order to report the finding of a lost item.

After about half an hour, it was our turn to be dealt with by the firm but polite constable. After carefully noting the required particulars on an appropriate form, he asked if we knew what was in the case. When we said that we didn't, he said, he would have to list the contents and get us to verify that the list was correct. When he opened the case which was not locked but tied up with a rope we saw, or rather smelt, that the case was full of filthy, stinking men's underwear and socks.

We were just about to ask the constable if it would not just be possible to describe the contents collectively rather than individually when a ruddy faced, stubble bearded man, smelling strongly of alcohol stumbled into the enquiry room. He shouted out that he had been robbed, that his suitcase had been stolen by some despicable unknown, illegitimate person who should be hung for the crime against such a law abiding person such as himself.

Spotting the case on the counter, he shouted, "That's it! That's me case. I only left it for five minutes whilst I went to get a cup of tea and when I returned, someone had stolen it!" I thought, tea today has an aroma strongly akin to alcohol.

Fortunately for us, the constable explained that it had not been stolen but handed in by a couple of concerned citizens believing it had been lost.

The constable did not ask for evidence of ownership and quickly closed the case and handed it over to the claimant who had to sign for it.

The man turned his bloodshot eyes on us and shouted, "In future, mind your own bloody business". Then in a sudden change of mood said, "I suppose you meant well" and taking a 50 pence coin from his grubby purse pressed it into Dora's hand and said "Here, buy yourself a cup of tea."

William

I suppose that I should have been suspicious when Tony took an interest in the condition of the paintwork on my house. He pointed out that the paintwork was beginning to look quite shabby and said that it was not like me to neglect it. It was quite true, when I was salaried I used to spend some weekends or part of my summer leave touching up and washing down the paintwork, which as a result was always spic and span. Tony had hit a sensitive point. I told him, that since becoming self employed, I was so busy that I did not have the time to attend to such things as the paintwork.

He then told me, that fortunately, he knew someone who could do the paintwork for me at a very cheap price. He said that often he was fully engaged but at present was free to do the painting. He said he would ask his acquaintance, William, to call on me and give me an estimate.

William's estimate was exceedingly cheap, he could, if I agreed, start work the following morning. His estimate was for labour only, I was to supply all materials and tools etc.. Dora pointed out, that at Willy's rate, it would not pay me to do the painting myself in the future, as on a time basis, I could earn much more at my own work.

Willy turned up sharp at 9am the following morning and I had already prepared the tools and materials he would require. A clean pair of overalls, an extending ladder, a painters kettle and hanging hook, an assortment of brushes, paint cleaner, a bucket, sponges, rags, scrapers, putty knife, putty, paraffin blow lamp, paraffin and methylated spirits, a box of matches, a bottle of shellac stopper, lead primer, undercoat and finishing paints.

Willy was very pleased with the provisions and said that he would start at the back of the house. After about half an hour I went out to see if there were any snags and saw Willy gazing disconcertingly at the blow lamp. He asked if I would rather that he used chemical paint stripper instead of the blow lamp. I said, certainly not and then asked if he had had any problem with the blow lamp which I had used myself many times. He confessed, that he had never used a blow lamp before and also that he had virtually no previous experience in house painting but, if I was to advise him, he would be only too glad to carry on. I duly showed him how to light the blow lamp and carefully supervised each stage of the work. He was keen to learn and was a willing and hard worker.

The next morning, he did not turn up and we thought that he had changed his mind but soon after lunch he came along, bright and cheerful and carried on working. He apologised and said that he had to see someone urgently.

The following day, a smart looking gentleman enquired if Willy was employed by us on painting the house and if his work was satisfactory. We assured him that we were so far quite pleased with him and would recommend him for similar work. The man went away, apparently satisfied.

A couple of days later, when Dora went round the corner to the greengrocer, she noticed that he had a nice colourful shop blind. When she commented on it, the greengrocer said that the man we had recommended had done it for him very cheaply. It turned out that it had been Willy who had canvassed all the shop keepers in the parade to renovate their blinds and using our name as a reference. He had told them all, that he was working for us.

When he had finished the preparatory work, he brought along a young lad who he said would help him finish the job. The lad also had had little experience in painting and was also keen to learn.

The day after the lad had started work, the same man who had made enquiries about Willy came back and made similar enquiries about the lad. This puzzled us and we asked Willy what it was all about. He apologised and explained that the lad was on probation and Willy had volunteered to employ him and as an aid to his rehabilitation. He assured us that we had no cause for alarm as the lad had not been convicted for any dishonesty. He said he was a 'lover boy' and tapped the side of his nose knowingly. He may have known why being a lover boy was not a dishonest crime but we certainly did not and still do not. He said that the man making enquires was most likely the lad's probation officer making sure that he was being gainfully and honestly employed. He said that he felt an empathy for the lad who was a close neighbour's son because he himself had been in a similar predicament when he was about the same age. He admitted that he himself had been in prison for petty thieving but had learnt his lesson. He realised that no temptation was worth the deprivation of freedom especially now that he had a son of his own. His wife had warned him that if he went to prison again, it would be the end of their marriage. He also mentioned the choice that he had whilst in prison of 'doing my bird soft or hard'. We never found out quite what he meant by this.

Whilst he was working on our house, several people asked for his telephone number and promised to contact him in the future. They took it, that if he was good enough to work for me, he was good enough to work for them.

One such person was Leon. He had arranged a labour only contract with Willy and agreed to supply all the materials and implements required and to leave them in the unlocked garage.

Willy turned up one day when Leon had gone away on business for a few days and started work on the house. He obtained the materials and tools as arranged from the garage and as there was very little preparatory work to be done, completed the contract in a few days whilst Leon was away.

When Leon returned, he was shocked to see the newly applied paint peeling and curling. To his horror, he found that Willy had used the wrong paint, he had used an interior emulsion instead of the gloss exterior paint. When he refused to pay Willy for his labour he received sinister threats which really frightened him.

Leon contacted a good friend he had in the Police who looked up Willy's criminal record. He found that in addition to the petty crimes in his youth to which he had confessed to us, he had a long list of convictions in his adult years for burglary and safe breaking in which he specialised.

His last conviction for which he had only recently been released was for attempted murder of a policeman. Willy never did carry out his threats to Leon.

One day, whilst Willy, who the police knew as Willy the Weasel was working for us, he asked if we would like to buy a lovely Chinese rug which was going very cheaply. We told him that we were not into such luxuries as we could hardly afford linoleum floor covering. He did not press the offer and said that he had only made it as he appreciated all that we had done for him and for the lad who was on probation.

When we next met Tony, we asked him if he knew about Willy's criminal record when he introduced him to us. He said he did, but was not concerned as Willy was notorious for not stealing anything unless it was first locked up in a safe.

He said that he had introduced Willy to us because Willy owed him money and he thought that if he did the job for us, he would have the money to pay for the lovely Chinese rug which he had recently sold to Willy and for which he had not yet paid.

The Burglar

Dora and I were both in a good mood because we had been to our dentist for our biannual check and he had not found anything wrong.

Just as we neared home, I spotted a black youth struggling with the weight of a very heavy suitcase. As it was a very hot clammy day I felt sorry for him and said to Dora, "I'll see if he would like a lift." Dora said, "It's dangerous to give lifts to strangers, you just don't know what you might be letting yourself in for." By the time she had finished warning me, we were alongside the youth who looked at me rather anxiously. I had no alternative by then than to ask if he would like a lift.

At first he declined my offer but before I could drive away he had a rapid change of mind and expressed his appreciation of my generosity. He said that even though he did not have far to go, the heat was making it very difficult.

He placed the case in the boot and I drove him to his bed-sitter which was only in the next road. He was most appreciative and said that maybe he will do the same for us one day. We were both impressed with his politeness and manner. A few minutes later we returned home glowing in the knowledge that we had not only escaped treatment by our dentist but that we had done a good deed and earned the gratitude of a neighbour. Dora said, "What a pleasant fellow, it goes to show that not all the youth today are bad."

As we got out of our car, we spotted an excited group of people and a police car in front of a close neighbour's house. When we enquired, we were told that the neighbour had only just popped round the corner to collect her widow's pension but when she returned she had found her front door smashed open and her video recorder and jewellery missing. In the short while she had been gone, she had been burgled. She was far from rich and the burglary was a great shock to her.

It was then, that we recalled the black youth and the heavy suitcase. We told the Policeman who was taking the details, about the black youth and told him where the youth lived. The next day, a detective called to see us to take details. He told us that they had called at the address we gave them and found not only the items stolen from our widowed neighbour but also many other items stolen from several nearby houses. What they had found was virtually an Aladdin's cave of treasures. It appeared that the youth had a girl friend living in a first floor bed-sitting room and she spent all day watching and logging the movements of the neighbours. When she felt it safe, she phoned her boyfriend who had a stolen mobile phone and told him which premises it was safe for him to enter. She then kept watch and in the event of any possible danger, she would 'phone him again in order to warn him.

Dora turned round to me and said, "I told you he looked dodgy and it was lucky that she had taken careful note as to where he lived."

The detective congratulated Dora on her astuteness and for being wise enough not to tackle the suspect as many might have been tempted, but by a clever ruse discovering where he stored his ill gotten gains and informing the police accordingly.

The youth was subsequently tried and found guilty and was sentenced to six months prison but the sentence was suspended on the condition that he did not visit his girl friend who lived in our street. Soon after, she moved out to an adjoining street.

Dora is quite the heroine among the neighbours now.

Esther and Jack

Esther was always vibrant and overwhelming. She had dark Gypsy eyes and luxuriant black curly hair. A loud voice and infectious laughter. She was well endowed physically. Even as a schoolgirl teenager, her bosom was rather larger that the average. Not that I particularly noticed as I was several years her junior and did not take interest in such things at the time.

I had very little to do with her as she was my elder sister's school friend and they kept themselves very much to themselves. However, I do remember that when she came to our house, my father would hide the biscuit tin away as otherwise, Esther would consume the lot. My father used to buy large quantities of broken biscuits. He knew of a shop in the east end of London that sold mixed broken biscuits at a very cheap price. Whether there was a factory that specialised in producing broken biscuits or they were the result of bad handling, I do not know.

I did not hear any more from or about Esther for many years until after the war. She 'phoned me up, quite out of the blue one day and said that she had heard that I was a surveyor. Actually, I was not a surveyor but as an architect I did know something about building construction.

She said that she was now married and had a young child and was in the process of buying their first house and would like me to have a quick look at it before they completed the purchase. It was a small two storey terraced house near the Hoe Street market in Walthamstow, east London. The vendor was still in occupation.

I duly reported back to her by 'phone and told her of several serious defects. She said that she did not consider the defects so serious and was intent on completing the purchase in any event. She said that her husband, Jack, was very handy and would remedy the defects himself. Some while after she had moved in, she 'phoned again and invited me and Dora to drop in for a chat any time we were passing. We need not make an appointment as she was at home most times.

One day, when Dora and I were in the district I decided to pay Esther an unexpected visit. It was obvious when she answered the door that she did not recognise me. The last time she saw me was when I was a young snotty schoolboy and now I was grown up and sported a large bushy moustache. She had never met Dora before.

Esther looked just the same as. before but much more so. The devil must have got into me and in a flash I contrived to play a joke on her. On the spur of the moment, I invented a name and said that I heard that the house had changed hands and that I wanted to pay a sentimental visit. I told her that my best friend had in past years occupied the house and that his young and beautiful wife had been unfaithful. The torment had driven him out of his mind and that he murdered her. I was able to tell a convincing story because I was able to describe details of the house that only someone who was closely acquainted with it would know. Of course, I knew, because I had done a detailed survey.

Esther lapped it all up and kept urging me to tell more about the sad romantic tale. Dora was taken by surprise as this was not pre-planned and I was so convincing that even she began to believe it. Just as I was getting into my final stride and improving on my imagination the next door neighbour came in and when Esther told her what she had just learnt the neighbour became most agitated. She had lived next door all her life and she knew that there was not a word of truth in my story.

Suddenly, my nerve gave way and I confessed the truth and who I actually was. The resultant laughter was terrific and at least one pair of knickers became wet.

After this episode we kept in regular if not frequent touch with each other. We visited her more often than she did us because we had a car and she did not.

Esther's husband, Jack, was just the opposite to her. He was diminutive, quiet and prematurely bald.

Esther described that she first met Jack when they both belonged to the same predominantly Jewish rambling group. The girls and boys could, for a few hours at the weekends get away from the smog ridden streets of east London and enjoy some healthy exercise walking in the fresh air of the nearby beauty spots such as Epping Forest. They could not get up to much mischief whilst they were walking and the brief periods for refreshments were devoted to mild flirting.

Esther said that she fancied Jack and tried to attract his attention but he never seemed to notice her. She was aware of her own failings and when one day Jack asked her what size shoes she took, she nearly fainted with delighted surprise. She considered her small feet her best asset and was overwhelmed that Jack had noticed them. She coyly said, "Size 4". "Good", he replied, "Here stamp out my cigarette". They were the first words he ever spoke to her. They were treasured because he spoke so little. Even when we asked him questions, Esther would reply on his behalf while he muttered under his breath.

She told us that she tried to encourage him to speak more, and once when he was feeling affectionate she demanded that he say something sweet to her. He replied "Tate and Lyle Syrup."

Jack did not earn much. Although he was skilled cabinet maker the trade was in virtual permanent depression, he was often unemployed and when he did have work, was poorly paid. Esther did not go to work but supplemented their income by doing dressmaking at home. One evening when we were visiting them, there was a knock on the door. Esther said to Jack, "You answer it, its dark and you are the man of the house." He returned a short while after and said there was no one there. If there had been someone there they would have rung the bell. A short while after there was another knock on the door and again Jack said that there was no one there. On the third knock Esther said, "It must be the kids, I'll deal with them." When she opened the door, there was a frantic voice saying, "Its me, Michelle." Looking down, Esther saw a midget girl, she was one of Esther's customers. After collecting a dress that Esther had altered for her, she explained that the girl's mother was normal but she had inherited the dwarfism from her father who was classified disabled due to dwarfism. Because of his disability he could not find work and consequently received several benefits including the free service of having his house regularly re-decorated throughout by Council paid contractors. What the Council did not know, was that the girl's father was a skilled decorator and earned good money moonlighting. He easily made up for his lack of stature by the use of steps and ladders.

Once when we were in their company, Esther complained of having a lousy headache. Jack immediately said "Take a Keatings." For those who don't know what a Keatings was, it was a well known anti flea powder used on pets. It appeared that she did not even hear him and continued in her loud conversation. She never considered that it was her loud voice that may have caused the headache. One sunny Friday afternoon, I bumped unexpectedly into Esther as I emerged from the Shoreditch branch of Barclays Bank. I had just cashed my monthly pay cheque and was in a hurry to get back to the office. Most unusually, Esther was subdued, her eyes were red and she was obviously upset. She said that she had just been to the nearby hospital where Jack was lying seriously ill. He had suffered a serious heart attack and she was afraid that he may not survive. She was also frantic with worry as she had no money and she had a child to feed and a mortgage to pay. She said that despite their low joint income, they had never resorted to public assistance or charity and she just did not know what to do. Someone had told her to go to the Sailors and Soldiers Relief Fund as Jack would be eligible because he had served in the Royal Navy during the war. She had gone there and they had interrogated her. Among the questions asked was did any member of the family have any savings. Esther told them that Jack had ten shillings (50p) in a Post Office Savings book which he received when he was Bar Mitzva'd and kept for sentimental reasons.

They said that the rules took it, that anyone who could save money before the war must be from a rich family and would therefore not be eligible for relief now.

Under the circumstances what could I do? I reached into my pocket and handed her the whole of one month's salary. She was so distressed, I don't think that she actually knew what was happening. What surprised me most was that Dora agreed with what I had done. I really expected a proper rollicking when I got home.

Subsequently, when Jack recovered, we visited him at home and took with the customary bunch of grapes. We asked what may have brought on such a heart attack. Esther said, "Plenty" and turned to Jack and said, "Tell them about your war experiences." No sooner had he started that Esther explained that when he was in the Navy, his boat was torpedoed twice. He was rescued from the water twice and on the first occasion found himself drenched in oil swimming among his mates who were also drenched in oil but most of them were dead.

On the second occasion he was on duty in the chain chamber. This is a small steel compartment in which the anchor chain is wound and the personnel on duty have to be sharp in order not to be enmeshed in the chain, especially when it was being released. It was a most traumatic experience being trapped in this steel sarcophagus knowing that the boat had been torpedoed and was sinking. These experiences had haunted him ever after and he was most reluctant to talk about them. Esther only found out when she spoke to some of his shipmates.

After the war, Jack vent back to his trade as a cabinet maker. The trade had somewhat changed. Most of the furniture was being made in large factories on unskilled labour production line systems. Post war restrictions confined furniture to what was called 'Utility' which was superseded by 'Whitewood' furniture which was sent out of the factory with no finish, to be painted by the customers. There was little call for the skills in which he had been trained. He was therefore thankful when he was able to obtain a suitable job in one of the few remaining old fashioned craft workshops. There was however a problem. The workshop was in a multi-storey Georgian house in Charles Square in Shoreditch which was not suitable for the purpose. It was a veritable fire hazard. It only had a single unprotected timber staircase and there were wood shavings, sawdust and chips of wood piled up everywhere.

A thick layer of sawdust covered everything. The electric wiring was old and most dangerous. Worst of all, was the polish spraying carried out in the basement. In order to obtain the highest quality finish, high volatile, spirit based varnishes were used. The use of such polishes under the prevailing conditions was actually illegal. The conditions worried Jack very much and it often gave him nightmares but there was not much he could do as he knew he was hardly likely to find suitable work elsewhere. One day, his fears came true. There was a terrific explosion. Jack was blown into the street through an open window with his clothes alight. Fortunately the flames were put out before he was badly burnt. Several of his workmates were badly burnt and the two owners of the workshop were both killed.

Jack was forced to take a job in a large modern furniture factory as an unskilled machine minder. The work was boring but it was comparatively safe.

One dark murky morning, when cycling into work he noticed what looked like a sackful of rubbish lying in the gutter being splashed and sometimes knocked by passing vehicles. When he got close he realised it was not a sack of rubbish but one of his workmates who had been knocked off his bicycle.

Esther knew it was this last experience more than any other that caused Jack to have his heart attack.

All the while she was telling us this, Jack himself was quietly murmuring and muttering incomprehensible comments as he bent over his workbench in the front bay window repairing an alarm clock. As part of his rehabilitation, he had been taught clock repairing which he could carry out in the peace and quiet of his own home. The front lounge was full of old clocks waiting repair or collection.

When Esther's sister died we attended the funeral out of courtesy. We had never met her, but out of respect for Esther we went despite the atrocious freezing weather.

Just as the coffin was being lowered into the grave, Esther gave out a hysterical cry, she said it was the wrong grave. She told the officiating rabbi that her sister had reserved a plot directly alongside the grave of her first husband and Esther had noticed that neither of the adjacent graves were those of her first husband. The gravediggers said that the ground was frozen too deep and too hard to dig another grave immediately. We would all have to come back in a few days.

The rabbi and near relatives adjourned to the cemetery office and checked that Esther was correct and that a terrible mistake had been made. Whilst we waited in the bitter cold, the correct grave was dug and the interment quickly concluded.

Whenever, Esther and Jack came to us, Dora always laid on a nice tea and insisted that the tea be made in a warmed china tea pot.

Esther always criticised the delay in making tea in this fashion. She herself always used instant tea bags. On one visit, we timed it very nicely and as soon as they rang our doorbell, we opened the door and thrust a tray with cups of tea already poured out to them. Jack immediately said, "What kept you?"

Once again we lost touch with them and recently their daughter 'phoned to inform us that they have both died.

Esther's daughter has inherited her Mother's dark Gypsy features but not her rumbustious character. She was small, petite and very reticent. In this respect she seems to have inherited Jack's nature.

We recalled the daughter's wedding which took place in a registry office on a Saturday morning. She was married in a registry office because her husband was not Jewish and therefore could not be married in a synagogue. For religious reasons she did not wish to be married in a church. She wore a full traditional bridal outfit and the groom was appropriately dressed in a smart dark suit. The two bridesmaids were very pretty and wore beautiful dresses made by Esther. The principal guests all wore appropriate sober clothes.

We were surprised, when, after the ceremony, on the way to the restaurant where the celebration were to be held, the cars stopped outside a church. The wedding party got out and posed for wedding photos in front of the church. This we presumed was for the benefit of the groom's family who could not attend.

Just at that moment a group of people on the way home from the local synagogue after the Sabbath morning service were amazed to see some of their synagogue members posing for photos in front of a church

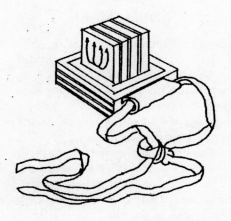

The Mongrel

Whenever I am in the vicinity and have the time to spare, I drop in for a chat with Hershel who runs the local Jewish book shop. He is also known as Hershel the Bershtel. Actually his name is Harry but prefers to be known as Hershel which is his Hebrew name which is derived from the word 'deer' but in its Yiddish diminutive form. Bershtal is a rhyming Yiddish word meaning little brush, no doubt alluding to his little black bristling beard. He is a devout Jew and apart from Jewish books both religious and secular, he also sells religious requisites such as Tallith (prayer shawls), candle sticks for the Sabbath candles, Menorah, nine branched candle stick for celebrating the festival of Chanukah which is Hebrew for 'dedication' which commemorates the ancient victory of the Maccabees over the Greeks and the re-dedication of the holy temple in Jerusalem which had been defiled by the Greeks. He also sold Yamulkas (skull caps), Yar Zeit candles which are used on the anniversary of the death of a near relative and many other religious objects including Mezuzoth (plural of Mezuzah) and Tefilin (Phylacteries) always in the plural form.

Mezuzoth are those things that one sees fixed to door frames in Jewish homes and other buildings. Tefilin are much less likely to be seen as they are normally only used by devout Jews during their early morning prayers.

Both Mezuzoth and Tefilin are cases for strips of parchment onto which learned scribes have meticulously written by hand extracts from the Old Testament, Exodus, Chapter 13 and Deuteronomy chapter 6 which include the words "Hear, 0 Israel, The Lord our God is one Lord; And thou shalt love the Lord Thy God with all thine heart and with all thy soul, and with all thy might. And these words, which I command thee this day, shall be in thine heart: And thou shalt talk of them diligently unto thy children and thou shalt talk of them when thou sittest in thine house, and when thou walkest by the way, and when thou liest down, and when thou risest up, And thou shalt bind them for a sign upon thine hand, and they shall be as frontlets between thine eyes. And thou shalt write them upon the posts of thy house, and upon thy gates."

The parchments within the Mezuzahs are the means by which Jews fulfil the writing upon the posts of their houses.

The parchments within the Tefilin are the means by which Jews fulfil the commandment to have them as a sign upon thine hand and as a frontlet between thine eyes. These commandments given by God direct to Moses on Mount Sinai are considered to be most sacrosanct and not to be deviated from by one iota. It is therefore, most important that the words be written most carefully by trained and skilled scribes. It is also held by some devout Jews, that even the slightest error in the wording could lead to terrible consequences.

Such an alleged error is claimed by some to have led to the tragic deaths of 36 Jewish children who were gunned to death by Arab terrorists when their clearly marked school bus was ambushed near Maalot, a farming village in North Israel.

Jewish scholars claim to have found an error in the schools Mezuzah which indicated the figure 36.

Scribes and vendors of Mezuzoth therefore feel that they have great moral responsibility to ensure that the parchments within the Mezuzoth and Tefelin they sell are 100% correct.

Hershel therefore, obtains the parchments only from scribes he has great confidence in.

This all leads up to why, when I last visited Hershel's shop, that I found him in an extremely excited and agitated state.

As usual, he greeted me in his friendly manner. After enquiring about my health and that of each member of my family that he was aware of, he asked. "Have you heard about Mrs Bloom's Tefilin?" In the good old Jewish manner I responded with a question, "Is this a joke?" He said "No its very serious" and went onto explain. Mrs Bloom had brought in a pair of Tefilin which she had not long before bought for her son on his Barmitzvah. The boy had negligently left the Tefilin on a chair after using them during his morning prayers. The family had recently acquired a stray playful young mongrel dog, who, not realising the sacred significance of the Tefilin exercised its teeth upon them. Fortunately, the Tefilin were rescued before they were too badly damaged.

Mrs Bloom had brought the damaged Tefilin to Hershel and asked if he could get a qualified scribe to examine the parchments carefully and if retrievable, to put them into new cases.

Hershel had immediately noted that the tefilin had not been supplied by him but agreed to comply with Mrs Bloom's request as she was normally a good customer and friend.

The scribe duly declared that even though the parchments had not been irretrievably damaged, they were, nevertheless 'posal', that is , not fit for use because they contained three errors in the text.

Hershel passed this information onto Mrs Bloom and asked her where she bought the Tefilin from. She said that she bought them through a local rabbi because she thought that they would be more reliable than if she had bought them from Hershel.

In a way, Hershel was pleased about this episode as there had been some bad feeling because Hershel thought that the rabbi in question was exploiting his prestige to gain commercial advantage for a religious charity trust he was associated with locally who sold similar artefacts as Hershel did. Hershel thought it was difficult enough to make a living without such unfair competition.

When Hershel explained the possible drastic consequences the errors in the Tefilin may have led to, Mrs Bloom, said that it was as though the Almighty himself had sent the stray mongrel their way so as to warn them of the potential danger. She said that she would take special care of the dog as a reward. The dog was consequently pampered by the family, but not for long. One day it slipped out and got run over by a lorry. Maybe the defects in the Tefihin had predestined the mongrel's fate.

When Dora heard about the matter she became concerned about the Mezuzah fixed to our front door post. I assured her that she should have no qualms about it. I fixed it myself when we moved in about 40 years ago and that no great tragedy had occurred since. Dora said that in 40 years the parchment and its wording could well have deteriorated and may lead to terrible consequences.

I told her not to be concerned in that respect, as there was no parchment what-so-ever inside the case. At the time, I could not afford to buy one complete with parchment.

Harry Berg

Harry passed over to the great boot sale in the sky many years ago. May his soul rest in eternal peace, that is, if he has not already sold it on to the second hand market.

I don't know if Harry based himself on the famous, artful TV car dealer character, Arthur Daly, or the other way round. There were many similarities between the two, both physical and in mannerisms. They were both about the same age, build and dressed alike; natty little trilby hat, camel hair overcoat, brown suede shoes, rose in lapel, flashy tie and gold plated teeth.

In addition, Harry had a squint in one eye that gave him a rather sinister look but he had a heart of gold which he would have sold if he could only have found a buyer.

He was a trier and having, rather unsuccessfully, tried making an entrepreneurial livelihood in many fields set himself up in the fast expanding bric-a-brac market in the 1960's.

Like most of the others in this particular commerce, he knew very little about it but was willing to learn and to use his intuition. Fortunately for him, there was an abundance of items around to buy and sell and those selling to him usually knew less than Harry did about the goods and so he was able to make a reasonable profit.

There was much he had to learn the hard way.

He opened a shop in a sunny parade in Walthamstow in east London. It is by far not a posh area and most, if not all, of his customers were local working class people. Fortunately for him at the time, there was an influx of Asian immigrants from India and Pakistan who were setting up home in the locality. They had little money to spend so keenly bought the second hand furniture etc. that Harry had to sell. They spoke little or no English but knew such phrases as 'How much' and 'Too much'. Sometimes, they brought with colleagues who could speak a little English to act as an interpreter.

One day an Asian lady and a companion came in to buy a used aluminium saucepan. They spent nearly all day 'how muching' and 'too muching' until he physically ejected them from the shop. That did not prevent them coming back the following morning for a repeat performance.

A more promising customer was an Asian gentleman who said he wanted to buy sufficient items to fully furnish a two bedroom flat that he wished to let off He bought up nearly every item Harry had in the shop but haggled over the price of each and every, item. It was hard work for Harry but he kept his temper. When the gentleman had finished buying, Harry totalled up the bill and then the customer demanded a large percentage discount for mass purchase. Having got over that problem without throwing the customer out of the shop, the gentleman said that he assumed that the final agreed figure included delivery. Harry explained that because he had to pay someone to deliver his goods he usually made a charge for delivery. Not wishing to loose such a good sale, he reluctantly agrees to make a free delivery. The Asian gentleman, thereupon wrote the address upon a piece of paper and said he will pay for the goods upon delivery. After he had left, Harry looked at the address and saw that it was in Birmingham. As far as is known, the Asian gentleman is still waiting in Birmingham to receive the goods.

Harry was that much wiser, so that when another Asian gentleman bought a lot of items, he gave a generous discount but only having first generously increasing the prices. He also insisted on the goods being paid for before leaving the shop and carefully ensured that the address for delivery was local. When the hired van arrived at the address, the purchaser pointed out that the flat was on the fourth floor but there was no lift. Harry delivered the goods but left them all on the pavement for the customer to carry up to the flat. Harry was very proud of his shop and always arranged the goods in an attractive manner. The previous occupant had formed a continuous shelf at cornice height all around the shop. On this shelf, Harry displayed his prize china plates, jugs and fine porcelain figurines. It had the advantage that customers could not easily reach them, with the possibility, of dropping them. Harry carefully handed down for inspection any of the items a customer may have been interested in. Unfortunately for Harry, he was superstitious so that when a young black cat wandered into the shop one day, Harry took it as a good omen. He made a fuss of the cat who enjoyed the attention and to display his appreciation purred loudly and rolled over on its back. When Harry stopped in order to serve a customer, the cat sought to attract further attention and leapt onto a chest of drawers and from there onto the top of a wardrobe and then onto the China display shelf. It thought it was a wonderful game to shove the plates and figurines off the shelf whilst Harry frantically tried to catch it. Lucky or not, the cat is no longer welcome in the shop.

As the shop was too small, carpets were unrolled and displayed on the public thoroughfare. On such occasions Harry had to be careful to stop passing dogs leaving their seal of approval on the display carpet.

One day, when we visited Harry's shop, he had a lovely Turkish carpet on display in front of the shop. It was reasonably priced as none of the locals were interested because it did not look modern. They preferred the rubber backed rubbish that is misleadingly sold under the description 'carpet'.

We bought it and told Harry not to bother to deliver as we had our own vehicle with us which due to economic reasons was a van with windows cut in the side.

It was not until Harry helped me to load the carpet into the van, that I realised just how heavy it was. Between us, with much groaning and puffing we got the carpet loaded. We next visited my parents and it was rather late in the evening by the time we got home and it was too late to ask our friend who lived across the road to give me hand in unloading.

I opened our front gate and door wide and also that of our kitchen which was opposite the front door. Between Dora and myself we loaded the rolled carpet onto my back and I started to totter towards the front door. My objective was to stagger into the hail and drop the carpet there until I could get help. As I tottered up the front path into the hall I found that the impetus was such that I could not stop. I continued, bent double with the carpet on my back until I was violently stopped by colliding with the kitchen door that led onto the rear garden. It was fortunate that the door was securely bolted otherwise I would have continued staggering into the rear garden. I collapsed with the carpet pinning me down to the floor. Our poor cat who had been patiently waiting at the rear door anxiously to be let out to do her toilet and to respond to invitations from local Toms disappeared and we did not see her again for five days. When she did return, she looked decidedly pregnant.

One day, a young couple asked Harry to buy their pride and joy, a very expensive, almost new gas cooker. They were splitting up. Harry paid them cash on the spot after inspecting their fully paid receipt. Their marriage had failed and they were separating. As soon as they received the money they divided it 50/50 between them.

The woman had been a terrible slut and even though the cooker was quite new, it was filthy. Harry got a local youth to give the cooker a thorough cleaning, both inside and out until it gleamed and shone like new. The cleaned cooker was put on display outside the shop and within a few days the man who sold it to him said he would buy it. His new girlfriend had seen it and liked it very much and the man said it was very much like the cooker his separated wife had chosen when they got married.

When we set up home, Dora and I bought a drab bed with a wooden head board. It was all we could afford at the time so when I spotted a metal bedstead at the back of Harry's shop I was very interested. The bedstead looked as though it was constructed of iron, it was entirely black. I liked the design and had visions of what it would look like when painted in white with features picked out in gold. Harry said I could have it for its scrap iron value of fifteen shillings which in today's money is seventy five pence and that included transport.

As soon as I started to clean it, I realised that it was not constructed of iron but of solid brass. It took me ages to polish and lacquer but now stands as a gleaming memorial to the departed vendor, may he never find out that it was brass and not iron and may his soul therefore rest in peace.

Selling is only one part of the problem in running a bric-a-brac business. In most businesses it is possible to stock your shop by ordering in quantity from a catalogue or from a travelling salesman and the goods are subsequently delivered to the buyer but it is not so in the case of bric-a-brac. Usually, one has to visit the premises where the goods are for sale and articles are purchased individually.

Harry was called to house of a dying woman by her sister. The dying woman was lying in bed groaning with pain. The sister showed some items that the dying woman wanted to sell in order to pay for her funeral. Each time Harry offered a price the dying woman croaked out "Not enough" between her groans. After a while Harry realised that he was on a wild goose chase and turned to the dying woman and shouted, "Have you got nothing better to do in your condition that to waste my time? Don't you realise that as soon as you have gone, your relatives will snatch everything and sell them for next to nothing and if they are not able to get that diamond ring off your finger, they will cut your finger off to get it!" With that he stormed out of the house.

One day, we were lumbered with a large, very heavy, chest of drawers with a marble slab top. It was constructed of Cuban mahogany and had two large doors enclosing the drawers. It is known in the trade as a commode but it is nothing to do with the receptacle normally associated with this name. It was a beautiful piece of furniture but we had no room for it. We asked Harry if he would be interested in buying it. He explained that there was not much call for French Empire 2nd Period style furniture in east London. He said that he knew a 'runner' that is a freelance agent who bought on behalf of posh antique shops in the West End and Chelsea etc., who may be interested. Harry told us, that if there was any potential, the 'runner' would ask us how much we wanted. If he did so, we would know that it was valuable and that we should not sell it to him as he would not pay what it was worth. If he is not interested, he will just walk out of the house. The 'runner' called looked at the item, shoved the marble top aside and walked straight out of the house mumbling "A waste of time and petrol." We found out later that our commode was a contemporary copy of one made by the famous French cabinet makers of the time and if it had been a genuine one, it would have had the makers' name branded on top under the marble slab, "Les Freres Jacques." In which case it would have been very valuable.

After we knew Harry for a while, he invited us round to his house for a coffee and to see the way he had decorated and furnished it. He told us with pride, that he had impeccable taste and had kept the cream of everything that passed through his shop for himself.

He showed us round the house, but even before we entered, we had a foretaste. His front garden was scattered with garishly painted concrete gnomes. On the roof was a black painted concrete cat stalking grey coloured concrete pigeons. The front door bell gave a long chime of several popular tunes before it stopped. Everything inside the house was garish and crude; unbelievably so. He was so obviously proud and kept asking us what we thought We kept saying "Very nice" or "Very extraordinary" etc., etc.

Suddenly, half way down the stairs he turned round and shouted, "You are taking the Mickey out of me!" He rudely shoved us towards and out of his front door. We never had the coffee and he refused to have anything further to do with us. May he rest in peace.

Honeymoon

If you think that I am going to describe in lurid detail the events on my honeymoon then you will be disappointed but I can assure you that it was most pleasant and successful.

Without any parental financial assistance what-so-ever, we had, out of our own very meagre means paid for the wedding reception, bought a house and furnished it. We had very little to spend on a honeymoon.

We spent the wedding night at a three star dingy hotel in the west end of London. Food was still on ration even though the war had finished three years previously. We had to queue for a tasteless, cold, meagre breakfast and considered ourselves fortunate that Dora's boss had used his influence with the management to book the room for us and that we did not have to surrender any of our precious food coupons. Dora's boss was a solicitor who had influence with the hotel management because he regularly booked rooms so as to enable his clients who wished to be divorced to be 'caught' by a private investigator in the room with a person of the opposite sex to whom they were not married.

Early the following morning, we caught a train to Combe Martin on the north coast of Devon overlooking the Bristol Channel. Combe Martin is a small village, some 200 miles from London and ten miles from Barnstable and five from Ilfracombe, situated on the edge of Blackmoor and not far from Morte Bay and Baggy Point. It is also not far from Lynton and Lynmouth which not long after our honeymoon was subjected to disastrous flooding.

We were to spend our honeymoon on a small isolated farm overlooking the bleak Blackmoor whose main asset, as far as we were concerned was that it charged what we could afford to pay, which was very little. In return, the fare was commensurate. From Barnstable railway station we took a dilapidated taxi to our destination. The taxi driver was equally dilapidated, dressed in shabby, dark suit, black tie, dirty shirt and peaked cap. Although he smelt strongly of beer he negotiated the winding bends in the narrow country roads very skilfully. On the way, he informed us, without removing the cigarette from his mouth, that despite the fact that London had been heavily bombed and burnt, they in Devon seemed to have food galore. No doubt, he intended to cheer us up. We never did ascertain what the farm where we were staying produced, but it would appear that a good part of the farms income was derived from paying guests such as ourselves. There was a family of six staying at the farm at the same time. To us, they were rich because they ran a car, a luxury to which we did not aspire at the time. The head of the family was a health fanatic and seemed to thrive solely on bread and jam and hot water. He was a picture of robust health.

The farmer and his wife were also a picture of robust health, somewhat in their early forties, and we were soon to learn that neither farming nor hosting were their primary preoccupation but having affairs. Our fellow guests who holidayed at the farm regularly filled us in with the full details.

There was one other occupant in the farm; an old lady who sat all day by the fireplace in which a fire continuously burnt even though it was September and the weather was fine and warm. She did not join in any of the conversation as she was hard of hearing and the metal trumpet she applied to her ear did not seem to help.

We were shocked to hear the farmer and his wife openly make disparaging and cruel remarks about the old lady and even our fellow guests were rude about her. We thought, that it was a good thing that the old lady could not hear or else, she would, undoubtedly have been most annoyed and insulted.

We had a most enjoyable holiday. The countryside around Combe Martin was most beautiful and varied and we had lovely weather the whole time.

On the day that we were leaving, we had our bags packed and were waiting for the bragging taxi driver to take us back to Barnstable railway station, we bade farewell to the old lady. None of the others were in the room at the time. As we shouted our farewell she put her ear trumpet down and looking round to make sure no one else was present said, "There's no need to shout, I'm not as deaf as I make out to be. I can hear what you say and also I can hear what the other's say to and about me." She shocked us, she spoke quite clearly. She continued, "I noticed that you were the only ones who were not rude about me and therefore I trust you." She took a large sealed and addressed envelope out of her large leather handbag and

304

handed it to us. She said, "Please post this when you get back to London, it is to my solicitors and it is about my Will, you see this farm belongs to me but my daughter and her husband think they are automatically entitled to inherit it from me but when I am gone. They are both in for a shock, I will have the last laugh on them."

Even though we were tempted, we did not open the envelope to see what was in it. We duly posted it as requested when we returned to London.

The Specialist

Some years ago, I tripped over a protruding paving slab and badly injured my left arm and bruised my face. The local Council's contractors who were in the course of re-surfacing the public footway had left their work in a dangerous condition overnight. When taking my early morning constitutional my foot caught on a projecting paving slab. I immediately went home and gave myself first aid, changed my clothing which had become damaged and returned with my camera. I recorded photographically the offending slab and the way the contractor had so cordoned off the street that there was no alternative but to walk over the dangerous section of footway.

The contractor's supervisor got to hear about the accident and offered an immediate cash compensation of £100. I told him that the damage to my clothes and wrist-watch alone was in excess of that amount. I also informed him that I would complain to the local Council and would make a claim for damages and compensation from them as they are by law responsible for the good and safe condition of the public footpath even though they may contract their work out.

I notified the Council that I would be making a claim against them. They replied that they had referred my letter to their insurers who would be contacting me.

When I received a letter from the Council's insurers I passed it to a solicitor who I had been told specialised in such cases.

Soon after the accident, I went to see my doctor who referred me to a Nose Throat and Ear Specialist because I had injured my nose when I fell. He also sent me to see an orthopaedic specialist who in turn sent me to have my arm x-rayed.

In due course, my solicitor sent me to both a private NT &E specialist and to a private orthopaedic consultant. The orthopaedic consultant sent me to have my arm x-rayed so that he could write a report in support of my claim.

His report was submitted to the Councils insurers who in turn sent me to see an ENT specialist about my nose and another orthopaedic consultant about my arm in order to ensure that my claim was not being exaggerated. Apparently, all the specialists agreed as to the extent of my physical damages as the insurers did not dispute the medical evidence.

Eventually, I was sent to see a private orthopaedic specialist in order to ascertain what remedial therapy I should undergo.

The specialist held his private consultations at his own home. He lived in a lovely ivy clad Georgian house overlooking a village green. His wife acted as his receptionist and let me in. He was sitting at an impressive desk but strangely he was sitting sideways on and spoke to me out of the side of his mouth. He examined my arm and told me to attend his private clinic where I would be shown by the therapist there, what exercises I should do.

As I went to leave, I noticed on a shelf in his consulting room six beautiful Burmese glass vases. I congratulated him on his collection and mentioned that I would have liked to have a similar collection but such glassware was far too costly for me to buy. He was quite pleased to have met someone who recognised and appreciated the items. He told me that he too, would not have been able to have purchased such costly items, but he had inherited then from his father who had been a keen collector of Burmese glassware. He saw me to the door and as he shook hands I noticed that he had a very dark brown skin. This confused me as up till then, I had the impression he was a white man. His posh double barrelled name and Oxford accent and his home, all gave the impression of a cultured, well educated, Englishman. Then I connected the Burmese glassware and in confusion thought that the man's father may have been Burmese and thus the reason for the dark skin and collection of Burmese glass.

The specialist sensed my confusion and explained that just up to when I called, he was stain varnishing a very tall bookcase. He went to put the steps away but forgot that the open tin of stain varnish was still on top of the steps. The varnish spilt and some landed on his head and ran down the right side of his face. He had instinctively wiped the stain and thus spread it further over his face He had to make a quick decision, whether or not to spread the stain to the other side of his face.

He decided not to and had hoped that if he sat sideways to me, I would not notice the stain on the right side of his face.

Scamp

The large Victorian house next door to
us had been converted into four self
contained single bedroom flats. They
were expensively finished and fitted luxuriously and looked very attractive. The
conversion work was executed under
the direction of a brilliant and charming
young architect.

As we lived next door, we took a keen interest in all stages of the work.
Only the best labour and materials were used.

We were, therefore, keen to see who our new neighbours were to be. It
was with great excitement that we watched the first removal van arrive and
unload. We were amazed to notice that instead of taking the furniture
straight indoors, they left everything on the paved forecourt parking area.

After an animated conversation, the removal men drove away leaving
the furniture and packing cases exposed on the forecourt of the house.

Moving among the furniture were two elderly ladies and two men, one
of whom frequently made frantic 'phone calls using his car telephone.
They were later joined by another man and all three men kept referring to
papers in bulky files that they were carrying. Eventually, curiosity overcame Dora who instructed me to ask if they would like a cup of tea and if
we may be of any help. They accepted the tea and biscuits which they consumed sitting on chairs set up on the forecourt. The two women were in a
very distraught state. They were sisters, one of whom was the purchaser of
one of the ground floor flats. They explained that it had been agreed
between the vendor's solicitor and the solicitor acting for the purchaser,
that a cheque for the full purchase price of the flat would be presented by
the purchaser's solicitor to the vendor's solicitor who would then hand over
the keys of the flat and the relevant legal documents. This was supposed to
have happened that very same morning. There was however, a problem.
The arrangement was that the requisite cheque was to be produced by the
solicitor acting for the local council who had agreed to loan the purchaser
the full purchase price. At the very last minute, the clerk acting for the

308

council's solicitor said that he cannot part with the cheque because he had discovered an inconsistency in the signatures on the legal documents. He said that on one of the documents the purchaser had signed her name as Eleanor Maria Northeast and on another she had signed E M Northeast. The purchaser explained that she was not consistent and sometimes signed her name fully and sometimes used her first name initials.

I was furious at the Council's clerk's stupid last minute obstructive heartless decision. He said that it was more than his job was worth to part with the Council's cheque when there was such a serious inconsistency in the legal documents. He seemed to relish in the aggravation he was causing.

When I told Dora what the situation was she said, "I will soon see to that."

She 'phoned a friend who was a senior Councillor on the local council and explained the situation to him and warned him that if the local newspapers got to hear of the situation, it would be front page news in the local press and possibly even the national press and TV would give such heartless bureaucracy full coverage. She also reminded him that the next local elections were not far off. Within 25 minutes a car pulled up and after a short and sharp conversation, cheque and papers and keys were exchanged and the men hastily carried the furniture and cases indoors.

This was our introduction to our new neighbour, Mrs Northeast, who for some unknown reason preferred to be known as Nellie. We were further amused because a Mr Southwest had recently moved into a flat a little further up the road. Nellie told us that she had recently lost her husband who had been a fireman until he retired. She had decided to sell her house and to buy a cosy small self contained flat to settle down in.

After a few months she missed her husband and felt lonely so she decided to get herself a companion, a dog. She acquired a Yorkshire terrier puppy. In her wisdom, as it was a small dog, she bought it a short lead and as a consequence when she took it out for a walk, she had to bend doubled up. It took her a few weeks to realise that a small dog actually required a long lead especially so, as Nellie was taller than average, she was about 6 feet (1800mm) tall.

It was possibly her height that attracted short men. On a dark evening, when taking Scamp out for a walk, Scamp was her dog's name, a short Irishman smelling strongly of beer tried to strangle her but had difficulty in reaching her throat. Whilst he was trying to kill her, Scamp was frantically biting her ankles.

On another occasion, when on a winter cruise to recover from the attack, she was amorously attacked by a short steward in the ship's lift. Despite keeping her right index finger on the emergency stop button the attack continued until the steward gave up in despair as he could not reach Nellie's lips.

She very rarely took Scamp out for a walk and when she did, it was usually just to the local shops, about 5 minutes away. The dog performed its natural functions in the small garden at the rear of her flat. The garden soon became covered with dog's mess and was a very unpleasant, weed ridden patch.

I felt sorry for the poor creature (the dog) and offered to take it with me when I went for my regular half hour early morning constitutional. The offer was gladly accepted by both Nellie and Scamp.

When I rang her bell sharp at 7am each morning, the dog would become hysterical with excitement. For the first five minutes of the walk it would appear that Scamp was trying to strangle himself by pulling so strongly on the lead. His hysterical tugging on the lead gave way to sniffing everything within the radius of the lead and without any prior indication he would dart in various directions and stop to sniff. Each time he did so, I also had to stop and wait until he had finished sniffing. My half hour walk thus became a one hour walk and the constant stopping and starting tired me out.

Apart from constant stopping to sniff, he often stopped without any prior indication to relieve himself. When it was to lift a leg and squirt, it was not too bad but he had the habit of suddenly squatting and emitting a foul smelling gluey substance on the footway. On every lamp post on the route that I took; there must be at least a hundred, there is a Council notice to the effect that anyone in charge of a dog that fouls the public footpath is liable to a fine of £400, that was roughly the equivalent to nine weeks of my old age pension!

I did a quick calculation and reckoned that in one week Scamp deposited at least £2800 worth of fines or the equivalent of more than a year's worth of my pension.

To add insult to injury, he once even did it on my brown suede shoes! But I don't know if the Council would count that as an offence as it was not on the public footpath although my shoe was at the time.

One morning when I popped into a local newsagent to pick up a newspaper, I tied him (the dog) to a pile of empty milk grates awaiting collection outside the shop. When I came out, he was not there, I saw him hysterically bolting up the street dragging the empty milk grate behind him. Luckily, there were no bottles inside. It took me quite a while to catch up with him. I am not physically built to catch up with hysterical dogs racing up the road dragging empty milk grates behind him.

Finally my nerves gave way and I had to explain to Nellie that if I continued to take Scamp for walks I could be made bankrupt and even have my house re-possessed in order to pay the fines for his misdemeanours, she accepted my resignation philosophically.

The fence dividing my garden and that in which Scamp used next door as his private lavatory was constructed of discarded wrought iron gates. It is very decorative. Whenever I went into my own garden, Scamp would rush over to the fence hoping against hope that I might relent and take pity on him and take him for a walk. Sometimes, he would rush towards the fence yapping madly with the hope that he would panic my cat and cause her to run up the old pear tree. He knew that when the cat ran up the tree, I had to get the ladder out and rescue her. It gave Scamp some satisfaction watching me carry out the rescue.

One day, when I went out into the garden I found Scamp whining madly with his head caught in one of the wrought iron gates. I tried to prise the two pieces of metal apart but was not strong enough to do so. I decided that I would have to cut the offending metal bars off but the sound of the saw only sent the dog hysterical and I was afraid that in his frenzy he would break his neck.

Nellie was not at home, so Dora came to the rescue by 'phoning the local fire brigade. One of their giant rescue appliances and six good, worthy and well trained firemen arrived with flashing lights and siren sounding away. They rescued Scamp using the same hydraulic tools that they use when rescuing people trapped in crashed cars.

It was Scamps hysteria that was to be his undoing. Nellie took him for a walk in a park near where her son lived. As there was no traffic in the park, she let him off the lead. No sooner had she done so, then literally quite out of the blue, there was a clap of thunder. That was a good enough excuse for Scamp to go hysterical and to run blindly out of the park and under the wheels of a passing lorry. The driver had no chance to avoid him.

Antique Clocks

It was with some great consternation that we heard that our friend, Andrew, had been seriously ill and for some time had been in intensive care. His wife told us that he had not fully recovered and was now convalescing at home. She said he would be glad to have some visitors, especially us, as we had known him for so many years.

We gladly accepted her invitation as we always liked to meet Andrew and his wife, a most charming couple but moreover, we loved to visit his beautiful home. When we entered the front door of his Georgian house in the quaint Essex village of Sawbridgeworth, it was like stepping back some 150 years in time. The furnishings were consistent with the period of the house itself. The atmosphere was enchanting. Andrew had been born into a poor but respectful family in the east end of London close to where Dora and I had been born, His father worked in the London docks and Andrew had left school at 15 years to be apprenticed to a tailor who specialised in making period costumes for stage and films. Through his study of the historical background to the costumes he helped to make, he became aware of the homes and furnishings of the periods.

At first, this interest was purely academic but as his knowledge grew, he began collecting and selling small antique items. In a few years, this hobby became so profitable, that when the firm he worked for got into financial difficulties, he was able to set himself up as a full time antiques dealer.

At first, he operated from a small shop in east London but as he was burgled so often, he started trading mainly from home.

His first house in Dagenham, east London was small and restrictive but as he prospered, he was able to buy his present home in Sawbridgewoth which was much larger. The pleasant, mellowed outside of the house was most deceptive because in a very clever unobtrusive manner, Andrew had virtually turned the premises into a fortress and was as practically possible, burglar proof.

The neighbours were not aware that Andrew traded from home, as he always loaded and unloaded his wares behind locked garage doors. The neighbours were mainly retired business and professional people and were far too polite to ask what Andrew did for a living and if they had, Andrew and his wife had a truthful but misleading reply prepared. We first got to know Andrew when quite voluntarily, out of the blue, advised us that some of the items we were selling at a charity jumble sale were worth much more than we were asking and to prove the point, he paid us his much enhanced valuation. In return, in future jumble sales we gave him first opportunity to buy before the public were admitted. He always volunteered generous prices for the items he was interested in. He explained, that he in turn, could get a good price for quality goods in which he specialised.

In the course of time, he concentrated more and more on quality antique clocks and barometers and became known in the trade for his specialisation. His knowledge on the subject was encyclopaedic. He would entertain us for hours describing the clocks and furniture he had retained for his own home. He would also tell us about the famous actors and actresses and opera stars he had met when he fitted their period costumes. He recalled, how, when the famous Bolshoi Ballet was performing in London, he was called upon to do running repairs to some of their costumes because they were so old and decrepit. Sometimes, he virtually had to sew the Bolshoi stars into their costumes. Apparently, despite their fame, the Bolshoi did not have the money to replace the disintegrating costumes.

Andrew had built up a very good reputation for supplying genuine, quality clocks and barometers and even though highly priced, his goods were in great demand especially so, in recent years, by very highly paid Yuppies working in the financial institutes in the City of London. They had the money and they wanted quality goods and they trusted Andrew to supply them.

We were received by Andrew and his wife in their usual charming manner. Success had not spoilt their attitude to old friends.

We asked Andrew as to how he had become so ill. He told us that some weeks previously, he had attended an auction in London at which he knew several excellent antique clocks would be on sale and which he needed urgently for his own business. He had bid high and obtained all the items he wanted. He was not unduly concerned about what he had paid because he had in his mind, at least one potential customer for each item who would be willing to give him a substantial profit.

The goods he bought at the auction amounted to over £150,000 which he paid for on the spot and loaded onto his old but reliable Volvo estate car. He used his old car for business in preference to his shining newish Mercedes so as not to attract attention to his activities. He, himself; was surprised that so little room in the car was taken up with £150,000 worth of goods.

He covered the items with a couple of old grey army blankets and started his journey home. All went well until a few miles from home when he was caught in a fierce snow storm.

All the traffic on the secondary road came to a standstill and the vehicles were soon engulfed in snow drifts. It all happened so suddenly.

After a couple of hours, the police came along and told the motorists that the local Council did not reckon to be able to clear that particular road until the following day. They volunteered to take all the occupants of the vehicles to a local village from whence they could make their way, home but they would have to abandon their vehicles until the road was clear.

Andrew thanked the Police for this kind offer but said that he would prefer to stay in his vehicle until the road was clear.

The Police kindly agreed to let Andrew's wife know the situation and that he was safe and well.

The night turned out to be exceptionally cold and Andrew was unprepared for such an eventuality. He had no food or drink in the car and even though he wrapped himself in the two army blankets he became increasingly cold. He, occasionally turned the car engine on in order to use the heater but could only do so for short periods as he was low on fuel.

Without realising it, he fell into a deep sleep and awoke the following morning frozen through and through. When he did get home, he realised that he had a severe cold which rapidly turned into pneumonia. He was rushed to hospital, where, for a time, he was in intensive care.

Dora asked him why he did not agree to be evacuated by the Police. Andrew said he could not because of the gear in the car. Dora asked why he did not get a car with an automatic gear like the one we had in our car.

Bert and the Bees

Mrs Norman and her lodger, Bert, were as different to each other as chalk is to cheese. It always puzzled us how it was that they got on so well as they did. Maybe it was because there was some degree of interdependence.

Mrs Norman was small in stature, some 4'6" (1370mm) in height and Bert was a strapping 5'11" (1800mm) robustly built young man about 35 years of age. Mrs Norman was old enough to be his mother.

Despite her shortage in stature, she was strong in character and most assertive. She had grown children, one son was about Bert's age but she had no husband. Whether she was a widow or not, none of the neighbours knew, but there were rumours about a difficult marriage. Both she and her son were committed Christians and were very active in the local church. She made no secret of her religious commitment and preached to all and sundry at each and every opportunity, even to the milk delivery man. Apart from her lodger, Bert, she lived alone in a large four bedroom house on the corner of the street which had the advantage of being only one of the four houses in the street which had a garage.

Apart from her much proclaimed religious conviction she was also a staunch Conservative Party supporter. At election times, all her windows would be plastered with large Tory party posters including the rear windows, kitchen and bathroom windows. However, there was one window with a small Labour Party poster and that was to Bert's bedsitter room.

Bert was not a Labour Party supporter. He was an ardent active member of the Communist Party but as they had no candidates, he tactically supported the local Labour Party at election times.

We don't know if Mrs Norman was aware of his political commitment but she should have known as Bert made no secret of his affiliation to the

Communist Party and of his hatred of the property owning bourgeoisie such as his own landlady. His feelings were that all landlords, and presumably all landladies as well, should be consigned to labour camps and their properties given to the working class of which, he naturally considered himself to be a member.

He was an atheist and scorned all religions. He had been married, and when we got to know him, he was either divorced or legally separated from his wife. One day, he showed us a photo of his wife and we noted that despite all his polemics the photo showed his wife in a white wedding dress whilst he was dressed in a smart morning suit and top hat. He confessed that he had married in a church but said it was only to please his wife's parents.

We got to know him fairly well because he liked coming into our house and doing DIY jobs. In return, he had his meals with us and he particularly enjoyed Dora's home Jewish cooking and my excellent wine. It was through the effects of the wine, that we learnt a lot of truths about him. It was after a couple of large glasses that he showed us his wedding photos. It would also be after an excellent meal and wine that he would expound on his political beliefs and declare that capitalists such as ourselves, that is Dora and 1, who gorge on such excellent food whilst millions of the working class starve will be forced to work, come the inevitable revolution.

We were curious to know, how it was, if he was a member of the working class, that he never appeared to be short of cash, wore Saville Row quality suits of which he had several, wore silk shirts and ties, expensive shoes, dined out at expensive restaurants, went to costly West End shows and drank heavily in public houses and wine bars and at the same time spent so much time at home, not working.

After the consumption of sufficient wine, he would reveal the secret. We already knew that he was a merchant seaman but he explained how the system operated.

No British Merchant Seaman was allowed employment on a British owned vessel unless he was a member of the British Merchant Seaman's Union. It was a closed shop. Seaman could work as and when they liked. If they wished to go to sea they would attend a special employment office where they would be told which boats would be departing in the near future and their destinations. The seaman would indicate which boat he would like to work on and if there was a suitable vacancy he would be assigned to that ship for that voyage. The office was run by the Seaman's' Union officials and the ship owners and officers had virtually no say in the matter. The Seaman's Union was dominated by members of the Communist Party.

As Bert was both a senior member of the Union and the Party he was always able to obtain the jobs that suited him.

He was qualified as a Quartermaster seaman which meant that his duties would include steering the boat. This was a very responsible job and required a lot of concentration and as a consequence he was required to work only two hours at a stretch and then two hours rest. The Watches were of eight hour shifts so he was only required to work four hours a day on a shift basis.

Normally Bert chose boats going on a long journey so that he would be away for a long period and he also chose boats that were scheduled to make several ports of call.

The working agreement between the Union and British Shipowners was, that each time a boat called into a port or left a port, the crew would each receive a £20 bonus. Considering that the basic seaman's wage at the time was £16 per week, this was very generous. In addition, as the working day was eight hours the remaining sixteen hours the crew stayed on board was considered as inevitable and unavoidable overtime and was paid at double rate. Another very generous bonus. As there were always additional duties to be performed on board that was not strictly those of seaman, such as painting etc., any such duties were paid for in addition to any other money earned.

Because there was virtually nothing to spend money on during the voyage, food and accommodation was free, the money accrued was out of all proportion to the basic wage.

An additional bonus was duty free goods brought back and consumed on each journey.

We also discovered by chance, another very generous tax free bonus that Bert enjoyed. When we were setting up home we avoided buying new furniture but responded to adverts in the local paper when people were disposing of surplus furniture or were emigrating. By this means we had acquired some very nice items at very reasonable prices.

It was in response to one such advert that we met Bert's mother. He was always going on about the deprived working class especially the poor old age pensioners and widows who were constantly on the verge of starvation and being evicted by greedy landlords. We were interested in acquiring a dining table and chairs that the advert mentioned. The address was in East Ham in east London. The house was luxuriously furnished and equipped with expensive TVs, video, dishwasher, washing machine, etc., etc.. It was obvious that the woman who owned it was living an opulent life. She told us that the table and chairs were only about a year old but she felt like changing it for another that she had seen in a shop window.

After we had paid her, she asked if we had far to go. When we told her that we lived in nearby Ilford, she said, so does my son and she gave the name of our road. It then transpired that she was none other that the woman that Bert had described to us as his poverty stricken old age widowed mother living in the east end of London. She was very proud of her son and told us that she regretted that he refused to live with her in her three bedroom house which she owned and presumably which Bert would inherit upon her demise. She told us that he was very clever, he was a top union official and was responsible for settling a lot of industrial disputes. She did not seem to be aware that he was also the cause of many of the disputes. She also added that he made her a generous allowance from out of his wages which the ship owners, in accordance with the Unions conditions, doubled at their own expense.

When Bert came home on leave, she handed him his allowance back and kept the tax free bonus. When the Seaman's Union called a total strike some years back and brought every British merchant ship to a standstill and consequently a halt to our export trade, Bert was one of the Union organisers. He denied being what Lenin had described as being 'a useful fool' and acting against the interest of this country on the instructions of the Communist Party and in the interest of the Soviet Union. He almost cried when he denied this saying that the British Seamen had to strike because they could not live on the £16 per week basic pay which they received and then only when they were working. He said that in order to ensure that the strike could not be ascribed to Communist influence, he and other members of the Communist Party on the Union's executive, had severed all connection with the Party for the duration of the strike. Although we had our doubts we accepted his earnest disclaimer because of the sincerity in which it was given. We eventually came to realise, that for his performance, he should have been awarded an Oscar. We discovered the truth, again by sheer coincidence.

We were leaving home one day to visit my mother when it started to rain hard and as we passed by Mrs Norman's house which was nearby, we saw Bert leaving. He did not have a car, so we stopped to offer him a lift which he surprisingly refused. He said he did not want to inconvenience us and he would go by bus. We then offered to give him a lift to the bus stop, pointing out that if he walked to the stop and then waited for a bus he would get soaked through.

We could not understand his reluctance as normally he welcomed a lift in our car. We asked him which stop would be the most convenient and when he told us we said that we were actually going in the same direction as the buses go from that stop.

He reluctantly agreed for us to give him a lift but as it was really raining exceedingly fast he acquiesced. After a mile or so, he asked us to drop him off at Burdett Road on the corner of the Mile End Road and said he would walk the short distance down the road to a friend's house. We told him that even in a short distance he would get soaked and insisted on taking him up to the premises he was visiting. We are not sure what the number of the house in Burdett Road we dropped him off at, but I believe it was number 24. He got out of the car hurriedly and quickly descended the external stairs leading to the semi basement.

We thought no more about it until several weeks later, we read in a national newspaper a description by an investigative journalist as how the seaman's' strike was organised and run by the British Communist Party from the premises we had given Bert a lift to. Harold Wilson, the then Prime Minister was certainly correct when he described the disastrous strike as politically motivated.

Some while after the strike was over, Bert came along to tell us how he had rescued his landlady from a swarm of angry bees. He heard cries of help coming from the garden and saw Mrs Norman surrounded by a swarm of bees. She had been hanging out some washing and for some reason or another had angered the bees. She ran into the house wildly waving her hands about which only seemed to anger the bees even more. Bert reckoned that the only way to get rid of the bees apart from smoking them out which was not very practical inside the house, was to immerse Mrs Norman in a bathful of water. He quickly turned the bath taps full on and shouted at Mrs Norman to strip off her clothes and get into the bath. She did so with great alacrity and enthusiasm despite the fact that Bert did not avert his glance.

When Bert had opened the windows and persuaded the swarm to leave, his religious landlady gave loud praise to the Lord for saving her from such horrible and mortal danger.

Bert did not return from his last voyage and we heard through a friend that on the journey to Australia, he had met a divorced woman and had married her. Her extremely rich father had set him up in business as a property developer and now he was extremely wealthy in his own right.

Come the revolution, he will, no doubt be consigned to a labour camp!

The Bat Mitzvah

I was a keen amateur photographer and found Israel to be a photographer's paradise. The country just simply abounds with scenes crying out to be photographed. The constant sunshine made exposure simple and reliable. The country is full of historic and monumentally modern buildings and the people from over 100 different countries are intriguing. Both adults and children loved to be photographed and to engage in conversation.

A photographer's problem is not to be too carried away by the atmosphere and potential subjects and thus run out of film.

People loved to exercise their knowledge of English and were naturally curious about our background and Israeli's are not reticent when it comes to asking personal questions. At first, we were shocked by their directness but soon realised that they did not necessarily expect truthful replies. We, in turn, abandoned our natural reserve and asked questions we would never dream of asking at home. It was through such open conversations that we got to know the background of some of those we met.

One person we got to know was Hanan. He was an insurance agent and was very easy to talk to, but strangely, it was not from him direct that we got to know his tragic story, but through a mutual friend, Hans.

Hanan was a boy of just 15 years when the Germans invaded and occupied his home country, Poland. At first, very little changed but along with the rest of the Polish people, his family suffered a terrible shortage of food. They just carried on with their normal life and hoped that the food supply situation would improve. They saw little of the German invaders. Occasionally, a German army vehicle would drive through their village.

One morning many German army lorries arrived and disgorged hun-

320

dreds of soldiers. One of the vehicles drove slowly through the village announcing through a loud speaker that every Jew in the village, of whatever age, must assemble in the square in front of the church by twelve noon. They should take with them a loaf of bread and their valuables in a suitcase. Any Jew failing to comply, for whatever reason, will be shot on sight.

Non Jews were warned not to assist Jews to evade this order, or they too, would be shot on the spot.

Hanan, together with his parents, ailing grandparents and his two sisters duly arrived in the square. For quite a long while nothing happened but occasionally they could hear shots in the nearby streets.

As it was getting dark, army lorries blocked off the exits from the square but still nothing happened except children were crying with hunger and thirst.

Hanan's father said to him, you don't look particularly Jewish, as soon the opportunity arises, slip away and go to the nearby forest where there is a band of Partisans operating and tell them what is happening here and see if they can get help, as I fear they are going to send us to some remote part of the country.

Hanan located the Partisans who said they were not in a position to help but if any able bodied men wanted to, they could join the Partisans but they will only be accepted if they bring a firearm and ammunition with them. Hanan returned to the village which was strangely quiet. The German army vehicles had gone and when he reached the square he saw it was strewn with bodies, adults, children and babies. Moving among the dead were some villagers looting the pathetic belongings of the slain, including their shoes and boots. He verified that his whole family were among the dead and then slipped away in case someone would point out that he was a Jew.

He managed to obtain a gun and spent the remaining war years operating with the Partisans against the Germans.

After the war, he emigrated to Israel where he married and had two children. Hanan introduced us to interesting people and showed us interesting places that most tourists did not see.

One day, he said that he would like to take us with him to visit a friend who lived on a kibbutz (communal farm) and whose daughter was being Bat Mitzvah'd that day. Bat Mitzvah ceremonies are not ancient but seem to have been accepted by world wide Jewish communities post war, as a parallel to the Jewish boys' Bar Mitzvah which is a very ancient ceremony denoting the boy's responsibilities under the Jewish Laws on attaining the age of 13 years.

We were naturally pleased to visit a kibbutz but queried the fact that we had not been invited by the family who might object to the intrusion of strangers. Hanan assured us that we would be most welcome. He said any celebration in a kibbutz is open to one and all. The more the merrier!

It was a lovely ceremony and festivity. Afterwards, Hanan told us about the history of the Bat Chayil's (the title of a girl undergoing the Bat Mitzvah ceremony) mother.

She was born on or about 1st September 1939, the day the Germans invaded Poland. When her mother heard about the slaughter of the Jews in surrounding villages, she asked a Christian neighbour to adopt her baby and to bring it up as her own until such time as the present troubles would cease. The neighbour, who could not bear children of her own was only too pleased to do so even though she was aware of the potential danger if caught. She undertook a terrible risk in order to save the baby's life.

By the time the war was over, the whole of the baby's family had been killed by the German's with the exception of an uncle who had fled to Palestine and survived. He returned to Poland to find his whole family destroyed except this girl who was by now six years old.

One can only imagine the emotions involved when the uncle claimed the one and only survivor of his family. All his own children had been slaughtered. On the other hand, the woman who had cared for the child at great danger to herself and through all the rigours of the German occupation regarded herself as the rightful mother.

Fortunately, the uncle and the woman reached an amicable agreement. They would jointly bring up the child and would do so in the kibbutz which we were visiting. By the time the girl's daughter was Bat Mitzvah'd both the uncle and the adoptive mother had died and were buried on the kibbutz.

Hans was born in Germany and remembers how in 1936 his younger brother went off as usual to school but was returned later in the day in a sack which was left on their doorstep with a doctor's certificate pinned on certifying cause of death due to heart failure. His body was covered in bruises. Possibly, he had been beaten to death by his school mates under the urging of a Nazi teacher.

Han's parents realised the danger to the rest of the family and they all fled to Palestine. Hans grew up there and during the war served as an auxiliary in the British army. After the war, he set himself up in business as a car body repairer.

It was Hans who drove us all down to the Kibbutz in his Jeep style vehicle. He told us that just before the six day war in 1967, at a coded signal on the radio, he had left the vehicle as pre-arranged, in a car park to be picked up by the Israeli army. He himself reported to an army medical unit.

After the six day war, the vehicle was handed back to him but there were several hundred miles added to the milometer.

We learnt recently that Hans had died from cancer. When he knew that he did not have long to live, he returned to the town in Germany where he was born and asked to be buried near his younger brother. He wanted his brother to know that he had not been forgotten and would no longer be alone.

Whilst we were on the kibbutz, we got chatting to an elderly lady. She told us that she did not know if she was a widow or not.

When the Germans attacked Poland in September 1939, the Russians had, under the German/Russian non-aggression pact occupied half of Poland. When the Germans broke the pact, the Russian occupying authorities told the inhabitants of the lady's village, that for their own safety, they will be evacuated to Siberia. In a way, they were not displeased because they had heard rumours of the atrocities being committed by the Germans in the other half of Poland.

They were loaded onto barges which slowly and painfully wended their way up the river in a general eastward direction. After several weeks they were told to disembark.

They had been landed in the midst of a seemingly never ending forest, hundreds of miles from any civilisation. They were given some primitive tools and told to build a logging camp for themselves using the surrounding trees as their building materials. They were told, that in exchange for logs, they would be supplied with food and medical supplies etc.

At the beginning, they had no food and had to survive by eating bark from the trees and wild berries etc. and a little meat they were able to trap. Many of the elderly and ailing died from hunger and cold.

Life was hard in the camp and rather lawless. She was young at the time and out of desperation for self survival went through a form a marriage with a young man whose main attribute was that he was physically strong and able to look after himself. It was a marriage of convenience as far as she was concerned and not of love.

The inhabitants of the logging camp became aware that not far away, there was another camp. It was one of the many notorious Russian forced labour camps and from what they got to know about the conditions there, made their own existence appear luxurious.

When the Germans were defeated and the war ended, the news soon reached both the logging camp and the Gulag camp. The so-called 'free persons' in the logging camp and the guards in the prison camp duly celebrated the event. There was plenty of home brewed Vodka available.

The guards celebrated excessively and they all to a man, became blind drunk. The Gulag prisoners could not believe their luck, they looted the camp and streamed out to freedom. When the guards sobered up, they organised search parties and recaptured many prisoners but they could not account for fifty or so that were still missing.

The camp commandant easily overcame this problem, he sent his guards into the logging camp and took fifty of the male occupants back to his labour camp to make up the missing number. Each of the newly acquired prisoners was given the identity of one of the escapees.

The lady's 'husband' was among the fifty taken as prisoners. She could never discover what happened to her 'husband' because the Russian authorities denied that they had a prisoner by that name.

When she made her way back to Poland, she discovered a strong hostile and anti-Semitic attitude to returnees. Her family's house was occupied by a non-Jewish family who claimed that they had always lived there and that she had no right to it. She decided to spend the rest of her life in Israel.

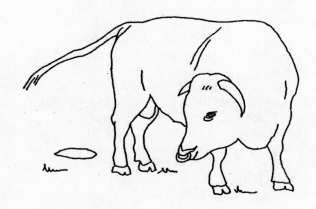

Putting My Foot In It

When it became obvious that war with Germany was becoming almost inevitable, the British government decided to put into operation its plan to evacuate children from areas that they considered would be most vulnerable to aerial bombardment. They anticipated that London would be particularly targeted.

I was still at school and normally, I would have been leaving at the time the evacuation was being put into effect but my parents decided that I should stay on and be evacuated with my school so that I would be able to keep an eye on my younger brother and sister who would be evacuated with me.

The evacuation, sometime in late August 1939 worked quite smoothly. Children assembled, class by class in the school's playground wearing a large luggage label with the child's name and home address on it. The child also carried on a string around its neck a cardboard box containing a gas mask which had been issued by the government a few weeks previously. The children had been drilled in how to don the mask in case of need. What no-one at the time realised, was that the filter in the mask contained a potentially dangerous asbestos fibre. They also carried battered suitcases containing change of clothing.

My school was the Jews Free Central School in Middlesex Street, east London in the heart of the predominantly Jewish district. On Sundays, an open air street market is held in Middlesex Street when it is more commonly known as 'The Lane'.

In those days, primary schools were not integrated so that the assembly consisted mainly of boys between the ages of ten and fifteen.

There was great excitement among the children who regarded the evacuation as akin to a school holiday in the countryside. Among the parents who came to see the children off were not a few with tears in their eyes and anxiety in their heart.

The destination of our coach was the village of Isleham in Cambridgeshire, whilst those of the other two coaches were the nearby villages of Soham and Fordham.

Our coach driver had some difficulty in finding Isleham as all the road signs had either been removed or deliberately repointed in the wrong direction. This had been done so as to mislead any enemy paratrooper or saboteur who may be dropped into the country. When the driver stopped to ask someone the way, they denied that any such village existed in Cambridgeshire and that he should try somewhere else. It was not that they did not know, but they had been instructed not to give information to anyone which maybe useful to the enemy. We realised later, that the yokels had great difficulty in differentiating between foreigners and Londoners who they regarded as foreigners in any case. We eventually found Isleham and disgorged from the coach to find ourselves in the midst of most strange surroundings. Some of the slum children had read about country life but suddenly finding themselves in the midst of it was a culture shock.

The village was very straggly and the centre quite small. There were no street lights and it only had one fair sized shop, the Co-op, which supplied virtually all the needs of the villagers. A few of the houses facing onto the high street, used the front rooms as shops selling sweets and other items. Some of the other houses, were licensed to serve alcoholic beverages in their front rooms and these served as the village social centres in the evening. The high street also contained the village's one and only church although there were several chapels dotted around the straggly village.

The houses and farm buildings were constructed of chalk blocks dug locally out of the ground and in places faced with flint stones. The roofs were covered with clay tiles fixed to undulating rafters constructed of unsawn tree branches. Windows were small and often askew.

For the first time in their lives, the children heard the sound of cows and chickens and breathed fresh country air and smelt animal odours.

The villagers had previously been canvassed and asked to volunteer to foster evacuees from London. Many had done so, there was no shortage of hospitality, but most of the villagers had had illusions of blond, blue eyed, innocent cherubic three year old cuddly girls but instead were shocked to be presented with much older scruffy boys with dark eyes and dark hair, speaking with Jewish cockney accents.

After the initial shock and disappointment, most of the fostering villagers accepted the children who had been brought to their front doors.

There had been a problem with finding accommodation for three of the least attractive children but eventually, these too were accepted.

The villagers were also shocked to discover that their evacuees were Jewish. None of them had ever before come into contact with Jews and some even remembered something about them that they had heard as children in Sunday school. Church and Chapel clergy tried to enlighten their parishioners, but they themselves were ignorant and confused with the Jews of today and those they read about in the bible.

Some of the Jewish children felt shocked at having to eat non-kosher food for the first time in their life but soon accepted this as a necessity.

I was fortunate to be billeted with a very nice family near the centre of the village. The family consisted of Mr and Mrs Patrick Murphy, Mrs Murphy's elderly small bad tempered mother and a young orphan boy, Eric, that they had fostered. The poor boy was badly bullied by Mrs Murphy's mother who used her walking stick as much to hit Eric with as she used it to aid her walk. I don't know why she had it in for the little boy.

Mr Murphy worked full time as a store keeper to the contractor extending the facilities at the nearby Mildenhall bomber aerodrome. He supplemented his income by the crop from a small apple orchard he owned and in which he kept bees. I was intrigued at the way he handled the bees and was delighted to eat honey straight from the comb and apples straight from the trees.

He also kept a large shed with about 100 chickens in it. We rarely ate eggs, he sold them all, and we only had chicken when any had to be slaughtered because they were ill and could not be marketed. He showed me how he killed the chickens by wringing their necks but he was not very efficient at doing so. Some of the chicken ran around in circles after he said he had wrung their necks. Mrs Murphy was very houseproud. Her house was better built than most in the village and had quite a bit of ground around it. She kept two dogs, one was a very old and sick mongrel and the other a young red setter of which she appeared to be very fond of but she would not allow either of them into the house except on rare occasions. Otherwise, they lived in a commodious kennel in the garden.

Like all the other houses in the village, it did not have piped water, or gas or electricity. All water had to be drawn from a well, artificial light was by a paraffin lamp, cooking was done on a paraffin stove or a wood burning boiler. Clothes were washed in a copper boiler heated by solid fuel. There was no bathroom. Baths were taken in a tin bath in a draughty barn which was torturously cold in the winter.

There was no water closet. The outdoor earth closet with no window but with a heart shaped vent hole in the door consisted of a wooden board with a hole cut in it over a deep pit into which everything fell with a splash. The smell was awful because the pit was emptied only once a year.

Even in the slums of east London we had water closets, gas mains, good clean drinking water from the tap and eventually electricity. Whilst we did not have bathrooms, we had access to municipally run public baths.

Early one evening, soon after my arrival in Isleharn when I was meandering down a lane on the outskirts of the village absorbed in the wonderment of nature surrounding me, I was ambushed by about six village youths. They started taunting me about being a Londoner and being ignorant about country life. Actually, they were correct on both accounts but I was somewhat apprehensive about their belligerent attitude.

One snatched my school cap and threw it over the nearby hedge. I deftly dodged them and quickly clambered over a five bar gate even though it had barbed wire strands fixed along its top edge. I did not stop to read the 'Keep Out' sign. I retrieved my cap and made my way over the grassy field so as to evade the gang who were standing near the gate shouting obscenities after me but not trying to chase after me. Whilst crossing the field I trod into some cow dung.

When I returned to my billet, Mrs Murphy noticed that I was in an upset state and that my trousers were torn when I climbed over the barb wire on the gate. She also noticed the smell of the cow dung. I told her what had happened. She assured me that the youths only acted out of ignorance, that they were ill educated mindless yobs. She said that she would repair my trousers and asked in detail where the encounter had taken place. When I told her she was shocked. She said that the field that I had crossed was one in which a fierce bull was kept and that I was extremely lucky not to have been attacked by it. Possibly, the shouts from the boys had distracted its attention from me.

She asked me if it was then, that I trod in the cowpat. I said I did not know what a cowpat was. She very circumspectly explained what a cowpat consisted of. Being an ignorant cockney, I said that it could not be a cowpat I trod in because there were no cows in the field only the bull. I naively blurted out what I thought it must have been, and I used a term that shocked her tender ladylike ears. She was a regular and ardent chapel goer and was the chapel's organist.

Emmanuel Knok

My father held his friend, Emmanuel Knok, in very high esteem. Emmanuel was several years older than my father and had emigrated to this country from Belarus several years before my father did, and in that period had picked up a good bit of the English language. Not only could he speak English, he could actually read it. He was also literate in the Yiddish language. Whilst all the recent Jewish emigrants from eastern Europe around the beginning of the century spoke Yiddish, very few were literate enough to read it. To be able to speak and read English was virtually unknown. It was whilst my father and Emmanuel worked together in the Jewish subterranean bakeries below the Jewish baker shops in the east end of London that Emmanuel was able to impress my father with facts that he had gained from reading both Yiddish and English newspapers. This information opened up a vast new world to my father.

Apart from not being able to read the newspapers himself, my father did not own a wireless set, which were very primitive in those days and even if he had listened to the crackling, distorted sounds that emanated from them, he would not have been able to understand a word.

Emmanuel also impressed my father by obtaining substantial damages from the local council as a result of an accident caused somehow or other by the council's negligence when carrying out road works. Because of the accident, one of Emmanuel's legs became paralysed and he was unable to continue working in the bakery trade which involved standing up for long hours. What impressed my father was that Emmanuel was able to obtain a substantial sum of money without working for it. This was an unknown phenomenon among the illiterate immigrant Jews in the east end of London. My father was also impressed when Emmanuel used the money to buy a house. It was unknown in those days for a poor immigrant to own his own house and not to have to part with a substantial portion of his hard earned money every Monday morning when the Landlord called for the rent. The money also enabled Emmanuel to send his clever son to the local Davenport Grammar School and eventually to qualify as a doctor.

My father was proud and honoured to have such a friend and was glad when he accepted the invitation to attend my wedding.

Emmanuel, in turn expressed his appreciation by presenting me and my bride with a cream coloured electric clock. When I plugged the clock in, it started to smoulder and give off smoke. I still have the clock as a fond souvenir of my father's close friend.

Although Emmanuel could not carry on working as a baker he exploited an artistic talent he had, combined with his literacy.

Because the secular calendar is based upon the movement of the earth around the sun and the Jewish calendar is based upon the movement of the moon around the earth, it is very complicated to co-relate anniversaries in one with the other. One very important date to all Jewish families is the anniversary of the death of a close relative when special prayers are recited and a 24 hour candle lit in their memory. To overcome this problem, Emmanuel used to prepare a chart, beautifully hand written giving all the anniversary Lunar dates for the coming 20, 40, 60 years on the secular calendar.

He also prepared beautifully coloured framed wedding certificates in combined English and Hebrew wording. He was very well rewarded for such works of art. This accomplishment added to my fathers admiration for the man.

One day, Emmanuel confided in my father and told him that he had accumulated a lot of money through this work and not trusting banks, he had converted the money into gold sovereigns which he kept in an iron deed box which he placed up one of the bedroom chimneys in which he never lit a fire. As he had not had an opportunity to inform his son about this cache since he went to college to study for his doctorate, he asked my father to tell his son about it should anything unexpectedly happen to him. His wife had died when their son was very young and Emmanuel and his sister had between them brought the boy up and they were both very proud of him. In those days, it was truly most exceptional for a poor immigrant's son to go to college.

When my parents and Emmanuel were elderly, I used to pick up Emmanuel in my car to take him over to spend an evening with my parents and then take him home again. In this manner, they were able to keep in touch with each other. I did not mind doing this, but what irked me was, each time I called to pick him up, his sister would insist that he changed his shirt and suit on the grounds that the one he was wearing was shabby. I was especially irked because the suit he changed into was not any smarter.

Due to illness and my own preoccupation, we saw Emmanual less and less frequently.

We heard that his son had qualified as a doctor and that his sister had died and because he could not care for himself, Emmanuel had entered an old persons home in Bournemouth.

One fine weekend, we visited some friends in Bournemouth and decided to see how Emmanuel was getting on. The home was lovely and Emmanuel was enjoying his stay there. His one and only complaint was that because his son was so busy, he very rarely saw him and when he did, it was only for very short visits.

A short while after, we had a letter from Emmanuel telling us that he had married one of the women guests at the home and he enclosed a wedding photo of himself in a smart morning suit, bow tie, top hat and carnation. His bride was dressed in a white wedding gown holding a large bouquet.

He told us that the home had put on a wonderful reception including a large wedding cake. He did not say where he had spent his honeymoon. He must have been at least 80 years old. I naturally sent him our congratulations and was very tempted to send him the electric clock he presented me with on my wedding and which I had kept for sentimental reasons.

Only a couple of weeks later, we had a letter from his son informing us that his father had died and was buried in the Jewish cemetery in Rainham in Essex.

About a year later, we were surprised to receive an unexpected visit from Emmanuel's son. He said that he knew that his father and mine had been close friends and asked if we would like a photo of his father as a souvenir. We accepted his kind offer.

We asked him if his father had left a will. He said that as the only living relative, that had not been necessary but a careful search of his fathers house before disposing of it did not reveal one. He turned deathly white when we asked if he had found the iron deed box with gold sovereigns which his father had hidden up the chimney. He said that he had no idea about the hoard and it was too late now to do anything as he knew that the new owner had had all the chimney breasts removed. If he had not found it, the builders most certainly had.

Some while later, when visiting my parents grave in the Rainham Jewish Cemetery, I passed a fairly newly erected tombstone dedicated to Emmanuel Kok. No one apparently had noticed the mis-spelling of his name or even cared if they had done so.

Sculptures

The Ashmore family who used to live next door to my father in-law were very peculiar but most friendly and pleasant.

The houses were part of a long terrace of Victorian style in StokeNewington, north London. When my in-laws moved in, the Ashmores were very helpful, obliging and neighbourly. They went out of their way to make my in-laws feel welcome. The two families remained good neighbours without ever a cross word between them.

Despite their friendliness the Ashmore's were rather reticent and reserved and preferred to keep themselves to themselves.

There were three members of the Ashmore family and they had a dog, a cat and a parrot. Their son, Michael, in his mid twenties was very shy and spoke very little. Mr Ashmore explained his son did not work because of a trauma caused by seeing his comrade in the army accidentally shot.

Apparently, a rifle was inadvertently fired in the barrack room and hit Michael's friend who was sitting alongside him. Part of his friend's brain was splattered onto Michael's face. He never recovered from the shock and consequently was discharged as mentally unfit from the army with a invalidity pension.

Because of that, the family could not watch television or a film in case a shooting is depicted which would upset Michael terribly.

Michael spent most of the day reading, painting in oil colours and sculpture.

Mrs Ashmore did not go out to work, she took their dog on long walks and did a lot of laundry, she also spent a lot of time studying antiques as she said that it was their ambition to open an antiques shop when Mr Ashmore retired.

Mr Ashmore worked for one of the large, well known antiques auctioneers in London. His job was to supervise the men who moved the various items about when they came in for auction. It was a very responsible job because the valuable antiques could so easily be damaged.

Because of his connection with the antiques trade, he was able to acquire suitable items very cheaply with which to stock his own future antique shop when he retired. His home was chocka-block with antiques, enough to stock several antique shops.

Most of the items were, to me, ugly, cumbersome, dark and depressing. They also had many large, dark and depressing oil paintings. The rooms were also decorated in dark and depressing colours which were accentuated by the permanently closed heavy dark red velvet curtains on the front windows. They explained that the curtains were kept closed in order to prevent the sun ruining the furniture.

The depressive atmosphere was increased by the use of very low wattage bulbs in lampshades that obscured the light.

This did not seem to worry them, as they went to bed very early in the evening.

Although they did not watch television they listened to the radio but mainly to heavy classical music. Sometimes, their dog came out into their rear garden and whined mournfully into the night air.

One day, Mrs Ashmore informed my in-laws that the dog had passed away after a long and painful illness. She said that Michael would make a sculpture of the dog and place it in the garden as a memorial. The sculpture, cast in fine concrete, rather larger than life size, was duly placed on a concrete plinth in the rear garden over the dog's grave. This was followed not long after by a similar sculpture of their cat which died of old age. Both sculptures were placed in a well kept Geranium flower bed which offset the sculptures.

The family was seen quite often to come out to pay their respects to their departed pets. They obviously missed them very much.

One morning, my in-laws noticed two additional statues at the bottom of the Ashmore's rear garden. They were of a man and woman cast in fine concrete, just a little larger than life size, placed in the centre of a newly formed flower bed.

Several weeks later, my in-laws remarked to Michael that they had not seen his parents for quite a while. For a change, he was very talkative and explained that his father had decided to take early retirement on a generous pension and that both his parents went up to Norwich to search for premises for their antique shop and also a dwelling. He said that they apologised for not bidding them farewell but would be in touch as soon as they had found suitable premises.

A few months later, my in-laws were amazed to see Michael and another young man loading the concrete statues into a skip. They asked Michael that if he did not want them, could they have them for use as garden ornaments. Michael said that unfortunately, the facial features were badly damaged and that was why he was getting rid of them. What also surprised my inlaws was the relative lightness of the concrete sculptures, the two young men were handling, them with fair ease. Michael explained that they were hollow, the concrete was only a thin skin reinforced with chicken wire. He did not explain why it was only the facial features that were damaged or as to how the damage occurred. He also amazed them with his loquaciousness and happy demeanour especially when in the company of his companion.

One day, Michael bade my in-laws farewell and said that his parents had found suitable premises and that he would be moving the house contents up to Norwich. The house was soon sold.

Although Michael had promised that he would let my in-laws have their new address, he did not do so. A couple of years later, when Dora and I were doing a car tour around England, we visited Norwich but did not find any antique shop run there by the Ashmores, nor were they listed in the local telephone directory.

Two Poles

During the German wartime 'Blitz' on the east end of London, my mother rented a cottage in the Cambridgeshire village of Isleham in order to look after my younger brother and sister who had previously been evacuated there and were being fostered by villagers. Having such a place in a relatively safe and quiet part of the country enabled other members of the family, including myself, who remained working in London to benefit from short periods of respite from the almost continuous aerial bombardment on the part of London where we lived. At times, we were actually homeless due to the bombing.

The cottage was off an unmade country lane not far from the village centre. It was one of a semi-detached pair. It had been vacant and derelict for a long time. The other cottage was occupied by Mr Clark, a ploughman who still used horses to pull his plough, his wife and his sweet 14 year old daughter, Edna.

The cottage was constructed, as many of the village houses were, of chalk blocks dug out of the ground locally, it had no damp proof course, the stone covered floor was some 450mm below the outside ground level. A narrow, steep staircase led directly from the one and only ground storey room up to two small bedrooms on the first floor. The first floor had large gaps between the floorboards and it was possible to peer through these gaps into the room below because there was no ceiling to the ground floor storey.

The undulating rustic tiled roof was supported on un-sawn tree branches. The wind was able to blow directly into the bedrooms through the gaps between the tiles. There were no gutters or down pipes. The cottage had no electricity, gas or water mains. Nice cold water was obtained from a well just outside the front door but at certain times of the year the water contained snails and slugs.

Cooking was done on a paraffin stove and artificial light was by candles or a paraffin lamp.

There was no kitchen as such and no bathroom or water closet. The outside privy consisted of a lean-to structure in which was a wooden board with a hole cut into it placed over a deep pit into which everything fell with a splash. The pit was emptied once a year. It was not much of a house, but it was a home, a refuge and the rent, including rates was 1/6d (7½ pence) a week. That was the going rate and the owner was glad to receive it. Life was primitive in Isleham, but dangerous in Stepney in the east end of London.

Due to rigorous war-time rationing and being away from the traditional Jewish shops, my mother had to adapt her style of cooking. She exchanged recipes with Mrs Clark next door. My mother started to cook such dishes as spotted dick which she called 'shmutter puddin' because of the cloth involved and Yorkshire pudding which she mispronounced 'Yockisher puddin' which loosely translated means Christian pudding.

On the other hand, Mrs Clark started to cook for her family, 'Simmas' which consists mainly of sliced carrots and 'Cholant' which is a slow roast consisting mainly of potatoes and dumpling.

Quite unexpectedly, early one Friday evening, two young Polish soldiers called at the cottage. They explained that they were Jewish and were stationed at a nearby army camp. They had heard that a Jewish family was living in this isolated village and came to make their acquaintance.

They could not speak a word of English and we could not speak a word of Polish but we were able to converse in the Yiddish language we all knew.

They told us that in September 1939, when the Germans invaded their home country, Russia, in accordance with a prior agreement with the Nazi government, occupied the eastern half of Poland. At the time, they were both serving as conscripted Privates in the Polish army. They said that they were lucky, because if they had been officers, the Russians would have killed them, but instead they interned them, in labour camps in Siberia. When the Germans broke their pact with the Soviets and invaded Russia, the Russian government allowed the interned Polish soldiers to emigrate to the west to join a Polish army in exile being formed by the Polish General Anders in order to fight the common enemy. That is how they found themselves stationed in a camp near the village of Isleham. They had no idea of what had happened to their families in Poland. They had had no contact with them since the Russians invaded and occupied eastern Poland. They said that even though anti-Semitism was rampant in pre-war Poland, they themselves, had not experience much of it because they lived in a predominantly Jewish village. However, since they joined the Polish army they experience it daily. Fellow soldiers blamed them as Jews for anything that went wrong as well as holding them responsible for the death of Jesus some 2000 years ago. They said that the officers were also anti-Semitic and gave us two examples.

One day, their battalion was paraded to receive award of a medal. An officer called out the names of the Jewish soldiers and commanded them to take two paces forward. A Colonel then came and pinned a medal onto all those still in line but omitting those who were not. Another example was when two stray dogs were caught in the camp. They were put into a sack and an officer commanded them to beat the dogs to death. They were sickened by this command but had no alternative but to obey. The officer then put the battered bodies of the dogs on display near the camp entrance and erected a notice nearby saying that 'these dogs were cruelly beaten to death by Jewish soldiers.'

They gladly accepted the invitation to stay and to participate in the Sabbath eve ceremony and meal. They openly cried during the ceremony as it was identical to their experience at home in Poland. They delighted in seeing the Sabbath candles lit and blessed and the blessing of the Sabbath chalah (bread). They said it was so much like home that they thought it was a dream from which they would awake. They said that even the humble home was similar to that of theirs in Poland. The meal which they partook in was probably not similar to that in Poland in as much as it included chicken soup with possibly more snails and slugs than chicken in it, Yorkshire pudding and spotted dick. We gave them a small Hebrew prayer book to keep and told them to call again. They did so once more to tell us that they were moving camp. We did not hear from them again and we do not know if they survived the war and if so, if they returned to Poland.

The Polish army in exile and men who served in the RAF served with distinction and suffered heavy casualties.

Faith

Malcolm had given up a promising career in an exclusive bank in order to serve his church as a minister. As a lay preacher, he was most successful. Whilst training for the ministry, he served his church as a social worker. Young delinquents were very influenced by him and abandoned their wicked ways. They idolised him and his charming wife, Beryl, who eagerly helped him and shared his beliefs and ambition.

He was fearless and did not hesitate to approach anyone he considered to be a sinner and ask them to repent. He tackled headlong groups of youths in the streets however fearsome and threatening they may appear, he begged prostitutes soliciting on the streets to give up their profession, he entered pubs in slum districts and preached against the demon drink. He picketed outside betting shops and preached to jovial inebriated crowds at fun furs etc. etc.

He was not afraid as he believed that the Almighty would protect him, whatever the danger, just as he had protected Daniel in the days of old. As far as I know, nothing untoward ever happened to him despite the many dangers he deliberately encountered.

Perhaps, it was his comical face that helped him to avoid physical harm. He had a long thin face and due to his extreme shortsightedness, he wore very thick lenses in dark, heavy square shaped frames. He also retained a fairly strong Lancashire accent although he had not lived there since he was a child.

Nothing could shake or make him doubt his faith one iota. In fact, his faith increased with the passing of time. Although he considered me as an irredeemable sinner, he never wasted any time or effort in trying to save my condemned soul. I've no doubt, however, that on the quiet, he did pray for my redemption. If he did, it must have been his one and only failure. My wife and I got to know him quite well as whilst he was training, he lived right next door to us in a bedsitter.

One day, there was a commotion in the street and looking out we could see Malcolm taking delivery of a second hand three wheeler car.

He proudly showed it off to us and said that he would get it insured that very same morning through the Church's insurance broker and if we liked, he would take us for a ride in the country.

We kindly declined his offer on the grounds that our religion forbade us to commit suicide. He assured us that there was no need to fear any danger whilst he was at the wheel and the Lord at his elbow.

We asked him when and where he had passed his driving test. He said that he did not need one as he already had a licence to drive a motor bike and that same sort of licence covered driving a three wheel car providing it did not have a reverse gear.

We further queried the fact that he was not wearing his glasses and asked if he was wearing contact lenses. He told us that he had thrown his spectacles away a few days previously when a voice from heaven told him whilst he was eating his supper that with faith, he would not need them any more. He assured us that he could now see quite normally without wearing glasses. We had our doubts as he was peering away, even at a short distance, to see who he was speaking to. He said that if I had faith, I too, could have my short short-sightedness cured instantly. I told him that I had faith in my optician.

In the afternoon, we heard the roar of his engine and looking out of the window we saw him, with his wife seated next to him driving up the road leaving behind a layer of exhaust fumes on the road.

About and hour later I heard a crashing sound and looking out of our window I could see that Malcolm had crashed his car into the double wrought iron gates to our forecourt parking area. The gates were badly buckled and one of the brick supporting piers partially dislodged.

I asked Malcolm what had caused the accident and he replied, "1 am sure I left the gates open when I left". I told him that he had done so, but the gates that he had left open were next door where he lived. I asked him for details of his insurance as I intended to claim against them for the damage to my gates. Malcolm said, "They won't like this, when I left about an hour ago, I went into the side of a double decker bus just on the corner of the road. I don't understand why I did not see it, it seemed to come out of nowhere."

A policeman attending the scene of the accident was very impressed when Norman had explained that his insurance certificate was in the post because he had only arranged for the insurance about an hour previously over the phone with the broker who acted on behalf of his church. However, Malcolm thanked the Lord that no one had been hurt in either incident.

His car was a write-off but he still made a handsome profit by dismantling the wreck and selling the parts to three wheel car enthusiasts.

He told me that I had acted immorally by claiming for new gates and repair of brick pier when I had not had the pier repaired but demolished and had not replaced the gates.

Scottish Holiday

Our first car which we bought in 1957 was a clapped out 1927 Austin Seven tourer. We did not have it long before we thankfully sold it. On reflection, I suppose, I should have had a guilty conscience running it because the contraption was a virtual death-trap, but in the period concerned, when new cars where almost unobtainable to the ordinary citizen, it was the accepted standard.

After we had disposed of it, Dora and I resolved that we would wait until new cars were more readily available and until we could afford to buy one. Our next car which we bought a few years later was new, but was not actually a car. It was a Ford 5cwt 'Thames' van which we had converted into a sort of shooting brake by having windows cut into the side and seats fixed on the floor at the rear. The object of this exercise was to avoid the still long list awaiting delivery of new cars and to avoid what was then called 'purchase tax' the predecessor of VAT. It was quite legitimate to buy a commercial vehicle which was not subject to purchase tax and to convert it into a car which would have ordinarily been subject to purchase tax. However, soon after, the Chancellor of the Exchequer put a stop to such avoidance of purchase tax, which I reiterate, was at the time quite legitimate.

In fact, whenever, I parked the vehicle, it often attracted curious and possibly envious inspection by members of the public.

Soon after its acquisition, we decided to make a grand tour of the United Kingdom.

Upon request, the Automobile Association provided us with a route, which as far as practicable involved secondary roads with picturesque views. It was quite easy to follow even for Dora who acted as navigator and who was hopeless at reading maps. Basically the route was northward from London keeping to the east of England and Scotland and then back down the west side of Scotland and England only touching parts of northern Wales. The route included the more historical, picturesque towns and cities.

To make the tour all the more economical and affordable we acquired guides, 'Where to stay in England' and 'Where to stay in Scotland'. They were both very useful and accurate. Where we could, we chose to stay in 'Bed and Breakfast' in private homes.

Our daily routine was to leave our nightly abode as early as we could after breakfast and then to motor for about three hours to our next destination. That would leave us plenty of time to find the next nights accommodation and to explore the locality on foot and also to participate at leisure in my hobby of photography. This generally worked quite well but one day as our three hour motoring period was expiring, we could not locate any private accommodation and so entertained the idea of staying at a hotel which we came across and which looked more like a castle than a hotel.

When we entered, there was no reception desk and only saw some elderly people hobbling into the dining room. Eventually, we managed to speak to a member of staff to enquire if we could lunch there. The lady said, "Certainly." and added "Lunch will be served shortly."

Soon after, a young lad in a kilt sounded a huge 1200mm brass gong in the entrance hall that caused our ears to ring for some while after. Despite this, one elderly gentleman asked us if the gong for lunch had sounded.

It appeared that the majority of the guests were elderly long staying residents who came from well-to-do families. The gossip whilst they waited for lunch to be served was spoken very loudly for all to hear and concerned some quite prominent people.

The meal consisted mainly of easily digested food including mashed and creamed potatoes, minced meat and tapioca pudding.

As with most buildings in Scotland to which the public had access it was smothered in tartans, the carpet, the wall papers, the table cloths, serviettes etc. etc. The walls were adorned with Victorian style highland scenes including the 'Stag at bay.' All the staff wore tartan but surprisingly, very few of the residents.

One day, when searching for accommodation in Pitlochry, Perthshire, we stopped to ask a man where a certain place was. He told us that if we wanted a nice homely, reasonably priced room for the night he could certainly recommend a certain lady and gave us her address. We duly booked in but soon after the very same man came in; he was the lady's husband.

In the course of conversation, he told us about a wonderful recently constructed dam nearby to which he had access because he was one of the watchmen. He offered to show us the way.

I was not a very experienced driver and the rough contractor's track that led to the rim of the dam was very steep and precarious. The sheep grazing on the hillside were obviously unaccustomed to seeing vehicles and panicked as our car approached. As they hurriedly scrambled away, they dislodged stones and rocks that came bouncing down in our direction in the form of a minor avalanche. I was really scared and my fear was transmitted to our guide who was obviously relieved when we finally and safely reached the summit. The reservoir was a very beautiful and tranquil sight.

Our guide said that he had very little to do when on duty and spent most of the time fishing in the reservoir. The dam had been opened by the Queen and he showed us a specially erected marble faced toilet in case she should require to use it during her visit.

I don't know whether it was because he just wanted a lift to work when he kindly offered to show us the dam, or whether he was too scared of my driving, but he refused my offer to drive him back down the contractor's track.

One night we stayed with an interesting couple in the remote hamlet of Kingussie in the Cairngorms. He was the retired butler and she a maid in a nearby hunting lodge which was let to world famous people. From their conversation we realised just how snobbish the servants were in such households and what intimate secrets they divulged about those they served but were not supposed to observe.

At the time of our visit, they were upset because they had heard rumours that two more cottages were to be built further along the lane where they lived which they felt would be akin to over-crowding when added to the six already there.

We were very impressed with Oban to such an extent, that we decided to stay a fourth night, especially so, in order to see once again the breath taking beauty of the sun set. Whilst we were there, we were enticed to visit a nearby island, the name of which I forgot. The ferry crossing in what was just a glorified rowing boat was very choppy and we got soaked through but as soon as we landed we were greeted by a mobile canteen serving piping hot tea already poured out. Nearby was a mobile shop selling the ubiquitous tartans. We were tempted to buy a tartan skirt for one of our nieces but we noticed it had several large moth holes. Inspection of other garments revealed similar defects.

Whilst we were hanging about waiting for the ferry to take us back, we observed a man with a powerful telescope looking at the approaching ferry and he called out to the woman in the canteen that the ferry contained so many adults and so many children.

The woman began to prepare piping hot cups of tea for the incoming passengers who were bound to be as wet and cold as we were.

In England, we have many beauty spots but in Scotland they have none but virtually the whole of Scotland is a breathtaking beauty spot which tempted us back twice more.

In those days, motoring was a pleasure and a relaxation with little traffic on the roads and much less tourist than there is today. Sometimes, we motored for a good hour before seeing another vehicle or person.

Shop Lifters

Whereas I dislike shopping very much; Dora loves it. I take advantage of this to get her to buy on my behalf, mundane items such as socks, batteries for my portable radio etc. apart from household shopping. I even get her to take my wrist-watch in for cleaning. Sometimes, I take her to the shops in order to bring heavy items home in the car, but I don't enter the shops with her. I wait outside in the car park or nearby street.

My dislike of shopping was recently reinforced by an unfortunate incident. When I realised that I was getting low on stock of wine and spirits I agreed to accompany Dora to re-stock. We are not alcoholics, far from it, but for medical reasons and for relaxation we do partake in a glass of whisky in the evening and we enjoy a glass of wine sometimes with our evening meal. In order to keep such shopping expeditions to a minimum I buy a fair amount on each occasion.

When we arrived at the supermarket, Dora said. "You had better come in and select the wine and spirits as I would not know what to buy." Dora told me to take a trolley as I would not be able to carry all the bottles in a hand basket.

I wheeled the trolley to the wines and spirits department which was at the far end of the large supermarket. Dora left me there while she went off to buy some groceries elsewhere in the store.

I asked the girl who was re-stocking the shelves for two empty cardboard boxes with the sub divisions so that the bottles should not rattle together. I began to select the drinks I wanted and put them into the cardboard boxes. Suddenly I became aware that the young girl who had given me the boxes and a young man were closely watching me from around the corner of some shelving. The young man I was later to discover was the manager of the wines and spirits department. Having picked up the groceries that she required, Dora re-joined me at the wines and spirits department. No sooner had she done so, that a giant of a young man in a security firm's uniform complete with cap and badges loomed up and told me that for security reasons I must remove the bottles from the cardboard boxes and place them loosely in the trolley. I told him that I didn't see the point of that, and if I did so, the bottles would rattle together and might even break. He said that the girl at the cash desk would not know what to charge if the bottles were not out of the boxes.

I told him that when I reached the cash desk, I would reveal the contents of the boxes to the cashier and if he had any doubts he could accompany me through the check-out and ensure that all the drinks were properly paid for.

Other shoppers, looked on curiously while this altercation was proceeding. The large security man was soon joined by the young departmental manager who explained that they had to be careful as people tried to obtain drinks without paying for them. He told me that only two weeks previously, he had watched an old lady conceal a bottle of champagne in her shopping bag and had tried to leave the store without paying for it.

I assured him that I was not an old lady, I was not trying to smuggle a bottle of champagne out of the store without paying for it; that I did not particularly like champagne and that it was an over-rated and overpriced beverage.

He then observed that two dozen bottles of alcohol was a large quantity. I told him that there were no laws or regulations restricting the amount of alcohol purchased in a licensed department of a super market and that I had adequate means to pay for my purchases. I told him that if he had any doubts he could accompany us out through the check-out to ensure that everything would be properly and fully paid for.

I duly revealed my purchases to the cashier under the watchful eye of the young departmental manager, the burly uniformed security man, the young girl who re-stocked the wines and spirits, the two adjacent cashiers who were distracted by the event and a cashier supervisor who saw that something out of the ordinary was happening. Such an event also attracted a few elderly shoppers who stopped to see what was going on.

Before setting out on our shopping spree, I had pre-arranged with Dora that she should pay for the drinks with her credit card and I would reimburse her when we returned home. After the cashier had duly priced everything, I pushed the heavily laden trolley through the checkout leaving Dora to settle the bill with her credit card. As I was heading for the exit door, I was stopped by the security man and the cashier supervisor who told me that there was a little problem. When Dora had presented her credit card the cashier pointed out that its period had expired and that it was null and void. Neither of us had brought any cash with us.

The cashier supervisor impounded the loaded trolley and chained it to a nearby rail.

The security guard suggested that I take a seat while the matter was being sorted out. Dora dashed out to her bank, which was not far away, to see if the card could be renovated or to draw sufficient cash to cover the purchases.

The bank clerk said that there was no problem and promptly produced a new card which she said had been ready and waiting for about two months to be picked up by Dora. She said that for security reasons, the cards were no longer sent through the post as previously. Dora said that at least they could have notified her that her present card would shortly expire and that a new one awaited collection.

The supermarket bill was soon settled under the watchful eyes of the young departmental manager, the uniformed security guard and the cashier supervisor. The young girl had already returned to re-stocking the depleted shelves.

Dora bitterly complained to her bank manager for the humiliation that we had both endured because his bank had not notified her that her credit card had expired as it had always done in the past.

He was very polite and humbly apologised for the way the supermarket staff had treated us.

Car Maintenance

Soon after passing my driving test in 1950, I enrolled on an evening class course on car maintenance. In those days it was quite common for car owners to carry out their own car maintenance and repairs. There were very few company owned cars and cars were constructed so as to need frequent maintenance, not just the once or twice a year affairs that pass for maintenance these days.

Most car owners would check their tyre pressures and radiator level daily, oil levels weekly and very frequent washing and polishing. Fan belts were checked for correct tension and lights for correct alignment.

Car owners were more to be found either under their cars or heads in bonnets than in the driving seat.

Never-the-less, it was quite a common sight at weekends to see at least a dozen cars at the road side on coastal routes with the owners busy changing tyres or trying to find out why the engine was over heating etc., while the family enjoyed a roadside picnic.

I was lucky in as much that the course I enrolled in was taught by a car mechanic with much practical experience and a pleasant natural way of teaching. I was also lucky in as much as most of the lessons took place in the garage where our tutor worked full time as foreman mechanic and most of the demonstrations were on cars bought in for maintenance or repairs by the garage's clients.

We were shown how to repair flat tyres, top up the anti-freeze in the radiator, repair a leaking radiator or hoses, check and charge the battery, check and change bulbs, clean and adjust sparking plugs, adjust fan belts, free a jammed starting motor, adjust a carburettor, make good damaged paintwork etc., etc.

We were not only shown what to do and how to do it but also carried out some of the work ourselves.

There were no more than ten pupils in the class, some of whom took advantage to have maintenance or repairs done on their own cars free of charge as part of the demonstration.

Most of the demonstrations took place in the garage where the tutor worked and commenced early in the evenings in order to take advantage of the daylight. Several of the students came straight from work and the tea and biscuits served by the tutor's wife were very welcome.

The tutor and his family lived in the flat above the garage's reception office and stores.

One evening when we were assembling for our lesson, we could see our tutor on his back under a car at the far side of the garage yard. We assumed that he was either finishing off a job for a client, or preparing a demonstration for us.

The tutor's wife did not greet us with piping hot tea and biscuits as she usually did, but after a short while her young son came out and said. "Mum's not well, I'll call Dad." He went out and shouted to our tutor to come urgently as "Mum has been taken very badly." The tutor had previously told us that his wife was very allergic to aluminium. The most minute trace of aluminium would have a disastrous effect on her. She could not eat out, in case any of the food was cooked in an aluminium pot, she could not even accept a cup of tea in a friends house in case the water had been boiled in an aluminium kettle. She could only eat food from containers which the manufacturers guaranteed were aluminium free. Life was most complicated by this allergy but she managed to avoid attacks except when by some mysterious means she had consumed food or drink that had traces of aluminium in it. It would appear that in such an event, she had to be rushed to hospital and detoxified in the intensive care unit.

When the tutor did not respond to his son's message we went over to make sure that he had heard, but we also could not get a response. We next hauled him out from under the car, which was not difficult because he was lying on one of those trolleys with small wheels. When we got him out, we were shocked to find that he was dead. He had been dead for quite a while and had died from a heart attack.

The Jardiniere

I was fairly surprised when Dora phoned me rather urgently. She had gone out as she usually does to buy her day-to-day shopping locally. She told me to come out at once to one of the local departmental stores where they had an offer; off-cuts of a superior carpet at greatly reduced prices. The off-cuts were the result of a contract to lay carpeting in a luxury cruise liner. Dora said that the quality and colour and pattern were ideal for our entrance hall which at the time was partially covered with lino and partially finished with black and white chequered pattern stone tiles which always looked grubby and were slippery in wet weather. I quickly took measurements of our entrance hall and hurried off to meet Dora at the shops. I knew that there would be hell to pay if I arrived too late and the carpet was sold to someone else. I was already in Dora's bad books because I had kept her awake for much of the night. It was not what you might think, but it was because of a self winding wrist watch I had recently acquired. During the first couple of nights, the watch had stopped. When I complained to the vendor, he explained that if I was sleeping restfully, the self winding apparatus in the watch would not function and the watch would stop. This played on my mind and the following night was a restless one and each time I awoke, I vigorously shook my arm about. The watch continued going throughout the night but Dora was very annoyed.

As I walked briskly down to the departmental store, I kept in mind the need to keep the watch moving so I energetically waved my left arm about as I walked along. En route, I was stopped by one of our acquaintances who asked me if I was alright. I assured her that I was but she told me that her late husband who died from a thrombosis used to throw his arms about like I had in order to improve his blood circulation. I assured her that I was not waving my arms about because of my blood circulation but because of my ticker. This explanation did not seem to assuage her concern.

Dora was right about the carpet. It was certainly first class quality and the colour and pattern, despite being a bit garish, was right for our entrance hall.

As there was no question as to who was going to lay the carpet, I got right down to it as soon as it was delivered.

The space in the hall was quite restrictive so I proposed to Dora that I would move the Victorian brass umbrella stand, the Yew wood coat stand and the lovely Moorcraft jardiniere on stand into one of the adjoining rooms. She said that would not be necessary as I could place them at one end of the hall in front of the street entrance door and then, when I had finished laying the carpet at the other end of the hail, to shunt them over whilst I lay the carpet at the front end of the hail. She said that this would minimise the risk of damage to the jardiniere which we both admired very much. As an extra precaution, she said that we could double bolt the front entrance door even though no one other than ourselves had keys thereto and the door would not be opened unexpectedly.

As I was working away assiduously at the rear part of the entrance hail, there was an enormous crash and looking round, I saw our beautiful jardiniere lying smashed in dozens of pieces on the hard black and white chequered stone tiled floor.

Dora immediately shouted, "What the hell have you done you idiot, have you been waving your arms about again?" I assured her that I had not done anything, I had not even hammered in a single tack, I had only been measuring and cutting the carpet. On closer inspection, we realised that the jardiniere had been pushed over by a free paper vigorously pushed through the letter box of the front door.

The Boxing Championship

I was greatly flattered, when, one humid summer's evening, Morry Goldstein confidentially put an arm around my shoulder and told me that he had decided to give me the opportunity to be the boxing champion of Clark Street where we both lived. Morry was looked up to by most of the kids as he was older than most and seemed to know so many interesting facts of life including where babies came from. He was also bigger than most of the kids in the street. His family occupied a two storey terraced house opposite our buildings. It was a two up and two down Georgian style house but the front 'parlour' had been converted to a 'workshop' where the whole family worked from early morning to late at night operating buttonhole making machines. Nearby tailor sweat-shops found it more economical to use such specialist workshops for button holes than forming them themselves by hand.

Morry told me that he had arranged a championship boxing match and that my opponent Monty Vyner did not stand a chance against me because he was smaller that me and also had a 'chicken heart' which caused him to quickly become short of breath. I already knew about Monty's heart condition because he boasted about it to everyone. Apparently, it was undersized and on the wrong side of his chest. This heart condition caused Monty to have vivid red cheeks which belied his true state of health.

Morry assured me that with him acting as my manager, I could not possibly lose. Monty's manager who was Solly Altman was much less experienced.

The selected site for the match was, fortunately out of sight of my family's home as otherwise, the bout would have been brought to a premature halt by my mother who was an ardent pacifist except when it came to

352

clouting me across my face for the slightest misdemeanour and especially so, if she suspected that I had been fighting. A small crowd had already collected to watch, especially so, because Morry had let it be known that the prize was a complete set of 'Players' cigarette cards depicting famous cricketers.

The 'ring' was drawn in chalk on the granite cobbled stone paved road. Morry had not overlooked such necessary details. He announced to the assembled spectators, that as he had promoted this match entirely at his own expense, he would naturally act as the referee. Nobody argued with Morry.

I, and my opponent were ordered to strip to our vests and were sternly warned not to punch below the belt even though neither of us wore belts. Our trousers were held up by braces. I was also ordered to take off my spectacles which left me at a slight disadvantage. There were no gloves, no kids in the east end of London owned such a luxury. It was to be a stand up bare fist fight.

Whilst my opponent's manager was instructing him how to dance lightly on his toes and to duck punches, Morry told me that I should keep stepping to the right in a circle around my opponent and each time he lashed out, his punches would miss me and in turn, I should punch him in the face.

Just as he was about to blow his whistle to indicate the commencement of the fight he reminded me to adhere strictly to the tactic of stepping to the right. Monty stood in the centre of the ring dancing lightly on his toes and ducking imaginary punches. Suddenly he lashed out and hit me straight in the face. I did not forget my manager's instructions and kept moving to the right. Each time I stepped to the right, Monty hit me in the face and soon my nose began to bleed. As soon as he saw the blood, Morry, acting as the referee, stopped the fight and declared Monty the winner on points and on a technical knockout.

Whilst I was putting on my shirt and trying to stop the flow of blood, Morry went over to my opponent's manager, Solly Altman, and demanded the set of Player's cigarette cards which he had promised to give to Morry if his protégé, Monty, was to win the fight.

Afternoon Nap

Quite often, Dora and I take an afternoon nap. Sometimes it only lasts 5-10 minutes before we are disturbed by the telephone or someone at the door, sometimes the nap takes as much as half an hour. Whatever the duration, we arise greatly refreshed and rested in body and mind. Dora likes to take her nap half reclining on our old Victorian Chesterfield horse hair stuffed settee, whilst I prefer to take it lying on top of the bedclothes on our Edwardian brass bed with a modern very firm mattress.

I lay down flat on my back fully clothed with the feather filled pillow acting as a small bolster in the nape of my neck and covering my ears so as to keep out extraneous sounds. I fold my hands across my chest and commence the dozing process. Having our naps in separate rooms avoids mutual accusations of being disturbed by snoring which we both deny.

I commence the relaxation process by thinking first about the top of my head and gradually and systematically working my thoughts down my body down to my toe nails. It is much more effective than counting sheep. I am thankful that even though I have very little hair, it has been neatly trimmed and recently shampooed using a very mild shampoo.

I next think of my scalp and am pleased that I do not suffer with dandruff and that it does not itch.

I am happy that I am not subject to headaches and that my brain is not agitated in any way what-so-ever. My eyes are relieved and my ear drums do not hurt or buzz. I do not have any nasty taste in my mouth and my throat is not sore and my catarrh was clear.

Thank goodness, I still have most of my own teeth and they are in fairly good condition.

I appreciate the relaxation the pillow is giving my neck. I am thankful for a healthy heart and lungs.

My stomach and bowels are comparatively trouble free. My bladder has been relieved and is relaxed.

My joints, thanks to 'Paracetomol' are pain free.

My thoughts continue to reflect on various organs and members with great relaxing satisfaction. I realise that most people take their body and its functions for granted until something goes wrong.

If I had been counting sheep jumping over a gate I would by now only have got bored and wished that one of them would fall over or something to relieve the monotony.

By the time my thoughts had reached my toes, I would be fitfully entering meaningless dreamlets, rapidly changing from one unrelated subject to another.

This afternoon, I had just reached this stage when I thought I heard through the pillow covering my ears, the front door bell ring but I was not sure if in fact it was the bell or part of a dream. I listened out to hear if the bell would sound again and it did soon after. I was now convinced that there was someone at the door and was making up my mind whether I should answer the door as we were not expecting anyone. The bell went once again and simultaneously Dora called out, "Can't you hear the bell? Someone's at the door. Put the chain on before you open the door."

I no longer had any choice. I quickly got off the bed and went down to see who was at the door. If it were the Jehovah Witnesses again, I would be most annoyed as they only called a few days before. When I opened the door, no one was there. I looked up and down the street and no one was in sight.

I went to tell Dora that whoever it was had not waited despite the fact that they had urgently rung the bell three times.

When I opened the lounge door, Dora was fast asleep and snoring loudly.

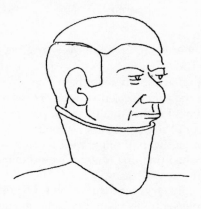

Broken Neck

Harry took his obsession of hypochondria very seriously. He spent many hours in the local council's reference library reading medical books and kept cuttings from newspapers concerning medical articles or reports of wrong diagnosis and treatments by doctors and hospitals. He assiduously watched every TV program involving medical matters. He was very concerned about a recently reported case where a woman with a broken neck had been sent home after being examined by a hospital casualty department following a road accident and being told that there was nothing wrong with her. He kept telling anyone that would listen that it was happening all the time.

It was dangerous to tell him about any accident or illness because within a short while he would report similar symptoms to his doctor, who not finding any corroborative evidence would give him a letter to see a specialist in a hospital. If the specialist also could find any such evidence, Harry would insist on having a second specialist's opinion. Sometimes, the specialist would keep him in hospital for tests and observations which pleased Harry very much as he loved the attention he was receiving.

On one occasion, a specialist agreed with Harry's self diagnosis and advised an immediate, urgent operation. Harry quickly discharged himself and left the hospital hurriedly and declared the specialist did not know what he was up to.

He loved attending hospitals and clinics and cross examining and telling doctors what was wrong with him. It was amazing just how many illnesses etc. a single person as himself could endure in one lifetime. There was hardly a part of his body that had not suffered, from psoriasis on his scalp to fungus on his toes.

Unfortunately for him, he receives very little sympathy from those who know him.

He was also a health faddist who insisted on doing the household shopping himself so as to ensure that only the most beneficial foods and drinks were brought into the house. Quite often, he has been seen carrying heavy bags of shopping despite the fact he claims to have a painful slipped disk.

He had been prescribed all sorts of medicines, pills, tablets and medical appliances by different doctors the consumption of which preoccupies him for a good part of each day. Apart from being a confirmed hypochondriac of long standing, he was also a terrible driver. He only passed his driving test after many attempts and driving his instructors crazy. He had so many accidents that he found it difficult to obtain insurance and ended up by having to pay a heavy premium to a small obscure company for 3rd party insurance only with a heavy excess clause. Even the motoring associations refused to renew his membership after a while because of his frequent demand on their services. Never-the-less, he persisted in motoring and blamed everybody else for his misfortunes. Most of his journeys were very local, either to his doctor, pharmacist, hospital, clinic or reference library.

It was when he was returning from such one of these journeys that he felt a searing pain in his neck which spread up the side of his face. As he believed in plenty of fresh air, he had been driving with his window wide open and the cold air had caused a reaction on his facial neuralgic nerve. Even though he did not have far to go to reach home, he panicked and pulled up on the roadside grass verge but not before lightly hitting a lamp post.

Recalling the recent report of the woman with the broken neck, he froze and tried not to move a single muscle.

After he had sat there absolutely immobile for a long period, a small boy came along and told him that he would be in trouble for parking on the grass verge. Without moving his head and talking out the corner of his mouth, he told the boy to phone 999 and get an ambulance. The boy told his mother about the man in a car who wanted an ambulance and before long there was one there.

The paramedics immediately slapped a neck brace on Harry who grunted and gave them all the symptoms of a broken neck which he had previously read about. The paramedics summoned the fire brigade and told them that they dare not move Harry out through the car door in case they aggravated a possible spinal injury. They asked the fire brigade to remove the car roof so that they could move Harry without danger of worsening any spinal injury.

As soon as Harry realised what was going on he tried to stop them but due to the neck brace and neuralgic pain he found it difficult to talk his way out of the situation he now found himself in. Every time he tried to talk they told him to relax and not move. He was whisked off to casualty in an ambulance with flashing lights and sirens sounding. After a most careful examination and tests, he was assured that he had no neck or spinal injury and that he could go home. They gave him a letter to hand to his doctor the next day.

He tried to convince his family that he had a broken neck but they preferred to believe the doctors.

A few days later, he received a letter from the local council telling him that they understood that a certain damaged car belonged to Harry and that if he did not remove the vehicle within seven days the council would do so and have it destroyed and any costs involved would be chargeable to him. They also said that in the near future, they would be sending him a bill in connection with the damage caused by his vehicle to the green verge and the lamp post.

The Valuation Surveyor

We were not particularly surprised when we received a communication from the local District Valuer's office informing us that a representative would be calling to inspect our house with respect to the revaluation of properties under so and so Act of Parliament.

This was a valuation on a national scale and had been much discussed in the news media.

When we phoned the Valuer's office they could not give us any date for the visit as they were overwhelmed with work and were very short of staff.

They did however explain that the inspection may not in effect take place as it was only necessary to inspect one or two properties in any one street that may be typical for the rest.

We thought this was a strange way to value properties because even though all the terraced houses down the street looked very much the same from the front, many differed considerably inside and at the rear. Some had enormous extensions built at the rear, some had the attics converted into additional rooms, some were converted into two, three or even four self contained flats, some had central heating and some had additional bathrooms added but none of these variations could be seen from the street.

Actually, our own house was very much as it was originally built some 90 years ago. It has not been extended or structurally altered, it retains the original fireplaces, doors and sliding sash windows.

Many weeks passed and we had almost forgotten about the possible survey when one morning without any prior notification or appointment a surveyor called. He was young, tall and extremely smartly dressed in a light coloured, obviously very expensive suit and bow tie and without any apology or courtesy of any sort announced that he had come to value our house

359

for rateable purposes. He did not ask if it was convenient or apologise for calling without a prior appointment and entered our home with the attitude one would expect of a sanitary inspector entering an unlicensed abattoir.

From his expensive looking brief case he took out a clip board and a gold propelling pencil and started to take notes.

He was very bumptious, pompous, arrogant, officious and curt to the extent of being rude.

He opened doors and entered rooms without asking permission and looked as though he found everything he saw as disgusting. When he left a room, he did not bother to close the door.

We found him to be the most disagreeable person we had ever encountered.

Finally, he said that he would like to inspect our basement. I told him that we did not have a basement, but we did have a small cellar. He said that he would never-the-less like to inspect the basement because when he had inspected a similar house across the road, he found that the basement was very extensive and virtually added an additional habitable storey to the house.

We opened the door leading down to the cellar and switched on the light. We told him that we do not use the cellar because it had been flooded up to 150mm for many months with ground water whilst the local council were diverting a local underground stream to enable a nearby motorway to be built.

He looked down the cellar steps and said I can't see any water. What had happened over the months was that a fine layer of dust had settled on the still surface of the water and in the dim artificial light did actually look like a firm cement floor.

He looked down at us, he was some 200mm taller that us and said, "I will go down and see if you are trying to conceal something from me, I am not that easily fooled."

He went down the cellar stairs and confidently stepped onto what he was convinced was a firm cement floor. He lost his balance and fell face down into the dirty water. His suit got soaked and it took him a while whilst he searched with his hands for his clip board and gold propelling pencil which he had dropped.

He hurriedly left without the courtesy of thanking us for our cooperation or even saying goodbye.

Several hours later, someone from his office phoned and asked if he had called at our home. They were rather concerned as he had not reported back to the office as he should have.

When I told him what had happened he laughed like mad and quickly recounted our story to those in his office. We could hear the hysterical laughter over the phone. The caller said, "It couldn't have happened to a nicer person."

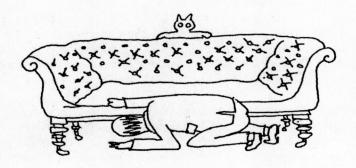

Blackie and the Vet

Blackie's first experience with a vet was when she was very young. She was spayed and deprived of the chance of motherhood even before she really began to know what sex was all about. What she did not have, she did not miss and therefore did not bear a grudge against the vet or her previous owner who arranged for the operation without consulting Blackie before hand. Her next encounter with a vet was several years later after she had taken up abode with us when we noticed that she was off colour, that is listless and not eating her usual vast portions. We took her to see a local vet who in a flash of a second had inserted a thermometer where Blackie reckoned he had no right to do. She had hardly got over the shock and the indignity when he gave her an injection without as much as a by your leave.

She did not forget this episode and resolved never to forgive him or any other vet.

For some reason or another, the next time she was ill we decided to ask the vet to make a home call. We thought that this would eliminate the distress of a journey to the vet.

He came just when we expected him to and I was holding Blackie on my lap. Dora went to let the vet in and no sooner had he said, "Good morning", that Blackie leapt off my lap and dashed under the heavy Victorian couch. She had recognised his voice, even alter several months since her visit to his surgery.

We tried hard to coax her out from under the heavy couch which we could not move in case we injured her. The vet did his best by getting down on all fours and shining his torch on her. He prescribed some pills to be administered three times a day. However hard we tried, we could not get her mouth opened to insert the pills. It seemed as though a pneumatic drill would not have been able to get her mouth opened.

Never-the-less, we still received a bill from the vet for a home visit.

Some while later, she showed signs of constipation and we considered this to be serious having regard to the vast quantity of food that she continued to eat. We were reluctant to consult a vet again but a neighbour told us that her cat had similar symptoms and her vet had prescribed liquid paraffin.

We resolved to give this remedy to Blackie even if she clenched her teeth together, by pouring the liquid through the gaps in her teeth. After a hard struggle, we managed to get a little of the liquid paraffin into her mouth and quite a quantity onto the glass topped table. I triumphantly released the cat thinking that she would make a dash for her refuge under the couch but to our amazement she eagerly lapped up all the spilt liquid paraffin and asked for more. She had much more than we intended her to have with very unpleasant consequences.

Her last encounter with a vet was when one evening we came home very late, about midnight, we found her coughing very badly. This alarmed us, as at the time, cat 'flu was very prevalent in the district. We knew that we had to act urgently and could not wait until morning.

It was too late to contact a neighbour to whom we had loaned our cat basket a few weeks ago. We knew that they went to bed early and would by now be fast asleep. We decided to improvise by lining the bottom of a cardboard box with one of my old woollen jumpers. Usually, we would not have any problem in getting Blackie into such a box. She would naturally regard it as a great game and cooperate. However, on this one occasion she was very suspicious and it was only with great difficulty that we got her into the box, closed the lid and secured it with a length of washing line.

For a while she was quiet and then began an unholy pitiful cry that nearly broke our hearts and awoke the neighbours.

We knew of a local 24 hour veterinary service and drove straight there. Dora sat on the rear seat of the car with the box on her lap. We rushed into the consulting room and placed the cardboard box on the stainless steel table. We told the vet what the problem was. He asked us to place the cat on the table. We undid the rope and opened the box but there was no cat therein. When we rushed back to the car, we found Blackie contentedly washing herself on the back seat but still coughing.

We grabbed her and rushed back into the vet's consulting room and triumphantly placed Blackie on the table. We were surprised how calmly she accepted the situation.

The vet said that he would have to take her temperature but as soon as Blackie saw the thermometer, she exploded into a black ball of fury, lashing out with all four legs, scratching, biting, swearing and hissing. As soon

362

as the vet let go, she became her usual placid self and commenced washing the orifice into which the vet had tried to insert the thermometer.

He said he was amazed. He had never before encountered such behaviour in a domestic cat. Thereupon, he handed me a pair of stout leather gauntlets and told me that I should put them on whilst he did likewise.

Between us we managed to hold the black ball of fury to enable her temperature to be taken.

The vet was surprised, the temperature was quite normal. He said that her cough was probably caused by a hair ball in her throat but as a precaution, he would give her an antibiotic injection. The all-in twoto-one wrestling match recommenced with me getting about half the dose intended for Blackie. Just as we were leaving, the vet asked for his fee apologetically explaining that the high amount was due to the high cost of keeping a fully manned surgery open 24 hours a day seven days a week.

As we went out, there were two persons waiting with cats on their laps. The cats were placid and quiet.

As soon as we returned home, Blackie vomited an hair ball, curled up and fell fast asleep.

Grandad

About 15 years ago, a church housing association bought a large Victorian house two doors away from us and converted it into four self contained flats.

The first tenant to move in was George, a tall, thin, bony, angular man, about 56 years old. He occupied one of the two ground floor flats. His flat had French doors which opened directly onto the rear garden.

It was obvious that he knew nothing at all about gardening but was eager to learn. I tactfully had to inform him several times that certain plants he was tenderly caring were actually weeds. He gladly accepted advice and spare plants and seedlings I gave him. As he was often obviously short of breath, he also gladly accepted the loan of a spare electric lawn mower.

He was quite successful in growing tomatoes. He spent many hours each day either tending his garden or relaxing therein. It would appear that he had never before had a garden of his own and enjoyed it as though he was in heaven.

We got on very well with him, in fact, as far as we knew everybody who came in contact with him also got on well with him.

We often wondered why a man of his age should be given a flat by a charity housing association. Usually at his age, men are often well established with a home of their own. We did not know if he was he married, widowed, divorced?

Did he have children, family, close friends of either sex? None appeared on the scene.

Had he been a homeless person or even someone just out of prison after a long sentence? Even though he was very friendly, he never gave a clue to these questions. One day we saw George being taken into an ambulance wearing an oxygen mask. It appeared that one of the other tenants in the house found George in a collapsed state and called the ambulance. He told her that he suffered with emphysema which he developed whilst working as a heating engineer. At last there was a crack in the wall that concealed the mystery of his past history.

He had no visitors but regularly, every Sunday morning a car would call and take him to a local church and then bring him home after the service.

About five years after he moved in, the flat above became vacant and was occupied by a girl of about 15 years of age. Nobody knew the reason why such a young girl had been given accommodation by the church housing association. This event was to have a profound effect on George who 'adopted' her and displayed a fond avuncular attitude towards her. She needed someone to rely on and confide in and he desperately needed company and someone to care for.

About 5 years after Joan moved in, she gave birth to a fine healthy boy who added to George's joy. The baby's father was a very quiet and shy young man and very little was seen or heard of him. George became very fond of the baby who grew up to regard and to call George 'Granddad'.

A couple of years later, Joan gave birth to a girl. Her one bedroom flat was then too small for her family and she was re-housed by the local authority in a first floor flat in a nearby district.

George was heart broken and nearly had a breakdown when Joan and her family moved out. However, he accepted the situation when Joan visited him regularly which was at least once a week. She also visited him daily whenever he was taken into hospital with his respiratory problem.

One of his attacks was fatal and he died in hospital. Joan was the only person at his bedside when he died. Everybody, including Joan herself had expected that George would make a generous bequest in his Will to her and her children, but despite an intensive search of his flat, no will or other instructions could be found. George had in fact died intestate. According to the law his estate passes onto his nearest living relatives or in the absence of any such relative, to the state.

The church that George attended regularly undertook to arrange his funeral and the disposal of his estate. They located a very elderly sister who lived in Somerset and who for some unknown reason had dissociated herself from George for about fifty years. She agreed that the church should arrange for George to be cremated but refused to accept the legacy. George's estate therefore automatically went to the state and Joan received nothing at all.

After the cremation, one of the church's members took George's ashes home with him and placed it on a shelf in his garage and told Joan that George had once declared when he was recuperating in the church's convalescent home in Devon that he would like his ashes scattered in the grounds of the home.

When Joan told one of the other tenants in the house about this proposal, the tenant said that George had often said that he would like his ashes scattered in the garden which he enjoyed so much. As she was so fond of George, Joan was very concerned about the proper disposal of his ashes. She wrote a very emotional letter to George's sister explaining her relationship with George and that because he had been a regular church goer, she felt that his ashes should be buried in consecrated grounds accompanied by a proper Christian burial service. The sister readily concurred and signed a prepared letter addressed to George's vicar requesting such a burial and service.

The vicar agreed and a funeral date set down. The ashes were handed to Joan who placed the urn reverently on the book shelf in her lounge.

When George died, Joan explained his absence to her little boy by telling him that "Granddad has gone to join Jesus in heaven."

The little boy was puzzled when he was subsequently told that Granddad was in the urn and in the near future he would be buried by the vicar. He wondered how such a big man like his Granddad could be in such a little urn. One day when his mother was preoccupied in the kitchen, he stood on a chair and took the metal urn down from the book shelf. He carefully opened it but could only see light grey coloured ashes. He poked around with his forefinger but could not feel anything. He took the urn onto the balcony where the light was much brighter but he still could not see anything. He then tipped the ashes onto the asphalt balcony floor but he still did not find anything. He decided that it was just like many of the other lies that his parents told him.

He shoved the small pile of ashes over the edge of the balcony with his foot, replaced the lid on the urn and quickly returned it to the book shelf. He did not say anything to his mother as he instinctively knew that what he had done was somehow not correct.

The funeral service was conducted with solemn dignity. Quite unexpectedly, George's sister had travelled from Somerset to be present

and pay her last respects to her brother to whom she had not spoken for fifty years. Apart from his sister, the service was attended by Joan and her husband and a small group from the church congregation and possibly also by George himself, in spirit form.

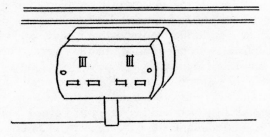

The Neat Electrician

Not long after moving into our existing house, we wanted to have an additional 13 amp electric socket outlet fixed in the rear ground floor room which we had decided to use as a guest room. It was a pleasant room with French doors leading straight onto the garden. It already had a wash basin with hot and cold water, a gas fire but only one electric plug which was situated in an inconvenient corner. The previous owner had, just prior to sale redecorated the room and covered the floor with bitumen felt that resembled linoleum. Because we knew that such felt tore easily when disturbed, we asked around for a local electrician who would be very careful.

As a consequence of these enquiries, John came to us most highly recommended. He was young, knew his job well, kept appointments, was intelligent, worked diligently, his prices were reasonable and he was very clean and tidy.

When we asked him to be careful when handling the flooring, he told us not to be concerned as he would not be disturbing it at all. We were incredulous and asked how he would get the wiring across the room without taking up some of the floor boards. He told us that our meter was in the cellar, he would supply and fix a new fuse box near the meter, run the cable across the cellar ceilings and through the 600mm space under the ground floor joists access to which is possible from the cellar.

He refused a cup of tea and got down to work straight away. He took his tool box and roll of cable down with him into the cellar but after about a quarter of an hour came rushing up, very excited and shouted that we should evacuate the house immediately because he had found a cluster of World War II incendiary bombs concealed under a sack in the space below the ground floor joists.

He told us that as he was drawing the cable along under the ground floor joists, he came across this sack covered obstruction. When he removed the sack he saw this cluster of incendiary bombs including the metal case in which the bombs were held whilst being stacked in the bomber. We knew that during the war, some people had kept unexploded incendiary bombs as souvenirs and we had even read about an old age pensioner who used a live bomb as a door stopper. John said that he took a keen interest in the war and had studied all aspects of it and was sure that what he had found was a cluster of magnesium incendiary bombs, hundreds of thousands of which had been dropped over London during the blitz. He said that after all this time, they may be in an unstable condition especially so, if he had disturbed the fuses.

Dora took our cat to a neighbour and asked her to keep him indoors until we had the all-clear.

I phoned the local police who sent two young constables round. They flashed their torched into the dark void under the floor and confirmed that the items looked like a cluster of unexploded incendiary bombs. The police phoned the army bomb disposal who promptly arrived as did several fire brigade appliances, and ambulances. The police sealed the street off and evacuated the occupants of the adjacent properties and their cats.

The bomb disposal team threw open all the windows and doors, tore the felt flooring away, ripped up the floor boards and dug a one metre deep hole in the middle of our immaculate lawn in which they said they would explode the bombs rather than take the risk of transporting them through the streets.

When the bomb disposal men had carefully removed the 'bombs' and took them into the rear garden in order to place them in the prepared hole, they said that the items were not bombs at all but looked like some peculiar light fitting.

They hurriedly left, so did the police, the fire brigade and the ambulances and our cat returned home.

I surveyed with great dismay the devastation they left behind.

The electrician completed his tidy work and in a way of consolation told us that not long ago, he had come across a dismantled piano in a nearby loft.

To add insult to injury, the local press had headlines about an irresponsible couple who hoarded live bombs in a local residential area.

Butch

I can't explain why it is, but several of our neighbours entrust us with the keys to their houses. Some do so on a permanent basis and others do so whilst they are away on holiday. Maybe, it is because we have honest faces or maybe, they consider us to be so simple or lacking in courage to do anything dishonest.

Possibly, the last is the more truthful explanation. In fact, we have a completely clean criminal record, not even a parking ticket has ever been issued against me or a fine imposed by the local authority for an overdue library book.

Of course, honesty is not the only criteria, there is also reliability and efficiency to be considered.

The ones who leave their keys on a permanent basis, do so in case they ever lock themselves out and otherwise, would have to resort to expensive and inconvenient service by a locksmith. In this respect, we have been able to assist several times.

When neighbours leave their keys with us whilst they are on holiday it is usually accompanied with a request that we feed their pets and, or, water their houseplants as well as to switch lights on during the evenings in order to make the house appear to be occupied. We don't mind in the least obliging our neighbours, whom, we are sure, would, if requested, do the same for us.

We place the keys on brass hooks on the inside face of a cupboard door and label them neatly, but in code so that, if they go astray for any reason, there would not be any obvious clue as to which property they appertained to.

Some neighbours inform us that they are going away on holiday but do

369

not leave their keys with us. They ask us to 'keep an eye on their house'.

We don't expect any payment or reward for helping our neighbours and putting their minds at ease and thus hopefully, enabling them to enjoy their holidays. Sometimes, we are rewarded by a token of appreciation. We were amused, when, one year, one of the neighbours who asked us to 'keep an eye on their house' whilst they spent a holiday in their home country, Greece, rewarded us with a nice box of Turkish Delight!

Last year, just as one of our neighbours (who asked us to water her plants whilst she was away) was leaving to catch a plane to Florida, informed us that she had smelt a bad leak of gas in the vicinity of her new gas cooker. She asked us to contact the Gas Boards emergency service to get it seen to.

The Gas Board were most efficient. We had hardly put the phone down, when their engineer was at the door. He located the leak to a poor connection between the newly installed cooker and the gas pipe. As a safety precaution, he checked all the other appliances in case of any other leaks before he left. We were very impressed with his efficiency and conscientiousness. In the evening, I returned to her house to switch lights on and to make sure no taps had been left dripping etc., when I noticed all sorts of lights on the cooker. Some I could see were electronic time switches and others were temperature indicators, and indicators showing which item on the cooker was in use. I was somewhat bewildered by this array of electronic lights and numerals but as far as I could make out, the oven was in operation. After much trial and error, I was able to open the oven and saw that it was hot and contained a potato that was half cooked. It took me quite a while to work out how to turn the oven off.

I congratulated myself on averting a potential disaster and thought that the householder was negligent in not turning the oven off before leaving. My opinion on the conscientiousness of the gas board's engineer was also greatly diminished considering that he had not noticed that the oven had been left on. However, my mind was not at ease and I later returned to the house to make sure that the gas leak had been totally eliminated and that the oven was truly out and cold. I was pleased to note that there was no smell of gas but I was shocked to note that the oven was still hot and the potato was still baking away.

I fiddled again with the knobs and switches until I felt certain that the oven was off.

About an hour later to put my mind fully at ease before I went to sleep, I returned once more to the house and noticed that the Gas Board's emergency notice van was outside the door. When I went in, I found that the neighbour's daughter, who I was told was away at college had returned home to make sure everything was in order. She had put a potato in the oven for a meal and had lain down for half an hour to rest after her journey.

When she came down, she found the oven off and the potato was only slightly cooked. She relit the oven and went to have a shower. When she came down again, the oven was once more cold.

She decided to call out the Gas Board's emergency service just in case there was some potential danger in the oven's malfunction.

You may very well be asking yourself, what the hell has a half baked potato got to do with Butch the smelly, half feral, undoctored tom cat. Well, nothing directly, but to show what onerous responsibilities we undertake when we promise to look after neighbours' houses whilst they are away having a carefree, enjoyable holiday. Another neighbour, Mrs. Hudson, told us that whilst she was going on holiday in sunny Spain, her husband would be away visiting a very sick relative in Wiltshire.

She said that she could not give us a telephone number where she could be contacted, but we could, in an emergency, contact her through her husband's sick relative whose telephone number she did have.

Whilst she said she would appreciate us keeping an eye on her indoor plants, she was most concerned that we should put out fresh food and milk daily for Butch the tabby, undoctored, feral torn cat which she had adopted. He was obviously a stray and greatly appreciated being fed daily. She said that we were to make sure that the conservatory door was to be kept open at all times but never to allow Butch into the house itself as he stank to high heavens and left his 'visiting card' wherever and whenever he could. He was very timid and would dash away if we were to approach him, she left a vast quantity of varied tins of cat food and the milkman had been instructed to leave two pints of full cream gold top milk for the cat every day.

We thought this provision extravagant and excessive but she assured us that Butch had a terrific appetite and thirst. In the corner of the conservatory was a cat basket on which the cat slept from time-to-time. Although, the generous portions of food and milk we left out for Butch each day was consumed generally during the night we did not catch sight of Butch until about eight days later. He was lying in the cat basket and was in a very bad state. He was panting and his body was covered in wounds. It was obvious that he needed veterinary attention urgently. To make sure that he did not escape whilst waiting for the vet, we closed the conservatory door.

The vet confirmed that the cat was seriously ill and said that he could not treat him in-situ and would have to take him back to the surgery. We were surprised, after what we had been told about him being very timid just how meekly the cat allowed itself to be picked up and carried out to the vet's vehicle.

A couple of days later, the vet said that despite intensive treatment, the cat had died from a pulmonary infection and asked what he should do with the body. We urgently contacted Mr. Hudson whom we had already informed of the cat's condition. He said that we should ask the vet to keep the body in a deep freeze until both he and his wife could return and arrange a burial. Meanwhile, the vet kept badgering us about the cat's body. He had placed it in his family's deep freeze cabinet but his wife was objecting very strongly to having a dead cat that had died from an infectious disease lying amidst her prime chickens and other choice meats.

The Hudsons returned within a couple of days, the vet solemnly but thankfully returned the cat's body. The cat was buried in the rear of the garden alongside the bodies of five other cats. After the internment, the burial party returned to the house for refreshments but were amazed to hear loud, pitiable meowing of a cat in distress. The sound came from the conservatory. Upon entering the conservatory they saw Butch staring in disgust at his empty food bowls and expressing his annoyance in no uncertain terms.

It was no doubt Butch himself. Apparently, the cat that had just been buried was a look-alike undoctored tom who, had, unknowingly for years to the Hudsons, been sharing the food and drink left so liberally in the conservatory.

Not long after, Butch failed to re-appear and his fate is unknown.

The Permit

Some while ago, Ruth, one of Dora's acquaintances, told her that she and her husband had been invited to a reception at the House of Commons by the local Member of Parliament to celebrate his recent reelection. Apparently, both Ruth and her husband had been very active on behalf of the MP during the election campaign and the MP wished to show his appreciation.

Unfortunately, her husband was not well and could not attend, so Ruth asked Dora if she would like to accompany her. The M.P's secretary had agreed to the substitution.

Dora had never before been to such an event at the House of Commons and readily agreed.

The two women travelled to Westminster by the London Transport underground train service. The trains, as usual, at that time, that is early evening, were crowded and the journey was uneventful.

Dora was very impressed by the reception and the ambience in which it was held.

After proudly entering the building through the St. Stevens gate, they were courteously directed to the room in which the party was being held but not before going through rigorous security checks. The celebration was taking place in a room at the far end of an enormous banqueting hall with hammer beam roof trusses.

There was an abundance of help yourself snacks and various drinks. Most of the guests already knew each other and the atmosphere was very relaxed and friendly. There were no formal speeches, just a few words of welcome and appreciation by the re-elected MP

Quite a number of the guests, like Dora, had never before attended such a reception at the House of Commons and they were discussing their experiences including the security arrangement.

Ruth pointed out that whereas many of those present know each other there were a few, like Dora, who were unknown. She said that although their handbags had been searched when they entered the building and although they passed through an electronic gate to see if they had any concealed weapons under their clothes, nothing was done to check their identities. This raised the point of whether electronic identity cards should be required to be produced by people especially when entering sensitive establishments such as the Houses of Parliament. Ruth pointed out that after entering the building, they had come in close contact with well known political figures, including some Cabinet Ministers.

Dora also pointed out that despite the fact that they had been searched for concealed weapons when entering the building, the reception room was filled with potential weapons freely available in the form of knives and forks and also beer glasses and bottles. It was a very interesting discussion.

As a whole, despite some reservations the general opinion appeared to be in favour of identity cards. Ruth also pointed out, that on the journey, the trains were filled with most peculiar looking people and if challenged, could easily give false identity and address.

There was talk of identity cards being a loss of personal liberty and others who declared, if you had nothing to hide or to be ashamed of, there was no harm in having one.

Strangely enough, it was the women who seemed to object more than the men. Possibly, it was because the cards may bear the date of birth.

The celebration was highly successful and ended about 9pm. Dora smuggled out two House of Commons paper serviettes as souvenirs of the evening. There were no security checks on the way out.

The two women were to return home, the same way as they came. They caught a District Line underground train at Westminster Station which is very close to the House of Commons and changed onto a Central Line train at Mile End Station. Both trains were only about one third full and there were plenty of vacant seats. Some of the passengers were sleeping and others were reading magazines or newspapers whilst others stared hypnotically at the boring adverts above the opposite passenger's heads. It had been pre-arranged, that when the two women reached Gants Hill Station, they would phone me and I would pick them up and take each to their respective homes. In the event of anything going amiss, they were to take a black London taxi cab from the rank just outside the station. The two women seated themselves at one end of a long row of seats. At the other end of the facing seats there was already seated a well dressed middle aged man assiduously reading his newspaper. He did not glanced up to see who, if anyone, had entered the carriage at the last stop and kept on reading his newspaper without turning the page. Ruth and Dora assumed he may have fallen asleep. Nothing untoward happened until the train reached Leytonstone tube station. Quite surprisingly, the automatic doors of the carriage did not open when the train stopped even though the automatic doors to the other carriages operated normally, allowing passengers to alight.

A young couple, further along the carriage tried unsuccessfully to open the doors by pressing the. 'open' button. The passengers in the carriage became concerned in case there was a mechanical failure and that their journey home would be delayed; that is all the passengers except the man opposite 'reading' his newspaper. His eyes were still fixed on the same page. After about five minutes, which in the uncertainty, seemed like an eternity, the door was opened from the outside by a uniformed railway official using a special key and a uniformed London Transport policeman entered accompanied by a flustered looking, middle aged woman.

He proclaimed in a loud voice that everyone should remain in place and remain calm. He then said in a loud voice for all to hear, "Would the gentleman who indecently exposed himself to this woman please leave the carriage." Everybody looked round to see who the culprit might be, that is, everyone except the man 'reading' the newspaper. He did not even look up and remained staring at the same page of the paper.

After a quiet consultation between policeman and the woman, she pointed to the newspaper reader. The policeman approached the man and said in a loud voice, "This woman says you indecently exposed yourself to her, would you please leave the carriage with me, I am a police officer."

The man still did not raise his eyes from his newspaper but slid a hand into his jacket pocket and produced an official looking identity card which he showed to the police officer without uttering a word. The policeman's demeanour immediately changed and profusely apologised for the incident to the man and ushered the woman out of the carriage.

The train continued on its journey with the man still staring at his newspaper. Both Ruth and Dora returned home safely and even until this day still wonder what sort of identity the newspaper 'reader' had produced in order to create such a reaction from the policeman.

Simon's Bungalow

Sometimes, when the weather is exceptionally nice, Dora and I go down to the local beautifully kept Valentine's Park. It is not generally known, but Valentine's Park in Ilford, Essex is the largest park in the London area, even larger than Hyde Park. Perhaps, because of its large size it does not get over-crowded.even on lovely days when people from adjoining boroughs come flocking in. It has many attractions and facilities including a boating lake, lovely flower beds, an Elizabethan house used for council offices, large fields, bowling greens, putting greens, children's play areas, a cafe, bandstands, ornamental lakes, toilets, a large field where visiting fairs and circus' set up and a field where first class and county cricket takes place. It is a credit to the local council and the rate payers who pay for it.

The paths are well kept and there are plenty of clean, sound benches upon which to relax and to watch the passing cavalcade of visitors.

It was while Dora and I were relaxing on one of these benches that we got into conversation with Simon. He was tallish (nearly everyone is tallish compared with me) and portly. We were surprised when he told us that he was one of the gardeners responsible for the upkeep of the park. He had an ample supply of cakes, sandwiches and bottles of drink of which he partook from time to time whilst chatting with us.

He said that he was on a works experience scheme for unemployed people and was enjoying himself but made it clear that he was not unduly concerned about being caught not working because the government had undertaken to reimburse his wages to the council for a period of six weeks. If the council wishes, after that trial period, they can employ him full time. Simon said that he was not worried about being kept on by the council as by then, the weather would have changed and when there were not so many visitors, he would not be able to skive for most of the day.

He told us, that since he developed a heart condition some five years previously, he could only undertake jobs that involved light duties.

This job was not the first he had under the government's works experience scheme which was designed to get long term unemployed back into work. He had also had a six weeks spell as a hospital porter but did not like it as he was continually on call.

He also found a government financed course in watch repairing which he did not complete because he found it boring, nor did he complete a course in plumbing as he found that too dirty.

He did however, get a full time permanent job as a driver of a light delivery van for a local stationer delivering small packages mainly to schools all over the county of Essex. He was warned that the van was not insured to carry passengers who were not employed by the firm. This, however, did not stop Simon taking his current girl friend with him on some of the journeys, especially when they involved deliveries to the seaside resort of Southend-on-Sea.

It was during one of these visits to Southend that Simon met an elderly man who complained about not feeling well and would like to be taken back to his wife. When Simon asked him where he lived, he said, "East Ham in east London." Apart from his other weaknesses, Simon was kind hearted and as the man reminded him of his late departed father, offered to take him home. He told the man that it was no trouble at all as East Ham is close to Ilford where he, himself, was living at the time. On the way back, the van was involved in a traffic accident and the return journey was delayed by police enquires and having certain essential repairs done to the van to make it road worthy.

When they finally arrived at the elderly man's house rather late in the evening, the door was opened by a very distraught young woman who said, "Where the hell have you been all day, mum is going crazy waiting for you to return to the boarding house." He apparently forgot that he was on a two week holiday in Southend with his wife.

Simon's own son had tried to help him by employing him as a general handyman/office junior in his solicitors office but had to dismiss him when he found that Simon spent most of his time reading confidential divorce files on local people he knew.

Once he started relating his work experiences, there was no stopping him even though the time was passing rapidly by.

We asked him what his basic trade or profession was before he developed his heart condition. He said that when he left school, his father who was a master tailor, had apprenticed him into the trade but as soon as he completed his apprenticeship he was conscripted into the RAF. He spent most of his time in the RAF altering and repairing officer's uniforms. He had no direct contact with flying machines, only sewing machines. He surprised us when he suddenly produced a thimble from his trousers pocket and told us that he always carried it with him as a symbol of his trade. When he was demobbed from the RAF, civilian clothes were still severely rationed and he found that there was little demand for his skills and he entered into a very prolonged period of trade depression and unemployment.

Having told us about his work experience, he started to tell us about his matrimonial situation. Apparently, despite his prolonged spells of unemployment, his first marriage had been a fairly amicable one and it produced a son who consequently qualified as a solicitor and ran a successful practice but eventually Simon's wife found his lackadaisical character unbearable and divorced him. His second wife, was, until she recently died of lung cancer caused by excessive smoking, a very rich and successful business woman. Simon had decided that it was his duty to share her opulent life style and to live a retired gentlemen's life without working, not that he evef worked much.

This suited his wife who in turn married Simon in order to gratify her excessive sexual demands. Simon found this ordeal unbearable and was quietly relieved when she passed away.

His great expectation of financial material benefit arising out of her considerable estate was not realised. She had so skilfully arranged matters so that he did not benefit by a single penny. He even had to vacate the matrimonial home.

Simon reckoned that it was through the physical strain of that marriage and the subsequent financial disappointment that he developed his present heart condition.

However, in order to avoid lengthy and costly eviction procedures, the executors of his late, dearly beloved wife's Will, offered to pay for a deposit on a modestly priced house and for him to take a few items of non antique furniture from the matrimonial home. Simon agreed with alacrity to this proposal and bought a small modern semi detached bungalow on the outskirts of the picturesque Essex village of LangleyWoods. He had often stopped off there with his present girlfriend for a drink in one of the quaint pubs.

Having expounded at length about himself without almost stopping to take a breath, he commenced asking questions about Dora and myself. Were we married, for how long, any children, where did we live, was I retired, what did I work at before retiring.

I told him that until I retired about five years ago, I was an architect in my own small, one person practice. When he heard this, he said that I possibly could be of considerable assistance to him. When he bought the bungalow his son had arranged for it to be surveyed by a local surveyor. The surveyor's report had caused great consternation but after some hard bargaining and negotiation, his son had arranged a suitable agreement with the vendor. Simon said that he could not understand what the problem was all about and said that Dora and I would be most welcome to have tea with him and his girlfriend in his newly acquired bungalow and whilst there, he would show me the surveyor's report so that I may be able to explain what it was all about in simple straight forward English instead of the incomprehensible legal/technical language in the report and subsequent correspondence conducted through his son.

As soon as he gave me his address I asked him if the basic problem with the bungalow was concerned with ground/heave settlement. He was amazed and asked me how I knew. I told him that the address itself indicated the problem, the bungalow was situated in Willow Tree Walk and the district was named Langley-Wood. As soon as we arrived we could see the source of Simon's query. A large, mature, beautiful willow tree in a neighbour's garden dominated the area. A quick glance at adjacent properties confirmed that the problem was not restricted to Simon's bungalow alone. The other bungalow to which Simon's was attached was obviously empty with three different agents 'For Sale' notice boards in the front garden. The previous owner had not been able to sell the bungalow and could not keep up his mortgage payments. The bungalow had consequently been re-possessed by his building society who re-sold it at a greatly discounted price to a speculator who was now trying to re-sell it at a profit. He was waiting for another Simon to turn up.

After I had explained to Simon the contents of his surveyors report and outlined the guarantee negotiated by his sons on his behalf we settled down to a nice relaxing tea which included home baked cakes and dainty sandwiches prepared by Simon's girlfriend.

Simon said that the owner of the adjoining bungalow was having great trouble in selling it because of the ground heave/settlement problems. Very few people had come to view it. Because the bungalows were in a cul-de-sac, all viewers have to pass his window so that he gets a good idea of how many that come and what sort of people they are. He was obviously most concerned to have nice quiet amicable neighbours.

He told us that he was presently on sick leave recovering from the trauma of a recent incident at Gants Hill underground station. Simon was waiting near the edge of the platform for the next train to arrive when he had a sudden blackout. The next thing he knew was when he came-to in the local hospital casualty department. Although shocked, he was relatively uninjured, just a few bruises. When he blacked out he fell down and rolled over the edge of the platform and fell in the pit between the rails. A quick thinking nearby platform porter realising that a train was due in at any moment, leaped in and pinned him down until the electric current was cut off. One wrong movement and both would have been electrocuted.

Simon was most grateful and full of praise for the brave porter and asked London Transport for an opportunity to meet the porter so that he could thank him personally. They said that the porter had been given special leave to ensure that he was not suffering from any trauma and as soon as possible they would ask him if he would like to receive Simon's personal thanks. Because of security, they were not permitted to give the porter's address or telephone number but they had given him Simon's address and telephone number and left it to him to arrange any meeting he wished to make. They did, however, reveal that the porter's name was Cohn Wilson.

Whilst we were chatting merrily away discussing Simon's miraculous escape and the unselfish bravery of the porter, Simon leapt up out of his chair and rushed to the front bay window. A black man had passed and with a paper in hand had walked up the path to the bungalow next door.

The man realising that the bungalow was empty hesitantly approached Simon's front door and rang his bell. He excused himself and said that he was looking for a Mr Simon Abrahams. It turned out that it was the hero himself, Cohn Wilson. London Transport had not only given him the wrong house number but also the wrong telephone number so he could not phone beforehand to let Simon know he was calling.

He was a very jovial man, kept laughing and spoke with a strong Jamaican accent.

Simon explained that he was no scholar and would not have been able to put into writing the words he wanted to express in appreciation of what Cohn had done. He said, "Apart from anything else, I owe my whole life to you".

After Cohn had left, Simon continued to praise him and said that during his service in the RAF, he had never encountered such bravery. He continued, "when I first spotted him approaching the next door bungalow, my heart sunk because I thought he had come with the intention of buying it."

Mark Baum

"It's a small, small world." This fact was brought home to me particularly when in 1962, I set out with my wife Dora to visit Israel. Because Dora was then scared of flying we went by boat. We travelled by the train to Marseilles and from there boarded the 'Moledet'. We shared a dining table with three other English speaking couples, all of us about the same age. We planned to stay as tourists in Israel for four weeks before making the return journey on the 'Moledet' which is Hebrew for 'Homeland'

We got quite friendly with one of the couples, Mark Baum and his charming but very shy wife, Helen. During the five day voyage we had plenty of opportunity to chat.

During a very stormy passage through the Strait of Messina we were the only passengers who were not sea-sick. Because very few of the sea-sick passengers turned up for their meals there was an abundance of food available. We were amazed at the vast quantity of food that Mark was able to devour. He was a big robust man with an enormous appetite. In contrast, his wife was dainty with a moderate appetite.

Mark told us that he was not always so healthy and hearty. In his younger days, especially as a child, he was very weak and sickly but after he grew up and especially after he married and moved out of the slums of east London to an opulent district of Glasgow from where his wile came, his physique improved considerably and now he enjoyed all forms of sport. He was now quite prosperous and was the owner of a very successful clothes factory in Glasgow employing several hundred people. Whilst his wife spoke with a strong Glasgow accent, he still retained his Jewish cockney accent.

One day, when we were discussing our backgrounds, I was amazed to learn that as a child he actually lived in the same bug ridden slum tenements as I did, known grandly as the Clark Street Buildings. Whereas I lived on the first floor of No 54, he lived only two doors away at No 50 on the second floor.

I recalled, that as a child, perhaps about five years old, I was friendly with a child who lived in that flat but his name was not Mark Baum but, Mike Mandlebaum. He said, that's me, I changed my name a little bit for business reasons. I liked playing with him because his mother used to give me slabs of chocolate. We excitedly exchanged memories of the Buildings and its occupants and life generally in that very Jewish part of east London. He had a fantastic memory for names and details. When we reached Israel, he went off to stay in a five star hotel whilst we went to look for some cheap Bed & Breakfast accommodation.

Before we parted, we agreed to meet again from time-to-time, which we did, especially when mark visited London in connection with his business.

During one of his visits to our home, he seemed to be particularly disturbed and distressed but I did not like to question him in case it was something personal. After a short while we learnt that the problem was when he suddenly asked if I had used some liniment. I told him that I had applied an embrocation to my back a few days ago because I was subject to attacks of lumbago and I was surprised that the smell should still be ascertainable. He said that he was extremely sensitive to the smell of liniment especially so, as it recalled a traumatic experience that had occurred when he was a very young child in his flat in Clark Street Buildings. He said that the incident concerned caused him to have re-current nightmares. He says that he recalls every little detail as though it occurred only yesterday even though it happened about sixty years ago when he was only about four years old.

His overworked and harassed mother had asked his eldest sister to assist with the housework by sweeping the living room floor. In those days, in the east end of London, carpeting was unheard of, but the room was covered with linoleum which in itself was a luxury because most of the dwellings in the east end of London just had bare boards which had to be scrubbed.

His sister was on the tubby side and lazily inclined and only commenced the chore after much coercion and threats.

The room was very crowded with furniture, even though it was the family's living room it contained two double beds, a wardrobe, a chest of drawers, a dressing table and several dining chairs. There were no armchairs or easy chairs as they too, were unaffordable luxuries. As his sister approached a family member sitting on a chair, she asked them to stand up so that she could sweep underneath. She similarly asked her grandmother, her mother's mother, to stand up and when the old withered lady went to sit down again, his sister snatched the chair away so that the old lady fell onto the floor. At first his sister found the episode very amusing and laughed loudly but soon she started to sob and whine when it was realised that the old lady had broken a leg in the fall. His sister vehemently denied having anything to do with the accident.

The local doctor was summoned. He charged two shillings and six-pence (twelve and a half pence) for an emergency or urgent home visit. He was Doctor Jaffa, a friendly, round, ginger haired man with a club foot. He had the advantage over other doctors in that he could communicate with the Jewish patients in Yiddish.

Mark recalls that tense atmosphere and the call for broom sticks to be used as splints. The grandmother was carted off by ambulance to the local hospital because she had suffered a compound fracture. A few days later she developed pneumonia and died.

I asked Mike if he told anyone about seeing his sister pulling the chair away from under his grandmother. He said that he could not. Even though he was about four years old, he was not yet able to talk coherently. It was this inability to communicate what he had witnessed that impressed the episode so strongly and lastingly on his subconscious mind.

He remembers his grandmother being brought home from the hospital in a plain, sawn pine wood coffin and placed in the living room but he was not allowed to go into the room. Two elderly stout ladies dressed all in black with black ribboned bonnets came to wash the body. They brought with them long wooden boards and trestles as well as a tin bath.

Soon after the two elderly ladies had entered the living room they commenced their task, he became aware of a very strong smell of liniment. He assumed that it had something to do with the corpse and even today, associates the smell of liniment with corpses. Upon his mother's insistence, the lid of the coffin was raised for her last farewell but all that resulted was a long and loud wail not only from her, but also from all the other women present. The louder they wailed, the stronger the smell of the liniment appeared to become until it was almost suffocating and overpowering.

All mirrors and photos in the flat were covered with white pillow slips.

He was not allowed to go to the funeral, but later heard that his mother had fainted at the grave side when she heard the first clod of earth being cast onto the coffin lid.

'Sheva' was sat. That is, that closest adult relatives went into seven days deep mourning, sitting on low hard stools or chairs. Friends and relatives came to console them and to hear how, due to her old age, she had a dizzy attack and had fallen over and broken her leg.

Every evening at 8pm, prayers were held in the living room where the 'accident' occurred. Only men were allowed in accordance with the Jewish religion to participate in the prayers.

Edith

My wife's cousin's wife, Edith is, or rather was until recently, a doughty, valiant and nononsense type of woman. She was born and bred in a Scottish village and after living in an east end London suburb for many years became quite street wise. Several of her friends had been mugged and she was determined not to be a victim herself. Her husband, that is, Dora's cousin told her not to resist any robber and to hand valuables over without struggle if threatened. She agreed that that would be the wisest thing to do and consequently whenever she went out, took with the minimum amount of cash and wore no expensive jewellery.

Never-the-less, despite her resolve and precautions she is now receiving counselling and in the near future may very well be subject to psychiatric treatment for trauma as a result of mugging.

Her first personal experience of being mugged was when she was shopping in a local supermarket. She had placed her handbag on the small shelf near the trolley handle and secured it to the hook provided and also kept a close eye on it. She had heard that several women had had their handbags snatched from such supermarket trolleys and considered that they must have been negligent. She had nearly finished her shopping when she took her eyes off her trolley to get some item out of a deep freeze cabinet. This only took her a few seconds, but when she turned round to put the item in the trolley, her handbag had gone.

She was amazed, she just could not believe it could have happened to her. There had been noone particularly close to the trolley at the time and she could not discern anyone in the vicinity who might have snatched her bag. She immediately set up a hue and cry but there was no sign of her bag which contained her shopping cash, reading spectacles, house keys, library

384

tickets, bus pass and pension book. On her way to the shops, she had drawn her week's pension.

The store's security supervisor took details and promised to let her know if her bag or any of its contents were found. He also allowed her to phone her husband to come with enough cash to pay for the shopping and to take her home in the car because she was a bit shocked and had lost her bus pass.

Her husband consoled her by telling her that she was lucky not to have been hurt physically. All the stolen items, even if they were not recovered could be replaced.

They immediately notified the local post office to put a stop on any further money being drawn on her pension book and an application was made for a replacement. The front door lock on their house was changed because the thief had her keys and address, the local council was notified about the stolen bus pass and an application for a duplicate to be issued. The police were notified and requested to keep an eye on the house in case a thief tried to use the stolen keys.

She felt angry and helpless and stupid at the way she had lost her handbag and resolved to be even more careful in future.

With one thing and another, she was kept quite busy as a result of. the theft. Friends, neighbours and relatives called and asked if they could be of help and to discuss the theft.

About a fortnight later, when she decided once again to go shopping in the supermarket, her husband suggested that he would accompany her as her minder. She declined his offer saying that he would only be an encumbrance and that she would make sure that her bag would not be purloined again.

On the way to the shops, she called into her local post office to collect her pension money. The Counter Clerk assured her that no-one had yet tried to cash any money on her stolen book and he is still keeping a sharp look-out for anyone trying to do so.

This time, Edith secured her new handbag in such a manner to the shopping trolley in the supermarket that it would take quite a while to remove it. She also kept a special extra eye on it.

Despite this, she became aware of a young man lurking about and surreptitiously watching a middle-aged woman whilst she went around the store loading her trolley. Edith noted that the woman had foolishly placed her handbag on top of the trolley and had not secured it. As the woman went from section to section, the young man followed her, watching from behind vantage points or pretending to be interested in certain items on the shelves. She noted that the man had no trolley or basket or even shopping bag with him and therefore had no interest in actually buying anything.

As soon as the opportunity presented itself, Edith excitedly brought the man's behaviour to the attention of one of the uniformed security guards. She thought that maybe the suspiciously acting man might be the person who snatched her handbag. The security guard, surprisingly told her not to be concerned and not to attract attention to the suspect. He told her that he was actually a plain clothes member of the security staff and that he might have reasons to suspect that the woman he was watching was not behaving properly. His suspicions proved correct as when she attempted to leave the store after checking out through the cash desk, she was found to have a huge quantity of expensive items she had not paid for.

It was then, that Edith realised, that in her distraction, she had failed to keep a close eye on her handbag but fortunately, it was quite safe.

By the next time she went out shopping, she had fully regained her confidence and once again declined her husband's offer to accompany her. She took the precaution of taking the absolute minimum with her and so loaded her bag only with her reading glasses and her replaced pension book. She even left her housekeys behind.

In accordance with her custom, she called in to the local post office to collect her week's pension and to ascertain if any effort had yet been made to use her stolen pension book.

It was shortly after she left the post office that she heard the sound of running feet and felt a sharp tag on her handbag strap. A young man was tugging frantically at the strap and shouting at her to let go. Despite her resolution not resist any handbag snatch, she held onto the bag desperately and screamed out for help. The attacker became quite alarmed and ran away sans handbag. Edith was quite shocked at the suddenness of the attack but what shocked her most was the horrid look of hatred and anger on the young man's contorted face. Someone nearby called the police on a mobile phone and they were soon on the scene.

Edith could not give much of a description of the attacker and several of the witnesses gave differing accounts. She declined the suggestion that she should go to the hospital for a checkup and a police woman kindly gave her a lift home in her car.

When she got home, she found that she was badly bruised on her right arm and shoulder. The assailant must have punched her several times in the attack.

She was severely shocked and after a nice strong sweet cup of tea lay down in the lounge on the settee to recover.

Early that same evening, her good friend, Elsie, came to see her and told her that the best therapeutic treatment for the shock of the attack and celebration for not losing her bag and pension was -a jolly visit to the local Bingo. Elsie was so assertive that Edith had no alternative but to agree and off they both went. Although her husband had his doubts, he knew just how much Edith enjoyed her visits to Bingo and agreed. He always stayed behind as he preferred a couple of pints of beer and to watch telly.

He was very surprised to receive a phone call later on in the evening from Edith who was phoning from the Bingo hall. She was hysterical with joy. She was laughing so much, she had difficulty in telling her husband that she had won £1000 on Bingo. She said she was nervous about coming home on her own with such a large sum of money and would he come and pick her up in the car. He said that he could not do so because he had been drinking and at the best of times disliked motoring at night. He told her to get a mini-cab and he would pay when she arrived.

When she did arrive a short while after, she was white and shaking violently and was obviously very shocked. She gasped in short breaths, she was cold and her face was covered in perspiration.

It was with great difficulty that he finally managed to elucidate what had caused her such a dramatic change in her attitude.

She said that soon after she and Elsie had got into the mini-cab she caught a brief glimpse of the driver in his rear mirror. She felt strongly that it was the face of her attacker but was not contorted as earlier in the day. She was determined to have a good look at him as soon as they got out and in the safety of her husband's presence. Her alarm increased because Elsie kept on blabbering about her good fortune and she was sure the driver was aware that she had such a large sum of money on her. She just could not stop Elsie chattering in her loud excited voice. The journey seemed endless and as soon as the car stopped she bolted indoors without having a good look at the driver.

The police were notified and soon traced the driver who had a cast iron alibi as to where he was at the time of the attack earlier in the day.

The police supplied a counsellor who suggested that Edith should undergo psychiatric treatment.

Eric

When we moved into our existing house some 40 years ago, Eric Petchey and his family were already long established residents in a nearby house. We never got to know his wife's name, but his attractive looking, well dressed daughter was known as Olivia. She had a very good administrative job in the local council's Borough Treasurer's department and apparently was well paid. We understood that she was divorced. Her grown son, Charles worked in a local solicitor's office. They appeared to be a nice, well behaved family and were good neighbours, in as much as they did not annoy anyone. But being human, they had their foibles and very much kept themselves to themselves. They were very pleasant and passed the time of day with anyone but never engaged in conversation.

Eric, for some reason or another had taken early retirement from his job as a sorter in the local post office but kept himself busy with regular and painstaking maintenance of his house and car. He appeared to be more often up a ladder painting his house than on terra firma. He lovingly tended his gardens, he had large gardens both at front and rear of his house and he washed and polished his car even when it was shining clean. He was ruddy faced and full of energy.

Our street is a friendly one and nearly every neighbour stops and chats whenever the opportunity presents itself but such friendship is not over done to the extent that it produces friction. Apart from the weather topic, pets are often the subject of light conversation. If any of the neighbours stopped to chat to Eric whilst he was polishing his immaculate clean car or watering his front garden, one of his vertical sliding sash windows would be flung up and a loud voice would yell, "EREEEK!". In an instant, Eric would drop any item he was holding and without a word of apology or

388

excuse to anyone who was speaking to him, would dash indoors.

This was disconcerting to most of the neighbours who would consequently discreetly avoid any conversation with Eric. Other, more mischievous neighbours, for devilish delight would deliberately try to engage Eric in conversation just in order to hear "EREEEK! I" being yelled from within the house but through an open window.

The first we knew of Eric's death was when a funeral cortege left from his house to the local crematorium. There were very few mourners. We would have gone to his funeral had we known about it and so would several other neighbours. It appeared that Eric's ruddy healthy complexion was actually caused by high blood pressure and this caused him to have a severe stroke from which he died. Presumably, his early retirement from the post office may also have been caused by his high blood pressure.

A few years previously, Charles had married and set up home on the other side of London. Eric's wife sold up and quietly moved into a 'granny extension' which Charles had had built onto the side of his house. She did not bid farewell to any of the neighbours, not even to the immediate ones.

Some years later we met one of her immediate neighbours who had in turn had some while ago moved away from the district. When she heard that Eric was dead, she decided to impart a secret which she had learnt in strict confidence from a midwife who was involved in Charles' birth. Olivia was not divorced, she had never been married. Eric was her natural father but he was also the natural father of Charles through an incestuous relationship with his daughter Olivia.

Whatever went on behind their front door, one will never know but it was obvious, that whatever it was, Eric's wife was determined that it should never be known. As Eric was a natural chatterer, she would make sure that he would not let slip to any neighbour the dreaded family secret. Whenever, he left the house in order to do any gardening or other domestic task, she would watch him, From the moment any conversation between Eric and any of the neighbours exceeded passing the time of day she would call him indoors by yelling "EREEEK!

Our informant told us that in turn, she herself had a secret which she had kept from Eric and his family.

On the day following that on which Eric and his family had moved into the next door house, she was hanging some washing in the garden when she noticed a big fat rodent entering her garden shed. Like most people, she had a phobia of rodents and hysterically called her husband and told him to get rid of it. He skilfully dispatched it with a single blow of his spade and promptly buried it.

They both naturally assumed that the rodent came from their new neighbours. They were disgusted as they had never before had rats in or near their house and as far as they knew, none of their neighbours down this respectable street ever had.

It was to their great embarrassment, when the next day, young Olivia asked them if they had seen her pet hamster which had escaped from its hutch.

Norman

As a child, Norman displayed no indication of his potential brilliant entrepreneurial genius. Yes, he was bright, clever and perhaps a little precocious but not more so than most other children. He did well at school, gaining admission to a well known grammar school, but then, so did many other pupils.

He started to distinguish himself when he gained entrance to a prestigious Cambridge University college and passed with a first in Economics.

As soon as the college results were known, he had attractive offers of employment from large reputable organisations. He accepted a job with a well known international firm of accountants who promised to train him and to help him qualify as an accountant. After a short while, he resigned as he found the work boring, and although prospects of promotion were good, it depended largely on stepping into 'dead men's' shoes'.

He threw aside the security of such employment and plunged himself into the wild, cruel world as a commission earning salesman.

He loved this life, he worked hard and did very well financially. He refused offers from his employers to act as a manager, supervisor or director. He just simply loved salesmanship pure and simple.

After some practical experience in this field, he decided to set up in business on his own account. He first entered the field of cavity wall insulation. When he sensed that the potential was reaching fulfilment, he sold out and started another firm dealing with double glazing. Once again, his brilliant salesmanship made this company very successful and when he found that the pressure of business obliged him to remain office bound in administration, he once again sold out at great profit. He also had a successful spell selling and installing electric powered showers.

His next venture was in computers with world-wide sales. As soon as he felt that the market was being saturated, he sold the firm.

He realised that there was a big potential in the market of domestic intruder alarms and home security. This was brought home to him by his insurers who pointed out just how inadequately his own home was protected against burglary and the rising crime rate especially in house breaking.

He set about setting up a firm specialising in intruder alarms and other securities with his usual enthusiastic energetic capability. His firm prospered and rapidly expanded. The potential market was increased when insurance companies began to insist on improved domestic security including intruder alarms.

He enhanced his reputation by raising his standards of installation and administration and was accepted by NACOSS (National Approved. Council for Security Systems) and BSIA (British Security Industry Association) as an approved installer.

He also impressed several regional police authorities who placed his firm on their approved list of installers to be recommended to the public who made enquiries.

His firm prospered and expanded. He was still young and because he was a workaholic he remained a bachelor. He bought himself a lovely bungalow surrounded by a large garden and furnished it tastefully with expensive antique furniture and porcelains. His particular hobby was collecting vintage fountain pens. He did not have a particularly large collection, but those he did have were very rare models and very costly. He was well known at vintage pen auctions for outbidding anyone else for such rare pens which he stored in discreetly concealed display cabinets at home.

When returning home one day, he was surprised to find his front and rear doors wide open when they should not have been. He suspected that someone had illegally entered his home and may still be in the premises. He phoned the police on his portable phone. They arrived very quickly and after searching the bungalow assured him that there were no intruders still on the premises. The sergeant in charge said that whilst he was there, he would take details of the robbery.

He was most surprised, when after Norman had made a careful inspection reported that no article was missing. The sergeant asked about cash and jewellery. Norman assured him that the concealed safe where he kept his valuables was intact.

The sergeant said that the burglar must have been very skilled to have been able to gain access without setting off the alarm. He had noted the many security devices on the premises. Norman then admitted that the apparent devices including the exterior bells, infrared detectors, control panel and video cameras were all dummies given to him by the manufacturers for demonstration purposes. Because they were useless dummies, they were not wired up. The sergeant was astonished. He knew Norman was involved in the security alarm business and it was obvious that the house contents were very valuable. He asked Norman why he had been so negligent in protecting his own home. Norman said that an alarm would not have been much use because the bungalow was so isolated that none of the neighbours would be able to hear if the alarm had been actuated. He had tested a siren and none of his neighbours, most of them elderly, had heard it.

One elderly lady who said that she thought that she had heard it, mistook it for her electric kettle boiling and made tea. She wondered why the tea was cold.

However, Norman said that the house was not unprotected because he had bought a highly trained German Shepherd guard dog in which he had great confidence. He knew that burglars were very wary of breaking into premises guarded by such dogs. The dummy alarms were to deter opportunist thieves. When the sergeant asked Norman where the dog was, Norman shamefacedly admitted that it was the only missing item. It must have been stolen along with its feeding bowl. Neither the dog nor its feeding bowl were ever recovered.

John 2:9

The early 1950's was a period of exciting and intense building activity in the east end of London which had been subject to concentrated bombing during the war. Virtually all of the building was the provision of housing for the local residents. It was not only dwellings that had been destroyed by the bombing that had to be replaced, but also many bug ridden, rodent infested, overcrowded homes had to be demolished and new modern dwellings provided in accordance with people's expectancy.

Whilst many houses had been destroyed or badly damaged by the bombing there were only a few sites that were completely cleared and ready for re-development. The strategy adopted was to build tall blocks of flats on the sites that were available, and then decant residents from adjoining areas into the new flats and thus making other sites available for development.

The local councils in collaboration with the LCC (London County Council) which was then the over-all authority responsible for the planning and re-development of the whole of the metropolitan area, devised neighbourhood development plans so that the initial haphazard developments were part and parcel of a comprehensive plan for the neighbourhood and in turn, the neighbourhood was to be part and parcel of a brave new invigorated, modern London.

Multi storey municipal housing was a new phenomenon because in pre-war years such council housing was usually low, dreary development in traditional brick construction. It seemed to have been accepted dogma that municipal housing should appear to be so and in order to appear to be so, had to look dreary.

Now there appeared to be a new psychological approach. Council housing was to be inventive, bright, imaginative and exciting.

And who were the people to plan this utopia? Pre-war, there were virtually no town planners and relatively few architects. Most of the pre-war architects went out of practice because, those who were fit were taken into the armed forces during the war and the others closed their offices as civilian building came to a total stand-still.

After the war, those architects who survived active service and who were willing to work again as architects could not find any private work because all building work was strictly licensed and licences were issued mainly to councils for housing purposes. These architects survived on work connected with repairing existing but war damaged premises.

The councils had to rely mainly on young architects, most of them yet unqualified, studying architecture in evening classes but bursting with enthusiasm to build a new environmentally clean, green London where prior to the war, green usually indicated damp mould, not grass and trees.

With practically no previous experience they produced utopian designs incorporating new untried methods of construction and materials.

They also had to cope with a terrific shortage of skilled labour and materials.

The atmosphere in such a council's architect's department was terrific, but human nature being what it is, there is always to be an odd character or two among the group of people however strong their common interest.

One such character was Dorothy. It was not that she did not comply and involve herself in the enthusiasm of the work but she tended to have a suppressive effect on the ebullient, buoyant atmosphere in the office. Although only in her mid 30s she was older than any of the other assistants in the office but it was not her age that caused a barrier between her and the others, but her high and mighty and more holier than thou attitude.

Among the highly ebullient members of the office, there was a fair bit of rude, friendly banter, most of which would be considered 'politically incorrect' by some today but quite acceptable in those days. All gave as good as received, that is, except Dorothy who showed and expressed her objection to much that was said or done mainly on the grounds of, as she saw it, religion.

She was a Church of England vicar's daughter, but had recently converted to Catholicism. She would have been much happier, I'm sure, if she had entered a convent rather that an architects office.

Out of respect to her age and her religious convictions, most of the other in the office would restrain themselves and refrain from saying anything profane within her hearing but, unfortunately, she had very acute hearing.

There were several other religious people in the office but they tended to keep their opinions and beliefs to themselves except possibly during the brief tea breaks in the office.

One lad who had a Welsh Presbyterian background would, from time-to-time burst out boisterously singing aloud some hymn, the words of which he reckoned would annoy her. In turn, she angered a young man who had very recently 'seen the light' and who objected to some of her dogma especially that concerning illness and death, as his own brother was seriously ill at the time.

The office was always noisy and one day, in order to keep out the noise of the general hubbub, I sang Psalm 23 to myself, "The Lord is my shep-herd." I don't know why I should have chosen that particular psalm. I am not religious, maybe I had heard it on the radio that morning before set-ting out for work and that it stuck in my subconscious. Despite the gener-al hubbub and the fact that Dorothy's own desk was at the opposite end of the office, she heard my tune and came striding over to me. She accusing-ly said that I was singing one of the Christian hymns. I was astonished and told her that the psalms of David were written in the Jewish bible centuries before the advent of Christianity. She did not appear to accept my asser-tion as fact. However, she kept most of her admonishments for the office junior and made his life a misery. She knew he was also a Catholic of Irish descent. She expected him to be an example to the non-Catholics in the office and reproached him for what she considered to be even the slightest of 'sins.'

He in turn, built up a fierce resentment against her. Matters came to a head between them in the week or so leading up to Christmas when Dorothy's religious ardour increased.

Because of the building boom, there was a constant stream of technical representatives calling at the architects office to bring the assistants' atten-tion to their firms particular product or service. Each interview with such a representative might take up to half an hour or even an hour. During the working week, such interviews would detract the assistant from his work for a total of several hours.

The chief architect therefore tried to discourage the number of such representatives calling and the time they spent in the office.

In the week or so leading up to Christmas, the representatives tried to carry favour with the assistants by presenting them with seasonal gifts and thus hoping that they would be granted interviews during the coming year.

The gifts varied according to seniority. It was known that most of the senior members would receive large, fat turkeys and cases of drink. Lower down the scale, the gift might be single bottles of drink or spicy picture cal-endars. The lowest yet, would be given pocket diaries with the name of the presenting firm on the cover.

Each person would be curious to know what his or her colleagues had received and in turn, each recipient would be reluctant to reveal what goodwill presents, if any, they had been given.

These seasonable gifts in the main, created more bad feeling than the goodwill intended. Nearly everyone felt that their gift was not good enough and as a consequence, interviews were more difficult to obtain.

Dorothy proclaimed loud and clear that the acceptance of such bribes, she called them bribes, not gifts, were both illegal and immoral.

In some instances, she upbraided the unfortunate representative for offering her a goodwill gesture, this was invariably when the offering was, say a pocket diary or a scale (special ruler used by architects) but on other occasions the gift was quietly accepted with words of blessing and the item swiftly locked into her desk drawer.

Her double standard was duly and carefully but prudently noted by the others present. Although, John, the office junior was not offered any gift by any of the representatives, Dorothy warned him sternly against even considering accepting any, even a pocket diary.

Her hypocrisy hurt him very much, because he knew as well as the others, that she herself had been accepting gifts from some of the representatives.

At the office party on Christmas Eve he became somewhat intoxicated and declared to some of the assistants that he had got his just revenge on Dorothy. One day when everyone had gone home, he managed to unlock Dorothy's drawer to see what gifts she had secretly kept for herself and discovered six bottles of various alcoholic beverages. He said he poured the contents down the lavatory pan, refilled the bottles with water and carefully re-sealed the caps. On hearing this, there was great hilarity and the boys could not wait till after Christmas to find out just how much Dorothy had enjoyed her beverages and with whom she may have shared them.

At the first tea break after the Christmas holiday, there was an air of expectancy; each waited for the other to raise the question.. After a while the intrepid lad from Wales delicately raised the subject by directly asking Dorothy if she'd enjoyed the drink that she had surreptitiously accepted from various representatives and concealed in her locked drawer. Dorothy said that she was glad to clarify the situation and appreciated that whoever had intruded on the privacy of her locked drawer had done so only with the best of intentions. She said that she had indeed accepted some gifts from representatives but only after she made it clear they were not for her personal benefit but would be passed on in the seasonal spirit of goodwill to the Mother Superior in her local convent in order to permit the impoverished nuns to share the goodwill enjoyed by the many in the celebration of the birth of our Lord. At this, she stared at me and repeated 'Our Lord.'

I did not remind her that her Lord was a Jew. She continued, I'm sure you would not begrudge the nuns this little comfort in their sacrificial life. She added that she had told the Mother Superior that the gifts were from everyone in the office and the Mother Superior promised to write and thank them.

John's face went a crimson red and possibly the words of his namesake, Saint John 2:9 may have echoed through his head.

GARRULUS GLANDARIUS

The Jays

We nick-named the young family who moved into the house whose rear garden backed onto ours, the Jays, because the initial letter of each of their first names was the letter J.

There was daddy James, mummy June and baby Jackie who at first we took to be a girl because he had lovely long blond hair and bright blue eyes. When he grew up, he was far from girlish.

In order to communicate more freely, we formed a small gap in the fence dividing our rear gardens so that we could slip into each others houses through the back doors.

June would often do so when she fed our cats when we were out and likewise, we did the same when they were out and their cats needed feeding. They did us the honour of naming one of their she cats after my wife Dora, and named a mangy tom-cat after me, Hissing Sid. We accepted the honour in the spirit it was given. Whilst we got on well with the Jays, our respective cats largely kept to their own territorial limits. Often, we would go on joint outings with the Jays which was made more enjoyable because of shared interests in ancient buildings, country houses, historical towns and photography.

James usually drove his own car because, whereas I am not fond of motoring, he loves it and as he said, he could ascribe the mileage on his business account.

He was a partner in a construction company and normally clocked up a high mileage for his firm. He was very fond of Jackie and we were surprised to learn that he was not the father. Jackie was the child of Junes first marriage which was a short and unhappy one. Now, she seemed to have struck it lucky with James.

399

June originated in Devon and by profession, was a doctor's receptionist, but only did part time work. She said that she did not really have to work as James earned very good money. She was of sallow complexion and had a mass of dark curly hair, bright eyes and was very vivacious. By contrast, James was pink skinned and had, surprisingly for his tender years, a mass of white hair. He said it was a common genetic defect among some Welsh people of whom, he originated, although he did not have the slightest trace of a Welsh lilt in his speech. If anything, he had a slight Essex accent.

One thing the Jays were adamant about, was that they would not socialise in any form what-so-ever on Friday evenings. They explained this by saying that June washed James' hair every Friday evening and that they liked to relax afterwards.

We were very impressed by such devotion by a wife to her husband. We had never heard of any other wife washing their husband's hair.

A lot later on, we were amused to learn that James was completely bald and wore wigs. He had several wigs each cut slightly longer that the other which he wore on successive days so as to give the impression that his lovely mop of grey hair had a vigorous growth. When he wore the one with the shortest hair, he would not fail to bring to attention the fact that he 'had had a hair cut.'

He spent a small fortune on these wigs and devoted Fridays evenings to their care. He certainly fooled us!

Late one Friday evening, there was a frantic knocking on our rear garden door. It was June, she was hysterical and clutching a sobbing Jackie. Her hair was dishevelled, she had a split lip and blood was oozing out of her nose.

She asked if she could have shelter for the night because James was in a violent temper and had beaten her up.

When she had calmed down, we were shocked to learn that James was a Jekyll and Hyde character. Normally, he was the pleasant, intelligent and amusing person that we knew, but when he had had a few drinks, he became a sadistic wife beater and a bully to anyone who unfortunately crossed his path.

Quite often, on a Friday evening, the senior members of his firm would have a few social drinks before parting for the week-end. That usually was enough to spark off the problem. On his way home, he would bully other drivers who he considered had not been courteous to him. He had even boasted to June that in such circumstances, he had killed two men, but he had not elaborated.

He had beaten her up many times for the most trivial of reasons but he had always taken sadistic delight in bruising her body where it would not show. On this particular evening, he had not cared and had punched her several times in the face. She said that his temper flared when she refused to eat a fairy cake. As we were obviously ignorant, she explained that what she meant by a fairy cake was a small cake into which cannabis had been baked. She had refused to eat it as she did not want to become addicted to it.

She also revealed that James was a regular participant of cocaine, which he sniffed. She said, that now he had shown a disregard about hitting her in the face that she realised that she had to leave him.

We made plans for her to escape from our house if James decided to come and fetch her. In the event, he did not come and the night passed uneventfully. In the morning, June returned to her own house accompanied by a policeman in order to collect her belongings before going to a women's' shelter.

To her surprise, she found her front door wide open and all her husband's clothes etc., including his treasured wigs missing. It turned out that he had realised that he had gone too far and absconded to his girl friend by whom he had fathered two children whilst being married to June. Later, June discovered that he had fathered many of the children in the village where he came from.

Apart from her matrimonial trouble, June also had maternal problems. Her mother had been one of nature's worriers. She used to worry about every little thing and as a consequence became deeply depressed. Eventually, she got into such a bad state that she had a brain operation to relieve her anxiety and depression. The operation had been most successful, in fact too successful. Her mother had changed her character completely. Now, she could not even care less about anything and treated everything and everybody light-heartedly.

Neighbours often phoned June to say that her mother had left the house and not bothered to close the door behind her. Several times, June had been called to the local Police Station because her mother had walked out of a super-market quite openly without paying and could not understand what all the fuss was about.

In the cold weather, she would go out without a coat and wearing her house slippers.

She became a constant worry to June but refused to move in with June so that a close eye could be kept on her. Often she would not replace the phone receiver so that when June tried to contact her she could not do so.

Eventually, all this problem with her mother together with the immense problems arising out of her husband leaving got the better of June and she became very morbid and depressed.

Because she became incapable of caring properly for little Jackie, he was taken into care and June was taken into a psychiatric hospital.

One day, when her mother came to visit her, she suggested that June have a brain operation to remove her depressed state of mind.

VAT Scam

I was innocently and very marginally involved in a big Value Added Tax racket expose that resulted in a lengthy and costly trial in the High Courts. The trial lasted for several weeks and was widely reported in the national press as well as in the local papers. Three prosperous local business men were the accused, but I was not mentioned at all. In fact I had been used by the authorities in order to bring those guilty to justice

It all began when a well know, respectable, well established estate agency manager contacted me. He told me that I had been highly recommended by a mutual acquaintance and he would like me to carry out a measured survey of his own premises.

Apparently, he had been approached by the local council, who told him that they were concerned that certain structural alterations had been carried out on the premises without official approval being given. They were most concerned about the means of escape in case of fire as the building was now multi-occupied.

The manager impressed upon me, that I must be most discreet and not to discuss what I was doing with anyone else because of security reasons. He explained that the building was owned by the estate agency but the three upper floors were leased to three separate professional firms who were, for reasons best known to themselves, very security conscious. The top floor was occupied by a firm of solicitors who often did conveyancing for the estate agents. The next floor down, the second floor, was occupied by a firm of finance consultants, who, when requested, arranged mortgages etc. for buyers of properties sold by the estate agency.

The first floor, the lowest of the three, was occupied by a firm of accountants who were sometimes, although very rarely called upon to explain to the Inland Revenue how it was that someone who was a declared bankrupt and with no visible means of income, was suddenly able to buy a luxury home for one of his daughters who was getting married.

The work that the three firms did to aid the estate agency was only a minor part of their activities which the manager said remained a mystery to him.

When any of their services were required, they sent a member of the staff down to discuss the problem in the interview room at the rear of the agency's ground storey shop premises. No outsider, not even the estate agency manager ever went upstairs to discuss business but because of the pressure from the local council, I was to be allowed to enter each storey and take the necessary measurements and details to enable me to prepare the detailed plans requested by the local council's officials. The alternative, was possible closure of the whole of the premises.

After I had completed taking the necessary details in the agency's part of the premises, the manager led me through a stout looking door which he opened by an electronic lock.

At each floor, he had to announce himself before we were admitted. Each office suite was an open plan occupied by about six persons who kept a careful eye on me whilst I took details of the structure. At the far end of each open office was a small secluded office occupied by the principal, who in turn, kept a silent, careful watch on me whilst I was in his office. The atmosphere was quite eerie.

Each landing on the staircase was fitted with a security video camera, which in turn, kept a careful watch on my activity. As far as I was aware, there were no prying cameras in the toilets, but who was to know?

I also took details of the iron fire escape at the rear of the building.

Access to the offices was normally through the estate agency's office but the principals had their own private access at the rear straight off the private car park. This rear door was also guarded by a video security camera and the car park was illuminated by bright security lights.

All the security arrangements seemed to me more suitable for premises in the Hatton Gardens dealing with expensive jeweller)' than just professional men's offices.

When I completed the plans, I handed them to the estate agency's manager who said he will let the local council have copies.

A short while after, I learned that two officials had visited the premises to check that the plans were correct. They were most meticulous in doing so and made careful notes of the security arrangements in relation to the means of escape in case of fire. What the manager, nor anyone else knew at the time, the two officials were not from the council, but from the Customs and Excise who were using my plans in order to decide the best means to carry out a search of the three office suites. The search was most successful and provided the information they were seeking to smash a highly organised and very profitable racket involving VAT re-payments on gold coins which never existed except on paper.

Apparently, each of the three professional occupants of the premises were involved. Their staff were not aware of what had been going on because of the extreme security involved.

Very little of the money fraudulently obtained was recovered. The solicitor and accountant each received five years imprisonment whilst the financier, who the judge held to be the evil ring leader received seven years.

Because they were model prisoners and because of their health and age, they were transferred to an open prison.

One day, when the financier was relaxing in the prison's recreation room, he got into a conversation with a young prisoner who was an obvious homosexual.

As usual, newly acquainted prisoners exchanged their experiences and the reasons for their incarceration. The young man told the financier that he was receiving lenient treatment because of his sexual proclivity which, in more strict prisons, caused him to be physically abused by other prisoners. He said that the lenient treatment was also because violence was not involved in his crime. He said that for a while, he had been the sexual partner of a very rich business man who despite his wealth, had been very mean towards him. He decided to blackmail his sexual partner by threatening to publicise certain photographs that would be most embarrassing to the rich man. Unfortunately, he was caught in a carefully laid trap and found guilty. The financier said that he deplored the use of blackmail to make money and in turn explained how it was that he himself was in prison and said that once he was very rich but now he was ruined.

The young man said that surely he could have employed clever solicitors and accountants to get him out of trouble. The financier said, "I did, and they put up a very complicated defence which was beyond comprehension but if you want to know the intricacies of the case ask them, they are over there, on the other side of the room playing table tennis."

Brutus

I first heard about Brutus when I called on an old acquaintance to collect some bric-a-brac she had donated for a charity jumble sale my wife was organising.

She was living with her son and had her own house up for sale since the death of her husband. It had become too large for her to live in on her own. She apologised for the scant amount of bric-a-brac and said that she had had a much larger and much better collection but most had been stolen by squatters who had taken occupation of her house before she could properly empty it of all its contents.

She said that the squatters had not only taken the bric-a-brac but had also taken much of the furniture and what they had not taken, they had broken and fouled up.

They had also done a lot of damage to the structure both internally and externally. The carefully tended front and rear gardens were ruined and littered with rubbish. The front garden was strewn with discarded car and motor bike parts and worn out tyres. She said that it will cost her a small fortune to put the property back into a saleable condition. The insurance company was refusing to pay any compensation on the grounds that none of the losses claimed came within the provisions of the insurance policy. Neighbours who had been disturbed by frequent all night parties and loud thumping rock music during the day had held her responsible and said that it was up to her to get the squatters out.

The police said that there was very little they could do because the law governing squatting was antiquated and favoured the squatters rather than the owners. The squatters had access to free legal aid and advice and knew everything to enable then to continue to occupy empty premises.

She had employed a firm of solicitors who were acknowledged to be expert in this very specialised field of the law. Up-to-date she had paid then a small fortune in legal fees but they had, after nearly a year, failed to get the squatters evicted.

As she did not appear to be too concerned or worried , I tried to comfort her by saying that no doubt the solicitor will be successful in the near future.

She said the squatters were already out, but not due to the efforts of her solicitors. She said that for just one hundred and fifty pounds paid in cash to Brutus, the squatters were out and she was confident that they would not return in a hurry.

Brutus was not actually his real name but he was known to all his acquaintances as Brutus and he preferred to be known by that name mainly for professional reasons. Officially his profession was 'unemployed', and had been so as far back as anyone could remember but he did, from time-to-time, supply his services as a 'hard man'.

He was fifty years old and came from Glasgow which he left as a young man but he still spoke with a strong Glaswegian accent.

His mode of operation if called upon to evict squatters, was first to collect his fee in cash and then, along with two other fellow Glaswegians to get well and truly inebriated on strong ale. When it was dark, all three would then stagger down to the occupied property and mask their faces but not before making sure that they were at the right property. Once, they had ejected the occupants of a property to which they had proper grounds to occupy. They waited till loud music blared out from the house and then burst in brandishing pick-axe handles or iron bars.

They gave the squatters five minutes to quit the premises and then proceeded to smash up any electronic equipment capable of making a noise such as radios, music centres, amplifiers, loud speakers and televisions. If any of the squatters were still in the house by the time they had finished smashing their audio equipment they just simply threw them bodily through a window which was not always open.

The whole procedure was completed within ten minutes and then they were away before any police arrived.

Everybody was pleased, even the squatters who usually had their eyes on another potential squat in case something like this was to happen or if their present squat became unbearably foul. Our acquaintance said that she could heartily recommend Brutus to anyone who may need his specialised services and not to waste money employing a solicitor.

When I asked for his name, address and telephone number, she said that she did not know how to contact him but if anyone wanted to, they could do so at a certain pub which she named. She added, that he would be very wary of anyone approaching him, and it would be best to do so through herself who he knew and could trust.

All she knew was that he was not married and was one of several male lodgers in a house owned by a Pakistani landlord.

It was only a few weeks later that I read in the local paper that a man known to his fellow lodgers only as Brutus had been battered to death by his landlord using a cricket bat. Apparently, there had been an altercation concerning non-payment of rent and noisy behaviour.

The landlord received a light sentence on the grounds that he was not guilty of murder but of manslaughter whilst acting in self-defence against a well known violent criminal.

The Quantity Surveyor

From time-to-time, we have a flurry of excitement in our street. One such incident occurred recently. Builders digging a trench to form a drain to a new garage they were erecting at the side of No 96, which is the last house in our street, came across some buried bones. The foreman thought that they may be human and reported the find to the local authority, who in turn, referred the matter to the Police.

The Police promptly stopped all building work on the site and sent the bones away for forensic examination. A short report in the local paper brought newsmen to the street from far and wide. They questioned the builders, the present owner of the premises and neighbours about the previous occupiers of the house.

The Police too conducted similar enquiries and it was not long before some of the neighbours directed them in our direction as they knew that I had had some connection with the immediate previous occupier, Robert Mason.

I told the Police that my contacts with him were purely professional. From time-to-time, I had need to use the services of a Quantity Surveyor in connection with my work as an Architect. As he was so close and as he was very experienced and fully qualified, I found his services very convenient.

I had not been in touch with him for at least ten years and at that time he was semi-retired, partially due to the onset of Parkinson's disease and partially due to having to nurse his invalid wife. The neighbours often saw him wheeling his wife to the shops but had little to do with them because of the peculiar attitude of his wife who spoke down to all an sundry. She apparently considered herself as being superior to the others because her husband was a qualified professional man with his own practice.

Robert Mason himself was quite pleasant but he was very neurotic and at times acted most strangely. Neighbours often heard him and his wife having loud shouting arguments. He refused all offers of help from neighbours with his shopping etc.. His house and gardens became increasingly neglected and shabby.

When neighbours noticed that he no longer took his wife out shopping in her wheelchair, he told them that her health had deteriorated and that she had been taken into a nursing home as he could no longer cope.

He continued living in his large four bedroomed Victorian house all on his own without any outside help.

Eventually, due to his own failing health, he put his house up for sale and went to live in a nursing home. He had no difficulty in selling the house which was on the corner of the road at the end of the terrace and had a large side garden on which there was ample room to build a double sized garage. Garages are in great demand in the locality. He left no forwarding address and all the neighbours including ourselves lost touch with him.

Apparently, he read the newspaper reports about the discovery of the bones and asked for a senior police officer to come and visit him at his nursing home as he wished to make a statement.

He astonished the Police by confessing to having killed his wife during one of their many violent arguments and burying her body in the garden. He described the exact location which coincided with the position that the bones were found. He said that he had buried his wife's possessions with her, including her wheelchair which he had dismantled into its component parts.

The Police were puzzled because no such artefacts had been found with the bones and because of his rather incoherent speech, they extended the search of the garden and found nothing to confirm his claim.

Soon after, the forensics laboratory declared that the bones found on the site were not human and it appeared that they had been buried for about 100 years.

There was one puzzle however that the Police could not solve, they could not, even after the most extensive enquiries and questioning of the incoherent Robert Mason, discover what did happen to his wife. She had just vanished from the face of the earth.

Tony's Suocera (Mother-In-Law)

My first regular job upon leaving school in April 1940 was as a junior in the Planning Office of a large internationally famous departmental store in Oxford Street, London.

This enormous store was part of a combine of other large famous stores in other parts of London and in provincial towns. The Planning Office concerned itself mainly with surveying and recording the many buildings that it owned together with all its fittings and furniture. From time-to-time, which actually was quite frequent, it replanned the various departments in the stores in accordance with the management's policies. The planning staff were all young, all were under the age of 18 years, the age when able bodied men were conscripted into the army. I was 16 years old, the youngest of the young. The only adult was the office manager who was a qualified architect and even though apparently fit, had not yet been enlisted for some unknown reason.

The Planning Office was situated in the ground storey of a large Georgian house at the rear of the store overlooking Cavendish Gardens. It was strict company policy that food and drink must not be partaken in any part of the premises except in the staff canteen. As this was situated in another remote part of the stores conglomeration of buildings, it took a long time to reach and by the time one was served, the refreshment break was over. It was, therefore, more convenient to take our short refreshment breaks in a nearby cafe run by Tony. He was of Italian parentage and even though born and bred in the centre of London, he spoke with an amusing Italian accent.

His customers consisted mainly of members of staff of the surrounding businesses which towered above his diminutive two storey building of which the cafe occupied the ground storey. He was very talkative and told us, that even though the war had adversely effected his business, customers had been conscripted or transferred to war work etc., he would not ever consider selling up because he anticipated that one day, one of the giant stores would require his premises to redevelop their own and he would be able to extort a fabulous sum for his premises.

He dreamt of retiring on the proceeds of such a sale to sunny Italy and possibly running a little restaurant there for British visitors.

Not long after he revealed his ambitions there was a drastic change in his situation. One night, the German bombers had changed their tactics from bombing the east end of London where I lived, to the west end of London, where I worked and where Tony had his little cafe. Both his potential nest egg and the large departmental store were burnt to the ground after being hit by oil bombs dropped by the German bombers.

Soon alter this destruction, I left the Planning Office and obtained work with the War Office in a drawing office attached to the Command of Royal Engineers. I next met Tony by chance several years later after the war, when I pulled into a service station to refill with petrol. He was one of the forecourt attendants. He recognised me immediately and arranged to meet me in a few days time at a nearby cafe for a chat about 'old times'.

We duly met and he told me that he actually owned the service station where we met and at the time was helping out on the forecourt because of shortage of staff and the rush hour.

We reminisced about his old cafe. He had not been able to retire yet to Italy because of complicated legal problems associated with the disposal of the bombed out cafe site. An adjoining departmental store had submitted plans to the local council for the comprehensive development of the area and his cafe site was included as part of a proposed combined car park. He had been threatened that if he did not sell the site voluntarily at a reasonable price, it would be acquired compulsorily by the local council and its value based on that of a car park. Such compensation would not be enough to fulfil his retirement dreams.

Whilst this problem was on his mind, he told me of a more immediate and annoying problem. During the war, his wife's father who was Italian had died and now that the war was over, his wife's mother who was also Italian had come from Italy to live with them until her dying day. At first, he welcomed her and in accordance with Italian tradition was pleased to offer his wife's widowed mother, hospitality and care in her old age.

However, things soon changed. His mother-in-law blamed the British for everything she considered to be wrong. Apart from the climate she said the food was atrocious. In some respects she was somewhat right. The climate was nowhere as sunny as in south Italy from where she came and for quite a long while after the war, food in England was scarce and rationed.

She implied that her husband would still be alive if it had not been for the wicked British invading peace loving Italy. No one could fathom out why she said this as the remote mountain village where she lived during the war had not been effected at all by the battles fought elsewhere. She said that the streets of London were full of foreigners and bandits that robbed and raped God fearing old ladies such as herself. Her dying wish was to return to her native Italy. She complained of high prices even though she did not have to pay for anything at all. Moreover, she complained of disturbed sleep. She said that because of disturbed sleep she suffered with all sorts of ailments for which there were no proper remedies in the English shops. Among the causes for disturbed sleep she blamed Tony's snoring, the dog barking, low flying aeroplanes, car doors slamming, nearby railway service, early bird song etc., etc.

She did not have a good word to say about anybody or anything. She said that she regretted the day she left her village to come to stay with her daughter in a north London suburb.

This annoyed Tony very much as he did his utmost to make his mother-in-law welcome and happy.

Tony told us, how early one fine spring morning, he awoke with the intention as usual of getting to work before the early morning rush hour began. He tiptoed past his mother-inlaw's bedroom so as not to disturb her and quietly descended the stairs.

Because he was still half asleep, he did not particularly notice that the staircase carpet had been removed. He did however notice that the front door mat was not in its usual place and assumed that his houseproud wife had removed it for cleaning.

He went into the kitchen to make himself a strong cup of coffee to wake himself up. The kettle was not in its usual place on the gas stove so he went to take a saucepan instead to boil water for his coffee. No saucepan - in fact virtually every item in the kitchen except the stove and sink was missing. The fridge, the deep freeze, cutlery, crockery and cooking utensils as well as all the food in the larder were missing.

In a flash, he was fully awake and at first thought that some elaborate joke was being played on him or perhaps, he was having a nightmare. He realised that it was neither a hoax nor a dream and awoke his wife. Not only had the kitchen been stripped but so had all the ground floor rooms. The TV and radio, furniture, ornaments, pictures, light fittings including bulbs were all gone!

When they checked the garage, all the garden implements and tools were gone and so too was the firm's van which the burglars had obviously used to cart their loot away.

They regretted the day they gave the dog away so as to assuage Tony's mother-in-law who said that the dog kept her awake all night with his barking and scratching.

Then suddenly, realising that amid all the hubbub she had not made an appearance, they dashed up to her room fearing that possibly, the intruders may have done her some harm. When they opened her door she lay fast sleep snoring loudly and steadily.

When they awoke her, she immediately complained about being woken so early and said she had not slept a wink all night because Tony's snores had kept her awake.

Sorry, Wrong Address

We live in a quiet residential suburb to the east of London. The two storey terraced houses in our street were built in 1904. They are double fronted with four bedrooms and three reception rooms. A few of the houses have been converted into four single bedroom flats. The front gardens are large enough to act as forecourt parking for three cars.

One of the houses, not far from our own, was the one in which Edith and Percy Thomson lived. Mr Thomson was murdered by Frederick Bywaters a young lover of Mrs Thomson and the consequent trial and executions of Mrs Thomson and Frederick Bywaters in 1922 became famous in the annals of murder stories.

The residents are very friendly; the atmosphere in the street is more like that of a village than a London suburb. We are on nodding terms at least with virtually everybody and chatting terms with quite a number of neighbours.

Residents are well behaved and considerate to each other. Children are polite and quiet. No loud all night parties and many would be only too pleased to baby-sit if required or to do shopping for anyone incapacitated. Houses are well maintained and a neighbourhood watch is in being although there is very little crime.

Because we have lived in the street for some forty years, we are among the oldest residents, that is, those who have lived in the street the longest.

Quite often, we are handed the keys of their houses by neighbours and asked to feed their pets whilst they are away and to "keep an eye" on their property.

As my wife and I are both retired, we often enjoy a lunch seated at our dining table in the living room's large bay window. From this window, we

414

can see the comings and goings up and down the street.

Yesterday, we were enjoying such a lunch which was enhanced by the appearance, or rather, near appearance of the sun which tried to burn its way through thin white clouds. The brightness was most welcome after weeks of dark depressive days with no sunshine at all.

We noted the coming and goings of various neighbours, delivery vans, window cleaners etc., and the meandering of neighbours' well fed cats.

Suddenly, we noticed a tall dignified looking man wearing a top hat and morning suit walking solemnly down the centre of the road in our direction. Following, slowly and sedately behind him was a shining hearse and three chauffeured driven limousines. The hearse contained a simple plain wood coffin with no embellishments and there were no floral tributes.

Being of the Jewish faith, we knew that the lack of floral tributes was an indication of a Jewish funeral but we were puzzled by the fact that apart from ourselves there were only two other Jewish families living down the street and as far as we knew all were alive and relatively well considering their ages.

We were astonished when the man leading the cortege stopped opposite our front door. The hearse and three limousines also stopped. The man then walked deliberately up the path of the house right opposite to ours.

The house was occupied by a very elderly Jewish lady and even though she had been very ill for several years, we had noticed her being taken out in a car by a young nephew only the day before and later on, being returned by the same person.

The funeral director rang the door bell with great aplomb but there was no response. After a suitable dignified period he tried again but once more there was no response. The third time, he used the door knocker but still no response. Although he did not seem to notice, but we did, the lace curtain to the adjoining bay window of the house twitched slightly and the elderly occupant peered out as was her habit when someone persistently rang her door bell. She would not answer the door unless the person was expected.

Obviously, the young man in his funeral directors outfit was not expected and she did not answer the door.

At this stage, I was debating with Dora whether or not, I should cross the road and try to clarify, the situation. Dora said that if Sybil, the elderly neighbour concerned, does not wish to open her door for whatever reason she may have, it would not be proper for us to interfere.

Before we came to a decision, that is before Dora finally decided, the matter was resolved when two middle-aged foreign looking gentlemen arrived rather breathlessly, and after a few words and gestures towards the bottom end of the street from which direction the cortege had come, the cortege moved off.

That same afternoon, we learned that another elderly neighbour had died about a week ago. We were not unduly surprised because he had had a stroke about five years ago and two subsequent operations as well as two broken hip joints. We had often exchanged the time of day with the elderly man and his wife.

They were both foreign and when we had tried to talk to them from time-to-time, we found it difficult because of their poor English and heavy accents.

As soon as we heard about his death, we went along to convey our condolences to his widow.

Despite the fact that she had lived in England for about fifty years, she still had difficulty in speaking and understanding English but despite this we learnt something about herself and her husband.

They were both born and bred in Czechoslovakia. He was born in 1913 and qualified as a doctor. When the Germans invaded Czechoslovakia he fled to this country as a refugee and joined the British army. He served in Montgomery's Eighth Army in Africa and Italy and after the war returned to this country and became naturalised. He met and married his wife and settled down lecturing in medical schools.

He had no desire to return to the country of his birth as it had been taken over by the Communists after the war.

Before settling down here, he had tried to go and live in Palestine, but the British Mandate Authority refused to grant him permission to enter. As he was determined to go, he went unofficially through clandestine channels and the boat he arrived in with hundreds of other refuge seekers was sunk by the British navy.

He was rescued from the sea, whilst hundreds of others drowned and he was taken to a harsh detention camp in Mauritius. After a while, having British citizenship, he returned and settled down to a quiet, if not wholly healthy life, here in the east London suburb of Ilford.

He kept in contact with relatives and friends who remained in Czechoslovakia and many came here especially for the funeral. It was actually, two of such acquaintances who approached the funeral director and clarified that the cortege was at the wrong house. For some unexplained reason, the cortege had called at No 47 whereas they should have called at No 74.

The deceased's widow explained, that whereas they were both not religiously inclined, she was born a Christian he was born a Jew. He had told her, even though he did not practice Judaism, he was, neverthe-less, born a Jew and when he died, he wished to be buried as a Jew.

Accordingly, she had carried out his wishes but due to her ignorance, she had had him cremated which is contrary to Jewish law and practice. Also, in accordance with his wishes, she is arranging for his ashes to be buried in a consecrated cemetery in Israel, the country he had once so wished to live in.

We told her, that in order to show our respects, and in lieu of a floral tribute which is not in accordance with Jewish tradition, we will arrange for five trees to be planted in a forest near to Jerusalem in his memory.

-When we returned from paying our commiseration we noticed an emergency ambulance outside No 47, that is Sibyls house. We subsequently learnt that when Sybil had peered out of her bay window to see who was ringing her door bell and who was persistently knocking, she was shocked to see a funeral director standing there and in the road was a hearse and three shiny limousines. The shock had caused her to have a stroke and that is why she was being taken to hospital. She never did have much sense of humour.

The Violinist

It is difficult today to describe the abject poverty that was universal in the east end of London during the 1920's - 1930's. Such poverty was not unique and no doubt equal or even, possibly worse poverty existed elsewhere in this country but I can only authoritatively describe what I personally experienced and saw.

My family, that is my parents, five children including myself and also my maternal grandparents lived in an 'apartment' at 54 Clark Street Buildings, Stepney, London E1. The apartment was situated on the first floor of a five storey slum tenement building. It consisted of kitchen/dining room on a mezzanine level and five steps up along an open passage was the sole bedroom and another room that served as a living room/bedroom.

From time to time, the 'apartment' also housed a lodger who slept on a sofa in the kitchen. There it was warm in the winter and hot in the summer.

In the summer, the 'apartment' also housed a host of very active, well fed bed bugs that swarmed over everybody during the night, especially on hot, suffocating, restless nights.

There was no bathroom and no WC. inside the 'apartment'. We shared a WC situated two floors up with three other large families.

The only sanitary facility was a sink served by a cold water tap in the kitchen. There was of course, no central heating or piped hot water supplies.

Lighting and cooking was by means of mains gas through a penny (240 pence equalled one pound) in the slot gas meter situated in the open passage way. There was no electricity, no radio, no fridge and certainly no TV.

This standard of accommodation was not unusual. It was the accepted norm.

Children were bathed in tin baths that were hung, when not in use, on the walls of the open passage way. In fact a lot of items were kept along the 'passage' which was an extreme fire hazard because it led off from the sole staircase which was of timber construction.

Adolescents and adults bathed in the communal baths which were situated in a converted house on the corner of the street. Ironically enough, the house containing these public baths is now a much sought after desirable Georgian style residence overlooking a compact public square which has now become gentrified.

I describe our 'apartment' because by comparison with the 'apartment' that the Bercovitch family occupied it was a luxurious palace. They lived in the semi-basement beneath our 'apartment'. By all rights, they should not have been allowed to live there as it had long ago been condemned as uninhabitable by the local public health authority and in those days, for the dwelling to be so condemned, it must have been bad, and so it was.

Being semi-subterranean, the walls were perpetually damp. The scant lighting and air was through a small well, the top of which was at public pavement level and covered with a cast iron grill.

The floor was dusty concrete and the damp walls had long lost their plaster.

As with our 'apartment' its only sanitary appliance was a kitchen sink served by a single cold water tap. They shared an outside WC. in a stinking yard with workers from an adjoining tailoring sweat shop.

There were several children in the Bercovitch family but I cannot remember how many, but no mother. She had been subject to fits of extreme depression and during one such fit had committed suicide by drinking undiluted carbolic acid. The children had witnessed her horrible death.

The father did his best to look after the children but he was inadequate to the task and refused all offers of help from neighbours and charities.

By profession, he was a violinist but unfortunately not good enough to compete in those days of economic depression for a job in an orchestra.

The children were well fed because the cost of good quality basic food was extremely cheap and sympathetic neighbours gave food direct to the children.

Because of the lack of facilities, the children were extremely dirty, not only their bodies but also their clothes. At some time, someone had given them pyjamas which they wore day and nights for weeks on end without being washed.

The poor residents of Clark Street felt sorry for the impoverished motherless family and helped them as much as they could.

The family could not afford such a luxury as artificial lighting in their dingy 'apartment' and only used candles when absolutely necessary and for welcoming the Sabbath on Friday evenings.

One luxury they could enjoy however, was music played on his violin by their father. Neighbours used to gather around the grating in the pavement through which the apartment was lit and ventilated, to listen to the music sometimes accompanied by the singing of the children.

Mr Bercovitch did try to earn some money by playing his violin in the streets but musicians playing their instruments in the streets were common place and earned very little money.

It was about this time, that one of the school teachers organised music lessons in my school and offered that for three pence a week, he would provide a suitable violin for participating children to learn on and would give free lessons. When I asked my father if he would pay the threepence, he refused saying he would not like to see me ending up playing the violin in the streets like Mr Bercovitch. Who knows what virtuoso was lost to the world by that decision?

One day, someone told Mr Bercovitch that he was wasting his time and talent in playing to the local impoverished residents and that he should play in a position where passers-by were more affluent and affable. Consequently, he took to playing his violin outside Bloom's and P. Strongwater's kosher restaurants situated just off Whitechapel Road and also nearby to the Jewish Palladium theatre in Commercial Road.

He indeed increased his income considerably from people frequenting the restaurants and theatre who either had a guilty conscience about their own relevant opulence or who came to take a liking to his pathetic character and his Jewish music.

He found that people gave more generously when he appeared to be playing for them personally. This pleased their ego and they paid accordingly. Regular admirers would stop to exchange friendly words of appreciation and encouragement. This so pleased Mr Bercovitch that he started wearing a tatty top hat and playing a bit of the clown. When any particular generous patron would approach, he would stand on one leg, like the pose of the Eros statue in Piccadilly Circus and play joyous lively music aimed at the patron's good lady.

This was appreciated most generously and Mr Bercovitch was doing financially very well.

Unfortunately, this did not last very long. Some people are born to be unlucky. One evening when he was performing his Eros pose and playing to the lady of the man who he knew was very appreciative and generous, he lost his balance, fell and broke the Femur bone in his leg.

This put a stop to his profitable enterprise.

I don't know what eventually happened to the family because just before the commencement of World War II, my family moved to a house which actually had a bath albeit that the hot water had to be heated in galvanised iron pails on the gas cooker.

I do know that at some time during the war, Clark Street Building received a direct hit by a German bomb and was badly damaged. I don't know if the Bercovitch family were still resident there at the time.

Some years after the war, I did meet a very successful and prosperous accountant who lived in a luxurious house in a salubrious suburb in N.W. London whose name was Bercovitch. When I mentioned that I knew of a family of that name who lived in Clark Street Buildings in Stepney, he quickly changed the subject.

Car Insurance

For quite some time now, scientists have discovered that we are what our genes make us

Our genes are determined from the moment of conception and are passed onto us by our natural parents. Our genes predetermined whether we will be tall, short, athletic, skinny, fat, clever; dull, handsome, beautiful, they will predetermine the colour of our skin, condition of hair, propensity to certain ailments both physical and mental as well as longevity

Recently, a scientist found that our inherited genes even gave us propensity to crime, wickedness, perversion, cruelty or deceit etc., etc..

Even though he did not say so specifically, it can reasonably be presumed that our genes also give us a propensity to honesty and kindness.

I believe, that it was my fortunate fate, with all due modesty to inherit genes that gave me a kindly and honest nature.

I am kind to animals and even to insects. I believe in live and let live. I would rather open a window to allow an annoying bluebottle fly to escape than to kill it with a swatter. I give generously to various animal welfare organisations but I admit, that I have not yet so far donated to any insect protection charity as I have not yet come across any. No doubt, somewhere, one does exist.

Being honest, that is in the truthful sense, I am not absolutely certain that my honest, that is in a non criminal or fraudulent sense, is due to having inherited an honesty gene but rather a cowardly gene.

Whenever I have been tempted to be dishonest, even in a most minor matter, I have been deterred by the fear of being caught and the consequences.

Being honest in the truthful sense, I must confess that I have on a few

422

occasions succumbed to the devil's temptations but only in minor matters. In most instances, honesty genes, or possibly my cowardice genes predominated and hopefully eased my path to a future among the angels.

By now you may well be asking yourself, what has all this pseudo scientific confessional soliloquising (whatever this word means) has to do with the essence of this story. You may very well ask and I will try to explain.

One of my weaknesses or virtues (depending on whether you are an insurance sales person or not) is my tendency to insure against virtually all eventualities.

Over the years I have expended a considerable fortune on insurance premiums.

Naturally, I have insured my house against all the standard risks including fire, burst pipes, lightning, vehicle impact, objects falling from the sky, foundation subsidence and damage due to ground heave (whatever that may be).

I have insured the contents of my home against all conceivable risks, even a bicycle which I do not own and also valuables etc. when on holiday. I always pay additional premiums to have excess clauses deleted or decreased.

For 36 years I had a private medical care insurance policy in effect both for myself and my wife. This was not for selfish reasons. As I ran a one man architectural practice with my wife as my sole assistant, I felt obliged to my clients, both legally and morally, to be available at all reasonable times even in sickness.

As an architect, I insured myself against any possible claims by clients or others for professional negligence and or incompetence. Even if completely innocent, it costs a fortune to prove one's innocence.

In these days with government funded legal aid willingly, easily and generously granted to any impecunious Tom, Dick or Harry, it is easy for legal actions to opened against architects but virtually almost impossible in most cases to recover the enormous costs involved in legal defence let alone to obtain compensation for loss of time and earnings involved.

By law, architects cannot shield themselves against claims by forming limited companies, they are personally responsible till their very last penny. If unlucky, they could even end up losing their savings, their house and home. It was, therefore, most prudent to be well insured against such claims even though the premiums were enormous.

One form of insurance I have always been very careful about is motor insurance. These days with crowded roads, it is so easy to be involved in an accident and your car can be damaged even when it is parked and you are not in it. Another big potential loss is the theft of your vehicle or its contents thereof. I am proud to say that in 48 years of motoring, I have only been involved in three minor incidents and none of which involved injuries.

In two of the accidents the fault was so obviously the other person's fault, that I did not lose my no-claim bonus. The third accident was also clearly not my fault but I did lose my noclaims bonus because the other party was driving uninsured. Since then, I have paid extra premiums so as to cover the possible loss of my no-claim bonus which is quite considerable.

Whenever I take out a new motor vehicle insurance, I closely examine the details and get obscure and ambiguous points clarified in writing before paying the premium.

With insurance policies, I tend to behave loyally to the insurers in the belief that such loyalty will be duly recognised and rewarded by lowered premiums and sympathetic treatment in the event of a claim.

Unfortunately, I have discovered somewhat late in the day that such loyalty is not programmed to be recognised by the computers which dominate the operation of the insurance companies these days.

The day I turned 65 years of age, my insurer's computer automatically as programmed, without any word of regret or explanation, doubled the premium on my health care policy despite the fact that in 36 years I was insured with them, I had not made a single claim.

Similarly, I realised recently, that the company I had my house and its contents insured with had for many consecutive years automatically raised their annual premiums disproportionately to rising values and costs. I discovered that by simply making a phone call, I could reinsure my house and its contents with another company at much better terms and much lower premiums.

My previous insurers did not even bother to ask why I was not reinsuring with them.

I had a similar experience with my motor car insurers. One day, in response to an advert in the national press, I picked up the phone and obtained an amazingly lower quote from a firm I had never previously had any business with.

I was amazed just how swiftly, politely, pleasantly, smoothly and efficiently the reinsurance was arranged.

Once again, my previous insurers did not bother to enquire why I had not re-insured with them. They did not even send a reminder after I had not responded to their renewal notice.

I had put the question of motor insurance out of my mind till recently when I disposed of the car I had been running for the past eleven years and acquired a much younger car albeit that it had had three previous owners.

I bought it on the recommendation of the garage owner where both my car and the one that I bought were regularly serviced.

Now, I am getting to the point of this story. My acquisition was in good bodily and mechanical condition but absolutely filthy both inside and out.

I engaged a car cleaning firm who came to my house and gave the car a thorough going over both inside and out. It took him four concentrated hours to complete but it transformed the appearance of the vehicle, most noticeably, the interior.

I could hardly believe my eyes and even Dora agreed that the car looked wonderful.

I was so pleased that I paid the firm more than we had contracted for although not by much.

The biggest surprise was the wonderful appearance of the cleaned seats. I had not realised what a lovely colour and texture the seat upholstery was until I saw them in their renovated state. Everything was pristine and looked new and smelt good.

The cleaner told me that the seats were the dirtiest he had encountered for many years and had spent a lot of time with his special mechanical shampoo cleaner to get them back to their new condition. He told me that because he had used such a lot of shampoo, the seats may take a while to dry out and advised me to leave the car windows partially open overnight to facilitate the drying and smell of the shampoo. The next morning, when I went to top up the petrol tank the upholstery appeared to have dried out. As I was leaving my driveway, a neighbour passed by and made a complimentary remark about how nice the car looked. This pleased me and I offered to drop her off at the local shopping parade on my way to the petrol service station. She readily accepted my invitation.

When I returned home and got out of the car, I realised that my clothes were soaking wet. I had to change completely.

Apparently, even though the upholstery surface felt dry to the touch, the underlying spongy interior of the seats had absorbed an enormous amount of the shampoo which was squeezed out by the weight of my body through the pores in the upholstery and thence into my clothes.

My dear wife, Dora, who apparently inherited genes of a concerned nature, asked what happened to the pleasant smartly dressed neighbour to whom I had given a lift. I told her that I did not know because I drove her off as soon as I had dropped her off at the local shopping parade.

Because she was so concerned, Dora phoned the neighbour who said that she had been most embarrassed. As soon as she had got out of the car she realised that her dress, especially round her bottom was soaking wet and clinging to her body. She had hoped that no-one would notice but she soon became aware that nearly everyone in the shopping parade and in the shops were looking or pretending not to be looking at her wet clinging dress. A few asked her if she was not well because she looked so distressed and one of her close neighbours offered to drive her home in his new car but on reflection quickly changed his mind.

Our neighbour said that she had to change all her clothing and she hoped that the soaking would not spoil her expensive clothes. She also told Dora that as she was very susceptible to colds and chest infections she was going to bed immediately as she could not afford being sick and away from work.

Whilst all this sounded genuine, I was alarmed that the incident may lead to a claim for damages and compensation. I was not sure that my motor insurance policy would cover such an eventuality. I quickly got onto my insurance company in a bit of a panic and reminded them that when I changed my car about three weeks ago, I had phoned them and gave them all the details that their computer required regarding the replacement car and that the lady who took the details had promised to let me have a cover note immediately. I told them that I had not received the cover note and I was most concerned in case something had gone wrong.

The lady listened patiently and sympathetically and entered the details onto their computer and solemnly promised to post a duplicate cover note to me that very same day by first class post.

When I had not received the duplicate cover note within two days I urgently phoned again and after a lot of questions and entries into their computer, the girl politely informed me that they could not issue a cover note as I was not insured with them.

She told me that I had not sent the premium requested in their renewal note and consequently, my policy with them had automatically lapsed. They had not sent me a reminder as she said it was not their policy to do so.

I had a sickening feeling that despite my pedantry concerning insurance, I had been breaking the law for the last three weeks by using a motor vehicle on Her Majesty's highways without being insured. However, I felt sure that I had not so long ago sent a cheque to the insurance company. I checked and there was an entry for a certain amount in respect of car insurance. I checked my bank statement; the cheque had been paid in. Next, I got my car insurance file out to check the renewal notice and to my horror I remembered that when I received it, I quickly made a phone call to another insurance company and changed my insurance. It had all been done without fuss and at a big reduction. Out of habit, I had phoned my previous insurance company about the change of car and they had not even bothered to let me know that I was no longer insured with them. A quick phone call to my new insurers quickly produced a cover note concerning the change.

I now wait with trepidation in case our nice, charming and pleasant neighbour submits a claim for spoilt expensive clothes and loss of earnings due to a severe cold in her posterior or possibly something even more serious.

The Shoemaker

When people exclaim "Its a small, small world" they don't usually refer to its physical dimensions but rather to a coincidence, the probability of which is remote.

One such event occurred to my wife and myself. Although it happened fairly recently, its origin commenced some 26 years ago, in 1970.

In that year, my wife and I became involved in a world-wide spontaneous effort, centred mainly in the USA and Great Britain, to "Free Soviet Jewry". In 1970, after many years of Stalinist oppression, the Jewish people in the Soviet Union began to demand their constitutional right to emigrate, mainly to Israel, which not long before has astounded the world in a brilliantly won war against overwhelming odds. The news of this victory and that there actually was a Jewish country stimulated and encouraged dormant Jewish hopes among the oppressed Jewish citizens of the Soviet Union.

Although it was their constitutional right to emigrate from the Soviet Union, to apply to do so, was an extremely dangerous decision. Like many of the Soviet constitutional rights, it was most laudable and worthy but in practise what mattered was what the dreaded Soviet Security Bureau, the KGB decided. They decided that any Soviet citizen who declared a desire to leave the socialist paradise of the Soviet Union were either insane of traitorous.

Many of the early applicants to emigrate were either incarcerated in horrific lunatic asylums or condemned to long sentences in the notorious Gulag hard labour prison camps in Siberia and other inhospitable regions of the Soviet Union. Some were sentenced to death on trumped up charges but after fierce protests in the democratic West, the sentences were commuted to long prison sentences.

When the news of the KGB re-actions to the applications to emigrate became known in the West, individuals or small groups spontaneously sprang into action and each according to their own ability, contacts, and initiative took appropriate, dignified, peaceful but effective action. This varied from person to person and ranged from letter writing to demonstrations. Individuals merged into groups and groups into national or regional organisations.

In the course of time, methods were refined to become increasingly effective.

The story of this movement is most interesting and I hope that it will be told one day as a record of an historical event in which some 1,000,000 Jews were extracted from the jaws of the KGB and led to freedom. This is an event which compares with the Exodus from Egypt as related in the bible.

Alright, already, I agree that there were some differences in the two events. In the recent exodus there were no burning bushes, no singular leader of Moses's stature, no ten plagues, no smiting of the firstborn, no darkness, no hail, no frogs, no blood etc., but the Russians had enough trouble of their own making to have noticed if any of these had occurred. True there was no dividing of the sea but the 'Refuseniks' left in air conditioned iron birds that flew through the sky and reached Israel within a few hours unlike the first Exodus journey which took some 40 years through scorching deserts.

Whereas most children are aware of the great Exodus of several thousand years ago, very few are aware of the even greater one of recent times.

Apart from participating in spectacular demonstrations organised by the 35's Woman's' Campaign for the Soviet Jewry under the brilliant leadership of Mrs Rita Eker, we, that is, my wife and I, decided on a letter writing campaign including, over the years, thousands of letters written with the aid of friends to those condemned to labour camps and to those who had applied to emigrate and waited in dread in case they will become one of those chosen by the KGB to be examples in order to discourage others from applying. Those, whose applications were refused became known as 'Refuseniks'.

After their eventual release, prisoners told us that even though they were never handed any of the letters or postcards sent to them in the labour camps, they were aware that something important was happening because of the improved attitude to them by the camp commandant and guards. Others, who were awaiting the KGB reaction to their application were encouraged to persevere when they received letters from the West, even if they could not translate them, they knew that someone, somewhere, was aware of their plight and was concerned. Many did not dare to ask acquaintances who knew English to translate in case the KGB became aware through the wide involvement of informers in the former Soviet Union.

We were told by one such 'Refusenik' that he was informed that a relief gift food parcel sent by us awaited him in the local post office and even though desperate for its contents they were too scared to go along and collect it.

The Soviet Union was a vast conglomerate of Republics including, Armenia, Azerbaijan, Belorus, Kazakhstan, Kirghistan, Moldova, Tajikistan, Turkmenistan, Ukraine, Uzbekistan and also the Baltic states of Estonia, Latvia and Lithuania as well as Georgia and Russia.

We wrote to the 'Refuseniks' in each of the Republics and so, we certainly had our work cut out. Each letter was individually written in as clear English as possible and a great many of the replies were written in Russian which we had to get translated by our wonderful, indefatigable volunteer, translator who worked like a Trojan. There are relatively few people in this country who can translate Russian into English than there are Russian people who can do the reverse. We were very lucky to have had the services of the excellent translator that we had.

I wrote the foregoing as an introduction to the main point of this story.

Although we wrote thousands of letters and sent nearly 2000 gift parcels we received relatively few replies. We attributed this to the fact that either our letters were not.being delivered or that the recipient's replies were being intercepted by the KGB or to the fact that the recipients could not read English. Sometimes the replies from a regular correspondent would suddenly stop and eventually we would discover that they had emigrated.

On our last visit to Israel, we met several of the 'Refuseniks' we had previously written to and to whom we had kept contact. But due to time limitation and language problems these were few and far between.

When we visit Israel, we do not stay in luxurious hotels or eat in expensive restaurants. We usually stay in Bed and Breakfast rooms in private residences.

The traditional Israeli breakfast is enormous and was normally sufficient to last us the day. We did not travel around in guided tourists' air conditioned coaches but by local bus services. This suited me fine as I am a keen amateur photographer and find this freelance form of travel more suited to my convenience and produces much more interesting and colourful photos.

When we were not dining in ex-'Refuseniks' houses, we often ate our evening meal in what in this country used to be called a transport café. Good and plentiful food at cheaper prices.

After a gruelling day's exploring and photographing in and around Beer Sheva which is situated in the middle of the Negev desert including the picturesque camel market, we popped into such a café in one of Beer Sheva's side streets for our evening meal before catching a bus back to Tel-

Aviv where we were staying. The café's tariff was written in scribbled Ivrit (Modern Hebrew) which was unintelligible to us. The café owner knew no English so we tried in turn, elementary French, German and finally Yiddish which although it utilises the Hebrew alphabet is quite a different language to Ivrit. As soon as the café owner heard Dora speaking fluent Yiddish, he clapped his hands and jumped with joy. He said that it was many years since he had heard such clearly spoken Yiddish. Apparently, his parents had emigrated from Russia before the revolution and they spoke to him only in Yiddish and Russian.

He wanted to know if we too were Jewish and how it was that a pair of English tourists could speak such excellent Yiddish. We explained that even though we had both been born and bred in London, our parents who were immigrants from Eastern Europe also only spoke Yiddish to us and that we did not know any English until we started attending school.

We asked him to translate the menu but he said in Yiddish that the Menu was irrelevant because we would have his speciality which was chopped chicken liver and chips.

He served the chopped chicken liver out of a large plastic washing up bowl and loaded the plates with delicious chips. As we were hungry, we immediately tucked into our meal.

The café owner, a tubby man with a bald head, about fiftyish sat down and continued the conversation. Whilst talking, he helped himself periodically to chips from our plates which he ate with great relish.

He neglected serving his other customers who did not seem to mind as they were listening intently to the conversation at our table although they could not understand a single word.

Soon a dark complexioned man of about 45 years and his son, about 10 years old also sat down at our table and started to speak to the cafe owner in Russian. He asked the cafe owner if we were from America. He was told that we were actually from England. He then asked the cafe owner to ask us if we knew the Mishpacha (family) Gabriel from Ilford in England. We knew that there were several families of this name living in and around Ilford, one of which, not related at all, lived a few doors away from us in our own street.

The inquirer however, clarified that it was actually us he was asking about. He explained that for about five years his wife, Nina, who was a teacher of English used to correspond with us regularly when they lived in Tajikistan one of the Soviet republics.

We remembered his family well and we recalled the wonderful family photograph they had sent us not long before their correspondence suddenly stopped.

The man whose name was Isak Yosef told us why his wife suddenly stopped writing to us.

They lived in the capital city of the republic which was mainly populated by Moslems whose religion like that of all other religions was greatly oppressed and discouraged by the central Soviet government who expounded their own 'religion' of Marxism.

The Moslems resented this repression and with the encouragement and influences from outside Moslem regimes began to rebel against the central government who sent troops in to suppress the rebellion.

At times, the fighting was quite severe and moved rapidly from one part of the republic to another in a guerrilla style of warfare.

One day, when Isak was travelling on a bus through a desolate desert area to another town, the bus was halted by a group of armed and masked Moslem guerrilla fighters who told the Moslems in the bus to remain seated and all non Moslems to get out and lie down on the ground. As he was not a Moslem, Isak got out along with a few men who likewise were not Moslems and lay on the ground, face down. He then heard the group's leader instruct his men to execute all the non Moslems as enemies of Islam. After two prisoners had been shot, he heard one of the group ask his leader to spare Isak's life as he recognised him as his shoe repairer and swore that even though he was not a Moslem, he was a good and respectable humble worker and was not anti Moslem. The group's leader agreed to spare him. Isak rejoined the other passengers on the bus and was conveyed to safety. His immediate family which consisted of eleven persons including three year old twin girls decided that they must emigrate immediately.

They sold everything they had and used the money to bribe the emigration officials to grant them the permission they were legally and constitutionally entitled to. At the customs, most of their personal belongings were confiscated including the booklet in which our address was written. Even though they had wished to contact us, they could not do so as they did not memorise our address or telephone number.

And now, by the grace of God, here we were, in this remote part of the Earth, both thousands of miles from the land of our births.

The cafe owner who had translated all this from Russian to Yiddish was emotionally moved and so too were the other cafe customers when they learnt what it was all about. Dora and I as tourists, and he, working as a gardener in the nearby Ben Gurion University.

To celebrate the occasion, the cafe owner asked us to join him in a glass of Bronfen which is my parent's home and that of Dora's, was the Yiddish word for Brandy. We gladly accepted this offer but the cafe's owner's idea of Bronfen was foul castor oil flavoured Gin.

Finally I was handed the heshbon (bill) which included for four large Bronfen.

The Five Kava£ires

All their acquaintances knew them as the 'five Kava£ires', a sobriquet which they themselves proudly invented for themselves. They never tired of explaining that the initial capital 'K' represented the metric symbols for thousands and the '£' letter is the symbolic initial of the Latin word 'Lira' which means pounds sterling and which is still in current usage.

They wanted people to acknowledge that they were proud, fabulously rich men worth at least thousands of pounds. In fact, each one of them was a multi millionaire.

Unlike many people in the their financial situation, they did not suppress the fact that they were exceedingly rich, they took every opportunity to express it even to the extent of some vulgarity which although frowned upon in this country, would have been applauded in the USA. All five had originated from very humble, impoverished slum homes in the Jewish east end of London.

Their parents had been penniless immigrants from eastern Europe not knowing a single word of English. They enthusiastically worked long hours in the sweat workshops in the slums in order to bring their children up in happier circumstances than their own. They had not only fled grinding poverty in their homelands but also cruel pogroms.

The five Kava£ires had first become acquainted with each other when they met in the same class in the Jews Free School in Bell Lane in the heart of the Jewish populated east end of London.

The school was called the Jews Free School because some Jewish philanthropists had undertaken to pay the one penny per day (240 pence to the pound) being charged by other schools for elementary education.

Thus, Jewish children were encouraged not to play truant in order to

432

alleviate their parents pecuniary plight as a penny a day for each of their children, possibly seven or more, was a big strain on their meagre income especially so, if the bread winner was unemployed.

Although there were over sixty children in their class, the five young embryo Kavafires were naturally attracted to each other and found a friendship that was to last them for the rest of their lives and possibly, even beyond.

Right from an early age they demonstrated their natural inborn entre-preneurial skills and enterprises. During play periods, dinner breaks and the short period just before school assembly, they did not join in the noisy boisterous games in the crowded playground but instead, concentrated on selling such items as second hand comics, children's magazines and ciga-rette picture cards to their fellow pupils.

As they progressed, they also sold luxury items such as second hand watches and fountain pens.

By these means they were able to earn more than they could have if they had played truant and worked in their parents sweat shops.

During the war, the school was evacuated to three small villages in the Cambridgeshire Fens but the five remained in London and soon after commenced work full time in the sweat shops even during the German blitz on their part of London.

Eventually, they were split up at the age of 18 years when they were conscripted into the armed forces.

The armed forces showed them a different world to the close, narrow one in which they had been born into and brought up. The forces taught them skills that were not available to them in the east end of London. They also saw how other people lived, in smog free suburbs, luxurious spacious houses, beautiful gardens, cars and various country pursuits.

They were determined to participate in this new way of life and realised the key to the door of this paradise was education.

Their parents could not afford, after the war when they were demo-bilised, to support them whilst they attended college, so they enrolled in evening classes and in the course of five grinding years of working during the day and studying at night they each, in their own sphere, qualified.

One qualified in estate agency, another in banking, one in business management, one in accountancy and the other in building construction.

After the war, they regained acquaintance and renewed their friend-ship.

All five joined the same ex-servicemen's' and ex-servicewomens' clubs, the same rambling clubs and simultaneously conducted courting from among the same group of eligible young women.

All five married and produced happy families but they still retained the bachelor type friendship.

At least once a month, they met alone without wives being present.

They became Freemasons in the same 'Lodge of Light and Honour' which was composed mainly of ex-pupils who had attended the Jews Free School in the east end of London.

They continued to enjoy the week-end rambles in the countryside even though their wives could not often accompany them due to family commitments.

Whilst this friendship grew and strengthened, so did their business enterprises until one day it suddenly dawned on them that they were exceedingly wealthy people.

They had each acquired a miniature mansion in a salubrious suburb in North London noted for its high occupancy of millionaires.

They had each acquired several luxurious cars including either a Rolls Royce or a Bentley.

The awareness of their accumulated wealth seemed to dawn upon them suddenly. Up till then, they had been too busy making money to appreciate what they had accomplished.

One evening, alter a splendid dinner at their exclusive club whilst they were savouring a glass of fine French brandy and an excellent Cuban cigar, they became pensive and asked each other, what is the point of all this?

Alter a long discussion they decided that there was no point in continuing making money which they could not possibly spend. Each had already amassed more than they could possibly spend in the expected remaining years of their lives.

They each decided to retire and enjoy life before they became too old, too infirm or too senile to do so.

They therefore agreed to name their little group the five Kavaℒires and to spend the rest of their active years enjoying themselves.

They all agreed that their families had been well and truly provided for and that during their successful years, they had given generously to charities

Next, they agreed upon a most spectacular and unusual agreement. They each agreed that they should not end up as one of the richest men in the cemetery but as one of the poorest.

They made a verbal agreement sealed with a handshake that in the event of one of them dying, their Will will be such, that their entire residual fortune goes equally to the surviving four and in the event of one of - the surviving four dying, his entire residual. fortune, including his share of the first inheritance, will be divided among the surviving three and so on until the last survivor inherits the fortunes of the other four.

Their next resolve was that the last survivor was to will his own and all the accumulated fortunes to a charity or charities of his own choice.

After the solicitors had finally drafted a sample Will which they all agreed to abide by, they made their decision known to their relatives and acquaintances. They were told quite clearly and firmly, that they had all been more than adequately provided for and that they should not expect any more from the estates of the five 'Kavaƒires.'

Their relatives and acquaintances received the information with stunned incredibility. They could not believe that such a naive plan would work in practice. They doubted that each of the five would honour the agreement after having received any portion of their friend's estate. They did not believe that all five would abide on such a plan that relied on absolute trust and the temptations that such large sums of money offer.. They believed that the chain of trust would he broken sooner or later, and sooner, rather than later.

The five also made provision for their burials. They decided that even in death they would not be parted from one another. They bought five adjacent burial plots in the cemetery where they intended to be buried and each had the inscription on the simple, modest headstone consisting only of their name, date of birth and provision for their eventual date of death. No sentimental messages of grief or prayers etc. was provided for.

They also intended to have the words "Here lies the remains of one of the five Kavaƒires" but the burial authorities would not permit it. They said it would be a precedent for other such irreverent words on other tombstones.

When the first of the five died, relatives and acquaintances were amazed that he had duly kept to his agreement and had left the whole of his residual estate to be equally divided among the other four. There was much gnashing of teeth and raised blood pressures among the relatives but lawyers assured them that the Will could not be successfully challenged in court unless any of the deceased dependant relatives had not been adequately provided for.

The lawyers further explained that the only possible chance of challenging the Will would be if any of the other four failed to abide by the mutual agreement, something they termed 'consequential. reciprocity'.

As the years rolled by, the remaining four survivors gave no indication of giving the lawyers the opportunity to prove their contention right or wrong.

They continued their agreement to enjoy life to the full. They spent much time caring for their health by staying at health farms, taking relaxing holidays, especially during the winter months, in Bermuda.

They were advised to play golf but each time one of them applied for membership in one of the prestigious clubs, they were black-balled. They overcame this problem by buying one of the clubs near their homes and appointing themselves life members. They them re-sold the club at an enormous profit. They had not, even in retirement lost their Midas touch.

After a few years of most enjoyable, healthy retirement, they did start to depart this world, one soon after the other. When one died, their will-power to continue seemed to evaporate.

In turn, as each one died, the relatives waited to see if they had abided by their original agreement. Most surprisingly, each one did until only one surviving 'Kava£ire' remained.

He had cancer of the bowels and it took him a very long time to die.

By now, there were many relatives, not only his own but those of the preceding four Kava.fires waiting to see what the provisions of his Will revealed.

His accumulated wealth amounted to several millions of pounds. Was he going to be loyal to his pre-deceased friends' wishes or was he going to dispose of the vast amount to his own kith and kin?

When, his Will was finally revealed, he had entirely complied with the agreement made with his lifelong friends and he left the whole of his estate to a charity trust to provide free higher education to those Jewish boys from impoverished families anywhere in the world who deserved such help.

After the last interment took place among the five modest (graves in a remote part of the enormous cemetery, the words 'Here lies the remains of one of the five Kava£ires' appeared mysteriously on each of the modest marble tomb stones.

Nobody knows who arranged for these words to be incised on the stones or who paid for the work 'to be done but possibly the fact that the Secretary of the burial society had been a close friend of the five may have had some bearing on the matter.

Nobody raised any objection to the wording or tried to raise them as a precedent as nobody seemed to be aware that they existed because no one visited the five forlorn graves.

Hannah

Consequent to my wife breaking her thigh bone in her left leg, I acted as her chauffeur, conveying her and her shopping to and from the local supermarket.

Whereas she loves shopping, I detest it very much. Before her accident, I even used to ask her to buy things on my behalf, such as clothes, toiletries and stationary etc., etc..

Now, I trundle a trolley behind her whilst she selects items from the supermarket shelves and places them in the trolley. It irritates me enormously at the way she carefully examines each item she purchases before placing them in the trolley. I know she is going to read the contents, the expiry date, the food values etc., printed on the containers; She also carefully examines items that I know she has no intention at all in buying and comparing aloud what she declares as being outrageous increases in prices.

Moreover, I am infuriated at the behaviour of the elderly dears who have the uncanny ability to crawl along or even completely halt just where their trolleys form a bottle-neck in the aisles. They seem oblivious to their surroundings and never apologise even in the slightest manner for the inconvenience they cause. When they do stop to take something off a shelf, they skew their trolleys at right angles to the shelves so as to cause the maximum obstruction and they often manage this when another old dear has similarly stopped on the other side of the aisle.

Why there is no outbreak of trolley rage at the supermarkets I do not know.

It was on one of such shopping expeditions, when my blood pressure was running high that I was suddenly accosted by a rather tall, well dressed elderly man (well, nearly every man is tall and well dressed compared with myself) who extended his arm in greeting and smilingly expressed his delight in meeting me.

There was no doubt, he knew me, and even though he was somewhat familiar, I could not recall who he was or under which circumstances I had previously known him.

He asked after my wife, Dora, who soon joined in the conversation. She appeared to know who the man was and being embarrassed, I also pretended to do so hoping that I would be able to identify him from something he might say. He told me that I looked well considering my age but I could not return the compliment truthfully because the man had a haggard appearance and his suit hung loosely upon his lean figure. He noted that our trolley was full and said that as he had also finished his shopping he would like us all to meet and to have a chat and a coffee in the supermarket restaurant after we had checked out. He said that the treat would be on him.

When he had departed, I asked Dora if she knew who he was, she said that she thought I knew, she was not sure but she suspected it was Arthur Goldsmith who was once, many years ago, one of my clients.

As soon as we entered the restaurant we saw Arthur sitting at a table with cups of coffee and plate of pastries waiting for us.

He immediately said, "Its good to speak with someone from the good old days. Very few people recognise me nowadays and many of those that do, are too embarrassed to talk, including those who still owe me money. Still, it doesn't worry me because I now realise that good health and good friends like yourselves are worth all the money in the world."

As he was speaking, his eyes sparkling and his face flushed, memories came flooding back to me. In the mind's eye I could see the Arthur of twenty years or so ago, when I first met him. He was tall, as he still was now, but in those days he was big and burly, the sort of person you did not lightly dare to annoy.

I noticed that he still wore as he did 'in the good old days,' an expensive, tailor cut suit, silk shirt and tie and an expensive Rolex watch, a heavy gold chain bracelet and, an even heavier gold chain around his neck from which hung a large gold medallion. I appreciated how, in the 'good old days' it would have taken a very brave or a very foolish person to have tried to mug him for these ostentatious gold items, especially so, as he was rarely without a most deterrent looking minder present. I also recalled his opulent, immaculately kept gold coloured Rolls Royce. It was no wonder that in those 'good old days' I had nicknamed him in my own mind, 'Mr Goldfinger' although I would never have called him that to his face.

From his present day frail appearance it would appear that even a child would be able to mug him for his gold accoutrements with ease.

When I knew him, he was a dealer in exotic, expensive vintage and rare cars. He specialised in Rolls Royces, Bentleys, Ferraris, Aston Martins, Bristols, Alfa Romeos, Porches, Lotus's, Mercedes and BMWs.

In those days, any dealer who could get their hands on any of these vehicles was assured of an easy and very profitable sale. Arthur did not seem to have had any problem in getting hold of such cars and with a long waiting list of eager would be buyers had no difficulty of a fast, lucrative turnover.

He came from very humble origins, his father was a farm labourer who also worked hard to bring up a large family during very hard times. Arthur knew extreme poverty as a youngster, had a hard time as a -private in the army during the war, but consequently revelled in his wealth which he proudly showed off ostentatiously.

His main asset in life was his amiable nature, quick wit and fantastic ability to memorise and to instantly recall the most minute details and a most uncanny shrewdness. However, very few were aware of his dark hidden secret.

I was introduced to him by a mutual friend for whom I had acted as his architect some years previously. He told me that Arthur who was a fellow member of his golf club, urgently needed the services of a good architect. He was having trouble with an extension he was having built to his palatial house in Gidea Park, Essex

Arthur picked me up in his gold coloured Rolls Royce and whisked me off to his house and showed me some trenches that had had weak watery concrete poured in to form the foundations for a proposed extension.

He told me that a short while before, his wife, Irene, who was much younger than himself had seen a photo of a country house illustrated in a glossy magazine. The house was named 'The two gables'.

She had been so enamoured by it, that she resolved to extend her own house so that it would have two gables and also be known by that name.

She was impulsive and impatient. She called in a builder whose sign board she had seen outside a neighbour's house. She showed him the magazine photos and asked him how much he would charge to build such an extension.

The builder thinking that all she wanted at that preliminary stage was an indication of the probable cost, gave a figure off the top of his head. To his utter surprise she accepted the figure and told him to start work the following Monday.

On the spot, on a rough piece of paper he wrote a confirmation of the quoted figure and a very crude description of the work to be done. What the description amounted to, was in effect, an open cheque to be made out to the builder.

Irene agreed that he could immediately have cash to cover the estimated cost of labour and material to be involved in the first week of work and a similar payment on each subsequent Friday. The weekly estimates were to be made by the builder himself.

When he asked about plans and specifications and who was to supervise the work on her behalf, she told the builder that plans were not necessary as all he had to do was to build an extension that looked like the one illustrated in the magazine. She said that she would not waste time making an application to the council as that would only delay the project. She assured the builder that her husband knew all the important people on the Council and they will not cause any problems. Also, she pointed out that her immediate neighbour was on the Council and she got on very well with him and his wife.

As to the employment of an architect or surveyor, she herself would supervise the work and on her husband's behalf., she would pay him the weekly advance payments which she said he could have in cash if he so preferred.

The builder promptly commenced work the following Monday, but unfortunately for him and Arthur, the immediate next door neighbour noticed the activity. He was indeed a local councillor and also happened to be the Chairman of the Town Planning and Building Committee.

Within a few days, council building inspectors called on the site and as a consequence of what they saw, an urgent stop notice was served on the site forbidding any further work being carried out pending approval of plans which were to be submitted to the Council.

The work already carried out was condemned as not being in accordance with the Building Regulations. As soon as the builder realised that there was going to be trouble, he whisked his men, materials and plant off the site and disappeared along with his advance cash payment, never to be seen again.

Irene was furious and because she was upset, so was Arthur. He told me to proceed with all due haste to meet the Council's requirements and to prepare plans and specification to comply with his wife's desire.

He, in turn, used his influence and the plans were approved in very quick time.

I helped them to get competitive tenders from several reputable local builders based on my plans and specifications. The extension was erected promptly, properly and fulfilled Irene's vision that had come to her in a glossy magazine. She proudly had stationary printed with the address as 'The two gables'. Everybody was pleased, especially Arthur because Irene was pleased. He was especially pleased with the way I had expeditiously executed my duties and promised to recommend me to others.

During our discussion in the restaurant, the subject of the extension arose. I asked Arthur if there had been any consequent problems. He replied, "I don't know, I don't live there any more". He went on to explain that not long after the extension episode he developed cancer of the lungs, caused no doubt through the excessive smoking involved in his business and social life. He had been very ill and was lucky to survive.

Just as he thought he was over that hurdle, he suffered a severe stroke and was incapacitated for a very long while. He had made a remarkable recovery but it had taken a very long time. It was during his illnesses that his business collapsed. His business was based on his personality and contacts. Whilst he was out and about making contacts and deals, the paperwork was done by an efficient office manager and the work on the vehicles was supervised by an extraordinary efficient foreman neither of who had an earthly idea as to how to buy or sell the vehicles he specialised in.

During Arthur's illness the business was changed mainly to the repairs and maintenance of quality cars.

Whereas Arthur was good at making money, Irene was good at spending it. When she realised that Arthur would no longer be able to earn the sort of money he used to, she started divorce proceedings and moved Arthur's office manager into the matrimonial bed and home now known as 'The two gables'.

When Arthur recovered sufficiently to care for himself, he was allocated a sheltered accommodation flat by the local council not far from the supermarket in which we met.

He said that he was not badly off financially. Even though Irene had been a big spender, he had been prudent and put aside sufficient to enable him now to live a modest and comfortable life.

He said that he will look forward to meeting us again as he had very much enjoyed our chat, although it was he who had done most of the talking.

He gratefully accepted my offer to give him and his two heavy bags of shopping a lift to his present home. He said that he had to dispose of his gold coloured 'roller' when the authorities refused to renew his driving licence due to the stroke he had suffered.

Even though he had voluntarily told us a lot, there was one problem that had always puzzled me. I suspected all along that, despite his success in life, that he was actually illiterate. This suspicion was aroused through actions like never reading any document I showed him on the excuse that he had forgotten to fetch his spectacles with him although he was quite capable of seeing other things at close quarters.

If any documents had to be signed, he would take it away and return it signed within a day or two.

He would not have been the first successful businessman I had encountered who was to some degree illiterate. One thing in particular puzzled me was when he returned any document or cheque, the signature read 'Hannah'. When I first noticed this, I queried it with him but he was evasive. He assured me that the signature was authorised and notarised and would be accepted as his, even on his cheques.

I took the opportunity of our chance meeting and the friendly atmosphere to raise the question of his curious signature again.

He smiled and said, "No doubt, you suspected that I am illiterate. You are right, I cannot read or write a single word, I suffer with a peculiar form of dyslexia. Most sufferers have difficulty in reading or writing because the letters of the words get mixed up and out of order. My form of dyslexia is that I can't avoid reading or writing words backwards. Its stupid and I can't explain why it is. I've tried hard enough to overcome it, but I cannot do so. That is why I used to take documents away with me so as to get my wife or office manager to read them out to me."

I told him that I appreciated his problem but I could not see why he used to sign cheques and documents with the name 'Hannah'. He smiled again, "Simple, because it's spelt the same way forward or backward!"

The Sub Collector

When I worked in the Architects' office of a certain local east London Metropolitan Council, it was the Labour Council's policy, that as a condition of employment, every employee, from the most humble to the very highest, had to be a member of an appropriate trade union. Loss of membership of a union involved immediate and automatic dismissal.

The Council considered membership of an appropriate trade union was more important than appropriate qualifications and or experience when selecting candidates for employment.

The Council, however, did make one concession, instead of a trade union, employees could belong to the National Association of Local Government officials; NALGO. Although NALGO was to all intents and purposes a trade union, the Council looked unfavourably on it because the members continually voted not to be affiliated to the Trade Union Council; TUC., the national umbrella organisation for all trade unions. The NALGO members as a whole, considered themselves superior to other trade union members and refused to be associated with them through the TUC. The majority of the white collar Council employees preferred to belong to NALGO but the lads in the Architects' Office to a man, expressed their Bolshie, rebellious nature by joining a far left union, the Association of Building Technicians; ABT..

Apart from anything else, it was cheaper and also expressed their superior attitude to the hum drum clerical staff in other Council departments.

It was one thing agreeing to belong to the ABT, but it was quite another to get them to pay their monthly subscriptions.

No one in the office was agreeable to act as sub collector but eventually, one of the more serious and studious of the assistants, Victor Newton, reluctantly agreed to undertake the onerous task.

On pay day, he went from desk to desk, imploring the reluctant members to part with their measly subscription. It was only after considerable arrears had mounted up and after he pointed out that arrears could mean cancellation of union membership and the consequential dismissal from employment, that part payment was made.

It needed someone of strong but placid nature to tolerate the monthly torment that Victor endured on each monthly pay day.

One of the reasons, and possibly the main reason that Victor endured this monthly humiliation was that he was keen to ensure that the ABT did not fail to maintain a strong membership. His enthusiasm was inspired by the fact that although he never did reveal it to his colleagues, he was a very active member of the Communist Party of Great Britain and the ABT was one of the front organisations of the Party although most of the members of the ABT were not aware of it.

Victor was a quiet and popular colleague among the Architect office staff who were aware of his extreme left wing opinions but not of his membership of the Communist Party. They did not object to his left wing views as the majority of them were likewise inclined but drew the line on actual membership of the Party.

Victor boosted his popularity by acting as unelected and unpaid social activities secretary. He organised some wonderful events. He hired a vintage, double decker London bus and organised an outing to Southend-on-Sea. He organised a trip on a paddle steamer down the River Thames to Margate; a visit to the Tower of London and a behind the scenes conducted tour of the workings of Tower Bridge was likewise very much appreciated. Also high on the list of activities were visits to the local Queens Theatre, where a bar on a balcony overlooked the stage on which crummy local talent tried their luck. All his events were most successful.

He also organised boozy visits to lively local pubs. Colleague's wives were sometimes permitted to accompany their husbands but very rarely.

As far as these activities were concerned, he had no problem in collecting payments.

It was the morning following one of the pub crawls that Victor came to work obviously in a terrible condition. It was not one of the usual hangovers that most of the revellers suffered with after a previous night's pub crawl. He was white, trembling like a leaf and mumbling to himself.

At first, he was the butt of jokes and leg pulling but it soon became clear that something much more serious underlay his condition, especially so, when he slumped over his desk sobbing uncontrollably. It was obvious that he was not fit for work and I was delegated to take him to the staff canteen in order to ascertain what his trouble was.

The canteen was not yet open but the staff were sympathetic and willingly made us cups of strong coffee and told us to relax for a while in a quiet corner.

The coffee certainly helped Victor to pull himself together a bit. He stopped sobbing and in a weak broken voice began to explain the reason for his condition.

Apparently, he got home late last night safe and sound although deeply inebriated but conscious enough to realise that he must not awake his wife if she should be asleep.

The house was in darkness. He peeped into the kitchen and saw that the breakfast things were on the kitchen table ready for the following morning. His wile normally arranged that just before going to bed.

He undressed down to his underwear and socks in the dark, in the entrance hall, and tip-toed up the stairs keeping tight to the handrail to ensure that he did not stumble and also to minimise the creaking of the timber stair treads. When he reached the landing he listened out for snoring.

Actually, snoring sounds came from both his bedroom and from the spare bedroom.

This rather upset him as this indicated that his hated mother-in-law had kept her threat and had come to stay with them for a week or two. He had intended to slip into the spare bedroom and thus avoid waking his wife who was bound to be annoyed with him for staying out with the boys and coming home in a drunken state.

If he could have kept out of her way till the morning, he could have avoided unpleasantness. As there appeared to be no alternative, he crept into the matrimonial bedroom and quietly as possible slipped into the matrimonial bed and lay as near to his edge as possible so as not to make bodily contact. He said that he must have fallen into a deep slumber almost immediately.

At some time during the night, he found himself in a passionate embrace. Thankfully, he thought that all had gone well and that in the morning, his late return home would have been forgotten and or forgiven.

Due to the large amount of beer he had drunk during the evening out, he went down to the toilet at least three times and each time he returned to bed, he was passionately embraced.

In his sleep he heard the pre-set electric alarm clock sound and most reluctantly he let himself gently out of bed. It was still dark and in appreciation, he did not want to disturb his wife, so he left the bedroom as quietly as he had entered the previous night. He relieved himself once more in the toilet, remembering again not to flush the cistern in case the noise disturbed his wife. He crept silently down the stairs and dressed himself with the clothes he had discarded in the entrance hail the previous night.

He decided to prepare his own breakfast before going to work. He was specially looking forward to a nice big, strong cup of coffee. When he entered the kitchen he was shocked to see his wife cheerfully preparing the breakfast.

She said, "Don't stand there looking like an idiot, sit down and have your breakfast". Before he could say anything, she continued, "I'm glad you had enough decency not to disturb me last night and had enough common sense to sleep your drunken stupor off on the couch in the front lounge"

Victor said that as though in a dream, he asked his wife, "Who was it sleeping in our bed". She replied, "It's my mother you dopey idiot, you knew she was coming to stay and I left a note on the hall stand to let you know that she was sleeping in our bed as the spare bed was too cold and damp for her rheumatics. It's a wonder you were in a fit enough condition last night to read to note. I slept in the spare bedroom but never-the-less, I heard you go to the toilet several times"

When Victor told his wile that he had slept with her mother, she treated it as big joke. Even when Victor said that her mother had not said a word she laughed and joked, "You know she is not on speaking terms with you"

His wile went into hysterical laughter when she fully realised the import of her own joke. Victor's face became increasingly flushed as he related last night's events. His eyes gleamed and asked me "What if my wile realises the truth? What if her mother confirms the truth?"

I told him to calm down and to treat the whole episode as a very nasty nightmare. I told him that his mother-in-law was not likely to confess to her own daughter that she had slept with her hated son-inlaw. I pointed out that if he kept shtumn (silent), the event will either be forgotten or treated as a big laugh.

He said that I was most likely right and thanked me profusely for listening so patiently and wisely and thanked me for my sound and sensible advice.

He said that now, he himself doubted whether it had actually happened and that he had had a most realistic nightmare.

He implored me not to tell the lads and not to tell it to anyone at all, not even to my wife.

He got up to return to the office saying, that he felt a lot better, and said, "By the way, you still owe me a month's union sub"

Parking

Recently, Dora said that she wanted to buy some items in the local Jewish delicatessen shop but as the items would be too heavy to carry home she wanted me to go with her in the car. So we trundled up to the local shopping parade in my old olive grey BMW 520.

I was fortunate enough to find a spot to park quite near the shop. I told Dora that I would wait for her in the car and if a traffic warden were to come along, I would drive round the block and return when the warden had gone. Needless to say, the only spot I found to park on was on a yellow line and the offence carried a fine of £40 or the car may be towed away and the cost of retrieval is £177.

Soon after Dora had disappeared into the shop I noticed a traffic warden approaching the line of illegally parked cars. I promptly drove off and lingered around the corner for about ten minutes and then returned to the shopping parade.

The warden had, as I anticipated, gone but the place where I had parked had been taken by another car, which by coincidence was the same model and colour as my own, and coming out of the car was a red faced, embarrassed Dora.

She had done her shopping quickly and coming out had quickly entered what she took to be my car, flung the shopping on the back seat and said, 'Quick, drive off, there's a traffic warden around.' She was shocked to hear the driver say, 'Sorry dear, I think you've got the wrong car.' To her extreme embarrassment she then noticed that the driver was a jet black West Indian with a large grin that displayed an array of gold capped teeth that matched his gold Rolex watch and gold chains around his neck and gold bracelets on his wrists.

Guide Dog

The blind girl who lived a few doors away hated the thought that people felt sorry for her. She said that nearly everybody had something or another wrong with them and some had conditions that were far more serious than hers. At least, she said, my condition is not terminal, it is not painful and otherwise I am quite fit. She deplored it when anyone spoke to her loudly or slowly as though she was deaf or daft. She was rosy cheeked, had a well-fed appearance and always looked fresh and cheerful.

She lived alone in a bed-sitter and went to work each day guided by her passive, faithful and well behaved guide dog. Each morning the dog would lead her down to the bus stop and make sure that no traffic was coming when they crossed a road. He would then lead her into the local railway station to catch a train to the city where she worked as a telephonist. In the evenings he brought her safely home to her bed-sit.

One morning things went very wrong. He guided her to the bus stop and then took her onto the local station but instead of stopping at the usual spot on the platform, he led her onto the railway line. Fortunately the rails were not live and no train came along. Both girl and dog were soon rescued and after the girl was checked at the local hospital both were taken home by ambulance.

The charity, which had trained the dog and supplied it to the girl, was very concerned. The dog was well trained and experienced. They took him back for a refresher course but when their vet examined him, he found that the dog was totally blind!

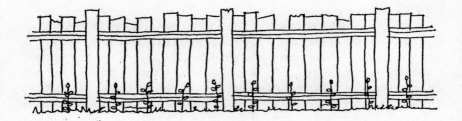

My Life
by the Green Dragon

My existence began about 70 years ago when the original owner of my house inserted a row of sprigs from a privet hedge. His intention was to form a dense hedge to conceal the front party close boarded, feather edged fence, which had stated to show signs of deterioration. The planting of those sprigs you might say, were my conception. Personally, I don't remember the event, but then, I don't suppose many are aware of the most momentous event of their existence.

In a few years those sprigs became a vigorous growth. The house owner was quite proud of his effort and regularly trimmed the tops of the growth so as to encourage more dense growth rather than height. Soon there was not much to be seen of the old wooden fence from my owners' side of the divide but the wooden fence continued to deteriorate and began to look very shabby.

Nothing much happened for the next 20 years and then, sadly, my owner died after a long illness. His heart had never been too good. It was reputed that he was closely related to a famous artist who ended his years in a mental home after murdering his father. The family did not speak about this connection.

His son inherited the house but did not give me the same care and attention that his father had. Through neglect, I grew very straggly and untidy. He not only neglected me but also both the front and back gardens and even the house itself.

About four years later I became alarmed when a man came and without a word of explanation to me, stuck a notice board up, 'For Sale'. At first, I did not realise that the notice was applicable to the whole of the

449

property not just to me alone. Other men came and quickly painted the exterior woodwork in order to make the house look less neglected. Several people came to view the property but none of them even gave a sidelong glance in my direction.

It was not long before the 'For Sale' notice was changed to 'Sold'. I was quite bewildered by the number of people coming and going. Furniture was removed, other furniture taken in; plumbers, surveyors, electricians, meter readers and all sorts of other people came and went. Then the new owners moved in. They appeared to be a nice young couple but at first I did not see much of them as they both went off to work early in the morning and did not return till late in the evening. I noted with satisfaction that they had brought a black cat with them. Black cats are a sign of good luck and people who like cats usually are nice people.

I am glad to say that they did not bring a dog with them. Dogs attract other dogs and all dogs are dirty, messy creatures. I won't tell you what they do all around me; it will only make you feel sick!

As the new owners moved in in the autumn, I did not see much of them until the following spring after they had settled in a bit. The male started to tidy up the gardens and one of the first things he did was to give me a thorough trim. I had by then become very straggly and unshapely. No longer was I the nice closely clipped, straight hedge. I was all lumps and bumps and holes. My new owner trimmed me very frequently which promoted vigorous new dense growth. I began to feel very much better, healthier and happier. He also removed the annoying weeds and dogs' messes around my stems, which used to irritate my roots. He also took away the remains of the dilapidated wooden fence that was also an irritant and inhibited my natural growth. I got to like my new owner very much and looked forward to seeing him, which was usually at weekends. I did not see much of his wife.

After a few years of our friendship, I noticed that my new owner had made no effort to restore my previous neat and straight appearance; instead I was neatly trimmed lumps and bumps, and then suddenly one day, after hearing what a passer-by had said, I realised that I was no longer an ordinary suburban privet hedge, but a full blown dragon! I was really proud of myself. I had grown in height and width but not in length. I was still about twenty feet long but at the highest point I was now about six and a half feet tall and about five feet wide. I was a magnificent sight and much superior to any other hedge I know of. Many people started to take note of me and make nice remarks. The local children called me 'Puff the Magic Dragon' after a famous cartoon character on TV. Not that I watched TV myself; I preferred watching the pretty girls walk past in their short, tight mini skirts, wiggling their little bottoms. Bless them!

I also liked adults of both sexes, especially when they stopped to admire me but not those who said, 'what sort of idiot did that?'

One day the local newspaper printed my photo on its front page and many more people came to look at me and to be photographed alongside me. From time to time, coaches with tourists, both young and old, came to view me. My fame spread far and wide. My photo was published in several national newspapers and one day a Japanese journalist asked my owner permission to photograph me. He said that the photo would be published worldwide and he would send copies but none ever came. I've got quite a fan mail from pen friends in various countries who want to know about me, so I am recording my life for the benefit of historians in years to come. It makes my very happy to bring joy into people's every-day, mundane lives. It is lovely to see the amazed looks on strangers' faces as they first notice me and then when the look of amazement changes to laughter. Regular passers-by often smile back at me with a kind word. One lady who has a lot of domestic problems often comes and confides in me but I won't tell you what her troubles are as I respect such confidences.

Only a short while ago, a funeral cortege passed by and as each and every car approached the glum faces of the mourners changed from sadness to happiness. Even the funeral director could not help smiling!

One day, two cars collided head-on right in front of me. They were both strangers in the road and both had had their attention distracted by my smiling face. I wonder how they explained the cause of the accident on their insurance claim forms?

My owner is very kind and considerate; apart from regular trims he often removes my eyeballs, which are made of rubber, because some of the local boys use them to play football. The youngsters today have no respect for their elders. After all, I am old enough to be their grandfathers' father. I wonder how their grandfathers' father would like to have his eyeballs used as footballs!

I was proud to learn recently that a person who trims hedges such as my owner does, is known as a topiarist.

I owe everything that I am today to my present owner and every time he goes out, I pray for his safe return. Every night, I pray for his well-being because I worry as to what will become of me if misfortune ever overtakes him. We have been associated for such a long time. If only it could last forever. Recently, he has been showing signs of old age, including an arthritic knee. Come to think of it, he must be at least as old as I am!

Anita

Jewel Street, in Stepney, east London no longer exists. It was bombed out of existence in the early summer of 1941 and its remains, after the war, were razed to the ground. Its granite stone road and York stone pavements were grubbed up and the site grassed over. The only solitary reminder was the stunted lime tree that grew in front of number 13.

An insipid, municipal three-storey block of flats was erected nearby and what the German bombs combined with the Council's bulldozers did not achieve was accomplished by the children from the adjoining block of flats. They destroyed the tree. Now there is nothing at all to mark the street where my family lived for many years.

It was quite a short street with about fifteen, two-storey, Georgian-style terrace houses on each side of the road. The houses were small with none of the modern conveniences that are taken for granted these days. Yes, they had rising damp, electricity and gas mains but no internal WC or central heating or hot water. Today, they would be described as slums but in those days they were luxurious, especially compared with the slum apartment in Clark Street Buildings where we lived previously. The rent of our house was thirteen shillings a week inclusive of rates, that is sixty five pence in modern currency but in order to obtain occupation, it was necessary to pay the managing agents fifteen pounds 'key money', which was about five weeks' wages for a man, if he was lucky enough to have a job at all.

The residents were mixed, that is, some were Jewish and some were not. I would guess about 50-50 but they all got on well with one another. Our two immediate neighbours were not Jewish and we were very friendly with them. Being a small street, everyone was at least on nodding terms with one another.

When the war broke out in September 1939, I was fifteen years old and because my school was evacuated to the country, I left school soon after in order to commence work.

For the first few months of the war, all was quiet in this country; the period became known as the 'phoney war'.

In early summer, 1940 however, things changed and London became subject to heavy bombing by the German air force, which concentrated its raids on the East End of London where we lived.

For weeks, bombs fell all around Jewel Street, wreaking devastation on the humble houses of ordinary working class people. One night, a 500-pound, high explosive bomb fell on the house opposite but because it had a time delay device, the brave men of the bomb disposal unit managed to take it away to nearby Hackney Marshes before it exploded.

Many incendiary bombs fell on the houses and these were extinguished by the combined efforts of the residents themselves using buckets of water and stirrup pumps.

Jewel Street became a war zone. Some of the families evacuated themselves to areas not subject to such intense bombing or to the countryside. Some, like ours, carried on as best we could even though all the glass panes were blown out and many of the roof slates blown off.

Among the few families that remained was one that lived up the other end of the street. I never got to know their surname but I knew their elder daughter, Anita, who was a year or two older than me but much more mature and sophisticated.

She was a beauty; slim, curvaceous, blond, fresh complexioned with rosy cheeks, usually cheerful; a veritable Marilyn Monroe.

After helping to extinguish an incendiary bomb in her family's roof, her mother made obvious suggestions that I should become friendly with Anita. This scared me more than the German bombs! I was naturally shy and very bashful, especially so where girls were concerned. I was no conversationalist and became tongue-tied if I spoke to a girl. I was also discouraged in taking up Anita's mother's suggestion, because every time I passed Anita in the street she would walk past as though I did not exist. She did not even respond when I timidly passed the time of day.

Apart from my personality deficiency and inferiority complex, I had other problems. I had not long commenced my first job as an office boy in an architect's office in the west end of London and was being paid the grand sum of fifteen shillings a week, gross (75 pence in modern currency). Out of this, I contributed five shillings (25 pence) to my parents towards my board and keep and out of the remainder, I had to pay my fare money to work, meals in the canteen, buy my own clothes and pay for my evening classes education. I had enrolled in a course of architecture in the

Regent Street Polytechnic, which was near where I worked.

Office hours were 9am–6pm weekdays, and 9am–1pm on Saturdays. Evening classes commenced at 6.30pm three evenings a week and ended at 9.30pm. By the time I got home, it was at least 10.30pm. On the evenings that I did not attend evening classes and also at weekends, I was obliged to do homework set by the tutors at the Polytechnic.

All this, plus being kept awake many nights by the air raids and my duty rota as a first aider - stretcher bearer in the local Air Raid Precaution First Aid Post - I had very little energy and time left in which to cultivate the friendship of Anita or any other girl. After all the essential expenditure out of my gross, meagre fifteen shillings a week, I had very little to spend on amusements, let alone taking a girl out.

One sunny Saturday afternoon, when returning home from work about 2pm, I found that during the morning a German bomber had utterly destroyed our house along with several adjoining houses and had badly damaged most of the remaining houses. Most fortunately, no one was killed or injured. I was left with just the clothes I was standing up in. I had to seek temporary shelter wherever I could until my family was re-housed by the authorities. We lost contact with the other families in Jewel Street, who likewise left their houses hurriedly.

It was not until some while after that I found out what had happened to Anita.

Anita's mother was bright and beautiful like her daughter, but she was married to a man who was much older than her and who was continually depressed and unemployed. Anita's brother, who was a little younger than her, was a simpleton and although always bright and cheerful, could only perform the most simple of tasks. He was unemployable. Her younger sister was a terrible flirt and seemed determined to get herself into trouble. Anita was the main breadwinner of the impoverished and pitiful family and she realised that the most practical way to escape from her situation was to marry a rich man. Fortunately for her, at that time London was bursting with seemingly young rich men, American servicemen.

In order to meet some of them, she attended dances in the west end of London where they particularly congregated in order to meet young, pretty English girls.

So as to look her best for one of these Saturday dance meetings, Anita had her blond hair coiffured on the Friday evening. When she emerged from the hairdresser she looked a real picture, a film star, enough to turn any boy's head and she knew it.

She walked boldly out of the hairdresser's into the street that was pitch dark due to the blackout. There were no streetlights, not even a glimmer from a window, pitch darkness and she walked directly into the path of a passing bus.

The bus driver did not see her because all the bus lights were dimmed and his headlights were fitted with louvered masks that made them almost useless. At the subsequent inquest, it was revealed that Anita was extremely short sighted and despite the fact that she was almost blind in the darkness, refused to wear her thick-lens spectacles out of doors.

Her beauty and her vanity combined with the war exigencies were the cause of her untimely demise.

The Dragon and the Foxes

Once upon a time, I may have been considered just another one of the many privet hedges adorning the front gardens of suburban houses. However, this resolutely changed when, after several years of patient exercise of the noble art of topiary, the current owners of my house metamorphosised me into a veritable dragon of impressive dimensions but of genial expression.

This transmogrification took place many years ago and has been recognised and acknowledged by many people as well as being pictorially recorded in the local, national and overseas' press. In fact, I am now an established celebrity in my own right.

Even though I may be somewhat immobile, it is not proper for any living creature, man or beast, to take advantage and to treat me to any indignity. I have never done any harm to anyone and, in fact, I have caused quite a bit of happiness and hilarity to many, both acquaintances and complete strangers. There are not many who can resist acknowledging my constant smile, whatever the weather.

Yes, I admit that there are some people who pass by and don't smile back at me but no doubt they have good reason to be pre-occupied with pressing personal problems. If they would only stop just for a few minutes to chat, I would alleviate their mental anxiety.

Many are the people I have helped in this way. 'After all, if I can help somebody as they pass along, my being shall not be in vain!'

I am a light sleeper and do not require many hours of sleep. This is fortunate as something or another often awakes me from my dreams. It's amazing just how many people pass by at all hours of the night. Some, by the regularity of the times they return home have, no doubt, been working;

456

some by their uncertain gait have been drinking whilst others, by their stealthy walk, have been doing something they should not have been.

In addition, there are constant comings and goings of cats and dogs. Each time a dog passes by, whether or not it is on a lead, I am apprehensive in case it deposits its mess in my vicinity. Because it is dark, they think they can do anything they like. What I say is, live and let live, but don't mess on my roots.

As to the question of fox hunting etc., I've always had an open mind. Till recently it did not really concern me because, apart from there not being any foxes in the vicinity, there was little I could do either way.

However, in recent times, urban foxes have appeared in the neighbourhood and increasingly so. I was quite excited when I first saw one but now they appear almost nightly.

So far, they have not messed around my roots but I have noticed how they tear open the black plastic bags left out by our neighbours to be collected the next morning by the Council's refuse collection men. They eat whatever tasty morsel they find in the bag but in the process, leave a nasty mess of refuse around.

I still had no decided views on fox hunting as I maintain, live and let live. This was so, until the other night when I was awakened by the noise of a nearby neighbour's refuse bag being torn apart by a pair of foxes and hearing their grunts and squeals of satisfaction on finding some nice items of food. As usual, they left a scattering of refuse around the torn bag.

Their movements were swift and restless, they darted back and forth and I was generally alarmed when they made their way in my direction. I knew they could not harm me but there was something sinister in the co-ordinated actions. They had an air of conspiracy about them.

It was a balmy night lit by a full moon that flitted from one small cloud to another. I kept a close watch but lost sight of them when they passed behind some parked cars. Suddenly they reappeared right alongside me and as though by some prearranged plan, one of them jumped up on my back just behind my head where I could no longer see him. He then deliberately walked the whole length of my back up to my tail, some twenty feet and then jumped off. When I say walked, it was more like wading in my growth up to his stomach. This seemed to give him some terrific delight as expressed in his squeals. The squeals were a signal or an invitation to his partner to follow suit, which he or she promptly did. They both so enjoyed the experience that they repeated the process. Possibly they would have continued doing so if some drunkard being led home by his faithful dog had not passed noisily by.

The foxes disappeared swiftly and silently into the night but I fear they will return. What pleasure could they derive from torturing me so? I have never done them any harm but I can now begin to see the point of view of those who advocate the control or urban foxes.

The next day, my personal resident topiarist noticed the wounds in my back and did whatever he could to straighten the damage, which was considerable. It will be several weeks before my appearance will again begin to look something like normal.

When my topiarist was discussing the damage with our next-door neighbour, he told them that no doubt foxes did the damage, as children would not have been around during the night. I could have told him that! He also told the neighbour that apart from tearing the refuse bags open the foxes had stolen his gardening shoes which he had left out over night to dry and they had removed the brown laces and eaten the leather tongues. What next will they get up to? The neighbour said that it was no doubt the foxes that chewed up the plastic nozzle of his garden watering can, rendering it useless.

Mugged by an OAP

Because of the fine warm weather on one of the few hot, sunny days in June 1997, I was wearing a pair of shorts and an open necked shirt with sleeves rolled up. Not the sartorial, opulent appearance that would convey the image of wealth.

I was standing outside a local estate agent's shop premises waiting for my wife, Dora, to come out. She had arranged with the estate agent to collect an autographed copy of a book on the history of the local borough of Ilford, written by his brother, who was an authority on the subject.

Actually, the book proved to be most informative and interesting and very good value for money, especially so as Dora had negotiated a two-pound discount.

Because it was such a lovely day, I decided to wait outside the estate agent's shop whilst Dora went in to do the transaction. As time is money, it would have been a lot more economical for the estate agent to give a free copy to Dora or even to pay her to take one without charge.

Whilst waiting, I noticed on the other side of the busy main road a large notice outside a public house advertising a special two-course lunch for old age pensioners at the reduced price of £3.25.

From time to time I was distracted by passers-by, many of whom were walking along talking into mobile phones, especially so, the younger pedestrians. I wondered how they could afford to acquire such luxuries and to make such lengthy, expensive phone calls.

I also observed the illegal parking of cars right along the road on both single and double yellow lines and delivery vans leaving their doors open whilst taking goods into local electrical shops etc.

It seemed to me quite easy for anyone to remove one or more of the cartons from the vans whilst the driver was in the shop and make off with them quite easily.

Whilst making my observations I was surprised by a spry, elderly, conventionally clothed gentleman approaching me quite swiftly and stopping very close to me, closer than one would normally expect on such a warm day and on such a wide pavement.

I did not see where he came from but I had the impression that he had approached me from the direction of the public house and was a little inebriated.

I expected him to ask for the time or the directions to somewhere but instead, he peered into my face and in a loud voice, as though he was aware that I was hard of hearing, said, 'I have a gun and I want all your money.' I had certainly not expected such a request from the elderly gentleman but I did confirm that he had his right hand high up under his jacket where one would normally expect a gangster to wear a shoulder holster. My initial reaction was that this was just a practical joke but I had always resolved that if I were ever to be mugged, I should swallow my pride and comply with the mugger's request. This prior decision had nothing at all to do with me being one of nature's natural self-preservationists.

As it happened, because I was attired in my summer outfit, I had no money with me. I told this to the mugger and turned out the linings of my trouser pockets to demonstrate my plight. I did not reveal that I did have a five pound note in my back pocket that I always carried in case of an emergency and that if he had requested it, I would have handed it over just so as not to get my summer outfit spoilt by blood.

In order to alleviate the tense situation, and as I was still not sure whether the episode was a practical joke or not, I said, 'I'm sorry to disappoint you but if you were to give me ten pounds, I would, in return, give you back five.'

He seemed to find this proposal quite amusing and began to laugh. He also pulled his hand out from under his jacket and showed that he was not holding a gun. Instead, he jokingly pointed his fist at me with two fingers extended in the way that children use to imitate a pistol.

He was most apologetic and said one must have a laugh now and then or life would not be worth living. I heartily agreed especially so about the living part. He asked if I was scared and if I was likely to have a heart attack. I assured him that my heart was in excellent condition but I had shat my trousers. I assure readers that this was not true nor had I micturated but was said in order to further relieve any remaining tension.

The repentant "mugger" found this further amusing and assured me that he meant no harm.

Having now assured myself completely that he was just a silly old fool,

I told him that if he continued to carry out such practical pranks, he might end up in the notorious Parkhurst Prison. This further amused him and he said that he had actually spent two years in Parkhurst, but as a warder not a prisoner.

In order to further alleviate the situation I said that it would have been better if he had been a warder in the Holloway women's prison. He seemed to imply that he had also served there and assured me that there was plenty of gratuitous sex to be had there, more than one could cope with.

He then sauntered away after assuring me that he meant no harm and only wanted to have a laugh.

Whilst I looked round to see if Dora had finished her transaction inside the estate agent's shop, the mugger disappeared into the crowd.

Nobody seemed to have noticed this episode, which I suppose could only have taken one or two minutes. Youngsters continued to pass by talking animatedly into mobile phones and van drivers were still loading and unloading goods whilst stationed on single or double yellow lines.

I did not think much more of this episode until a couple of weeks later when I read in a local paper that an OAP had been arrested and charged with trying to rob another OAP in the local high road. He was also charged with being in possession of a loaded revolver, which he wore in a shoulder holster whilst attempting the robbery.

Fire Alert
or
A Cold Heart

It was one of the worst, possibly the most embarrassing, episodes in my life.

The event that led up to it commenced over two years previously when, Dora, my wife, read an article in one of the national daily newspapers written by a doctor who advocated that people, particularly men who were experiencing heart and or circulation problems, should take an aspirin tablet once a day as a preventative measure against their condition worsening. The article emphasised that one aspirin tablet (300mg) could do no harm but only positive good.

Despite my protestations that, thank goodness, I had no heart or circulation problems she insisted that I take the doctor's advice. If I had not concurred, her anticipated insistence may very well have created such problems in me.

I duly took an aspirin a day until a few weeks after when I noticed blood emitting along with my stools.

When I reported this to my doctor, he said it was regrettable that I had this reaction to aspirin but as the daily consumption of aspirin is highly recommendable, he advised that I should reduce my daily intake to a quarter of a standard sized tablet, that is, 75mg. He said that such a minute dose, whilst being helpful, could not possibly do any harm.

I duly accepted his advice, which Dora heartily endorsed. It did not have any obvious side effects and the haemorrhage stopped immediately.

Recently, whilst I was consulting my doctor about prescribing an

462

embrocation for a painful arthritic knee, he suddenly looked me straight in the face and asked if I had anaemia. This caused me some confusion as that very same morning I had been buying plants for bedding-out in my garden. These days, garden nurseries take fiendish delight in describing plants on sale by their Latin botanical names instead of the good old-fashioned names like snapdragons, lupins, lilies etc. In my confusion I could not recall having bought any anaemias and thinking that he might be angling for some plants for his own garden I told him that I had a couple of spare dahlias.

I immediately realised my stupid error and answered that I was not suffering with any undue loss of memory. Even though this amused him somewhat, he remained serious and said he thought that I may be anaemic and prescribed iron tablets, ferrous sulphate, 200 mg to be taken three times a day. He also handed me a note and told me to take it as soon as possible to our local general hospital for me to have a blood test.

When the doctor received the result of the blood test several days later, he told me that I had severe anaemia (low red haemoglobin concentration). He said that he would urgently arrange for me to see a consultant haematologist and that meanwhile I was to continue taking the blood pills and not to do any work.

Needless to say, this alarmed me quite a bit and it caused me to wonder how, in the first place, my doctor saw something in my face that caused him to suspect anaemia.

Even though I normally look in the mirror several times a day I had not noticed anything untoward. I looked again specially to notice any signs or symptoms.

I was shocked to see that both my earflaps were as if they had been moulded in white candle wax; the sort of ears one might expect to see on a corpse. I wondered why nobody else had noticed this phenomenon. Maybe they were too polite to tell me that my ears appeared to belong to a dead person.

The seven days wait to see the consultant haematologist passed most anxiously.

His examination consisted mostly of questions concerning my excrement and any matter from various orifices and my diet and habits.

He also had a look up my rear passage but could not find anything untoward. I was tempted to ask him if he could see my tonsils. He finally came to the conclusion that the cause of my low blood count was due to my daily intake of aspirin. He advised me to stop taking aspirin, however small the dose, but to continue taking my three iron tablets a day. I felt very relieved at his conclusion, as needless to say, all sorts of fears had crossed my mind. He said, that in order to eliminate any other possible cause, he would arrange for me to have an X-ray and a barium test. These would not be possible for another few weeks.

After his verdict and after the swift beneficial effect of the iron tablets, I felt a lot happier and lot healthier, a lot less weak and a lot less tired. My earflaps returned to their normal pink hue.

As I was feeling so much better, I readily agreed to accompany Dora to a local jeweller. She had been asked by a neighbour, aged 95 years, to get a ring valued for probate purposes as she intended to leave it to a favourite niece. It was a very old ring, with a beautiful fire opal and a lot of brilliant diamonds.

Many of the local jewellers have now become pawnbrokers and Dora did not consider them suitable to value such an item. She decided to try the jewellers in the local shopping mall where there were several good-class jewellery shops. They were mainly concentrated on the upper floor.

The first few we tried suggested a value of £200 - £250 but refused to give a written valuation. The last shop we tried commenced with a similar figure but constantly upgraded it whilst Dora kept them in conversation. Finally the jeweller suggested a figure of £2,500 and said that he might know someone who would be interested in buying it. Eventually, he agreed to give a written valuation, 'for insurance purposes' but it would take about an hour to process. We told him that we would return in about an hour.

After we left the shop, we became rather concerned, as we had not asked for a receipt for the ring. If we returned and the jeweller denied having accepted it, there would be nothing we could do and we would have a most embarrassing experience explaining this to the old lady who had entrusted us with her most precious ring. We impatiently waited for the hour to pass and to pass the time away we decided to have a coffee and a pastry in a nearby cafeteria within the mall's precinct.

I ordered a milky coffee in order to quell the stomach upset caused partly by our failure to obtain a receipt for the ring and partly to the scratch lunch we had before setting out on our venture.

Our lunch consisted of various leftovers from previous meals and included a couple of bhajis (highly spiced Indian-style fried vegetable patties containing curry and goodness only knows what else, but very tasty), some boiled broad beans, mushy peas and diced boiled potatoes in salad cream mixed with chopped up onions. I should have known better than to have devoured such a potentially explosive mixture.

Soon after our coffee, I suggested to Dora that we walk around the mall for a while before returning to the jeweller.

The shopping mall is faced with beautiful, smooth marble slabs, marble slab floors and consists of an atrium and various galleries and is roofed by domed and arched glass structures. It is a lovely building but has the disadvantage that sounds echo and re-echo until the accumulative noise is almost unbearable.

It was with this background noise in mind that I decided to relieve the internal pressure on my stomach walls by expelling some of the excess digestive gases that had accumulated therein. Normally this should not have presented any undue problem as with over 70 years experience, I am normally able to perform such a task without any problem and without anyone noticing.

As it was a very humid and hot day I had come out dressed in just a tee shirt and loose fitting shorts.

As this point I must explain that one of the side effects of the ferrous sulphate iron pills is that they cause the stools to come out jet black and also when micturating the liquid is also a dark grey colour. There is no harm in these side effects as normally, no one except the patient is aware of them. There is however, another side effect (even though other people will not normally be aware) in that gastric gas emitted from the back passage is also deeply discoloured. Not a lot of people know that! I only discovered it by chance in the bath one day.

What happened, as we walked through the noisy, crowded gallery where the posh jewellery shops were situated, was that I attempted one of my quiet emissions but the effect of the lunchtime meal caused it to emit much more voluminously than I intended and rather noisily.

Dora glared at me and walked ahead at quite a fast pace to as to dissociate herself. In turn, I glared at an old man nearby hoping to deflect the cause of the rude noise onto him, but suddenly, right behind me came the shrill voice of a little girl who cried out in a penetrating voice, 'Look, Mummy, that man's trousers are on fire.' I looked round and true enough the digestive gas, instead of being invisible as normal, was emitting from my shorts as what appeared to be smoke. I hoped that the 'smoke' would not be sufficient to set off the sensitive fire alarms.

I ignored the child as though she had not spoken and sped up to reunite with Dora just as she was entering the posh jeweller's shop. We retrieved the ring and paid for the valuation.

The Window Cleaner

When Dora and I moved into our present Victorian terraced house about 45 years ago, we found that with it came a window cleaner.

Not long after we had settled in, we were suddenly startled to see the face of a young man appear at our first floor window.

He explained that he had always cleaned the windows of our house for the previous owner and that he would be glad to continue doing so for us. He told us what his charge was, which we thought was very cheap and we naturally agreed. We were very pleased as we had not yet got round to thinking about a window cleaner, there were so many other things that needed to be attended to that were more urgent.

He told us that he was not keen on doing the insides of the windows, nor was he keen to do the windows at the rear of the house very frequently.

We found that the reason for this was that he had the contract for nearly every house on our side of the street, and having climbed his ladder on the street frontage at one end of the terrace, he was able to proceed right along to the other end simply by stepping from one wide window sill to the next. By this means, he avoided having to move and climb his ladder repeatedly from house to house and from window to window. This applied both to ground and first floor windows. One of the snags I soon discovered was with his service to me; I was obliged, by being mid-terrace, to replenish the water in his bucket. As he was such a nice chap and was a fellow lover of cats, I was pleased to oblige even though he kept me talking for a long while and this prevented me from getting on with my own work and earning a modest living.

He said that we should call him George, even though that was not his real name. He tapped the side of his nose knowingly whilst telling us this; he said it was for business reasons really.

He did not come too frequently but this suited us because each time he did the outside of the windows, I was obliged likewise to do the insides which, because of curtains and furniture, were not so easy as the outside, uncluttered window panes.

This state of affairs continued until about a year ago when George, who like ourselves had aged over the years, turned up one day accompanied by a young man who was young enough to be his son but was not related.

We had noticed that the windows had not been cleaned for a long while and George explained that one day when he was traversing at first floor level from house to house, from sill to sill, he had fallen down and badly injured his leg. Fortunately, he had landed on a privet hedge that had broken the impact of his fall but had not prevented his injury.

He told us that as it might be a very long while before he anticipated being well enough to carry on with his window cleaning, he was handing his round to Ray, who accompanied him. He highly recommended Ray and said that Ray, which by the way was, for business reasons not actually his real name, would carry on, on the same terms as previously.

We happily agreed. Ray did turn up a few weeks later to do our windows but it was obvious that he was completely inexperienced. He did not have George's confidence and had to continuously move his ladder from window to window and from house to house. That was the last time we saw Ray and our windows went uncleaned from then on. Despite the vast number of reported unemployed in the district, no one seemed keen to take over the window round. Still, it does not worry me because, in turn, I am not obliged to clean the insides of the windows.

The film of grease and dirt on the windows has the advantage of filtering out some of the scorching sun that we have been enjoying recently, and in the winter will act as an additional insulation against heat loss. These old Victorian houses are so cold in the winter that the additional insulation will be most welcome to keep our heating costs down.

One day, we were telling this to a visiting friend, Sam, who is a builder. He said, 'What a shame that my father died recently, he was a window cleaner and he would have gladly taken over this window round.'

I was surprised and reminded Sam that his father was very elderly and lived at least 12 miles away. I knew that he did not drive a vehicle and got around on a pedal bicycle when he was transporting his window cleaning ladder and bucket.

Sam said that his age and the distance would not have deterred his father. He told us that even though his father was 76 years old when he died, he never gave up his work and cycling 12 miles even to clean the windows of a single house was all in a day's work for him.

He also told us something that we had not previously been aware of because his father did not like it being discussed. Even Sam had not been aware of the fact that his father had an artificial leg. Sam did not know how or when he lost his leg, and even today, he does not know how his father managed to climb up and down ladders all day and also cycle along carrying his ladder and bucket. The only indication of anything untoward was that his father developed a slight limp as he got older. It was only by chance that one day in his local pub, Sam learnt from a fellow imbiber, who knew his father, about an amusing incident involving Sam's father.

One day, when his father was cycling to work, his artificial leg fell off. He lost control of the bike and fell off. As he was lying in the roadway, his drinking friend's sister, who was passing by, went to help him. She first had the presence of mind to pop her head into a nearby shop to ask the shopkeeper to phone for an ambulance. When she went over to Sam's father, who was sitting up on the roadway, to tell him that an ambulance was on its way and that he should remain still and calm, she saw that he was holding his artificial leg, which she thought, was real. She fainted on the spot and when the ambulance arrived soon after they took her to the hospital whilst Sam's father, who had meanwhile reaffixed his artificial leg, insisted carrying on cycling to his work.

Sam told us that even when there was mass unemployment, his father always found work however hard it may have been and however far he had to travel by bicycle to get there. He was very careful as to how he spent his money. He lived very frugally and saved hard, 'for his old age'. Although Sam and his brother were never seriously deprived, they both never enjoyed new clothes. Their outfits were purchased at jumble sales or in charity shops and Sam constantly inherited the clothes his elder brother, Joshua, grew out of.

Sam's father never employed anyone when he could do a job himself. He did all the maintenance on their semi-detached house in Hornchurch, Essex, and taught Sam his trade as a builder.

He had an allotment on which he grew a lot of the fruit and vegetables that the family needed. He even kept chickens for both flesh and eggs.

His father never took a holiday but on some weekends, he would take his sons into the nearby countryside to pick wild fruit and mushrooms.

Over the years, by working hard and being economical with his expenditure and also investing wisely but safely, he had accumulated quite an appreciable nest egg which he put aside 'for old age' but would never acknowledge that the late autumn of his years had already arrived.

Sam constantly urged his father to give up work and to enjoy the fruits of his labour but after a lifetime of hard work and stringent saving he could not change.

He told Sam he was very happy as he was. He did not want to go on a world cruise, he did not like foreign food nor did he know any foreign language. He would not feel at ease in a posh hotel doing nothing all day but being waited on by foreigners. He was quite happy as he was and would be glad if he were not nagged into doing something he did not want to do and which would only make him unhappy.

He also refused Sam's suggestion, that if he did not want to go on holiday, he should spend money on modernising his house to make it more comfortable.

Same even offered to do the building work free of charge but his father refused to have his kitchen modernised, central heating or hot water installed, double glazing to cut out the cold draughts, better lighting or adequate electric socket etc.

He also refused to have a modern radio and colour TV. Sam felt very sorry for his father who had worked so hard and saved so consciously all his life and now refused to have the most elementary essentials of life that so many layabouts took as being their natural right.

Sam's brother said that Sam should stop annoying and nagging their father as he was obviously quite happy as he was. If he did not want to spend his savings, that was up to him.

Sam could not appreciate or understand his father's attitude. He told his father, 'If you don't spend your money whilst you are still live and capable, I will only splash it out on extreme luxuries and boozing when I inherit my share.'

Little was Sam to know what effect this was to have on his father. When his father died and his will was revealed, Sam discovered that he had been cut out of his father's will completely. The solicitor administering the will read out a letter dictated by Sam's father explaining that he loved him as much as he did Sam's brother, but that there was no point in leaving any money to Sam because he would only waste the lot on luxuries and booze. Sam's elder brother inherited the lot and is now spending it on luxuries and riotous living!

Sam did not even inherit his father's artificial leg and never did discover what happened to it when his father was cremated.

The Gardener

A few years ago I suffered a bad and prolonged period of lumbago and was not able to attend to either my front or back gardens as I usually do.

It was late autumn and there were several urgent jobs that had to be done before winter set in. As I was unable to do these tasks myself, I decided to call upon the services of Ron, who I employed from time to time to do odd jobs such as tree lopping, fence repair and carting away garden rubbish that the Council bin collectors refuse to do. He was usually very obliging and efficient.

I dialled his usual number and found that he had acquired an answering machine on which I duly left a message asking if he would be kind enough to do some urgent gardening for me.

A couple of days later, a young coloured man rang my door bell and told me that he was now Ron's partner and as Ron was busy at present he would do the gardening work for me. At first I was inclined to refuse his offer mainly because he was so ugly. It may be foolish of me, but I always associate ugly men with criminals.

However, I overcame my first instinctive prejudice and realised that I was being irrational and that if I refused to employ him he may think I did so because he was coloured. I don't discriminate on the basis of colour. I accept or reject people just as I find them, good or bad, white or black, tall or short, educated or ignorant.

He was very keen to start immediately and this impressed me. I like people who prefer to work rather than scrounge or swindle.

I noticed that he had not arrived in a vehicle. Ron usually came in an old, clapped out, open-top lorry and brought his own equipment with him. I asked Paul, (the young man's name), what he was going to do about a lawn

470

mower and hedge cutter etc. He replied that that was no problem; he would borrow them from another customer who lived just around the corner.

I told him not to bother his other customer as I had all the implements he may need in my garden shed.

He thanked me and said, 'You are a marvel, really,' and almost kissed my hands.

We agreed a rate of pay; he took his jacket off, hung it up in my hallway and started work.

He said he would start with the front privet hedges and did I have an electric hedge trimmer? I told him that there was one in the shed but it was almost new, it was very expensive and that he should be careful using it. He told me not to worry, as he would treat it as if it was his own. This struck me as rather ambiguous. After I had plugged it in for him, I left him to get on with the job.

It was not long after that he rang my front door bell to inform me that he had accidentally cut the electric lead. He said that he could not understand how it had happened. He suggested that if the lead had been orange coloured instead of white, he would not have damaged it, as it would have been more prominent.

I told him that he was lucky not have electrocuted himself because I had taken the precaution, when plugging the lead in, of using a micro-current isolator that cuts the electric current off immediately and does not rely on a fuse, which is not so efficient in preventing electric shock.

He apologised profusely and said that I was a "real gent", and would I please let him have some electric insulating tape so that he could join the cut lead ends together.

The cut was not far from the hedge trimmer itself and a bodged repair in that position could be most dangerous. I told him to get on with some of the other work whilst I went to the local electrical shop and bought a proper junction adapter and fixed it.

Even though he was not on piecework, he was being paid by the hour; he did all the work in a rush as if to get it completed as soon as possible. As a consequence, the result of his labour was shabby, the front hedges were jagged, the lawn was lumpy, the flowerbeds were rough and many of the weeds were cut down rather than pulled or dug out.

When he told me that he was finished and could I pay him, I pointed out that he had not bagged the hedge clippings or the weeds or the grass from the lawn. He quickly bagged the leaves etc., but left many lying around for me to clear up afterwards.

When he next asked for payment, I pointed out that even though he had bagged the garden refuse, he had not carted this away as we had agreed initially, also I pointed out that he had not replaced the several implements that he had borrowed from my shed and that he had not cleaned them.

He cleaned the implements and threw them back in the shed and took the six bags of garden refuse out and placed them in my front garden, assuring me that he would return within the hour with Ron's lorry and cart the bags away. Upon this assurance, I paid him. He retrieved his jacket from the hall stand and hurriedly went away, almost at running pace as though his life depended on spending the money as soon as possible but not before telling me, 'You are a wonderful person.'

When I looked out in the front garden shortly afterwards, the six bags of garden refuse were gone. I was glad that my trust had not been misplaced. Later the same day, Paul returned with a bin liner full of unwashed laundry. He asked if I would be kind enough to put it through my washing machine. I told him that my wife was in hospital with a broken leg and that I had no idea at all as to how the operate the machine.

He told me not to worry, he would find out and operate the machine himself. Having had the recent experience of the way he used my hedge cutter, I told him that it would not be convenient and asked why he did not use his own washing machine or the nearby launderette. He mumbled something about his landlord having fixed a pre-paid electric meter and he did not have the money to use the launderette.

He went away in a very angry mood and this time, he did not tell me what a wonderful person I was.

The same evening he returned once more with a pair of ladies' shoes and asked me if I was interested in buying them. I refused because they were not Dora's size, they were far too small and I was suspicious as to how he may have come upon them.

He then asked if I would run him, in my car, to someone who lived about ten minutes away and whom he thought would be interested in the shoes.

When I told him that I did not wish to take him to his destination in my car he said he did not see why not, he would pay me for the petrol.

I told him that I was not running a mini-cab service. At this, he turned really nasty and said, 'Typical Jew-boy'. This flabbergasted me as it came from a black youth and in all my 74 years experience I had never before had anyone express such outright anti-Semitism to my face. He promptly turned around and walked swiftly away. Unfortunately, this was not the last repercussion to arise from my employment of Paul.

The next day I saw a very irate neighbour placing six bags of refuse in my front garden. When I asked him why he was doing so, he said that he had found out that it was my gardener who dumped the bags in his front garden when both he and his wife were out at work.

472

The Cache

Harry Jacobs was born with a withered left arm. He was very self-conscious of this defect, which caused him to be introverted. Apart from this deformity he was also less than average height for his age. At school he was bullied by other boys and scorned as being inferior.

When he left school in 1930, at the age of 16 years, he could not find any employment. Because of mass unemployment, employers could pick and choose from the many applicants for each vacancy, so why select an undersized cripple who could be a liability for the firm?

He overcame this disadvantage by exploiting his interest and ability in repairing old radio sets, which were commonly known in those days as wirelesses. Non-functioning sets could be acquired for very little money, and more often than not, for nothing at all.

People who felt sorry for him gladly gave him their old sets or asked him to repair their wirelesses when they broke down, which in those days was quite frequently. Quite often the sets were not economically viable for repair and he sold the owner a similar wireless that he had cannibalised from other non-functioning sets.

Repairing and selling such wirelesses became quite profitable and Harry took it up professionally full-time, and stopped looking for paid employment. His hobby had become his livelihood.

At first, he carried out these repairs in his small bedroom at the rear of his parents' house but after a while the room became too small for this purpose and he built himself a spacious shed at the bottom of the long, neglected garden at the rear of the old, end-of-terrace Victorian house where he lived with his widowed mother who was not pleased at the large number of people who called on Harry in connection with his radio business.

473

His parents had had a profitable men's wear shop locally and by comparison with the neighbours they were 'well off'. Apart from the luxurious carpets and expensive furniture and light fittings and the silverware on display, they also had the only central heating and hot water system in the street. This made his mother self-conscious from the security point of view and she was very unhappy with some of the types of people who called on Harry and who she deemed to be potential burglars.

When Harry moved his business into the shed she was most relieved because his customers needed no longer to come through the house but could obtain direct access to Harry's shed through the side gate and through the neglected and shabby rear garden. Working in the isolated shed also had the advantage that the noise made by the radios did not disturb the neighbours.

When Harry discarded a wireless set as being unrepairable, he carefully dismantled it and stored valves and condensers etc. in the commodious cellar under his parents' house.

In the course of time, Harry married and had children of his own and he ensconced himself in his parents' spacious house. His father had died when Harry was quite young. Just as Harry had not taken any interest in his parents' business, so too, Harry's children took no interest in his radio business which steadily kept expanding.

As a dutiful son, he took on the responsibility of caring for his decrepit, widowed mother who seemed to be a walking catalogue of serious illness. Harry became well known nationally for his expertise in restoring old wireless sets and for what appeared to be an unlimited supply of scarce spare parts especially thermic valves, which in the course of time had become superseded by transistors.

As time went by, old wireless sets continued to be in demand by people who wanted them to decorate a room with period items, by people with sentimental recollections of such sets in their parents' or grandparents' home when they were children, and by people who suffered with tinnitus who preferred the mellow sounds of the old sets to the harsh sounds of transistor sets. Many professional musicians also preferred the mellow sounds of the old sets worked by thermic valves.

Harry received orders from all over the United Kingdom and even from overseas. He advertised his goods and services in trade magazines and even formed a club for people whose hobby was collecting and repairing old wireless sets.

As business expanded so did Harry's concern about the security of his home.

When he first started his business, his street was occupied mainly by middle class, skilled artisans and business people but in the course of time the type of people who moved into the large Victorian houses were the unemployed who did not appear to have any shortage of 'partners' who were unemployed and unemployable because of their criminal records. The character of the street changed completely. Police raids on premises in the street took place quite frequently and loud, raucous parties disturbed virtually every night.

The more Harry did to make his own house secure, the more it became obvious that there was a reason for it. Security lights and an intruder alarm only served to make the premises more obvious as a potential target. His mother refused to move. She insisted on staying on in the house and she also wanted to be near her friends who she had known nearly all her life. As it was legally her house, there was nothing he could do but to grin and bear it. He could, if he had wished, have bought a modern house in a salubrious suburb but he could not bring himself to abandon his elderly, decrepit mother in such a hostile environment.

Harry acquired a large, iron safe that he installed in his workshop shed. Anyone who called on business could not but notice this prominent piece of security. Eventually, the inevitable happened. One day, despite all the security precautions taken by Harry on the insistence of his insurance company, the shed was broken into.

Fortunately, nothing of value was stolen, as the valuable spare valves etc. were stored in the cellar below the house. An attempt had been made to remove the safe; it had been unbolted from its concrete base and, despite its heavy weight, moved toward the door, which Harry had so constructed as to be too narrow to pass the safe through. In disgust at their failure to secure anything of value, the burglars, who could not have been professionals, vandalised the shed.

In accordance with his insurance policy's conditions, Harry notified his insurers of the intrusion and vandalism even though he did not make a claim for any loss. He did not wish to prejudice the chance of having his insurance renewed and in any case there was a heavy excess clause in the policy.

The insurance company sent one of their inspectors down to report on the incident and to recommend further security to minimise any future attempt at intrusion. The inspector asked Harry why he did not try to conceal the safe, as it was obvious to anyone visiting his workshop or office. Harry said that it was intentional that the safe should be obvious as it was only a decoy. He did not keep anything of value in it and he definitely kept no money in it. He told the inspector that he kept all his money in a safe and obscure place outside the shed but did not elaborate.

The attempted burglary was quite a shock for his mother, who in addition to all her other ailments suffered with high blood pressure. One day, soon after, when she was out shopping she suffered a slight stroke and collapsed in the street. She was taken by ambulance as an emergency to the Royal London Hospital in Whitechapel Road, East London. Upon arrival in the emergency casualty department, the nurses started to remove her clothing so that the doctor could examine her.

They first looked into her handbag to see if they could identify her and were glad to find not only her name, address and telephone number but also her son's name and telephone number citing him as next of kin.

They were also especially delighted to find a postcard on which was neatly written all her ailments, the details of her doctor and a list of the drugs and medicines that he had prescribed for her. This was most useful for the doctor who was making his diagnosis.

The staff at this East London hospital was quite used to discovering the unexpected when examining casualties brought in as emergencies; very close by was a large Salvation Army hostel for homeless people, a large proportion of whom were hopeless alcoholics or suffering with mental ailments.

The doctor was however puzzled by the heavy crepe bandaging on both of Mrs. Jacobs' legs, which extended from her ankles up to her knees. No mention had been made on the medical details found in her handbag of any ailment of her legs and this type of bandaging would normally indicate open varicose veins.

He asked the nurses to remove the bandages so that he could examine her legs and they were astounded to find, not varicose veins but hundreds of crisp five-pound notes. A fortune by any standard!

So this was the cache that Harry had referred to when speaking to his insurance company's inspector!

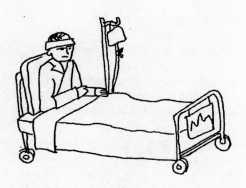

The Eye Witness

Arnold finishes his coffee, dons his heavy, warm donkey jacket and says, 'I won't be long,' to his wife.

She knows that he is going to do a short spell in his black taxi at the rank outside the local train station which serves both the electrified railway from Liverpool Street Station in London, to Southend and the District Line tube service from central London to the terminal at Upminster in Essex.

He times his nightly shift to coincide with the last few trains from London, knowing full well that there will be quite a number of late night revellers who have spent the evening in London's West End and will be returning homeward in a good and generous mood.

From Arnold's, and also from his colleagues' point of view, the cold, dismal, drizzly weather was ideal, as none of the arrivals would wish to spoil a nice evening out by walking home in the atrocious weather.

There was no rivalry between Arnold and his colleagues as there were usually plenty of punters to satisfy them all. Their only concern was the occasional pirate, unlicensed mini-cab predator waiting to snatch one of their customers. He was happy to be only second from the front of the taxi queue in the rank.

Just as he expected and dead on time, the surge from one of the late night trains started pouring out of the station and at the head of the crowd was an early middle-aged man accompanied by a brassy, giggling blonde, both of whom appeared to have had a good time in London and now were intent on further enjoyment and obviously not of participating in a game of chess.

Arnold was sorry he was not the first taxi in line as, no doubt, the man would be a good tipper unlike most of the city businessmen who tipped very meanly.

The couple made their way towards the first taxi but before they could reach it, a couple of toughs who had been loitering about pounced on the man, silently and ruthlessly beating him up and stealing his wallet and valuables before handing a bundle of money to the blonde, who they appeared to know. They jumped into an unlit car, which had slid up unobserved in front of the first taxi, and drove off furiously. The blonde tried to get into the car with them but they refused to let her in and instead she jumped into the front taxi, which drove off.

Arnold was amazed to see this Chicago-style gangster action enacted right in front of his eyes. Without thinking, he dashed over to the victim who was groaning in agony on the station forecourt. Other people walked right past him as though he was not there, maybe they just thought he was drunk and they did not wish to get involved.

The man was still conscious and between his groans asked Arnold to get him a taxi. When Arnold explained that he was a taxi driver, the victim asked him to take him to the local emergency casualty unit, which was not far away. He refused Arnold's offer to phone for an ambulance or the police.

Arnold dropped him off at the local hospital. The man said that as he had been robbed of all his money, he could not pay his fare but he would make a point of returning to the taxi rank as soon as he was able and to reward Arnold generously.

He asked Arnold what had happened to the blonde he was with and Arnold said that she had gone off in a taxi.

The man said, 'I know where that tart hangs out and I will let her have what she deserves,' and added, 'She set me up for this; she's dead meat.'

A couple of days later, the police contacted Arnold and asked him for a statement concerning the incident. He described the events as truthfully as he could. The police said that he was much more helpful than his colleague in the first taxi who claimed he saw nothing and could not remember anything, not even where he dropped the blonde off.

Arnold agreed to attend an identity parade if the police required him to, as he was sure he would be able to identify the assailants if he saw them again.

A couple of evenings later, the victim did turn up at the taxi rank in a flash Mercedes sports car and rewarded Arnold most generously for his help.

When Arnold told him that the police had been in touch with him and that he had readily agreed to attend an identity parade, the victim said, 'Don't bother, mate. They won't be in a fit state to take part in an ID. I know who they are and I'll find them.'

A few days later, a brutish looking thug called at Arnold's house and told his wife that it would be better for Arnold and his family if Arnold did not attend any ID parade. This was said in such a threatening tone that Arnold's wife was quite shocked. When she told Arnold of the visit he was shaken and uncertain as to what to do. He reasoned to himself that the threat may or may not be carried out, but if he refused to co-operative with the police, his next application for renewal of his black taxi driver's licence could be refused on the grounds that he was not co-operative with the police in dealing with street crime. He would lose his livelihood.

After much soul-searching and long discussions with his wife, he took the brave decision to act as a good and conscientious citizen and to attend the identity parade to which the police had invited him.

The police's case against the two assailants whom they had arrested was based largely on Arnold identifying them. He had agreed with his wife's advice that in order not to fall out with the police and thus lose his valued black cab driver's licence, he would attend the parade, but would deliberately pick out the wrong persons. By doing this he would remove the ominous threat by the assailants' accomplice.

On the appointed day for the parade, Arnold decided not to travel to the police station in his own black taxi cab but to go by the District Line underground train service to the station where the incident took place and from there, to take the first cab in the rank to his destination. He feared that if he went in his own taxi, the gang may arrange for him to have an accident en-route.

Arnold's wife waited anxiously at home for Arnold's return but was shocked to receive a phone call from the police to inform her that Arnold was in the local hospital casualty ward, badly injured.

She naturally assumed that the assailants' accomplices who, at that stage were not to know that Arnold would not identify their comrades had beaten him up on his way to the parade.

She rushed to the hospital and to her horror saw her husband in bed heavily bandaged, one arm in a sling and on a drip feed. Despite his condition, Arnold was able to describe what had happened to him.

When he reached the underground station, he rushed out of the concourse towards the taxi rank intent to get into the first cab before he could be waylaid in the station's forecourt. With his eyes firmly focused on the first cab in the rank, he recognised one of his colleagues as the driver. He dashed up to the glass exit doors to the concourse not noticing a sign, which said, "Doors out of action. Please use side doors." He expected the glass doors to open automatically as he had noticed so many times when he was picking up passengers.

The doors did not open and despite being armour-plated, they shattered, under the impact of Arnold's fourteen stone weight, into fragments but did not disintegrate.

Under the circumstances, the police forgave Arnold's non-attendance at the parade; in fact, they were most apologetic as they considered themselves partially responsible for Arnold's accident.

The thugs were pleased, as Arnold's non-attendance had forced the police to drop the charges against them. They left the police station with threats to sue the police for unlawful arrest and harassment.

Arnold said to his wife, 'All's well that ends well.'

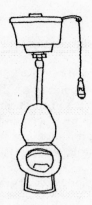

Atomic No. 56 Element

Atomic no. 56 element is more commonly known as barium and is used medicinally in the form of barium sulphate to facilitate taking X-ray images of the digestive tract.

The name is derived from the Greek word for "heavy". It is silver-white in colour and almost as heavy as lead, which everyone knows is very heavy. In all fairness, I must now advise all readers of a sensitive or prudish nature not to proceed any further as what I am about to reveal is not for the eyes of genteel people.

I've no doubt that you all have precluded yourselves from the foregoing genre as otherwise you would not be reading this, so now be prepared for a few crude shocks.

When my doctor suspected that I had anaemia, he arranged for me to have an immediate blood test, the result of which caused him to have quite a shock. My blood count was dangerously low.

On my behalf he urgently phoned the local hospital and made an appointment for me to be examined by a consultant haematologist immediately. The consultant could not find any obvious cause of the anaemia but suspected that it was caused by a daily dose of a quarter of a tablet of aspirin (75 mg) which I had been taking for over a year to lessen the chance of blood circulation problems.

In order to eliminate any other possible causes, he arranged for me to have two barium X-ray examinations, each two weeks apart.

So far I've written nothing to shock even the most sensitive person, but I will soon be reaching that stage. You have, once again, been warned.

In the past even the most miserable and complaining individuals, who had barium examinations, only said that they did not like the chalky taste

481

of the barium. I was therefore completely unprepared for what I was to experience.

I turned up bright and early at the hospital on the appointed day for the first of the two examinations hoping to get through it quickly without any delay. I was actually the first one to be examined and was asked by a nurse to strip completely except for my shoes and socks. Who was I to refuse such an invitation, even though it took place in a booth with a flimsy curtain for privacy directly off a mixed sex (that is men and women) waiting area?

I was next asked to don a floral cotton gown done up at the rear of my neck with a pair of white ribbons. This was quite tricky, as I could not see the ribbons and the bowknot that I had tied soon came undone as I left the booth and walked through the mixed sex waiting area, exposing my posterior in a most embarrassing manner.

The nurse led me to a room at the entrance to which was an illuminated sign saying, "No Entrance – X-Rays in Progress", or words to that effect.

As soon as I entered the room, a young, pretty nurse asked me, "remove your socks and shoes for me". I certainly could not see any reason to remove these items as I was only expecting to have my stomach X-rayed.

As I am not the argumentative type I duly complied. Next, she asked me to, "lie down on the couch for me". At first I thought that I was mishearing things but she clearly repeated her request with a sweet smile. I willingly complied with this invitation. She next removed my hearing aid and spectacles (no, this is not a spelling mistake) leaving me at a great disadvantage. Without these items, my vision and hearing are greatly impaired.

Out of the corner of my right eye I saw the figure of a white-coated doctor enter the room and take up position behind a glazed screen, which I presumed was X-ray-proof.

The nurse told me that the doctor had arrived and the examination would now commence. She wheeled a contraption that looked very much like a drip feed stand close to the couch. At the top of the contraption was a plastic bag containing, I would guess, about two pints of white liquid.

Next, she asked me to "turn over onto your left side for me", and no sooner had I done so than she inserted a tube that led from the drip feed-type of contraption into my back passage. It was not painful or uncomfortable, but most undignified.

She next explained that the doctor would keep asking me to change positions on the couch while liquids and air were pumped into my intestines. Whilst doing so, the doctor would ask me to keep absolutely still when he took X-ray exposures. She also told me that I would experience a strong urge to empty my bowels during the examination but I was told to resist the urge to the utmost. Because my hearing aid had been removed I had difficulty in understanding the doctor's instructions, which had to be repeated several times, and which prolonged my discomfort.   .

After about half an hour during which at least thirty X-ray exposures were taken at various angles, the torment was over. The tube in my posterior was removed much to my relief.

The nurse handed back my hearing aid and spectacles and told me that I might put my shoes and socks on again. I was assured that despite my hearing difficulty I had been a most co-operative patient.

The nurse led me back to the mixed-sex waiting room and told me to re-dress in one of the booths. I was further told that the X-ray exposures would be passed onto the haematologist who was due to see me again in three weeks' time.

I was advised to drink a lot during the next few days but I was not given any warning about the consequences that were to occur but which I feel duty bound to warn others about in advance.

As I had not eaten, in accordance with prior instructions, for 36 hours before the barium X-ray, it was not for a long while before I had the urge to visit the toilet. As usual, when I had finished I pulled the chain, (yes, we have a very old WC cistern that is operated by pulling a chain on the end of which is a white porcelain handle marked, "Pull"), and glanced down the WC pan to ensure that the contents had been cleared away. To my surprise I saw what appeared to be several white, rough-faced stones. I repeated the flushing process several times but the "stones" would not budge.

When I asked my wife if she had thrown any unusual items down the WC she reacted quite angrily. She said that as there were only the two of us who used the toilet, the culprit must be me, as it was not her. It was a logic that I found hard to counter.

I tried budging the objects with a stick but every time I manoeuvred one of the objects to the back of the pan and into the outlet it just simply slid back. This was not solving the problem, so I next tried to break up the objects by using the stick. After much hard work I broke up the objects to the size of small pebbles but still they would not flush away. I continued breaking down the now pebble-sized objects to a sandy consistency, which turned the water in the pan to milky white, heavy silt, but it would still not flush away.

Even after ten buckets of water were sloshed down, and a hosepipe played on it, the sediment persisted.

It was only when I used a stout rubber plunger did I manage to clear the silt from the base of the WC water seal. This problem recurred for several days each time I used the toilet and at times I even had thoughts of calling on the services of Dyno-Rod, as there was a danger of the drains clogging up.

A fortnight after my first barium X-ray examination I returned for a second one. This time I only had to strip down to my waist and swallow some crystals, which tasted pleasant, and swallow a small quantity of barium, which did not taste at all unpleasant. The X-ray exposures were taken whilst I was in an upright position. I had the opportunity to observe the fantastic machines in the X-ray room, which was one of several such rooms. The machines appeared to be there from a science fiction film set.

Unfortunately, the WC problem recurred for the next few days but this time I was prepared for it and I hope that those readers who have persevered with this account will also be prepared if they should ever have the misfortune of having to have an enema barium X-ray in the future.

I have written this account before returning to see the haematologist who will be able to tell me whether or not there is any underlying cause for my anaemia.

Wish me luck.

The Raincoat

The group consisted of boys who initially became acquainted with each other before World War II when they were in the same class at the segregated Central Jews' Free School, situated between Bell Lane and Middlesex Street (known on Sundays as "The Lane" market) in the East End of London.

Although the school's name incorporated the description of "Jews", it was not a religious school but, like all state schools, its syllabus included religious assembly and instruction. Virtually all the pupils were Jewish boys living in the slums of east London. I only knew of two boys in the school, both coincidentally in my class, who were not Jews; one was named Stanley Hilton and the other, Fred Becket.

They said that their parents wanted them to go to the school as they considered the standard of education there to be superior to other local schools.

I met Stanley Hilton again by chance several years later outside an estate agents' office in Poplar, east London, where he was employed as a surveyor.

Quite a large percentage of the teachers at the school were not Jewish, especially those teaching technical subjects such as carpentry, metalwork, electricity and draughtsmanship etc. The school's name included the words, "Free School". This was because it was founded when pupils attending school were required to pay one penny (240 pence equalled one pound) per day for their education. This may not appear to be much, but in those days, it was a considerable amount. One penny a day meant five a week, which multiplied by, say, six children, amounted to 30 pence a week. This was a terrific burden for families whose income, if they were lucky enough to be employed, was about two pounds and ten shilling (£2.50) per week.

The old age pension was ten shillings (fifty pence) per week and so were the average rents for slum apartments.

When the family breadwinner in those days was unemployed or ill, he could not afford to send his children to school and thus many were, as a result, under educated. In order not to let Jewish children in the East End of London be educationally deprived, some rich Jewish philanthropists paid the penny a day fee on their behalf.

Subsequently, all elementary and primary education became totally free in all schools but this school retains the description even today, when it has been relocated outside of the East End of London in a modern building and still maintains a high and envious standard of education.

In August 1939, just before the war broke out, the school was closed down and many of the boys and teachers were evacuated for their safety to the villages of Isleham, Soham and Fordham in Cambridgeshire. I was evacuated along with most of my classmates to Isleham but when the anticipated bombing of London did not occur soon after declaration of war, many of the boys returned to their homes and as they were of school leaving age sought and found work.

I lost touch with most of my classmates during the war but some came together again as a group, which gathered together in the home of Henry Sugarman. The group formed a spontaneous, unofficial club, which socialised together and flirted lightly with other boys' sisters who were about the same age group.

However, three of the boys were not present as they died during the war. Morry Goldstein, who was a very talented artist, died at the age of 17 years when a bomb, by a million to one chance, fell down a ventilation shaft at Bank underground station where he and his family sought shelter during the German blitz on London. The bomb exploded in the concourse where hundreds of people were assembled.

Bank underground station was considered to be possibly the safest in London because it was hundreds of feet below ground level. At the time, the City of London's financial centre was not being bombed and Bank station was not far from the East End of London.

Keith Koskovitch was killed on 'D Day', when his landing craft was sunk in the English Channel not far from the Dieppe beach-landing site. His body was never recovered.

Issy Abrahams was killed by a Japanese sniper in the Burmese jungle.

Among those who survived the war and joined the group, was Mad Mark, who declared he was sent crazy when he served in the artillery. He was stationed on a very isolated island on the north west coast of Scotland.

The island had previously been uninhabited; in fact it was uninhabitable but was set up with heavy guns to protect shipping in the area. For weeks on end, he and his comrades sat by their guns ready for immediate action, which never occurred. The weather was continuously atrocious and their only company was the screeching sea gulls. One of his comrades was driven, by the sheer boredom, to commit suicide and Mark said that he, too, nearly did so.

Another was Lenny Burns, not his real Jewish-sounding name, which he changed when he joined the Air Force in case he was shot down and captured by the Germans, was still in uniform. He was an observer/gunner in a heavy bomber but did not see any action because the war ended before he finished his training in South Africa.

Solly Josephs, who had also served in the Air Force in the Far East, joined the group for a while but then went to live somewhere in India where he became, to the horror of his family, a drug addict and a follower of some obscure guru.

The group met in Henry Sugarman's flat. He was a tall and handsome chap and the target and desire of all the girls who could not net Henry. Although Henry yearned to be allowed to join the Air Force and become one of the glamorous "Brylcreme" boys, he was not permitted to because he found himself in what was termed a "reserved occupation". The firm he worked for as a draughtsman produced and installed refrigeration plant in food producing factories. During the war food was in very short supply and what was available had to be carefully preserved.

Among some of the other club members was Eddie Cohen, who was not actually an ex-Jews' Free School boy but a friend and close neighbour of Lenny Burns. Eddie had also been conscripted into the Army but had not seen any active service.

His father, who died of a heart attack when Eddie was very young, had been a master tailor. His workroom was situated off the ground floor flat's tiny backyard, which also housed the dustbins. In the good, old-fashioned manner, Eddie's father sewed his garments by hand, sitting cross-legged on a large wooden table. His one and only assistant was his dutiful wife. They both worked day and night in order to give their two sons a good start in life. Eddie's younger brother was, unlike Eddie, very active, noisy and naughty. The father was never short of work in the days of high, depressing, degrading unemployment. High class and expensive Saville Row tailors in London's West End sub-contracted work out to him but only paid him a fraction of what they charged their customers.

When her husband died suddenly, Eddie's mother had to take over the role of the family's breadwinner and resorted to her pre-marital trade of hand-rolling cigarettes for a large, well known firm of cigarette manufacturers. As she had to care for her two fatherless sons at the same time, she was allowed to roll the cigarettes at home on a piecework basis. No equipment was required, just a small timber board and the dexterity of her fingers. Often, Eddie would sit alongside her helping to fulfil her quota. They both sat working silently for hours at a time whilst the younger son played noisily in the street outside.

Being silent was no strangeness to Eddie. He was by nature the strong, silent type. He was extremely shy and very rarely spoke, but when he did it was with a masterful use of the minimum of words. Even such an effort made him blush in embarrassment. He was very placid, smiled a lot and was liked by his friends because he never uttered an unpleasant word to anybody, in fact, he hardly uttered a word at all.

He was most awkward in company and clumsy when dancing and could never, ever flirt with a girl or even carry on the most simple of conversations. When there was a lively conversation or discussion, he contributed nothing.

His appearance was quite good; tall and well built, fair-haired with soft pink skin, which blushed even at his own thoughts. After army service, he resorted to his own trade, as a master tailor, which he had been taught as an apprentice in order to follow in his father's footsteps.

He was actually an excellent tailor and in order to advertise his skill, took great care in tailoring his own suits and coats and in selecting only the very best in shirts and shoes etc.

In contrast to his more shabbily dressed friends, he was outstanding and attractive to the girls, before they found out that his shyness and lack of verbal communication made flirting with him impossible.

The item that Eddie was possibly the most proud of was the gabardine raincoat that he had made for himself.

One of the girls, who was attracted by Eddie's fine build and immaculate clothing was Lillian Berk, who lived nearby. Her name was originally Lilly Bercovitch but she abbreviated it when she found it was a hindrance when seeking employment outside of the East End of London. Her widower father was bringing her up as her mother had died of tuberculosis, which was rife in the slums of east London before the war.

Her father found it very hard to manage to bring up both Lillian and her sister, who was loud, rude and rebellious. For a time both the girls were placed in an orphanage but were returned to their father when they reached the age of 13 years.

Their first floor slum tenement was filthy, which was not helped when their father, who was a rag-man, returned in the evenings with his sack of old, dirty, stinking rags to sort out before he took them to his dealer. By this method he eked out a miserable existence. As soon as the girls turned

14 years they left school and earned whatever they could to help out financially.

Lillian was ambitious, she wanted to get out of their miserable poverty, and by sheer determination, natural charm and beauty as well as some economy with the truth, secured a job as a junior assistant in the cosmetics and perfumery department of Peter Jones departmental store in Sloane Square, west London. There, she came under the influence of the departmental manageress who took a liking to Lillian and helped her to improve her speech and appearance.

Lillian started to talk with a "posh" London accent and dressed herself most expensively. It helped to be able to buy good quality but slightly soiled or damaged goods from the store where she worked at very low prices. Such soiled goods were not available to the general public.

When she left for work each morning from her filthy slum residence, she looked like a model from the Vogue fashion magazine. Conductors on the buses taking her to work wondered what such a posh lady was doing in the East End of London.

Apart from anything else, she was eager to get to know Eddie better because as a master tailor he was earning very good money which she hoped eventually may help her to escape from the engulfing and overpowering poverty into which she had been born. She made her desire known to Henry who did not wish to get involved too deeply with any of the local girls who adored him, not even with the posh-speaking, well-dressed Lillian herself. He promised to help her in her desire.

Eddie was overcome with joy when Henry told him that Lillian had taken a liking to him and would be most pleased to go out with him one evening in order to get to know him better.

Henry arranged the rendezvous and told Eddie to put on his best clothes as Lillian very much admired the way he dressed. The rendezvous was to be at 7 pm at the entrance to the nearly Whitechapel underground station.

When Henry met Lillian the following day he asked, with a twinkle in his eyes how everything had gone.

'Disastrous,' was the reply in a very posh voice, 'It could not have been worse.'

She went on to explain how she had dressed herself in her most attractive and expensive clothes, spent ages putting her makeup on and used her most expensive French perfume. In her mind she had rehearsed what she would say that would impress Eddie and what carefully worded questions she would ask.

She went on to tell Henry how, despite the steady rain she had turned up right on time, not too early, not too late, to find Eddie already waiting for her in the station's entrance. She said that when she saw him she was shocked. Instead of the well-dressed man she expected to escort her for the evening, there stood Eddie dressed in shabby clothes. He could easily have been mistaken for one of the tramps that lodged in the nearby Salvation Army hostel.

She had a mind not to notice him and to return home but the alert Eddie noticed her arrival and acknowledged her with a faint smile but no words of greeting. She was so disgusted at his appearance that she asked if something had happened to him. He muttered something about not wearing his good clothes in case the rain spoilt them. When Lillian reminded him that she had seen him wearing a lovely, smartly-cut gabardine raincoat he replied that he could not risk that being spoiled by the rain and had borrowed his bother's old raincoat.

She told Henry how Eddie had bought the best tickets for the Odeon Cinema in Leicester Square and sat still and rigid right through the programme whilst all around them young couples were kissing and cuddling and not even looking at the screen. After the film, he took her, as instructed by Henry, to the nearby Lyons Corner House restaurant and bought her a nice salad meal followed by a luxurious ice cream desert and coffee. He was very generous.

All during the meal he hardly said a word despite her attempts to make conversation or in reply to her carefully prepared questions. The few words that he did utter were mumbled and he kept blushing away at each effort. All the time she was conscious of what other people would think of her being accompanied by this man who looked like a tramp.

She was glad when he finally bid her farewell at her door without even the slightest effort to kiss her goodnight or to arrange a further meeting.

Henry assured her that she had not done too badly if she had managed to get him to speak a few words. He asked if she would like him to arrange another meeting with Eddie.

Her unprintable reply was not uttered in a posh voice.

Crocodile Skins

This story does not have much to do with crocodiles or crocodile skins but I have titled it such because I could not think of a better one. Perhaps, after you have read it, you may think of a more appropriate title. If anyone is considering architecture as a profession for their son or daughter, forget it, unless they are willing to accept the fact that it is one of the lowest, if not actually the very lowest paid of all professions.

The training leading to qualification is long and arduous, vacancies in architects' offices are few and far between and the salaries for the first few years are miserably low.

Architects operating their own practices find much competition from unqualified and unregistered people blatantly advertising their services in local papers and undercutting the fees, however low, architects have to charge to make even the most modest of livelihoods.

Registered architects are not permitted to advertise and thus are at a great disadvantage against unregistered impostors in obtaining commissions. Even large corporate institutions and borough councils employ non-qualified people as their staff architects. Unfair competition is rife and depresses architects' incomes and status. On the other hand, a lot of blame for shoddy architecture carried out by unregistered and unqualified practitioners is generally blamed, in ignorance, on the genuine architects.

In addition, genuine architects have powerful restraints placed upon them by town planners, building inspectors, company directors and private clients with bad taste. It is a very daunting prospect but nevertheless, with indomitable spirit an aspiring architect could enjoy his profession by virtue of its many challenges and the satisfaction of mastering so many problems.

For 30 years, until I retired, I was a qualified and registered architect running my own, one-man practice, and when I say one man, I mean that I did everything except the typing which my devoted and dear wife did for me.

Being a single person general practice, I was involved in a wide variety of projects and met a wide variety of clients, most of whom were pleasant and who, I believe, eventually appreciated my services and possibly, commiserated with me on the pitifully low, miserable fee they paid me.

The projects I undertook varied greatly and included rear house-extensions, surveying properties on behalf of prospective purchasers, internal alterations of residences, small blocks of flats, supermarkets, offices, cafés, conversions of large houses into flats, private schools, medical clinics and private hospitals, factories etc.

In this story, I wish to describe one particular residential project in Hendon, North West London. Hendon is one of the more salubrious suburbs of London and the particular road in which this house was situated was one of the most prestigious in the district. Anyone owning a house in this road was automatically regarded as a millionaire or a wealthy bankrupt. In fact, it was generally known as "Millionaires' Row".

The actual two-storey detached house was situated at the end of a short, wide road leading to a municipal park, the entrance to which was adorned by a large ornamental gate. The back garden of the house overlooked this beautiful, well cared for park, which further enhanced the property's attractiveness. I cannot be more specific because of professional confidentiality.

As architects are not permitted to advertise, I was introduced to this client by another satisfied, enormously rich client who strongly recommended me for ability, conscientiousness and pitiful fee.

My clients on this project were a young couple who had been given the house by the husband's rich father who made a very good living as an importer and merchant of crocodile skins. He imported the skins because outside of zoos in this country there are no crocodiles to be shot. He sold the skins to manufacturers of shoes, handbags and high-class luggage. His one and only beloved son assisted him in the business.

My client's young and vivacious, very attractive wife was the dominant partner of the pair and she made all the decisions on his behalf. All he was required to do was to sign the appropriate cheques.

My client's father bought the house cheaply at an auction because the previous owners had become bankrupt whilst they were having the house extensively altered and because the local council had put a stop to all work on the premises as the owners had not sought nor obtained approval for the alterations.

The house was in an awful state with gaping, boarded up openings and Acrow props supporting the frontage. My client's instructions, or rather, those of his wife, were to reinstate the frontage and to floor-in the minstrel gallery to form two additional bedrooms with en-suite bathrooms in the space over the two-storey high lounge. She also wanted two new en-suite bathrooms off the master bedroom to be formed within the adjoining spacious roof voids. One of the bathrooms to be entirely in pink for herself and the other in blue for her husband. All the work, including the tricky plumbing was complicated.

When I submitted my initial, informal application to the town planners, they said that my proposals for the frontage, however nice, could not be accepted as the house fell within a conservation area. I would have to reinstate what was there previously even though they did not have any record. I thereupon submitted a sketch showing the boarded-up, gaping openings with the attendant Acrow props and asked if that was what they wanted. The proper application showing my true proposals was duly approved.

Normally, after I had prepared specifications and obtained competitive tenders from suitable building contractors, I was required to supervise the building works. However, on this occasion, after the building contract was signed, my client's wife said that as she was, apart from other things, a building expert, they would not be requiring any further service from me as she would supervise the building work herself. My fee was accordingly reduced and fortunately paid promptly by her husband.

She said that she had acquired her building expertise whilst watching builders erect a garage extension at her father's house. She said that no builder would be able to pull the wool over her eyes. However, she did make a proviso that she might call upon me to advise should any unforeseen problem arise, which in the course of events occurred quite frequently.

On one such site visit to sort out a plumbing problem, I asked the electrician where I could find the plumber. He replied in a manner of fact voice, 'He's in bed with the missus, he shouldn't be long.'

The next time I called, the plumber told me that the electrician was in the bedroom with the "missus" sorting out some problems.

During another visit, I noticed blood spots all over the premises. The carpenter told me that the clients had had another of their violent rows about the rapidly rising cost of the project and that she had chased him around the house stabbing him with a kitchen knife. He told me that they were now in their bedroom sorting out the problem.

When they eventually appeared, they both seemed quite composed and she said to her husband, 'Dinner will be ready soon, it's in the oven.'

He was covered in sticking plasters. When she left the room, the husband said that he was not gong to pay another penny to the builder. I duly warned him of the consequences contained in the contract should he default. I warned him that the builder could, under the contract, walk off the site and sue for any money due to him and for loss of profit.

He did not care as the works were nearly completed in any case. In fact, he did pay and the works were duly completed, including the vast number of extras and alterations ordered by his wife.

During another of my several site visits, I noticed several broken windows. My client told me that the damage had been caused during a violent fight between his Swedish au-pair girl and her lesbian lover.

Not long after the works were completed I heard that the couple had split up and the house was up for sale at a greatly enhanced price.

A very desirable purchase in a very envious position all paid for on the purchase and sale of crocodile skins, hence the title of the story.

The Dahlia Man

When we first moved into our existing terraced Victorian house about 48 years ago, the house directly backing onto our rear garden was occupied, as far as we could ascertain, by only a sprightly, middle-aged man. We never got to know his name but consequently we nicknamed him the dahlia man.

In the course of time, we did confirm that he was living all alone in the large, four-bedroomed house. Of course, we conjectured about his marital status, wondering if he was a confirmed bachelor, a divorcee or a widower. No woman was ever seen in or about the house, just the dahlia man himself.

We took up residence in the late autumn and were preoccupied with many tasks within the house. There were bookshelves to be erected for our large collection of books, carpets to be laid, cupboards and wardrobes to be fitted, curtain pelmets and rails to be fixed and a host of other tasks to make our house into a home for our convenience.

It was not until the following spring that I was able to get out and attend to our rear garden, which had become quite neglected and unkempt. It was hard work and the dahlia man who chatted to me over the rear garden fence frequently interrupted me He was an expert gardener and gave me a host of advice about the garden. He told me that he specialised in the cultivations of dahlias, of which he was an acknowledged expert. He told us that the flower was named after a Swedish botanist, Andrew Dahl. Hence our nickname, the dahlia man. He exhibited his dahlias far and wide at flower shows and won many prizes.

We were promised some tubers of his prize dahlias only on the condition that we did not pass any on to anyone else.

Later in the year, when we saw his dahlias growing, we were most impressed but however hard we tried to carry out his advice, we could not get our dahlias to match the quality of his. He explained that it would take many years to achieve his standard because, "the secret is in the soil" and I would have to improve my soil but it could not be done overnight.

I enjoyed my frequent chats with him and wondered how it was that a man much below retirement age could spend almost all day, every day in the garden. He never seemed to work and did not appear to be a rich man. The thought that he may have won the football pools crossed our minds but the chances of that were remote. It never even entered our minds that he might have been a professional burglar, but the truth eventually did emerge.

'Mr Dahlia' was actually employed by the local council as a bricklayer and he had volunteered to work at nights on emergency work. Apparently there was a great demand for such a bricklayer, mainly in the repair of main sewers, manholes (now termed access or inspection chambers for political correctness purposes), repairs to sewage pump works and refuse disposal depots, etc.

Of course, there were not always emergency jobs to be carried out but this suited the dahlia man as he could get a good night's sleep and so be refreshed to work all the following day on his dahlias in his garden.

There was no rush from any of the other council bricklayers for such duties and being on his own this suited the dahlia man down to the ground, so to speak, if you will kindly excuse the pun. His skill as a bricklayer was most evident in features in his garden.

He was also an accomplished amateur artist and proudly showed us some of his oil paintings, which were most impressive. Some of his paintings depicting dahlias were reminiscent of Van Gogh's "Sunflowers".

Maintaining and improving his large, Victorian house was also one of his activities.

He was always full of energy and joy of life. However, towards the end of the summer we noticed a marked change in his demeanour. He was much less communicative and neglected his prize dahlias. We thought that he had contracted some serious illness working in the sewers but eventually he revealed the reason for this change.

He told us that he was actually married. His wife was alive but had for the last 20 years or so, been confined to a mental home. Her mental illness apparently was genetically inherited, both her mother and maternal grandmother had also suffered similarly and until recently her illness had been considered incurable.

He had dutifully visited her every Sunday afternoon and had noted a steady deterioration in her condition. Most times she did not even remember who he was, except he was the man who regularly brought her flowers and chocolates.

When he had visited her recently, the medical staff told him that they proposed to treat her with a new drug that promised great hope of improvement in her condition. The drug certainly worked and she became a completely different and improved person.

The medical staff told him that in the near future they would be able to let her return home for final rehabilitation but this would be on a gradual basis beginning with one day at a time, building up until she could return permanently.

There was only one small snag; she would have to remain indefinitely on the drug, which he would have to ensure that she took three times a day after meals.

They were teaching her housework and cookery so that she could once again run the household.

When we told him that we were glad to hear the good news he said, 'You don't understand, after 20 years she has become a stranger to me who I dutifully visit every Sunday. I have lost all feelings for her as a wife. I am so used to my own routine in the house that I would not be happy to have what will really be a strange woman doing the housework and cooking for me. I would also have to give up my night-work duties and will not be around during the day to care for my garden.'

He said that the prospect was driving him crazy and he feared that when his wife returned home he would be certified (sectioned, as it is now termed) and confined in a mental home.

When we saw him a short while after, he seemed much more cheerful and told us that he had sold his house and would soon be moving out. He said that it was with the greatest of regrets that he was abandoning his beloved garden and dahlias, it was like losing a dear and beloved child, but without a home of his own, the health authorities could not send his wife back to him.

The new occupants of the house simply neglected the garden of love and joy, which now stands overgrown with weeds. His prim little shed and beloved greenhouse have fallen into disrepair and are now dilapidated.

Every time we see a dahlia in some garden or park, our minds go back to the dahlia man and we wonder what he is doing now, maybe tending everlasting dahlias in the heavenly Garden of Eden.

What made me recall this sad episode after so many years was the phenomenal growth of a dahlia seedling I had planted this spring, adjacent to the fence separating my garden and the dahlia man's garden. It has grown vigorously and is now about seven feet high and five feet across with at least 30 giant sized blooms at any one time.

Maybe the spirit of the dahlia man has become embedded in my soil or perhaps the demolished reinforced concrete air-raid shelter that lies beneath that part of the garden has something to do with it.

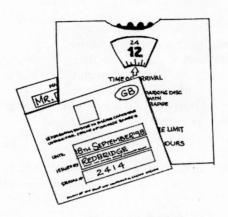

Orange Badge

Our friend and close neighbour, Andrew, is in his mid-fifties and already retired. He is a very rich man, doubtless in the millionaire class, who made his fortune in property development. He did not go to university; he was largely self-educated but very shrewd and wise.

He told us that he could have gone on making even more money but said, 'What would be the purpose if I did not have time to enjoy what I already have?'

From his modest, unassuming appearance and manner there was no indication of his wealth. The only indication of his wealth, which was known only to his most intimate acquaintances, was his two hobbies.

One of these was the care of his veteran Bentley motorcar that he kept in his centrally heated garage and which he only drove when attending specialised rallies, including the London to Brighton run. This annual event was the highlight of his and his wife's lives. The car he used for everyday journeys was a modest Ford Fiesta Ghia.

His other hobby, or rather his passion, was the collection of antique and rare books. He attended every book auction both in this country and overseas and was known to other enthusiasts and to members of the trade as a keen and knowledgeable buyer. He never sold or exchanged any of his beloved books.

From the outside, his house and detached garage gave no indication of the valuable contents. His books alone were worth hundreds of thousands of pounds. The only indication that the premises might contain valuables was the intruder alarm box on the front of the house and the security lights, but then, many of the nearby houses also had such precautionary installations. Andrew's intruder alarm installation was quite

498

complex in order to comply with his insurance company's requirements.

It was of the "silent" type, that is, the alarm did not sound during the first five minutes after being activated so as to give the police time to reach the premises without the intruder being aware that a central monitoring depot to which the installation was connected by a telephone line had alerted them.

Andrew and his wife consciously set the alarm each time they left the premises, however short their intended absence, and also when they retired at night.

The alarm was set by punching in a four digit number which was only known to the couple and was not known by anyone else, not even the installers, the insurance company, relatives or the police. In order to cancel the setting it was necessary to punch in the same four digits in the same sequence in which they were inserted.

The installation only allowed 20 seconds between re-entering the premises and inserting the correct four digits in the correct sequence before the alarm was activated. In order to facilitate memorising the four figures and the sequence Andrew and his wife agreed between themselves to use their telephone number.

On reflection, they realised that this was not very wise as any burglar who knew this telephone number would try it in order to cancel the alarm setting but on the other hand, burglars are also aware that apart from random numbers the householder may have chosen the birth date of himself, his wife or children etc. and he only had 20 seconds in which to enter the premises, locate and reach the control unit and insert the correct numbers in the correct sequence.

Therefore, professional burglars find it most useful to know the correct information beforehand and to Andrew's dismay this did actually happen and indirectly I was responsible even though, like everyone else, I did not know the secret number.

I became indirectly responsible when some while back; I advised him that because of his arthritic hip joints he would be eligible for an Orange Badge.

I explained that if his doctor certified that he could not normally walk more than a reasonable distance in order to visit shops etc. he could apply for an orange badge, which, displayed on his dashboard, permitted him to park in places where non-badge holders are not permitted. Such a privilege is subject to certain restrictions. Also, most supermarkets and hospitals etc. reserved parking spaces in their car parks near their entrances for the holders of such badges. In these days of difficult parking it is a most useful item to have and also, it is free of charge.

Obviously Andrew was most pleased because despite all his wealth he did not enjoy such a privilege. One day, when he parked his Ford Fiesta in one of the allocated spaces in a local supermarket he noticed a young man checking his orange badge. When Andrew asked him why he was doing so, he replied that he was employed by the company responsible for the parking and was taking note of anyone abusing the parking facility for disabled drivers.

Andrew did not take any offence as he himself had noted on previous occasions that some obviously young and fit drivers had parked in these spaces. He was also unconcerned as his car was fitted with a very efficient anti-theft alarm and it was comforting to know that there was an alert, responsible person nearby to take action should anyone tamper with his car.

Andrew had carefully displayed his orange badge, which actually was in two parts. One part had a revolving dial to record the time of arrival because parking was limited to two hours and the other part was a card on which Andrew's full name and other personal details but not his address were boldly written. The card also bore the name of the local council that had issued the badge and Andrew's passport-type photo.

When Andrew returned home, he found to his horror that his house had been burgled and noted that the intruder alarm had not been activated. Some cash and his wife's jewellery had been stolen but which, to Andrew's comfort, was covered by his insurance policy. However, to his dismay his lovely collection of antique and rare books had been tipped onto the floor and every drawer had been taken out and the contents strewn about. The intruder alarm installers were most concerned and sent their most senior technical inspector to ascertain why the intruder had not activated the elaborate alarm. His conclusion was that the installation was in perfect working order and the only possible explanation was that the intruder knew the code number.

Andrew protested that that was impossible, as only he and his wife knew the number, which they had not even written down anywhere.

His insurance company was also most concerned as the installers were on their approved list and had sent one of their senior assessors down to ascertain whether Andrew's claim for compensation was valid or not.

Andrew explained that there was no way the burglar could have known his secret code and insisted that there must have been a defect in the alarm system which he was sure he had set before leaving the premises. He was sure that he had set the alarm as it was his habit when doing so, to leave a birthday card with his birth date on it on the hall table to remind him that the alarm was set and that he only had 20 seconds in which to cancel it. The card was still as he had left it.

The assessor closely questioned Andrew and his wife but when recalling the events of the day, Andrew told him about the young man in the car park but said that there was nothing on the orange badge or in the car that would have informed the young man about his alarm code. A quick call to the supermarket security officer confirmed that the young man was bogus; he was not employed by the company that managed the car parking or by the supermarket themselves.

The insurance company's assessor said that they recently had several such cases and they deduced by the modus operandi that it was the work of a single gang, possibly, not more than two persons. One would note the name of the badge holder and look him (or her) up in the local telephone directory and then contact his accomplice on a mobile phone giving the victim's name, address and telephone number.

The accomplice would then go immediately to the victim's address knowing full well that the victim was likely to be at least 30 minutes shopping and returning home. In any case, the car park spotter would advise him by phone when the victim had emerged from the supermarket and possibly was on his (or her) way home.

All the intruder had to do before entering the premises was to ring the doorbell to ensure that no one was at home. He could then confidently search the house for hidden valuables at his leisure. If the house had an intruder alarm, he would immediately enter the victim's telephone number on the control panel as that is used by a high percentage of households. Should that not work he would not waste any time and beat a hasty retreat, grabbing anything of any value that was easily to hand.

The gang was difficult to trap because they did several houses in one district in a day and then moved onto some other district using the same MO.

When Andrew told me this and said that he would not be using his orange badge in future I told him that a simple expedient would be when displaying his badge was to place the disc badge so as to conceal his name but not the other details. Without his name, the scam could not be used. Once again Andrew was thankful for this sensible advice and welcomed it because he found that the use of the badge was so very convenient.

It was not very long after, that a disgruntled Andrew told me that he had received a parking ticket when he parked his car in a permitted manner displaying his orange badge as I had advised.

Apparently, if the holder's name is not displayed then the badge is not valid and the motorist has committed a road traffic offence as though he had no orange badge at all. Andrew said that in light of this latest experience he would definitely stop using his orange badge.

I felt very sorry for him as I know that his disability would make it most difficult for him to walk any great distance to visit shops etc.

However, my nimble and agile brain, the only part of my aged body that is so nowadays, and then not on every day or all day, came up with another foolproof suggestion which has worked so far, but which I will not reveal here because criminals are likely to find a weakness therein and exploit it. Andrew's insurers were impressed when they heard about it and have condoned it.

The Preacher Man

Stuart and his wife were joint partners in a local bric-a-brac shop. They were both honest and hard working and as a result their regular customers, who largely relied on them to buy and sell items at reasonable prices, trusted them.

Apart from their casual or occasional clientele the bulk of their business was with professional buyers. These consisted of "runners", that is people who visit local bric-a-brac and antique shops spotting potential bargains and selling them directly onto to expensively priced antique shops in fashionable districts, and also specialist dealers involved in war memorabilia, rare books, pianos, numismatics paintings, antique furniture, clocks and watches etc. Whenever Stuart got hold of any item that he knew a certain specialist would be particularly interested in, he would not put it on display in his shop but phone the specialist who would come post-haste to view the item and give his specialised opinion thereupon.

Thus began the dealer-to-dealer circuit of items that would steadily increase in price as they passed through several dealers' and restorers' hands before being sold to a member of the general public at an enormously inflated price. Stuart was not a specialist but he instinctively knew when a certain object had potential and would research it in the vast library he kept in a room at the back of the shop. His wife also had an excellent knowledge of the value of books, which proved to be useful from time to time.

Sometimes, local people would bring in some object to sell in order to raise some ready cash. These objects might consist of a pair of brass candlesticks, a silver framed photo, an oil lamp or an old clock. However, their main source of goods was derived through a regular advert in the local

503

weekly newspaper offering to buy for cash jewellery, watches etc. and also to clear houses. These house clearances were generally very profitable, as the contents were not priced individually but collectively. The total amount was usually very enticing to the vendors, who might have inherited the contents or who were a young couple either emigrating or separating. A quick deal settled in cash was usually most acceptable.

Normally, the goods were removed the very same day leaving the premises vacant and immediately available for disposal. A quick clearance was often essential as otherwise other relatives or claimants would come and snatch items that they considered to be either legally, morally or sentimentally theirs. Such items, coincidentally, would often be the most valuable.

Stuart and his wife were often up against stiff competition from other dealers and had to offer a good price in order to clinch a deal. Sometimes one item alone proved, after a bit of research, to be worth much more than the price paid for the whole lot.

At first, Stuart and his wife found some of these house clearances very sad and depressing but after a while, just like undertakers, they became somewhat inured to the pathetic circumstances. If they did not perform this important service other, possibly less scrupulous, dealers would.

They were, therefore, not surprised when one morning they had a response to their weekly advert in the local paper. A crisp and precise invitation was cordially extended to them to come and give an estimate to purchase the contents of a local residence. The voice was that of an educated, businesslike woman.

When Stuart and his wife arrived at the detached house, which was situated next door to a defunct, depressing, dismal, dilapidated church that had been badly vandalised and neglected, it was easy to guess that the residence was or had been at some time, the vicarage, but it too had been sadly neglected and looked shabby but respectable.

Whereas the house was in the ecclesiastical gothic style, all the other houses in the street were typical two-storey, semi-detached, inter-war style houses with prim front gardens, largely paved over in order to provide parking for highly polished family cars (the cars, not the families).

The front garden of the vicarage was full of overgrown, dark, depressing looking laurel shrubs with a neglected gravel path leading up to the front door porch. As there was no functioning doorbell, they rapped loudly on the heavy cast iron doorknocker.

For quite a long while there was no response, only deathly silence, but then, loud measured footsteps were heard upon a hard-tiled floor. The door was opened by a tall, thin, gaunt looking elderly woman in deep mourning black. She did not utter a word but stared hard at the callers and

504

only responded after Stuart had introduced himself and his wife. After looking them up and down she seemed to approve of their appearance and beckoned them in. She reeked of carbolic soap and naphthalene moth repellents.

The dark dismal entrance hall, containing a dark-stained oak-cased grandfather clock with a painted dial and other items of dark-stained but highly polished oak, smelt overpoweringly of musty dry rot and woodworm infestation (merulius lacrymans and anobium punctatum, to be a little more precise).

The woman told them that she had already obtained estimates from other dealers so they should not waste valuable time by quoting a ridiculous figure. She led them from room to room whilst Stuart made a mental note of the value of the contents. He noted the unfashionable dark-stained, uncomfortable furniture, the moth-eaten carpets and rugs, the threadbare curtains, the cheap ornaments, discoloured lampshades, framed photos and faded print pictures, the uninteresting leather-bound books containing selected sermons, the lives of the saints, historical sites in the holy land etc. These items were just not saleable and he would most likely end up paying the local council to take them away.

However, there were three items of interest to him. One was the grandfather clock in the entrance hall, which dealers would not be interested in because it was dark oak and had a painted dial but an ordinary member of the public could well be interested. The other two items were an oak rolltop desk, which is very collectable these days by people carrying on a business at home, and a particularly interesting glass fronted, flamed, Cuban mahogany bookcase in which the uninteresting books were stacked. Stuart reckoned that the bookcase might even be of Georgian vintage and would be very much sought after by the owners of the posh shops in Belgravia and Chelsea.

He based his overall offer mainly on the value of these last three items and was surprised at the alacrity with which the vendor accepted his quotation. He paid her cash on the spot and sent his wife to bring the van round to take the items away before the vendor changed her mind or before anyone else came to claim any item which they may consider to be rightfully theirs. It is amazing just how many forgotten and distant relatives suddenly appear to claim sentimental mementos of the deceased!

Whilst he waited for his wife to return with the van, he started to move items into the entrance hall so as to save time loading. Whilst he was doing so, the vendor explained her predicament. She told him that the Church Commissioners had rented the house to her husband when they returned after many years serving as missionaries in several West African countries. She met her husband when they both sang in a local church choir and they married soon after. They were both still quite young when he started to train as a teacher, specialising in art and music. She trained as a nurse. It was a hard period for them financially and life became additionally difficult when soon after their marriage they found that her husband was sterile. They therefore had no children of their own but sought solace in her serving as a nurse in a children's hospital and he, as a teacher in a religious school where he concentrated on art and music.

For some reason which she could never understand but which she reckoned was due to incompatibility with the headmaster, her husband, suddenly, in mid-term, resigned and got another job in a different district. This problem occurred twice more before her husband said that he had had a message from God that his true vocation in which he would find peace and satisfaction was to become a teacher missionary in Africa. With the aid of the Bishop he was soon to find a suitable posting where she too was able to work as a nurse with sick native children.

For some inexplicable reason her husband felt it necessary at times, to change from one mission to another and from one African country to another.

Finally, when he reached the age of 60 years, he retired and returned to this country and the very same Bishop who helped him to seek satisfaction in Africa arranged for him to rent this ex-vicarage for the rest of his life or until it was required for development. Now that her husband had found eternal peace the Church Commissioners had asked her to move out but had arranged for her to be re-housed in a modern, supervised flat specially built for elderly people and managed by a church housing association where she could live out her natural years.

She did not need to take any furniture with her as the new flat was fully furnished by the previous tenant who had died intestate. She only wished to take with her a few personal items including a framed photo of her late husband taken whilst serving in Africa.

She said that he was a God fearing man but people who he worked with could not get on with his strict religious outlook and practices. He was not slow in condemning outright and loudly any unchristian behaviour and strongly condemned some of the recent liberal trends in the Anglican Church. He was also very strict with the children he taught but he loved them and they in turn respected him.

In his retirement, he was not idle; he became choirmaster, acted as a lay preacher, served as a governor on the board of a local church school and used his artistic talent to illustrate several different church magazines. In addition, he devoted himself to publishing a children's bible, fully illustrated, in colour and which could be used to educate illiterate children and even adults in Africa. He did all this without receiving a single penny in recognition. Some people were jealous of his talents and in the course of time made matters so difficult that he had to resign and find employment elsewhere. She added that he was an unrecognised and unappreciated martyr in his devotion to the children he taught.

Tears welled up in her light blue eyes as she unburdened her heart to Stuart. She added, 'If that is the cross that we were destined to bear, so be it.' Even Stuart after his many years of experiencing tragic reasons for home clearances was touched by her pathetic story.

He was relieved when his wife returned with the van so that they could commence loading. As usual, they started with the bulkiest item, which was the large, mahogany bookcase cabinet. They removed the books from the shelves and placed them in tea chests. Next, they started to ease the bookcase forward so that each of them could get a good grip of the heavy item. As they moved the bookcase forward they discovered stacked behind, four cardboard folios, each about 600 mm x 400 mm containing many sheets of illustrations.

The vendor immediately exclaimed, 'I looked everywhere for them and could not find them!' She said that she knew her husband had hidden his illustrations for his planned picture bible in case a burglar stole them. In such an event, his work would take many years to do again. She eagerly undid the tapes of the first folio to see what her husband's illustrations were like. He had not shown them to her as he wished them to be a surprise when his bible was published.

When she turned the sheets of illustrations over, their beauty and the messages they conveyed overcame her. Her joy was overwhelming and she hoped that the other three folios would contain sufficient illustrations to warrant the bible being published and to serve as a memento of his lifetime devotion to his beloved religion and the sacrifices he had made on its behalf. She exclaimed that he was both a genius and a saint.

When she expectantly opened the next folio she uttered a low and long moan, followed by, 'The f...ing, rotten, filthy sod, he swore on our beloved Holy Bible that he had given up his perverted fantasies that had bedevilled all our married life... How could he?'

The more she looked at his illustrations, the worse her language became. Stuart and his wife were shocked to hear such words that even Stuart, though he had been brought up in the docklands of east London, had never heard before. Her torrent of abuse of her recently departed husband increased in foulness as she continued to view his perverted illustrations. She said that she could not possibly let them take the illustrations away. She, herself, would burn them and she hoped that as she did so, his soul would burn simultaneously in hell to where he, no doubt, had been consigned.

The Parrot

Enid was found dead in her bed, clutching a brass crucifix with her eyes wide open and bulging as if in terror.

At the foot of her bed lay a parrot, also apparently dead. The police had broken into her small, two up, two down, old, neglected, Victorian terraced house in East Ham, not far from the London docks. They had been called when a meter reader could not obtain access to empty her coin-operated gas meter. He had noticed that there were several bottles of milk on her doorstep and in accordance with standing instructions from his employers he had notified the local police of the possibility of a dead or severely ill occupant.

The police broke in after confirming with neighbours that a single elderly person occupied the house. A doctor called in by the police confirmed that Enid was indeed dead and had died several days previously. The postmortem, which is normally held in such circumstances, confirmed that death had been caused by a heart attack, possibly aggravated by the extremely cold weather.

Enid was one of those people who believed in sleeping with her bedroom window wide open whatever the weather. The night that the doctor calculated to be the night of her death had been bitterly cold. The thermometer had dropped to minus ten degrees Centigrade. Even the inside surfaces of her bedroom windowpanes were coated with ice.

Her doctor's records showed that Enid was 67 years old and had suffered with angina, a potentially fatal heart condition. Despite her doctor's advice, she did not keep herself warm and avoid violent exertions. She was of the generation that considered that self-denial, frugal food, plenty of fresh air and hard work never did anyone any harm. She refused any form of charity or public assistance, supplemented her meagre pension by doing a part-time job as a waitress in a local café and was a devout, regular church attendee.

When her mother became a widow many years earlier, Enid gave up a good, steady job as a bookkeeper in the City of London and devoted herself to caring for her bedridden, invalid, ungrateful mother. Nevertheless, when her mother died, Enid was heartbroken. She never married and continued to live in her late mother's house until her own untimely, tragic death. Her lonely, unhappy, impoverished life was made endurable by her deep religious faith and devotion. She felt that the simple, dark-stained oak wooden cross fixed to the wall over the head of her bed and the small brass crucifix, which she wore at all times on a chain around her neck, were assurance and consolation enough for her deprived life on this earth.

Every night before going to sleep she would read a passage or two from her bible and say a prayer whilst kneeling at the side of her bed. Having thus prayed, she felt relaxed and slept peacefully. However, this was not destined to be so on the night of her tragic death.

Having read her bible passage and said her prayers, she slid under the blankets with a hot water bottle, one of the few luxuries she allowed herself when the weather was exceptionally cold. In next to no time she fell into a deep sleep that was suddenly and violently broken in the middle of the night by screeching, squawking and the fluttering of wings. Ornaments were knocked over and broken. She had been dreaming, or rather having nightmares, about Hell and the Devil in which she was being accused of having sex with a handsome young curate on the church's altar. Still half asleep, her nightmare continued into reality when she perceived in the gloom, the vague shape of a winged creature, screeching and squawking on the rail at the foot of her Victorian, iron bedstead.

In her confused state of mind, she took the creature to be one of the Devil's demons sent to punish her. She wanted to deny accusations about her having sex with the curate but found that her voice box was paralysed. She broke out into a cold sweat and felt a searing pain in her chest and down her left arm. This she accepted as being just punishment for profaning the sanctity of the church's holy altar and for the sinful sex with the young curate. She clutched the brass crucifix that hung around her neck, stared at the horrid looking and dreadful sounding Devil's servant and died.

The creature that she saw at the foot of her bed was actually a parrot that had escaped from its home a few doors away and eluded capture during daylight hours. When the night turned very cold, it sought shelter and warmth by fluttering in through Enid's wide-open bedroom window. By the eerie light of the bright moon it perceived a human form lying on the

509

bed and sensed the warmth of the hot water bottle. It was a spoilt pet and demanded attention, fuss and food from the human being lying on the bed and did so in the only way it knew, by squawking and shrieking and repeating its best remembered phrase which it had learnt from its owner's cricket loving boyfriend, 'Another one for Len Hutton'.

When Enid heard this she thought that the Devil's messenger was noting her for a particular tormentor in Hell. Poor Enid was not a cricket enthusiast and did not know who Len Hutton was. She regarded all forms of public entertainment as the Devil's work for idle people. The parrot continued to demand attention until cold and hunger finally overcame it and it collapsed near the cold feet of Enid's corpse. A sad fate for both Enid and the parrot.

After the doctor had pronounced Enid as being dead, two policemen waited in the house for local undertakers to remove the body to a mortuary. Whilst waiting, they closed Enid's bedroom window and in order to warm the house a little, lit the gas oven and left the oven door open to allow the heat to circulate around the house. One of the policemen decided that out of respect for the dead, he would remove the parrot from the bed, but as he did so and as a prank he placed it in the warm oven saying that he would serve it up at Christmas instead of a turkey. Both policemen were startled when a short while after a bewildered and angry parrot flew out of the oven shrieking and squawking and flapping about. It finally settled once again on the rail at the foot of Enid's bed shouting, 'Another one for Len Hutton'.

When Kate Nazip, a close neighbour, heard that a parrot had been found in Enid's house, she recognised it as her own, which had escaped from her house a few days previously. Both she and her boyfriend, Stuart, who was a cricket enthusiast, were overjoyed to have the parrot back as they both loved it very much. They both fussed over it and laughed until tears ran down their cheeks when it loudly and clearly kept repeating, 'Another one for Len Hutton'.

The Elderly Couple

Most motorists, especially so the male of the species, are eccentric creatures of which, I suppose, I am one.

During their lifetime, most motorists spend more on buying their cars than they do on acquiring their homes. When buying a car, perhaps every two to five years, they unstintingly spend thousands of pounds and quite often the purchase price of the car is at least half of their annual net salary! Extra luxury fittings can also add many hundred of pounds to the acquisition cost. Many harassed wives go to work just in order to help to support this financial caprice.

In addition, the motorist has to pay heavy insurance premiums, road tax, fuel purchases and maintenance charges. In ever increasing numbers, the motorist spends this enormous outlay without much thought or reluctance. A lot of time and energy is spent in proudly cleaning and polishing the vehicle in order to maintain its pristine appearance, but to impress whom?

In sharp contrast motorists display a completely different attitude when it comes to paying a paltry sum for the privilege of parking their pride and joy on a public highway or in a car park. I've noticed owners of very expensive cars parking illegally in order to avoid paying a modest sum at a parking meter. They become most annoyed if they get a parking ticket for such unsocial behaviour. I suppose the reason for such meanness in paying a parking fee is the thought that through general taxation, purchase tax, value added tax, road tax and local council rates the motorist reckons, even sub-consciously, that he has paid for the highway or car park and that it is an imposition for him (or her) to have to pay just for parking on what they have already paid for!

511

The Elderly Couple

In truth, I must confess that I belong to this specie of motorist. Whenever I can, I try to avoid paying to park at kerbside parking meters or in a car park. I too, take chances in order to avoid such payments even though my second-hand, or more likely, fourth-hand, car does not come within the price bracket of most of my neighbours. Also, now that I am retired, my annual mileage is extremely low, unbelievably low. In fact, I am tempted to wind my odometer on a bit when I resell my cars because otherwise, potential buyers suspect that because of the low recorded mileage, I have wound the clock back.

Most of my journeys nowadays are down to the local supermarket, to the doctor or to the pharmacist. Actually, it was one day when I went to get a prescription dispensed that I became involved in an unfortunate incident.

Not far from the local pharmacist's shop I know of a spot where I can legally park without feeding a parking meter. It is situated in a short stretch of road in between two batches of parking meter bays. This short stretch of road does not have parking restrictions because the adjacent pavement has a crossover leading to a detached garage.

One day, I noticed that a local shopkeeper was using the garage as a storeroom for his stock. I asked him if he would object if I parked my car there whilst I did some local shopping including in his own shop. He said that he would not mind at all because he did not himself use the garage for vehicles. I confirmed with a traffic warden that I would not be parking illegally because there was not a yellow line along that short stretch of gutter between the two batches of parking bays.

I often found this free parking space most useful and very rarely occupied by other motorists. Even if I had wanted to use one of the parking bays, they were rarely vacant.

One day, when I took my wife down to the local shops, I neatly parked in what I had begun to regard as my own private parking place. I noticed that all the adjacent parking bays were occupied and congratulated myself on my local knowledge. We had not been gone for long when we returned to our car. As we approached we saw an elderly couple taking details of our car as though something was amiss. As soon as they confirmed that I was the owner/driver of the car, they informed me that they were taking details because when I had parked in what they described as an illegal manner, I had reversed and broken their front licence number plate.

They showed me a broken number plate and told me that a young man had seen me cause the damage and that I had not, in accordance with the law, exchanged details or left my name and address under their windscreen wiper.

He said he would regret getting me into trouble but he would have to do something because they could ill-afford to pay £20 for a new number plate or alternatively lose their no-claim insurance bonus. I was quite confused as I was sure that I had not caused the damage but I was scared that even so, if he produced the young man who he claimed had seen the incident, I would be in difficulty.

The elderly couple looked so distressed and pathetic that even though I was sure that I had not caused the damage, I felt sorry for them. Visions of having to complete piles of forms for the police and insurance company filled my head. I decided that in order to avoid such unnecessary trouble and because I felt sorry for the pathetic old couple, I told them that even though I did not accept responsibility, I would pay them £10 on the spot provided they withdrew their allegation. They readily agreed to this proposal and I was glad to drive away, especially so as it was cold and it had started to drizzle and I was not wearing a coat. The elderly couple were overwhelmingly grateful. I noted that their dark blue Ford saloon car with an 'A' registration, making it about 16 years old, even older than my own car, was in impeccable condition, highly polished and obviously their pride and joy.

Upon reflection I considered that under the circumstances I had acted sensibly and honourably, even Dora agreed!

A few days later, I had need to visit the local shops again and when I approached my "private" parking space I noticed that it was already occupied and the driver was exchanging details with, to my amazement, the same elderly couple. I first thought, what a coincidence, but a certain suspicion crept into my mind. My suspicion was confirmed when on two subsequent occasions there were the pathetic looking couple exchanging details with embarrassed motorists who had had the temerity to park in our "private" parking space!

I often wondered if I had been the elderly couple's first victim, I certainly was not their last. I thought that they had deserved my £10 even if only for their wonderful acting.

Friday Night

I thought that it was very much out of character for Lenny Schneider, who nowadays likes to be known as Leon Taylor, to have tried to commit suicide.

The whole episode was wrapped in secrecy. In fact, it was not until someone passed the rumour onto us that we became aware of the event at all. When we, that is my dear, beloved wife, Dora, and myself phoned the family to express our sympathy and to enquire as to Leon's condition, we were firmly but politely given vague and evasive replies. Our suggestion that we would like to visit him was also avoided and we were told that at present he was not in a suitable condition to receive visitors. Our inform- ant said that he received his information from someone who had read a report in a local newspaper, which did not actually say that he had tried to commit suicide, but the inference was clearly there. The report said that a man known as Leon Taylor had been found badly injured in his pyjamas on a concrete path in the early hours of the morning at the approach to a block of council flats in Stoke Newington, North London.

It appeared that he had either fallen or jumped from a first floor win- dow, which was still fully open. The caretaker who phoned for an ambu- lance discovered the injured man. The caretaker said that the injured man was not a resident in the flat concerned. The report, along with the evasive behaviour of his relatives, made us think that perhaps he had tried to end his life but we could not think of any possible reason. As the saying goes, no smoke without fire.

Leon was a happy-go-lucky, successful street trader. He was happily married and was proud of his two children who were both doing very well at university. He had a lovely bungalow in Ilford, not far from where we live.

Although he was an extrovert, he was also serious and in recent years had become increasingly religious. He said his morning prayers before breakfast every day and he looked forward to attending synagogue services every Sabbath eve on Fridays and Sabbath morning services on Saturdays. He especially loved attending these services with his father-in-law who lived in Stoke Newington. These were special to him because they were held in a shteibel, which is a private home and where the congregants are ultra-orthodox Jews. Leon just simply loved the special atmosphere and the devotion and piety of the participants, which he felt lacking in the more traditional, larger synagogues. He told us that he felt transcended to another world whilst he was at one of these shteibel services.

Because travelling by any means of transport is forbidden in the ultra-orthodox Jewish religion, he arrived at his in-laws' flat, usually once a month, on Friday afternoon, before the Jewish Sabbath, which commences at sundown, and stayed the night there, along with his wife. On the following morning, he would rise early and accompany his father-in-law to a local shteibel.

About the only points of dispute between Leon and his wife were his incurable smoking habit and his love of classical music. She would not allow him to smoke his pipe indoors nor to listen to his classical gramophone records unless he listened to them through earphones so that no one else could hear them.

Whereas Leon's wife was a sound sleeper and snored a lot in her deep slumber, he was a very light sleeper and often had his sleep disturbed by his wife's nocturnal cacophony.

He only needed a few hours sleep each night and he got into the habit, in all seasons, to slip out of his bungalow's bedroom window without switching on the light and to creep into his garden shed where he would while away a few hours smoking his pipe to his heart's content and listening to his beloved classical records. He would then slip back into bed without his wife being aware of his harmless night's activity, although it was no secret.

Many months later, when Leon had fully recovered from his multiple fractures we did eventually meet him and rather cautiously approached the delicate subject as to how he had sustained his serious injuries. He told us that both he and his family at first felt so foolish and embarrassed about the cause that they did not like to discuss it. He confessed that one hot and humid night when he was staying in his in-laws' first-floor flat, his wife's snoring and snorting woke him up and he could not get back to sleep. He decided that in order to overcome his discomfort he would, as he so often does, slip out and have a good smoke and an earful of music.

He then looked at us sheepishly and said, 'In my confused state, I forgot it was Friday night and that I was not at home in my bungalow.'

Cars

In a few months' time, I will have been the proud holder of a full British driving licence for 50 years with not a single blemish on it, ever. No endorsements not even a single parking offence. There can't be many people today who can make a similar claim.

I must, however, confess that during the last 50 years, including the period during which I held a learner's licence, I did have a few minor accidents, but in each case my insurance company accepted the fact that I was not at fault.

During the last 50 years I've seen a lot of changes in motoring and motors. When I started driving there were far fewer vehicles on the road and motorists were much more courteous to one another and to pedestrians. There were no motorways but there were a few of what were called arterial roads on which there were no speed limits. There were no yellow lines, no parking meters and few one-way streets. If you wanted to visit a particular building, you simply pulled up outside and went in.

Motoring was so much simpler, more convenient and more pleasant. Petrol was cheap, even as a newly married student architect earning only five pounds a week I was able to buy petrol without great hardship. Petrol pumps were not automatic as they are today but were operated by attendants who expected a tip for operating the pump for you and for wiping your windscreen.

There were of course disadvantages. In 1948, when I began motoring, just two years after the end of World War II, new cars were not available to the general public. After six years devoted to war production, factories were slow in changing to civilian work and the few cars produced went either for export or to VIPs and you had to be very important to be so privileged.

This state of affairs persisted for many years after the war. Nearly every car on the road was a vintage model that had been laid up in its owner's garage during the six-year-long war. When they were put back on the road, they often over-heated or otherwise broke down. Flat, worn-out tyres were commonplace. There was no MOT test in those days.

The adventure of taking one of these clapped out jalopies on the road was one of the pleasures for the fortunate few who owned them.

It was during such a period that I bought my first car, an original Austin 7 tourer, registration number, MT 5576. How I managed to run such a car for about six months without injuring myself or any passenger or pedestrian I shall never know. Just to start the engine involved the dangerous procedure of cranking the engine with the small fixed starting handle at the front of the car. After many arduous turns the engine would suddenly spurt into action by violently turning the starting handle back against the starter's arm. If you were not quick in withdrawing your arm, you ended up with a badly bruised or broken forearm and that was just for starting the car!

Stopping the car was another hazard because once having got the car moving it was very difficult to stop it, as the brakes were mostly ineffective. There were no mechanical or electrical indicators so all signals had to be by hand and in the winter such signals resulted in frozen fingers. Each driver had his own idea for signalling so in many cases it was difficult to know if the driver in front intended to turn left or right or whether he intended to slow down. It is strange to think now that there were virtually no female drivers. Women were not considered capable of driving such contraptions. Any such vehicle surviving today is a much sought after vintage motor.

Being a bit of a nervous disposition, or in other words, an unmitigated coward, I soon disposed of my Austin 7 and in lieu bought myself a brand new Ford, 5 cwt., Thames van. This was achieved as a close neighbour worked for a Ford main dealer and through his influence I was permitted to buy a commercial vehicle, which were more readily available than new private cars. There was an additional advantage to such a vehicle inasmuch as it was not subject to purchase tax and was therefore much cheaper than a private car. My good neighbour then again used his influence to persuade his garage to cut windows in the sides of the van and to fix passenger seats onto the floor. The rear passenger seats were not very comfortable but they were better than none. So this all goes to show just how advantageous it is to have an influential neighbour.

Many were the envious glances when I drove the vehicle through the largely car-less streets of east London. The government, who is always one step behind tax avoiders, soon stopped the dodge of converting a non-purchase taxed commercial vehicle into a passenger car.

I ran this vehicle for five happy years and then, because of the imposition of purchase tax and the rapidly rising prices of new cars, I was able to resell the vehicle for about the same price as I paid for it five years previously. The man who bought it from me was so pleased that we became firm friends until he died a few years later.

My next vehicle was a third or fourth hand luxury Rover saloon car with a long bonnet and two musical silver horns on the front. It was a beauty of a car and I am sorry even today to have parted with it. It was a very prestigious-looking car, the type used by VIPs, including government ministers. In fact, one day when I was parked near the local Conservative office building waiting for Dora to return with some shopping, a distinguished looking man opened the rear door of the car and sat down. I asked who he thought he was and he told me that he was some Minister of the Crown and had mistaken my car for his own official vehicle, which was waiting for him a short distance away.

Those were the days when cars were so comparatively few that the sprucely uniformed AA patrol officers smartly saluted members who displayed the AA badge. Because my car looked so important and because I kept it immaculately polished, I got extra smart salutes. Little did those AA patrol officers know that I was just a junior assistant in the east London, Poplar Town Hall architects' department.

With the passing of time, I do not remember when or why I sold the vehicle or what my next vehicle was but I do know that after my very pleasant experience with that car, several of my succeeding cars were also made by Rover until their standards rapidly deteriorated.

In the 1960s, when I had established myself as an architect in my own practice, I was advised by my accountant to buy a new car every two years in order to claim tax relief on the loss of the value when reselling. This was sound advice in principle but difficult for me to achieve in practice. I always kept my cars in immaculate condition with a low mileage, so when I came to sell my cars, these factors combined with the fact that new car prices had risen rapidly meant that I made very little loss. This infuriated my accountant who considered that I was hopeless.

Except for two instances, other than the one I have already described, I can't remember whom I sold my cars to. Most likely they were sold to dealers in part exchange.

One of the two outstanding cases that I do remember was a Welshman. It was at the time of the Suez oil crisis when the sale of used cars and also new cars came to a virtual standstill. This was because very little petroleum was being imported into this country of the crisis, and as a consequence the Government imposed severe petrol rationing. Only those considered to be on essential work were allowed a petrol ration. At the time, I was the architect for a factory producing precision instruments for the Ministry of Defence and it was necessary for me to make weekly site visits. Because this was considered essential work I was allocated a petrol ration.

This was all very well but because of the difficulty in selling new cars, my regular car dealer informed me that a new car that I had not anticipated receiving for several more months, was now available immediately. I could not refuse delivery because in the past the dealer had been very helpful in enabling me to get new cars without an undue waiting time. I did not mind having the new car but because of the sale difficulty, he did not want to take my existing car in part exchange. I did not need nor did I want to be the owner of two cars at the same time. I advertised my car widely and normally it would have been snapped up but on this occasion there was not a single response. I knew that the longer I kept the car the more the price would deteriorate and also I would have to continue with the overheads, such as the road tax and car insurance.

When I discussed this with my handyman, he asked why I was advertising my car in magazines and newspapers where hundreds of other people were advertising. He said I should advertise in a magazine that did not normally display adverts of cars of that quality. He suggested that I advertise in the "Exchange and Mart" magazine. I thought that I would be wasting my time and money if I did so, but as I was desperate I did place an advert in that magazine. To my utter surprise I received a response the very next day after the advert appeared.

Early in the morning I had a phone call, the speaker had a strong Welsh accent and he asked if he could come and see the car. He confirmed that he came from Wales. I asked him when he expected to arrive and he said in half an hour. I was immediately suspicious. I knew he could not possibly get from Wales to Ilford in Essex in half an hour even if he came by jet plane. It crossed my mind that I was being subjected to a practical joke but as I was so desperate to sell the car, I took the chance and asked him how he intended to get to London in just half an hour. He told me that he did not need to get to London as he was already here and actually he was in a guesthouse in Ilford not far from my home.

He duly came and brought his wife and two children with him. He said that he had travelled up from Wales the previous day and wanted to make a quick purchase in order to get back to Wales before it got dark. He said he was a builder and lived in a small village and urgently needed a reliable vehicle such as mine for his family use. I invited him to inspect and test drive the car but he said it would not be necessary, as he had seen it in the driveway when he came in. He produced a chequebook and wrote out a cheque for the full asking price. I told him that I could not part with the car without first getting the cheque cleared. He said that he must have the car to return to Wales because he and his family came up on a one-way ticket only.

Two thoughts crossed my mind. Either this was a crude attempt to obtain the car by deception, or it was a very elaborate joke. To balance either of these events was my desperation to sell the car. I knew of at least one person who would go to such lengths to get his revenge for a practical joke I played on him and I would hate him to succeed. If it was a genuine sale, I did not want to lose the opportunity. I looked at the cheque again and noticed that the signature was William Smith, a most unlikely name for a Welshman. I was just about going to say, 'Okay, joke's over, who put you up to this?' when my dear lady wife, Dora, asked if he had any proof of identity.

Unfortunately, he had none that was acceptable but said, 'Why don't you phone my bank manager, he will vouch for me.'

He gave me his bank manger's name and phone number. I went into the next room and on an extension asked telephone directory enquiries to give me the phone number of the bank. The number was the same as Mr. Smith had given me. Now, some doubt began to evaporate. I phoned the given number and asked for the name of the manager, which tallied with that given by my potential buyer. I thought that either this was a most elaborate set-up or I was in luck. I was put through to the manager and I asked him some questions about Mr. Smith but another problem arose. The man who claimed to be the manager of that particular branch said that he could not possibly discuss details of one of his clients with a stranger especially so over the phone.

When I told Mr. Smith, he said, 'Let me have a word with the manager.' After a short conversation, he persuaded the bank manager to give me the necessary information which in essence was if the car is as good as Mr. Smith's cheque then he had a very good purchase.

Oh, what a relief to hear such comforting words. I agreed that Mr Smith may drive my car away and I told him that I would send the logbook on by registered post as soon as his cheque was cleared. In order to clear up the final doubt in my mind, I asked him why he was so keen and so sure that my car was okay and why he did not buy one nearer home. He said he would not buy a car that had been used in Wales because the salt they used on their roads in icy weather rotted the chasses of cars and as he found out that I was a professional man, he relied on my honesty. The cheque was cleared quickly and I despatched the logbook as I had promised.

The other sale that has remained clear in my memory was of a lovely, metallic red, Mercedes 250 CE coupe car. I put it up for sale because my accountant said I would be silly if I did not. I now wish that I had ignored his advice.

I advertised it in one of the motoring magazines and immediately I had a phone call from a doctor in Surrey who said it was just the car he had been looking for for ages and could he come straight away and see it. He said he would be coming by public transport and asked me to promise not to sell the car to anyone else before he arrived. As soon as he saw the car he agreed to have it at the advertised price. I told him that I could not let him drive the car away until his cheque was cleared. He said there was no need for that. He took the full asking price in five pound notes out of a plastic carrier bag he was holding and placed them in neat bundles on the dining table.

Reluctant Payers

During the 33 years I was in general practice as a self-employed architect, I was commissioned by many clients on a wide variety of projects. Not only did the projects vary but also did the clients, several of whom became, and remained, friends.

Architects are not allowed to advertise themselves and so they have to rely largely on the recommendations of satisfied clients. I'm pleased to say that on this basis I was never short of work during the whole of my professional career. However, there were two unfortunate exceptions who I discovered late in the day were what I termed professional non-payers. They did not pay any obligation as a point of principle even when extremely satisfied with goods or services received. They only paid up when they were forced to do so through legal means, which many find inexpedient to resort to, and even then they only agree to pay virtually on the Court's doorstep. I presume they find this policy to be profitable.

For professional reasons, even though I am now retired and these incidents occurred many years ago, I will not refer to these culprits by their real names but will call the first recalcitrant, Mr. Aybury and the second, Mr. Becroft.

Mr. Aybury phoned me one day and said that he had been recommended to me by a mutual acquaintance, Mr. Seebag, an electrical subcontractor whom I had used several times very satisfactorily on various contracts. He said that he had acquired an old house on a prime site overlooking a picturesque village green. He wanted me to design a new residence on the site for his own occupation and money was not to be any impediment to his desires.

He willingly signed the Royal Institute of British Architects' standard form of contract for employment of an architect. He did not quibble at any of the conditions or the fees to be paid which were to be based on a percentage of the building costs.

He outlined his requirements and showed me photos and drawings of antique works of art and statuary, which he wanted me to incorporate in not only the design of the house but also in the garden. He was very pleased with my proposals, which I then submitted for Town Planning and Building Regulations approval and which I obtained.

He said that he would not need my services to supervise the construction because he had a friend who was a high-class builder and who would be carrying out the work for him. I duly submitted my account but got no response despite several polite reminders. Eventually, I realised that he was not prepared to pay and I referred the matter to my Professional Indemnity insurers whose policy included for legal action to recover unpaid fees.

There was a lot of correspondence between my insurers' solicitors and my client's solicitor but eventually and quite unexpectedly I was paid in full, in cash, which arrived by registered post.

When I was next in contact with Mr. Seebag, he was very surprised that I had received my fee. I asked him if he was aware that Mr. Aybury was a bad payer. When he replied in the affirmative, I asked why he had recommended him to me. He said that he did not know anyone else who would be able to satisfy him and he was scared not to make a recommendation. He explained that his fear was based on the knowledge that Mr. Aybury was a top member of a notoriously violent gang of villains.

My other unfortunate encounter with a reluctant payer was with Mr. Becroft, who was a furniture manufacturer. In the 1950s there was a huge demand for new furniture following the many years of non-production during the war and the restricted post-war manufacturing. As a consequence, his business was prospering and he urgently needed to extend his factory in the east London borough of Shoreditch, the then centre of the furniture industry in this country.

It was the local council's Town Planning policy to discourage manufacturing in the borough and they refused to grant him planning permission to extend his factory but in collaboration with the government offered him a vacant site on one of the industrial estates being established on the eastern outskirts of London.

At that time, I was acting as the architect for several other furniture-manufacturing firms who were likewise being relocated and possibly he came to know of my association with the trade. As far as I can remember, I was not recommended to him by any of my acquaintances.

He willingly signed the RIBA's standard form of contract to employ an architect and I handed him a copy of the RIBA's booklet that described the minimum fees payable under the contract.

Before getting down to work, he took me in his Rolls Royce car to view a nearly completed factory an acquaintance of his was having built under the council's relocation scheme. He told me how much a square foot it was being built for and instructed me to design a factory that would not cost more and would be up to the same standard of construction. He was astounded when I informed him that the cost of his acquaintance's factory was some 30% more than a factory I had recently had constructed on a nearby site, and that I would never consent to being associated with such a deplorable standard of work.

He asked me what was wrong, as I had only had a quick glance at the construction. I pointed out that the steel stanchions were not vertical and which could easily be verified by lining a row of stanchions through. A minimum of at least 75mm out of vertical could be noticed. I also pointed out that the concrete floor slabs were tilting and in places were 50mm above or below adjoining slabs and the concrete floors had no dust-proof finishings. In addition to other obvious defects and omissions I pointed out that the factory had no office or toilet accommodation and that the front gable wall was not buttressed. This last observation was proved to be only too true when the wall was blown over soon after. Fortunately, no one was on site at the time. I told him that I would no doubt find a lot more wrong if I had the time but I did not wish to get involved in criticising another architect's project.

Mr. Becroft told me that no architect was involved. The project had been undertaken on what is known as a 'Design and Build' basis. The firm supplies the site, the design and supervises the construction for a simple fixed sum agreed in advance.

I proceeded with Mr. Becroft's instructions and obtained Town Planning and Building Regulations approval. A quantity surveyor prepared detailed Bills of Quantities, which, in conjunction with my plans were used to obtain competitive tenders from six well-established building contractors, each of which had a good reputation. I presented the lowest tender to the client for his acceptance and upon which I was ready to prepare contract documents. The tender figure was indeed much lower than that which his acquaintance had paid for his deplorable factory.

I was shocked when Mr. Becroft told me that he did not intend to employ the firm who had submitted the lowest tender but he was going to employ a friend of his who was not among those who had submitted competitive tenders but who was prepared to carry out the works at 10% below the lowest figure tendered. I told the client that he was honour bound to accept the lowest competitive tender. He adopted a bullying attitude and told me to do as he instructed and to prepare the necessary contract documents and to do so speedily because his friend was all ready to commence work on the site the following Monday morning. I told him that I could not be a party to such an arrangement and that I was resigning as the architect immediately. He replied, that in that case I could whistle for my fees. His actions and attitude enraged me and I decided to take immediate action.

Fortunately, I knew where every copy of my drawings and the Bills of Quantities were. I quickly collected all these in and then told Mr. Becroft that they would not be issued to his builder until my fee was paid in full. I apologised to the six competitive tenderers for unwittingly having used them in such a deplorable manner and told them that as a protest, I had resigned as the architect.

Mr. Becroft blustered, threatened and raged but eventually paid as requested in full by a banker's draft.

It was soon after this episode that I heard of another reason why Mr. Becroft had paid up. He was involved in another, much more serious matter. Apparently, it was his practice, once a week, to send a van full of furniture up north to the Midlands. The driver would drop off items at certain shops en-route and then return back to the factory when he had completed his deliveries.

On one such journey, when he had nearly finished, the few undelivered items on the van were stolen whilst the driver was having a snack in a nearby café. Mr. Becroft was furious and bullied the driver into making a false declaration that the van was fully laden when the contents were stolen. He provided the driver with false documents to substantiate the claim. Mr. Becroft obtained compensation from his insurance company based on the driver's assertion and the false papers. All went well for a short while until the driver, who was a religious man, driven by a feeling of guilt, made a confession to the police. As a result, Mr. Becroft was charged and stood trial in the High Court.

He was found guilty on all charges and sentenced to four years in prison but the sentence was suspended because of an emotional appeal by his defending barrister and because of his declared ill health.

Ahh, such is life!

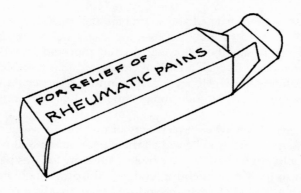

Medical Aid

By nature, both my wife and myself are of a charitable nature. We donate to charities generously according to our means, which because we are now old age pensioners, is not very great. We are happy in the knowledge that despite our modest income we are still able to contribute to worthy causes.

Despite our charitable nature, we resent the practice of door-to-door collections and street collections, which we feel are intended to embarrass people into donating. Some of these collections are in aid of some obscure, unknown charity and others are for well known, well-advertised, over-subscribed, enormous organisations whose main activity appears to be promoting propaganda in order to raise even more money for their inflated balance sheets. The only practical application for their activities appears to be to make even more propaganda to raise even more money, a large proportion of which goes to paying a large professional staff in a central London office building.

Our instinct is to support small charities, some not even registered, run by a small number of enthusiastic, unpaid volunteers who work energetically for their cause and which is often in aid of animal welfare. They give unselfishly of their time and own meagre resources with full heartiness. They use their own homes as their offices and premises and most of their expenditure is paid out of their own limited incomes. They have no time for propaganda or making street or door-to-door collections.

Apart from our own modest financial contributions we also give invaluable practical help and advice based on many years experience in running a charity of our own. We help these small charities to raise funds by assisting them and advising them on organising jumble sales, bric-a-brac stalls at festival events, bring and buy sales, garden parties, garage sales, charity shops, plant sales, book fairs and collection of used postage stamps etc.

These events bring in much needed funds but need careful organising to ensure that there are adequate volunteers for the day, appropriate transport of goods and personnel, payment of rentals, public liability insurance and preparation of posters and banners, circulars and advertisements.

Collection of bric-a-brac has to be organised well in advance. Our spare room is more often than not choc-a-block with all sorts of saleable oddments brought to us all the year round. We hand these items out as required to various charities to augment their own collections.

We also collect knitting wool for an enthusiastic, not so young, group of women who knit garments for refugee babies and children. Their knitwear is a work of art and very much appreciated by the recipients.

Some while ago, we heard of a group who were collecting unused and surplus medicines to be sent to the former Soviet Union where modern drugs are almost unobtainable, and if they are available, are sold by the Mafia on the black market at enormously inflated prices.

Through our many contacts, we put out an appeal for people to let us have any unwanted drugs etc. that they had stored away in the backs of cupboards and drawers and for which they no longer had any use.

It was not long before supplies came flooding in. All sorts of medical items arrived; pills, tablets, capsules, sprays, linctuses, lotions, ointments, ampoules, creams or all sorts, sizes and quantities. There were also spectacles, hearing aids, false teeth, plasters, lint and bandages. There was enough to fill a chemist's shop.

When we examined the items, some had the labels removed so that the contents could not be easily identified, some were years beyond the use-by date, some had not even been opened and there were several unopened containers in the same person's name. They had obviously been obtaining repeat prescriptions when they did not really require them. Anything for nothing! Normally this is just a sheer waste, but in this instance, most useful.

Where labels had not been removed, we obliterated the person's name for confidentiality's sake but kept the other details intact. We also examined the contents of jars of ointment to see whether they were dried out and therefore useless. We also tested tubes of cream to see if any were dried out and therefore not worthwhile passing on to the charity concerned.

It was when I opened a packet purporting to contain a tube of anti-inflammatory painkiller gel for rheumatic relief, that instead of a tube of gel, I found five, tightly rolled up ten pound notes. Presumably, someone, possibly an elderly person who had since died, hid away their savings without informing their next of kin. We had no idea who the packet had come from as the label had been removed and there was no other identification. Eventually we passed the money to the group who were organising the despatch of the medicines to help defray the costs.

If, after reading this story, there is someone who thinks that they were, or knows someone who was, the donor of the packet of money and wish to claim it as being an inadvertent donation, they will have to provide a vital piece of evidence that has not been revealed in this story but is an essential missing link.

In any case, it's only a story.

The Piccadilly Office

For some reason or other, best known to themselves, the mandarins in the War Office placed people with defective hearing in a low medical category. As I had lost the hearing in my right ear when I was a child, after five mastoid operations, the medical board who examined me when I was conscripted in January 1942 at the age of 18 years, decided to place me in Medical Grade IV, which in practice meant that I was not fit to serve in any of the armed forces.

The war against Germany in 1942 was going disastrously wrong and so the War Department in Whitehall, London, decided that the only way to reverse the course of events was to second me as an architectural assistant to the District Command, Royal Engineers, NW London. From then on there was quite a noticeable improvement on all war fronts and no doubt it was also a severe psychological blow to the German High Command in Berlin when they got to hear the news. However, the Germans knew that I was in London, and so they carried out intensive and continuous bombing in a vain attempt to eliminate me.

Even though it took me four more years, we eventually defeated the evil Nazi forces and peace was declared.

Having won the war, Great Britain had another problem to overcome, i.e. the tremendous shortage of housing caused by intensive bombing and the deterioration of the remaining housing stock due to six years of neglect when labour and materials were not available for building maintenance. The Government realised that something had to be done urgently to overcome this tremendous problem.

Building materials and skilled labour were in great shortage and one of the methods used to overcome this problem was to employ red-hot technology. One of the solutions was for the War Department to release me from my vital war service so that I could apply my enterprising skills in developing the new technology of pre-fabrication.

As soon as it became known that I was available on the civilian market, I was quickly employed, in March 1946, by a firm of architects situated in Piccadilly, in the heart of London, in developing prefabricated asbestos-sheet-clad housing. This prefabrication was a technological revolution in the building trade. It obviated the need for skilled building labour and the use of traditional building materials such as bricks, timber and tiles. All that was needed on bombed and levelled sites was to lay a 150mm thick concrete slab covered with 18mm of hard mastic to give a dust proof and moisture-tight finish and then to clip prefabricated asbestos cement panels thereupon to form a modern, instant bungalow that did not even need time to dry out, as traditional building materials do.

These homes were never intended to be permanent but even today, after more than 50 years, some are still happily occupied by proud tenants. This proves the old saying that there is nothing so permanent as a temporary expedient.

I was happily employed in this architects' office for about twelve months before deciding to move onto new pastures where more traditional building materials were being employed and the designs were more progressive than pre-war architecture. The architects' offices where the prefabricated bungalows were designed were situated in Piccadilly, London opposite Green Park and conveniently near to Green Park underground station.

The principal architect was no less than a Lord of the Realm and it was through his contacts and personality that a lot of work was introduced into the firm. He was a ruddy faced, rotund, jovial sort of person who entertained clients and potential clients in his luxurious office. He did not engage in the actual design process itself. He had a junior partner who attended to the administrative and financial side of the practice who in appearance and manner was just the opposite of him. It was a case of Lord Nice and Mr. Nasty.

There was a large staff, both clerical and technical. The technical staff was housed in a large drawing office under the direct supervision of the Chief Architectural Assistant who slept most of the day seated on his high stool with his elbows resting on his drawing board and his head cupped in his hands as though in deep contemplation of an intricate technical problem. He was a pleasant and clever chap but you had to wake him up to ask him a question.

In a small office partitioned off from the main drawing office was a person whose duties were obscure to the rest of us, but Mr. Nasty spent a lot of time with him, especial so soon after lunch breaks. We only met this mysterious person when he joined us at tea breaks. He rarely spoke and when he did, he did so with a peculiar nasal lisp.

All the architectural assistants were, with the exception of one middle-aged man, young men who were, like myself, working for a living and studying architecture at evening classes.

Because we were not yet qualified, the pay was not very good and an indication of this was that even though I did my own shoe repairs, I often could not afford to buy the leather to carry out the repairs. Many were the times when I stuffed cardboard into my shoes when the soles were worn right through to my feet in order to prevent my socks being worn out on the concrete paving stones. Even then, I was continually darning my socks to keep up appearances and to keep my feet warm.

As the Chief Architectural Assistant was often asleep at his drawing board, discipline was fairly lax but discreet. One way we used to amuse ourselves was to rub the silver foil caps from milk bottles onto half crown pieces (12.5 pence coins) to form an image of the coin and then to place the worthless images in the gutter in front of the building. We obtained our amusement by watching smartly dressed men on their way to a nearby exclusive gentlemen's club stooping to pick them up. One day, we even saw Lord Nice himself stoop to pick one up.

The architectural practice did not rely on the design of the prefabricated bungalows only. Through Lord Nice's contacts, the office obtained, among others, a contract to design the conversion of multi-storey, terraced houses in nearby Eaton Square, Belgravia, into luxury flats. The houses were enormous and each could easily be converted into six commodious and luxurious flats.

Before any design could commence, each house had to be surveyed and plans drawn to scale. All the houses were vacant, as the occupants had evacuated themselves to their country estates during the London bombing although few bombs fell in that part of London.

The basement floor of one of the houses had at some time been occupied as a Fascist Party headquarters. Nazi posters adorned the walls, inflammatory, racist leaflets were stacked on shelves and there was also a storeroom full of plaster busts of Sir Oswald Mosley, the leader of the Fascist Party. In a drawer we found ledgers listing local sympathisers' names and addresses and their generous donations and subscriptions. There were many titled people among the names listed. A young Welsh boy whose father was a local councillor somewhere in Wales methodically smashed all the plaster busts with a hammer and took the ledgers to his local Labour Party headquarters.

In another of the grand, vacant houses I had a strange and frightening experience. I went along with the middle-aged Architectural Assistant to help him survey one of the houses. On the outside it looked just like any other in the terrace but as soon as we entered we realised that it must have previously been owned by a mentally disturbed person who was obsessed with the creation of optical illusions, which are commonly known by cockneys in the East End of London as Trompe l'oeil.

It was not long before we were completely confused and disorientated. What appeared to be doors were just timber panelling, some doors just opened onto blank brick walls, what were actually doors had the handles on the same side as the hinges, some cupboards were doors to rooms, some windows .were only clever paintings. There were stairs that led nowhere, what appeared to be sloping floors were actually level and mirrors gave false impressions of openings.

On this survey, my task was to measure the distances between windows, the widths of windows, distances from doorways to corners, thickness of walls and height of rooms. Whilst I called out these measurements, the middle-aged Assistant recorded them on paper. When we had completed measuring the periphery of one of the large panelled rooms we went to go out but there was no obvious door. The door by which we had entered was identical to all the timber panels in the room and had no obvious handle or hinges. The Assistant worked out from the plan he had sketched which panel was actually the door but there did not appear to be any means by which to open it. We tried for what seemed like ages to get out without any success. It was getting dark and the electricity was not connected. There was no point in shouting for help as the house was empty as were all the adjoining houses. The street was void of people.

Panic had started to set in because it was late Friday afternoon, the office was due to close down for the weekend and no one would notice our absence until Monday morning and then they would most likely think that we were both away sick and that we would return to work in due course. Neither of us was married and so there was no one to raise the alarm even after a few days. Fortunately, the Assistant remembered reading about a similar situation in a comic in his youth and recalled that the trapped hero found a certain concealed section of the dado rail that could be pressed to release the door. After a short search, we found the release and swiftly left the house with the survey unfinished.

One of the empty houses had a caretaker. She was an elderly servant of the owner who was permitted to stay on to keep an eye on the premises whilst the owner and his family were evacuated to the country. She was the biggest snob I had ever met!

One day, Lord Nice came into the main drawing office during tea break and called the staff together declaring that he would like to hold a consultation meeting. He was very pleasant as usual and asked if anyone had any point to make that would help in the day-to-day running of the office. Everyone was silent, as they could not think of anything. I then ventured to suggest that it would be helpful if office hours could start a half an hour earlier in the morning at 8.30 am and finish half an hour earlier in the afternoon at 5.30 pm. I explained that this would mean travelling on the crowded underground train service would not be such a crush in the morning and in the afternoon, the half hour would give those attending evening classes the opportunity of travelling to the polytechnic and getting some tea in the canteen before classes started at 6.30 pm.

Lord Nice said that such an idea would not suit those who did not travel to work by the underground train service and also those who did not attend evening classes. Nevertheless, he pleasantly thanked me for suggesting such a helpful idea.

A few weeks later, an article appeared in the Royal Institute of British Architects' Journal written by Lord Nice in which he described how his office democratically held regular office meetings during office hours when the staff could discuss with management such things as convenient office hours.

That teatime meeting was the one and only office meeting held during the 12 months I worked there.

The Wedding Guest

About 15 years ago, my wife, Dora and myself received an invitation from an acquaintance to attend the wedding of their daughter. The happy union was to take place in a picturesque village several miles away in Hertfordshire. The girl was marrying a very rich, successful city trader. They were both deeply in love and it all seemed like a dream event.

The ceremony was to be held in a quaint old church that had been the bridegroom's family's church for generations. The reception was being catered for in the grounds of the bridegroom's parents' palatial country mansion. A suitable marquee had been erected for the occasion in case of rainfall and a military band engaged to provide the music. All was to be carried out with great pomp and ceremony. Money was no object.

We were surprised to receive the invitation as we were not very close to the bride's parents and we had in the past made it widely known that we did not care to attend any function of whatever type where there was likely to be more than just few people or a noise. Such gatherings are a torture to me because of my tinnitus. Anyone who is subject to tinnitus will appreciate my dislike of such occasions. Because of what is to me an intolerable noise, I have, in the past, had to leave places rather prematurely.

Normally, I usually refuse such invitations, explain the reason for doing so and in order to show no ill feelings, give an appropriate gift. However, on this occasion we could not refuse to attend because the invitation was not actually addressed to us, but to our sleek, black female cat, Blackie.

On the back of the expensive invitation card was a note saying that if Blackie wished, she might bring us along as her chaperons ('shlaperons', as my dear old mother used to say in her broken English). In a subsequent telephone conversation, the bride's mother explained that they were very superstitious and believed that it was essential to have a black cat and a chimney sweep at a wedding in order to ensure good luck to the married couple.

Chimney sweeps nowadays virtually don't exist but she had arranged for an actor to come along dressed as such. As we were the only people she knew who had a jet-black cat with no white markings whatsoever, she was desperate that we should bring Blackie along to the wedding. If we did not, she would be most disappointed and unhappy.

In the circumstances we, on Blackie's behalf, felt obliged to accept the invitation. As the appointed day dawned, it promised to be lovely and sunny, just right for a garden party reception. In this respect, Blackie had certainly appeared to bring good luck, as up to then the weather had been horrible.

Our next problem was to keep a careful eye on Blackie as on such fine days she had a habit of disappearing into neighbour's gardens and houses for hours at a time. After her morning's toilet, we managed to trap and keep her indoors.

We dressed appropriately as the chaperons of the important wedding guest and put a colourful new collar around Blackie's neck. This naturally caused her to become suspicious and she became really alarmed when we carried her into the car. This was accomplished with great difficulty accompanied by loud yells of protest from Blackie who usually associated rides in the car with unpleasant visits to the vet. When she saw that we were not taking the usual route to the vet, she relaxed somewhat, although remained quite apprehensive.

When we arrived at the church, I remained in the car with Blackie whilst Dora attended the ceremony. It was just as well, as even a solemn church service can be torture for my tinnitus.

The reception was really a wonderful affair. The beautiful, well-nurtured, extensive grounds were a lovely background to the joyous celebration. The military brass band added to the happy atmosphere. The music did not annoy me as most of the time I kept within the house so as to keep an eye on Blackie in order to ensure that she did not stray into the garden and possibly show her prowess in killing a songbird or two in front of the guests.

Once she realised that she was not on her way to visit the vet, she relaxed and started to show off. She rubbed herself against anyone who stopped to exchange greetings with her and rolled over in order to have her belly stroked. She chased imaginary mice around the antique furniture. Children found her most amusing and kept her entertained by throwing paper balls for her to catch and play with. She disregarded the cat food that we brought with us and instead consumed all sorts of food fed to her by the children. Food that she had never before tasted or even knew existed. The more she ate, the more the children gave her. Finally, the inevitable happened. She vomited all the unaccustomed food out onto a lovely genuine Chesterfield couch covered with very expensive embroidered brocade silk upholstery.

Soon after, we took our leave but not before Blackie and the "chimney sweep", together with the happy couple had a group photo taken by the official photographer on the lawn.

We never received a copy of the photo but we still have the wedding invitation. As far as we know, the couple lived happily ever after.

Dan, the Bric-a-Brac Man

For many years before I finally retired, I was a self-employed architect working from home. I had a fully equipped, quiet office in a first-floor room at the rear of my suburban house overlooking a beautiful garden. I had no employer and no employees, and my dear wife, Dora, did my typing. Otherwise, I did everything myself including sticking stamps and sealing envelopes.

I really enjoyed those years and treated my work more as a hobby than as a profession. Not having any overheads was quite a relief. Also I did not have to endure the daily journey to and from work. I carefully kept to regular office hours, 8.30 am to 5.30 pm, with a one-hour break for lunch, five days a week. I was able to get a lot done in those hours because I had few of the interruptions that those who work in larger offices have to endure.

I was also careful not to accept more commissions than I was able to cope with in my self-imposed office hours. However, come 5.30 pm, I welcomed closing my office and taking a 15 minute stroll down to the local newsagent to buy an evening newspaper. I also took the opportunity to pop into the adjacent bric-a-brac shop to browse around his intriguing objects and books for sale.

I had many interest conversations with the shop owner, who was very knowledgeable on every item he had for sale. Everybody knew him just simply as Dan. No one seemed to know his surname or where he lived. Several times he told me about the problems he had both when buying and selling his bric-a-brac. Some of the items he acquired were when people responded to his permanent advert in the local newspaper. He assured me that he always bought at a fair price that was often confirmed by the vendors who informed him that other dealers had offered much less. He believed in paying a fair price and selling at a reasonable profit for a quick turnover. He did not like having the same stock in the shop for a long while. I always found him to be very frank and honest. He said that because there were a number of rogues in the trade, all dealers had a bad reputation, but there were also many naughty "punters" as he called members of the public. He tried to avoid buying goods that he felt were dodgy, that is, not legal.

When youngsters came into the shop and tried to sell him an article of which he was suspicious, he insisted that they returned with a parent to confirm that the item was indeed properly being sold. Very rarely did such youngsters return with an adult.

On one occasion, a young, well-dressed man entered his shop and offered a large silver bowl for sale. He said he was desperate for the money and would accept any reasonable offer. Something did not seem right and Dan said he was not prepared to buy the bowl unless the young man could produce proper evidence of ownership, such as a receipt. The young man hurriedly left the shop but very soon after two policemen entered and demanded to know if Dan had bought a silver bowl from a well-dressed young man. Dan suspected that the young man may have been an "agent provocateur" and said that life was complicated enough without such problems.

He was also annoyed at the number of respectable-looking people who tried shoplifting, quite often silly cheap items, which they could well afford to pay for.

He recalled how, one day, he got an urgent phone call asking if he would be interested in buying an antique double size brass bedstead. The caller explained that she knew that the bed was old because her elderly mother had used it as the matrimonial bed all her married life and that she had inherited it from her mother. As it sounded interesting, Dan took his van and went round to the address soon after. When the vendor showed him into the bedroom he was shocked to see her mother's corpse still lying on the bed. The vendor excused herself explaining that she expected the undertaker to arrive at any moment and if he would be kind enough to wait just a short while he could remove the bed provided a suitable deal could be arranged.

On another occasion, when he arrived at the deceased's home to estimate the value of the contents, the corpse was lying on the floor. The whole house stank horribly because the body had lain there for several days in hot weather whilst the family squabbled about their claimed inheritance and who was to be responsible for arranging the funeral. Dan felt sick for weeks afterwards and kept imagining that he could still smell the stench.

Some of the calls to clear homes were in cases where young couples, sometimes not even married, were splitting up, but many were instances where the sole elderly occupant had either recently died or had been taken into an old people's home. In nearly all cases, the circumstances were sad and it took him a long while to become inured. Despite this, some of the transactions were quite amusing and illuminating.

One day, whilst he was negotiating for a lovely pair of Imari vases he found that the vendor, who was selling them on behalf of her very old mother, knew all about them and the haggling was quite intense. Dan was keen on acquiring the vases because he knew of a collector who would love to have them, but each time he raised the price he was offering, the elderly mother, who was sitting, heavily wrapped up, on an old oak armchair, would say in a high-pitched, piping voice, "not enough". When Dan made his final offer, above which he knew he would not be able to resell the vases at a profit, the old lady piped her usual "not enough", but the daughter said, 'Not this time mother, we've got a good price.' This did not stop her mother from periodically piping, "not enough" even when the weather was being discussed.

A woman who wanted to sell an oak bookcase said that Sotheby's had valued it several years ago at £600. When Dan offered her £40, which was nearer to its true value, she said, 'Can't you make it £45?'

Dan did not like to buy large items of furniture as they cluttered up his modest-sized shop and they were difficult to sell as well as cumbersome to handle. When two elderly sisters offered him a heavy, three-seater couch and two matching armchairs, all he could offer was £30. The sisters said that they would rather burn them than accept such a measly amount. However, three weeks later they phoned to meekly accept the £30, presumably after having approached other traders.

He told me how, several years ago, he hit the "jackpot". He had successfully tendered to clear the house of an elderly lady who had died. It's strange, but in his experience, it was almost always elderly ladies who died, rarely elderly gentlemen! The person arranging the clearance lived far away and was in a hurry to return home. She handed the keys to Dan and made it a condition that everything was to be cleared that same day, including anything in the loft, garden shed and garage. To his absolute surprise and delight he found the garage crammed tight with unopened cartons of expensive luxury goods.

Dan had a parallel experience when he was called to clear the effects of a deceased woman in a Council flat. He was amazed to find that every room was crammed tight with thousands of women's garments of all sorts and sizes and household linen. Most were still in their wrappers. It was difficult to enter any of the rooms because of the goods, even the kitchen and bathroom. He could only assume that the previous occupant had been a kleptomaniac. All means of identifying the origins of the goods had been meticulously removed.

Some vendors have no real intention to sell unless they are offered some fantastic amount and then they suspect that they have an unidentified treasure and consult one of the big, well-known auction houses for a valuation. Their true motive in approaching would-be buyers is to take the opportunity to talk to someone and to unburden their hearts. Whilst they are pathetic, they are terrible time wasters and, as the saying goes, time is money.

One woman spent ages extolling her dear long-departed husband and eulogizing her wonderful children and brilliant grandchildren, none of who appeared to visit her, so she relied on strangers to chat with. She was annoyed when after a while she was reminded that the actual purpose of the visit was to buy some item that she said she had for sale.

Although traders in the second-hand market have, along with car dealers and estate agents, a bad reputation, there are many members of the public who are not beyond a dirty trick or two. Quite early on in his career, Dan found that it was advisable to take away with him any goods that he had agreed to buy. In one house, he agreed to buy a lovely Georgian bookcase, but when he returned a short while later with his van, he found that the bookcase had been substituted with a much inferior Victorian oak case of much lower value. The vendor vehemently claimed that it was the one agreed in the sale.

On another occasion, a lovely Georgian bracket clock by a known London maker had been substituted with a similar sized 1930s oak mantle clock. When this was pointed out to the vendor, he said, 'What's the difference?'

Another, tearful woman, tried to sell Dan a plait of golden coloured hair which she said was that of her dead daughter who died many years ago of pneumonia. Upon close inspection, Dan noticed a small label with the words, "Made in Taiwan".

Once, Dan made the mistake of paying for his purchases before collecting them. He paid cash as he usually does for some nice porcelain figurines and a lovely Turkish carpet. He returned after a while with his van to collect the goods only to be told by the vendor that a man who claimed to be Dan's partner had already collected them. Dan strongly suspected who it was because he had mentioned the deal to a fellow trader who knew that Dan would be delayed in his shop before he could return to collect his purchases.

A woman who tried to sell a pair of brass candlesticks declared that they were over a hundred years old; they had belonged to her grandmother who had brought them out with her when she emigrated here from Tsarist Russia at the end of the Nineteenth Century. When Dan looked under the base, it was marked, "Made in England". This wording was not in use until 1920.

In the 1970s there was a sudden upsurge in the volume of bric-a-brac trading and many who knew little or nothing joined in the bonanza. After a while, as with all such booms, the trade worked itself out and became stagnant. A lot of the traders who rode the crest of the wave departed for other promising pastures.

It is now difficult to make a decent, honest living in the bric-a-brac trade but nevertheless it is most exciting and interesting.

The Piano

When you have lived in the same house as my wife, Dora, and I have for over 45 years; you get to know some of the neighbours, at least on chatting terms. So it was with Mrs. Hudson who lived further up the street. She was a widow and although elderly, still worked as the manageress of a local dry cleaner's shop. She described herself as the manageress although she was the sole employee, but from time to time farmed out small repair and alteration jobs to other local women in order to oblige customers.

It was when we were chatting to her one day that she asked if we would do her a favour. The house that she lived in had been converted, in a crude manner, into two flats. The conversion had been done in the immediate post-war years when rented accommodation in the district was very scarce and the local authority deemed it expedient to ignore such infringements of Town Planning and building byelaw regulations in order that the number of available dwellings in the borough was increased.

She told us that an elderly widow, the sole occupant of the ground floor flat in her house, had died some while ago and the landlord had asked Mrs. Hudson to get the contents cleared out as he had plans to leave the seaside residential home to which he had retired during the war and to return to live out his remaining years in the flat. He told her that he realised that the contents were not worth much as they were old and shabby and he would be glad to receive whatever she could get for them, however little. He promised her a commission for doing so.

She had already contacted a few people who advertised in the local press as house clearers but when they viewed the contents they were not interested unless they were paid to take the items away. However, a local bric-a-brac shopkeeper had promised to view the contents and to give an

542

estimate but because of her commitments at her place of employment, Mrs. Hudson could not take time off and she asked us whether, if she were to let us have the keys to the ground floor flat, we would be kind enough to let the bric-a-brac man in to view the contents. As it was, we knew the person quite well and assured Mrs. Hudson that if anyone was to give her a fair price, it was Stuart, as we had known him for a number of years and had done several deals with him.

Mrs. Hudson then told us that there was a problem. When the house was converted, the ground floor flat was fully furnished and no account was taken to allow large items of furniture to be moved into or out of the flat subsequent to the conversion. The sliding sash front windows had been removed and large, fixed panes of glass were fixed direct to the frames with only small opening sashes to provide a minimum of ventilation. This not only spoilt the appearance of the terraced house but also infringed the building byelaw regulations. Also, in order to provide the flat with its own access door, a small lobby had been formed. The lobby was so small that it was impossible to move large items of furniture such as tables and wardrobes through it. In addition, the doors to the lobby were only 680 mm wide. Mrs. Hudson was concerned that anyone who agreed to clear the contents would not be able to move out the larger items without breaking them up and thus making them more than worthless.

When Stuart, and his wife who was his business partner, turned up, we duly let them into the flat. They said that the contents were worthless except for the grand piano and that such instruments were a specialist item not saleable locally. He said he would have to consult a dealer who specialised in pianos before he could give an estimate. He returned a few days later with such a specialist who identified the piano as being by a well-known maker.

We asked Stuart just how he intended to get the piano out of the flat without costly structural work on the lobby or front window. Without telling us how he was going to achieve it, he promised to clear all the contents of the flat and to pay Mrs. Hudson the sum of £200 in cash.

As he could not give us a precise date or time in which he would do the clearance, we handed him the keys to the flat. Two days later, he returned the keys and handed us the £200 in cash to pass onto Mrs. Hudson. When we checked, the flat had indeed been cleared of all its contents and there were no signs of damage to the entrance lobby or the front window.

It was only after much persistent questioning that Stuart finally revealed the secret. He reminded us that the room in which the grand piano was situated was a through-room, that is, it stretched from the front of the house to the rear. The front of the room had the inaccessible window but the back of the room had a pair of French doors opening directly onto the rear garden. We pointed out that getting the piano into the rear garden would still not have solved the problem. He said, 'Quite right, but it is the first step,' and then went on to explain that the next-door house was occupied by an Irishman who, in return for a bottle of whisky, agreed to let him transfer the piano and other large items across his rear garden into the rear garden of the next house which was vacant and up for sale.

His wife had arranged with the estate agent to view the property and whilst she kept him engaged in conversation at the front, Stuart and the piano dealer swiftly transferred the piano and other large items of furniture across the garden and through the side gate which led directly onto a side street in which they had parked a removal van. Stuart's wife then told the estate agent that the house was not suitable because the side gate made the rear of the premises vulnerable to intruders and that she would not, therefore, feel secure.

Mrs. Hudson never did find out the secret and her landlord did not live long enough to move back into the empty ground floor flat.

The Voice

Sophie was a distant relative on Dora's side of the family; so distant, as to be difficult to define. Although her name was Sophie, she was more commonly known as "The Voice". Even as a young child she had a very loud voice, always louder than any of the other children she played with. Teachers tried without success to get her to speak more quietly. Perhaps she had impaired hearing and did not realise that she was speaking so loudly and had to do so in order to hear herself talk. In those days, when there were 60 or so children in a class, the teachers and social workers had no time to assess such matters even if they did suspect something was wrong.

Because of her loud voice, even as a child she tended to dominate any conversation or activity. School reports repeatedly mentioned that she was noisy and spoke too loudly. She loved to sing, she had a nice voice, she was musical and she sang upon every possible occasion. This was also confirmed in her school reports. She was always selected to sing at school concerts. In her teens she joined her parents' synagogue's choir where she eventually met Hymie, who was to become her husband. He was a fine, professional violinist and also the unpaid choirmaster, a position of great honour in the community. He helped Sophie to train her voice but however much he tried, he could not subdue her forti multo soprano voice.

Rather disconcertingly, her powerful voice dominated the choir and when the choir accompanied the Chazan (the leader of the religious services) her voice also overpowered his. At social gatherings, such as wedding celebrations, her conversation could clearly be heard above the general hubbub of all the other guests and it was for this reason that many came to know her as "The Voice", although not unkindly.

A few years after her marriage, she bore a child, Arnold, who by nature took after his father and was as quiet as his mother was loud and domineering. She fussed over him in all respects and people felt sorry for him because she suppressed any attempt on his part to express individuality. Her constant fussing over every little detail in his dress and behaviour embarrassed onlookers and he, in turn, was embarrassed in front of his peers and strangers.

Suddenly, at about the age of 18 years, Arnold secretly withdrew all his savings, sold all his personal belongings and left home without giving any indication whatsoever of his intentions or whereabouts. Occasionally, he would send his father a picture postcard from the last place he had been simply saying that he was having a good time and that he was in good health. The postcards arrived from all parts of the world. Sophie and her husband were frantic with worry and spent a lot of money employing specialist agencies to trace him in order to implore him to return home. After several years, Arnold was eventually traced to a hippy commune in California where he was living with a male friend as a dropout from society. He absolutely refused to have anything at all to do with his parents but did accept the money that they regularly sent him, without any acknowledgement or thanks.

His father was heartbroken and died, quite a young man, of a massive heart attack. Even though Arnold was notified by telegram in good time, he did not attend the funeral or send any message of condolence.

About a year after her husband's death, Sophie met and married an elderly widower. Before retiring, he had been a very successful clothing manufacturer in Manchester and was reputed to be a multi-millionaire. They lived in a grand mansion with servants and gardeners and rode about in a chauffeured Rolls Royce. He had been a local Mayor and enjoyed a lively social life. People who knew her were pleased at her fortune and to some extent were secretively envious. Along with her husband, she attended social events and whenever the opportunity presented itself, she sang to an appreciative audience. The power of her voice had not diminished with time.

Her new husband was very proud of her but most unfortunately he died within a few years of their marriage. Relatives and friends naturally expected her to inherit a fortune when his Will was read but she received absolutely nothing at all. During his first marriage, which was most unhappy, he had transferred his business to his sons and tied up all his other assets in trusts, so in effect he was penniless despite his opulent lifestyle. Even his mansion and its valuable contents were part of a trust which agreed to allow Sophie to stay as a lifelong, rent-free tenant provided she paid all outgoings on the premises. As Sophie's only income now was her meagre widow's pension, she could not possibly accept this proposition. Because she had effectively become homeless, the local council re-housed her in a flat in a run-down shabby council estate where crime and drug-dealings were rife. The chauffeured Rolls Royce returned to the sons' business from where it had been on loan to her late husband.

Although her voice was still strong, she now had little opportunity or inclination to exercise it. Whenever she did sing, the neighbours did not appreciate it and told her in no uncertain manner to shut up.

After a short period in her impecunious state, she died a lonely and sad death a long way from her family and friends in London. Arnold was promptly informed of his mother's demise but made no effort to attend her funeral or to visit her grave or to arrange for a memorial stone to be erected. As next of kin, he came to England to claim her estate but was bitterly disappointed when he found that it consisted of virtually nothing. He had heard that she had remarried a fabulously wealthy man and expected to inherit a bonanza. He promptly returned to his commune in California.

The family heard no more news from or about him but before leaving, he left a strange message on his mother's kitchen table. On the back of a picture postcard he wrote in capital letters, "THE BEGINNING IS THE END, THE END IS THE BEGINNING, ETERNITY IS INFINITY AND INFINITY IS ETERNITY".

The council employee who cleared the flat of her pitiful belongings threw the postcard along with other odd items into a black plastic refuse bag.

Narrow Escape

Our local London Borough of Redbridge is generally considered to be a relatively law-abiding district, at least in respect of violent crimes. It is therefore somewhat alarming to read in each week's editions of local newspapers of a number of street crimes, several committed in broad daylight. Upon reflection, I suppose that on an average there may be, perhaps about five a week. This may not appear to be a lot, but nevertheless it is quite alarming.

At the average rate of five a week, the street crimes would amount to about 300 a year and over a five year period, this would amount to about 1500 crimes involving 1500 victims! I'm not particularly a physical coward, but I would certainly not wish to be a digit of such statistics. Upon reflection, I consider myself to be fortunate that in my 55 years sojourn in the borough that I have only been involved in two potential, but not actual crime incidents.

One such incident, which occurred about a year ago, was when an old age pensioner approached me in the street and demanded money. He was warmly dressed in a heavy overcoat and wore a hat even though it was a very hot day. He claimed he had a gun but I saw no sign of it. I treated the incident as a joke, which perplexed the elderly man who rapidly walked away. I did not report it to the police as I regarded it as a practical joke. I would have completely forgotten the matter if I had not read later in the local press about an old age pensioner who had been caught with a loaded revolver in an attempted street crime.

The other incident occurred more recently near some local shops. I had agreed to buy an antique chest of drawers from a local dealer and promised to return later in the day with the cash. As the dealer did not know me too well, he insisted on being paid in cash. I went to the bank and withdrew the required sum, which for me was quite a considerable amount.

As I approached the dealer's shop, two young black men passed me. Being aware of the considerable amount of cash on me, I was rather nervous and tensed up. My apprehension was increased as while they were approaching me they exchanged quiet words between themselves and then looked meaningfully in my direction. They were tall, much taller than me and athletic in appearance but they passed me by, one each side of me and all the time looking at me as though sizing up a side of beef hanging in a butcher's window.

I was very relieved when nothing happened and I was able to settle my account in cash with the antique dealer. Never before was I so pleased to part with such a considerable sum of money and not only because I was pleased with my purchase. When the dealer delivered the chest of drawers later in the day, he said that I had just missed a lot of excitement near his shop.

He told me that soon after I had paid him, two young black men had threatened a nearby shopkeeper with a knife and robbed him. I then realised just how near I had possibly been to being another crime statistic In a recent newsletter to local residents, the Council stated that the current population of Redbridge was 231,817 persons of all ages who dwelt in 90,000 households. There were also 2,000 businesses. I'm no statistician but I calculate that based on this population figure, and my estimate of some 300 street crimes a year, the odds of being a victim is 773 to one and the proclaimed chance of winning the National Lottery each week is 14,000,000 to one! Each National Lottery punter dreams of winning the jackpot but few realise they have a much greater chance of being mugged. The chances are possibly even greater because I doubt if all street crimes are reported.

Frost Bite

About 30 years ago, we had a sudden, very cold and snowy snap of winter weather in late December. It was very unexpected because the forecasters had not predicted it. It came, as you may say, "right out of the blue". Well, not exactly out of the blue, because the weather changed during the night. When the temperature fell sharply, it started to snow heavily. By dawn, there was at least 600 mm of crisp, virgin, brilliant white sparkling snow. In some places, the snow had drifted to over a metre deep. The sky had cleared, the sun shone brilliantly and the air had a feeling of mountain purity. It was a picture postcard scene.

Because it was a Sunday morning, there were no people about and the snow lay undisturbed. As the roads had not been cleared, there was no traffic. By mid-morning children appeared and started playing in the street, building snowmen and throwing snowballs at each other. I tried to clear our front path but gave up after a short while because the snow was too deep and a strong wind just blew the snow back into the trough I had started to form.

I remember the day very well because we had our young niece, Katie, staying with us for the weekend. She was about ten years old at the time and was very excited because it was her first time of being away from home on her own. It was quite an adventure for her, especially so, as this was also her first association with such deep, undisturbed snow. It was like a wonderland for her. No doubt, her parents must have been just as anxious as she was excited.

After a hearty breakfast and muffling up well, she ventured out to join the fun with the other children in the street who were having a fantastic time. Even our cat, Taffy (may his soul rest in peace), joined in the fun for a while, trying to catch the snowballs which the children threw for him but soon gave up when he found he kept sinking deep down in the snow with the danger of being buried alive. Our other three cats wisely decided to watch his antics through the lounge window, in the warmth.

After about an hour, Katie came in crying her eyes out. Her right hand had gone completely numb from frostbite. She was hysterical as she sensed that something was seriously wrong. Dora my dear wife, who always acts decisively in such moments of crisis, immediately instructed me to do something about it. She quite rightly said that we could not possibly return Katie home to her parents without a right hand, they would, no doubt, be extremely annoyed.

While I pondered as to what to do, Dora reminded me that I had been a volunteer first-aider/stretcher bearer during the German blitz on the East End of London during the Second World War. I was nearly tempted to retort by saying that the Germans did not bombard us with snowballs and therefore, treating frostbite was not within my wartime experience. Before I could suggest what action to take, Dora said that she would get a bowl of hot water and bathe Katie's frozen hand in it. I then recalled that at some time during my young school days, I had read in an adventure comic how rubbing the affected hand in snow had successfully treated someone with frostbite.

Dora said that I was being stupid but nevertheless agreed to try this remedy when I said that too rapid thawing of Katie's hand might cause permanent damage, just like defrosting meat straight from the deep freeze. Dora yelled that I should carry out the snow remedy but to do so quickly before Katie's right hand fell off. I dashed out into the garden and brought in a plastic bucket full of snow. After about a quarter of an hour of massaging her hand in the snow, the blood circulation returned and she stopped crying. By then, my own hands had become extremely cold but fortunately I did not suffer frostbite.

When it was all over and the atmosphere had reverted to normal calm, Dora said that it was fortunate that Katie had suffered the frostbite in such cold weather. She added, 'Where would we have been able to get a bucket full of snow if she had got frostbite during a heat wave in the summer?' When the cold spell was over, we were able to return Katie to her parents in good health and complete with two hands.

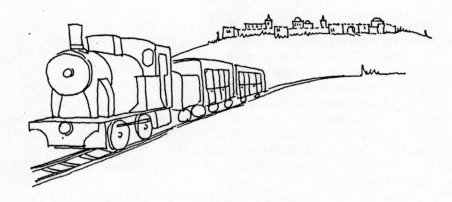

A Train Journey

A most memorable train journey my wife, Dora, and I experienced some 40 years ago during our first visit to Israel was recalled to mind by the recent hot weather, with temperatures up to 28 degrees Centigrade, or reverse the digits, 82 degrees Fahrenheit.

We were staying in Tel-Aviv and were eager to visit Jerusalem. Our host told us that the most picturesque route was by railway, which ran direct from Tel-Aviv to the Holy City. The service consisted of one train, which departed very early in the morning to Jerusalem, and one return journey late in the afternoon.

The alternative was by a slow, crowded, non-air-conditioned bus or by a "Sherut", which is a private taxi, seating seven passengers sharing the fare, but more comfortable and only slightly dearer than the public Egged bus service run by a co-operative company owned by the staff themselves.

When we got to the station well on time, the platform was already crowded. The booking clerk advised us that the Third Class carriages were always very full and as we were tourists, we should book First Class. We accepted his advice, as the difference in cost was minimal.

Our impressions of the station and the waiting train were reminiscent of what we imagined were those of British Mandate times or even the previous Turkish Empire Period. We were amazed when we entered the elegant First Class compartment to find that we were the sole occupants and we were pleased that we had gone to the slight extra cost of such a luxury and privilege.

After much banging of ancient carriage doors in the Third Class compartments and loud hooting and whistling, the train slowly chugged its way towards the Holy City. No sooner had the train left the station than a horde

552

of Third Class passengers accompanied by large items of baggage, which virtually included the kitchen sink and some live chickens, poured out of the adjoining Third Class carriage and into ours.

Each of these passengers seemed to speak excitedly in a different language, or more correctly, shout, in a different language. We were rather fortunate because we had seated ourselves near the open windows, which permitted us to get a good view of the wonderful scenery, and some fresh air mixed with smoke from the ancient steam engine. Our faces were soon covered in soot from the smoke.

Our fellow passengers immediately extracted spicy smelling food from packets and pockets and spent the whole journey heartily eating, drinking and talking.

The scenery was indeed most picturesque and we were emotionally moved when we realised that the surrounding countryside was virtually the same when journeyed through by the great and famous names in the bible, not that any of our fellow passengers seemed to notice.

We had plenty of opportunity to admire the scenery, as the train's progress was very slow because the route was uphill all the way. It was only afterwards that we learned that part of the route was through Jordanian-held territory and that at times, they occasionally took pot shots at the trains just to remind the authorities that they were still technically at war with Israel and that the train was being allowed through their territory by their good grace.

Our first visit to Jerusalem, or more correctly to West Jerusalem, was most impressive. At the time, East Jerusalem was occupied by the Jordanian Army and as we had Israeli visas in our passports we were not allowed to enter or visit many of the sacred sites, such as the Western Wall of the Temple Mount and other sites of great biblical interest.

Whilst passing a narrow ancient street in West Jerusalem with houses built with the traditional gold-coloured Jerusalem stone, I caught a glimpse of the Old City Wall. The view was an absolute delight to a keen amateur photographer such as myself. The street was too narrow for traffic and was filled with happy children playing in small groups. Just as I lifted my camera to eye-level to record such a wonderful sight, I was tapped on my shoulder by an Israeli policeman who told me that it was very dangerous to take photos of the Old City Wall because behind the wall battlements were Jordanian Army snipers who took such actions as being hostile and often took shots at the photographers. Being the sort of hero that I am, I accepted his advice but the impression of that view still lingers in my memory even today.

As we realised that there was only one return train a day to Tel-Aviv we arrived in good time at the station, and being that much wiser through our recent experience we booked Third Class but found the carriages nearest to the First Class were already full. Our return journey in the Third Class carriages was hot, crowded and airless because we could not get seats near the open windows. The seats themselves were wooden slats, which after a short while became torturous whichever way we shifted about.

We could not see the scenery and were looking forward to the end of the journey when the train came to a halt at a little railway station. The guard told us to get out and to wait on the platform. After a short while we found a railway employee who understood a little English and he explained by pointing to the ancient steam-enveloped engine that it was "m'cholla", which is Hebrew for "ill". We understood what this word meant because it is also a Yiddish word.

The station had no buildings apart from a toilet and the village, which we believe was called Kafar Habad, extended right up to the station platform. Villagers were seated in nearby open-air cafés looking on with mild amusement as though the breakdown was a common occurrence. What amazed us was that the village appeared to be totally ultra-orthodox and both the people and the scenery looked just like a setting for the film of the "Fiddler on the Roof". We would not have been at all surprised if Tevyeh the Milkman with his horse and cart had rolled up and started a song and dance (Tevyeh, of course, not the horse).

After a short while, two Egged buses pulled up and a railway official announced that the remainder of the journey would be by bus. All the passengers crowded onto the two buses but when we saw how dangerously overcrowded the buses were, we refused to get on. After the buses had departed, we told the railway official the reason for our refusal. He heartily agreed with us and observed that the other passengers were all "meshuggar", that means "crazy" both in Hebrew and Yiddish. We were to find our knowledge of Yiddish most useful, as we knew no Hebrew at all. The official arranged for another bus to take us and an elderly, crippled man onto Tel-Aviv. At last we were to enjoy a little luxury although the rest of the journey was not long, that is if the bus did not break down!

We took all our future journeys to Jerusalem by "Sherut" taxis, which run in parallel to all regular bus routes.

Post-Mortem

In my old age, I often think about death and its consequences. Naturally, I don't want to die, but I realise that death is inevitable to everyone, including myself. Already, several of my peers have died and no doubt it will be my turn soon. I don't believe in an afterlife and so I try to be philosophical and stoical.

I have already made arrangements for my funeral inasmuch as I belong to a synagogue burial society to which I make annual contributions to cover a basic, standardised, utilitarian funeral and burial, including the burial plot. My wife is similarly covered by the same contributions. What is not covered is the provision of tombstones.

I would not wish that any of the twaddle that appears on many tombstones appeared on mine. Words such as "Deeply Mourned By" followed by a list of insincere relatives would be offensive to me. I would also not want the usual incomprehensible Hebrew words and abbreviations to appear. They are meaningless except possibly to a small handful of fast-diminishing religious people who would not care a toss for me. I certainly don't understand them and don't want them. In any future life, in which I don't believe in any case, I am sure that I will be able to manage without them (famous last words). Nor will I miss anyone saying the traditional Hebrew memorial prayer for my soul (God help me). If necessary, I will plead with the Creator on my own behalf, not that I think that anyone except possibly a paid cleric will say the memorial prayer for me. No, I am not being morbid, just realistic.

What brought on this mood was a recent experience. My wife and I were leaving our house in our car one drizzly, dull morning to go shopping when we saw a near neighbour walking down the street in the same direction. She was dressed all in black and was accompanied by a man who we did not recognise and who was also dressed in black. It appeared as if they were on their way to a funeral. Normally, she dressed in harmonised, colourful clothes and as we knew that she did not have a car of her own, we asked, out of neighbourly politeness, if we could give them a lift. She said that a lift to the local bus stop would be most welcome especially so as the weather was so wet and that they would have to change buses a couple of times to get to where they were going. When we asked if they were going to a funeral, they said that they were actually going to a local cemetery to dispose of her father's ashes. He had died a few weeks previously and had expressed a wish for his ashes to be interred in the family grave.

We knew the cemetery they were going to and, as it was not far from the shopping centre that we were aiming for, we offered to drop them off near the cemetery gates. When we reached the cemetery, I remembered a long-held desire to view a particular tomb which a braggart we knew claimed to be her family's tomb and where she wished her remains to be interred when she died. Apart from being a snobby, braggart we also knew she was an inveterate liar. She had described the elaborate tomb in great detail and also showed us a photograph of her and her first of four husbands standing in front of it. He had died many years previously and was already buried there. It was the most prominent tomb in the ancient cemetery.

We told our neighbour and her companion, who turned out to be her brother, that we would also go into the cemetery and would wait to take them home if they would care to accompany us on our shopping trip enroute.

We easily found the braggart's prominent family tomb and were quite impressed with its well-maintained marble sculptures.

It took our neighbour quite a while to locate her family's grave, which was fairly neglected, and overgrown. When we rejoined them, they had just disposed of her father's ashes through a small gap in the ground adjacent to the slab formed by settlement of the earth or by an animal boring into the grave for shelter. She explained that she had done so because the cemetery authority had demanded several hundred pounds to raise the slab and then to re-fix it after the ashes had been deposited in the grave. Although her father had expressed a desire for his ashes to be interred in the family grave, he had not left any money to cover the cost and so she had carried out his wishes without incurring any expense.

Whilst we were chatting, her brother, who was smoking a cigarette, nonchalantly flicked some of its ashes into the same hole through which his father's ashes had been passed. As he did so he said, 'Here, Dad, have this one on me."

We were still suspicious about the claim of our braggart acquaintance and we subsequently telephoned the vicar who had the records of ownership of all the tombs and graves in the cemetery. He confirmed that the prominent tomb was indeed that of her first husband's family but the current owners had left written instructions in the file that on no account were her remains to be interred in the tomb. When she died, she was cremated and her ashes are still in storage on a shelf in the crematorium storeroom, as none of her family, not even her one and only daughter, are interested in disposing of them.

Life can still be interesting, even post-mortem!

The Hearing Test

Mark Berg has been a friend since we both attended secondary school in the East End of London some 60 years ago. He is therefore well acquainted with the hearing problems I have endured ever since I was a child. He also knows about the additional hearing difficulties caused in recent times because of my Meniere's attack. As he was also acquainted with the fact that I had read a lot about hearing difficulties he approached me about a rather delicate problem he was experiencing personally. He felt that he could confide in me and that I would not laugh, as he suspected other people would. He strongly suspected that his wife's hearing had recently deteriorated. This in itself was not the actual problem but the fact that his wife, Helen, would not admit that her hearing was not as good as it should be.

Whenever he broached the subject with her, she would angrily reject the very idea and told him that he should have his own ears examined, attack being the best form of defence. He described to me how she often did not hear the telephone ring or the doorbell. When he mentioned that someone was ringing the doorbell, she would ask him to see who it was as she was busy. Also, when she did not hear the telephone she would tell him that she had heard it but thought the call was for him.

Often, when speaking to her, she would ask him to repeat a sentence or give an answer to something else. She blamed his false teeth for him not speaking clearly and for not understanding what he was saying.

She had all the hallmarks of impaired hearing and was also too proud to admit that, due to age, one of her five senses was no longer as it was years ago. Psychologically, it is hard for a woman to acknowledge this fact.

Mark asked for my advice. I told him that first he must confirm that her hearing was actually poor and as she would not consult her doctor or a commercial audiologist he could carry out a simple but convincing test himself that I conjured up on the spot and described to him.

About a week later, a very worried looking Mark came back to report to me the result of the test. As I had suggested, he had stood several paces behind his wife when she was busy at the cooker. In a normal voice he asked her if dinner would be ready soon. No reply. He then advanced nearer and repeated the question. Still no reply. He repeated this experiment twice more until he was very close to her.

At the fourth attempt when he asked in a normal voice, "Will dinner be ready soon?" She replied, "For the fourth time, the answer is yes, and stop pestering me when I am busy."

Ding Dong Dell...

The old English nursery rhyme, which commences, "Ding dong dell, pussy's in the well. Who put her in? Little Johnny Gryn. Who pulled her out? Little Tommy Snout", does not always invoke in my mind a vision of the traditional English country cottage well, but quite a different picture.

Nowadays, even in the most remote hamlets there are few such functioning wells, consisting of a deep brick lined circular pit, the bottom of which is below the water table level. A low wall of brick or stone surmounts the pit and there is a rope-operated hoist to lower and then raise a bucket full of fresh, clean, cold water. Piped or even pumped water from a borehole is now available to even the most isolated home in the country. The few old-fashioned wells that do exist are mainly sentimental souvenirs of a bygone age, although they were not that uncommon up to some 60 years ago in villages.

However, the nursery rhyme does bring back to my mind an experience that my wife and I had in the early 1960s during our first visit to Israel. In those days, tourism was not very well developed, so we tended to explore and find our way about the country on a hit or miss basis on our own.

For economic reasons, we travelled everywhere by public bus service, Egged, which was cheap and efficient, although not all that comfortable. Despite the fact that we could not speak or read the official language of the country, which was Hebrew, we coped rather well because all public signs, including bus routes, road names etc. were always in Hebrew, Arabic and English as a legacy of the English Mandate period. Also, quite curiously, for some reason or another, nearly all the bus drivers spoke English. Just imagine bus drivers here speaking Hebrew!

In those days, tourists from England were a rarity and most people were only too glad to converse and help us find our way around the country. Sometimes, it was most embarrassing, as the people were most curious about life in England and were not inhibited from asking what we considered to be the most personal questions, but we soon got used to that.

One of our first such unaccompanied expeditions was to the town of Beersheba in the midst of the Negev desert. In those days it was more like a large, sprawling village rather than a town. It had about 50,000 residents, a little industry, some shops, some municipal and administrative single-storey buildings, a bank and a medical clinic to serve both the residents and the nomadic desert inhabitants.

Adjacent to the town was the embryo of the newly founded University of the Desert, named in honour of the first Israeli Prime Minister, David Ben Gurion and in the nearby desert, a flourishing agricultural communal farm, a Kibbutz, named Sde Boker, which means Morning Field.

The town is named in the King James translation of the Bible in Genesis 21:31 as Beersheba, but the original Hebrew name, as written in the Old Testament, is actually, Beer Sheva. The translators were obviously confused by the fact that the Hebrew letter "B" is identical in shape with the Hebrew letter "V". In Hebrew, the work "Beer" means a well, and Sheva can mean either an oath or the number seven.

The Old Testament describes how the patriarch, Abraham, dug a well in the vicinity over which there was a dispute with the King of Gerar, Abimelech (which in Hebrew means the King's father). When the dispute was resolved, they swore a covenant of peace and thus, the well was know as the Well of Oath, Beer Sheva. Alternatively, because there were six other wells in the vicinity, this one was called Well Seven, Beer Sheva. Pay your penny and take your choice.

Beer Sheva, or Beersheba, was strategically placed at a crossroads in the centre of the Negev desert and was also an important market town for a very large catchment area. It was originally a Stone-Age settlement.

Although we caught the first bus very early in the morning from Tel-Aviv, it was already getting very hot by the time we arrived. It was mid-June, which is not an advisable month to engage in active tourism. To our western eyes, the town and the market were very exciting and I took a lot of coloured photo slides. In the market, there were a lot of kneeling camels and robed Bedouin Arabs. The Arabs appeared to be more interested in buying and selling Mercedes saloon cars than camels. One small, excited group were most interested in a Royal Enfield .303 British Army rifle. We were told later than the Bedouins needed such weapons to protect their flocks in the desert from marauding predators.

After photographing the market, and visiting the university and the kibbutz, Sde Boker, where David Ben Gurion and his wife are now buried, we had a very interesting and surprising encounter in a small café where, right out of the blue, we met for the first time a Russian refusenick with whom we had corresponded in Tashkent in the former Soviet Union for many years. We did not even know that, at last, he and his family had arrived in Israel.

Before returning to Tel-Aviv we decided to visit the famous well dug by the biblical patriarch, Abraham, some 3000 years ago as recorded in the Old Testament. We finally located it after much trouble. Everyone we asked had heard of it but did not know where it was. When we finally came across it, we were most disappointed. Instead of an awe-inspiring, impressive structure, all we could see was a dusty sign in Hebrew, Arabic and English saying that this was the well mentioned in Genesis 21:31. All we could see was a steep sloping path down to what looked like a crudely dug tunnel entrance. As we gazed forlornly at the dark tunnel entrance, we saw an Arab woman gesticulating excitedly into the tunnel entrance from which could be heard the loud mewing of a cat. We could not understand a single word she was shouting. We assumed she was asking us to enter the tunnel to rescue the cat, which sounded very much in distress. It was our natural instinct to do so, but caution prevailed. What if it was a trap to entice us into the tunnel where we could be robbed or even murdered? We looked around to seek help from someone who could speak English but there was not a single person around except the Arab woman. As we stood there, the mewing got louder and louder until it sounded quite unnatural. We then suspected that it was a man-made sound and decided not to enter the dark tunnel until some English speaking person arrived. None did, there is never an English speaking person around when you need one! It was mid-afternoon by now and every sensible person except mad dogs and Englishmen were taking the traditional siesta - even the mad dogs.

We reluctantly decided to leave the scene for someone else to resolve and to return to Tel-Aviv after a most tiring day during which we hardly rested despite the intense desert heat. We still don't know if there was an actual cat in the well and if there was, who put it in or eventually who pulled it out. It was certainly not us, nor, as far as we know, Johnny Gryn or Tommy Snout.

The Letter

Post arriving on a Monday morning or the day following a Bank Holiday usually consists of circulars from commercial firms or from various charities. For some reason or another, post from overseas also arrives on such days. The Post Office offers inducements of reduced postal charges to bulk dispatchers if made just before or during weekends and Bank Holidays.

On the particular Monday morning concerned, I received six such circulars, which are easily recognisable as such, and an obviously private letter with what appeared to be semi-literate handwriting on the envelope. As is my normal custom, I opened the circulars first as they are normally easily and swiftly dealt with. Not all are put into the waste paper bin straightaway, as some may be from charities I support. Most of the circulars are sent to me because my name and details were published in professional directories even though I retired about twelve years ago. What a waste when one considers that there are thousands like me who retired years ago and have no use for such circulars, which are expensive to produce and circulate. I pass on a few of the circulars to friends who I know are interested in particular items.

Having dealt expeditiously with the circulars, I next turned my attention to the private-looking letter. At first, I assumed from the handwriting on the envelope that a foreigner overseas wrote the letter but then I noticed that it bore a British postal stamp and that the cancellation mark was that of our local sorting office. The letter must have been posted fairly locally late on Friday or early Saturday for it to be been delivered on Monday morning. Curiously, the flap was sealed down with Sellotape for extra security and bore no identity of the sender.

Normally, I like receiving private mail as it affords me the opportunity

563

to indulge in a form of gratifying fetish or ritual. Whereas some people can't start the day without first saying a prayer or doing some physical exercise or taking the dog for a walk or reading a newspaper etc., I like to start the day by writing a letter, preferably a private one; it stimulates my brain. I therefore anticipated replying to the letter immediately but on re-reading the address, I was shocked to notice that what, at a glance I had initially accepted as being the capital initial letters of my professional qual-ification after my name, the letters actually formed a crude word whose first letter, "F", and which was the same letter as my qualification. I thought it was in very poor taste especially so as our regular post-lady may have noticed it.

When I started to read the letter itself, I was amazed. It appeared to be the ranting of a mentally deranged person with some form of grudge against me. The letter was, of course, anonymous and concluded with a challenge to discover who the writer was. There were several clues, as the writer appeared to have a very good knowledge of my family and me going back many years. He or she either knew me very well or knew someone who knew me very well. Some of the facts and incidents in the letter, which were crudely and cruelly recounted, were from the dim and distant past. It appeared that the writer had been brooding on insignificant events and had held resentments, possibly through jealousy or envy. Apart from expressing the writer's pent-up resentments I could not see the point in the anonymous letter except as a challenge to discover his or her identity.

The letter was written on a sheet of lined paper cut out of a school exercise-type of book, quite a contrast to the expensive paper I use when writing private letters, and was written with a ball point pen, again a con-trast to the vintage fountain pen with a script gold nib, which I use. I write my letters in carefully composed paragraphs using a flourishing, flowing script, the result being most distinctive these days.

I often recall one incident when I was still practising as an architect; I was involved in a complex project extensively altering and extending a state-aided private school. Because public grants were involved, the Council's Chief Education Officer's approval was required. In response to his request for certain details, I wrote to him and awaited his reply, which came in the form of a joint invitation to myself and the Chairman of the Board of School Governors to meet him in his office. The Chairman fore-warned me to expect a hard time, as the man was notorious for being dif-ficult to satisfy. Quite to the contrary to what I had been led to anticipate, the Chief Education Officer was most courteous and agreeable. Without any objections, he approved all the points I had made in my letter to him. The school Chairman was amazed and after a while, suspecting some sort of a trap, he suspiciously but with great circumspection asked the Chief

Officer why he was being so unusually agreeable and co-operative. The Chief Officer pointed to my letter, which was before him on his imposing desk, and explained that day after day, he dealt with a mass of letters, all of them, almost without exception typed, whereas my letter had been compiled and written with great care in beautiful script handwriting. It had been such a pleasure to receive it that he almost cried with joy. Therefore, he was only too glad to agree with its contents. This, together with other pleasant incidents encouraged me to continue to handwrite many of my letters in preference to having them typed.

I apologise for having digressed somewhat from the subject matter, but I only wanted to contrast my handwriting to the poorly presented and written anonymous letter I had received. Someone possibly laboriously trying to disguise their normal handwriting wrote the badly formed words. Both Dora and myself pondered long and hard in an endeavour to work out who the culprit was because many came under suspicion but we came to no definite conclusion. Even Dora with her woman's instinct could not be definite. It was frustrating and baffling.

I should have just torn the letter up in disgust and thrown it into the waste paper bin as a stupid and crude joke but the challenge remained to discover the perpetrator.

A few days after receiving the letter whilst we were calmly watching a soap on TV, Dora suddenly exclaimed, "I know who wrote that letter, it was you! Nobody else except you and I would have known all the details in it and it was certainly not me." She also added that the spelling mistakes were obviously mine.

I congratulated her on her power of logic and expressed my surprise that it had taken her so long to tumble my joke.

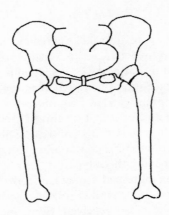

Fractured Femur

It is said that most accidents happen in the home and it is no wonder. The average home is filled with the most dangerous items such as sharp knives, scissors, high voltage and amperage electrical gadgets, poorly guarded electric heaters, toasters, food blenders, liquidisers, mincers, kettles, electric knives, unguarded gas cooker burners, pans of boiling water, slippery floors and a host of other dangerous items and that's only in the kitchen! In the bathroom there is the risk of scalding water in the bath or shower or slipping and even drowning in the bath or on the wet floor as well as dangerous drugs in the cabinet or electrocution by an improperly installed heater.

All over the house there are of 13 amp electric socket outlets and also sharp sewing needles and pins. Even an innocent kitchen chair or stool can be the cause of a serious accident by tempting someone to stand on it to adjust a curtain or change an electric light bulb. In addition, there is the profusion of do-it-yourself jobs that seem so easy and simple yet are full of potential dangers with powerful electric drills, saws, planes, sanders, strippers etc. all operated by untrained enthusiasts. Also in the garden there are lawn mowers and vicious electric hedge cutters with unguarded blades. The use of most of these items by amateur persons would constitute a serious offence under the Factory and Workshop (Safety) Acts under which, employers would be subject to serious penalties.

In addition, there is also the fire risk from "romantic" or "aromatic" candles, nightlights and unextinguished cigarette ends and dangerously old electric wiring, badly fitted staircase carpet and loose rugs. The list is almost endless. What is most surprising is that there are not more serious accidents in the home!

It was none of these potential dangers that caused Dora to suffer a serious accident in our home. Actually, there was no apparent cause for her to fall and break her left thighbone. She was not dizzy, she was carefully carrying a small, light carton of wine glasses from a rear ground floor room to the entrance hall when she lost her balance and fell. There was no defect in the carpet and the lighting was good. She just simply fell and broke her left femur. Nobody else and nothing was to blame. At the time I was quietly reading a book in the lounge when I heard the crash of her falling and the sound of breaking glass. I rushed to see what had happened and saw Dora lying on the entrance hall floor not far from the foot of the stairs. She had not fallen down the stairs. The first thing that she said was, "I think I've broken my leg, help me to get up and sit down on the lower step of the stairs." I had a grounding in first aid and told her that if she had broken her leg, she should not move and I would get medical help.

However, she insisted on standing up and walked the few paces to the foot of the stairs and sat down. I assured her that as she could walk, she could not possibly have broken a bone in her leg.

I phoned the doctor's emergency service but as it was a Saturday evening his surgery was closed. When I spoke to his receptionist and explained the situation she said that in the circumstances, I should dial the Emergency Service 999 and ask for an ambulance. She said that in any case it would be prudent to have Dora's leg X-rayed to ascertain the actual damage. The 999 Service did not quibble, and said that an ambulance would be sent as soon as possible. Dora was not in pain but insisted that she had broken her leg. I wrapped her up warmly even though it was not a cold evening and we waited for the ambulance, which we expected to arrive within 10 to 15 minutes. Actually, it did not arrive for more than half an hour. The crew apologised for the delay and explained that the local ambulance station was inundated with calls and that they had come from an adjoining district. Because they were not acquainted with the local roads and also because the roads were congested with traffic, it had taken them longer than it should have. They were so apologetic and pleasant that it was impossible to be annoyed with them, but it was lucky nevertheless, that Dora was not in pain or in a life-threatening situation.

They did not dispute that Dora had broken her leg. They splinted it up and carried her carefully into the ambulance. They allowed me to accompany her to the hospital. They put me in a seat reserved for sitting patients and strapped me in, in case I fell out and injured myself during the journey, which took longer than it should have because of the congested roads.

They carried Dora through the hospital's Accident and Emergency Department entrance and told me to enter and report to the reception through the adjacent Outpatient Department entrance. I don't know why they were so pedantic. I soon joined up with Dora who had been placed in a curtained-off cubicle on a trolley, which was in fact a narrow, comfortable hospital bed on wheels for easy perambulation.

A nurse assured her that someone would see to her soon and meanwhile took her temperature and asked if she would like a painkiller, which Dora declined. The nurse returned about very 15 minutes and took Dora's temperature and each time asked if she would like a painkiller and each time Dora declined saying that she was not in pain. After a few such visitations, the nurse said that Dora had not been registered and that I would have to do so and collect a chart so that her temperature could be recorded.

Dora's cubicle was one of several to the side of a large reception area where the bulk of the casualties were patiently waiting to be seen. Several of the casualties were apparently, quite lively. They appeared to be a party of highly inebriated youths who were using wheeled trolleys as battering rams good-humouredly against each other in a running battle. Nobody intervened except a small, young nurse who told them that as they did not appear to be injured, they should leave the Casualty Department immediately. This stern admonition seemed to be effective as the more boisterous ones did leave sheepishly.

In a corner there was an elderly couple in their 70s lying on adjoining trolleys, both with badly bruised faces, groaning and cursing each other like mad. It appeared that they were Saturday night regulars. When they had calmed down, they were treated and taken home, still cursing each other. Other casualties were fearfully and patiently waiting to be seen to.

After about two hours, a doctor came to see Dora and apologised for the delay. He said that Saturday evenings were always very busy but this evening they were especially busy as a coach had been in a collision and several badly injured passengers had been brought in just before Dora had arrived, two requiring urgent operations which had kept him and other staff busy. He said that Dora would have to have an X-ray to ascertain the nature of her injury. He showed us the X-ray plate, which indicated a very clean fracture through the femur close to the hip joint. He admitted Dora for an operation for the following day when suitable personnel would be available. Once away from the noisy, chaotic Casualty Department, the atmosphere was peaceful and reassuring. Dora slept like a log for the rest of that night.

When I had seen Dora safely settled in, at about 2 am on Sunday morning, I decided to make my way home. At that time of night there was no public transport available and so for security reasons I telephoned and ordered a black taxi cab and waited at the Casualty Department entrance to be picked up. Whilst I was waiting, a mini-cab driver asked in very broken English if this was King George Hospital, despite all the large signs, and if so, where was the Casualty Department. Right in front of him was a large, brightly illuminated sign declaring, "Accident and Emergency Department".

After a short while, a black taxi pulled up opposite the entrance, the driver eyed me but did not signal me even though I was the only person in sight and was obviously waiting for transport. After a while I approached him and asked if he was the taxi I had ordered. He said no, he had been ordered to pick up a woman. I convinced him that I was indeed the person to be picked up and told him my destination. He consulted a road map but soon lost his way, but I eventually got home and I too slept like a log.

The next morning, Sunday, I started to inform people who should know about the accident, including the six members of Dora's family who were due to make their periodic visit to us that very same day. Dora had spent much of the previous day getting ready for their visit and had prepared a plethora of delicacies which they so much liked and anticipated and which were not available where they lived, such as pickled herring, brown bread with caraway seeds, shmaltz herring, matzos, salt beef, plava cake and many other Jewish delicacies washed down with iced grape juice or sparkling wine. It was a shame that due to Dora's most unfortunate accident they had to forgo this treat but as all clouds have a silver lining, the provisions stood me in good stead for the following week or so.

When Dora came home, she was incapacitated for a couple of weeks during which I had to do the housework, cooking and shopping which she normally did.

I seemed to manage fairly well except that I had some difficulty with the shopping. Dora gave me a detailed list of what to buy and where but because of my hearing problem, I could not catch what the shopkeepers were asking above the background noises. I tried to overcome this problem by offering a ten-pound note in each shop and pocketing the loose change. After about two weeks of such shopping, I had an enormous amount of small change.

Dora's leg is now fully recovered and she is back to normal and doing her own shopping.

The Estate Agent

From time to time, because I was an architect, I used to be asked by friends and relatives to give my opinion on a property they were considering buying. Although a fee was not mentioned it was mutually understood that I would not make a charge for such a service and naturally, I would do so gratis for the sake of family and friendship. I was often told that I need not do a full and detailed inspection as they were either paying a fee to the building society who were making the loan or that they were employing a "proper" qualified surveyor but nevertheless, my observations would be welcome as an additional safeguard.

Sometimes, I would be asked for my opinion, unpaid of course, on a structural report prepared by such a "proper" qualified surveyor. They wanted my explanation on some possibly technical/legal phraseology used by the surveyor in his written report. I often pointed out just how little such reports were worth because of the cautious wording imposed by the surveyor's insurers. Such phrases exempted the surveyors for responsibility for not reporting on concealed parts of the structure such as foundations, drains, embedded pipes and wiring, floor joists and plastered brickwork as well as differential settlement, ground heave, disguised rising damp, dry rot, wet rot, woodworm infestation, central heating and electrical wiring deficiencies. I know such excluding phrases only too well as they had also been imposed on me by my professional practice insurers over the course of time. I don't say that such structural reports are useless, but they do safeguard surveyors and their insurers against consequential legal responsibilities for any negligence or incompetence.

When I agreed to look over a property, I often had the additional problem of having to make it appear to the vendor that I was just an acquaintance who had accompanied the purchaser and was only giving opinions on possible future improvements. I was also expected to give a running commentary on technical points whilst making notes for future discussions away from the property. Although I gave such services non-professionally, that is, unpaid and with no written report, I was conscious of the enormous responsibility involved should I fail to detect any defect.

On one occasion, it came back to me that one person who availed herself of such a service, complained to others that I had failed to warn her that there was woodworm infestation in timber used behind a fixed bath panel. This was not discovered either by her paid "proper" surveyor who would in any case have been covered by an exclusion clause in his report but came to light many years later when a plumber removed the panel to carry out a repair, neither did she make it clear whether the infestation was dead or alive.

Not all my friends and relatives who bought properties availed themselves of my unpaid services. Some did not consider my advice was worth asking for, whilst others did not get an inspection at all but quickly came to me, as if it was my fault, if they found any defects after buying the property.

I did three free-of-charge full surveys for one particular relative. She did not proceed with the purchase of the first house because of my adverse report; she was gazumped by the vendor on the second property but did buy the third one. One day she gave me £30 towards my travelling expenses which I felt was quite generous considering that none of the others had compensated me in any way whatsoever but it was only later that I discovered that the vendor who had gazumped her had given her £300 towards her surveyor's fee!

It was with some trepidation that I accompanied a relative who had decided to buy a bungalow and welcomed my (free) opinion. The property was empty, as the vendor had been moved to a nursing home. I noticed a large amount of old floor covering piled up in the front garden and new floorboards in several rooms, a sure sign of distress in the ground floor timber construction. I also noticed obvious signs of differential floor and wall settlements as well as defects in the damp-proof course. It was while I was explaining my fears that a small boy from the next-door property entered the bungalow and attached himself to our little group listening most attentively to what I was saying. He was only about 10 years old and during a short pause he started to speak. His demeanour was very serious and we realised that he was repeating verbatim some of the tings I had been saying and what other people had said when visiting the property previously.

He said, quite authoritatively, "Look at the wonderfully spacious rooms with grand views through the elegant Georgian-style French doors over the beautifully tended garden, the graceful character of the period architecture, the carefully preserved original features such as the tiled fireplaces and hearths, the ornate picture rails. The mellowed varnished woodwork is as original." He then looked at us to confirm that we were paying due attention and continued, "If they should ask about the cracks in the walls, tell them it is due to shrinkage caused by the exceptionally hot and dry summer and that they will not be noticed when the rooms are redecorated."

There were other interesting snatches of conversation. The child obviously had a wonderfully phonographic memory of what other viewers to the property had been saying. When we asked the boy's mother if she would be kind enough to loan us a pair of steps or a ladder so that we could look into the loft, she excused her son, saying that he was a right chatterbox and always loved to enter the empty property when there were visitors, she just could not keep him out.

The potential purchaser gathered more useful information from that boy than he did from his professional surveyor's report or my verbal one.

Gabrel v Gabrel

About 40 years ago, not long after I had moved into my present house, the owner of the next-door house introduced himself and made a business proposition. He explained that he had not only recently become a widower but he had also recently retired as a handicraft teacher and now wished to retire to his seaside home. He said that his house had for many years been let as four fully furnished flats, two on the first floor and two on the ground floor. The flats were not self-contained inasmuch as they all shared one first floor bathroom/WC and one outside WC in the garden. They all shared the main entrance hall and staircase and had no proper self-contained security.

He had also become increasingly concerned that there was no adequate fire separation or secure means of escape in case of fire. None of the apartments had central heating and the widespread use of open fires and paraffin and electric heaters created a dangerous fire risk. Because the provisions were sub-standard, his rents were very low and therefore very popular and in great demand among newly married couples and young persons living away from home, including nurses and teachers.

He was sorry to have to give up what he had found to be a pleasant and profitable supplement to his teacher's salary but he realised that soon he would not be able to do so for medical reasons. He now proposed to seek official town planning and building regulations permission to convert the house to four high standard, self-contained flats and to sell them on long leases to the same types of people who now rented them.

He knew that I was an architect; actually, at the time I was not yet qualified, and asked me if I would be willing to prepare the plans for the official applications. I willingly agreed to do so as I would be able, in my spare

573

time to supplement the meagre salary that I earned as a local authority trainee architect.

However, there was a snag: because he was a pensioned schoolteacher, he was not flush with money and he would be hard pressed to finance the scheme out of his savings and pension. He therefore proposed doing most of the building work himself; he was still quite fit and being a handicraft teacher he knew enough to carry out most of the work himself and would only employ specialist trades such as electricians as and when required. Due to the shortage of ready money, he proposed that instead of paying my fee in cash, he would transfer the freehold of the property to me. He explained that he proposed selling the four self-contained flats on 99 year leases and as the freeholder, I would be entitled to £25 ground rent per year from each of the four leaseholds, paid yearly in advance. Each leaseholder would own their own self-contained flat for a period of 99 years but I would own the freehold in perpetuity and when the leases finally expired, I would be able to repossess the four flats and resell or let them at the current prices.

I willingly accepted, after all, I would received each year in advance for 99 years what I would have charged just for doing the plans for cash and in addition, I would be the freeholder in perpetuity!

Everything went through as they say, "according to plan". The town planning and building regulations applications were passed without undue problems, the flats were sold and I received the freehold deeds of the property. Before receiving the deeds, I had to pay a solicitor a hefty fee for doing the conveyance for me. I had not anticipated this expenditure nor had I anticipated receiving a demand from the Inland Revenue for Capital Gains Tax on the freehold, which they estimated at the value, if I remember correctly, of £1,000, which at the time was more than two years of my then gross salary! I could not possibly afford to pay such a fantastic sum. I protested most strongly but the Inland Revenue were adamant, either I pay up promptly in full or they would take me to court and obtain possession of the property plus a penalty tax, plus accrued interest and also plus their legal costs. If I failed to pay their additional extortions, they would obtain possession of my own house. I frantically arranged a loan with my bank to meet the Inland Revenue demand to be repaid plus interest over a ten-year period. My bargain proved to be most expensive.

To add to my anguish, soon after, I received an income tax demand in respect of the unearned ground rent income of £100. No relief is allowed on such "unearned income".

Over the course of years, I paid my commitments and am now the proud freeholder of the next door property of four leasehold flats from each of which I continue to receive £25 per year less the agent's fee for collecting the ground rents on my behalf.

Not very long ago, I decided to improve the potential value of my own house by building a single storey rear extension to line through and to match the existing extensions on both adjoining properties. I don't really know why I decided on this project as I neither needed the extra space nor intended selling. Dora kept on about all our other neighbours having rear extensions built; some even had two-storey extensions. I engaged a local builder who agreed to build the extension very cheaply provided I was in no hurry because he had so many other orders. I said that this suited me and we agreed a very reasonable price on the understanding that I would not pay him anything until the job was completed. Despite this, he started almost immediately although he took many unexplained days off, especially during fine weather. It was on such a fine day that I looked out of the rear window and saw Taffy, one of our four cats, happily using the soil from a partially dug foundation trench as his toilet. No sooner had I looked away than I heard the rumble of freshly dug earth falling back into the trench. There was no sign of Taffy. I jumped into the partially filled trench and dug away frantically with my bare hands to find Taffy before he suffocated to death. I dug and dug but there was no sign of him. Absolutely exhausted and out of breath I looked up and saw both Taffy and Dora peering down on me. Dora told me to stop messing about and to mow the lawn if I had nothing better to do.

When the walls of the extension had reached roof level, one of the lessees of the next door ground floor flat told me that my new structure had caused damage to his nearby drains and he was having to have expensive emergency repair work carried out. He told me that he was claiming on his insurance policy. Soon after I received a letter from his insurers asking me to pay them for the damage caused to my neighbour's drains. I disclaimed responsibility, telling them that I was aware that he had had problems many times, even before work had commenced on my extension. They persisted, saying that as the freeholder of the adjoining property, I was in any case responsible for damage to the drains on the property as they were shared by all the leaseholders. Fortunately, I had taken the precaution of insuring myself against such claims. There was a lot of correspondence between the two insurance companies which resulted in a court writ being issued against me headed, "Gabrel the Plaintiff versus Gabrel the Defendant". I was therefore the Plaintiff as the freeholder of the adjoining property and the Defendant for my own house extension.

After many more months of correspondence between the solicitors representing the two insurance companies, during which the local water supply company, who was legally responsible for the maintenance of the communal sewer, became involved, it was decided to withdraw the writ and each party was to bear its own costs.

The neighbour still gets his drains blocked periodically and my insurance policy premiums were subsequently increased enormously by much more than the annual ground rents that I receive.

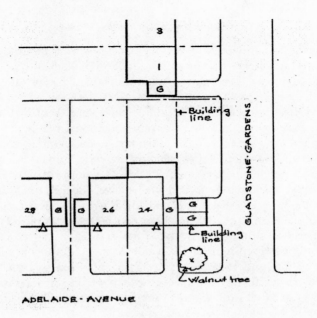

Double Garage, Double Trouble

It is now some 14 years since I retired after a long career as an architect. When I first qualified, I worked as a salaried architect for an Inner London council designing blocks of flats to replace desperately needed housing that had been destroyed in bombing raids during World War II. The flats were designed to be let at low rents and therefore had to be built very economically. Building materials at the time were in very short supply, especially timber. It was a good and enjoyable experience involving novel forms of construction.

When I considered that I had enough expertise and confidence, I opened my own, one-man private practice. It was a bold and risky venture; I had no capital, no useful contacts and, as a qualified architect I was not permitted by my professional institute to advertise in any way whatsoever. I had to obtain commissions through the merit of my work and the recommendations of satisfied clients. My earliest private projects were small domestic extensions, which involved complicated work and small fees. It was when I had designed a kitchen extension in a north west, prestigious and affluent district of London for a man who I will refer to as "Mr. A", for professional and confidentiality reasons, he was so impressed at the efficient way I handled the complicated project that he commissioned me

577

to design a new multi-storey factory for him in the Hackney district of London. The factory was for the production of high-quality furniture, a supreme luxury in those days of rationing and utility production. Mr. A was most satisfied and pleased, as the factory was built within the contract time and the contract figure. My fame soon spread through the closely-knit furniture manufacturing fraternity and soon I was being engaged to design similar factories for other furniture manufacturers and associated industries and warehouses. Not glamorous work, but very satisfying.

It was through such a contact that Mr. B, whom I shall not name so as not to embarrass him if he should still be alive, engaged me. What I did not know at the time was that Mr. A and Mr. B were business rivals and thoroughly disliked each other. When I had successfully completed Mr. B's factory, he was so pleased that he asked me to design a garage extension on his recently acquired house in Adelaide Avenue, a most desirable street. I was not keen to undertake such a domestic extension, as I knew from previous experience that such projects inevitably led to all sorts of difficulties that were out of all proportion to the fees involved. However, in the circumstances, I could not very well refuse.

By sheer coincidence, Mr. B had bought the house quite knowingly from Mr. A. I was later to discover that the reason Mr. A sold his house to his arch rival was that he was aware that Mr. B intended to erect a large garage extension on the extensive piece of land adjoining the existing garage in order to house his prize possession, a beautiful vintage Rolls Royce. Mr. A gloated in the knowledge that the local council had previously rejected a similar application, as in order to gain access to the new garage, it would be necessary to remove an old walnut tree on which a preservation order had been served. The application was also refused because the proposal would have infringed the building line of the houses in the adjoining side street, Gladstone Gardens.

When I made preliminary consultations with the council's officials, they apprised me of the previous rejection. Nevertheless, they agreed with my contention that the building regulations only required complying with the building line to the frontages in Adelaide Avenue in which the house entrance was situated and not also to the frontages to the houses in the side street, Gladstone Gardens. I thereupon prepared plans that conformed to the building line in Adelaide Avenue but projected considerably in front of that in the side street, Gladstone Gardens. The Town Planning staff agreed with me that it would be preferable to have a firm visual stop to the line of houses in Gladstone Gardens so I took the opportunity to add an additional garage and a first floor extension over the three garages to house a granny flat for the applicant's elderly widowed mother.

Needless to say, Mr. B was exceedingly pleased when full Town

Planning permission was received. He boasted about my brilliant success in the close-knit furniture manufacturing fraternity especially in the Vapour Bath Club to which most of them belonged.

It was not long before I received a most irate telephone call from Mr. A accusing me of gross treachery and making him appear to be an idiot. All his colleagues had previously heard him boasting about the way he had sold his rival a useless plot of land and now the laugh was on him. He said he would no longer recommend me and that there were many more architects to choose from. He ended the diatribe with a firm, "GOODBYE".

The Packet of Biscuits

I was 16 years of age and had just left school when I got my first job as a junior draughtsman in the drawing office of a large, well known, multi-departmental store in Oxford Street, London, the one that proclaims, "Never Knowingly Undersold", whatever that may mean. It was a small office housed in a beautiful Georgian house at the rear of the store overlooking a lovely enclosed square.

Not long before I joined the company in 1940, it had acquired a string of multi-departmental stores all over the country, the most well known was in Sloane Square, London, another in south London and others in Windsor, Peterborough and elsewhere. The manager of the office was a qualified architect in his early forties and the next most senior was in his late 20s and who it was rumoured had not been called up for military service because he had TB (tuberculosis). The other six occupants of the office were all under 18 years of age because anyone over that age had been conscripted into the armed services. It was the firm's policy that when men were conscripted, they would make up the difference in the wages. It was very generous of the company and fortunately for them, the difference was usually not very great. They did not pay the difference if anyone volunteered to join the armed forces and so there were very few volunteers.

My job mainly was to visit these recently acquired departmental stores, take careful, meticulous measurements of the structure and shop-fittings and upon return to the office, and draw up the plans to scale. The purpose was to record what the company had acquired and then to re-plan the layout of the stores to accord with the policy of the company.

I welcomed such survey expeditions to provincial cities for several reasons. It enable me to get out the boring office routine and to see cities that

580

I had never visited before, but most of all it enabled me to get away from the nightly bombing raids on the East End of London where I lived.

The German Air Force intensively bombed this district of London both by day and night in an effort to break the morale of the citizens and to damage the docks and ships that brought desperately needed supplies to the capital. During one of these raids, my family's home was razed to the ground and I lost everything I owned except the clothes I was wearing at the time. The raid took place on a Saturday morning when I was at work. Fortunately, my family (except my father) had previously evacuated to the country for safety. My father also survived because for the very first time in his life he worked on a Saturday, the Jewish Sabbath.

We were homeless and absolutely impoverished. We obtained shelter in a local school where pupils and staff had been evacuated to the country. We slept on the hardwood-block floor of the school's assembly hall along with about 40 other bombed out people. There was no privacy whatsoever. The lights were on all night. Children were crying and some adults were rowing. Despite this, we slept fairly soundly. In the morning we were served bowls of hot porridge cooked by the cheerful, hard-working members of the WVS (Women's Voluntary Service). They were obviously not local women as they spoke very poshly. We could have as much porridge as we wanted and also large mugs of sweet tea and thick slices of bread and jam.

The breakfasts were most welcome and filled me up until lunchtime when I could get a good subsidised lunch in the firm's staff canteen. Later on, I usually had a snack and a cup of tea in a cheap café. Weekends were the worst because I could not get lunch in the firm's canteen and I could not afford to eat out. My total income was only fifteen shillings a week, less National Insurance (fifteen shillings = 75 pence).

Whilst I was homeless, I could not supplement these meals with the meagre rations which civilians were allowed because, being homeless I was not entitled to a ration book. I welcomed the provincial surveys because I could charge the cost of café meals and hotel expenses to the firm, especially so, if these surveys covered the weekends.

One of the surveys was in Peterborough, about 85 miles from London. My train journey commenced at Euston or King's Cross railway station, I can't now remember which. As I had some time to wait for my train, I joined the queue for the station buffet. Not unusually, there were several soldiers in the queue. Railway stations were always busy with servicemen coming and going to and from their barracks. The majority of travellers in those days were servicemen; civilians were discouraged from travelling with posters that proclaimed, "Is your journey really necessary?" The servicemen were not only British, a large number were from overseas and who had volunteered for the British services, their shoulder flashes indicated that they came from such diverse countries as Australia, South Africa, Cyprus, Malta, Norway, Canada, Poland, Czechoslovakia and others.

I noticed that when the servicemen ahead of me in the queue ordered tea, they were also served with a small packet of biscuits. I had not enjoyed the luxury of tasting biscuits since before the war commenced; they were not normally available to civilians, not even on ration. It was therefore with great relief that when I asked for a cup of tea, I was also allowed to buy a small packet of biscuits. I noted that the biscuits were made by a well-known firm and were specially packed in waxed paper for sale in railway buffets. Possibly, it was old stock they were unloading onto passengers.

I hurried to a nearby group of small circular tables to enjoy my unexpected fortune in relaxed comfort. I sat down on one of the few vacant chairs and noticed that sitting opposite me was a soldier with a Czechoslovakian shoulder flash. I politely nodded to him and he returned my courtesy by indicating that I was welcome to share the table with him. I put my cup of tea, packet of biscuits and newspaper down on the table and gratefully relaxed on my chair. I placed my case alongside my chair and half turned to carefully hang my gas mask box on the back of the chair. All citizens, including children had been issued with gas masks and were required to carry them, in the cardboard box provided, everywhere they went, including school and work. It only took a few seconds but when I turned back to relish my unexpected luxury I saw that the soldier had opened the packet and was consuming one of my treasured biscuits. I just could not believe my eyes. I was momentarily dumbstruck. I pointed at the packet and firmly protested but all the response I got was a big smile showing his gold teeth and a finger indicating that I may have one of the biscuits. It was obvious that he had not understood a word of my protest. When I hesitated, he held the packet out to me and insisted that I take one of the biscuits. What on earth was I to do? I took one of the biscuits and bitterly chewed it with tears of frustration welling up in my eyes. This seemed to please the soldier who deliberately took another biscuit and heartily consumed it. Every time he brazenly took a biscuit, he offered me one until the whole packet was consumed. When the last biscuit was eaten, he gulped down his tea and with a big smile he said something in a foreign language, clapped my shoulder in a goodwill gesture and walked swiftly towards the ticket barriers. I felt sick but at the same time I felt some sympathy towards this young man, thousands of miles from his home and family, who had volunteered to fight in our desperate struggle for survival against the German enemy.

I still had some time to spare before catching my train, so I decided to read the Daily Herald newspaper that I had bought, price one penny, on my way to the station. Not that there was much to read, it consisted only of one double folded sheet and would be filled with bad news from all fronts except for the air war over south east England where the British Spitfire pilots were taking a heavy toll of German planes. When I lifted the newspaper, I was astonished to see laying beneath it my precious unopened packet of biscuits!

Gladys Whiteson

As soon as Dora caught sight of the hat she recognised it as belonging to Gladys Whiteson, even though she had last seen it some 50 years or so ago in the immediate post-war austerity years in Britain. At the time, Gladys was the personal secretary of the Town Clerk for a neighbouring London Borough council. The borough has since been amalgamated with others to form a larger entity and the exalted position of Town Clerk had been changed to Chief Executive Officer.

Gladys was a powerful and awesome figure in the Town Hall. All appointments and interviews with the Town Clerk had to go through her. All visitors to the Town Clerk had to be vetted and approved by her before being allowed to pass her desk, which was outside the door to the Town Clerk's office. She opened all the Town Clerk's post, even if marked, "private and personal" and decided whether or not to pass it on to the Town Clerk. It was also she who made all the Town Clerk's appointments without even consulting him first.

Everyone, from the lowest to the highest, held her in great esteem and respectful fear. Among the lowest was my dear wife, Dora, who at the time was employed by the Town Hall as a humble shorthand typist and who at Gladys's instructions typed the Town Clerk's letters many of which were dictated to her by Gladys on the Town Clerk's behalf.

Anyone who knew Gladys in those memorable days would have been impressed by Gladys's hat, which she constantly wore both indoors and out, providing the weather was fine. It was rumoured that Gladys had inherited the hat from her mother who possibly had inherited it from her own mother. It was a masterpiece of millinery. It was tall, with fine feathers, bunches of various fruits and an abundance of flowers and jewelled

584

hatpins. It was her badge of office, just as the Mayor's ermine-edged robe and gold chain was his.

At first, Dora thought she was seeing a ghost. If this was truly Gladys Whiteson herself, then surely she was well into her nineties and yet she only looked about 65. For a moment Dora thought that maybe this was Gladys's daughter who had inherited the hat but then she remembered that Gladys did not have a daughter. However, as soon as their eyes met, they definitely recognised each other and embraced as old friends despite the great age difference.

Gladys immediately remembered Dora's name and also remembered signing a card congratulating her on her marriage to me. They both recollected names from the old days and events including office scandals. It appeared that Gladys was aware of certain happenings in the Town Hall and which it had been assumed that she was ignorant of. Somehow or other, she had kept up to date with retired colleagues, those who had died and what illnesses they had died of, those who had remarried and where they were now living and those who were in nursing homes and also those who had gone a bit doo-lally. As she spoke, the feathers in her hat quivered in excitement and the faux jewelled hatpins glistened in approval.

They were both very excited and promised to meet again but when Dora offered to write down her address and telephone number, Gladys assured her that it was not necessary as she already knew and rattled off the up-to-date details precisely, even though our telephone number is ex-directory. Goodness only knows how she knew.

She revealed that after she retired, she married one of the Council's retired structural engineers and that they now lived not far away in a luxury bungalow in a very select area. Their combined pensions and income from prudent investments enabled them to live very comfortably and to participate in their respective hobbies. Hers apparently was attending to their large garden and his was collecting and restoring antiques. Dora told her that I too was interested in collecting antiques and that recently I had acquired some Meissen china. The feathers in Gladys's hat immediately quivered and she declared in her authoritative voice of old, "I would never allow Harold to fetch mice into the house and in any case we have four cats that would soon put a stop to any such nonsense." The feathers in her hat quivered once again in agreement.

Dora tried to explain but her words seem to fall on deaf ears and Gladys asserted, "China yes, but no mice thank you."

Time had soon passed and Dora said that she had better be getting back as otherwise I might start worrying. Gladys asked Dora if she had a car and if so, did she drive. Dora explained that I had recently sold our old car and had decided not to renew it. Even thought she must have turned

90, Gladys said she was considering getting a car as she could easily afford one on her income. Dora was amazed, she asked Gladys if she had a driving licence but Gladys said that it would not be necessary as she would get one of the self-drive cars she had seen advertised.

Dora then realised that Alzheimer's disease had begun to take its toll on this indomitable woman.

The Prostate Ward

Some people, including myself in the past, confuse the words, prostate and prostrate. Although they sound similar they are vastly different. All male human beings, and possibly some other species too, are born with a small prostate gland within the bladder near to its exit. It does not appear to have any function and is unaccountable for in the evolution of mankind. However, in many men, after the age of 50, for unknown reasons, it begins to enlarge in size and restricts micturation, the passing of liquids out of the bladder. It is not painful in itself unless it unfortunately coincides with cancer of the gland when there is some pain and passing of blood in the urine. The rate of enlargement is very slow and insidious.

I first began to notice my increasing frequency of urinating many years ago. At first I just ascribed it to a personal physical weakness but eventually, when I found that I was visiting the toilet about every half-hour I decided to consult my doctor. After just a few questions he diagnosed that I had an enlarged prostate gland and gave me a letter of reference to a urological specialist at a local hospital and who had an excellent reputation for treatment of this condition. My doctor forewarned me that I would most likely have to have an operation to remove the gland but which he assured me would be simple and painless.

The hospital informed me that there was a six-month waiting list for patients to see that particular specialist. I resigned myself to wait. It's amazing, that when the subject is mentioned, just how many people have personally had the same operation or know someone who has had it.

During the six months' wait, I was directed to have examinations and tests in various clinics. In one clinic, I had a rate-flow test where I had to pee into a contraption that electronically recorded in graph form, through a complicated looking machine, the rate of flow whilst a nurse looked on, presumably to see that I did not cheat. Her only comment was, "Is that all?" One test was an internal bladder inspection through what looked like a submarine's miniature periscope. The next test in a different clinic was a scan. I had to lower my trousers, raise my shirt and lie on a padded couch while a young blonde nurse passed a contraption back and forth over my bladder. This was most uncomfortable and embarrassing because I had not been to the toilet for over half an hour and I was bursting to relieve myself before there was an involuntary emission on her hand and instruments. Another test involved a young doctor asking me many questions and then inserting his index finger into my rectum to check that my prostate gland was still there and its size. What some people do for a living! I also had a cardiogram test, which assured me that there were no circulatory problems. All this in addition to blood and urine tests.

The six-month waiting period soon passed and I was summoned to see the great man himself. Actually, I did not see him but one of his registrars who accepted me for an operation, but because my condition was not considered urgent and due to heavy demand, I had to wait a further 18 months during which I underwent further tests and examinations. I decided that I had no option but to wait, especially when a neighbour told me that he had had a similar operation privately without having to wait and by the same specialist but it had cost him £6,000. I thought it would be less painful to wait than pay such a large sum of money.

In the event, I did not have to wait 18 months because after 16 months I received an invitation to enter the hospital for the long-awaited operation. I was given three days to accept or to go back to the end of the waiting list. I accepted.

I duly reported to the In-patient reception area and was directed to a first floor ward. On reflection, I find it strange that proof of identity was not asked for, as anyone who was mentally deranged could have reported in my stead. No doubt, there are some people who would undergo such an operation just in order to seek attention and sympathy.

The reception nurse apologised that there was not a vacant bed in the appropriate ward but if I did not mind I could have the private isolation room normally reserved for private patients or those with very serious illnesses or a very infectious condition. I was flattered and felt most fortunate to be offered this single bedroom with en-suite bathroom. Unfortunately, the door to the room was wedged fully open and faced directly onto the reception and enquiry desk, which was a hive of activity and noise both by day and night. Not only were there at least six medical staff present but also a steady steam of visitors, all of whom through curiosity looked into my room to see who merited such a privilege.

A nurse erased the name of the previous patient from the notice board above the head of the bed and wrote in my name with the initials, "NBM after 4 am". I later found out that NBM stands for "Nil by mouth". This is standard practice before an operation. I was then asked several personal questions which were duly recorded on a form: name, date of birth, next of kin, religion, any special dietary requirements, did I smoke, medical conditions, medicines normally taken etc. Next, I was asked to sign a form consenting to be operated on.

Despite the noise and bustle all night just outside the open door to my room, I slept quite soundly except for my usual regular visits to the toilet. Just before 11 am the next morning, two young men dressed in green-coloured gowns and with green caps came into the room accompanied by a nurse and told me that they were taking me to the operating theatre for my operation. They wheeled me along endless corridors and over several covered bridges accompanied by the nurse who had my file with her. After a very long journey we arrived at the operating suite in the old, Victorian part of the rambling hospital. As far as I could see, there were three operating theatres with a large reception room and a large adjoining recovery room. The atmosphere was of quiet, efficient, conveyor-belt activity. I was the third patient waiting to enter an operating theatre. My turn soon came. I was asked to confirm my signature on the consent form. I was then asked to remove and hand over my hearing aid by one nurse and soon after another nurse with a foreign accent said, "We will have to remove your spectacles." This shocked me because I could not hear what she said clearly due to my hearing difficulty but when she motioned towards my spectacles I realised with great relief what she actually said. After all, I had heard about wrong kidneys being removed or even the wrong leg amputated. I was thankful for small mercies.

Next a doctor, complete with green gown, green mask, green cap and red turban, asked me whether I preferred a general anaesthetic or a local one, adding that he personally would prefer the local one. Not wishing to give offence, I agreed to the epidermal injection anaesthetic. I only felt the gentle dap of an antiseptic pad in the middle of my back and very soon after my legs started to become numb. In a very short while the whole of my body from the waist down to my toes felt like that of a corpse. Just no feeling whatsoever. I was then wheeled into the operating theatre and swiftly transferred from my trolley bed onto the operating table.

There were several men in green coloured gowns and caps wearing green coloured masks around the table and with quiet, practised efficiency erected a green coloured screen across my chest so that I could not see what was going on. One of the men assured me that I would not feel anything. He was right. The operation commenced sharp at 11 am and I was

589

surprised when, an hour later, I was informed that it was all over and that I could return to the ward after a period in the recovery room. Because of the screen, I was not able to see what was going on but I could see the electric clock over the door. I could not hear anything except very muffled sounds because my hearing aid had been taken out.

After a short while in the recovery room I was wheeled back into my "private" room and then I could see that I had tubes going into my left arm and in and out of my most private parts. For another four hours I could not move my legs and the lower part of my body still felt dead. Slowly, feeling returned to my legs to my great relief.

Later in the day I was informed that a bed was available for me in the general ward. I was wheeled into ward number 1 and placed in bed number 1. The other five beds in the ward were already occupied but none of the occupants took any noticeable interest in my arrival. They either continued sleeping or blankly stared into space.

I could now ascertain that two of the clear plastic tubes led from two clear glass containers marked sodium chloride 0.9% and led to a catheter which fed direct into my bladder. Another clear plastic tube exited from the catheter and discharged into a large plastic bag clipped onto the side of my bed. Discharging through the exit tube was a deep red liquid in which were suspended small particles, which looked like pieces of minced meat. The first night, the tube became blocked with these particles, which caused me great discomfort. Liquids were entering my bladder but their exit was blocked. The night duty nurse perceived my distress and by deftly twisting and squeezing the plastic tube cleared the blockage. Periodically, a nurse would empty the plastic container, as and when it became full, into a plastic bucket kept under the bed. It was the contents of this bucket that interested the visiting doctors.

I had daily samples of blood taken for examination and a nurse frequently took my blood pressure and took my temperature by way of a nozzle placed in my ear.

One thing that was very noticeable in the ward was the background noise. Even though the patients were very subdued and quiet, the noise came in through the open corridor. The ward, like all the other wards that opened off the corridor, was not partitioned off and noises from far away were carried in and reflected off the hard, gloss-painted walls and ceilings and highly polished floors. Apart from several simultaneous loud conversations there were also the noises from squeaking trolley wheels, trolleys of all sorts, dinner trolleys, tea trolleys, medicine trolleys, trolleys conveying patients' files, newspapers and snacks trolleys, cleaners' trolleys and also wheelchairs. They were all fitted with loud, squeaky wheels. The staff had to speak loudly to be heard above this background noise that continued night and day.

The ward was light and airy, fully open at one end onto the open corridor and through wide French doors onto a large verandah at the other, which was the roof of the ground floor rooms below. Also noticeable, was the complete absence of flowers or potted plants. Whether this was because they were not allowed or because the ward was mainly for elderly men, I do not know.

The bed immediately next to mine seemed to be reserved for transient patients who only stayed for one day and then were wheeled elsewhere. They mainly arrived during the night and were gone by the evening.

One of the patients, unlike most of the others, was young with a shaven head, rings in both ears and in his nose. He glared aggressively at everyone and occupied most of his time perusing illustrated catalogues for guns and other deadly weapons for sale. A middle-aged couple, that I presumed were his parents, came to visit him. They seemed very nice, respectable people. In the bed next to him there was an elderly man who wore an oxygen mask all the time except when he walked, as though in his sleep, to the toilet which opened directly off the corridor opposite the ward. He then drifted dreamily back to his bed looking neither right nor left and re-donned his oxygen mask. He wore a long nightshirt instead of pyjamas.

Opposite him was Trevor who, apart from bladder trouble had an open, ulcerated leg that would not heal. He told me that he had been in the ward already for six weeks but had been told that same day that he could return home. One day, a man of about his own age visited him and handed Trevor a brown paper bag of sandwiches, which he devoured with much relish. He told me that in a way he was sorry to be going home because his daughter was in the very next ward and he had been able to visit her every day. He did not say what was wrong with her.

The day before I left, a middle-aged man with a Greek sounding name occupied the bed next to me. Apparently, he was in agony with kidney stones. I wondered what he worked at because he had obviously extremely strong arms but a flabby body.

Directly opposite me was Frank Butcher, about my own age. He told me that even though he could not drive a car, he was a tank driver during World War II. We had a friendly competition to see who could pass most urine and whose urine was the reddest. He won on both counts and even though he had had his operation the day before me, I was discharged before him. So he was welcome to his Pyrrhic victory.

One of the patients told me that he had been in that ward 17 times in recent years. I did not like to ask him what his problem was.

When I arrived in the ward, an elderly gentleman who gave the impression that he was a dignified, retired Air Force officer already occupied the bed between Trevor and Frank. This impression was reinforced by the fact that he was perusing a pile of magazines dealing with World War II aeroplanes and their crews. By their magazines thou shall know them! I did not get around to confirming my impressions because he was discharged the next morning. His bed was immediately taken over by Albert, a very fit and healthy looking elderly man with a deeply tanned, ruddy complexion. A group accompanied him, presumably members of his family who all talked very loudly and continually laughed hilariously. My impression was that he was a farmer. He brought an enormous amount of luggage with him as though he was going on a long overseas visit. In fact, there was so much luggage it encroached on the space around the two adjoining beds and made access to all three beds difficult. As soon as his family left he drew the curtain around his bed presumably to undress privately but when he opened it again, he had only taken off his jacket and boots. He lay down on the bed and donned a pair of earphones, which he plugged into a portable radio. The look of ecstasy on his face was wonderful to behold. I discovered later that he was profoundly deaf but refused to wear a hearing aid.

All members of the staff, both medical and auxiliary were excellent. They were hard working, willing, kind, considerate, obliging and efficient including the young nurse who removed my catheter the day before I was discharged. The medical and auxiliary staff was of several nationalities. One West Indian nurse was highly amused when my wife referred to the tubes and urine bottles as paraphernalia. The next day she brought along a student nurse especially to point out the paraphernalia.

However, despite my interesting experience, I was glad when I was able to return home. It was the first time I had been an in-patient since I was a child, some 70 years ago. Now, four weeks after the operation, I am still visiting the toilet frequently, although slightly less than just before the operation, and someone who has had the same experience has assured me that a marked improvement won't be noticeable for another eight weeks.

A few days after my return home, I read in a newspaper that a new tested and approved drug, Finasteride, is now available for prescription to the public (men only) and which shrinks the size of the prostate gland without the need for an operation. It has the added advantage that at the same time it restores lost hair. If only I had waited the full 18 months for my operation, I could have avoided the inconvenience and discomfort of the operation after-effects.

Fire-Fighter Sid

It was recent reports in the national press of a threatened series of 48-hour strikes for increased pay by fire-fighters (it is not politically correct these days to call them firemen) that recalled to mind my own illustrious career as a fire-fighter some 60 years ago.

My family home at 13 Jewel Street, Stepney, in the impoverished East End of London, had been razed to the ground by enemy bombing in September 1940. Most fortunately, there were no casualties, not even the dog or family cat was hurt. My mother and my siblings, except for an older sister, had previously been evacuated to the country for safety. For a while, my father, sister and myself, the wage earners, were homeless and sought shelter in a nearby school building, sleeping on the hardwood-block floor of the assembly hall until we were re-housed in what was then considered to be a safer part of London, Holborn, which is almost in the centre of London adjacent to the commercial centre known the world over as the City.

For strategic reasons, the Germans had up until then concentrated their bombing on the East End of London in which were situated the docks upon which the country depended desperately for overseas supplies of food and other essentials. The impoverished East Londoners had bravely and stoically taken the brunt of the German onslaught. However, no sooner had we, my father, sister and myself, been relocated at 23 Coram Street, Holborn, London WC1, than the German High Command decided to switch their bombing to central London, the City itself. Their tactics included the dropping of hundreds of thousands of incendiary bombs and giant oil-filled bombs that caused oil to seep through building structures, spreading the fire with it. The result was devastation, which was assisted by the fact that at night, when the air raids mainly took place, the City was virtually uninhabited. There was very little residential accommodation within The Square Mile, as the City was known. Urgent calls went out for volunteers to act as fire-fighters to do duty at night and at weekends in the deserted City and surrounding districts, including Holborn.

The conflagrations were most spectacular and destructive. My family, who had been evacuated to Isleham in Cambridgeshire, some 70 miles from London, could clearly see the red glow of the fires and said that they looked like sunsets.

I duly volunteered and was accepted as a fire-fighter by the Metropolitan Borough of Holborn's Air Raid Precaution Department. I was issued with a steel helmet, a pair of dungarees, a pair of rubber gumboots and a military style respirator. I was also issued with a card which certified that "Sidney Gabrel is a member of a voluntary fire fighting party which is recognised by the Holborn Borough Council and possesses the powers of entry and of taking steps for extinguishing fire or for protecting property, or rescuing persons or property from fire, which are conferred by the Fire Precautions (Access to Premises) Order, 1940." So far, so good.

The fire station I was allocated to was situated in the Council's cleansing depot. I reported for duty one evening and found four men playing cards in one of the rooms that served as an office. No one seemed to be in charge. I was asked if I could drive. I told them, no, I was only 17 years old. They said that in that case, as there was no driver present, they would not be able to answer any calls. When I declined an invitation to join them at cards, they said that I might just as well go to sleep in the next room, which served as a dormitory. The dormitory was in total darkness, lit only by eerie moonlight. There were six camp beds and only two seemed occupied. Well, actually one, because two young men kept hopping from one bed to another accompanied by much giggling and squeaking of bedsprings. The pranks only stopped when one of the two men yelled out, "You've broken it". The other man seemed to disbelieve him. I never found out what was supposed to have been broken.

I slept very soundly that night and in the morning, I was informed that there was no rota and I could report for duty whenever I liked but training only took place on Sunday afternoons. Being keen on becoming an efficient fire-fighter I reported soon after lunch the following Sunday. There were about ten volunteers present, all keen to be trained although the instructor wasn't very experienced himself. He showed us the fire engine, which consisted of an old open-top lorry with a wooden bench for passengers along one side and a wooden ladder tied onto the outside. The ladder was only tall enough, even when fully extended, to reach a first floor window. There was also a petrol-driven water pump, some coils of hoses and several red painted buckets labelled, "Water", but containing only sand. This was to be our conveyance to any incident, provided a driver could be found.

The training was quite exciting. We uncoiled the hoses, connected them to a street hydrant and squirted water onto an imaginary fire. It was amazing; it took three of us to stop the hose from recoiling backward. It was like an untamed beast. We also practised placing a bucket of sand over an imaginary incendiary bomb whilst lying flat on the ground in order to avoid the explosive charge that the incendiary bombs carried in their tails. Also, we were instructed to crawl with our faces at floor level through a wooden shed filled with smoke to demonstrate that even in a fierce fire, there is sufficient air at floor level to breath. We entered through a small, dog-kennel-type entrance at one side of the shed and out through a similar opening at the other end.

There was a bit of panic when the last volunteer was due to exit the smoke filled shed. After each one of us had successfully gone through the exercise, we rushed round to the exit opening to welcome the next volunteer. However, the last volunteer, who was rather stoutish, chickened out when it was his turn and quickly rushed round to join the others unnoticed. When he did not appear at the exit opening there was a moment of panic until we realised what had happened.

One bright, moonlit night when I was on duty, we got a call to attend a roof fire in a nearby warehouse building. When we got there, we found the front door to be heavily reinforced with steel bands and the windows were all fitted with burglar bars. We had no axe or any other implement to break into the building and had to wait until the regular fire brigade arrived. They soon put out the small fire caused by an incendiary bomb. The next call I attended was to an office building in the City itself. The caretaker who had made the call unlocked the front door to let us attend to the fire. Just across the road there was an emergency water reservoir formed in the basement of a fire-destroyed building but when we lowered our hosepipe into it, we found it to be dried out. The nearest fire hydrant was too far away for our hosepipes to reach. Once again, we had to wait for the professionals.

I did eventually assist in extinguishing two small fires but never got round to heroically rescuing anyone from a smoke-filled burning building or even of using the wooden ladder.

Early one morning, we were called out to assist the regular fire brigade who had been up all night fighting raging fires in a nearby City street. When we got there the fires were already out but we were amazed to see huge icicles hanging down the front facades of the burnt-out, Victorian office buildings. The night had been so cold that despite the heat of the raging fires, the water that the fire-fighters had squirted onto the buildings had frozen and had formed the giant icicles which would, when they began to melt, form a danger to anyone nearby. As the fires were already out, we volunteered to help by rolling up the many hose reels, some partially frozen and also to sweep up the many shards of broken glass and other debris. Pedestrians and traffic were not allowed through the street until the icicles had partly melted and dropped to the pavement.

After about three years living in Holborn, the authorities decided that it would be comparatively safe for us to quit our flat and move back to east London that no longer was subjected to heavy bombardment. I duly handed my gear back to the Holborn authorities and took up residence with my family in Stratford, east London, just in time for the next stage of German terror, the V1 doodle bug bombs and V2 rockets, one of which landed on the corner of our street soon after we took up residence.

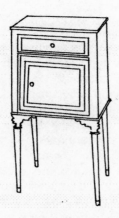

The Bedside Cabinet

In September 1954, we moved home from the semi-detached 1930s house in Becontree Heath, Essex, to our present, larger, double fronted terraced house in Ilford, Essex. The move was supposed to have been a temporary one in the steps up the housing ladder, but after 50 years we are still happily ensconced here. We are now the longest continuous residents in the street. All the other residents who were living in the street when we moved in have gone away, sadly some feet first.

When we moved into the house it had been converted, by the previous owner, into two self-contained flats. This suited us fine because we desperately needed, for financial reasons, to let the ground floor flat in order to meet our greatly increased commitments, for which even our combined salaries at the time were not sufficient. Fortunately, the previous owner had not removed the curtains from the largish windows and had also left some items of furniture that would not fit into his newly built, small bungalow. He, no doubt, thought that he had pulled a fast one on us by leaving what he considered to be undesirable, old-fashioned items that he would otherwise have had to pay to be removed. Actually, what he left was very useful to us in helping to furnish the otherwise empty ground floor flat.

Whilst the furniture he had left was helpful and welcome, it was not sufficient to fully furnish the flat. In those days, it was most important to let accommodation furnished in order to circumvent the draconian tenant protection legislation of unfurnished flats. In any case, a higher rent could be charged for a furnished flat than an unfurnished one. As far as we were concerned, the more, the better.

Even though it was nine years since the end of World War II, there was still a great shortage of new furniture in the shops and what was available

597

was flimsy, badly designed and comparatively expensive. We therefore decided to buy or otherwise acquire second-hand furniture and fittings.

Some of our acquisitions were gifts from various acquaintances who were disposing of what they considered to be unwanted, old-fashioned stuff that they would otherwise have had to pay someone to remove for them. The unwanted stuff they gave us was truly old at the time but with care the items eventually became treasured antiques.

One of the items was a genuine Chesterfield couch with the original, although somewhat tatty, embroidered brocade covering and horsehair stuffing. It is now worth over £2,000 but we would not part with it because it is so comfortable. We know it is original because it has Mr. Chesterfield's signature branded on the timber frame. Two of the settees that the donor had replaced it with have disintegrated and been thrown away.

Apart from some fine furniture and carpets that we were given there were some ornaments that over the course of time have turned out to be valuable porcelain from famous potteries. It was certainly worthwhile helping people to get rid of unwanted clutter.

Apart from these most useful gifts, we needed to supplement the contents of our furnished ground floor flat by buying second-hand goods. We toured the second-hand junk shops and carefully scrutinised adverts in the local newspapers and in newsagents' windows. In this manner, we finally furnished the ground floor flat and also supplemented the furnishings in our own first floor flat.

Not long after we moved into the house, I noticed a lovely Hepplewhite worktable lying in the front garden of a neighbour's house. I timidly asked her if she would like it removed. She gazed at me as though I was an escapee from some mental home and said that I might remove it as long as I did not make a mess. We still have that lovely, delicate object, which is not only elegant to look at but also very utilitarian.

We had a succession of tenants occupying the ground floor flat who were most grateful for being afforded the opportunity of renting a comfortable flat at an economical rent. In this way, we made several friends and at the same time helped to relieve our impecunious cash flow problem. After several years we stopped renting out the ground floor flat and incorporated it as an integral part of our home, if only to store and display some of the lovely antique furniture and other beautiful articles that we had accumulated over the years.

Among such items was a very handsome bedside cabinet. I can't remember where or from whom we obtained it. Perhaps it was from a local bric-a-brac shop which is now closed and whose owner recently died. We placed the cabinet at the side of our bed, the side that I sleep on, and placed a table lamp on it as well as a clock radio. The cabinet is of

The Bedside Cabinet

Edwardian style, about 1904, which is the same age as the house itself. It is very sturdily constructed of mahogany timber with a starburst marquetry design on the cupboard door. The top is finished with embossed green leather. The legs are finely tapered and fluted with ormolu mounts. The cupboard is lined with polished white marble, presumably to house a chamber pot. Above the cupboard is a drawer which is useful for keeping items that a gentleman may need during the night, such as a torch, cough sweets, headache pills and manicure scissors.

Quite recently, I noticed that the drawer was getting stiff to open and close. From experience with other drawers in the past, I knew the remedy was to rub candle wax on the runners. I pulled the drawer right out and as soon as I applied the wax the drawer immediately ran smoothly in and out. Whilst it was out, I noticed that the drawer was about four inches shorter than the depth of the cabinet. I used the torch that I kept in it to see if there was any reason. There was indeed a four-inch space at the rear of the drawer and in that space were two small packets wrapped in grubby towelling material. I immediately opened them. In the first were two small multi-coloured glass marbles, rather the worse for wear and one shirt cuff link and four collar studs that were used in the days when collars were not commonly attached to the shirts. In addition there were two, enamelled lapel badges, one with the words, "Workers Circle Friendly Society" and the other, "President, Jewish Tailors and Tailoresses Trade Union". These I would guess date from the 1930s when lapel badges were very common and proclaimed the wearer's association with various organisations such as sports clubs, schools, regiments etc.

When I unwrapped the other small bundle it contained a wristwatch with a leather strap. It had several small dials showing the date, day and month as well as the traditional hour and minute hands and seconds' sweep hand as well as a moon-phase dial. It was the sort of watch I had always yearned for but never possessed. I was as pleased as Punch, especially as, after a few winds, I noted that it still functioned although after a few minutes it stopped when held at a certain angle. I assumed that after a long incarceration at the back of the drawer, it needed some cleaning and oiling. I did not recognise the name of the maker, "Vacheron et Constanin, Geneve" and the dial had the word, "Tourbillon" on it. At the time, none of this had any meaning to me. The dial also contained a cut-away to show a regulating flywheel with a ruby stone. I also noticed that the leather strap had very little wear. Either the watch had not been used much or the strap had been renewed.

As the watch was not functioning properly, I put it aside until the next visit to us by Peter, who dabbled in second hand watches and knew several good watch repairers. After several weeks, Peter did turn up for one of

599

his periodic social visits and I asked him if he could recommend a reliable watch repairer to clean and oil the watch. As soon as he saw the watch he became very excited. He exclaimed that it was a Toubillon Vacheron and that it was worth thousands, possibly £20-25,000. At first I thought he was having me on but I soon realised that he was in earnest. He recommended that I did not allow any watch repairer to dabble with it but to sell it in its present condition. He advised that I sell it at auction through a well-known auction house. He said that he knew several collectors who would give their right hands to get such a watch. After some thought I agreed with him because if I declared the watch to my insurance company they would immediately raise my insurance premium and impose stringent security measures and restrictions. I realised that it was not worth hanging onto the watch. I also realised that it increased the risk of being mugged if I wore in it public.

A short while after, I saw a newspaper advertisement by a well-known auction house, Bonham's, asking people to submit clocks and watches for their forthcoming auction. I carefully wrapped the watch in a padded envelope and sent it by registered post to Bonham's asking them to submit the watch in their forthcoming auction. About a week later, the watch was returned to me through the post with just a compliment slip bearing the name of the person in charge of the department. I did not know if this was the usual procedure for submitting watches for auction so I phone the person concerned who said he remembered receiving the watch but he had returned it to me because Bonham's do not deal with fake watches. He said that it was not worth much and that I should enjoy wearing it as a talking piece with my acquaintances. He agreed that it was not worth being mugged for.

I wonder if the person who concealed the watch was aware of this?

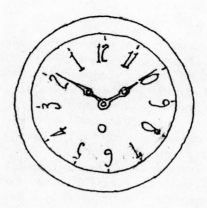

Vice Versa – Asrev Eciv

Several years ago, just a couple of weeks before my birthday, which occurs towards the end of January, my wife came home from shopping and gave me a most welcome and unexpected gift. It was unexpected because she rarely remembers my birthday but nevertheless expects me to remember hers. The gift was a lovely, heavy, hand-knitted, high neck woollen jersey. It was only a coincidence that it was just before my birthday as she had in mind that I could wear it when gardening during the cold winter. She had spotted the jersey in a charity shop window and bought it because it was so cheap.

It was just the right size for me but the pattern and colours were unimaginative and drab. Whilst trying it on, I accidentally turned it inside out and to my delight, I discovered that the colours on the wrong side were bright and cheerful so I decided to wear it inside out even indoors. The seams were conspicuous but formed an interesting pattern. It was not long before some of my more observant acquaintances discreetly pointed out to me that I was obviously wearing the jersey inside out. I told them that there were no instructions as to which was the inside or the outside and I had chosen the inside to be the correct side. I also pointed out, because none of them had noticed, that I was wearing it back to front.

Eventually, after much hard wear and warm and cosy loving comfort, it peacefully, with the aid of some friendly moths, passed away and was respectfully laid to rest in eternal peace in the dustbin. Farewell, dear inside out and back to front friend.

I thought that the exposure and display of seams could be developed into an art form with elaborately decorated seams being the main features of clothes. This could give a new meaning to the phrase, "the seamy side of life". Another advantage of wearing clothes inside out is that famous makers' labels could be displayed adding to the wearer's prestige. Price labels and washing instructions could possibly also be a feature.

One cold winter day, after I had done some arduous gardening, I came indoors for a rest and refreshments. As my shoes were somewhat muddy, I immediately commenced to change into my indoor shoes but before I could complete the change, there was a ring on the front doorbell. As I was near the front door, I went to see who it was. A neighbour had sent her young son with a message for Dora. Before he could pass the message, he noticed that I was wearing odd shoes. This so dumbstruck him that he forgot what the message was. However, his face demonstrated his astonishment.

This incident made me realise just how brainwashed we have been into being conventional. Nobody, however impoverished, would dream of wearing odd shoes. There is no logical reason why we should wear matching shoes. Sometimes, the shoe on one foot wears out before the other. Sometimes, the lace on one shoe breaks before the other. It is wasteful to cast away a pair of shoes just because one becomes unwearable before the other. If even only one fashion mogul decided that it was cool to wear odd shoes, everyone, especially those fashion conscious people would proudly wear odd shoes. However, I doubt if the shoe industry would welcome such an idea. No one seems to have marketed shoes that could be worn on either foot.

There is no reason why socks and stockings should match. It would be much more fun to select odd socks and stockings to go with odd shoes.

It is conventional for black garments to be worn at funerals etc. even if only in the form of a black tie or armband. Black is a sign of sadness, which would indicate that the wearer believes the deceased has not been worthy enough to gain admittance to Heaven and possibly whose soul has been assigned to eternal torture in Hell. On the other hand, white garments would indicate that the wearer believes that the deceased's soul has been received in Heaven for his good and righteous life on earth despite all his trials and tribulations. It is interesting to note that in Western countries, where mourners wear black, the deceased is clothed in a white shroud. It would be more logical if the reverse were the case. Actually, Islamic peoples do wear white as a symbol of mourning, according to tradition.

It is conventional, even in this day and age of equality, for a newly married wife to forsake her own family's surname and to take that of her husband. Why is the reverse not the case, even for a change, or why don't the couple adopt a joint surname?

Some while ago, whilst I was waiting to have a well-worn pair of shoes repaired in a local "While You Wait" shop, the wall clock puzzled me. I just could not make out what the time was and then I realized after consulting my wristwatch that it was working in an anti-clockwise direction. Because I, along with everybody else in the civilised world, was brought up with traditional clocks, I just could not read the time. The shoe repairer, who, by the way, also cut keys and engraved identity tags for cats and dogs, assured me that most people, including himself, had a similar difficulty and it was just as well, as it confused them when calculating how long they had been waiting for their shoes to be repaired.

This set me thinking, why do most clocks indicate the time with English or Roman numerals; why not use English alphabet letters? So, instead of saying ten past eleven, we say B past K. In any case, when we say ten past eleven the minute hand actually points to the figure two. The alphabet system would be much less confusing especially to young children learning to tell the time.

It is interesting to note, that in Hebrew, there are strictly no numerals in the language and often, but not always, the letters of the Hebrew alphabet are used in numerical order in the alphabet. This becomes very complicated when multiplication or division is involved.

A friend who collects old clocks has an unusual grandfather clock that he calls a Regulator. I suppose it is called a Regulator because its timing is regulated by a large brass pendulum. Its unusual feature is that instead of the traditional clock face, it has three separate dials, each the same size and each with a single hand, one of which indicates the hour, one the minutes and the third, the seconds. It sounds simple enough but reading it confounds most people who have been brainwashed by always having read the traditional clock face.

It is anachronistic in this digital, computer, information technology age that time is still traditionally based either on a 12-hour or 24-hour clock. It is far more logical for clocks to be on a 20-hour basis. This is bound to come sooner or later and the old 12-hour clock faces will be considered antique curiosities. A change to a decimalised 20-hour clock would also avoid confusion as occurred recently when I told my wife that a message had been left for her on the answer phone at 22.10 pm. She said that couldn't be correct as she was present at twenty to ten and the phone did not ring. Fortunately, this small misunderstanding did not enlarge into something big.

Convention insidiously dominates our daily existence and its constant repetition can be inductive to boredom. In order to enliven our lives, it would be exciting to break with some conventions, such as saying "goodbye" instead of "hello" when meeting someone. Saying, "I'm sorry to hear that" when someone says that they are in good health. Proffering the left hand when shaking hands instead of the right hand. Even asking someone what's wrong when they obviously look healthy. Such unconventional behaviour would add interest to boring repetition and invigorate the brain. Books could also increase interest in their contents if they were to be printed with lines reading from right to left and the spelling of words reversed and even the pages printed from bottom to top and also beginning at the traditional end of the book and proceeding to the front. What purpose one may ask if only to stimulate the brain and increase interest in the subject matter? Books could also be more interesting if they were printed on coloured paper with coloured ink to reflect the subject mood. More children could be induced to read something colourful rather than the traditional black print on white paper.

Just for the fun of it, dictionaries and encyclopaedias could commence with Z and end with A. A much more difficult matter would be to do arithmetic with numerals written from right to left. Just try a simple addition or multiplication to see how difficult the reversal of convention can be. The brain needs exercising just as the body does, that's why people do crossword puzzles.

Bank statements and other accounts could start with the balance in hand or final figure and work backwards. Biographies could commence with death and work backwards towards birth. It would be more logical for postal sorting purposes if envelopes were addressed in the reverse order to the conventional manner. The country of destination would be first, the province or county next and then the town and postcode and finally the street and number followed by the addressee or organisation. This already applies in many countries.

For privacy, ground storey windows of buildings could be glazed with dark-coloured tinted glass rather than shielded by curtains or blinds. It would be more interesting and practical if houses were built with their backs facing access roads. The housewife in the kitchen would be able to watch events in the street whilst working in the kitchen and have quick access to the front door when necessary. On the other hand, the access to the rear garden would be more pleasant directly off the lounge. Some people would find it more convenient if houses were built with lounges and spare bedrooms on the first floor and primary bedroom, bathroom and kitchen on the ground floor, especially the elderly and infirm. In any case, first floor rooms generally are brighter and sunnier than those on the ground floor.

With the rapid increase in traffic on our already congested road, accidents are on the corresponding increase despite much improved safety measures and car design. This was brought home to us when we recently heard that someone we knew had been seriously injured in a head-on collision on the nearby motorway. I explained to Dora that the speed limit on motorways is 70 miles per hour but when two cars collide head-on the combined force is equivalent to 140 miles per hour and that is what happened to our acquaintance. Dora has always been good at applied mathematics and physics. She asked why doesn't the traffic drive 70 mph head-on in one direction and in reverse in the other direction at the same speed. She quoted Einstein's Theory of Relativity, which states that when a positive force meets a negative one of the same magnitude, the resultant impact is Zero. She wondered why nobody else had thought of applying this theory to traffic accidents on motorways.

I was recently registering at a local hospital to have my right knee X-rayed when I noticed that the young girl taking down my particulars was writing with her left hand with a decisive backward slope. This recalled to my mind my first-hand experience with a person with the left hand difficulty. It was over 70 years ago in the local infants' school and it was our first lesson in writing with a pen and ink. The pen was a steel nib mounted on a varnished, ink-stained wooden handle with the impressed letters, LCC, which stood for London County Council. The class was all boys because in those days even the infants were separately educated. The teachers were all spinsters or World War One widows. Married women were not employed as teachers although married men were. The teacher's name was Miss Pearce and she was rather elderly. One of the boys, his name was Bernard, chubby with curly hair, was writing with his left hand. When Miss Pearce spotted this, she scolded him and told him to write properly with his right hand. The result was an ink-splattered sheet of paper with illegible words. He was told that he was being very naughty and was reduced to tears. His torment was increased when the other boys nicknamed him "stinky monitor" in contrast to the favourite boy (not me) who was promoted to "ink monitor". The ink monitor's duty was to refill the desk inkpots with black ink poured from a brown glazed jar with a spout and large cork. This duty was about the highest in the class. At the time I did not realise the symptomatic significance of this incident but over the years, I have become aware of the terrific disadvantages and prejudice endured by left-handed persons.

A census has never been taken of this problem, the largest minority group in the world. It has been reckoned that between 11% and 16% of the population in this country, 6.6 million to 9.6 million people, predominantly males, are left-handed. Most suffer with an inferiority complex and try to conceal their disability. Even though it is their natural instinct to proffer the left hand when greeting someone, they deliberately proffer their right hand. However, in an emergency situation, they will instinctively use their left hand to give signals.

The condition is something to do with the development of the brain as a foetus. In most people, the left side of the brain controls the skills predominantly to the right hand. Even in the womb, most babies suck the thumb on their right hand. The reverse is the case in left-handed people. Left-handed people are thought to be unusually creative, especially so in music, mathematics and languages but are also likely to be subject to stuttering and clumsiness. It is not known if the condition is genetic, whether left-handedness runs in families and whether it is inherited. It is not known if left-handedness is connected with dyslexia. It also not known if twins are subject to the similar condition. It is also not known how many people are naturally ambidextrous, that is, skilled equally in the use of both hands.

Left-handed people are considered by many people to be clumsy. In French, the word "gauche" means both left and clumsy whilst the Latin word "sinistra" from which the word, sinister, is derived, means left.

The sobriquet for a left handed person is "Lefty" which is usually used in a derogatory, contemptuous manner, whilst there is no equivalent appellation for a right-handed person. There is no known medical therapy treatment for the condition. Toilet flushing handles and chains are standard on the right hand side of the cistern. This makes it most awkward for left-handed persons to operate. Wristwatches always have the winding and adjusting knob on the right-hand side. To realize what this means to a left-handed person, just try adjusting your wristwatch with your left hand.

Left-handed persons can't use ordinary scissors. They have to acquire specially made left-handed scissors. Left-handed draughtsmen have to be equipped with special drawing board and tee-squares. This discriminates against them when applying for jobs. Starting switches on cars are on the right-hand side of the driving wheel. This makes it most awkward for a left-handed driver.

Institutionalised anti-left-handedness is embodied in English literature and its usage. "Left behind" indicates inferiority. In the armed services, salutes are always given with the right hand and the order to march is given by "by the right, quick march" insinuating the "by the left" would be "slow march". Legally, the terms, "right of way", "a person's rights" etc. are commonly used. In court witnesses are obliged to place their right hand on the Bible when swearing to give evidence. This suggests that the left hand is associated with untruthfulness. In the English language, the word "right" is associated with morally good, in accordance with justice, proper, correct, true, right side of material, right angle, good condition, right mind, correct decision, to set thing right, legal rights, Right Honourable Gentleman etc. etc. This all insinuates that left is the opposite. Even the Holy Bible is strongly prejudiced in favour of the description, "right". It said that the righteous will sit on the right-hand side of God, the honoured side, and presumably the left-hand side is reserved for the non-righteous.

The Holy Bible, both Old and New Testaments include the words Right, Righteous, Righteousness and Rightly, 878 times always in a positive sense whilst, in comparison, it includes the word Left only 208 times, mainly in a negative sense.

Throughout the ages, left-handed people have been most stoic and passive and uncomplaining but surely they have a right to form a world-wide organisation to care for their needs and to state their case.

I suggest that it may call itself the "Federation Against Rightism Tyranny" or some other resounding title.

Printed in the United Kingdom
by Lightning Source UK Ltd.
100856UKS00002B/25-300